This is one of my most favourite books on Wattpad. I recommend this to anyone looking for something special, unique, beautiful and amazing. This book brings light to many important topics that need light shed upon. The plot and characters are beyond amazing! I love Carmen and Asa with all my heart and a day never goes by where I don't think about them. I got a lot more to say but there are no words that could describe how special this book is to me as a person.
–Dima, *Goodreads*

Through Your Eyes is the kind of book that rips open your heart and makes a home. A book that you eventually crawl back to no matter how many times you've read it.
–Anisha Singh, *Goodreads*

This book is one that I suggest everyone to read. The author really knows how to touch a person's emotions. Once you read it, you'll want to read it again and again. I got addicted to it, I hope you too get addicted to this amazing story!
–Aisha Khan, *Goodreads*

Talent is something we all crave for. Whether it is in any form. By reading Through Your Eyes, I got a taste of what people meant by "God gifted talent". I am so glad to have the opportunity to read this book again and again which I am going to use to its fullest.
–Urooj Ibrahim, *Goodreads*

This book has always held a special place in my library and is my all-time favourite online book. The author is gifted with a talented and graceful style of writing that genuinely conveys emotions. I have unashamedly laughed and cried with the characters in this book. The author should be so proud of her incredible work, and we're all excited for her to share her work on a professional platform.
–Ishika Dhatariya, *Goodreads*

Typewriter Pub, an imprint of Blvnp Incorporated
A Nevada Corporation
1887 Whitney Mesa DR #2002
Henderson, NV 89014
www.typewriterpub.com/info@typewriterpub.com

ISBN: **978-1-64434-067-7**

DISCLAIMER
This book is a work of fiction. The characters, incidents, and dialogue are drawn from the author's imagination and are not to be construed as real. While references might be made to actual historical events or existing locations, the names, characters, places, and incidents are either products of the author's imagination or are used fictitiously, and any resemblance to actual persons living or dead, business establishments, events or locales is entirely coincidental.

THROUGH YOUR EYES

ALI MERCI

To all those who had it in them to love me
during the moments I looked like war, smelt like heartache, and tasted like
poison;
Thank you.

FREE DOWNLOAD

Get these freebies when you sign up for the author's mailing list!

ali-merci.awesomeauthors.org

01.
Asa

Asa's grandpa had once told him that his rash nature and tendency to act on impulse would get him in trouble one day.

It got Asa in trouble, all right. More than just once.

And it seemed like today was just another one of those days.

It wasn't Asa's fault. Not really. He just didn't like it when Hunter Donoghue spoke. Or moved. Or breathed for that matter.

"Take that, *pinche pendejo*!" Asa's fist landed on Hunter's jaw with a sickening crack, and the linebacker stumbled several feet backwards, thrown off-balance. He was still standing and not sprawled out on the ground, though. Not what Asa would've preferred.

Hunter's eyes flashed dangerously and, within the short space of two breaths, he lunged forward in a half-bent posture, ramming his head into Asa's stomach.

Asa groaned, all air knocked out of his lungs for what felt like an eternity. Both of them stumbled to the ground, Asa's back hitting the tiled hallway floors of Reichenbach High with Hunter's heavy body pinning him down.

Without a moment's hesitation, Asa shoved Hunter's body off of him, muttering a string of colourful words in the process.

"You absolute piece of garbage." Asa wheezed, his breaths coming in gasps. He clutched his abdomen where Hunter's head had collided.

"Oh, grow the hell up," Hunter sneered, his lips curling back over his teeth in a nasty snarl. "Trying to be the hero isn't going to get you anywhere."

"But bullying will?"

In answer, Hunter lunged at him again, but this time Asa had prepared himself. He used one of his feet to hook itself behind Hunter's shins, sending him to the ground.

Hunter hit the ground with a strangled yell but it was soon cut off when Asa pounced on him, driving a fist into his gut in retaliation for head-butting him earlier.

"Dude, what's your problem?!" Hunter grabbed a fistful of Asa's collar and struck him with a closed fist across his face.

Asa's head whipped to the side, but he only laughed in response to the question. "You," he spat. "People like you are my problem. What the hell is it to you how much someone eats?"

Hunter struggled, but he eventually managed to throw an aggressive Asa off him, quickly moving back a few steps as the latter did the same.

Both of the boys kept their eyes fixed on each other, their well-muscled frames tensed in anticipation of another round of punches, kicks and blows.

"She piles her plate every goddamn day with food enough to feed an army!" Hunter rolled his shoulders back, a gleam in his eyes as he watched Asa with a smirk. "I was only asking her to leave some for the rest of us." He shrugged, oozing with nonchalance and arrogance. "She could do with shedding off the extra weight. I mean, look at her."

Asa's eyes tore away from cautiously watching Hunter and landed on the girl standing a few feet away from them, curled up by the corner of the wall and the lockers, scared and terrified. His gut clenched at the sight, only adding more fuel to his hatred for the boy standing in front of him.

It had been right after English period, just as the lunch bell rang, when Asa had heard Hunter's mocking voice from the other end of the

2

hallway He'd known in his bones by then that the prick was up to no good.

He'd arrived just in time to hear Hunter's less than pleasant words to the girl, the kind that echoed in someone's mind for days, corrupting it so that, later, it would shape the way they saw themselves.

The familiarity of it all had hit Asa somewhere deep in the chest.

And then came the blinding rage, and suddenly, fists were flown and profanities were spewed out from each other's mouths. It was a wonder nobody heard them and a crowd didn't congregate around the two boys yet.

Asa looked back at Hunter's unapologetic eyes. "She looks fine to me," he said. "More human than you, anyway."

Hunter looked prepared to lunge at him again, but a shrill voice—that often reminded Asa of the whistle of the Hogwarts Express— cut through the tense air.

"What's going on here?" asked the screeching voice.

He hated *that* voice.

The boys shook off their predatory stance, lowering their fists and unclenching their palms. Mrs. Cromwell, their disciplinary head, was someone on the list of school authorities one simply did not mess with.

"Still having trouble keeping your fists to yourself, San Román?" Cromwell's beady, soulless eyes looked down from her nose at Asa as she took in the bruises and the cuts on him.

"Me? You're blaming *just* me? You don't even know what he did—" But Asa's retort was cut short by that same nails-on-walls voice.

"Mr. San Román," she curled her lips when she said his name, "I think it's pretty well-known how you can be biased towards anything that involves Mr. Donoghue, so pardon me if I don't take your account of what happened seriously."

Asa snorted. "And what? You think the animosity is one-sided? How is his version of events going to be any more honest?"

"Well, I guess you're just going to have to live with that, Mr. San—"

3

"Oh, for god's sake!" He stood to his full height and scowled at Mrs. Cromwell. "It's *Asa*. San Román is the family name. I get that you seem to like using that name, but would you mind?"

Mrs. Cromwell's cheeks coloured, her hands shaking by her sides, as if she wanted to smack Asa's head

"Watch it, young man. I do not appreciate being told what to do by the apes that come to this school."

Asa raised a brow. "Does that include you too, Ma'am? I mean, you *do* attend this school, too." From his peripheral view, Asa could see Hunter's shoulders shake with silent laughter as he tried to suppress it.

"Detention!" she boomed, her voice echoing throughout the deserted hallway. "For the rest of the week."

Asa's scowl deepened. He opened his mouth, ready to tell the stupid disciplinarian what had happened, when his eye caught the girl's movements. She shook her head, the gesture quick and short, but he knew what it meant. Most of the bullied didn't want to be dragged into the spotlight. Not 'till they were ready to tell someone.

"You're going to stick us together?" He scoffed, changing the course of what his words was going to say in a breath. "It's probably just going to lead to him opening his stupid mouth and saying something that pisses me off."

"You seem to be under the ridiculous idea that Mr. Donoghue is also receiving detention, Mr. San Román."

Asa's eyes narrowed into slits. "I wasn't fighting with air, Cromwell! He was in it as much as I was. In fact, he initiated it—"

"Enough!" she snapped. "You're not in detention for the fight, Mr. San Román. You're in detention because you were mouthing off at the disciplinary head and implying that she is an ape."

Asa knew—he really did—that he needed to shut his mouth. But when did he ever stop himself?

"Honestly, Cromwell. If I knew your feelings got hurt so easily," he said, grinning at the woman, "I can assure you I think you're prettier than an ape, if that is any consolation."

4

And Asa earned himself an extra week of detention.

02.
Carmen

Carmen woke up with a start, her breaths coming in harsh gasps, her heart a wild, restless beast within her chest.

"Just a dream," she mumbled, her hand coming to rest on the hollow of her neck. "Just a dream, Carmen." She soothed herself, just like she always had to do the past years.

But she knew there was no falling back to sleep now. Not after seeing the horrid images flash through her mind.

It was the dead of night, and it was so quiet out here in her bedroom. But in her head, it was so loud up there, where the sun never rises.

Carmen wanted to know what it felt like to have light inside.

Her hands twitched and her fingers throbbed, her body looking for a way to scream. But she'd always been a quiet person, finding her sanctuary in art, like her very own art journal.

With that thought, a smile graced her face. The instant her eyes landed on the spiral hardcover book sitting on the floor of her room, along with the pens, markers and sketching pencils strewn about, she slid her legs off the edge of the bed and headed towards her haven.

Art, she'd long since realised, made up for her lack of light.

•　　•　　•

"Want me to give you a ride today?"

Carmen looked up at her father, her hands pausing in its fidgeting with her necklace.

She smiled, kind and warm, just like how she always smiled. "No, Dad," she said with a slight shake of the head. "You know I prefer the walk."

"It's September," he muttered. "It's chilly out."

"But it's also the best time of the year for me to collect stuff for my journal," she pointed out gently. Autumn leaves, specifically. Carmen just loved how September made the leaves blush in shades of red and orange.

She heard her father sigh, but done with affection. "You and that journal of yours," he muttered, almost to himself, shaking his head. Carmen watched as his eyes lit up with his soft smile then grew distant as if remembering a hazy memory from another lifetime. She had to tear her eyes away once she saw pain flood into her father's.

Pain, pain, pain.

There was so much pain. But, Carmen realised, if she could smile and find some ounce of peace in her mind when the battles within them had calmed for a brief moment, then the world wasn't so bad a place, was it?

The world hadn't robbed her of her smile. Not yet. She supposed she could be at least thankful for that.

"I love you," she suddenly said. Because within that second, in that tiniest of infinities, she needed him to know.

Surprise sparked in her father's eyes, albeit brief. But it was there, along with a smudge of joy as a smile crept back in his face.

It warmed Carmen's heart. Her heart that, despite everything, was still capable of empathy and love.

And Carmen believed, in that moment at least, that was perhaps the most powerful defence she had against her own head.

•　　•　　•

Carmen was in the school office during lunch, filling out the details on a form for her student ID card (she'd lost her previous one—

7

much to her dismay since she had had it ever since freshman year) when the door flew open and a disgruntled Mrs. Cromwell stormed in.

She did not look happy.

"Smart ass," she mumbled harshly under her breath. "Prettier than an ape, my foot!"

Carmen wrinkled her brows, confusion sweeping through her at the disciplinarian's odd muttering. For a wild moment, she wondered if Mrs. Cromwell had hit her head somewhere and was harbouring a slight concussion.

"Everything all right, Martha?" One of the administrators in the office asked.

"As long as Asa San Román exists, no," she snapped, malice inserted in every syllable of the person's name. Carmen wondered what it was like to feel so much hatred in one's heart. Surely, it brought no happiness, did it?

"Don't you think you're being a little hard on the boy?" the daring administrator asked and Carmen's eyes flew to her name tag: Miss Willoughby. Carmen decided Miss Willoughby was quite a brave soul if not flinching under Mrs Cromwell's venomous glare was any indication.

Sensing that the disciplinarian was about to give Willoughby a piece of her mind, Carmen quickly finished with the form, handed it over and left the office, saving the administrator from the embarrassment of getting chided in front of a student.

She walked down the hall with a ghost of a smile on her face, ready to give it to somebody who came her way. Truly, she never knew who might need a smile that day.

The thought didn't finish crossing her mind when her eyes landed on a slightly pudgy girl nearby. She was standing by the lockers, alone, while people walked past her. Little bits of food littered around her feet and created a small trail towards a trash can nearby, where a whole tray of an uneaten meal was dumped.

Carmen was confused as to why anyone would want to waste a whole lot of food, but her curiosity didn't matter once she took in the sad eyes of the girl.

So Carmen smiled at the girl. The girl blinked in disbelief, but eventually smiled back, too. And as those frowning lips curved up and the sadness dissipated from those lovely golden eyes, Carmen also felt warmth flood over herself in a gentle wave.

But as she walked past the girl, the warmth faded.

The unwelcomed and unwanted coldness swept in, reminding her of a memory she'd tucked in the farthest corner of her mind: that she was born with blood on her hands and no amount of smiles or waves of warmth were flushing that away.

03.
Judgment

After Cromwell had thrown him one last revolted glare and stormed away with Hunter following behind her, Asa let his muscles relax and cursed under his breath.

Which brainless disciplinary head did not listen to two sides of a story? The one that worked at his high school, apparently.

He was going to have a hard time explaining this to his mother. God knew how many times his thoughtlessness and brash attitude had landed him in detention over the past few years. The only reason they didn't resort to expelling him from the goddamn school was probably because his father was on the school board. There was also the fact that Asa was an asset to them, what with him winning the all-state swimming championship last year for the under-eighteen category.

Hell, the first reason was most definitely the only thing this school thought mattered about him anyway.

Needless to say, Asa was in a pretty shitty mood for the rest of the day, scowling at anyone who even so much as made eye contact with him.

By the time lunch rolled around, his mood had worsened along with his gut where Hunter had attacked him with his head. Asa was quite certain there was a bruise already formed on his abdomen.

He didn't finish that thought when he rounded a corner and somebody ran into him—somebody much shorter. As in this somebody's shoulder was low enough to knock into his bruising stomach—of all places—sending a flare of pain up his entire body, making him hiss and recoil.

"Watch where you're going, asshole," he ground out through gritted teeth, waiting for the flash of pain to fade away from his abdomen.

"Excuse me?" a girl's voice answered and the venom in her tone made him look at her wearily. He wasn't in the mood for a fight.

"You don't pull a goddamn Usain Bolt around a bend in the hallways," he said, glaring at her. "The person on the other side can't see you, genius!"

She looked thoroughly unimpressed, and her hazel eyes—which Asa found hard to look away from—flashed with annoyance. "Listen here, Ace—or whatever the hell your name is." Asa realised she was probably a new student. "I've heard enough on my first day here to know the kind of tool you are. And maybe the entire student population here is okay with Mr. Popular walking them over, but I'm not that girl, all right? I don't take bullshit. From *anyone.*"

. He was staring at her, completely discombobulated and at an utter loss for words, then the girl shot him one last glare and stomped away.

What the actual hell? When had he ever walked over anyone in school, let alone the entire student population?

This day was just turning out to be one great train wreck. He couldn't wait to just get home and drown himself in a book.

•   •   •

As it turned out, Asa couldn't go home just yet. The detention imposed upon him was staying after school and helping put the library back in order.

Having an unparalleled love for books, however, made this task seem rather welcoming than exhausting. For once, he found himself being thankful that people normally assumed the worst of him; it came with the popularity. Because he was sure nobody knew he was actually a

11

bookworm; he was dead certain it wouldn't have even occurred to them that he knew how to read.

To them, he was just the airhead with a pretty face and a nice body whose saving grace was his athletic abilities.

"Hi." He heard a familiar voice say from near the librarian's desk. "I want to fill out a form for my library card? Can I..." Then he heard the sound of ruffling paper and pen scribbling across it. "Thanks."

Stepping out from around the shelf that housed the non-fiction works, where he was stacking the books in alphabetical order, Asa saw the girl who'd run into him earlier today.

She was sitting by one of the library tables, hastily filling out details on the library's pale green form. Her hair fell around her shoulders in wavy locks, the deep chestnut colour complimenting her hazel eyes.

He must have been standing there too long because she then lifted her head and looked at his way. Instantly, her shoulders dropped and a groan left her mouth.

It amused Asa, really. He didn't expect her to fall at his feet or to be mesmerised with him at first glance—he knew most girls had more self-respect than that—but the way she just seemed to dislike him with such vehemence intrigued him. Especially for someone he hadn't crossed paths with before.

"What are you doing in a library?" she asked him. "Not here for some payback because someone actually had the guts to stand up to you, are you?"

He frowned. "What the hell are you talking about?"

She gave him a roll of her eyes. "Please." She scoffed lightly. "I know your type. Popular boy with the school at his feet, breaking hearts left and right because he thinks girls are toys."

Asa didn't correct her. What was he to do? Drag her along with him as he went about his day and force her to stay by his side just to show her how wrong she was? This shouldn't bother him anyway. It came with being at the top of the social hierarchy. This was typically what anybody assumed of him, and it was okay.

12

It had to be okay. He could brush it off and learn to live with it, right?

"But you didn't answer my question," she pointed out. "Why are you here in the library?" She cocked her head to the side curiously before a horrified expression settled on her face. "Oh my God, please don't tell me you use this room as one of your quickie spots!" She sounded so full of disgust that Asa actually debated between feeling offended or laughing out loud. "You don't make out with people in libraries, it's just wrong—"

"Calm the heck down," he muttered, rolling his eyes. "I'm just here on detention."

She visibly relaxed, but that look of disapproval in her eyes didn't go away. Asa wanted it to go away. He didn't like disapproval.

"Either way I was right." She shrugged, getting out of her seat and walking to the librarian to hand her form over. Miss Garcia shot the girl a warning look and told her to keep her voice down. Asa watched as the girl's cheeks grew pink.

"Right about what?" he asked once she came back to the table to collect her bag and pen.

"You being in the library for no good," she said, slipping on the strap of her bag on one shoulder. "I mean, what do testosterone-filled jocks like you know about books anyway?" She sniffed and tilted her chin up, daring him to say something. Then she walked out of the library with a triumphant face when he didn't.

Because what could Asa have said, really? She'd painted such a picture of him in her head already. And she'd called him a jock. *A jock.* That was stereotyping at its finest right there.

But Asa had spent so much—*too much*—to get to where he was now. He'd dragged himself from out of the mud and up to the top to earn the goddamn respect he knew he deserved, but here was someone he just met, throwing it all away like it was nothing.

Like Asa was nothing.

13

But Asa knew what it had been like to be nothing for so, so long. And he didn't want to feel that way ever again.

He decided he was going to change her mind. It didn't matter how he did it or how long it took, he was going to do it. Asa would get the girl, whose name he didn't yet know, to see him in a different light.

And if there was anything Asa loved as much as books and swimming, it was the chase. The challenge.

Maybe his grandfather's words about his rashness should have occurred to him then. It should've served as a warning. He'd always told Asa that he'd have to end up sleeping in the bed he made.

But Asa's heart was already in the task he'd set out for himself and there was no taking it back now. Asa's impulsiveness and his need to just be seen was his own catalyst.

And nothing was going to be the same again.

04.
The Hazel-Eyed Girl

When Asa stepped into the living room, his mother gasped when her eyes fell on him, the smile instantly dropping from her face.

"*Qué pasó?!*" She rushed to him with a horrified expression, her tender hands holding his face as she took in the bruises and the cuts on him.

"*Es nada*, Ma," he mumbled, gently prying her hands away.

"It's not nothing!" she exclaimed, her dark eyes shining with fury. "Was it that Hunter boy again? I must do something! This is becoming crazy—"

"*Déjalo.*" He sighed, cutting her off, as he dropped his bag on the couch and sat down with a sigh.

"You're always asking us to let it be." She frowned, looking about ready to storm out of the house with a baseball bat in search for Hunter.

Asa chuckled softly. "That's because I can take care of myself, Ma." He smiled. "It's not like before. I can hit back now. In fact, you should've seen his face—" then he grinned devilishly "—it was worse than mine."

"Not making me feel better," she muttered grudgingly. Her eyes, however, softened as she came closer to him and inspected his face again. "Does it hurt?" she asked gently.

Not as much as seeing the terrified look in the eyes of the bullied girl, he wanted to say. But he didn't. Instead, he shook his head. "Not the face, just the stomach. Goddamn *puta*, he head-butted—ow!" Asa rubbed his forearm that his mother had just slapped sharply.

"Language!" she snapped, eyes flashing. "What have I said about language? Not in this house, not around your parents!"

Asa's cheeks flushed in humility, scratching the back of his head. "Sorry Ma," he mumbled. "It just slipped. Hunter's just a pain in the a— butt. In the back, neck. Just wherever, you know."

His mother cracked a smile, shaking her head fondly, as she watched her son. "Get cleaned up then. Made some of your favourite *pozole rojo*."

Asa's eyes lit up, his stomach acting on reflex at the mention of his mother's impeccable cooking as it growled. Both he and his mum dissolved into fits of laughter at the sound.

"I'll be down in a few minutes," he said as he got up from the couch. "Don't finish it all yourself." He smirked, knowing she had an appetite bigger than him and his father's combined.

"Just go, Asa." She sighed exasperatedly.

But he saw the affectionate smile on her face as she turned away.

•   •   •

Asa found the hazel-eyed girl in his AP English Literature class the next day, during third period. But he didn't approach her until the bell had rung and the class let out.

He should've turned around and just walked out, but he found his feet carrying him towards her desk, where she was packing away her things. He wondered if her eyes would hold that same smudge of disapproval when she sees him.

He hoped not.

"Look at what the cat dragged in." He grinned as he stopped right in front of her desk.

16

She groaned at the recognition of his voice before lifting her head up to glare at him. "If I throw you a bone, will you go away?" she asked him scathingly, the corners of her mouth turned down.

Would he? He didn't think so. But he wondered if his behaviour was indeed comparable to that of a dog. But here he was, wagging his tail in hopes that she'd get rid of that disapproval, that she'd see him as an obedient golden retriever than a rabid stray.

He felt pathetic for a moment there, maybe ashamed even. He was weak, wasn't he? He didn't want to be weak. He'd been *that* before, and it hadn't done him any good. And yet, he still stood there in front of the hazel-eyed girl.

"Probably not," he replied, making himself grin and play off the words casually.

"Right." She snorted. "Because guys like you don't know how to take no from a girl. What's wrong? Blow to your ego?"

"Girls don't really say no," he muttered thoughtfully. Of course, Asa had made out. A lot. With many girls. He didn't think they were weak because of it, though. He knew they'd just been looking for a good time, the same thing as he had. It didn't put him above those girls; didn't create the notion that his ego needed to be inflated each time he came in physical contact with one. And that was why the girls that came to him probably chose him—because he didn't trash them for it.

But, like everything else about Asa, the hazel-eyed girl misinterpreted this, too.

"Wow, you're so full of it." She laughed incredulously, her head shaking in mild disgust.

This one was going to be hard to crack, he thought. But when had he ever backed down from a fight?

"How did you survive in this school so many years with this guy around?" She turned to ask her friend (Asa assumed) who was sitting at the desk next to her.

The other girl looked startled, not expecting to be dragged into the middle of their argument.

17

"We've never really interacted, you know," the girl eventually said, her voice even and steady, not carrying a single trace of her startled reaction earlier.

"Lucky you," hazel-eyed replied. "Why can't luck be on my side for once?"

The other girl didn't reply and just looked away uneasily.

"Are the three of you planning on staying here the whole day?" Mr. Edward's voice cut off any further arguing. "My class has been over for some time now. Get to your fourth period classes. Go along now."

The other girl slid out of her chair soundlessly, as if she'd never even been there, and walked out of the class. Hazel-eyed, on the other hand, stared Asa down for a good few minutes, which only caused him to widen his smile before she gave up and walked away, too.

Asa was just about to move away when his eyes caught something sticking out from the pocket underneath the desks. He reached for it, pulling out a hardcover spiral book, with a plain, dark-blue texture.

He grinned. Now he had another excuse to approach hazel-eyed.

Fingers gingerly trailing down the edge of the book, he opened it. *Carmen West.*

The name was written on the front page in an elegant calligraphic style. *Carmen*, he tested it out on his head. He didn't know what to feel about the name. Somehow, it didn't suit hazel-eyed and he felt a flicker of disappointment, as odd as it was.

Not that it mattered now; he had something of hers. And she'd have to converse with him somehow. Asa's lips curved into a wicked grin at the thought.

"Carmen," he murmured to himself, feeling the syllables roll off his tongue in a gentle manner. "Carmen." He smiled.

He could get used to that name.

05.

A Broken Mind

Carmen watched Asa while she nibbled on her grilled cheese-and-ham sandwich during lunch. She didn't know why she found it hard to look away while he sat there with a bunch of other guys and girls. Maybe it was his good looks, or the way he kept shaking his left knee when he got uneasy or bored. Maybe it was the way his nose was slightly crooked, a consequence of being in one too many fights.

She didn't know, but she just couldn't look away.

Carmen realised her eyes kept marvelling at the golden hue of his skin. It was the kind of tan girls went to the beach for but could never get to their heart's satisfaction. And then there were those long eyelashes—eyelashes that she couldn't help but feel were simply wasted on a boy. It didn't look so wasted on Asa, though—not in Carmen's eyes, at least.

Her eyes swept over his slanting cheekbones, landed on his eyes that reminded Carmen of the coffee she sipped at night when things got too loud in her head. And her gaze travelled upwards, watching as his bruised knuckles from a recent brawl ran through his dark cinnamon hair.

Her fingers throbbed. She needed to draw something. She needed to sketch. To fill in another page of her journal. Maybe it'll be a coffee stain this time. Maybe grounded cinnamon blending into the sand, the way Asa's hair fell across his forehead. She just needed to get it out, before shades of brown and golden were all that occupied her mind.

19

Carmen reached into her shoulder bag, her fingers feeling around for that familiar smooth but hard texture of her art journal. When her hand came up empty, she tore her gaze away from trying to memorise what it looked like when the sunlight shone on Asa's eyes as it streamed through the canteen windows.

She placed the bag on her lap, opening it wide and peering inside for her journal. The movements of her hand turned frantic when her eyes didn't spot the book right away. Abruptly standing up and almost knocking back her chair, she pushed away her lunch tray and took off down the hall, ignoring the calls behind her.

She needed that journal. She needed it to breathe. To find some quiet.

She was so used to screaming in those pages, so used to yelling and shouting and throwing her emotions in a hellish tantrum through wild splashes of colours, mundane sketches and just nonsense doodling.

It was part of her; it carried her heart and her soul and the broken shards of her dreams and fragments of an old life.

Carmen wasn't Carmen without it.

Panic bubbled in her gut as she ran back into the empty classroom where she'd had AP Literature. Her lungs inflated, ready to release the breath of immense relief, but when she crouched down to check under her desk and found it empty, her chest constricted itself blocking her breathing.

It wasn't there. The realisation pounded through Carmen with each frantic beat of her heart. It wasn't there. It wasn't there. It wasn't there.

Thud. Thud. Thud.

It wasn't there.

She shut her eyes, as if blocking her sight would keep away the pain, and rested her head against the edge of the desk.

If her art journal fell into the wrong hands, they'd see no sense in it and label her crazy.

20

And if it fell into the right hands, in possession of someone who could understand it and hear her strangled screams through every dent and stroke and curve on those pages…

Well, they'd still label her crazy too.

And Carmen would rather have someone think she's insane out of misunderstanding than out from the knowledge that her mind was truly broken.

06.
Art Journal

Asa had a spring in his steps as he walked out of his last class for the day.

Time to meet Carmen.

The name sounded so foreign even when he said it in his head. Like it didn't belong there, not with him. It was just so out-of-sorts.

Carmen. Carmen.

Asa was driving himself crazy, that was for sure.

"Asa," Hunter greeted with that usual disdain in his voice as Asa walked past him.

"Asshole," Asa greeted back, not even sparing him a glance.

"You know…" Hunter's voice was right behind him, falling into step beside Asa deliberately. "You seem pretty chipper today," he remarked, that typical sneer ever-present in his tone. "What? Mum said she'd make you tacos once you got home?"

Oh, lovely. The stereotypical Mexican jokes now. Hunter's ability to sink lower and lower never ceased to amaze Asa.

"I don't even like tacos, you prick." Asa threw him a dirty look.

His reply seemed to only earn a smirk from Hunter. "Right," he drawled with the same old vicious glint in his eyes. "I forgot. You need to feel like one of us, to pretend you belong."

Asa froze, his back going rigid as the words found their way into his skin and crawled up his bones, leaving their imprint on his insides. Just like those words always did. Like a seal had stamped across his heart, his head and on everything that made him Asa.

And he hated it—absolutely hated it—that Hunter knew his way around him, that he knew which buttons to push, which bandage to rip open, and which wound to pour more salt on.

What Asa hated even more, however, was that he always let the poison in. And it sat there inside him, brewing in the pits of his stomach until it slipped into his bloodstream and flowed throughout his entire being.

He just wanted to stop letting Hunter win. To stop letting the part of this world that Hunter represented win.

Asa felt Hunter step closer, put a hand on his shoulder and dig his nails into the flesh. It had no effect on Asa, the pain just fading away and giving into the simmering of his blood in his veins.

And then he heard Hunter's voice next, quietly saying into his ear with so much loathing and disgust, "You'll never belong here, Asa. Not with us."

The hand on his shoulder tightened for a split second, trying to hurt him further—as if physical pain was still necessary after the cruel utterance of those words—and then it fell away and Hunter walked past him, knocking into his shoulder on purpose.

Asa could feel the blood pounding in his ears, his breath faltering, as he let the words build a home inside his head. As he let the words poison him yet again.

Because Asa knew, despite all his efforts and tears and pain, he was still an outsider.

And as long as he was an outsider, there was no finish line for him. There was no end in his efforts to prove himself to others.

He would always be under at least one scrutinising eye, and he'd have to prove their mindset regarding him wrong, or he might rather not be there at all.

•　　•　　•

With the wheels in his head spinning endlessly, Asa walked out the school doors.

"What, no *hi* this time?"

Asa paused in his tracks at the sound of the familiar voice, shocked that she was the one initiating the conversation this time. He smirked as he turned to face *her*, the sag in his shoulders dissipating as he straightened himself into that confident and devil-may-care posture, remembering that he couldn't let his exhaustion show. Not here. Not anywhere that wasn't home. And especially not around somebody else who thought he didn't belong and to whom he needed to prove otherwise.

"Did I hurt your feelings, Carmen?" He cocked his head to the side, narrowing his eyes at her. "Thought I hadn't noticed you?"

At the mention of her name, the girl's eyes widened with surprise and she scoffed. "Wow." She shook her head in incredulity. "And here I thought you only mixed up the names of the girls you rolled around in the sheets with."

She stormed away, looking like he'd wounded her pride somehow, and there was nothing he could do but stare at her fading figure as she put more distance between them.

Confused as hell, he pulled out the journal from his backpack and flipped to the front page.

No, Asa hadn't misread anything. It still had the name *Carmen West* printed on the smooth off-white paper.

Had she been playing him, then? Maybe she was just caught off guard at the fact that he discovered her name—

"Oh, there it is!" a serene and steady female voice called out behind him. The vaguely familiar voice held such immense relief that Asa would've thought the girl had stumbled across her long-lost child or something along those lines. "My journal, hello! Asa!"

Asa whipped around, a bewildered expression on his face as his eyes landed on the girl that had been sitting next to hazel-eyed one during

24

AP Lit, the one that had looked startled when she was dragged into their argument. "What?" he asked, blinking like an idiot.

She reached for the book in his hands, and he reflexively took a few steps back. What the hell was she doing?

The girl frowned. "That's my journal," she said slowly as if talking to a person mentally incapable of understanding her words. "Please hand it over. Now."

"No, it isn't," he blurted out.

Her frown deepened. "Yes, it is," she replied, her stupid voice still as stupidly calm as ever. "My name's written on the first page."

"It says Carmen on the first page."

"Yeah."

"Carmen isn't your name."

She raised her eyebrows at his, looking truly surprised and worried for Asa's mental state. "I think I'd know what my name is," she said even slower, eyeing him wearily. "Pretty positive it's Carmen West. So, my journal. Give it to me, please."

Asa's mind was a goddamn jumbled mess.

"But—but she—that girl you were with—her name—"

"Is Willa Bonham," the girl who claimed to be Carmen said. "New student, joined only yesterday, I think." He thought of her wavy chestnut hair and hazel eyes. Yes, Willa seemed like a more appropriate fit. It sort of made sense, the way he had first thought the name "Carmen" didn't suit her.

Asa's eyes took in the girl standing in front of him. This one, on the other hand, he decided, definitely looked like a Carmen.

Pretty wasn't the first word that entered his mind—not the way it did when he had run into Willa.

Carmen had long, flowing black hair—or was it the darkest shade of indigo?—almost like the endless night sky. Definitely not his type; she was someone he would not call pretty without batting an eye.

Her eyes reminded him of the sky just before it was about to rain, grey clouds bleeding into the white ones. That stretch of calm before the sky poured down in torrents. Also not his type; not what he'd call pretty.

And then there was her name.

Carmen, Carmen, Carmen.

Definitely not his kind of name either.

"My journal," her voice floated to him and he bit the inside of his cheek. Even her voice wasn't his type; like the autumn breeze that played with his hair before letting it fall back, or the gust that brushed past his ears in a whisper and then faded away, it starts off claiming his attention before lingering in the air and vanishing into nothing.

Carmen was out-of-sorts, a mismatch of everything that fitted together. If that even made sense.

"Asa?" His name tumbled out her mouth in exasperation. "Asa, my journal. I want it."

"No," he said, acting on impulse. Like he always did.

"What do you mean no?"

"I—she's your friend, yes?" He tucked the journal into his backpack, watching her as her eyes followed his movements. "Willa? You're friends with her?" he urged.

"Yes." Her tone was cautious, as if preparing herself.

Something inside Asa coiled in discomfort but he disregarded it; he wanted this. "Help me," he found himself saying, his mouth working and forming the words before his mind could catch up to them. "Help me with—with Willa. I just, I need…"

What did he need? But Hunter's words were there, pumping in his veins along with his blood, blending with the oxygen in his lungs and fuelling the fire that was burning in the pits of his stomach.

Asa could belong. He *will* belong.

And so he steeled his resolve, fortifying it and leaving no room for empathy for this Carmen.

"Just help me out," he looked her in the eye, knowing she was his last way to get through to Willa, "and you'll have your journal. So what'd ya say, Carmen?" Asa cocked his head to the side. "Do we have a deal?"

07.
Blackmail

Carmen should say no, she really should. She knew that what Asa was doing was uncalled for, that he had no right whatsoever to be bargaining with her, using something so intimately personal as leverage.

But Carmen's sense of self-preservation far outweighed any sense of logic or reason in her.

He did not realize that he was holding her everything—her lifeline—in that backpack of his. He was dangling her chance to reclaim the very thing that held souvenirs of her soul in front of her face, and Carmen would sooner die than let the chance slip away.

"Fine," she bit out, her voice trembling with restrained fury. She wanted to say more, say something that would send a dagger through his heart, but there was that hint of desperation in his eyes she'd seen in others before.

Seen before on Asa himself. On the overweight girls, on the queer boys. The kind she'd seen in her own eyes a few times when she stared into the mirror. The desperation of someone struggling to just coexist with everybody else. The plea for them to just be. To fit in.

But why the hell would *Asa* want to fit in? The question nestled into the corner of Carmen's mind and stayed there, undoubtedly plotting to nag at her sometime later.

She decided Asa was a paradox; someone with sad eyes filled with the need to belong yet also someone with a happy face that sat on top of the school's food chain.

"Fine?" he repeated, sounding genuinely surprised. As if he honestly expected her to put up a fight. Carmen mentally scoffed at the thought; there was nothing she wouldn't do to keep herself sewn tightly at every single edge, and that art journal had all the means to undo her.

And that was too great a power she'd let anyone have over her. If Asa wanted her help with Willa, as he put it, then so be it.

Carmen, though quiet, was no means ignorant. She'd observed Willa as she interacted with Asa. And it didn't take her long to realise that the new girl actually enjoyed the banter. Willa seemed to like the attention Asa was giving her.

That fact alone helped curb whatever guilt Carmen felt, knowing that she wasn't shoving into Willa's face something the girl wanted absolutely nothing to do with.

"You'll actually do it?" Asa asked for clarification. "You're okay with—"

"No," she cut him off vehemently, her eyes piercing into his, making her feelings very clear. "I am far from okay with this. You do best to remember that."

Carmen watched his posture soften the very slightest bit, and she wondered if some part of him hated doing this. If there was guilt eating him up on the inside—even a smudge of it.

But his eyes remained resolute; determined. He had set his course and didn't seem to have any intention of budging.

She could sympathise with the probability that his reasoning stemmed from a troubled place inside his heart—but that, in no way, meant she had to be okay with this. With any of this.

Carmen didn't have to pay for Asa's battles. But she also wondered if perhaps this was the universe punishing her. If it was life's natural course of payback. Karma. Or whatever it was that they call it these days.

It was taking away what she held most dear, and dropping it into the mercy of a stranger.

Just like how she herself had ripped away what her family once held most dear.

08.
The War Inside His Head

Asa deserved the coldness that was radiating off Carmen in waves. He knew that. She shouldn't have to be a casualty in the war that was raging inside his head. And he was just an impulsive heartbeat away from handing her the journal, apologising profusely and then promising to never show her his face ever again. He couldn't do it, though. Not when she'd already caved in to his offer. *Except it wasn't an offer*, the nobler part of him realised, *it was an unfair bargain. A blackmail.*

He averted his eyes, feeling the shame crawl up the back of his neck.

But it's just a godforsaken art book, the rasher part of him argued, *not her heart on a silver platter.*

"Well?"

Asa's inner ramblings came to an abrupt stop when she spoke, snapping him out of his stupor and bringing him back to earth.

"What?" He blinked, staring at her. This was the second time she'd caught him off guard, and he was starting to feel like an idiot. She didn't shoot him a condescending glance, though, or make any gesture that implied she thought he was an idiot, too.

"I literally just met Willa," she went on. "Like, yesterday, when she joined. But, of course, you already know this. So tell me how I'm supposed to help you. It's not like she and I have become best friends or something."

"No?" Asa's lips twitched, as he peered at her. "Doesn't the loner girl and the new girl just automatically hit it off and become best pals?"

"You're implying that I'm a loner," Carmen stated rather than asked, her brows furrowing.

Now Asa felt truly uneasy. "Well, aren't you?" he muttered, scratching the back of his head.

"No."

He shifted on his feet, resisting the urge to bang his head against the concrete.

"Right." He nodded, swallowing the embarrassment. "Right, sorry. I just…I thought—"

"Exactly. You *thought*," she pointed out. "Not knew."

"Sorry," he squeaked out again.

Carmen just sighed, and her eyes turned weary. "You let me know when you've come up with a plan on how I'm supposed to help you." She stood there, just staring at him a little while longer before her feet began moving soundlessly, walking away.

She was just walking away? No fight? No lecture on how he was holding her property against her own head? Asa didn't know what he'd expected—not that he had any time for expectations since he'd just jumped at the notion of getting Carmen to help him—but it certainly wasn't this.

He wondered just then, how much exactly the art book or journal or whatever mattered to her, if she was just willing to succumb to his whims this way.

09.

Take The Ugliness Away

Asa forgot whose house it was. Forgot the name of the boy hosting the party. All he knew were the red, blue, and green disco lights, the loud beat of the music and Marlene's hands, lips and legs on him.

Marlene wasn't someone he'd classify as a friend, despite being someone Asa had known ever since sophomore year. Over the course of their acquaintanceship though, they'd blurred certain lines, both of them enjoying each other's presence in a way that they've become so comfortable with each other that they didn't need a label. And tonight was another one of those times, with Marlene's hands tangled in Asa's hair, and her lips leaving a trail of hungry kisses down his throat.

It felt good. This felt good. Asa felt good.

Marlene let out a moan, her hands wrapped around his biceps, legs straddling his lap, as he sat with his back pressed against the wall, his legs stretched out in front of him.

Her fingers trailed down his arms, her body writhing against his with want and pleasure. Asa could feel the way her breath was rushed and heavy, as if she couldn't get enough of him. As if she thought he was irresistible. As if she truly believed he was beautiful.

Because Marlene liked his skin, and his eyes, and his hair, and that slight Spanish accent in his voice he couldn't get rid of despite his attempts. Everything that was a testament of where Asa came from,

Marlene liked. So had that girl from last week, and all the girls before that. They liked the way he looked, the way he spoke. Just as he was.

They didn't tell him he didn't belong.

With them, his skin felt beautiful and Asa had a tendency to drown himself in whatever took the ugliness away.

• • •

"Ace."

Asa stopped stuffing books into his locker and looked up at Isla, in all her cherry-stained lips and platinum crowning glory.

"Asa," he corrected with a sigh although he knew it was only futile. Isla was never going to grow out of calling him Ace.

"So, Ace, I was thinking—"

"Whoa." Asa held up a finger. "You sure that isn't hazardous to your brain or something?"

Isla only shot him a flat look in response, choosing not to dignify the gibe with a reply.

"I'm kidding, I'm kidding," Asa mumbled as he went back to doing whatever he'd been doing. "You know I love hearing about your thoughts. Your dreams, goals, if your stars have finally aligned." He glanced at his best friend sideways and shot her a cheeky grin.

"Sometimes I forget how much of a dick you can be," Isla said, but there was amusement in her tone. "And then you remind me."

"Yet you still put up with me."

Isla only grunted in reply.

Asa had learnt a long time ago that Isla wasn't the kind to have heart-to-hearts, and she stuck to grunting or making some sort of noncommittal noise in the back of her throat whenever the conversation ventured into any possible emotional territory.

So it wasn't a surprise, really, when Isla didn't say something sentimental that ran along the lines of *Of course, I put up with you, Ace, you're my best friend.*

It didn't matter though; Asa knew her grunt was more out of affection than discomfort.

"So, what's up?" Asa asked instead.

"I…" Isla's voice trailed away as her eyes focused on something else in the distance, past Asa's shoulders. And then Isla's posture stiffened. "Donoghue incoming," she muttered under her breath, her icy blue eyes narrowing the slightest bit. As much as Isla didn't get into touchy-feely topics, she *was* quite protective of Asa.

Hunter approached, and Asa didn't need to turn his head around to know it was him. He could detect that cold, hateful aura radiating off Hunter anywhere, any time.

Asa held his breath, waiting for another snide comment that would send him spiralling down a road in search of self-validation. Down a road where he gave in to his impulsive nature far too easily just so that he could feel better. Feel assured.

To his surprise, nothing came.

No gibe, no bitter remark, not even a deliberate shove of the shoulder.

"Maybe hell finally froze over," Isla suggested once Hunter was out of earshot. Apparently, she'd been thinking the same thing as Asa.

"Nah, I think it's you," he said instead. "I have a feeling you intimidate him."

"I intimidate all the guys," she muttered bitterly, looking away and into nothingness.

Asa shut his locker and turned to face his friend. "Shut up," he said. "If they can't accept your being unafraid to voice your opinions, then that's their problem." He threw an arm around Isla's shoulders and began steering them towards the school doors. "You'll meet someone who's man enough to appreciate you, until then—"

"—keep slaying," she grinned, bumping her hips with his in a nonverbal *I-love-you.*

"Atta girl." He smiled back, because even if Asa's insides were in a constant state of turmoil, there was nothing he wouldn't do to give those he loved a sense of peace.

After all, Asa had an abundance of quiet in his head, and he didn't mind sharing it with those who disliked the noise.

10.
Muse To Her Artist

Carmen sat down next to Lottie, an old acquaintance, during lunch that day. The chatter in the canteen was loud, but for once she didn't mind. Instead, she found herself revelling in the noise—it helped curb the intensity of the loudness inside her. It was only when her surroundings were silent that it became too profound; unbearable. And without her art journal, without her means to scream, this was the only way. Making sure she was surrounded by noise.

"So I'm guessing that's the popular table?" Willa asked, her eyes focused on a table somewhere past Carmen's shoulders.

"Totally," Lottie nodded her head vigorously. "Hunter's one of the linebackers on the football team and—"

"Hunter's the brunet with the blue eyes, right?" Willa asked, taking a bite of what looked like a Nutella sandwich.

"Yup," another girl, with a single purple streak in her brown hair (who Carmen knew was called Joyce and had always wanted to interact more with), chimed in. "He's so drool-worthy." She sighed dreamily.

"He's a bully," Carmen spoke, her eyes fixed on Joyce, and ignoring the bitter taste those unplanned words left in her mouth.

Joyce blushed, feeling embarrassed, and shifted in her seat uncomfortably. "Well, yeah, I know *that*," she mumbled. "I was just saying…"

"Aren't they all bullies though?" Willa snorted, eyeing the large group of boys at the table with her nose wrinkled in mild disgust. "With inflated egos just because they have all the girls in this school falling at their feet?"

"You have a very disturbing perspective of the female population." Carmen frowned, narrowing her eyes at Willa. "How can you think so low of your own gender? It's been just a few days since you've joined, how would you know all the girls at this school have no shred of dignity?"

Willa laughed as if she couldn't believe Carmen was asking her that.

"Really." She scoffed. "Look at those guys! Hunter and Asa, and all the other athletes and popular ones." Willa gestured at them. "They've got the looks and the influence on the students. You can just tell by the way they walk that they're players, thinking they're too good to settle down on just one girl."

Carmen wanted to say something. Something vehement. Something sharp enough to pierce through the new girl's mind and remain there. Instead, she chose to take a few seconds to breathe. To remind herself that the world was a better place when she gave away a part of her heart rather than a piece of her mind.

"Warren's the quarterback and is actually having a steady relationship," Carmen said calmly, keeping her tone light and pleasant. "And Grady, captain of the basketball team, has been eyeing this girl from my Art class for a while now; I'm positive he genuinely likes her." She took a bite of her grilled cheese sandwich, swallowed and spoke to Willa again. "I don't know about the other guys, but I think it's safe to say not all of them play around."

Willa stared at her long and hard, but Carmen only lifted her chin into the air, with an unwavering smile on her face.

"Not all of them are players, then?" Willa asked, her tone suddenly taking a cautious tone.

Carmen smiled. "No, Asa isn't like that," she said.

Willa's cheeks grew pink. "I didn't ask about Asa!" she retorted, glaring at Carmen.

"You didn't have to." Joyce giggled. "The way you rant about him ever since your first day here is pretty obvious."

"That's because he pisses me off!"

"Why though?" Carmen tilted her head to the side, searching Willa's eyes with curiosity.

"I don't know!" she groaned, exasperated. "He just does. His stupid smirk and his stupid face. Ugh."

"Asa has a very nice face." Joyce smiled, letting out a sigh of longing.

"Amen to that, sister." Lottie grinned.

Carmen didn't say anything. What was there for her to say? Could she agree with them, when all they could say about Asa's face was nice?

To her, Asa's face was more than nice. More than pretty. More than...

Just *more*.

His cheekbones and jawline were something artists would spill blood over to sketch. Asa himself was a thousand shades of brown and gold. The boy with coffee eyes and rich, dark cinnamon hair that made Carmen's hands shake with the aching need to draw him.

Asa wasn't something as ordinary and simple as nice, no. He was the muse to the artist in Carmen. And she could sketch his face an infinite amount of times, but would never learn to perfect it.

II.
A Frozen Sun & A Broken Moon

Asa emerged out of the school's pool, his palms pressed flat against the floor of the swimming complex to haul himself up.

He loved it here. The building was cut off from the main school building, housing the huge indoor pool of Reichenbach High which meant a lot of privacy from the other students.

The water dripped down from his body, his swimming trunk clinging to him like a second layer of skin, as he grabbed a towel from a seat in the bleachers nearby.

Someone whistled from behind him.

"Sure you don't want to just walk out of here like that?" Isla's familiar voice said. "I'm pretty sure a lot of students would appreciate the sight."

"Don't you have anywhere better to be, Isla?" Asa asked, drying his face and hair with the towel to hide his smile.

"A million places, actually," she countered. "But you know how it is. When you're the queen, you've got to spare some of your precious time for the peasants too."

"Ha, ha, ha," Asa dragged out dryly, opening his drawstring sports bag and grabbing his set of dry clothes to take with him inside the locker room. "Seriously though," he said, meeting her eyes, "everything okay?"

She smiled, soft and warm, a rare sight. "I'm fine, relax. Just wanted to borrow your history book. Lord knows I don't pay the slightest attention in that class."

Asa chuckled, then nodded towards his backpack sitting next to his sports one. "You'll find it in there. It's the blue notebook."

Isla zipped open his bag, her hands slipping inside as she searched book after book.

"Hmm," she said, sounding curious. "What's this?" And then she pulled out a familiar-looking hardcover spiral book.

Carmen's art journal.

All humour drained away from Asa's face.

"Put that back." It came out sounding like an order, abrupt and firm.

Which was obviously the wrong way to address Isla because she only raised an eyebrow in defiance. "Was that an order?" She smirked. "You're telling me what to do, Ace?"

Asa pinched the bridge of his nose before staring at her right in the eye. "Isla. Seriously. Put that back. Right now."

Her eyes only gleamed in response, and her fingers flipped open the book, watching him challengingly. Her eyes dropped down to the journal. "Carmen West," she read, before looking up at him. "What is this?"

"For god's sake, put it back!" Asa snapped at her, his heart racing in fear of the tiny possibility of her going through it and his inability to snatch it away from her in case he tore any of the pages.

He may have taken it from Carmen and, he did hate himself for doing it, but he was not going to invade her privacy by actually going through the contents of her journal.

Isla flinched, clearly taken aback at his tone. Something like hurt flickered in her eyes before she masked it with anger.

"Fine, whatever." She scoffed, throwing the book onto the bleachers. It landed on Asa's towel. "What the heck do I care, anyway?"

41

She turned around, storming away with her head high and her eyes narrowed into slits.

Asa sighed deeply, wanting to go after her and offer some sort of explanation. Maybe apologise even. But he'd been around Isla long enough to know that she wasn't the type of person who wanted someone to chase after her when she was mad.

Deciding to just go and take the shower he'd been planning to before he was interrupted, he absentmindedly pulled at his towel. He felt something heavy slide along with it and realised too late that the journal was on top of it, the book falling to the floor with a slight thud and opening to a random page.

He bent down, hand outstretched in front of him, his fingers almost brushing the edge of the pages. Then his eyes caught the wild splash of colours inside and there was no longer looking away.

The page seemed to be separated into two by entirely different settings. The left half of the page was painted in thick strokes of black like the night sky, a bright moon . The moon was drawn with a crack right down its centre as if it was broken and hanging there in the dark sky, ready to fall down any second. No stars were there.

The right half of the page looked like it was supposed to represent the day time. Except it couldn't be. Because the sun wasn't yellow—no, it was an icy blue, with white smudges around the edges of the sun as if frost was slowly spreading over its surface. The sky and everything around it was blank, just white. And the flowers at the bottom were wilted, their petals all shrivelled up in their dying state.

But right in the centre of the page was a drawing of a girl. She had no eyes, no nose, and no mouth. Just a body, an empty face and long, endless black hair flowing to the side and blending into the night sky and the other contrasting against the bland white of the daytime.

One girl drawn against two settings, each half of her belonging to a different time. Scribbled in the bottom corner, in silver ink and in thin, cursive writing were the words:

And, like the moon,

42

she had a side of her
so dark, even the stars
couldn't shine on it.
She had a side of her
so cold, that even the sun
couldn't burn on it.
– A quote by Abigail J.

Asa was vaguely aware that his lips were ajar, if the slight dryness in his mouth was any indication.

The drawing was…

It was… It just *was*.

And it pulled on his heartstrings that he thought they were going to snap painfully.

Swallowing, he quickly reached that extra distance and grabbed the journal, snapping it shut like he never wanted to lay his eyes on it ever again. He felt…guilty. There was a prickling sensation along his arms and neck as if he'd just stumbled across something so profoundly intimate. Something he could never *un*-see. Something that wasn't meant for his eyes.

It was more than guilt, whatever this was that was twisting the insides of his stomach into a tight coil. He felt like he'd just dived into a pool with unbelievable depth. A depth he wasn't prepared for. And if he, Asa, was finding it difficult to swim above it and breathe again, he didn't even know if he could begin to understand the intensity of the person behind the painting, the person who was actually drowning.

That person being Carmen West.

12.
QUEEN BEE

Asa walked into school the next day, with Carmen's art journal tucked into his backpack as usual, and felt like he was carrying boulders on his back instead of books.

When he saw *her* down the hallway, standing in front of her locker and smiling to herself, he had to turn around and walk the other way.

He felt wrong. He felt like he'd walked in on her stripping off every single piece of clothing. Felt like he walked in on her shedding off her outer skin and flesh. That he'd stolen a glance at something sacred. He didn't know why he felt that way, but he just did.

Someone bumped into his shoulder as the person walked past him, and he immediately recognised the familiar blonde head of his best friend.

"Isla, come on—"

But she'd already turned into a corridor and was out of earshot.

"What'd you do?" Willa's voice reached his ears as she stopped in her tracks and stood next to him. "Told her that her eyeliner wasn't on point?" She snickered.

Asa furrowed his eyebrows, looking at Willa questioningly.

She rolled that pair of amazing hazel eyes. "Oh, come on." She grinned, and Asa would be an idiot to not acknowledge how goddamn attractive this girl was. "I know the type. Head cheerleader, queen bee of the school, and also an alpha bitch."

Asa nodded, his fondness for her softening his eyes. Not that Willa seemed to notice. "That's Isla Martin for you." He grinned. Because, God, yes, was Isla the queen bee. And an alpha bitch, too. But Asa wouldn't have her any other way. She put him in his place when he got out of hand and gave him a good piece of her mind when he needed to hear it.

And he knew how much she worked her ass off to maintain her position as head cheerleader and how she poured into every practice session with her squad. In Isla's eyes, cheerleading was just as prominent a sport as any other, and no one could convince her otherwise. The girl had a true passion for it.

"See? What'd I tell you?" Willa shook her head. "I've read enough of chick-lit to know how the whole social hierarchy thing works."

"I'm still not following," Asa said.

Willa sighed, glancing at him with an air of long-suffering patience. "The littlest thing about her appearance can set her off. She and then her posse—"

"Posse?" Asa cocked his head to the side.

Willa nodded, seeming utterly sure of herself. "Her little group of minions, you know? The self-deprecating girls that hang on the queen bee's every word and do whatever she says, following her around like lost puppies? Yeah, them. Tell one of them their eyebrows look out of shape and see them take off running faster than me when Nutella is around." She shuddered in disgust at the very thought. "So pathetic if you ask me."

Except I didn't ask you, Asa wanted to say but held his tongue. Something about the way Willa spoke of those girls rubbed him the wrong way. He didn't feel okay with it.

Wasn't she being a little too judgemental? Especially for someone who joined the school only recently?

"Isla takes pride in how she looks," he said instead. "She likes to always appear at the top of her game."

45

"Yeah? What game is that?" Willa scoffed. "How many guys she can score as another notch on her belt?"

Asa didn't really know what to say to that, because, yes, Willa was right. Isla liked the casual flings, the whole no-strings-attached ordeal. He couldn't see what the problem was with that.

"It's her life," he eventually said, for the first time wanting to get away rather than grasp at the chance to have a conversation with Willa. "And her body too, by the way."

She didn't respond to that and just eyed Asa carefully like she was trying to figure something out.

But he was no longer interested in continuing that particular conversation with her and found himself walking away without blinking an eye.

•　　•　　•

"Asa."

Asa's head jerked up at the unexpected voice, his startled eyes landing on grey ones.

No. Wait. Not grey. They were more silvery now that he looked at them properly.

Silvery. Was that even possible? He didn't know.

"Yeah, Car—?" he paused abruptly before he said her name, feeling weird for some reason, "—men?"

Her forehead crinkled ever so slightly as if trying to understand the subtle break in her name. She must be painting a hundred different theories in her head already.

"I was wondering whether you'd decided on how you want me to help you get the girl," she said, voice as smooth as her straight black hair. Or was it the darkest shade of indigo?

"Get the girl?" he repeated, like an idiot. Carmen always made him look like an idiot, he realised.

"Willa," she said.

46

It felt like a crime to describe everything that left Carmen's mouth as "said". It seemed too simple. Too ordinary. Too shallow for someone with as much depth as her.

Jesus, Asa thought wildly, *I am losing my freaking mind.*

"What about Willa?" He tried making out her eyes, the way those pools of silvery grey blended into the white of her eye. They looked almost like the first few dark clouds on a rainy day moving into the sky, floating in front of the white ones.

"I thought you liked her?" she said patiently. "And that you really needed my help to get to her."

Did he like Willa? Asa didn't think so. And he certainly didn't deem it necessary to explain to this girl why he was doing what he was doing. He didn't think he could put what he felt and why it drove him to do pretty stupid things into words.

Sometimes he'd think he was an absolute idiot for needing to wash away the disapproval in Willa's eyes. But then he'd see Hunter and remember the prick's words, resonating in his head. Over and over and over. Like a broken record.

Not just the words from a few days back and not just from Hunter but a lifetime worth of them—from a few classmates and even from strangers sometimes when he bumped into them at supermarkets or malls. Different people but with the same shunning message. It was always like that ever since Asa could remember. Freshman year, sophomore year, junior year. And this year too.

"Right," he muttered, face blank. "And you're just really eager to help me?"

"No." She narrowed those eyes of hers. "I'm just really eager to have my journal back."

Her journal. Broken moon. Starless sky. Frozen sun. Wilted flowers. Faceless girl.

Goddamn, her journal.

"Right," he said.

"So, what is it that you want?"

Asa stared at her, frustrated beyond belief that he couldn't figure her out. She was just... Ugh, she was just so *Carmen*. She spoke tonelessly, stared expressionlessly and walked aimlessly. It's like she just existed. Nothing more, nothing less. Asa wanted to throw a godforsaken book at her face. Maybe that'd get a reaction out of her. Some reaction. *Any* reaction.

When he didn't answer and just continued to stare at her like he was trying to peel away the skin from her head and peer inside to see how her mind worked, she sighed.

"You haven't come up with anything yet?" She tugged at the chain around her neck. "Fine. How about you join our table for lunch today?" she suggested. "Under the pretence that we're friends, you and I."

Asa merely nodded, wondering where his energy had run off to. This was supposed to be him coming up with the ideas, with ways to get to Willa. But somehow, he wasn't feeling the thrill of it all today.

He was somewhat grateful, though, that Carmen could pick up the pieces that he'd thrown around and string them together to form an actual plan while he seemed to be completely out of it.

"That sounds great," he mumbled, finding this situation suddenly too awkward and just wanting to bolt out of there. "See you at lunch then."

She just stood there, right in front of him, her head tilted to the side very slightly as if there was something she needed to look at past his flesh and bones. The way she stared at that space was like she was looking right through him and seeing things he didn't want her to see.

"Bye, Asa," she murmured, finally tearing her eyes away, and headed in the opposite direction.

13.

The Storm Inside

Carmen's mind was a wreck.

Her muscles, nerves—everything—seemed to be coiled into a tight ball in a never-ending worry. Worry that Asa might not be half the decent person she thought he was and that he might have crossed the line and gone through her art journal.

Yes, Carmen was quite the observer, and she liked noticing the little things about the people she came across. It helped her a lot in deducing someone's character even before she got to know them. That didn't mean she was a profiler, though. She could be so wrong about a person as well, she knew that. And right now, it was grinding away at her insides.

Before, she could confidently say she liked Asa. As a person, that is. That she'd noticed his random acts of kindness, his strong stance against bullying and his fearlessness that radiated off him when he defended the bullied. Now, she didn't seem so sure.

She didn't appreciate the position he'd put her in. She didn't like what he was doing to her—making her pace around her bedroom like a madwoman, wringing her hands together like she was her own lifeline because the one thing she truly depended on was in his hands. In Asa's hands. A boy who she'd watched and ached to draw, but also a stranger to her.

Carmen might have given into him, wanting to get back her journal irrespective of the cost, but that didn't mean she was going to let him take his sweet time with it. She would just have to speed up the process of Asa and Willa hitting it off together, leaving no room for him to have her journal any longer than necessary.

She could feel her senses buzzing with anticipation of lunch period today. Once it was over, she'd be that much closer to getting back the only thing capable of calming the storm that was causing havoc inside her.

• • •

Before Carmen knew it, lunch had rolled around.

"Everything okay?" Lottie asked as they waited in the queue.

"Perfect." Carmen beamed at her. "Why do you ask, Lottie?"

"Because you—you look…" Lottie furrowed her eyebrows and scrunched up her nose as she looked hard at Carmen, trying to put into words how she exactly looked right then. "I don't know. It's your cheeks, I think? They're flushed? Something like that. I don't know. Just—they just look alive. Like you're pleased about something."

A beat of silence passed, and something dawned on Lottie's face. Like it only just occurred to her what she had just said.

"What?!" Lottie muttered to herself, looking absolutely flabbergasted. And then her accusatory eyes snapped to Carmen's. "How do you keep doing that?"

Carmen blinked, taken aback. "Doing what?"

"That—that thing!" Lottie gestured wildly. "Always getting people to say the silliest things around you. Like saying stuff that literally runs through their head. It's crazy."

Carmen blushed right then. "I don't know." She tugged at her chain. There was another pause, and she decided to answer Lottie's previous question. "I'm pleased because things feel like they're falling into place today."

"What things?" Lottie inquired.

The boy in front of Carmen finished paying for his lunch, and she stepped up to the front of the line. She offered a warm smile at the lunch lady to which the grumpy woman didn't return.

"What do you want?" the lunch lady asked in a flat tone.

Carmen placed her order, the smile still on her face, unfazed by the woman's hostility.

"Just things, Lottie," she eventually said, after collecting her tray of food. "Just things."

14.
Petty Best Friends

As soon as Asa stepped into his history class, his eyes automatically landed on the seats at the rightmost corner of the room, where he and Isla usually sat together. But Isla, being the petty little shit that she was, had some other girl sitting next to her.

In Asa's chair.

Rolling his eyes at the inevitable scene his best friend was going to create, and bracing himself for it, he moved towards her. He knew she was aware that he'd approached their desk by the way her shoulders straightened, as if daring him to say anything.

"Hey, Isles." He grinned, knowing it'd only infuriate her further. "I might be wrong, but you seem to be avoiding me as of late."

"Joyce," Isla said rather loudly, keeping her eyes fixed on a healthy eating magazine in her hand while she addressed the girl seated next to her. "Can you turn that down, please? That cawing sound is getting on my nerves."

Asa spared a glance at who he concluded was Joyce—a girl with a purple streak on her dark hair —sitting uncomfortably next to Isla. The poor girl looked like she wanted the ground to swallow her whole.

For a fleeting second, he was reminded of Carmen when Willa had dragged her into one their arguments right after that AP Lit period. Despite her initial surprise, Carmen had remained calm and undisturbed by it. But this girl, Joyce, seemed to be scared out of her wits.

Asa guessed it wasn't just guys that Isla intimidated.

"Hey, Joyce." Asa flashed her one of his charming smiles and watched her cheeks grow a slight shade of pink. He knew what he was blessed with, and he wasn't shy about using it to his advantage. "Do you mind taking your usual seat?" He cocked his head to the side for further effect, feeling a pathetic but undeniable flash of confidence when it seemed to be doing the trick. "Isla's kind of my best pal. I usually sit with her."

There was a huge snort from next to Joyce.

"Oh yeah, totally," Isla said sarcastically, whipping her head towards Joyce. "Best pal, indeed. That is, if your definition of best pal is someone you are unnecessarily rude to without bothering to apologise to them for, like, forever."

"Shut up, drama queen." Asa snorted. "It literally happened just yesterday."

"And apparently being a best pal also means having the liberty to belittle your uncalled-for behaviour on the basis that, in this so-called best pal's words, it only happened yesterday," she went on, still looking at Joyce.

Joyce looked like she was ready to cry.

"Isla, you're scaring the girl." He sighed.

Isla's eyes narrowed, and she shoved her face into Joyce's. "Is he right?" she demanded. "Am I scaring you?"

Joyce began to nod—to which Isla glared—and quickly began shaking her head instead.

"Joyce, why don't you find another seat?" Asa suggested.

"You keep your ass glued to that chair, Missy."

Joyce swallowed, eyes dashing between Isla and Asa like she was about to faint, and then, without any warning, she shot out of her chair and hurried away while clutching her bag in a death grip.

Isla's mouth dropped open in utter disbelief, watching as Joyce seated herself on the furthest corner of the classroom, a good distance away from the two of them.

"Well, there goes my faith in humanity!" Isla scoffed, flipping her platinum blonde hair over her shoulder. She set her face into a stony expression, facing forward and not acknowledging Asa as he lowered himself into the vacant chair next to her.

"I wanted to apologise," he said.

"By scaring my friend away?"

"Come on, Isla. We both know she was no friend. You definitely forced the poor thing to sit next to you."

She snapped her head to the side, glaring at him with such venom in her eyes. "Is this your version of apologising?"

He grinned and threw an arm over her shoulders, pulling her head towards him and rubbing his knuckles against the top of her head.

"Let go of me. Ugh! Let me go, you asshole!" she growled, slapping at his arms and shoving him away with as much force as she could muster.

"What're the magic words?" he teased in a singsong voice.

"Your bloody eyes," she snapped, "once I've clawed them out!"

He clicked his tongue, messing her hair up further. "Wrong answer, *chica*."

"Do *not chica* me you filthy pig, I will castrate you and—"

"Settle down, class," the teacher's voice boomed as he walked in, ten minutes late. "That goes for you guys too, Mr. San Román and Miss Martin. You wanna have a wrestling match, hit the gym after school."

A few students snickered, but Asa only rolled his eyes good-naturedly and let go of Isla.

"Asshole," she hissed under her breath, fixing her hair and straightening all the stray strands, her long fingers slipping into the silvery mane.

Asa noticed it wasn't the darkest shade of indigo. Or as endless as the midnight sky. He shook the weird thought off.

"That still doesn't sound like you saying you forgive me," he said, keeping his voice low so that the teacher wouldn't hear them.

"Well, duh. '*I forgive you*' and '*asshole*' don't sound alike at all."

Asa sighed, losing the grin and turning serious. "I'm really sorry though." He nudged her side slightly. "I shouldn't have snapped. It's just…It wasn't mine, that journal. And I was scared something was going to happen to it. Sorry."

She stared at him, searching his face for a few seconds before losing her rigid posture and sighing in defeat. "Yeah, whatever," she mumbled. And then she nudged him back, a small smile on her face.

"Why did you have Carmen's journal, though?" she asked, disregarding history period like she always did.

"Long story." He grinned. Then turned serious again. "Wait. You know her?"

Isla nodded. "Carmen's that girl everybody knows exists, you know? The girl that's always just…*there*, I guess. She's pretty nice."

"Hmm." Asa thought of the eyes that reminded him of the calm before the storm, and hair that blended with the midnight sky. He saw flashes of a cracked moon, a frozen sun, and wilted flowers.

And Asa knew. Finally, he knew what he needed to do.

15.
Blondes & Brunettes

"So…" Asa shifted on his feet as he waited for Isla to gather her things. History period was over, and it was lunch now. "You spending lunch with me….or?"

"Why does it sound like you're wishing I be somewhere else instead?"

Asa rubbed the back of his neck, feeling uneasy. "I was just wondering." He shrugged. "Because you usually skip lunch to go and entertain yourself with whoever catches your eye."

Isla smirked. "Speaking of boy toys, I haven't gotten any recently."

Asa shot her a deadpan look. "Must be an existential crisis. My heart bleeds for you."

"Shut up, Ace." She laughed. "What's up, really?"

"Well." He paused. "There's this new girl—"

"Not the bitch who gives me the stink eye?"

"Um, her name's Willa?" he asked tentatively.

"Aye, that's the one." Isla groaned as they walked out of the classroom together. "What do you want with her now? If you ask me, I truly believe she's got some big diabolical plan against platinum blondes with blue eyes. "

"Seriously, Isles?"

"Don't you hear about serial killers and them having a type? You can never say these days."

"I have heard that one actually." Asa chuckled. "They kill people who have a strong resemblance to the actual target of their hatred."

"I wonder what my look-a-like did to her," Isla mused.

"Maybe you remind her of the person who killed her pet chihuahua."

Isla snorted loudly before breaking into laughter, and Asa joined in just as they stepped into the cafeteria.

"I'd ask you to string her along and crush her judgmental little heart, but we both know you're too much of a softie to do that."

Asa glanced sideways at Isla and saw the semi-hopeful look in her eyes.

He shook his head. "You know I can't do that." He smiled, but his voice was firm. "I *won't*."

She rolled her eyes in response. "Figured as much," she muttered darkly. "Just would love to see someone put her in her goddamn place."

Asa merely shrugged, feeling that small knot of uneasiness in his gut whenever Isla got this way. As much as he adored her and valued their friendship, he found it hard to digest how ruthless she could sometimes be.

"Come on." He tugged her towards the lunch queue just as he saw a flash of midnight hair leave the line and float towards a table.

Broken moon. Frozen sun. Dead flowers.

He cleared his throat, hoping it'd clear his head, too.

"The crowd's gone," he said, moving forward as if he didn't want to stand there and keep looking at the girl with hair the darkest shade of indigo and wonder what it'd feel like to run his fingers through those silky locks.

"I'm buying, by the way," he said as they reached the counter.

Isla rolled her eyes. "You already apologised in class, you don't have to —"

Asa shook his head, cutting her off. "This is kind of a plea, kind of an advance apology."

Her brows rose warningly. "What for?"

"Since I'm too good of a friend to ditch you, I thought you'd like to tag along."

"Tag along where?" Isla's voice was cautious like she didn't want to hear what he had to say.

"Oh, we're spending lunch with Willa today." Asa grinned, appearing as if he didn't know this would undoubtedly piss his best friend off.

"Oh, hell no." Isla took a step back.

"Woman up, Isles."

"You can watch me woman the fuck up when I stick the carrot from my salad so far up that brunette's —"

"Jesus, has anyone told you what a mouth you've got," he muttered.

"I. Am. Not. Goi—"

"Carmen will be there," he suggested hopefully.

Carmen, Carmen, Carmen. Goddammit, her name.

Isla threw him a dirty look. "What the heck am I supposed to do with her? She's—she's just Carmen."

Asa didn't know how anyone could call Carmen as *just Carmen*. God knew he couldn't. She was the girl with the midnight hair who had thunderclouds in her eyes and separated herself into the half that was too cold for the sun and the half too dark for the moon.

Carmen wasn't *just* Carmen.

Carmen was the girl who walked like she had no destination in mind, with her head tilted the slightest bit to the side as if she was perpetually questioning the purpose of everything her eyes landed on. She was the girl who spoke not to be heard but to listen, like that was her role in life. The girl who wore no expression and yet always had a smile on. Carmen wasn't just Carmen.

And it made Asa want to shake her 'till she spilled **whatever she kept bottled up inside**.

Asa decided he was losing his mind.

"Please?" He sighed.

"You know this would be so much better if you just liked Carmen instead of Willa." Isla huffed. "Carmen I think I could put up with."

Of course Carmen was easier for Isla to put up with—for anyone to put up with really. But there was something about her... something more than just that lack of judgement in her eyes whenever she looked at Asa. Something that appeared more like understanding—like empathy. As if she somehow saw past his award-winning grins.

That was somehow scarier than the possibility that he would never be able to rid Willa's mind off all the assumptions she had about him. So here Asa was, going along with the choice that *didn't* make his heart leap to his throat.

"Just pretend Willa doesn't exist then." He offered her his best smile, not bothering to correct the fact that he didn't like Willa *that* way. "Come on, you know you like seeing me happy."

"Never take no for an answer, do you?" Isla muttered, shoulders dropping in defeat.

"You know it." Asa winked.

Asa was impulsive. Asa was rash. Asa didn't know how to take no for an answer and couldn't back down from a challenge.

Maybe it'll end up breaking him. And maybe, just maybe, it'll end up making him.

•　　　•　　　•

With a very, very reluctant Isla by his side, Asa strode confidently towards the table where Carmen, Willa, a girl with dark hair and a purple — *good lord, was that Joyce from history?* — and another girl with earphones dangling around her neck, were seated.

59

"Mind if we join you?" Asa asked, feeling completely in his element, the words flowing from his mouth with ease.

Joyce looked like she wanted to cry again. The girl with the earphones seemed to find the ketchup stain on the table top interesting all of a sudden and Willa just full-on gaped at his arrival.

Carmen beamed at both Isla and Asa, her cheeks glowing faintly, and pulled out the empty chair next to her and patted it in a welcoming manner. Isla practically jumped at the offer, obviously not wanting to be stuck on the other vacant seat which was next to Willa.

"Why ask if you're going to join anyway?" Willa asked Asa, raising a brow at Isla who had just made herself comfortable next to Carmen.

"I'm sorry, were you speaking to me? I couldn't tell." Isla shot Willa a sickeningly sweet smile. Too sweet.

Oh boy, Asa couldn't help but think.

"I don't know." Willa smiled back with that same over-the-top sugary niceness. "Do you even have the required intellectual capacity to have a conversation with another human being, let alone *me*?"

Oh boy, oh boy, oh boy. Asa found himself shooting a glance at Carmen for unknown reasons. When he found her eyes already fixed on him, there was a jolt in his chest, right at the centre. Asa decided, again, that he was losing his mind.

"Considering you have an IQ the size of your boobs, I'd say even a squirrel can have a conversation with you," Isla shot back.

"Um..." Asa wanted to say something. He knew he was supposed to because they were starting to gain attention from amused students. But damn Carmen and the thunderclouds in her eyes. It felt like they were shooting lightning bolts into his eyes as they maintained the eye contact.

Willa's face went red at Isla's remark about her body, touching on a sensitive spot. "Where'd you rip off that comeback from? How-to-pull-off-not-being-a-total-blonde dot com?" She sneered, throwing Isla a meaningful look over her blonde mane for emphasis.

"You got a haircut." Carmen's voice snapped both Isla and Willa out of their heated exchange. Meanwhile, Asa was stuck, wondering why Carmen's voice reminded him of his cousin Mirabelle's violin recitals during the family bonfires—serene and out of this world.

Asa was losing his godforsaken mind.

"*What?*" all four girls asked in unison, wearing identical expressions of have-you-lost-your-goddamn-mind on their faces.

"Your hair." Carmen smiled, nodding at Isla. "It's different now. Did you get a new cut?"

To Asa's amazement, Isla's cold demeanour seemed to soften a bit. She actually looked mildly flattered at Carmen's observation.

"Yeah," Isla said. "You noticed?"

Carmen nodded, that same effortless smile ever-present on her face. "It falls around your face differently now, makes your cheekbones look more prominent."

Isla's eyes widened, and she turned her body around to completely face Carmen. "It does, doesn't it?!" She smiled widely, looking excited, and Asa felt himself relax now that her mind was diverted from having a spat with Willa. "I thought the exact same thing when getting the haircut. But nobody else mentioned it, so I figured it must not have made that much of a difference at all."

Carmen opened her mouth to respond, but Asa didn't catch what she said because Willa had turned to speak to him.

"You planning on standing there for the rest of lunch?" She smirked, raising her brows at him.

Asa grinned back, dragging out the chair next to her and flopping down on it. "If you wanted me seated next to you, you could've just said so," he said.

Willa scoffed. "Please. Take that ego down a few notches. I'd sooner inhale polluted air than willingly have you close to me."

"Whatever helps you sleep at night, *mi amor.*"

Asa felt Carmen's eyes flicker towards him at that and then look away.

"Is that my nickname now?" Willa's hazel eyes lit up with amusement. "*Mi amor*?" she said, testing it out on her tongue. Asa couldn't help but notice how plump her lips were, coated in a coral pink colour.

He shook his head. "You don't really say it that way, like they're two separate words," he told her. "It kind of just rolls off as one word, like *miyamor*. You know, just naturally."

"Well, duh, coming from you, it naturally would."

"True, my first language *is* Spanish."

"I wasn't talking about *that*." Willa smiled slyly. "I was thinking more along the lines of how many girls you have already addressed as *mi amor* for it to become second nature to you."

Asa rolled his eyes. "Shut up," he muttered, thinking of the girls he'd whispered sweet nothings to. The girls he'd made giggle with his terms of endearment. He'd just wanted to make them feel beautiful, the way they made him.

But those words never meant anything, did they? He'd always grinned at them when he called them something sweet; he'd always said it with that teasing edge to his voice so that they knew he wasn't leading them on. For a brief moment, Asa wondered what it'd be like to actually mean those sweet nothings. What would it feel like to call a girl *mi amor* like he truly meant it? Like she was the love of his life?

A laugh broke Asa out of his haze and his eyes landed on a laughing Isla—*a laughing Isla.* Because of Carmen. She'd made the ice queen laugh.

Warmth flooded him at the realisation that Carmen had gone out of her way to make Isla feel comfortable there, despite the clear hostility displayed by Willa. She didn't have to do that, Asa knew. Carmen didn't have to do anything but pave the path to Willa for him, and yet she'd gone that extra mile.

Her kindness was a rarity, he had to admit, especially given the common misconceptions surrounding Isla's character.

His mind went back to what he'd been thinking of all through history period, about what he knew should be the right thing to do. Right now, he was surer than ever.

As soon as school is over then, he made a mental note. Lord knew Carmen deserved some of her kindness back.

16.
An Act of Kindness

"I think you were being a little harsh on Isla today, Willa," Carmen said as the last bell rang, ending school for the day.

Willa snorted as she stuffed her books in her bag. But before she could say anything, Joyce spoke up.

"You must be the only girl in this school that thinks that," Joyce said, shaking her head disbelievingly. "You're too nice, that's what you are. Who the heck could like a bitchy queen bee like Isla?" She shuddered.

"I do," Carmen replied, smiling. "I like her."

Willa threw her an exasperated glance. "Maybe you dig the whole I-will-destroy-anyone-who-gets-in-the-way-of-claiming-my-man vibe, but as for me, I think she's delusional and needs a reality check."

Carmen slipped the strap of her bag over her shoulder, standing up. "What on earth are you on about?" She looked confused. "Who is Isla claiming as her man?"

Willa looked at Carmen like she'd just grown another head. "Well, isn't it obvious? Asa! She thinks she's entitled to him, or something like that—"

"No, no, no." Carmen shook her head, her long hair swishing against her back. "Isla sees Asa as her best friend and nothing else. It's easy to tell by just the way they interact. There's nothing intimate there— at least, not in a way that's not platonic."

"Oh, come on, Carmen." Joyce huffed. "It's the typical queen bee staking her claim on the hottie of the school. I mean, why else would she be so hostile towards Willa in the first place? Because she knows Willa's caught Asa's attention! She's insecure about it, just like any girl with zero self-esteem would be."

Carmen wanted to say she believed Isla had a pretty strong sense of dignity and self-esteem. She wanted to say that perhaps Isla was so cold towards Willa because this new girl had just barged into her territory and was marching about with an air of superiority after having already decided what kind of girl Isla was just because she was a pretty and popular cheerleader who liked her fair share of boys.

Carmen wanted to say that maybe the reason Isla couldn't stand Willa's presence was because the latter let the former be defined by all those things mentioned.

But Carmen was tired. And she was beginning to think that no amount of reasonable argument was going to change the mind-set of people like Willa. Sometimes society drilled the stereotypes so deep inside one's head that there was just no other way for them to look at life except through a narrow-minded perspective.

She would know. It was society and its delusional sense to exercise a "right" to slap a label on anyone, that tore apart her life into shreds.

Carmen simply offered the two of them a smile and a wave, then walked out of the classroom towards the main doors of the school.

She'd made a promise to value kindness above everything, and she'd honour that promise 'till her last breath. And so she defended Isla, because God knew the girl didn't deserve being looked down on like a piece of gum stuck under someone's shoes.

No. That was Carmen. She was the one who was supposed to be looked down on. She was the one who'd ruined lives with her own. And Lord knew Carmen didn't deserve even an atom of the kindness she'd shown to anyone throughout her entire life.

•   •   •

"Carmen."

She stopped in her tracks across the parking lot and looked over her shoulder to see Asa jogging towards her.

God, he made her name sound beautiful, like there was a constellation waiting to be named after her. Or maybe his voice was just music to her ears, and it beautified every word that left his mouth.

"Yes, Asa?" Did she make his name sound as beautiful too? Did the way "Asa" fall past her lips let him know she saw him in shades of brown and gold?

Asa slowed down his pace as he drew closer, casually slipping his hands into the pockets of his jeans. He kept his thumbs out, using them to draw circles on the dark grey material of his pants.

"Hey," he breathed. Why did he *breathe* out the word?

"Hi." She didn't know how she sounded.

"Um." He stopped. "I...I guess I wanted to say thanks?" He looked away, his thumbs now tapping on the outside of his pockets. His eyes landed back on hers. "Yeah, I wanted to say thanks."

Carmen could've smiled and said it was her pleasure. But it wasn't her pleasure, was it? She was doing it at the expense of her means to get her emotions out. At the expense of her stress reliever. Her journal.

"There's really no reason to thank me," she said. "I did it because I had to."

He looked away, and guilt flickered in his eyes.

"No, I wasn't thanking you for that." He sighed. "Not for having me over at your lunch table."

Carmen adjusted the strap of her bag on her shoulder. "Okay?" She tilted her head, her long hair slanting to the side with the motion. "What else did you want to thank me for, then?"

Asa smiled at her then. At Carmen.

Smiled.

How much that word simplified the gesture Asa offered her. No, his lips curved up at the very corners, lifting the slant in his cheekbones and pooling his eyes with warmth.

That's what warm coffee should look like, Carmen thought to herself.

"Thank you for sticking up for Isles," he said. "I think the whole school, except for me and her cheer squad, has a very strongly misguided idea of who she is."

Carmen's lips parted, and something close to a sigh but without any sound, left her mouth. Or maybe it was just that she couldn't breathe in that second. She was always nice to people; she always defended the misjudged. This was the first time someone watched from the side-lines and picked up on it. And definitely the first time that someone had thought she needed to be thanked for it.

It felt…oddly nice.

"Carmen?"

She wondered if he thought of stars when he called her name, because Carmen didn't know how else to explain the way her name felt special when he uttered it.

"Yes, Asa?"

"Say something?" He cracked a smile, but his eyes looked guarded.

And so she smiled, wiping away the hesitation in his eyes.

"Not the whole school, I hope," she said softly. "I'm certain there are a lot more who see past the label she's been given. They just haven't spoken up yet."

"You did," he said and God, did Carmen's breathing falter.

"Yes." She averted her gaze. "Yes, I did."

"Kind of puts you in a whole new light," he muttered, scratching the back of his head. "Or rather, I'm just seeing you properly only now."

Asa's words were paintings Carmen could never create; a drawing she'd never be able to sketch. And yet—yet, she knew in her bones his speech was that: art.

"I'm not following," she told him.

"Here." He pulled his hands out of his pocket, using one to hold his backpack, and the other to dig inside for something. Then he pulled out the one thing that made Carmen's hands throb and ache with longing.

He was holding her art journal.

And then he stretched his hand out towards her. The hand that was holding her journal.

"I don't understand…" Her voice was quiet, but she reached out and let her fingers touch the familiar hard cover of the book anyway. And God did it feel like coming home again.

Her heart thumping inside her chest, she gingerly curled her fingers around the spiral edge and tugged, wondering if it was a cruel joke and Asa was going to pull it away any moment now.

But he didn't. Asa didn't. And Carmen could breathe again.

"I should never have done that to you." He sounded ashamed, and Carmen let him feel that way. For now, at least. She needed to know he felt guilty. She needed him to know how much the journal meant to her and just what exactly it was that he'd taken away.

"No, you shouldn't have," she said to him. Her eyes dropped to the journal, her fingers caressing the surface like a long-lost friend. She lifted her gaze back to him. "But this…this I did not expect. I didn't…"

He cocked his head to the side, eyebrows furrowed as he waited for her to get the words out.

"This is a rare act of kindness," she finally murmured. "I can't tell you how much this means to me."

"Like I said, it didn't feel right. I couldn't go about leisurely chatting up Willa when your journal felt like a ton in my bag." He chuckled, easing the intense atmosphere that had suddenly wrapped around them. "And speaking about rare acts of kindness… you deserve it. Especially after Isla. Haven't you heard of the saying what goes around comes around?" He grinned, and it looked like the sun had shone down on Carmen.

"I *have* heard of that saying," she eventually said, her chest constricting. That saying had defined Carmen's life, and would continue to do so. Because the pain that she'd inflicted, the anguish that she'd sent around, was going to come back around to Carmen. It was going to make its way back to her.

68

And she was just floating, existing, until that wave hits and she's swept away in the tide forever.

17.

A Touch of Galaxies in Her Veins

When Asa's eyes followed Carmen's hands gripping her journal with the air of a mother finally finding her child, he felt guilt claw at his insides.

He'd been rash and had acted on an impulse when he had struck the unfair bargain with her. Now, seeing her reaction and realising how personal an object he'd been keeping away from her, he wished more than ever that he wouldn't always act in the heat of the moment and instead would actually think things through. His mother would be so ashamed of him.

"I *am* sorry, Carmen," he said again, resisting the urge to yank his own hair.

She met his eyes. They weren't exceptionally pretty like Willa's hazel ones, but, God, did they send lightning bolts his way.

"I know." She smiled softly. "Apology accepted."

He nodded, smiling back at her, before it began to grow awkward again.

"Right." He paused, looked away, and then back at her. "Guess I better get going now."

"Bye, Asa." She lifted her hand in a small wave and dropped it back to her side, but she didn't move right away. Just like last time, she looked at him wordlessly for a mere heartbeat longer—but what felt like an infinity to him.

An infinity in which he saw a pale moon with a crack splitting it into two, a magnificent sun frosting over and sucking the life out of flowers, a girl with no face but long, flowing hair as dark as the starless sky.

That was the thing about Carmen, he then realised. She was a masterpiece who made other masterpieces and went about with her head tilted to the side like she was painting a whole new one in her mind.

And Asa wanted to take a peek inside. To see if her mind was truly as beautiful as her name. *Carmen, Carmen, Carmen.* It must be so colourful inside her head, while his was just a blank slate.

"How are you leaving?" the words left his mouth as soon as a particularly strong gust of wind blew past them. It sent a shiver down his back, and he wondered if she was going to walk in this chilly weather.

"By foot," she answered, the ghost of a smile on her face. Asa had come to realise that Carmen's lips always carried a trace of a smile, like she was just waiting for the moment when she would have to offer one to somebody. As if it was her god-given duty to smile at any breathing, living thing that walked past her.

He wondered then, if more than being colourful, whether her mind was a very sad place instead. A place where none of the smiles she sent everyone's way existed.

It made him want to send a smile her way every second of every day.

"It's cold," he pointed out with a slight frown. And then she did something that set off a grenade in his chest.

She laughed.

No, wait. Not a grenade. Because the feeling in his chest was something light and fluttery, zooming through his chest and his heart in a single strike. Too light to be a grenade, he thought, but also too peaceful to be a firecracker.

He thought of a shooting star then. Just passing through the midnight sky in a single strike, leaving a trail of glowing light in its wake.

71

He wondered then, if Carmen had a touch of galaxies in her veins.

"My dad said something similar last week," she said, her voice carrying faint traces of her laughter. "I told him I preferred the walk."

"You like the cold?" he asked. Stupidly, of course. Like the idiot she always turned him into.

"I like the autumn leaves," and right as she said it, a leaf broke away from its branch, fluttering around in the breeze, and landed on her hair.

It was a sight. Carmen, with her head tipped backwards and her lips stretched into an open smile as her fingers fought to untangle the leaf from her hair.

God, it was a sight.

Asa was losing his mind.

"You collect it for your journal?" he guessed.

She managed to pull the leaf out and then shook her hair, the strands flying around her face before settling down into an endless black river against her back.

"Yeah." She grinned and it was like the full moon glowing down at Asa.

Carmen, he'd wanted to say right then, *how could you ever believe the moon was cracked?*

"I'll drive you home," he said, the words leaving his mouth as if he was reading off a script because God knew his mind was too occupied with dark nights and starless skies illuminated by a single full moon.

Surprise flickered in her eyes before her lips curved into a smile again. "You don't have to—"

"I'd like to." He shrugged, stuffing his hands back into his pockets. "You're not even wearing a sweater. And neither am I so I can't offer you any."

"You have a very nice *mind*, Asa," she told him then, and Asa thought he'd burn by the way she was looking at him.

"Nice mind?" he repeated.

72

Carmen nodded. "Always looking to help." She tilted her head and Asa's world tilted with it. "It makes me think you have a beautiful heart."

Asa laughed then, because every other logical response had flown right out of his mind. "Come on, we've been standing here way too long. We gotta get going."

But when he'd checked his watch, he realised that only seven minutes had passed since he'd walked out of school and caught up with Carmen.

Seven minutes. And yet Asa could swear he'd caught a glimpse of what infinity felt like.

18.
Everything She Touched

Asa knew he was supposed to focus on the road while driving, but he couldn't help himself from sneaking sideway glances at Carmen who was smiling to herself in the passenger seat.

"What are you smiling about?" he asked, unable to stop the question.

"This leaf is so beautiful." She sighed, twirling the dry, pale red leaf between her thumb and forefinger.

"It's a leaf," he said dryly.

She laughed then, and he could swear another shooting star was born somewhere in the cosmos. Or maybe it was just inside his chest, near his ribcage.

"But don't you…" she started to say then trailed off, her eyes narrowing slightly while the wheels in her head turned. "When you see this leaf, or any red leaf for that matter, doesn't it feel like—like they're blushing? As if the September wind whispered something so intimate to the trees that they blushed so hard and their leaves turned red?"

Carmen, he'd wanted to say. *Carmen, Carmen, Carmen.* As if saying her name would make him understand the way her mind worked any better. But Asa realised he couldn't stare at the leaf in her hand and see it as just a leaf anymore. And it made him wonder then if Carmen had a way of taking the galaxies in her veins and pouring it out through her fingertips, if she knew how she was giving something as mundane as a leaf an element of wonder just by her touch. Maybe everything Carmen looked at turned into a thing of magic. Or maybe, Asa decided yet again, he was just losing his mind.

"No," he eventually said. "No, I've never looked at it that way."

She turned her head towards him, offering him a crooked smile, and goddammit, he's supposed to be focusing on the road. "That's good." She nodded. "It must be nice, just seeing the world for what it is."

Carmen, he wanted to say. *Are you out of your mind?* Because now Asa didn't want to see the world for what it was anymore. Now Asa wanted to see it through Carmen's eyes. Maybe then, when he stared into the mirror, he'd see himself as magic too. Maybe then, if he touched his cheek, his skin would have that element of wonder too. Just like everything Carmen looked at, just like everything Carmen touched.

Silence had fallen over them, but Asa didn't know if he could describe it as either a comfortable or an uneasy one. Because she was undoubtedly thinking of something—no, not thinking—probably painting another theory inside her head, and he was battling against watching the road and watching her.

It was silent, yes, but with neither of them acknowledging it, there might as well have been noise.

"Why do you like her?"

The question startled Asa, who'd been lost in thought of her midnight hair and her ivory skin.

"What?" He blinked. God, was he an idiot?

"Willa." She smiled. "Why do you like her? If I'm right, you really don't even know her yet."

Did Asa like Willa? He didn't think so. But it would take a lifetime for him to explain.

"I just need—she's got the wrong idea of me." His fingers tapped the steering wheel, eyes scanning the vehicles in front of him as they stopped at a red light.

"There's always someone out there who's got the wrong idea of you." Her eyes narrowed a slight fraction. "Always going to be."

75

Asa clenched and unclenched his jaw. "And I'm okay if that someone was Hunter," he said. "Or Cromwell. Don't see why it's necessary to add another name to that list."

The silence grew thick and uncomfortable for him as he continued to feel Carmen's eyes burning holes into the side of his face, studying him. There was this sudden urge to just rip the steering wheel off and chuck it out through the windshield. Maybe then she'd look away.

"She *does* have a wrong impression of you," Carmen finally said, looking away as the light turned green and Asa started driving again.

"What makes you say that?" He shot her a glance and then turned his attention back to the road in front of him.

"At lunch the other day, Joyce and Lottie were giving her the rundown on the social hierarchy of our school."

"And?"

"I guess she had it in her head that you're a player." Carmen's voice was steady as it usually was, the words flowing from her mouth easily in a conversational manner. She spoke like she had all the time in the world to say whatever she wanted, and that fascinated him for some reason. "I kind of set the record straight."

He shot her another glance from the corner of his eyes. "Set the record straight?" he repeated, lips turning down into a small frown. "What do you mean?"

She turned to look at him then, pulling her eyes away from the road outside. "Well." She paused. "You aren't a player." It didn't sound like a question, and it didn't sound like she was uncertain about her words.

No, Carmen said that like she was stating the sky was blue and something in Asa's chest—right smack dab in the middle of it—lurched forward as if being hurled from a cliff.

"No?" he asked, his truck coming to a slow stop in front of her house. His eyes quickly scanned the address plate on her front gate, making sure he'd gotten the right house.

"No," she said. And then she pulled her eyebrows together, wrinkling the skin on her forehead. "What? You're not sure of yourself?"

"No, it's just…" he trailed off, eyes fixated on the floor of his truck, seeing but not caring about the empty gum packet he'd carelessly discarded there. "It's only natural for people to assume that of me, given my popularity and looks and whatnot."

But you didn't, he wanted to add. *Why didn't you, Carmen?*

"I don't much care for assumptions," she mumbled, averting her eyes when he looked up at her.

"It's not like the assumptions are too far off," Asa quickly said, feeling restless for some unknown reason. "I mean, I *do* fool around—"

"Why are you doing that?" she cut in sharply, her lips twisted into a scowl and eyes narrowed into slits.

Goddamn, he thought, *her eyes*. Gone was the calm; it was pure storm now.

"Doing what?" he asked, looking away because her stare was too intense. *Carmen* was too intense.

Again, not Asa's type. Asa liked simple.

"Justifying what they label you!" Her voice shook with the strong undercurrent of anger, her eyes wild and passionate and, in that moment—in that fleeting, almost insignificant moment—Asa saw the artist in her. He saw the girl who had the ability to soak and engrave the pages of her journal in colours and strokes of her emotions.

Or maybe, he just saw Carmen.

"I'm not justifying it," he muttered, feeling edgy now and just wanting to get the heck out of her presence. "It's just—it comes with getting to the top of the food chain. They see Isla, they see a slut. They see Hunter, they think he's the bad boy with a heart of gold." Asa scoffed, wondering if Hunter even had a warm, beating heart in him. "And they see me, and think I'm a player, a manwhore too egotistical to be settling down for one girl." He met her eyes, his ordinary brown drowning in her stormy ones.

"So what? You think it is okay for them to get away with it just because it's the norm?"

"Hey, I offered to drive you home out of kindness but I didn't sign up for a goddamn game of twenty questions," he snapped, shooting her a glare but to his immense bewilderment, Carmen just smiled with a tangible softness.

"Thank you for that, Asa." She opened the door of his truck and twisted her body around to get out of the vehicle. Adjusting the strap of her bag and smoothening down the front of her shirt, she met his eyes one last time. "Thanks again. I'll be out of your hair now."

Shooting him another small closed-lipped smile, she turned around and started walking away, never even bothering to close the passenger seat door.

Sighing in half exasperation and half amusement, Asa leant across the seats and closed the door himself.

In the process of doing so, however, his nose caught a whiff of something lingering in the air. It was subtle and yet strong in its own way. In fact, it reminded him of his kindergarten days when the teachers used to make him paint and he'd always ended up making an utter mess.

Paint. It struck him in full force and he wondered how he could've missed it. But it made sense now. Carmen was an artist and it appeared that she left traces of that fact wherever she went.

So, with faint traces of paint smell and the scent of his watermelon-flavoured gum mixing together as one in his truck, he began his drive back home.

19.
Beneath Skin & Bones

Carmen thought her shoulder blades had turned to dust and that her spine wasn't some heavy bone but a river of still water because of the way she felt so light and unburdened.

Her lips stretched into a wide smile as she strolled into school the next day, seeing past the bodies walking in front of her and instead replaying the scene in her head of when Asa had reached into his backpack and handed over her art journal.

How simply wonderful and terrifying was it that when she'd defended Isla, she'd believed she didn't deserve any of that kindness back? But hours later Asa had walked up to her and told her exactly the opposite. He'd said "What goes around comes around" like he was telling her that *It's okay, Carmen, I've seen you be kind to everybody and here's some of it for you.* As if he was blind to the chaos she carried in her bones.

Don't kid yourself, Carmen, she told herself. *Asa didn't notice your act of kindness because he was watching you from the sidelines; he only noticed because he happened to be right there that day in the cafeteria, and he must have felt obligated to do something in return.*

Carmen couldn't expect everyone to be like her, could she? Just because she admired his brave heart when he took a stance and stood up for the things he believed in, it didn't mean he did the same for the same reason. She observed, yes, but that didn't necessarily mean she was being observed in return.

But, for the most part, she felt relieved. She felt this unusual sort of bliss. Because Asa hadn't turned out to be a complete jerk. He actually had decency, and even though what he did must have been just a random act of niceness in his eyes, it was much more for her. She found herself wondering if perhaps Asa's heart was made of the same beautiful gold his skin was painted in.

For one painful moment, a vision of his eyes flashed before hers. Eyes that were anything but an ordinary brown. She recalled that hint of desperation, that look of exhaustion when he thought no one was looking. The kind of exhaustion that was more than just a need to sleep. It was the kind of exhaustion that ran bone-deep and drained one's soul dry.

Despite her better judgment, Carmen turned around and began walking towards the direction of the lockers. Who was she to question Asa's feelings for Willa? If he wanted her help, then she was willing to offer it. More so now than ever.

If his heart-warming act of doing the right thing at the cost of what he wanted were any indication of the kind of person he was, then Carmen would like to be there for the entirety of it. She'd like to be there to see what he looked like beneath his skin and bones.

20.
Only Human

Asa had one of his worksheets tucked between his lips as he tried—but failed—to clear away some of the clutter, in what looked like an aftermath of a hurricane, inside his locker.

"Hey," someone said from next to him. He knew the voice belonged to Carmen, but when he turned his head around to face her, his mouth fell open anyway, and some of the paper from his mess of a locker fluttered to the ground in a slight *whoosh*.

He was prepared for the midnight hair and the thundercloud eyes, but goddammit, Carmen was *grinning* at him. Her teeth was a little crooked, a testament of her being human and not celestial like she seemed to be, and that knocked the breath right out of him.

Carmen was only human. *Human. Human.*

"H-hi." He blinked, opening his mouth to ask her how she was doing, but how do you force yourself to speak when no arrangement of the twenty-six letters from the alphabet seemed adequate in her presence? She was all mismatched things that fit together. How do you ask someone like her how they are doing? Which *part* of her would he be asking?

Asa didn't know what the hell was wrong with him. Yes, he was a bookworm. Yes, he read. Yes, he was normally good with words. But Carmen seemed to have crushed his literacy then and there which was just the most ridiculous and amazing thing that he could've ever imagined happening to him. A week back, he wouldn't have even spared this girl a second glance if he'd brushed past her in the hallways. But the minute—no, the second—he'd picked up the art journal, that had changed. Because now that he knew of her existence, she was all that seemed to be there. As if Carmen West held the core of the entire universe within herself and commanded his soul to sing to her tune whenever she was within reach.

There he went again, with those damned words. As if every fibre of his being knew too well than to simplify her into mere words, so that every single thing she did was automatically turned into poetry. He might just top his AP Literature class with Carmen by his side; he might be able to create masterpieces instead of the same old mundane papers he wrote for assignments.

"Um, Asa?"

Her voice brought him back to the now, pulling him out of his thoughts gently, the way his mother sometimes tugged at his chin to turn his head her way. It was oddly comforting.

"I'm sorry." He smiled then dropped it. How was he supposed to act whilst talking to her? His hands felt useless too and were just hanging down by his sides. So, he tucked them into his pockets and leaned back slightly against his open locker, the edge of one of his squeezed books tickling the nape of his neck. "Were you saying something?"

"Well…" She bent down, picking the worksheet that had slipped from between his lips. He had totally forgotten about in the mere heartbeats that had passed since she called him. "I was wondering if, you know, you still wanted me playing matchmaker?" She smiled almost teasingly at the end, a playful glint in her otherwise guarded eyes, making warmth flood him at the fact that he, Asa, had somehow evoked that emotion in her.

But then her words registered, and Asa would've choked had he been consuming anything.

"*What?*"

She tilted her head to the side slightly, and he almost tilted his head too in order to match her gaze. But he caught himself just in time.

There was no need to make himself look like a bigger idiot than he already was in front of her.

"Sometimes painting gets boring," she said. *"Said" was too shallow a word for someone with her depth, though,* Asa thought. "I don't mind playing cupid once in a while."

"So, you've done this before?" he asked with wide, awestruck eyes. *Get a grip,* he chided himself, *she's just a girl, not the view of a sunrise from a hilltop.*

And God help him, she laughed. She *laughed.*

Carmen laughed and there was another shooting star brought to life in the empty spaces of his ribcage, making him feel a little more whole in that tiny moment.

"Of course not!" She shook her head, traces of the laughter left in her voice, her smile, and her eyes. "But, if we're being serious, I really appreciate you giving me back my journal. So…" She shrugged, looking away, her eyes sweeping slowly over every single student that were loitering towards her left, lingering on a couple giggling and towards a boy angrily typing into his phone, before landing back on Asa.

They said eyes were windows to the soul and the way Carmen looked at him made him believe in that without a doubt as she sent lightning bolts his way, piercing through his skin and bones and touching something buried way deeper into his being.

But Carmen was only human, he reminded himself. And one human cannot hold that much power: her actually being able to see him, *all* of him.

"I did that because it was the right thing to do," he said, softening his tone, "and because you stood up for Isla. I've told you that. And you don't need to repay me for something that doesn't deserve it."

"It's not a repayment, Asa." She sighed, and goddammit, was it *his* name that spilled out of her mouth just now? How did she string three letters together and make it sound like it was one of her masterpieces she painted in the dead of the night? "I… I just." She paused, and Asa waited. "I would like to surround myself with beautiful things. And when I say things, I also mean people." Asa didn't think he was breathing anymore. He couldn't be. It should be a sin to be able to breathe after being spoken to like that by Carmen West. "And like I said when you drove me back home, you have a very nice inside, and if you don't mind, I'd like to be in your presence from time to time."

Silence was all that was there even though the bell for the first period just rang. Asa knew that students were banging their lockers shut, some of them were still talking, others exchanging hurried goodbyes and promises to catch up with each other during lunch. Despite all the extra noise, he couldn't hear them.

"Um," Carmen started, her mouth opening and closing like it was fighting with itself. "That is, you know, if you don't mind. Is it because of the way I speak? Too weird? Lottie once told me I spoke too intensely, that it was sometimes creepy, so I'm sorry if it—"

"No," he said firmly, snapping out of his dazed state within a blink of an eye. "It's not creepy in the slightest bit. You wouldn't be Carmen if you didn't speak the way you do." There was that fire coursing through Asa's veins again, wanting to defend this girl he knew but didn't know, because he didn't want her to feel uncomfortable in her own skin.

But then his words registered, and when she beamed at him like he was a beacon of light, he felt his cheeks burn. He knew he could be too passionate in his speech. He wanted to slap himself for letting himself get carried away just now.

"I mean, you know," he straightened himself, clearing his throat, "it's cool."

"That's great." She smiled, her fingers reaching for the chain around her neck and tugging it. "So, see you in class, I guess."

He shut his locker and grabbed his bag off the floor, throwing it over his right shoulder as it hung crookedly against his back.

"Yeah, we have AP Lit in fifth period, right?"

"Actually, I was talking about third period. Mr Kyung's class."

Asa's brows pulled together as his lips parted slightly, his mind racing through any memory he may have of that particular class. "We have AP Cal together too?"

Something in Carmen's eyes seemed to deflate the slightest bit. Asa thought it was nothing but a trick of the lighting in the hallway. "Of course," she said, voice as steady as ever and the smile not wavering in the slightest. Maybe he'd only imagined it. "I sit behind you since we're assigned tables according to our last names."

Asa wanted to bang his head against concrete so badly.

"So there's no one with last names starting with T, U, and V?" He smiled uneasily, feeling like he'd committed some kind of a crime in secret and that it was only coming to light now.

Did he really sit in front of this girl and not have been aware of her presence?

"Guess not." She smiled at him one last time and then began walking away.

The warning bell rang, but it just fell past Asa's ears, not making its way through to him as he watched Carmen walk with that subtle tilt to her head as she let her eyes drink in anything and everything as if she was painting another masterpiece now. As if she was pouring all her heart into something else not another soul will ever know about.

21.
Black Rose

The thing about speaking to Carmen, Asa realised, was that while you were so caught up in every single world that fell past her lips and every single thing that she did, you wouldn't really realise what she was saying until she'd gone away and taken that spell she cast over you along with her.

And as Asa sat in his second period class, all he could think about was the words "matchmaker" and "cupid" and everything along those lines that unsettled him for some reason.

He didn't want Willa in that way, did he? Yes, he was a guy and no, he wasn't blind to her looks and maybe it could actually go that way with her but…*but what, Asa?*

But Willa didn't *see* him yet, not in the way he wanted—past the popularity, the easy smiles and that smooth attitude he had.

He just couldn't figure out why Willa stood out to him; why it was her approval he craved so much. He just hated it when people assumed the worst of him, but what he detested even more was the restless part of him that couldn't be at peace with it. The part of him that wanted to satisfy and prove people wrong whenever they thought of him in a certain way that he knew wasn't true. That part of him that was a little boy, craving for affection and appraisal, seemed to drive away every other sense of logic in him.

But Asa was also a very passionate person, his blood always burning with one emotion or another, setting his veins on fire. He was a heart-over-head guy whose impulses fuelled almost every decision and choice he made, often leading to the most exhilarating or devastating circumstances.

In Asa's world, there wasn't room for reasoning, for logic. So, who was he to question why it was that he was ready to go to any lengths to feel validated by the girl with curly chestnut hair and incredible hazel eyes?

• • •

"How'd I do?"

"Consistent as the July heat in this town," Wyatt said. "Thirteen seconds, exactly."

Asa nodded and hauled himself out of the pool, where he'd just finished practicing his backstrokes.

"Keep going and you might end up being titled national champion this year, too." He grinned. "Except, it'd be for the under nineteen category instead."

Asa chuckled, grabbing his towel off the bleachers and wiping his face with it. "I appreciate the encouragement, buddy, but maybe boost yourself, too? You could go and claim that title as much as I'm capable of it."

Wyatt waved a hand in the air nonchalantly. "Don't care which one of us gets it as long as it's someone from this school. *Our* school."

"Yeah, well, I don't think the others feel the same way," Asa muttered, referring to the other Reichenbach High swimmers.

Wyatt sighed and dropped down next to Asa, letting his towel sit around his neck as he clasped his hands together. "Look, man, for what it's worth, I still got your back just like I've had since day one." He pinched the bridge of his nose, shutting his eyes for a few seconds. "But I can't speak for the others, okay? They need to learn to put their differences aside and learn to accept that you're part of this school and more importantly, part of the swimming squad here. And one of the biggest assets we've got on top of that."

Asa cracked a smile and looked at his friend from the corner of his eyes, finding yet another reason to appreciate the day he'd run into this boy during freshman year while trying out for the school's swim team. He was more than just glad they'd hit it off instantly and maintained that friendship. "Are we going to hug and cry on each other's shoulders now?" Asa laughed. "It'd be an epic finish to that speech."

"Screw you, San Román." Wyatt grinned, shaking his head as he stood up and chucked the towel at Asa's face. "See ya around, ass hat."

"See ya," Asa called over his shoulder as he began walking to the changing rooms in the opposite direction, the ghost of a smile still lingering on his face.

• • •

"Asa!" Isla's hands grabbed his and began yanking him towards a corner in the hallway whilst all the other students began making their way to the cafeteria.

"Yeah, what is it?" he asked in a bewildered tone, letting her drag him away as she made their way through the crowd, knocking into bodies while he kept throwing out apologies like confetti.

"So," she breathed out heavily once they'd managed to weave their way through the throng of students and stop in a less crowded area. "You and Carmen are kind of buddy-buddy right?"

"Uh…"

"Right, so—"

"What? No, wait, I don't even—"

"Asa," she hissed, eyes narrowing beseechingly as she folded her arms across her stomach.

He sighed. "What do you want?"

"Well…" she started, dragging out the word as her eyes widened slightly. "She has an art journal, right?"

"I'm not pinching it for you if that's what you want."

She slapped his arm so hard, the sound echoed throughout that hallway. Asa winced, fighting the impulse to drag her away and dump her into the school's pool just to infuriate her. *Bitch*, he cursed in his head as he examined the reddening of his skin.

"What the hell do you think of me?" She glared at him, annoyed. "Now, *don't* interrupt and let me speak!" She pushed away strands of her hair from her face and fixed her eyes on him. "That means she's good at this drawing stuff, right?"

"I haven't really had a conversation with her regarding her talents, but I'll let you know once I do."

"For fuck's sake, will you be serious for a minute?" She sounded exasperated now.

"I *am* being serious!" he exclaimed, his stomach growling due to the hunger that had been building ever since he'd used the pool with Wyatt during the free period they had after AP Cal.

"Well, then, ask her or something because I need a favour!"

"Why can't you?"

"Because—" She came to an abrupt stop, her words catching in her throat as the fire that was burning so brightly in her eyes dimmed a little. She looked away with an air of dejection.

Asa stopped rubbing his forearm angrily and felt his posture soften as he looked at his best friend more carefully. "Because what, Isles?" he asked, softly now.

"Well, you know, she'd do it for you," Isla mumbled, her voice sounding scratchy, devoid of all that fire that made Isla who she was. "You're, well, *you*. And people don't really think that much of me. I mean, Carmen's nice, and all but she's also *good*, you know? The righteous kind of good, and I don't want her looking down on me."

"Isles, she's not going to look down on you," Asa told her softly. "It's Carmen."

"Well, I don't know her like you do!"

"I don't really know her, either," he admitted, his forehead creasing as he really thought about it. Did anyone know Carmen, really?

89

"Well then, all the more reason for you to ask her. Just say you want a portrait done for your parents' anniversary, and if she says she'll do it, I'll give you a photo of mum and dad and you can just hand it to her, yeah?"

"I think Carmen would know the difference between Caucasian and Hispanic parents, Isla," Asa said, his lips twitching as they fought off a smile.

Isla's eyes widened at that, and she cracked a smile of her own before she dissolved into full-blown laughter. Asa grinned that his best friend didn't seem so disheartened anymore.

"I'm such an idiot," Isla muttered once her laughter died down, and she let out a huge, deep sigh. Her eyes flickered up to Asa's. "She'd do it for me then?"

Asa thought of her, of Carmen; of the girl who wore a ghost of a smile on her face every second of every day as if it was her duty. He knew what her answer would be.

"Yeah, Isles." He smiled, throwing his arm over her shoulder and steering them towards the direction of the cafeteria. "Just ask her. Trust me. She doesn't bite."

And when they stepped into the eating area, Asa's eyes searched—for just that one tiny moment—for a girl with hair the darkest shade of indigo who created masterpieces in her head.

He found her then: sitting at one of the ordinary tables, in an ordinary school's ordinary canteen, with other ordinary students, like she belonged there. Like she— Carmen West— could fit in with the rest of them.

But that was the difference between him and her; she stood out like a single black rose in a garden full of red ones, whilst he stood out like a pesky weed.

22.

Willa Bonham

Willa was holding an ice pack to her left eye, the cold temporarily numbing the painful throb that had spread over her cheekbone. Despite keeping the pain at bay, she knew it was going to bruise and turn a nasty shade of purple in a few hours.

"Is it any better?" Carmen asked from behind her, the left corner of her bottom lip tucked under her teeth in slight worry as she watched Willa.

"Oh yeah, it's fantastic," Willa responded sarcastically. "I can totally feel the pain disappearing into thin air like I didn't just take a freaking hit to my face while playing basketball!"

"You mean *attempting* to play," Lottie cut in, stifling a laugh. "You were so horrible at it I wanted to cry."

"Sorry," Carmen muttered, looking away and fixing her eyes on some graffiti on one of the doors of the bathroom stalls.

Willa sighed and lowered her hand, ignoring Lottie as she placed the ice pack on the sink for a brief moment. "No, I'm sorry for snapping," she said, looking at Carmen through the mirror and offering a small, tired smile. "It wasn't your fault."

And just like that, the dejected look left Carmen's eyes and she smiled at Willa with everything in her.

Carmen did that a lot, Willa realised. She was always so ready to smile and ask people how their day went and always help and give away her heart to a complete stranger. Willa shook her head to herself, scoffing slightly under her breath. *People like Carmen didn't last in this world,* she thought to herself, looking at Carmen, *not with that naïve mentality and idealistic tendencies, which was a shame, really, because Carmen was nice.*

Willa was realistic. She knew the way the world worked, and you didn't survive in it by setting yourself on fire so that others could use your flames as a source of light.

"We ready to leave?" Lottie asked after a few more minutes had passed.

"Yeah, I'm just going to walk though," Carmen said.

Willa resisted the urge to roll her eyes at the thought that Carmen probably chose to walk in order to not pollute the air with car exhumes or something along those lines.

"It's chilly outside, man," Lottie told her, looking at Carmen like she was crazy.

Carmen cracked a smile for some odd reason. Willa could never understand how that girl's mind worked. She was always walking around with an infuriating smile on her face like nothing could possibly go wrong in the world.

"That's okay," she murmured, adjusting the strap of her bag on the shoulder. "I don't really mind all that much. You kind of forget about the cold when you take in everything else."

"Everything else?" Willa asked despite herself.

"It's autumn," Carmen replied, a twinkle in her eye. "It's perfect."

"It's *cold*," Willa grumbled, leaning away from the sink and grabbing her backpack off the marble surface as she did so. "You're crazy."

Carmen only smiled in response, shrugging slightly. "I think it's beautiful."

Lottie sighed and opened the door of the washroom as the three of them began piling out. "You think everything's beautiful, Carmen."

Carmen didn't say anything; Willa noticed her hand reached up to the chain around her neck, tugging on it slightly.

"Hey," Willa said lightly, nudging her elbow as they fell back a little from Lottie. "We should go bowling sometime. I haven't checked out the arcade yet. Or the mall. Or any of the diners." She laughed lightly.

Carmen's face seemed to brighten at that, and despite Willa believing that Carmen was living in an ignorant bubble, she felt a sort of warmth at seeing her face light up like that.

"Oh, yes, we should do that." Carmen nodded enthusiastically. "We should bring Asa along, he'd know—"

Willa choked on her spit and shot Carmen an incredulous look. "What on earth for?"

"Well, he'd be a better guide than me, and more fun too. Plus, I want this wonderful place to leave the best first impression on you when you take your first tour, and Asa would guarantee that."

"But why Asa?" Willa asked, bewildered.

"Well, for one, he's a friend," Carmen paused, "...sort of. And because he's full of energy and passion—don't you see it in the way he speaks? If he loves this town and any particular landmarks, he'll make you fall in love with it, too and that's exactly the kind of first impression we want for you." Carmen grinned, her long black hair almost shimmering under the dying rays of sunlight once they stepped out of the school building and stood in the parking lot.

"Yeah, I guess that does sound fun," Willa responded, grinning ever so slightly at the idea.

"Right then." Carmen clapped her hands, her chin grazing the top of her intertwined fingers. She offered a small, serene smile at Willa. "We'll do it this weekend? Or Friday after school?"

"Friday sounds about good," Willa said, anticipation already simmering in the pit of her stomach though she tried not showing it to Carmen.

Carmen would think it odd that she felt sort of thrilled at having Asa show her around whilst she'd been keen in making it abundantly clear that she couldn't stand the sight of him. Willa didn't want to come off as a hypocrite. But she knew whatever this was, whatever she felt that was starting to brew in her guts for Asa San Román, it had to stop. She had to extinguish that spark before it grew into flames. Boys like Asa weren't the kind to think with their hearts. Willa knew she was worth more than being just another notch on a manwhore's belt.

23.
A Crack in The Glass

Asa had just stepped out of the main doors of the school and was walking towards his beaten up red truck when he noticed a familiar chestnut head disappearing inside a sedan before the vehicle began driving away, leaving another familiar head—midnight black, this time—standing by herself on the sidewalk for a few seconds before she too began walking away.

"Carmen," he called out, his voice carrying over to her easily in the silence of their surroundings. She turned her head around though her feet kept moving forward, only coming to a gradual stop once those piercing eyes took in Asa's figure.

She blinked once, then smiled. "Asa." His name tumbled out of her mouth like she was taking her very first breath. "Hi."

"Hi," he said back, momentarily forgetting why he'd called her name. What was it that made him forget? What was it about making contact with those eyes of hers that sent static through his head, wiping out anything that had been there? What was it about looking into those mini universes of grey that turned his conscious mind into a blank slate?

But her eyes were thunderclouds and Asa should've known anybody could get their minds sent into overdrive when lightning struck.

"Asa?" She was smiling as if letting him know she was used to his tendency of zoning off into space whenever he was trying to have a conversation with her.

He cleared his throat. "Yeah, sorry. Just, um, spaced out for a moment there." He let out an awkward chuckle, bringing up one of his hands to massage the nape of his neck in a weak attempt to be doing something rather than looking like an utter fool.

"Okay." She nodded.

"Okay?" he pulled his brows together, perplexed.

"Okay, I understand you spaced out," she explained, smiling at him again.

"Right," he said. "Right, of course." His hand stilled in its movements against the back of his neck, and he brought it down slowly, curling his palm into a fist, wondering why the heck she was the easiest person to approach and yet the hardest to have an easy conversation with.

For God's sake, Willa was new and he felt more at ease with her than this girl in front of him who went to the same school as him for years, and heaven knew how many classes he'd shared with her without his knowledge.

"It's nice to talk to you, Asa, however short our conversations might be," she spoke so smoothly, her voice as calm and steady as ever. "But I do really need to start walking home. So…"

And within the blink of an eye, he remembered.

"AH, YES!" he exclaimed, forgetting the volume of his voice and startling Carmen as her eyes widened at his outburst. "Sorry, but I just remembered what I was going to say when you mentioned walking back. Uh, I can drive you back, actually. That's what I wanted to say. Or ask, rather. You know. If you wanted a ride. Like last time."

Asa balled up his other palm into a fist too, wanting more than ever to just slam his head against the concrete. Did he not know how to speak without sounding like a malfunctioning record player? Why did he keep punctuating every few words with an awkward pause?

"Don't you have detention though?"

Oh, lovely. She knew about that, too, Asa thought. "Finished serving my sentence last week. I'm a free man now."

Carmen cracked a smile at that last bit he said, and despite wanting to return the smile, he didn't know if he could because when he said Carmen cracked a smile—he meant that she *cracked* a smile. As in, her mouth was still pressed together in the right upper corner the way it would be in a closed-mouth smile, but her lips were slightly parted towards the leftmost corner of her mouth, giving a lopsided edge to her half-grin, the way a crack in a wall might look like: jagged, and crooked; starting from one end and widening as it stretched on.

Or maybe it wasn't like a crack in the wall at all, because that would mean comparing Carmen's half-smile half-grin to a flaw, and Asa couldn't find a bone in his body that believed what his eyes were drinking in was a flaw.

No, not a crack in the wall. It was a crack in the glass—a crack in the glass of a window, to be more specific. And it didn't matter if that window was bolted shut and had its opening screwed to the windowsill. It didn't matter if the window had tinted glass to keep the light out—that crack was still there and through that crack, light from the outside filtered in.

And that was what watching Carmen with that crooked, jagged smile felt like. Like a flaw had the power to illuminate, if you just let it.

As if Asa's skin could be the embodiment of the sun's rays if he let it. As if his eyes could be reflections of a sunset if he just let it. As if everything that made him Asa San Román could be beautiful if he just let it.

Asa wondered then, for a split second, if this was what interacting with Carmen would always be like. If, when he wanted to speak to her and hold a conversation that would have taken a maximum of two minutes with any other person, he would end up analysing every sigh that escaped her lips, every blink of her eyes, and every flutter of her eyelashes.

He wondered if he'd always come up to her with the intention of offering her a ride and end up catching another glimpse into infinity instead. And despite the constant awkwardness, maybe Asa didn't really mind it that much because even though he didn't know exactly how many minutes and how many seconds had passed since he called out her name, Asa knew all that he'd asked her so far was if she wanted a ride and he'd spent the rest of that time marvelling at everything and anything that was simply Carmen West.

24.

Everything Beautiful About You

Asa backed out of the school's parking lot, the engine of his truck coming to life with a soft groan despite its age, while Carmen sat comfortably on the passenger seat like it was made for her.

Carmen had a way of turning every place she graced her presence with into home, and it always amazed Asa. It made him want to look at her with awestruck eyes again, the way a kid would if they witnessed a shooting star for the very first time in their life.

Asa felt stupid—and giddy.

He'd just turned into the main road when he snuck another look at her from the corner of his eye and saw her open her journal on her lap. The corners of her mouth dropped into a frown at the red leaf taped right at the centre of a fresh page. He'd never seen those lips of hers tugged into something that wasn't a smile. It didn't feel right.

"What is it?" he asked, forcing his eyes to look bored and his tone to sound casual. Like he didn't really give a damn, as if he didn't want to stop the truck right then and there and turn her frown upside down.

"I'm good with paintbrushes and pencils, you know," she said. And Asa wanted to tell her he *did* know. He did know because he'd accidentally seen that entry into her art journal of the frozen sun and the broken moon.

"I figured," he replied, smiling slightly. "That's why you'd have an art journal, right? Instead of a diary? Because you're better with colours."

His eyes were fixed on the road ahead of him, but something told him Carmen was smiling. Maybe it was the half-smile-half-grin thing she was doing. Maybe it was illuminating his worn-out truck, flooding the rickety old thing with light in all its dented areas.

"Right. Better at colours than words," she emphasised.

"Is that the problem, then?" he asked, forehead creasing in thought. "You want to add some text into that too?"

She sat up straighter. Asa's eyes followed her movements as she kicked off her faded shoes and brought up her bare feet on the passenger seat. She turned her body sideways to face him as she leaned her side into the seat, tucking her kneecaps under her chin. She really *did* make it look like that seat was made for her; as if it was only her body that could fit there and hers alone.

"Yeah, usually I just add in some quotes I've stored in memory for these purposes, ones that seem fitting to what I draw or paint..." she trailed off for a moment, hugging her knees and clasping her hands in front of them, "but, I don't know. Nothing comes to mind for this one."

"The leaf, you mean?"

"The very leaf, Asa." She was grinning, he could tell without having to look.

"You don't mean to say you've held on to that same one from last time?" he asked in a bewildered tone. But when he had to stop at a red light, he cast his eyes over at the journal laid open on the dashboard and the leaf that was taped to it had that same tear down its left side like the one that had fallen in her hair the first time he drove her home.

"Of course it is," she replied as if it was the most obvious thing in the world. "There's a reason I took it with me and didn't just chuck it away." She let her hands fall apart and twisted her body towards the front again, sitting crossed-leg on the seat now. "I put the leaf in there as soon as I went home, but I've been trying to add some sort of quote or something and I can't think of what."

"Why are you telling me this?" Asa asked, genuinely confused and realising how odd a conversation this actually was. Were they actually talking about a goddamn leaf? What bothered him more was how amusing he truly found it— how simple and warm what she spoke about was while it contrasted immensely to her intensity and rawness.

"Um…" she trailed off before laughing lightly. "I actually don't know?" She scrunched her nose as if trying to figure out herself why she was telling him any of this. "I don't know. It's just nice to talk to you."

"Oh." Asa blushed, forcing his eyes to stay on the road, while his bottom lip curled into his mouth in an attempt to bite down the idiotic smile that threatened to take over his face.

"Yes, I've actually wanted to talk to you for some time now," she went on, and Asa felt his cheeks grow hotter. "Never really knew what to say though. I couldn't very well just walk up to you and ask you how your day was going."

He only grunted in reply, not daring to speak, not daring to stop biting down on his lip in case it stretched into a megawatt grin that he certainly didn't want her to see. Why the heck did he want to grin anyway? He felt so ridiculous right now. It was ridiculous to even feel this ridiculous.

Oh God, he thought and mentally kicked himself. He was losing it.

He just wanted her to stop talking about him—*of* him. Of how she had wanted to strike a conversation with him and she had been thinking about it for a while. It was twisting Asa's insides, and he didn't like the feeling.

There was something undeniably terrifying of knowing that Carmen West, the girl who had a touch of galaxies in her veins, had been paying him attention long before he was even aware of it. As if Asa was something to marvel at even though she was a masterpiece herself.

"I think I actually have a quote," he found himself saying, wanting to talk about something else. *Anything* else.

"Oh, what is it?" She leaned in a bit, a grin tugging at the corners of her lips just as Asa stopped the car in front of her house.

And he opened his mouth to respond because, yes, he did actually have this quote about how autumn was a season of the soul than of nature (or something along those lines, anyway) by Friedrich Nietzsche. But the moment he looked away from examining their surroundings as he instinctively did, and landed his gaze on her, the words got lost somewhere up in his throat.

Carmen was looking at him eagerly, her eyes alight with something he couldn't name. Her lips were stretched into a smile, offering him a tiny peek into her white but slightly crooked teeth. A strand of her hair had fallen in front of her face, the tip of it resting against the hollow where both her collarbones met.

Asa had decided a long time back that Carmen tended to make him lose his mind, so he wasn't too shocked when he lifted his hand and brushed that strand of hair away, his fingers sweeping over her collar and neck in a single stroke. Gently, hesitantly; the way an amateur artist would when holding a paintbrush for the first time.

"*No spring nor summer beauty hath such grace as I have seen in one autumnal face,*" he murmured, transfixed by everything that was Carmen. "It's by John Donne," he continued, losing himself a little more into the universe she held in her eyes, "From The Complete Poetry and Selected Prose. It was quite a good read."

"Why are you whispering?" Carmen asked and Asa thought someone had set him on fire by the way his cheeks and neck was burning.

"Because I'm an idiot." He sighed, leaning away and putting some distance between them. "You're welcome for the quote, by the way."

"Oh, yes, thank you." She smiled sheepishly. "It's a beautiful quote."

Asa grunted in reply, his mind racing and blood pounding in his ears.

"I'm not really surprised that it came from you," she said.

Asa swallowed, ignoring that jolt in his chest. What was worse was that she wasn't even hitting on him, or trying to be smooth. She was just being Carmen, and he only admired her more for it.

"Technically, it didn't come from me," he muttered, scratching the back of his head. "I was just repeating someone else's words…"

"…Who probably died centuries ago but your mind remembered it anyway."

"Well, not—"

"Asa, will you please just stop trying to twist everything beautiful about you into something else?" she asked tiredly. "Can you, for once, just take my compliment and be happy with it?"

Asa's mouth dropped open, and he could swear he was about to say something in response but, God help him, he couldn't. What would he say to that? What *could* he say to that?

"Good boy." She patted his cheek in the most patronising way possible, albeit with the cheekiest twinkle in her eyes, then she pushed the door open, jumping out of the truck barefoot. She grabbed her art journal from the dashboard and tucked it into her bag, before leaning down and grabbing her pair of worn-out shoes.

"See you tomorrow then, Asa." She told him over her shoulder as she walked towards the door of her house, her backpack clutched in one hand and shoes dangling in the other.

She hadn't bothered closing the passenger door this time, too, but Asa's mind was a million worlds away to care.

25.
Bruised Knuckles & Bleeding Hearts

"Hey, Dad?" Carmen asked through a mouthful of slightly burnt waffles, tapping her fork on the edge of her plate. "Can I—"

"Swallow first," her dad said with slight disgust. "Don't speak with food in your mouth like that."

She nodded vigorously in half apology and half agreement, before gulping down the food hastily and speaking again. "Tomorrow, after school, can I not come home directly? This girl who just transferred in our school recently needs a tour."

He raised a brow at Carmen. "And you volunteered? Being a tour guide doesn't sound like you."

Carmen only shrugged in response. "Somebody else will be the guide. I'm just tagging along, playing the role of the Good Samaritan and welcoming her here with open arms." She grinned at the end, making her father chuckle and shake his head.

"Yeah okay, go ahead and have fun," he replied, smiling slightly. "Don't stay out too late, though."

"Oh, don't worry, we'd probably be back by ten, maybe even before that."

"That's good." Her father nodded, staring at her for a while with fondness before his eyes recognised his wife's features in his daughter's and he had to turn away.

Carmen saw his heart break one more time, the way he had to avert his eyes from looking at his own daughter for a time longer than he could take. In that moment, all she wanted was to stop being a living reminder of the dead woman.

•   •   •

Carmen's bones felt a little heavy that morning as she walked through the school gates, across the grounds, and into the building. But it was more than exhaustion in her bones—it felt deeper, more intense somehow. Like she was tired in her soul.

"Carmen, wait!"

Her head turned towards her left, and her eyes landed on Isla who was walking up to her from behind with a tight smile on her face. Immediately, she pushed away her own exhaustion and lit her face up with a welcoming grin, hoping it'd take away the weariness that seemed to be present in the electric blue eyes of the other girl.

And it did. Carmen saw it in the way Isla's posture instantly softened and in the way her tight smile eased into a relaxed one instead.

Miraculously—even though Carmen didn't believe in miracles— she felt her own exhaustion lessen in its volume. As if lifting someone else's spirits with a mere smile had succeeded in nipping away at the heaviness in her bones and making her feel a bit lighter somehow.

"Hello, Isla." She resumed walking when the other girl had caught up with her. "How can I help you?"

"Um," Isla began. "Well, see…you're…"

Carmen placed her hand on Isla's, bringing them both to a gentle stop in their walk down the hallway. "I don't bite, Isla." She smiled softly. "What is it?"

"Why are you so nice to me?" Isla blurted, yanking her hand away from Carmen's hold and folding her arms across her chest, her body going into a defensive mode within the blink of an eye.

Carmen's lips parted, but she didn't know what to say right then. The hostility hardening Isla's eyes wasn't understandable, not to her. "I…I

105

don't know why that's upsetting you," Carmen said quietly, her hand reaching for the chain around her neck and tugging at it.

Isla closed her eyes for several seconds, breathing heavily, before she opened them and looked at her with slight weariness. "I've never been on the receiving end of it that much," she admitted, voice clipped and palms clenched into tight fists. Carmen winced at her balled-up palms, worrying about the nail indents that might be engraved into her skin later on.

Carmen thought of going home today and draw palms with crescent like indents on them. Maybe she'll paint a heart that was cracked into two halves the way her own heart was breaking now listening to Isla's words about not having others be nice to her.

"I'm sorry to hear that," she said honestly. "I don't understand people sometimes." Or maybe she did. Maybe Carmen *did* understand people and how twisted some minds could become. In a way, it was that what scared Carmen the most.

"It's all right." Isla shrugged, but Carmen didn't see the nonchalance conveyed by her shrug there. No, Carmen's eyes saw the weight of the world sitting atop Isla's shoulders. She saw the struggle when Isla lifted her shoulders as if it weighed too much, and the exhaustion when the girl dropped them back down, as if she was being pulled under yet again. Isla wasn't all right as she claimed to be.

Then again, how many times had Carmen smiled and said she was fine herself when in reality all she wanted to do was go to sleep forever?

Forever. It seemed like a nice idea. Eternity wrapped up in a pretty little bow until you pulled one end of the knot, and everything came undone.

"Actually, there was something I wanted to give my parents as a going away present," Isla explained, smiling slightly as her hard exterior softened up again and she let her arms fall to her side. "And I need your expertise for it."

Carmen blinked, surprise dawning over her features. "Are you switching schools?"

Isla just laughed, shaking her head. "Of course not, but I will be going away for college, and it's so far it might as well be on the other side of this world. I won't get to see them as often as I'd like, so I want to leave behind something for them to remember me by." She ran a hand through her blonde hair, shooting Carmen a quick smile. "Tell anyone I'm a sentimental fool, and I'll kill you in your sleep."

Laughter burst out of Carmen, causing a few sleepyheads to snap in their direction as if they were wondering which sane person could be so jovial this early in the morning.

"But what do you need me for?" Carmen inquired once her laughter had died, and the ghost of it lingered in her voice. "And we've only begun senior year. Why are you planning a gift this early?"

"Those two go hand in hand actually," Isla replied. "I have a bunch of photographs that I need you to sketch because I want a few alterations made to them—all in one single book like a photo album, you know? Something like your art journal."

Carmen's shoulders stiffened, and the smile dropped from her face instantly. "How do you know I have an art journal?" she asked, frowning slightly, a haze of vulnerability enveloping her and heightening her senses. *Had Asa told her?*, she asked herself.

Isla blinked, as if debating with herself, before slowly responding, "Well, I found it in Asa's bag the other day."

"Oh," the word tumbled out of Carmen's mouth with a breath of relief. So maybe Asa hadn't deliberately shown it to his best friend after all.

"Yeah, we even got into a stupid fight because of it." Isla laughed, waving her hand in the air dismissively. "I didn't know it was something private like an art journal. I just saw your name on it and was curious, but he just went batshit crazy." She chuckled at the end as if reliving the memory in her head.

107

Carmen's heart swelled, and she found her lips stretching ever so slightly into a soft smile. Asa was like the sun, she realised. He might not be always near her, but he still found a way to shower her with warmth.

"Oh," she said again, but this time it was because she couldn't put into words something she wanted to paint instead.

"Well, that's what I want, anyway. To make something like a photo album but with sketches of those photographs instead of the images itself. Think you could do it?" Isla bit down on one corner of her lip, looking hopeful.

"Sure." Carmen smiled. "It will take time though, especially since you said you have enough photographs to fill an entire album."

Isla nodded. "That's why I'm coming to you as early as now. So that by the time senior year's over and it's time to head over, it'll be ready."

"Of course, Isla. You'll have it by then."

The bell for first period rang, cutting through the air and reminding everyone their day is far from over.

"See you around, Carmen," Isla said, smiling and waving as she turned around and headed in the opposite direction. As she walked, Carmen noticed Isla's shoulders straighten, and her back become rigid. As if she was preparing herself for battle.

Carmen saw herself in Isla in the way she braced herself before stepping into the ring as if their minds were chanting *today you fight, today you fight, today you fight* in hopes that one day they could just go to sleep without bruised knuckles and bleeding hearts.

Carmen had walked in with heavy bones and a tired soul today. But seeing Isla's smile made her bones a little lighter and Asa's warmth burning her soul a little brighter.

Perhaps that was the key to unravelling Carmen: understanding that she wasn't just Carmen, but a combination of many different worlds. She was made up of the people she crossed paths with. The people who broke her, the people who fixed her, the people who left her, and the people who were nothing more but a memory from another lifetime. Even so, they lived on forever in Carmen's heart.

Because whether they'd done right by her or wronged her, she'd once loved them. Loved their bones, loved their hearts and loved their souls. And when Carmen West loved, there was no going back. She carried pieces of everyone inside her.

And she was yet to decide if they served as an anchor that brought her home, or just deadweight that dragged her down.

26.
Boys Don't Break

It was lunch time, and Asa had a startling realisation while walking with a spring in his steps towards the cafeteria: he was looking forward to it.

He hadn't had a class today that he shared with Carmen so far, and now would only be the time—the first time—that he'll get to see her.

It wasn't like in the sixth grade when he had a silly crush on Hayley Woods. He'd used to excuse himself from his third period a few minutes just before it ended every Tuesday under the pretence of using the washroom. He'd lounge by her home-econ class so as soon as the bell rung, he would be able to catch a glimpse of her as she left the room.

It wasn't like when he had first decided to go and tell the school's swim coach that he liked swimming and wanted the training to officially play the sport on behalf of the school. He'd look forward to doing it after school, mustering up the courage and walking up to coach's office before he lost all confidence and walked away.

It wasn't like when he'd found Carmen's art journal and mistaken it for Willa's. He'd thought it would be the perfect excuse to have a run-in with the chestnut-haired girl again. He had anticipated the opportunity then to take away that judgement she held in her hazel eyes whenever they landed on him.

No, looking forward to seeing Carmen was more than the silly hopes of a twelve-year-old to catch a glimpse of his crush. Looking forward to seeing Carmen was more than the excitement of an awestruck fourteen-year-old who wanted to participate in a sport he'd always loved. It was more than the desperation of a confused almost-eighteen-year-old who didn't know how to love himself and went searching for validation and approval in the hazel eyes of a new student/.

No, looking forward to seeing Carmen was realising that someone he hadn't even spared a glance until two weeks back had somehow found her way into his bloodstream and there was no flushing her out of his system.

And Asa couldn't remember the last time he'd felt so terrified.

•   •   •

"You look distracted," Isla commented as they paid for their lunch and began walking away to their usual table where their mutual friends would gather.

"Mmm," Asa responded, eyes landing on Carmen without having to search the area, as if his body and mind already knew where she was.

And there she was. —Carmen West in all her ethereal glory.

Asa didn't know when he'd stopped in his tracks, but there he stood, towards the leftmost centre of the cafeteria, consumed by the girl who reminded him of the full moon's glow when she smiled.

Carmen was leaning back in her chair, her torso fully pressed against it that Asa's heart skipped at the fear that she might topple it backwards. Her chin was tilted upwards as she listened to Lottie ramble on about something. One of her arms was wrapped around her own stomach, and the other was toying with that chain around her neck.

She was nodding every now and then, completely engrossed in whatever her friend was saying. Asa knew that was the most normal thing anyone would ever do but something about watching Carmen behave like she was just another ordinary being made his lips twitch and stretch across his face in a secretive manner.

Maybe his lips knew that there was a smile that should be reserved for Carmen and her alone.

111

Maybe his senses and his organs were already tuned into everything that was Carmen West and finding her was becoming as natural as breathing.

Asa didn't know. God, Asa didn't know, but all he was certain of was that his world was one thing before Carmen and something else entirely once he'd laid eyes on her midnight hair and thundercloud eyes.

Asa was seventeen years and eight months old, but today he realised his life would no longer be measured by the years but by lifetimes instead. He was lucky to say he lived two different lifetimes: the world before Carmen West and now the one with her.

There was a sharp jolt to his arm, snapping Asa out of his trance. He realised he'd been recently falling frequently under it. His eyes landed on an annoyed Isla who was shaking his arm rather violently.

"What are you doing?" he asked her in confusion.

She snorted, gaping at him incredulously. "Are you for real? I've been asking you that exact same thing this entire time. You've been standing here in the middle of nowhere like a madman!" She dropped his hand and threw her arms into the air. "What are *you* doing?"

His cheeks started to grow warm, and all he could was nothing but a shrug.

Isla raised her brows. "The heck is wrong with you?"

Asa was grinning because right then, he just realised he didn't have detention anymore which meant another car ride with Carmen after school. Another early autumn evening of witnessing Carmen make herself at home in the passenger seat of his beat-up red truck—right next to him. Another day of driving himself back home from hers with the smell of her paint..

"Oh, my God." Isla squeezed her eyes shut, pinching the bridge of her nose and taking deep breaths as if to restrain herself from punching Asa's face repeatedly. When she opened them back again, the anger there reminded Asa why the shade of blue in her eyes was called *electric* blue, and he wiped the grin off his face immediately, sobering up.

112

"I'm sorry," he quickly said. "You must be hungry and I've kept you waiting. Let's go."

Just as he started walking in the direction they were originally headed to, Isla's hand shot out and wrapped around his forearm, stopping him in his tracks.

He sighed. "Look, I really am sorry, you don't need to have a go at me—"

"Do you want to sit at *that* table?" Isla asked, cutting Asa off as she looked at him with a seriousness he'd never seen her wear before.

"With our friends?" He pretended to misunderstand, referring to the table they usually sat at. "Yeah, sure. We sit there almost every day."

It was Isla's turn to sigh now. She shot him a deadpan look. "You know which table I'm talking about," she told him in an accusatory tone. "Now, do you want to sit there or not?"

He shrugged, rubbing the back of his neck as his eyes once again fell on Carmen, and slowly drifted towards Willa. "I know you don't like it there, Isles."

"Yes, but with the way you're staring at that place just seconds ago like a wounded pup is making me consider it."

He ignored her gibe. "I don't know. What if they find it weird?" he asked, his free hand curling into a fist like it did whenever he felt lost like he did right now.

"You're Asa San Román," she reasoned. "They'd welcome you with open arms."

Asa smiled, but it didn't reach his eyes, because not even his best friend understood him.

Isla had called him Asa San Román and it was the same thing as if she had told him *But you're so hot, why should you ever feel self-conscious?* Like that part of him was enough to make him feel accepted. But he was more than that, wasn't he? Asa wanted to believe he was more.

"You should go." She gave him a gentle push in the direction of where Carmen sat.

"You're not coming?" he asked, voice tinged with slight panic.

"Asa." She smiled knowingly. "Come on. You don't need me. Plus, my presence there would only make the situation really bad. I can't keep depending on Carmen to keep myself in check around that troll."

"Her name is Willa." Asa sighed. "And she's not a troll. She's a girl like you. Like Carmen."

"Don't defend her," Isla snapped, eyes flashing. "She looks at me like I'm the gum under her shoe."

"I'm not defending her, Isles," Asa said patiently. "I'm just saying there's always two sides to every story. As is with everyone."

"What's that supposed to mean?" Asa could sense she was going into defensive mode now.

Asa pressed his lips together, unsure whether it was a good idea to tell her exactly what was on his mind. But he thought that maybe Isla needed to hear it, and she was most likely to react less drastically if she heard it from him.

"You're not exactly innocent either, Isles," he said gently. "You've said pretty cruel things to the people you dislike too. Heck, Isles, you've *done* harsh shit to people."

"They deserved it," she said coldly, her eyes glaring at Asa with pure venom. It hurt him somewhere deep in his chest to have his best friend look at him that way.

"Don't you think that's the same mentality Willa has?" he asked, softening his tone even further but not backing down. "Don't you also think that in her perspective *you* deserve it?"

There was a stretch of silence, and Asa noticed the way Isla curled her palms into fists, as if truly making an effort to not hit him right then.

"Isles, you're my best friend," he said quietly. "And I love you. I do. But maybe I've turned a blind eye to all the shit you've pulled and excused certain aspects of your behaviour out of blind loyalty. It needs to stop."

"You're taking her side? Really? That ogre?"

Asa was aware they were attracting a little attention now, considering that both he and Isla were standing in the same place without moving.

"I'm not taking sides, that's what I'm trying to tell you," he explained. "I've only ever stood on your side of the line all this time. But that day, when we all had lunch together, hearing both you and Willa interact, made me think about how that other side of the line looks like. About how our side looks from theirs."

"Well, congratulations. I'm so fucking happy that you have a conscience Asa," she snapped. "You can go ahead and join the rest of them with holier-than-thou attitudes. I never needed you anyway. Not the way *you* needed *me*."

Time froze for Asa right then. His heart stopped beating and his lungs ceased functioning as well.

"What?" he whispered.

"You can't even walk up to Carmen because you're so fucking afraid of how she'd look at you," she hissed, throwing daggers with her eyes and twisting them further into him with her words. "You wag your tail behind Willa like some pathetic lapdog, looking for affection and approval in a place where you're never going to find it.

"You're so fucking insecure and unsure of yourself you can't even see that it's Carmen you're falling for. But if you think for even a second you deserve her, then you're wrong." She jabbed his chest with her forefinger, stabbing him over and over again with the dagger he'd handed to her on a silver platter when he'd claimed her as his best friend to love and cherish with all his heart.

His heart that she was shredding to pieces mercilessly right this moment.

He realised that he did deserve this no matter how much it hurt. Because how many times had he allowed her to rip to shreds the dignity of other students who pissed her off? How many times had he just watched on the side and done absolutely *nothing* just because she was his best friend in the whole goddamn world?

"You cling to me because I make you feel good in your own skin. *You're* the one who's always needed me, Asa," she went on, not done with burning every single bridge of self-love he'd struggled to build over the years. Until there was nothing but the charred remains of it, ashes and smoke filling him up on the inside, choking him. Suffocating him. Constricting his lungs and burning his chest.

Until there was nothing left. Until he was nothing.

"Maybe in some twisted way in that mind of yours, I was an armour for whatever Hunter threw at you. Because you couldn't just be a guy and let go of his remarks."

Asa was a guy.

I am a guy, Asa thought. *I need to have thick skin. I am a guy. I shouldn't let harsh words build a home in my mind. I am a guy, and I'm supposed to be stronger. I am a guy, and guys don't break.*

"No, you had to be a crybaby about it," she spat. "Guess what, Asa? There are other people with issues and insecurities, so run along and find someone to play house with. Because I'm sick of being the one for you to lean on."

And then she walked away with her head held high and her shoulders straight, leaving his maimed and burnt heart lying on the dirty floors of the cafeteria.

As if his heart was always supposed to be walked over and trampled on.

27.
The Road to Self-Love

"Asa?" a familiar voice called softly from behind him, just as he was about to turn around.

Just then the bell also rang, the sound unforgiving to his ears just like how everything around Asa was right now. It sliced through the tensed air in the cafeteria, where everyone knew something had gone down between the two best friends but didn't exactly know what it was about.

If there was anything Asa could appreciate in all this, it was probably the fact that Isla had kept her voice down the entire time instead of yelling it all at the top of her lungs. That would have been humiliating.

But somehow, he thought it was worse that Isla had kept the volume of her voice in check, because that meant she'd been in control. She'd been in control of her tongue and she'd decided to rip him apart anyway. How much more if her anger had fully erupted?

"Asa."

It was Carmen's voice now. He turned around to face her, and everything else faded into nothing when his eyes met Carmen's.

She was looking at him—at *him*—like he was worth looking at, and for the first time, he questioned it. Maybe it was just his mind creating illusions. For all he knew, Carmen was probably just looking at him the way she'd look at anyone, and like Isla had said, his twisted mind was imagining it to mean something else.

His eyes registered Willa's figure standing next to Carmen, and he realised it was probably her who called out his name the first time. But she didn't have the power to break Asa out of his cloud of misery the way Carmen's voice did. Willa called his name the way it was supposed to be called, but Carmen called him like she was thinking about a new masterpiece she was going to paint.

Maybe Asa was imagining that as well. There was probably nothing extraordinary about the way his name fell past Carmen's lips. Maybe he was just looking for something in her that he wasn't going to get, that he didn't deserve.

He *felt* her take a step closer to him before he *saw* her do it, and that was the moment Asa knew he was in way over his head when it came to this girl with midnight hair.

"Asa," she said softly, and one of her hands came to rest on his cheek.

Asa's heart had stopped beating when Isla had spoken. His lungs had ceased to function, and he'd forgotten how to breathe. But Carmen's fingertips were grazing his cheek like she was touching a fragile work of art that belonged in a museum.

He could breathe again. That was what Carmen always did to him. She reminded him to take a step back before taking everything in. To breathe.

And if he wasn't careful, Asa could fall in love with her for it.

But Carmen was the girl with a touch of galaxies in her veins, who could turn everything she looked at and touched into magic. So who the hell was Asa to think he deserved to be on the receiving end of her attention let alone her kindness?

Hadn't Isla told him just minutes ago that Carmen was the one he didn't deserve?

Maybe that was why a part of him always went running after Willa, because deep inside, he knew the way she looked at him with disapproval and weariness was what he truly deserved.

If there was something he was worthy of, maybe it was that judgement. Maybe he was born to be condemned before given a fair trial, so what good was there in trying to fight it? So as much as he wanted to lean his face into Carmen's palm and get lost into the universe she held in her eyes, he pulled away, stepping back and ignoring the flash of hurt in those pools of silvery grey he'd grown fond of.

He turned to Willa instead, who was looking at him in weariness and concern. There was no judgement in her hazel eyes for now, but he knew—like the others did—it'd return later. It always did.

And that was okay. He needed to learn to accept that. People will always look down on him. He only needed to be a guy and just toughen up and live with it. He needed to have a thicker skin and learn his place. Because even if Isla's words were knives in his chest, they'd held an ounce of truth.

Maybe he was a coward, after all, just like she'd said. Maybe his issues with his identity and his skin held no significance and they were all in his head. A figment of his imagination. Something that had no place in the real world.

God, he was a mess. And he'd actually entertained the idea of letting Carmen nestle herself into his chaotic mind.

"Are you okay?" Willa asked and he knew instantly it was out of courtesy's sake. He was sure he didn't look okay.

But Carmen didn't ask him that. And without having to ask her why, Asa already knew it was because Carmen didn't have to. She didn't have to ask him if he was okay because she knew he wasn't.

"I'm perfect." He grinned, squaring his shoulders and dusting his shredded heart under the rug, away from prying eyes.

Willa smiled back, though hesitantly, like she could tell he was lying but didn't want to push him. And that was okay. Because guys didn't talk about their issues. Guys were tough. Guys needed to have a bulletproof armour for a skin. He needed to learn to not let the words penetrate his flesh and engrave themselves into his bones.

Goddammit, Asa wanted to scream. He wanted to scream his lungs off so hard so all of the poisonous words Isla had poured in his veins would go out and never flow though his system again. But guys don't scream. They're supposed to take the hits and blows and dust it off and get back up like not even a falling skyscraper could hurt them.

"Well, then, shall we head to class?" Willa suggested, smiling up at him genuinely for the first time ever. She must have decided to go easy on him today. "We have AP Lit now, don't we? All three of us?"

He felt Carmen's eyes on his face, burning through his flesh and probably seeing his raw and bleeding heart despite his attempts to cover it up. A part of him believed that with her, he could scream. Maybe with Carmen, he didn't need to wear the suit of armour.

But Asa would never know.

"Yeah," he replied to Willa, not looking in the direction of the other girl, and no longer having an appetite for lunch "Yeah, we're already running late, so let's get going."

•　　•　　•

The day wasn't rushing by as Asa wanted. It took its time, dragging out the minutes in an excruciatingly slow manner.

Asa had once heard someone say that time heals all wounds, but his cuts seemed to only grow wider and deeper as each hour passed, with his wandering mind taking pleasure in inflicting more self-torture by allowing salt to be poured on all his reopened wounds.

He'd honestly thought he was getting better—that maybe he was actually starting to be okay with himself, with where he came from, with who he was. He'd thought he was learning the art of loving oneself he'd so often hear people preach about. Asa could've sworn he was getting there.

But right now, he felt like he was back at square one. Like all his efforts, all his coaxing to himself and all the sweet nothings he'd whispered into his own skin was no longer significant. It no longer mattered because he'd been torn down to his very core. All those stitches and Band-Aids keeping his old wounds together had been ripped off his skin without warning. He now needed to stitch himself whole all over again.

Was this how it was like? Self-love?

Was it building up yourself brick by brick despite the cracks and the crevices and planting seeds in those dark places so that every time you cried, your tears will make flowers bloom and bring to life the parts you deemed ugly?

Was it watching someone who has stood by your side for so long take a sledgehammer and break down your walls of self-worth like it was just a house of cards built? Was it watching that same person violently pull your flowers out of those corners until there was no life there, and everything just remained dead?

Dead, dead, dead.

Asa didn't think he had anything left in him to give away to bring those flowers back to life. He no longer knew how else to light up those ugly parts, to fill up those cracks and crevices. To think that he had honestly believed that he'd reached that light at the end of the tunnel.

But he was a guy, and guys don't have cracks and crevices. No, they had abs and a killer smile and the ability to brush everything off.

At least, that's what they're supposed to be—what *he* was supposed to be.

•　　•　　•

Asa didn't see Isla for the rest of the day, but then again, he wasn't looking for her either. He considered himself lucky that he didn't have history that day. It was the one class he shared with her.

And as for Carmen, he avoided her rather successfully.

"Hey, Asa, wait up!" Willa called from behind as she picked up her pace to fall into step beside him.

"Hey," he muttered, throwing her a quick glance over his shoulder just as she reached him, wanting to just get home now that school was done.

"You all right?" she asked, pulling her brows together.

"Why wouldn't I be?"

121

"Because you were just on the receiving end of the Ice Queen's wrath earlier. I doubt anyone would be okay after that."

Asa clenched his jaw and stopped walking abruptly, causing Willa to stop as well. She looked up at him in surprise.

"Is this another attempt of yours to take a dig at her?" he asked with a stony face, feeling the last few threads of his patience come undone and dangle around aimlessly in the air.

"I'm just saying I've dealt with the likes of her before," she replied cautiously, apparently taking into account Asa's emotional state.

"Isla's done nothing to you so far," he snapped impatiently. "In fact, I don't get why the two of you are always at each other's throats."

"I didn't say it was Isla," Willa said through gritted teeth, growing more agitated by the second. "I've just had the misfortune of having someone like her in my life, and I know how badly the words that leave their mouths can sting." She narrowed her eyes at him and stepped forward. "Go on. Tell me I'm wrong. Tell me there wasn't some poor, unsuspecting, vulnerable girl that used to walk down these halls whom Isla had never done something horrible to."

Asa swallowed, averting his eyes because of the guilt he felt clawing at the walls of his mind. An itch he could never get rid of.

"The girl's name was Valerie," he found himself saying, recalling a certain sophomore who was at the receiving end of Isla's wrath one too many times. "She had to move away because she couldn't take it anymore."

"Yeah, I heard about that." Willa snorted and looked away into the distance, her eyes hardening and her mouth twisting into a scowl. "And that's exactly why I will always look at Isla like she's trash because in my eyes she can be nothing else, Asa."

Asa sighed, knowing this fight was a lost cause. "You don't think she can redeem herself, I get that. But I do see the good in her, Willa. That's where you and I don't see eye to eye."

Willa let out a low, hollow chuckle. "There's no good in her," she said, turning around to meet Asa's eyes again. "There can't be."

122

"Why do you say that?"

"Because I was a Valerie once," she whispered, her eyes fixated on the ground. "Back in my old school. The girl with braces and baby fat. I was that. And we had an ice queen there too." Willa ran a hand under her eyes angrily, looking back up at Asa with fire in her hazel eyes. "And I had to move away to this town. To this school. Just like how—I'm sure—that girl Valerie must have done as well, packing up her life and moving somewhere else too. But I will never be that girl again. So if that means condemning Isla before she's had a chance to have a go at me, or any other girl for that matter, then so be it. I don't care how it makes me look; I vowed to put myself first and that is never changing."

"But Willa." Asa pulled his brows together, his forehead crinkling as he stared at the girl. "You don't build yourself up by stepping on the shards of someone else's remains. That's not glory; you won't feel better about yourself by putting somebody else down."

Willa let out an aggravated noise, throwing her hands into the air in disbelief. "Are you deaf?" She was seething. "I basically just told you how my entire school life has been nothing but—"

Asa shook his head, cutting her off before she could ramble on. "I'm not talking about Isles." When he used that affectionate nickname for her, something twisted in his gut. "I was talking about me."

Willa blinked. All the frustration left her face, replaced by utter confusion. "I don't understand."

He offered her a small, sad smile. "When you first met me," he reminded her, "did I deserve that treatment? Honestly?"

"I—"

"I can understand where you're coming from," he went on, "and I can see that this is all nothing but a defence mechanism. Maybe in a twisted way, your hatred towards Isla holds justification. But Willa, you're so wrapped up in your loathing and all that anger that you don't see Isla's not the only one you're condemning. And if you can't see that, then you're no different than her. In fact, the two of you could hit it off better than

123

anyone else." With a small shake of his head, he turned away and proceeded to exit the school.

Maybe the road to self-love was paved with baby steps—and maybe, just maybe, one of those tiny steps was acknowledging that you were treated in a way you weren't supposed to be. Perhaps the bigger step would be letting that person know just like what Asa had done with Willa.

Perhaps Asa could be more, if he just freed his mind and body and soul from the shackles that he and he alone allowed people to imprison him with.

Perhaps.

28.
Just A Boy With Awestruck Eyes

Carmen's head snapped up and her eyes landed on him, as if her senses were aware of his presence before she herself was.

How was that even possible? It couldn't be considered normal for her to be so attuned to someone's state of being. It couldn't. It shouldn't.

It made her want to both run in the other direction when her eyes sought him out amongst a crowd, but also towards him. Towards Asa. Always *towards* Asa. She pushed herself off the tree she'd been leaning against as she waited for him to walk out of those school doors. He'd taken so long that she'd wondered if he had already left. But there he was now, his rich cinnamon hair glinting with a touch of copper gold-like as the setting sun's rays bounced off his messy strands. And then, as if the universe itself had commanded it, his eyes found hers.

Amongst the crowd in the parking lot, through the tiny gaps separating the several bodies walking between them, their eyes had met. Everything else ceased to exist.

Carmen felt her lips part and her nose inhale air, like that tiny moment before she'd start to say something. But words failed her. There was nothing she could have said, because right then, one of the clouds moved away, allowing the sun to shine a little brighter, its rays hitting Asa's eyes, rendering them into a degree too painfully beautiful to be put into words.

Carmen felt her lungs collapse into a heap inside her. What was breathing again? She was sure she'd perfected that particular art over the course of her life, but here was a boy with the sun's glow in his eyes who made her forget all that.

So, she did the one thing that would calm the hurricane in her ribcage, the one thing that reminded her to breathe again. She called his name.

"Asa." It left her mouth in an exhale, as if she'd finally managed to swim above the waves for much-needed air. Because that was what getting lost in Asa's eyes was like. It constricted your chest and ribs for there was no possible way to understand such raw beauty completely. It both rendered one immobile and yet, that very same beauty itself also served as a reminder to live, to breathe.

Breathe for another day, because if this one person alone could hold such wonder, then surely there must be so much more in this world to appreciate. Carmen would do anything to see it all.

He must've read her lips as she called his name, because he was beginning to walk in her direction.

He was walking towards her. Towards Carmen.

Asa was making his way to her, and Carmen wished, in that moment at least, that he'd learn to make his way to her in more than just the literal sense of the phrase. But that would take a miracle, and Carmen no longer believed in them.

When there was only a few more steps left for Asa to take to reach her, she began to walk over to cover the distance. Then they met, with the clouds moving in to cover most of the sun again, taking away the gold-like tinge to Asa's hair and the sparkle in his eyes.

Even in the dull shade, she still saw Asa as a painting—a thousand shades of brown and gold. In that moment, Carmen realised how grand a museum she'd already built for him inside her mind. That should've frightened her, but seeing him as a work of art seemed to bring Carmen some quiet in her otherwise loud mind.

She'd always believed, right down to her soul, that art made up for her lack of light.

But here was that light: Asa.

But Asa was more than that. Asa was the embodiment of the sun in all its glory. Carmen wondered how close she could get to him without setting herself on fire.

"You called me?" he asked after a while, one of his hands fidgeting with the locks of his hair near his forehead. Pulling it then flattening it down, only to mess it up again.

She opened her mouth to respond, but a beat passed and she still couldn't say anything. What was there to say? "You've been avoiding me since lunch," she pointed out, not entirely certain whether she should have said that.

His hand froze, as if not expecting her to call him out on it so brazenly.

"I didn't think we had anything to say to each other." He sighed, running a hand down his face, looking tired in a way that Carmen was all too familiar with. Eyes so weary as if the exhaustion ran way deeper than he was letting on. Carmen knew exactly how that felt.

She also knew no amount of rest was going to cure that.

"Maybe you didn't," Carmen said, her heart doing rounds of nerve-wracking bungee jumping, plummeting down to her stomach and being yanked back up before it could hit the ground. On and off. On and off. On and off. Again, and again.

"But I have a few things to say to you," she told him quietly, her fingers picking at the loose threads on the sleeve of her other arm.

Asa sighed, dropping his shoulders, too tired to pour any more energy into pretending he could carry all the weight on his back. "Can't it wait?" he asked. "I'm really not in the mood."

"But I won't get to speak to you until tomorrow."

He raised a brow in question.

"I don't like it when someone I care about has to go to sleep with a heavy heart," she said, chewing on the bottom of her lip because her heart was *falling, falling, falling.* Falling into that bottomless pit of uncertainty and fear that always appeared whenever she spoke with her heart and soul on her tongue.

She didn't know what to expect, but maybe it wasn't the way Asa's hand froze midway as he ran it through his hair. Maybe it wasn't the way his coffee eyes zeroed in on hers like he was seeing something precious there that he hadn't found anywhere else. Maybe it wasn't the way he swallowed, as if he needed to feel his Adam's apple move in order to make sure he wasn't dreaming.

It certainly wasn't the manner in which he was looking at her now, like he'd witnessed something fall from up above and land right in front of him.

He called her name like there was a constellation waiting to be named after her, and now he was staring at her as if she herself was a celestial being. It pained Carmen to know that he was just a guy with awestruck eyes who thought she was a falling star when in reality, she was nothing but a meteor who only caused havoc and destruction, bringing nothing but pain.

"Don't..." His voice was hoarse, and his eyes looked conflicted. So conflicted, in fact, that if eyes were indeed the windows to one's soul, Carmen would see the war raging on inside him. "Don't say—don't talk to me in that way." He was struggling, and it was plain to see.

Carmen saw it in the way his palms kept curling into ironclad fists in order to hide the fact that his hands were trembling. His eyes stayed stuck on hers despite how his shoulders and jaw looked tense, as if he was about to take off running.

In that moment that had somehow turned into yet another one of their infinites, Carmen found herself wanting something she'd never wanted before from another person. She wanted half of Asa's weight— half the struggle she saw him carrying on his shoulders but wearing it as a cape instead.

"In what way Asa?" She cocked her head to the right slightly, narrowing her eyes and furrowing her brows. "I didn't mean anything bad by it."

He shut his eyes, as if her words troubled him deeply, and he couldn't bear to *look* at her and *hear* them at the same time. "I know, Carmen," he said in a pained voice. Oh how she ached to rip away the hurt from his veins. She wanted to flush it out of his system and remind him that pain had no business flowing through his bones when he had a heart made of a gold that rivalled the radiance of the sun itself.

He opened his eyes, and they looked so intense that Carmen felt her heart flutter in her ribs, wanting to spread its wings and fly, no longer comfortable with being caged.

"I know you didn't mean anything bad by it," he said, his breathing sounding uneven even to her ears. "But that's the problem." His fists clenched tighter if that was even humanely possible. Carmen pressed her lips, wanting to force his palms open; she was sure he was hurting himself. "You shouldn't—you shouldn't be speaking to me that way. I'm not... I'm *not*." He stressed on it, as if there was no better way he could explain himself than that. "And you *are*."

To Carmen, it made sense. It made more sense than it ever would if he'd tried explaining himself further. She offered him a small smile as she walked closer and then slowly, but without any hesitancy, her hands found his. She let her palms cover his own, as her fingers fought to uncurl his fists. Her eyes were greeted with the sight of pale red crescent-like indents on his skin.

"Why do you hurt yourself, Asa?" she murmured, her thumbs running over the indents on both his palms.

"It doesn't matter," he muttered. He didn't pull his hands away and, for some reason, it warmed Carmen's heart.

She tilted her head up, meeting his eyes and frowning at him. "Don't say that. Why—"

But she couldn't continue because right then, Asa had pulled one of his hands away from hers and shakily brought it up to her face. His fingers trembled like he was preparing to touch something that wasn't supposed to exist, and he just needed to make sure it was there.

His hand came to rest on one side of her face, his thumb grazing the skin just beneath her bottom lip. Carmen knew she didn't believe in miracles, but how else was she going to explain the way Asa's hand stopped shaking once it had touched her face? It was as if that was all it took to calm him.

"You're frowning," he murmured, tapping his forefinger on one corner of her mouth. "I hate it when you frown. It makes me want to tear to pieces whatever has upset you."

"Then tear down that armour, Asa," she told him, leaning her face into his palm. His hand was starting to feel like home, and it terrified her but also brought her peace. "Tear away that outer skin, and wear the one you were born with like its gold, because it is." She brought up her free hand to cover his that was holding her face. "Because right now, that is what's upsetting me."

And when he smiled then, it was different than all the other times she'd seen him do so.

When Asa smiled then, it was like the crack of dawn after a long, sleepless night.

When Asa smiled then, it was like the blooming of the first ever flower, signalling spring's approach.

It was watching something coming to life in his eyes, and Carmen felt a little bit of that blood on her hands get washed away. She may have taken away a life from this world, but something about bringing light into Asa's eyes made her feel more whole than she ever had in years.

He didn't just make her whole. He helped *her* make herself feel whole, and that was *everything* in Carmen's world.

29.
Home Is Two Hands & A Beating Heart

Asa knew he shouldn't be doing this, but what was *this* exactly?

He swore on his life that he was doing nothing but touching her face and yet… yet, it felt so much more.

So, *so* much more.

Everything with Carmen was always more. *She* was more. And she kept filling up Asa in the places that he thought were empty, like those cracks and crevices that he believed would forever stay dark and hollow.

But here she was, holding his hand and illuminating the parts of him he didn't have the energy to light up by himself today. Maybe this was the other step in the road to self-love; perhaps it was knowing when to allow your body to give in and rest because it can get tired sometimes. Perhaps it was knowing when to let someone else be your wings while you tend to your aching shoulders that felt too burdened by the world to lift you up anymore.

And that was okay. That was okay. Because Asa was allowed to take a break every once in a while. The art of learning to love yourself wasn't some masterpiece that had already been painted and hung behind a glass somewhere where everyone can take a peek at.

No, this art was a different form altogether. There was no original. There was no guideline. Like his, everyone else's wasn't fully painted yet, waiting for the angry strokes, the colourful ones; for stains, scratches and every single element that made each person's completed canvas unique. But Asa was far from being a finished piece. He was a work in progress, and he'd come to realise Carmen was a work in progress too, and that was okay. It was okay. What was the hurry, anyway?

Maybe Carmen and he could add the finishing touches to their canvases together. One day they could both stand shoulder to shoulder, hand in hand, and admire their completed canvases hanging on the museum walls he was sure she'd constructed in her mind.

"I thought you weren't good with words." He chuckled, looking at her fondly because he couldn't bring himself to move from the current position he was in. "And that art was your strong suit."

"It is," she agreed. "But, I don't know. Maybe it's just you." She smiled then in such a soft way that if Asa died right then, he'd die in pure bliss. "You make me say the kind of things someone usually writes down in their personal journal."

And there went Asa's heart, doing somersaults in his chest. He had to bite the inside of his cheeks to stop from grinning so wide that his face would've combusted. God, she made him feel like a kid. It was unreal.

This couldn't be true. This couldn't exist. There was no way it could. One single person couldn't just light up flares and illuminate all your dark parts and guide you home. That was too much emotional power for someone to have over you.

He'd given his best friend that kind of power, and in return had gotten his heart handed to him on a silver platter with a dagger sticking out from the middle of it.

And that was just Isla, his best friend. Giving Carmen West such power would probably have consequences on a cosmic level. It would be too much. *Too much, too much, too much*, Asa thought. That kind of intensity frightened him to no end.

"Actually, I was just sweet talking you into giving me a ride back home today." Carmen grinned then, and even though it was supposed to steal his breath away, Asa found himself laughing. "Look at you." He rolled his eyes. "Trying to sound funny."

132

"Considering the fact that you did laugh, I'd say I'm pretty darn funny."

"Mmm...hmm," he mumbled, his heart beating fast all of a sudden. He could never explain it when it came to her but he always found himself going insane in the moments where she was her simplest self.

That was the thing about Carmen, he then realised; she had a way of taking the most ordinary moments and turning them into some of the most extraordinary ones.

Or, maybe, he just found her the most extraordinary in all the moments of his dull life.

"Asa." She laughed, and he swore another shooting star was born. "We can't stand here forever. We're, like, the last students here. Even the janitors are starting to leave."

But I want to stand here with you, Asa wanted to say. *I want to hold your hand and touch your face forever.* Carmen made him want to cut open his chest and put his heart and soul on display for her eyes, but he didn't know how to do that without allowing other people access too.

So he remembered his place and took a step back, dropping his hand from her face and pulling away his other palm from her grasp.

"Yeah, we better get going," he said, keeping his tone casual, and averted his eyes before he could see her reaction. He made sure his shift in his attitude was subtle, but he was sure it wouldn't have escaped her notice. Carmen saw everything. He didn't want to know if pulling back had hurt her in some way.

He'd just had his heart shredded, and he didn't think he was quite ready to go around handing it to someone else in its raw state before it was fully patched up. Even if that someone happened to be Carmen West, the girl with midnight for her hair and thundercloud for her eyes.

Minutes later, Asa found himself with his hands on the steering wheel of his truck, and right next to him, where she belonged, sat Carmen. His eyes swept over her art journal sitting on the dashboard, her faded sneakers with one of the logos peeling off tossed carelessly on the floor of the vehicle, and then finally Carmen, landing on the seat with her feet tucked underneath her as she made herself at home in the passenger seat yet again.

And, for the first time in his life, Asa felt like home wasn't necessarily four walls with a front lawn, but maybe two hands and a beating heart.

30.
The Definition of Beautiful

"Oh, by the way. Asa?" Carmen spoke after a long stretch of silence, her voice blending with the tranquillity of it rather than piercing the calm bubble.

"Yeah?" Asa asked in response, his mouth automatically curving upwards into a smile. He just felt so goddamn happy whenever she spoke to him. It was pure madness now.

"I forgot to tell you about our plans for tomorrow," she said, colouring something in her art journal that Asa made a point not to take a peek at.

"Plans?" His brows furrowed together. "What plans?" He turned to face her just as he stopped right in front of her house and noticed the way she pursed her lips, as if she was being cautious about something.

"Well," she started and that was enough to instantly put Asa on his guard.

"What'd you do?" he asked wearily.

Her head snapped towards him, her grey eyes widening in innocence. "I didn't *do* anything," she defended. "Well, I mean, not anything *bad*."

"Carmen," he said warningly. "Out with it now."

She let out a deep sigh that Asa could swear almost had a dramatic touch to it, as she shut her journal and turned her body around completely on the seat to face him.

"Okay, so, Willa hasn't been around the neighbourhood yet. She kind of needs a tour around the place."

"Okay?"

"Yeah, so, you know." She shrugged. "I told her you'd be happy to be her guide."

Asa choked on his own spit, immediately sitting up straighter, as he looked at Carmen like she'd spoken in pig Latin.

"Why would you do that?"

"Because...I thought it was a good idea?" She pressed her lips further that her mouth was almost invisible now.

"What on earth." He closed his eyes, breathing deeply as he tried to make sense of her logic. "Made you think that was a good idea?"

"You're the one who told me you needed help to set you up with Willa," she pointed out.

"What?!" He asked, his mouth gaped open. "When did I ever say *that*?" He didn't like Willa in the romantic sense of the way, did he? Of course not. So, what was Carmen going on about?

Carmen sat straighter, looking at Asa like he was the one who'd grown another head now. "You kept my journal from me for it," she reminded him, incredulity and confusion settling into her eyes. "That's what you said I had to do in order to get it back!"

"I never said I *liked* her!"

"Yes, you did," she responded calmly, and that drove Asa insane. It always got under his skin how she could just remain so unfazed. He had that annoying urge again—to grab her shoulders and shake her hard until she spilled out her actual thoughts.

"No, I didn't," he said through gritted teeth, shooting an unimpressed look at her.

"Oh, goodness," she huffed, placing her journal heavily on the truck's dashboard. "You said I could only get my journal back if I helped you with Willa."

136

"Yeah." He raised a brow, emphasising on his point. "But I never said to *set me up* with her. I never even gave the impression that I like her in *that* sort of way."

Carmen blinked, as if finding it hard to understand the words leaving Asa's mouth. "But that's what you implied," she said slowly. "What else could those words have meant?"

Asa shrugged helplessly, throwing his hands into the air. "Literally anything else! It could've just meant that I wanted a way to interact with her."

"Yeah, exactly! Why else would you've wanted my help to find a way to interact with her unless you weren't interested?"

"You're not making any sense, Carmen." He sighed, pinching the bridge of his nose in frustration. She was driving him mad.

"*You're* not making any sense! Are you even listening to yourself right now? You're making my head messier than most of my doodling with all this confusion."

"*Por Dios,*" he swore under his breath, shoulders slumping in defeat, this nonsensical argument draining him of all energy. "Carmen," he said slowly, stressing on each syllable like a teacher would speak to a kindergarten kid. "I do not like Willa in that way, okay? The rest is history."

But Carmen didn't seem to be satisfied with his explanation, and she didn't appear to be leaving his truck either. She folded her arms across her stomach and nestled her side further into the seat.

"But then, why did you—I don't understand." She shook her head, completely ignoring his words about everything else being history.

"It doesn't matter," he muttered. "It was nothing but a moment of impulse anyway. I was being stupid and an absolute idiot."

He watched her pull in the rightmost corner of her bottom lip, her eyes never leaving his face as they searched and searched for something that would explain what he couldn't find the words to.

"To whom doesn't it matter?" she asked finally.

Asa blinked. "What?"

"You said it doesn't matter," she pointed out. "So, does it mean that it doesn't matter to you? Or did you mean that your explanation wouldn't matter to me?"

His lips parted because maybe his mind knew this was the time to say something—to respond somehow. But his heart was sending a different message, because words failed him right then. And Asa had always been a heart-over-head guy.

God, Carmen *heard* him. She heard him the way someone who'd been trapped in solitude and bound by shackles to cold concrete walls would want to be heard when their screams ripped through their vocal cords.

Carmen *heard* him, and somehow, that was everything.

"Your silence kind of answers that question," she said, offering him a small smile. "Want to tell me why you think what you have to say wouldn't matter to me?"

Asa swallowed, knowing he could just dodge these questions and get the hell out of there. Away from her. Away from Carmen West. because she heard him when he didn't expect anyone to, and if Asa wasn't careful, he could fall in love with her for it.

Despite that, he stayed put in his seat and only reached forward to kill the engine, realising that he might be here for a while.

"Because," he paused, "it's... stupid?" He couldn't meet her eyes. He wouldn't. "Yes. Stupid. Actually, it's even stupider to be talking about it, so you should probably just get going, Carmen."

"Why do you think it's stupid?" Her eyes stayed fixed on his face, never faltering. Never wavering. She didn't push him with her words or urge him on with her gaze. She just waited, and waited, and waited.

Carmen just sat there, her eyes patient and warm on Asa's face as if she was ready to make the whole world pause on its axis if it meant that he'd have more time to formulate the war raging on inside his heart into words.

Asa noticed this. Again, he reminded himself that if he wasn't careful, he could fall in love with her for it.

"Because...Well... I mean, when I first ran into Willa, she just..." he trailed off, creasing his forehead as he tried to explain something that had been building up ever since that moment in his predominantly-white primary school he'd attended in this predominantly-white city he lived in when one little girl had tapped her mother's hand and pointed at Asa, exclaiming loudly that he had different skin and that he spoke with a different accent.

Asa must've been five or six at that time, same as the little girl. But the mother had still turned her daughter's face away and shot her a disapproving look.

"Stick with the others in your class, honey," she'd told her, tucking a strand of the girl's red hair behind her ear. "It's for your own good, okay? And stay away from that one, too." The woman had then gestured at another boy whose mother had come to drop him off.

Asa hadn't seen anything odd about the boy's appearance because, unlike Asa, he had the same fair skin as the little girl's, but then he noticed the boy's mother with a cloth wrapped around her head, covering her hair, and he wondered if maybe that had been the problem.

Asa hadn't been able to see anything wrong with it, though. He'd just seen himself in that boy, scared as all hell to start first grade at a new school. He had also seen other kids his age, with the same fear on their faces. He hadn't seen them by the clothes their parents wore or the colour of their skin; he'd just seen the same frightened expression on each and every one of those students. Despite everything else, they'd all felt the same emotion.

Perhaps that moment was the stepping stone in Asa's wondering why he wasn't born in a way that everyone considered normal. And every other moment after that was just a chain reaction. A snowball effect. A snide remark here, a cruel comment there, a few nasty looks tossed into the mix. They'd all gathered as the years flew past, piling atop one another until it no longer suffocated Asa but became part of him.

And maybe it was a more open world now, maybe it being 2018 meant that things were different for this generation, but that luck was reserved for the kids born now. Asa's damage had already been done years ago, when bigotry dominated every fibre of too many beings.

"Asa?"

Carmen's voice snapped Asa from his walk down memory lane, bringing him back to the present. Bringing him back to this place, where the girl with midnight hair sat right beside him and didn't look like she was in a hurry to leave.

"She had the wrong idea of me," he found himself saying. "Willa, I mean. She thought I was an airhead, that all I had going for me was a pretty face. That I tossed girls aside like it was just another sport."

"And?" Carmen asked gently.

"And," he paused, not really knowing what to say. "I don't know. I just…I guess I wanted to please her?" He ended up questioning himself rather than stating something to Carmen, as if he himself was discovering this small part of him only now. "She didn't just think of me wrong. She *looked* at me wrong. And I guess I just wanted that to go away."

"You thought that maybe you could change how she saw you if you befriended her," Carmen murmured, no longer looking at Asa but getting lost in thought as she frowned to herself.

"You're frowning." Asa sighed softly. "Am I making you upset again?" he asked quietly, his eyes finding the courage to look away from nothingness and at her.

The creases on Carmen's forehead smoothened, and her gentle gaze met his. "You don't make me upset, Asa," she told him. "The world does."

"I used to think the same." He smiled in an almost nostalgic manner. "That the world was a cruel place. But then I look at my parents and I remember that when people like them exist, not all hope is lost, you know?"

140

"*You* exist too, Asa." She smiled then, illuminating the cracks in Asa's heart some more. And when she leaned forward and laid her palm on his cheek, his chest felt so full he thought it would explode. "And when you find yourself thinking the world is a cruel place again and if even looking at your parents don't seem to help, look at a mirror. You owe yourself that much."

Asa was sure school had taught him how to arrange the letters of the English alphabet into words, and words into sentences. He was sure he'd been taught to pronounce these words and voice out these sentences. Hell, Asa was pretty darn sure AP Lit was one of his favourite subjects and that he was a die-hard bookworm. Words were his strong point; they'd always been.

But Carmen...*goddamn*. Carmen robbed him of his speech every single time she spoke with her heart on her sleeve and her soul in her eyes. Words would never suffice, not when it came to her.

"You can't mean that," he whispered.

She moved her thumb against his cheek in small strokes like she was blurring the edges of one of her charcoal drawings. "I can." She dropped her hand and leant back. "And I do."

He didn't know what to say. He didn't. There literally was nothing he could say that would show her how much his heart swelled with an emotion so profound that it made him want to bring down the moon to her fingertips.

But a part of him already knew that Carmen would never ask for the moon to be plucked out of the sky. And that was what made her the phenomenal being that she was. She loved everything and everyone as they were.

Asa wouldn't say Carmen was pretty; she didn't have Willa's incredible hazel eyes that could catch anyone's attention at first glance. She didn't have Marlene's sharp facial features that made guys turn their heads when she passed them. Neither did she have one of those hourglass figures like Isla that made everyone in the hallway do a double-take in wonder when she walked past.

Asa wouldn't say Carmen was pretty.

Because Carmen West was, in every definition of the word, *beautiful*.

She was beautiful right down to her bones and her soul, and that made everyone else pale in comparison.

And if Asa wasn't careful, he could fall in love with Carmen for it.

He could.

Oh, he could.

31.
Clipped Wings

Carmen had only ever known noise. Up there, in her head, it was always so loud. *Too* loud, even. But here, in the passenger seat of Asa's truck, which was beginning to feel a little like home, there was only silence. Asa brought that calm with him, silencing the chaos that stirred up storms in her mind and easing the turmoil in her heart. In his presence, she found some quiet. She'd only ever thought that art had the power to bring her peace.

Then again, hadn't she always believed that Asa was a work of art himself? It was only obvious then that he could bring her the kind of solace she often looked for in the pages of her art journal.

"Hey, Carmen?" he spoke after a long stretch of silence.

"Mmmm?" She averted her eyes from where they were staring blankly at her shoes tucked in a corner and met Asa's inquisitive gaze.

"Can I ask you something?"

She nodded in response, and right then, she felt an odd sense of content wash over her.

"The first time I drove you home," he said and paused, "you told me you didn't think I was a player."

"Yes." She smiled.

"Why'd you say that?"

"Honestly, Asa." She playfully rolled her eyes, attempting to put him at ease. "For someone who loves words so much, you're pretty dense when it comes to definitions."

She saw his eyes widen in mild surprise but watching the grin that crawled over his face brought her relief after hearing him spill his heart out to her just minutes before.

"What's that supposed to mean?" He chuckled, and that sound alone lit a spark in Carmen's heart. She knew it would only grow into a fire which she'll never be able to extinguish.

Carmen didn't mind, though. Those flames will keep her warm on the nights when everything else fell apart and abandoned her on the cold concrete.

"A player, by definition, is someone who plays around with feelings and hearts. And correct me if I'm wrong, but I don't think you actually fit into that category. You don't string along anyone, do you?"

"Of course not," he said softly. "I just meant that I understand why it was an assumption everyone made…but somehow, *you* don't."

"I told you." She looked away from him, too scared he'd see something in her eyes when this topic came up. "I don't assume. I don't care what other people think."

"Yeah, I remember. I'm asking why you take such a strong stand against it…it just feels like there's something more there. Like you take it very deep to heart whenever anyone's being judgemental."

Carmen couldn't remember the last time she felt such panic take hold of her heart, almost squeezing the life out of it. But she'd mastered the skill to remain unfazed a long time ago when she had to be the shoulder her father had to lean on when it became too much for him to walk without the ground beneath him cracking wide open.

She'd long since learnt to slip a smile on her face and crinkle the edges of her eyes so that it looked genuine enough to make it easier for those around her to break without wondering if maybe she was breaking too, if not already broken.

And that is what Carmen did then; she offered him a soft smile as if she didn't feel herself slipping further and further into the abyss that always came calling during such moments of vulnerability.

"I could ask you the same thing, you know," she deflected his question subtly, but also genuinely, as she was also curious and wanted to ask Asa this question for a while now. "You defend Isla when they label her a slut, but you don't stick up for yourself when they pass their judgements on you." She frowned, wondering why Asa believed he wasn't worthy of being defended. "What makes you think they're all wrong when they ridicule her but that you're expected to tolerate it when the same is done to you?"

Asa just stared at her, not saying anything. He did that a lot these days, Carmen realised. It was as if he no longer knew how to use his voice.

"I mean, I've seen you defend so many kids who get bullied time and time again, but instead of defending yourself, you're trying to beat and bend yourself into the shape everyone wants you take form." She bit the corner of her lip, continuing to stare at him with worry swimming in her eyes. "And Asa, there's only so much you can bend yourself before you break."

"I guess I never thought it mattered enough," he admitted quietly.

"You mean you never thought that *you* mattered enough," she emphasised. "Not *it.*"

He cracked a small smile, looking at her sideways in an almost secretive glance. "Don't go getting all philosophical on me now."

"Hey, I was just giving you a pep talk on vocabulary and definitions." She held her hands up in a teasing manner. "It was you who took the conversation down this road."

He laughed then, and Carmen's heart felt a little more alive again. That abyss that seemed to suck the joy out of her spirits seemed to not be so overpowering anymore. She'd live to fight another day not to succumb to it.

"So, where were we?" Asa asked, grinning. "Ah, right, your ingenious decision to make me play tour guide."

Carmen pulled in her bottom lip, stopping herself from smiling because of that ridiculous sense of happiness that flooded her when she was reminded that Asa didn't see Willa in *that* way.

Carmen always saw things as more than what they were, looking past people's exteriors while searching for who they were right down to the core of their beings. But with Asa, she was reminded of the simple joys in life. Like what butterflies felt like.

She'd lost herself to the flames of intensity time and time again, that she never knew how much she actually craved for simplicity and the little, ordinary things until Asa had smiled at her for the first time and made her heart flutter in a way that she was sure was common amongst any teenager out there.

It felt nice knowing that she could be just one of them too.

"It wouldn't be so bad," she said. "Even though I don't know what exactly happened in the canteen, I know you're pretty sad about it and that it's still bothering you despite having this conversation. Maybe tomorrow will get your mind off things."

"Actually." Asa blinked, a look dawning over his face as if he'd just realised something himself. "I didn't once think about the incident throughout our conversation." He grinned then, so wide that the sheer joy radiating off it nearly blinded Carmen.

Watching him smile in that manner was probably just the same as staring at the sun for too long that once you looked away from such magnificence, it took you a few moments to compose yourself and your sight to adjust to your surroundings again.

"Oh," was all Carmen could say. Was it really her own presence that had distracted him from his troubles?

"Thank you," he said, sounding surprised himself.

She laughed, slapping his arm lightly. "It's not like I did it intentionally."

"Wouldn't be surprised even if you had," he told her quietly, his face turning serious.

She only shook her head with a small smile in response, "So, we'll see you there tomorrow?"

"Wait, you'll be there too?" Asa asked, sitting up a little straighter. Somehow, he didn't look so weary of tomorrow anymore.

Carmen nodded. "Yeah, she initially wanted me to show her around, but I figured adding you to the mix wouldn't be too bad."

"I'm sure," he muttered sarcastically. "Not bad at all."

She grinned at him cheekily. "Oh come on, it would be fun. Besides I'm always either holed up inside my room or walking around the neighbourhood alone. It'd be a nice change for me."

He cocked a brow. "And your true intentions have been revealed, after all," he declared dramatically. "You planned this entire thing so that you'd have an excuse to have fun, huh?"

Carmen let out a deep sigh, looking forlorn as she dropped her gaze to the floor. "Alas, you have discovered my diabolical scheme! Whatever shall I do?!"

"Oh, wow, you're terrible at this." Asa laughed unapologetically as Carmen just gaped at his blunt remark.

"Well, someone knows the art of flattery," she muttered.

"Oh, shut—" Asa's words died in his throat, as his eyes seemed to register something behind Carmen at the exact same time she heard someone tap on the passenger seat window she'd pressed her back against.

Despite knowing who it could be, she turned around anyway and found her father standing there with one palm lying flat against the glass as he looked at her with a curious expression.

Her hands fumbled against the surface of the door as she tried to find the handle, and swung it open after struggling with it.

"Hi, Dad." She grinned, feeling the faintest bit awkward, which was only heightened when Asa didn't say anything but just sat there in a dazed state.

147

"Hi," her father responded with an uncertain smile. "I thought you'd be walking home as usual."

"It was cold," Asa spoke up then. "I didn't want her to walk all the way in this weather. Despite telling her last week, she still won't wear a sweater."

"Thank you," her father nodded courteously, "for looking after her."

Asa shrugged awkwardly. "It was no problem." There was an uncomfortable pause. "She's actually quite entertaining."

Carmen's eyes snapped to Asa's whose cheeks seemed to grow slightly pink when he realised what he'd just said.

"Yes," her father replied dryly. "I figured as much considering you've been parked outside my house for a total of forty-five minutes now."

"Dad." Carmen chuckled uneasily. "Relax, we were just talking."

"Of course." He smiled, turning away his calculating eyes from Asa and looking at her with fondness. "Was just stating a fact, that's all."

"Of course, you were," Carmen replied, shaking her head slightly as she gathered her things and got out of the truck. "Bye, Asa. See you tomorrow?"

Asa looked away from watching her father cautiously, and something in his expression instantly softened the second his eyes landed on Carmen. "Of course, wouldn't want you to miss my first go at being a tour guide."

"You'll do great, wise one." She grinned, slamming the door shut and waving as he rolled his eyes and drove off.

"Tour guide?" her father's voice interrupted the almost giddy bubble that had begun to envelope her. "So, he's the one you'll be hanging out with tomorrow? Along with the new kid?"

Carmen turned around to squint at her dad. "Yeah. That's not a problem, is it?" she asked quietly, pulling in her bottom lip and chewing on the rightmost corner of it.

Her father sighed, placing a hand on the back of her shoulders and urging her forward as they walked back to their home. "No, it's not a problem. I'm just worried, that's all. It's a dad thing, honey. Don't think too much about it."

"You're sure, right?" she asked hesitantly.

"Pretty sure." He smiled down at her, opening the door and leading her in before entering the house himself and letting the door shut close after them. "He just seems like one of those jock types. I don't want you to end up hurt. Or worse."

Carmen froze in her tracks on the way to her room.

"That's not fair," she whispered, her voice trembling and her eyes blinking back angry tears. "That is so not fair, Dad. You of all people should know not to jump to conclusions."

"Keeping you safe is my priority," he said, unfazed. "I don't care about the rest."

"I don't want to be kept safe at the cost of putting someone else down," she said slowly. "If we ourselves won't adapt an understanding mind, how can we expect for anything to change with our world, Dad?"

"I owe this world nothing," he told her, his sea-green eyes boring into her own with so much pain in them. Carmen never wanted to die more than she did in that moment. "All it has done is *take*. And *take*. And ta—" His voice cracked, and his eyes immediately fell to the floor.

It was one of those nights again, when everything was falling apart. When the ground beneath her feet was shaking so violently like it was going to spit back out all the horrifying secrets this house had to bury along with her mother's coffin into the ground.

Her mother remained dead, but the terrible things that led to her demise didn't. It was alive in the hibiscus bushes that her mother had planted along the edges of their front lawn. It was alive in the absence of her face in any of the family photographs that sat on the mantelpiece in the living room.

It was alive in the way the look in her father's eyes held the remnants of a heart that was broken forever. It was alive in Carmen's existence itself, in the way she was never born whole but with a fractured soul that she was always trying to fill up with something that would take the horrors away.

It never worked, though. Nothing ever filled her up.

It was just one of those times again, when she thought this world was indeed a cruel place. She wanted to just set it on fire and watch it burn to ashes and dust. But she recalled her conversation with Asa and continued towards her room, where she stood in front of the mirror and looked at her reflection.

But it didn't work. She saw herself breathing, living, *existing*. And it had the complete opposite effect on her. She might've told Asa that he needed to use his own self as an anchor when things got too much, to remind himself that his existence was something that made this world seem less cruel, and she'd meant every single word. She *did*.

But looking into the mirror never worked when the problem wasn't with the rest of the world but with you.

She looked into that mirror, and she loathed what she saw there.

When the rest of the world was asleep, she would find herself on the floor, lying helplessly as everything around her crumbled to dust yet again, with her heart dying again along with her mother.

She'd been the wings of too many broken people who were weighed down by burdens that weren't theirs to carry, but she'd never learn to grow a pair herself.

Her wings had been clipped off long before she could even fathom the concept of flying, and it'd always remain that way.

32.
What Falling In Love Feels Like

All the way back home, Asa couldn't help but think about how much Carmen's dad's sand-coloured hair and sea-green eyes contrasted with Carmen's midnight hair and stormy grey eyes.

They looked nothing alike. Even their facial features were completely different that there was no way, really, to tell that those two shared the same blood, let alone be parent and child.

Was she adopted? Asa didn't really know, and despite sharing a few emotionally intimate moments and blurring the lines of their friendship recently, he still thought it was too soon for him to ask her something deeply personal like that. Hell, he didn't think it would even be acceptable to *ask* such a question, regardless of what the relationship between two people were.

But, goddamn, Carmen was *everything*, and he wanted to take his time peeling back layers after layers of her soul and memorising every single curve, edge and vertex of her existence.

Existence.

She'd said that his existence was proof enough that this world wasn't too terrible a place.

Something exploded in his chest and seeped into his veins, running through his bloodstream like its sole purpose was to flush out the poison Hunter and the others like him had poured into Asa's being. As if it was on a mission to wash out the venom that had manifested itself in him as Isla's words—and others'—had pierced into his flesh and his bones.

Carmen believed he made this world seem less cruel. Carmen *believed* that.

Asa wondered if she also believed that she turned everything she looked at and touched into magic, because he swore she'd left her imprint on his skin where her palm had made contact with his cheek in the gentlest of gestures. For the first time in forever, he was looking at his reflection through the rear-view mirror like there was something worth looking back at.

If Asa's existence dimmed the world's ugliness, then he was pretty sure it was Carmen's presence that lit it up in all its beautiful places.

She lit it up with the touch of galaxies she carried in her veins, and the constellations she weaved with her fingertips whenever they brushed against something that nobody else would spare a second glance to.

Just as he pulled his truck into his driveway, his eyes snuck a glance at the empty passenger seat next to him.

She wasn't seated there right now, but there were loose threads hanging from the edge of the seat where her fingers had been picking at it without her being aware of her actions. Asa's eyes had drunk it all in though.

She wasn't by his side right then, but she still left traces of her in his truck. Whether it was a strand of her dark hair that was lying on the headrest, or the belt buckle she'd tucked further into the seat, or even a few pieces that'd fallen off one of her shoes' peeling logo.

Asa had been completely oblivious to her existence before he'd taken the journal, thinking it belonged to Willa, but now that she'd planted herself in his world, there was just no going back.

Carmen had built herself a home in his very being and he didn't know how to burn it down without setting his own heart on fire.
She was everywhere: a few seats down in his AP Lit class, right behind him in AP Cal, the ghost of her touch in the vacant spot in the passenger

seat of his truck, the table at the leftmost corner of the cafeteria that his eyes always found against his permission, in the paint stains he'd find on the bottom edges of the school walls and even in all the scattered autumn leaves that decorated the city's streets and pavements.

She was everywhere without needing to be physically present; she just left pieces of herself in every nook and corner of Asa's world. There was no going back, not unless Carmen herself plucked her presence out of Asa's life and left without another glance back.

• • •

"Ma!" Asa called out as he let the front door slam shut to announce his arrival. "I'm home!"

"Great!" he heard her yell back from the living room. "You can see yourself out!"

Asa's grin slipped off his face, and he quickly kicked off his shoes, taking huge strides towards the direction of her voice.

"Why on earth would I do that?" he asked, staring at her in bewilderment. His mind raced through the past few days, trying to pinpoint any particular incident that he must've taken part in to annoy his mother.

"Oh, hey," a familiar voice reached his ears and Asa looked past his mother's shoulders to see his father descend the stairs and come into view. "You're finally here. I had to listen to your mother go on about how you don't want to come home anymore." His father rolled his eyes and gestured towards her. Obviously he only had the guts to do so because he was standing behind her and not in her line of sight.

Asa bit back a smile and averted his gaze back to his mum.

"That's not true," he defended himself, scoffing. "I always come home directly after school."

"Look at the time, *tonto*," she snapped, "wh—"

"No swearing in this house," both Asa and his father chanted in unison, an identical gleam of mischief in their eyes.

His mother's head whipped around to fix her steely gaze on his father, and Asa saw the grin freeze on his face.

153

"Don't take his side," she chided. "It makes me look like the bad guy."

"I'm just an hour late, Ma." Asa sighed. "Papá's not even making a fuss."

"Papá wouldn't bat an eye if you said you wanted to go skydiving," she shot back. "He doesn't worry about anything."

"But…" Asa grinned. "What if I *did* want to go skydiving?"

"Not while I'm still breathing." His mother narrowed her eyes. "So, why have you been coming late these days?"

"Relax," his father said lazily as he walked forwards and dropped down on the couch. "He's a boy. It's normal."

"And if it was a daughter instead of a son, you'd be the one firing a hundred and one questions and getting your shotgun ready in case there were boys involved," his mother retorted. "He's still my kid, and I want to know what he's been doing after school lets out. *Por Dios*, it's a very simple question. I don't know what you're making such a huge fuss about."

"Whoa, whoa, whoa." Asa chuckled. "Okay, calm down, Ma. It's honestly nothing to worry about, I—" He stopped mid-speech abruptly.

He was *blushing*.

Well, at least, he thought he was. Because he was going to say that there was this girl who wore no sweater in this chilly weather, and he didn't like the idea of her walking home in it.

But his lips had curved into a stupid, stupid grin, and he could feel the slight tingling sensation in his cheeks. *Goddamn*, what was she doing to him? Couldn't he even speak about her without feeling the ghost of her laughter pull at his heartstrings?

This was utter madness now. There simply was no other explanation to it.

When he snapped out of the trance and zoned back in to his surroundings, he found both his parents staring at him with an odd mixture of expectancy and confusion.

"You okay, *mijito*?" his father inquired, furrowing his eyebrows.

154

"Ye—" Asa cleared his throat and stuffed his hands into his pockets, adapting a nonchalant demeanour. "Yeah, I'm great. Anyways, what I was saying was that I'm late because I had to give a ride to a friend." He shrugged. "Gave her a ride past few days too, so that explains it."

"'*Her*'?" his mother raised her brows.

"Well, now that you're satisfied he hasn't been strolling the streets butchering people, maybe you can let him off the hook," his dad suggested, earning a nasty look from his mother.

"So who's this girl that's been keeping you from coming home early and spending time with your poor mother?" she asked, smiling slightly to show that she was only teasing.

"*I* spend time with you," his father muttered, making a face.

"It's not like that, Ma," Asa mumbled awkwardly, "she's just a—" *Don't you dare say it, Asa San Román! Don't you dare say she's just a girl.* Carmen was more than just a girl; she was more than *just*. She was *more*. "—a friend," he said instead, smiling slightly.

"It normally takes you fifteen minutes to reach home once school is over." His mother said. "Nowadays it takes you about forty minutes, and today you're a whole hour late! I'm guessing that means her place is out of the way. And you're telling me you go all that distance to drop off someone who's just a *friend*?"

"What can I say, Ma?" Asa lifted his shoulders in an innocent shrug. "You and Papá raised a gentleman."

"You keep those gentlemanly qualities in mind the next time I ask you to do the dishes and you start sulking," she muttered, wiping the triumphant look clean off Asa's face as she nestled into his father's side on the couch and they got engrossed in a conversation of their own.

He watched them for a moment, wondering if his father viewed the moments spent with the woman beside him as infinites and not minutes or hours. He wondered if his mother's smile planted seeds in his father's ribcage and if her laugh made them bloom into flowers that filled the spaces between those bones.

He wondered if that was what falling in love felt like.

He also wondered if perhaps falling implied that there was a landing somewhere, and if it would hurt too much to hit it.

33.
Beacon of Light

The next morning, Asa was up bright and early.

In fact, it'd be pretty safe to say that he'd barely slept through the night because of the knowledge that today, once school was over, he'd be hanging out with Carmen.

Of course, Willa was going to be there, but he figured that was a blessing in disguise because Lord knew he'd be tongue-tied for the most part of the evening if it was just him and Carmen hanging out. He could almost picture himself just staring at her with awestruck eyes while she told him about probably another reason why autumn was beautiful.

Somehow, it was different than the one-on-one moments they shared during the rides back from school. Which meant that today would be marked as the first time he would be officially spending time with Carmen outside of anything related to school.

It sort of made him giddy. It also sort of put him in an unusually bright mood that he was up before his parents were and even went all the way and prepared breakfast for the three of them.

He'd just turned around to place the last plate on the table when his mother stepped into the kitchen with a baseball bat in her hand. Her jaw dropped open the exact moment Asa's eyes widened in shock.

"*Qué estás haciendo?!*" both of them barked at each other in unison, looking at the other like they'd sprouted another head.

"What am *I* doing?" his mother asked, looking offended. "What are *you* doing?!"

"Geez, Ma." Asa let the sarcasm thickly coat his words. "You tell me. What does it *look* like I'm doing?"

She narrowed her eyes, and wagged the bat at him. "You keep running that mouth of yours, and you'll find out just how handy a baseball bat can be."

Asa's nose scrunched, and he frowned at the object in his mother's hand. "Wait, why do we have a baseball bat? Nobody in this house even watches the damn sport."

"Watch your mouth." She glared, obviously sick of asking him to speak in a decent language.

"Do you know how innocent the word *damn* is compared to the words other teens speak?" he asked wearily.

"You are not those other teens," she said in a matter-of-fact tone. "And neither am I their mothers. Now, what is all this?" she gestured with the bat towards the breakfast table.

"Breakfast?" Asa answered.

His mother closed her eyes and pinched the bridge of her nose. "I can't deal with you sometimes."

"He actually gets it from you," his father piped up as he too entered the kitchen.

"The two of you are always teaming up against me," she muttered. "But, what I meant was, why are you awake this early? And all this food—don't tell me you prepared it!"

Now it was Asa's turn to look offended. "I'll keep that in mind the next time I think of doing something nice for you guys."

"Hell is freezing over," his father declared, dropping down on one of the seats and serving himself. "But if we're all going to die today, it might as well be on the one day that our *mijito* prepared breakfast for us."

"Very funny, Dad." Asa rolled his eyes, pulling out one of the chairs and sitting down too. "The sixties called. Apparently, they want their joke back."

158

His father shot him a deadpan look while his ma just burst into laughter, joining them at the table once she'd set the baseball bat aside.

"You know," Asa said after swallowing a mouthful of food, "you never told me why you came in with that thing in your hand."

"No reason." She brushed it off.

"She thought it was a burglar when she heard sounds coming up from the kitchen," his father answered, earning a glare from his ma. "I told her there was also the smell of food being cooked so it was only you, because burglars don't normally break in to cook themselves breakfast. But when does your mother ever listen to me?"

"Is it that hard to believe I'd do this?" Asa asked, frowning. Maybe he needed to do these simple gestures of affection more often.

"Of course not, *cariño*." His mother smiled softly, blinking once in assurance. "We're just pulling your leg, your papá and I."

Asa only grunted in response, before he suddenly remembered why it was that he'd been in a good enough mood to wake up without his mother needing to yell at the top of her lungs.

"Oh, by the way, Ma," he paused to take a quick gulp of water before swallowing and setting his glass back down, "just a heads up. I'll be running late today too."

"Yeah, yeah." She sighed dramatically, shooting him a sideways glance. "You've got other priorities now."

"Oh my God," Asa muttered under his breath. "She's a friend. I told you that already."

"That's what they all say in the beginning," his father said in a serious tone.

The beginning.

Goddamn, the beginning. When had that been, again? Asa felt that it was a lifetime ago, as if everything else before Carmen West simply ceased to exist.

Did the existence of a beginning foreshadow the existence of an ending? Because he didn't think he'd bear to live through it. There could be no end to the phenomenon that was Carmen—there just couldn't.

"There he goes." His mother's voice reached his ears. "Zoning out again."

"I'm here, I'm here," Asa said hastily, ignoring the warming up of his cheeks and neck. "Anyway, it won't be like the other days. I'll be even later than usual."

His mother stopped lifting the spoon to her mouth, and set it down as she frowned at him. "And why's that?"

"Umm." He rubbed the back of his neck uneasily. "We're kind of hanging around the place."

"Hanging around?"

"Yeah." He shrugged. "There's this girl who joined our school a few weeks back. I'm just gonna show her around."

"The same girl you've been giving a ride?" His father furrowed his brows.

"No, that's someone else."

"So, there are two of them?" His mother looked at him with a bewildered expression.

Asa choked on his water, sputtering and coughing, as he tried to speak amidst it all. "No, Ma!" He looked at her with incredulity all over his face. "Of course not!"

"Okay, calm down," she said, struggling to contain her laughter. "I was just kidding."

"Willa's the one who just joined recently, and she's only a friend. Nothing else."

"So, your mum was right then," his father piped up. "Willa's only a friend but the other one who you've been driving home is more?"

Asa let out a gigantic sigh, all his energy and positive aura from when he'd woken up slowly dissipating now. "You know what, I need to get going." He stood up, pushing his chair back and grabbing his plate and glass from the table.

"*Mijo*, you know we're just joking right?" His mother spoke while he washed his hands. A few seconds later, he felt her familiar warm hands wrap around his torso from behind and her head rest against his left

160

shoulder. "There aren't many mothers out there who can proudly say they have a son who actually spends most of his time indoors, enjoying the company of his parents." Asa heard her sigh softly and step away from him, dropping her hands to her sides. "I'm just cherishing it."

"I'm not mad, Ma." He sighed, placing one hand on her shoulder as he leaned in and kissed the top of her head. "Maybe the slightest bit annoyed, though." He grinned, and his mum rolled her eyes and knocked his hand off.

"Go on," she said, giving him a slight nudge. "I don't want you getting late for school."

Asa grabbed his bag from the floor, where he'd set it down beside one of the tables' legs, and swung it over his shoulders. "*Adios, Papá*," he said, patting his father's arm. "Bye, Ma."

"*Te quiero*," both his parents called out in unison, the words falling on his ears just as he stepped out into the chilly autumn air and proceeded to shut the door behind him.

A strong gust of wind blew past, rustling the leaves of a tree by the sidewalk on the edges of their front lawn. One of its branches stretched far enough that it hung low over their house, and he watched as a leaf struggled and eventually broke away from the branch, fluttering around in the air before landing a few feet away on the ground.

A smile graced his lips without him even being fully conscious of it. He walked forward, remembering what Carmen had said once about the wind whispering something intimate to the leaves that turned them into different shades of red and orange.

He picked it up, the fragile stem held gingerly between his thumb and forefinger as he twirled it around and around, staring at it as if it was going to sprout wings and fly itself back up.

Carmen, he sighed mentally. He just couldn't look at the world the same way anymore—and maybe, just maybe, he didn't even *want* to.

The world through Carmen's eyes seemed like a more beautiful perspective.

• • •

161

"Ace?"

Asa's hand froze, his fingers tightening around the copy of *Harry Potter and The Half Blood Prince* that he was stuffing inside his locker. All that giddiness he'd felt ever since he'd woken up this morning vaporised into thin air, leaving a trail of coldness and misery in its wake.

"Asa," he corrected, finding his voice after a few minutes of internal struggle.

"Potato, potato." Isla grinned. Asa wasn't looking at her, still keeping his eyes fixed on the interior of his locker, but he recognised the grin in her tone. He would always know without needing to look. Just like how he knew that it was false bravado keeping her chin up and shoulders ramrod straight right now. Just like how he knew it was uncertainty and worry that made her curl her palms into clenched fists that she tried to conceal by folding her hands across her chest.

Asa didn't have to look at Isla to know. They were best friends. At least, they had been.

"Wow," she said, and he heard her chuckle. "Harry Potter again? You've read the series, what, eight times already now?"

He knew that keeping his face turned away would come off as immature, but for the love of God, he couldn't bring himself to look her in the eyes. All her words came crashing down in torrential waves over him, dragging him under a little more as each second ticked by. His breathing quickened and then faltered as he felt his chest constrict, the knife she'd stuck in him twisting further into his flesh as a brutal reminder that it was still planted in him and would probably never come out.

She thought he was pathetic. His best friend—his best, *best* friend in the entire goddamn world believed that about him. Was that how she'd always seen him?

Had she stood by him out of pity's sake, then? Had it always been a one-sided friendship with her?

Asa felt sick. His lungs shrank and the walls closed in on him as he found it increasingly harder to turn towards her. God, he felt pathetic.

"So, there's this party…"

162

Shut up. Shut up. Shut up. He wanted to scream at her, but his ears won't take in her words anymore. His throat was dry, and words weren't coming to him. It was a different kind of speechlessness, though. Not the kind that Carmen cast over him—

Carmen.

Her name slammed into his head, ricocheting off the walls in his mind and resonating throughout his entire being. It played on his heartstrings like it was a long-forgotten tune that his soul had missed so, so much. And just like that, his chest stopped constricting. His lungs expanded, and he could breathe again.

Asa could breathe again.

Carmen reminded him to breathe and, in that moment, Asa wondered if it was people like her that you held close and never let go of. The ones that reminded you to breathe rather than those who took your breath away.

Carmen was like the moon, he then realised (though he felt sort of idiotic for even coming up with that analogy). She wasn't anywhere near him but she still found a way to be a beacon of light for him in the dark.

And all those seeds her smiles had planted in the spaces of his ribcage, all those seeds that her laughter had bloomed into flowers, was now wrapping around him like a shield. Carmen's words were paintings on his skin, and he felt them burn into his bones as if they were coating his entire being with a layer of protection that no poison could infiltrate ever again. No knife could pierce through it ever again, even if there was one already buried deep inside his chest.

And it was with this newfound strength that Asa found it in himself to face Isla, to look her right in the eye without flinching or letting his mask slip.

"Sorry," he muttered. "I lost track there. You mentioned something regarding a party?"

"Yeah, it's tonight." Isla grinned, her whole set of perfect, shiny white teeth on display.

But Asa found himself picturing Carmen's slightly crooked ones instead.

"It's down by the beach actually," Isla continued and Asa just stared at her, wondering how she could just stand there and speak to him like she hadn't just ripped his heart out and tossed it over her shoulder like it was just another thing on her to-do list. "There'd be quite a crowd. And I know it's pretty chilly these days, but there'll be a bonfire and all that, so you should come."

"Can't," he said, his tone blunt. "Hanging out with Carmen and Willa."

At the mention of Willa's name, he saw Isla's eyes narrow into slits and her mouth form a thin line. He braced himself, waiting for her next verbal attack.

He made this world a better place—Carmen had told him that—and it was slowly getting easier to accept it, easier to even *consider* believing it. Carmen believed he made this world a better place, and that meant that whatever Isla had to spit at him wouldn't be true in the least bit. And in that moment, Asa felt ten-feet-tall.

"You can't be serious," she said through gritted teeth, the calm façade slipping off. "You've got to be fucking kidding me."

"No, Isla," he said, squaring his shoulders and drilling his eyes into hers. "I'm not." He slammed his locker shut and tightened his hold on his bag. "Must have something to do with the fact that I'm—what were your words, again? Ah, yes, a pathetic lap dog who goes looking for affection and approval in places where I'm never going to find it."

Isla's face was set in a stony expression, but her eyes betrayed her. Asa read the regret in them like an open book.

"I mean, those were your words, right?" he asked, his tone calm and guarded, not giving anything away. He couldn't see himself opening up to her in the way he used to. Not anymore.

Silence dragged on, placing another brick on the wall that had begun building itself in the space between them. Adding more distance between the minds that had once ran along parallel lines. Severing yet another of the few remaining threads that connected two hearts that had once felt one another's joys and grievances.

"Just let Carmen know I'll give her the photographs once school is over," Isla muttered, before turning around and walking away.

Asa watched her go as she took with her a piece of his heart that he was never going to get back. Perhaps that was his biggest flaw: he placed all the best parts of himself in all the wrong hands. Perhaps that was another step in the road to self-love. Maybe it was acknowledging the fact that it was okay to keep your heart under wraps like it was made of ceramic instead of iron and only letting those with cautious hands to handle it.

As he walked down the hallway, wanting to use the pool in his spare period, Asa found himself thinking of when Carmen had held his face with her hands and how he'd wanted to lean into her palms because they'd sort of felt like home.

Carmen's hands were cautious. Carmen's hands were a safe place to put his heart in.

And if he wasn't careful, Asa could fall in love with her for it.

34.
Take My Hand

Waking up was an accomplishment rather than just an ordinary task for Carmen that morning. Each shift of her muscles was the movement of a mountain, and swinging her feet off the bed and placing it on the floor of her room was stepping on a bed of needles. Her bones weighed as heavy as her heart did that morning, and she didn't know how she could walk without her feet buckling underneath her, but she did. She managed to walk towards her bathroom, get herself ready even though every inch of her body and mind screamed at her to go back to bed. Back to sleep. Back to that place where everything was just blank and nothing could touch her.

She didn't want to die, but she also wouldn't mind if she never woke up from her sleep one of these days. And that was supposed to terrify her, but it didn't. In all honesty, the idea of an endless, undisturbed sleep seemed welcoming to her.

Too welcoming.

Minutes later, she found herself seated on one of the stools at the counter, her father right across her.

She had observed him, saw the bags coating the skin underneath his eyes as if they were bruises his tears had left behind. She saw the dishevelled state of his hair, as if the demons from this house had sat up all night with him running their claws through it.

She wondered if she was a demon too, in her father's eyes. A demon in flesh and blood. The one that he'd never be able to escape when he'd somehow managed to drive away the ones in his head. The thought made her sick to the stomach, and suddenly, she couldn't eat anymore.

"Dad?" she called out after some time, her voice sounding scratchy even to her own ears.

He looked up, meeting her eyes, and Carmen knew it wasn't her mind playing tricks on her when she saw the warmth flood in them. She knew she wasn't imagining the soft turn of his mouth into the smallest of smiles.

"Yeah?" he asked softly, not touching his food either.

"I think I'd like a ride to school today," she told him, feeling no shame in admitting to herself that today was just one of those days. One of those days when she needed a little help. One of those days where she simply couldn't find the energy to even enjoy the walk to school because every nerve, bone and muscle in her body just ached too much.

"Sure, love." He smiled, nodding once before pushing his chair back while he stood. "Seeing that we're both not hungry, we might as well get going now."

Love. He called her *love*. Carmen wondered if he truly meant it.

Many times, she didn't see how he could. She couldn't understand how he found it in himself to look at her with warmth in his eyes, and a smile on his face, and love in his voice. She couldn't because how could he possibly love her when she wasn't even his own? How could anyone, really? Her own mother had forsaken her before she'd even learnt to walk.

So, Carmen would love. And *love*. And *love*. She'd love with all her heart, handing it out like it was extra change that sat in the back pockets of her jeans. She'd love because she knew what it was like to be unloved, and she'd do so without asking for even a fraction of it in return.

•   •   •

It was after second period that Carmen found herself walking down the corridor and into the main hallway where the lockers were located. She had a spare now, and like always, she was planning to spend away the minutes in the art room that Miss Cassidy had said was always open for her at any time of the day.

Just as she was getting out her art supplies though, her eyes landed on Asa a few feet away, standing at the other end of the hallway where another row of lockers were located.

She was about to approach him—she had no idea what she was even going to say to him except for a greeting of some sort—but there was that sudden rush of emotion in her, bringing her back a little more to life from the listless state she'd been in ever since last night. It made her abandon any sense of pre-planning for a conversation and turn around to walk towards him, only to stop dead in her tracks when she saw Isla herself approach him.

Carmen felt something tighten her bones, making her fingers throb with the need to hold his hand and remind him that she was there. That she'd always be there. It wasn't something as petty as jealousy, or something uncalled for like annoyance. It was more.

It was always *more*, like that surge of protection she felt the other day in the parking lot when he looked so crestfallen about what had gone down between him and Isla. That need to shield him from all the curveballs this world threw at him. That unexplainable want to dig her fingers into the very depths of him and flush out all the pain.

Pain that she knew Isla had caused him, even if Carmen didn't exactly know how. She liked Isla, she did. But it was hard not to be weary of her presence when every bone in Carmen's body seemed to shout out battle cries in Asa's defence.

She watched his shoulders stiffen and square up as he turned to face Isla, saw his body plant itself right there as if he was begging the ground to be his anchor and not split into half underneath his feet.

Goodness, how bad had Isla hurt him? she thought. Carmen didn't know. She didn't.

She wanted to, though. She wanted to know exactly how much hurt was coursing through his veins so that she could shower him with everything that was good in this world worth tenfold of all that pain.

Why couldn't she take it when he was hurting? *Why?* She felt his sorrow as if it was part of her own and funnily enough, it didn't add to her burdens or bring her down, but made her feel like she now held something precious in her hands and wanted to look after whatever it was for as long as time was on her side.

It was only when Isla muttered something and took off in the opposite direction that Carmen began walking towards him. Towards Asa.

Always *towards* Asa.

Before she could reach him though, he started walking down the hallway, a faraway look in his coffee eyes as he lost himself to whatever was swimming around in his head.

Carmen picked up her pace, shooting out a hand just before he turned around a bend in the corner, and wrapped her fingers around his palm to bring him to a stop.

His head swivelled around instantly. His wide eyes fell on their joined hands, blinking repeatedly, as if he had a hard time believing it was her hand sitting cosily in his. As if he was looking at his thoughts materialising into reality right in front of him.

Carmen allowed herself to wonder, for a fleeting moment, if perhaps Asa had indeed been thinking of holding her hands in his.

"Asa," she said. But she didn't *say* it, did she? She more than just *said* it. It was somewhat of a sigh, a breath of relief. The mere calling out his name felt so, *so* right on her tongue.

"H-hi," he said, still in a slightly dazed state before he came out of it. Carmen watched as his shoulders relaxed, as if she herself somehow had the power to take away what knitted and coiled his bones into heavy metal rather than the weightless nature they were supposed to be.

"What class have you got right now?" she asked, about to pull her hand away but his fingers tightened around hers, as if he'd seen what she was about to do.

169

"Nothing. You?"

She grinned. "I've got a spare too, actually."

"That's one coincidence I won't complain about." He smiled back.

"Do you believe in coincidences, though?" Carmen asked, knitting her brows together as she resumed walking towards the art room, pulling Asa along with her.

"Well," he paused, as if giving it some actual thought for the first time in his life, "I don't really know. I've never thought about it that way, I guess. But it is what it is, right? Coincidences are just that: coincidences."

"I guess so," Carmen mumbled, feeling a little stupid. Why was she always trying to look at the bigger picture? Why was she always on a mission to look past the surface and dig deep inside as if there was more to what meets the eye?

"Why?" Asa asked then, startling her. "What do you believe of coincidences?"

She quickly shook her head. "It's noth—"

"—*Not* nothing," he cut her off, looking down at her through the corner of his eyes, and that sideways glance made her heart flutter for some reason. It was such a normal gesture but something about the way his eyes burned when it fell on her seemed to heat up her insides, too.

"Okay." she smiled softly. "Okay." She stepped a little closer to him, her shoulder brushing against his arm, and the proximity made her pull in her bottom lip to bite down on the grin that threatened to explode across her face. "Um, it's just that, I kind of believe in a higher power, you know? Like, there's a reason everything happens. Every leaf that falls, every scrape of the knee, every chance encounter even if it's just a Tuesday afternoon and its someone who you've spilt your coffee on and you'll never see ever again, I just feel like there's some reasoning behind it. Something bigger that the naked eyes don't see."

"I can relate with that," he murmured. "Except for me it wasn't a Tuesday morning or spilt coffee but a chilly autumn afternoon and an art journal." He grinned down at her. "I'm kind of hoping I do get to see her though, rather than never crossing paths with her ever again. That'd be tragic."

Oh, Asa. She wanted to lean in a little closer, much closer, and bury her face in the crook of his neck and never let go.

"We would have still crossed paths, Asa," she told him as they entered the art room, dropping her bag on the floor as if this was her second home. Spotting the easel in its usual place at the corner of the class, she dragged it out towards the centre where it had the perfect lighting and flipped the page of the large drawing book hooked onto it to a new, fresh sheet.

She heard the sound of something being dragged along the floor and looked over her shoulder to see Asa pull one of the stools towards her until it hit the back of her thighs. His hands took a gentle hold of her shoulders, pushing her down onto the seat. He then proceeded to bring the table with all the paint supplies closer to her so that she'd have everything within hand's reach.

"Thanks," she mumbled, touched at the kind gesture.

"Don't mention it," he replied somewhat uneasily, rubbing the back of his neck.

"You're always fidgeting when I compliment you on something," she said out loud, squinting at him and pursing her lips in deep thought.

He stopped rubbing the back of his head, and his eyes met hers, emotions flashing through them in volumes that seemed even way out of Carmen's depth.

"You…" he said and seemed to hesitate, clenching and unclenching his fists, before he closed his eyes for a few seconds and reopened them. "I'm used to getting compliments on how good of a swimmer I am, or how I have nice cheekbones and an even nicer body." He slipped his hands into his pockets and seated himself on the edge of the supply table, his feet still hitting the floor due to his tall frame. "But whenever you say something nice, it's always on something that no one else bats an eye to. On the parts of me that is deemed irrelevant."

Carmen pressed her lips together even tighter, her brows furrowing harder as she observed him. It was a while before she responded. "You know Asa," she said thoughtfully. "Maybe if more people paid attention to the inside rather than the outside, this world would be a happier place."

"Basically, we just need a few more *Carmens*," he said nonchalantly, twirling a paintbrush he'd picked up from the table in his hands as if he didn't just utter words that struck a long-lost chord in her; as if he didn't just make her heart soar even though she was convinced she'd been stripped off her wings the second she was born; as if he didn't just imply the thought her perspective of beauty and this world mattered and was of significance.

Did Asa even know there was a museum in Carmen's head with walls that were painted in shades of brown and gold with his name embedded in the frames of each masterpiece he inspired her to create?

Maybe if she told him that, he might not let everyone else's words into his heart and let them colour him with shades of hate and cruelty.

"Hey, Asa?" she spoke just as she averted her gaze and picked up a brush herself, hovering her hand over the palette of colours on her left.

"Yeah?"

She pursed her lips and dipped the brush into the darkest shade of blue her eyes landed on. "Do...do you want to tell me what happened the other day?" Her hand began moving in wild, unrestrained strokes against the blank white of the paper. "With Isla?"

There was a long stretch of silence, but it didn't worry Carmen because neither was it an uncomfortable one or the kind that implied it was the calm before a storm. It just felt like he was contemplating how to phrase his words.

"She was having a go at Willa, I guess," he finally said. "And I tried to reason with her. Make her see that maybe there was just more to the story; that the two of them always being at each other's throats was stupid and tiresome to everyone around them."

172

"Oh."

"Yeah, obviously a dumb thing to do because it pissed her off," he mumbled, his tone growing distant and uncertain. "I had the same conversation with Willa that very day when school was over, but she's as stubborn in her opinion of Isla as Isla is about her."

"It's exhausting," Carmen agreed. "I feel like I'm the only one sticking up for Isla when Lottie and Willa are talking about her behind her back. But you know what, Asa? I've come to the conclusion that, at the end of the day, you and I don't owe them anything." She picked up another brush, dipping it in a sandy brown shade this time. "We've done our part as not being ignorant bystanders; the rest is up to them."

"It's just that…" Asa trailed off, and Carmen's hand stilled in its movements, her eyes finding his with the desperation to grab at the opportunity of him opening up to her in some way.

"What, Asa?" She coaxed, her tone gentle.

"She said some pretty harsh shit," he muttered, looking away and training his eyes on the nonexistent patterns his feet drew on the tiled floor of the room. "And…and I don't know if that's how she's always seen me, you know? I mean, they say drunk words are sober thoughts, and I'm wondering if that applies to words fuelled by anger, too."

Carmen's hand lowered on its own accord, placing the brush next to the paint palette as her feet lifted her off the stool and began moving towards him. Towards Asa.

Always towards Asa.

She came to a stop just inches away from him, standing between his outstretched legs as he continued to keep his gaze fixed on his shoes.

Sighing softly, she took a gentle hold of his chin and titled his head up to meet her eyes.

"I don't think that was the case, Asa," Carmen murmured. "Despite the fact that I only spoke to Isla for the first time ever during that lunch period we all sat at the same table, I knew her long before that. People think that just because I'm quiet, I'm blind, too. But I'm not." Her thumb drew circles on his chin, right below the curve of his bottom lip.

"I've seen Isla when she's all fired up and ready to go into attack mode. She's the kind who goes in for the kill, but you should already know this more than me, yeah? I think she knew she had power over you because of her knowledge of your weak spots, and she wasn't shy about pushing those buttons. That was malicious, yes. But I don't think Isla's always seen you in any way other than being her extraordinary best friend that she loves. She let her anger get the best of her, but that doesn't define who you are, okay?"

His lips twitched, before lifting up at the corners into the faintest of smiles. "All right."

"It speaks more about her character instead," she said, offering him a smile of her own.

He didn't speak, didn't so much as blink an eye as his eyes burned into hers with a kind of intensity that Carmen could only relate to the sun. And then, slowly, he lifted his hand and stretched it towards her, turning his palm outwards.

Carmen stared at it, her mouth opening to ask something— anything. But for the first time, she realised that there was nothing she could say to overpower the sensation that flowed through her at how inviting the surface of his calloused palm looked.

So, she lifted her own hand, placing it in his with uncertainty and a slight tremble in her fingers because it was so much more than just letting him hold her hand in his. So, *so* much more.

As soon as her palm met his, she felt his fingers cover her hand and tug her forward, until their chests were just a mere breath away from making contact.

And his eyes. His *eyes*. Oh *goodness*, his eyes. They had to have been carved from the sun itself because the way they burned into hers should've left her blinded. Instead, she only found it harder to look away and when his other hand came up to brush away her hair from the left side of her face, she felt her heartbeat accelerate.

Her heart that'd felt a little too dead this morning was so full of life right now. She feared she might actually explode into a million little

174

stars because that was with it was like to have Asa San Román look at you that way; it felt like you were more than just human. Like you were capable of being made of tiny little galaxies in his eyes.

That is how Carmen felt when his eyes swept over her face like he had all the time in the world; she felt like she held stardust in her veins and that through Asa's eyes, she probably was beautiful in a way she'd never seen herself as.

He learnt forward, his thumb turning her face to the side at the same time, and before she could ask him why he was turning her face away, she felt him press his lips on her cheek.

Time stilled. Or, maybe, time still passed. And the world still went on. Maybe it was just Carmen's heart that had ceased functioning for a tiny infinity right then.

"Thank you," he mumbled into her burning skin.

She swallowed, her hand trembling in his. "For what?" she asked quietly, her voice hoarse.

"For existing," he replied, and she felt his lips curve into a smile against her cheek, causing her own mouth to lift upwards.

She thought back to this morning when she'd thought it would be a release if death just claimed her in her sleep. But now, standing here, with Asa's legs on either side of her, her palm in his, and his lips pressed against her cheek, she was glad to be alive today.

She'd thought her death seemed like a welcoming thought, but here was a boy thanking her for being alive.

35.
Broken Things

Carmen's hand in Asa's was probably the only thing that held him rooted to the spot instead of him crumbling to the floor because his lips were on her cheek, and his nose was inhaling her scent even though it had no particular flavour like vanilla or spice, but *Goddamn*, she was in his veins, and there was no denying it.

She didn't even smell like paint, though his senses picked up on a very faint trace of it lingering around her. No. Instead she smelt like the sudden gust of wind that blew past him when it disturbed the peace of the scattered autumn leaves on the sidewalks, carrying the smell of damp earth and a pleasant coldness with it.

And then it finally clicked in his head. She smelt like a late afternoon in the fall. Somehow that was simultaneously the vaguest and yet most accurate way to describe her scent.

The realisation made him smile against her skin again.

"Carmen," he suddenly said, pulling back, but not moving his hands from where they were; one holding her palm, and the other cupping a side of her face.

"Yeah?" she replied, her voice slightly strained and eyes blinking really fast.

"What did you mean when you said we'd have met each other anyway?"

Her forehead crinkled. "What?"

"You said that you believed in coincidences being much more than just coincidences. That there was a reason why every single thing happened, including us meeting each other. And when I told you it'd have been tragic if ours was just another chance encounter where we never got to see each other again, you said we'd still cross paths." Asa's eyes followed his fingertips as they trailed down the side of her face and along the curve of her neck, not stopping as they ran along her collarbones and over the hollow right at the base of her throat.

"Yeah," she whispered, her hand still slightly trembling in his.

"What'd you mean by that?"

Carmen blinked, and Asa watched as the wheels spun in her head, causing her brows to knit together and her mouth to drop open as if she was finally about to respond.

But he wouldn't learn her response because the door to the art room swung open right then. Carmen flinched, jumping back a few steps. At the same time, Asa's back straightened and he swung his head towards the intruder.

Hunter walked in casually, one hand in his pocket and the other tapping away at his phone as he smirked at whatever he was seeing on the screen. He must have sensed that he wasn't the only one in the room though, because his head snapped up, and he instantly froze in his tracks when his eyes landed on Asa fist.

His mouth twisted into a scowl, "Ah, San Ro—" but Hunter didn't continue with his sneer when he noticed Carmen standing a feet away, his cold eyes zeroing in on their joined palms.

Asa didn't know what he was expecting, but it certainly wasn't the way Hunter's thin lips curved upwards into a calculating, malicious smile.

"Carmen," he said quietly, eyes gleaming with the euphoria that was found in the eyes of a predator who'd just sought out its new prey.

Asa felt Carmen's fingers slowly loosen their hold around his hand, as if all the energy was being sucked out of her with each second that Hunter stood there.

"Nice to see you, dear cousin." He grinned at her, no traces of mirth or affection in his gesture. "I see you've met our resident saviour." Hunter nodded in Asa's direction, keeping his eyes fixed on Carmen. "If you're ever having trouble in school, apparently he's the guy to go to. A huge softie on the inside and all that shit."

"Shut the fuck up," Asa snapped, shooting up from his seat on the table's edge and rising up to his full height even though his mind was spinning from the discovery that Hunter Donoghue was actually related— by *blood*, no less—to Carmen.

But Carmen was saying nothing, and that rubbed Asa the wrong way. He'd never experienced a confrontation with her beside him, so he didn't really know how she'd normally reacted to one, but the aloof demeanour she was slipping into just didn't seem right.

It only further confirmed his suspicions that something was very wrong when she pulled her palm out of his grasp completely and folded her arms across her chest, pursing her lips together until they were almost invisible.

"Come on, Carmen," Hunter coaxed. "You're hurting my feelings now. Aren't you going to say hi to your favourite cousin?"

Silence stretched on for a few painful moments, before Carmen cleared her throat and looked up at Hunter. "Hi, Hunter," she muttered, her voice shaking the tiniest bit.

"See, that wasn't so hard." He shrugged, watching her for some time before averting his devious gaze towards a confused and lost Asa. "Damaged goods, that one," he said, motioning with his thumb towards Carmen who just closed her eyes as if the words were too painful for her to take in. "But if you like broken things…" He let the sentence hang in the thick, tensed air before grinning once again and turning around to walk away.

"I actually came in here looking for an empty classroom to skip History, but now that it's been infested with the two of you, I guess I need to find another place to hang out now," he called over his shoulder, sounding slightly annoyed, before stepping out the door and disappearing from their sights for the rest of that day.

Silence. The silence was deafening, and it crawled up Asa's spine like an unwanted insect, making the hair on the back of his neck stand up.

The air was filled with so many unsaid words and jumbled thoughts, but none of them uttered a word, and to Asa's horror, he could feel a barrier come up between him and Carmen. As if she was pulling away and placing rocks with jagged edges in the place where she used to be, right by his side.

Jagged edges that was cutting into him when he kept trying to step closer to her while she continued to stagger away.

"Carmen, listen—"

"You need to leave."

The words were a punch to his gut, and it took everything in Asa not to double over in pain and heave for air.

"What?" he asked after a few breaths, uncertain if he'd heard what she said.

Carmen cleared her throat and stepped further away from him and closer to the canvas she'd been working on. "You were heading somewhere else for your spare, right?" she asked, picking up a brush and fidgeting around with a paint palette nearby. "Before I caught up with you in the hallway? So you better get going before you have no time left to be wherever you'd wanted to be in the first place."

"This is where I want to be, Carmen," he told her, clenching his fists by his sides.

"No, it isn't," she said calmly, slipping into her unfazed state. As if there was nothing that could shake her.

"How would you know?" he shot back, glaring at the back of her head.

He heard her let out a deep sigh as she carried on painting. Asa had a strong urge to tear the canvas in half and force her to look at him. "Fine then. But you know what I *do* know, Asa?" she asked. Asa noticed her knuckles whiten as her fingers gripped the brush tighter. He noticed

179

the strokes in her painting become angrier, more forceful. "I know that art is my thing. It's my state of peace, and I don't like sharing it with anyone. If you would please be so kind as to let me have my alone time, I'd really appreciate it."

Asa swallowed, keeping his feet planted to the ground and not letting her push him away. "You're the one who dragged me into the art room with you, Carmen. *You* wanted me here, in your state of peace." He took a few steps closer, holding his breath. "So, what happened within the space of a few minutes?"

"I changed my mind," she said matter-of-factly.

"Don't do this," he said quietly, his voice almost getting lost in the space between them. "Don't push me away."

"You should probably let Willa know that I won't be able to make it today after school," she continued, ignoring his plea.

Asa scowled, the hurt now being replaced with annoyance. "Are you really going to be like that?"

Carmen didn't respond, but her hand grew more frantic as she painted, her shoulder shaking violently with each stroke, as if she was pouring everything she was feeling into a painting that Asa's eyes and mind could never decipher.

His eyes followed her hand, landing on an ocean the darkest shade of blue that it was almost black, which met with the sand that was a shade of gold he'd never seen before. He hadn't the faintest clue what Carmen was intending to paint but a part of him could swear the ocean reminded him of Carmen's midnight hair, and the golden sand, his skin.

Shaking his head and hoping it'd also somehow rid his mind of the thoughts that revolved around her, he grabbed his bag and walked out the door.

•　　　•　　　•

Lunch was painfully awkward.

Asa was seated at his usual table with all the other swimmers and athletes surrounding him as they engaged in their own conversations. Some of the guys were laughing boisterously and slapping high fives, while the girls were huddled around a mobile screen, grinning about something they saw there.

Isla was at the other end of the table, playing around with her food as if there was no more energy left in her, as she just nodded along to whatever the vice-captain of the cheer team was saying.

Hunter was nowhere to be seen, so maybe that was one thing Asa could be grateful for.

But the air was still tensed, because everyone at the table knew Isla and Asa weren't on the best terms right now, and it appeared as if everyone was forcing themselves to cover up the awkwardness by having unnecessarily loud conversations.

It also certainly didn't help that a few of them kept sneaking glances at Asa and Isla every now and then.

"So, when's the meet going to start?" Hayden, one of the basketball players, asked.

"What meet?" Isla frowned, looking at Hayden with confused eyes.

"The swimming meet," Carson Williams replied. He was one of the lead swimmers, always on a tight competition with Asa.

Asa had enjoyed it at first, having found someone who was as good as he was, someone who he knew was a worthy competitor and made the sport all that more thrilling for Asa. Until he realised that the good-natured rivalry was only one-sided and that Carson hated him with all his guts.

Carson was a darn good swimmer but had a very poor sportsmanship. Last academic year, when the interstate swimming meet was held, Asa had hoped it would be himself and a swimmer from another school who'd be on the lead. Unfortunately, the meet allowed more than one swimmer from a school to participate, and it ended up with both Carson and Asa fighting for the championship.

Their strained acquaintanceship only hardened and turned bitterer when Asa had won the title.

"As in, the interstate one?" Isla inquired, snapping Asa out of his thoughts.

"Yeah," Carson nodded, before his eyes met with Asa's. A slow, spiteful smirk crawled over his face. "Didn't you know already? That's funny, you know, considering you've been to all of Asa's competitions and meets."

The chatter around the table came to an abrupt stop, like a truck forced to pull the brakes before a red light whilst driving in full speed.

"Shut the hell up, man," Wyatt muttered in a bored manner, but Asa noticed the way his friend's shoulders tensed, as if bracing himself for all hell to break loose.

"What?" Carson blinked in feigned innocence. "It was just an observation. I mean, come on. Who else at this table isn't shocked at the fact that the lovebirds are having a little spat?"

"Shut your face, Carson," Isla snarled, stabbing her plate with the fork in her hand, letting the sound rip through the cafeteria. "We're not lovebirds."

"Cool, you're not going out then." He shrugged. "Just rolling around in the sheets with each other."

Asa curled his palms into fists on his lap, taking in deep breaths and reminding himself not to cause a scene—that he couldn't give into his impulsive nature and pound his fist into Carson's face as he liked.

"Shut it," Asa warned. "or I'll make you."

"Stop it now," Lyra, one of the players from the girls' basketball team, spoke up with a scowl on her face, placing her palm on Asa's balled up fists in an effort to calm down. "And leave Isla alone." Despite Lyra and Wyatt knowing each other all their life, Asa had only began interacting with her during the end of junior year. So it was safe to say it came as a pleasant surprise for Asa to hear her put Carson in his place.

Ronnie, point guard of the boys' basketball team, chuckled. "What? It's no secret Isla's made her way through half of the guys in this school, probably even the teachers. You really think she hasn't done it with Asa of all people?"

182

Why wasn't Isla fighting back?

Asa's eyes landed on her, and something twisted in his gut when he noticed the exhaustion in her eyes. It made him angry—not at her, but *for* her. It made him want to react in a way that would surely earn him another detention.

"Well, Ronnie," Carson started again, but there was the edge to his voice that got under Asa's skin the wrong way and made his blood simmer. "Maybe she didn't bang him just yet. Maybe she never will. Maybe—" Carson's grin widened, "—it's just that she prefers a certain *type*."

The air went still, and it was as if everybody just froze in their place, even in their miniscule actions. As if all their lungs had taken a break while they held their breaths for whatever came next.

"*What*," Asa's voice was steely, his narrowed eyes lethal enough to turn anyone into stone, "is that supposed to mean?"

"Just that she must like guys with a certain allure, you know," Carson replied in nonchalance. "For example, guys who actually *are* from this country."

Nobody spoke.

Nobody moved.

Heck, nobody even seemed to be batting an eyelash or blinking.

They were all just waiting, waiting, waiting. Preparing themselves, bracing themselves for something they all knew in their minds was going to unfold pretty soon.

"Is there something you want to say, Carson?" Asa's deathly calm tone was that moment just before the storm roared to life. It kept everybody's feet planted to the spot, rendering them too afraid to even twitch.

"Yeah, *Asa San Román*," he spat out the name like it was poison on his tongue. "I have something to say—"

Wyatt butted in. "Okay, Carson, you need to calm the heck—"

183

Carson ignored Wyatt, pinning Asa down with a venomous glare and getting out into the open what he probably was itching to spit out ever since their rivalry began to grow into something more malicious.

"I am so *sick* of people like you walking into this goddamn city like you actually belong here, as if this is your fucking home," Carson snarled. "Stealing our jobs, stealing our titles, our scholarships. What? The hellhole you come from isn't good enough for you? Is that why you infest our—"

Whatever else was spilling out of Carson's mouth was drowned out by the protests of the others at their table, which in turn caused all the other tables in the eating area to look in their direction with bewilderment and nervousness.

All those who Asa was sitting with were chastising Carson, bombarding him with angry remarks and telling him that they no longer lived in an era where people were separated by their race or the colour of their skin. But it all fell on Asa's deaf ears.

He was too busy staring at Isla who'd just shrunken further into her seat, unable to meet Asa's eyes, choosing to be blissfully ignorant.

"What the fuck is wrong with you?" Hayden thundered at Isla, his grey eyes narrowing in disgust at her. "You're not even going to say something?"

"What's there to say, Hayden?" she asked in a bored tone. "If Asa wants someone to pacify him and tell him it's all going to be all right, he can go running to his mother."

Lyra snorted, making Isla's eyes snap towards her while all the others were too busy putting Carson in his place.

But Asa didn't care about Carson. He didn't care about putting the asshole in his place.

All that kept bouncing around in his head was that nobody had ever dared to say anything of the sort to him in front of Isla, and on the rare occasion that they did, she'd have given them a sharp piece of her mind. But now she just remained seated there, as if there wasn't even an atom of her being that cared about Asa anymore.

184

A part of him knew this was just Isla being her defensive, detached self when she was feeling particularly nasty. But he was beginning to wonder if the cruelty was justifiable after the numerous times he'd had her back and punched the shit out of anyone who'd ever shamed her.

He didn't need her to stand up for him, but knowing that she wouldn't defend him made him falter in his resolve to defend himself.

"You ungrateful piece of shit," Lyra spat at Isla. "The number of times he's had your back even when you weren't around to defend yourself!"

Isla cocked a brow. "Yeah? Well, did I ask him to?" When Lyra didn't reply, Isla just scoffed and rolled her eyes. "I'm out of this stupid place." She pushed her chair back and walked away, her heels clicking on the floor as the commotion around the table only grew louder.

Watching her walk away snapped something inside Asa. Gone was the hurt. All he felt now was anger simmering at the pit of his stomach—red hot anger that was quickly growing into a raging inferno.

Anger at Hunter's words earlier that'd made Carmen push him away; anger at Isla's lack of courtesy to apologise instead of continuing to give him the cold shoulder; anger at Carson's inability to digest not being as great a swimmer as Asa and using that bitterness to kick him below the belt instead.

"Well, I'm sorry that you're too much of a sore loser, Carson," Asa found himself saying as he turned his attention back to the idiot, causing everyone else to stop yelling. "I'm sorry that you can't take a loss with dignity. Sorry that you expected to win—"

"What I *expected*, you unwanted piece of trash," Carson bellowed, "was to never see your fucking face in my city again when they said a wall was gonna be built."

And all hell broke loose.

It was as if Wyatt already knew what Asa was about to do, as he moved to jump in front of him to block his way. But Asa was faster, and he lunged at Carson, one hand wrapped around his neck, as he slammed the other guy's back on the floor.

All the screams and yells from behind him did nothing to sway his anger or his growing need to use Carson as a punching bag. Blinded with rage and years of torment, he drove his fist into whichever part of Carson he could find.

Pow. Pow. Pow.

He was sick of the hate, sick of the judgments. Because if he wasn't the Mexican in a very conservative city that had the lowest amount of people of colour, he was the popular athlete who whored his way around school.

Asa was more than that. He will be more than what they told him who he was.

So he let his anger fuel every bit of his impulsive nature, letting them know that he won't be beaten down to nothing so easily.

Pow. Pow. Pow.

And the blood trickling down Asa's knuckles actually felt good.

36.
Fighting Hate With Hate

Asa's knee bounced as he tapped his foot nonstop on the tiled floor outside the principal's office, where he was told to be seated 'till Mr. Hendrickson could see him.

A barely conscious Carson had been taken down to the infirmary with two guys having to support him from either side.

Asa knew that if it had been Hunter, the outcome wouldn't have been the same. Hunter wouldn't have needed to be taken to the infirmary and would've probably done equal damage to Asa.

Carson, however, despite being built, wasn't as skilled at throwing punches the way Hunter was. Asa barely had any bruises except for those on his knuckles that he knew would be more evident by tomorrow morning.

"Hey."

Asa stopped shaking his leg and looked up as Wyatt approached him, dropping down on the seat beside Asa.

"Hey," Asa muttered, throwing his head back until it hit the wall and stretching his legs out in front of him.

"Feel any better now?" Wyatt asked, sarcasm evident in his tone. "Now that you've all but bashed his face in?"

Asa snorted. "It wasn't that bad."

"Get down to the infirmary and take a look for yourself," Wyatt snapped.

"What the hell is *your* problem?" Asa sat up straight and whipped his head towards Wyatt, glaring at him. "What, you're mad because Carson was one of us? Part of the swim team? Sorry that I attacked someone that you seem to care so much about—"

"You unbelievable asshole." Wyatt scoffed, shaking his head as he stared at Asa with incredulity. "You're such a goddamn prick sometimes, you know that?" He shot up from his seat and glared down at Asa. "I don't give two shits about Carson! You think I'm here for *him?*" He balled up his fists. Asa stared at them wearily, not really fancying another round of punches. "I'm here because I happen to care about *you*, dumbass. And I wanted to see if maybe you needed me to be here or even accompany you inside when they called you in. But, seeing that you're behaving like some rotten brat, I think I'll leave."

"Then leave!" Asa retorted, eyes flashing with all the anger that'd been building up ever since Isla had turned up at his locker this morning with the sheer audacity to ask him if he was going to the beach get-together, as if things were perfectly fine between them.

There was a flash of hurt in Wyatt's eyes, but it was gone as soon as it had appeared.

Asa's heart sank to his stomach. He wanted to take those words back because he was pretty certain he didn't want his friend to leave.

"I get that you're dealing with feeling hurt by turning it into anger," Wyatt said quietly. "But I can't be your friend if you're not going to let me be one. And yeah, Asa, you *still* got friends, in case you don't remember. So when you're ready to realise that you're too focused on Hunter and Carson and the other idiots like them that you've become completely blind to Lyra and I who've always been nothing but good to you, come find me."

Wyatt threw Asa one last glance over his shoulder and began walking away, turning around the bend in the corridor, leaving Asa by himself with nothing but silence as company.

This was different than watching Isla walk away. This was different that standing helplessly while Carmen pushed him away. This time, watching Wyatt leave, Asa knew it was no one's fault but his own. And maybe it was a wake-up call for him. Maybe something was trying to tell Asa that he needed to stop losing himself to all the hate and start focusing on all those who loved him instead.

•   •   •

Asa had entered Principal Hendrickson's room, waiting and sitting in awkward silence for about eleven minutes or so, when his parents had walked in. Asa felt his heart—which had dropped to his stomach when he'd made Wyatt leave—sink further down to his feet.

"Papá?" he called, panic apparent in his voice, as his eyes darted between his parents. "Ma? What are you doing here?"

"I called them of course," the principal spoke for the first time since Asa had entered the room. "They need to be here."

Asa's head snapped towards Principal Hendrickson. "No, they don't!" Asa said through gritted teeth, wanting the ground to split open underneath his feet and swallow him whole until he was lost beneath the earth.

The last thing he'd ever, ever wanted to do was have his parents called down to the school. The shame ate away at him in huge chunks, and he felt himself grow smaller and smaller with each bit that was taken away.

"I don't understand. What's going on?" his mother asked quietly. Her forehead was creased with so much worry, and that hurt Asa more than anything else that had happened so far today.

"Why don't you take your seats, Mr. and Mrs. San Román?" Principal Hendrickson gestured towards the two vacant chairs on Asa's right.

His mother took the seat right next to Asa, slipping her hand into his while doing so, and the tight knot of worry in his gut came undone at the support she was giving him. The principal started with his agenda and went on, debriefing both Asa's parents on what had transpired in the cafeteria until the other boys had managed to break up the fight in hopes that a figure of authority wouldn't see them.

It didn't really work out that way, seeing as how Cromwell had marched into the canteen with a thundering voice, barking out commands that sent most of the students scrambling away. Of course she hadn't kept her mouth shut, making snide comments at Asa that made him want to punch her too.

He'd stormed towards the principal's office, not waiting for the stupid woman (who was supposed to be a just and fair disciplinarian) to lead the way. He'd also made it a point not to glance at the table where he knew a certain girl with midnight hair and thundercloud eyes sat.

Something inside Asa hurt when he recalled the way they'd been lost in their own world, Carmen and he, when he'd kissed her on the cheek and everything had just felt so right.

And now they couldn't even meet each other's eyes.

It was as if Hunter always had a hold on the reins that controlled Asa's emotions. And he, Asa, was growing beyond sick of it. He wanted to stop succumbing so easily to his rashness; he didn't want to give himself over to that raging inferno inside him that Hunter always found a way to fuel. Asa knew he was and could be better than that.

Asa *needed* to be better than that.

"...your son did quite a number on the other kid," Principal Hendrickson was saying when Asa tuned his ears back in. "So, I'm afraid to say this has taken a serious turn."

"He deserved it," Asa muttered, shoulders squared and chin raised, not backing down.

"Did he?" Hendrickson cocked a brow. "Want to tell me how you came to that conclusion?"

Surprise flickered across Asa's face but he quickly composed himself. In all honesty, he didn't expect the principal to offer him a chance to explain. Cromwell never had.

But maybe not all the figures of authority in this school were as biased as her. Maybe Asa would get to tell his side of the story after all.

"He was making derogatory comments," Asa said in a cautious tone, not knowing how else to phrase it.

190

"Derogatory comments?"

"Yes."

Principal Hendrickson sighed and leaned back in his chair, holding his chin and observing Asa with a slight frown on his face. "Care elaborating on that, Asa?"

Asa blinked, his tongue not cooperating as it twisted into a knot and stopped the jumbled mess of words from falling past his lips. "Well…" he stopped speaking and clamped his mouth shut, because he didn't know. He didn't know. He didn't know. And worst, he didn't know what it was that he didn't know.

But Asa just didn't know.

He knew he was supposed to say something; to shed light on the reasoning behind his actions; to explain himself which was something not many people ever gave him the chance to do.

"He was just saying stuff, you know…" Asa trailed off, the previous tough exterior slowly crumbling away at the edges until bits and pieces of it fell to the floor like ashes, revealing the boy underneath. His armour was cracking open, and Asa didn't like the sudden rush of vulnerability that was seeping into his skin and leaving his bones cold.

"Okay." The principal nodded slowly. "What stuff?"

Why was it so, *so* hard for Asa to just say it? What was that rock which had lodged itself in Asa's vocal cords, not allowing him to let the words pass? This was supposed to be easy. He was supposed to explain himself, await whatever action the school thought was necessary and live with it.

But he was Asa San Román, the popular heartthrob who had a killer smile and supposedly had the entire student body eating out of his hand. He was Asa San Román, the defending champion of the interstate swimming meet who supposedly had the world at his feet and nothing got to him. He was Asa San Román, the boy who got into notorious fights for defending the bullied and was supposedly never bullied himself. He was Asa San Román, a guy, and as per an unsaid rule, guys don't get knocked down by words, but only with punches and kicks.

191

Did admitting it to himself make him any less masculine? Did letting his parents and the principal know that he didn't have it in him to take such discriminatory remarks make him weak? Pathetic? Less of a guy?

Did it, really?

"Asa?" his mother's voice tugged him out of his stream of thoughts. "*Mijo*, want to tell us what happened? Please?"

He closed his eyes, letting out a heavy breath, before he opened them back again and looked at the principal with defeat in his eyes. "He was giving me shit for being, well, *me*. He was saying that I didn't belong here, not in this school or this city, because of where I come from— because of my birth place. And I lost my temper."

And maybe that was another step in the road to self-love and acceptance. Maybe it was acknowledging that not only standing up for all those who'd had their hamstrings severed and kneecaps bashed in with cruelty and hate who couldn't stand for themselves was pretty good, but standing up for yourself mattered, too.

Maybe it was having enough respect for your own soul and mind that you learn to admit to yourself that what was happening to you was a form of bullying too, and it didn't matter how strong society deemed you were. You were allowed to say that it was hurting you.

The air in the principal's room was very still as both his parents stared at Asa in shock, obviously only hearing this now. Mr Hendrickson, too, seemed to be at a loss for words.

"You're not telling me that students of this school make racist comments?" the principal asked uncertainly, with the corners of his mouth twisted into a deep frown, his eyes looking truly troubled.

"I think that's exactly what my son said," his dad snapped, apparently still reeling from the shock that Asa had never mentioned any of this before.

"*Papá*," Asa quickly said, trying to tell him through eye contact to remain calm and not snap at the principal.

Principal Hendrickson ran a hand down his face, looking like he aged five years within the span of five minutes. "How long has this been going on for?"

"For as long as I've been attending Reichenbach High," Asa replied, shrugging. "It just…I guess it never occurred to me to say anything because it had just become part and parcel of school life."

"Oh, *mijo*," his mother murmured, running her hand through his hair. The skin on her forehead was still creased, and her eyes were unfocused, lost in the thoughts that were undoubtedly swimming around in her mind.

"How come the school does not know of such serious issues?" his father asked, jaw clenched and eyes hardened into slits. "They just turn a blind eye to bullying now?"

"I wasn't bullied," Asa hastily said, averting his gaze from the three adults and looking down at the floor instead. Shame crawled up his neck and left a trail of heat in its wake.

He didn't have to look up to know that all three pairs of eyes were on him; the sudden shift in the atmosphere and the sensation of holes being drilled into his skull were evidence enough.

"You, silly boy." His mother shook her head, sounding pained. "Always looking out for others but never yourself. Now you can't even tell that it's not okay for someone to say such things to you."

"I did defend myself," Asa muttered, not looking up just yet. "That's why Carson's in the infirmary."

"There's no point in punching the daylights out of someone if you can't even admit to yourself that what was happening was a form of bullying, Asa," Principal Hendrickson said slowly, as if his words were cautious footsteps on a road paved with eggshells.

The silence dragged on, loud and restless, awaiting the arrival of Asa's heart in all its raw and vulnerable glory. Because that was what Asa had to do, right? He needed to take down that armour he thought he was required to wear, and just let it all out.

He had to let all that poison out, because the hate and anger he felt brewing in the core of his very being towards the people that wronged him would eventually consume him too. And he'd be damned before he let them take that away from him as well.

"Why didn't you come to us sooner?" his mother asked quietly, breaking the silence that weighed on all four of them like a thick, suffocating blanket.

Asa still didn't look up even then, shutting his eyes closed, as he tried to level his breathing. "Because boys don't get bullied, Ma," he finally said, the words leaving his mouth which caused his heart to hammer away in his chest, creating havoc in that small space inside his ribcage. "At least, not the popular ones." He swallowed, feeling his Adam's apple bob up and down his throat as he tried to remain nonchalant. Opening his eyes, he continued to drill holes into the tiled floors of the office, not having the energy to face any of them just yet. "Definitely not the star athletes who seem to have everything going for them."

"That is a load of crap," Principal Hendrickson said. "I don't understand why you students let yourselves be bound by shackles that exist in no other place but your heads. Tell me something, Asa, half that weight you place on your shoulders, is it even yours to carry?"

Asa didn't reply, but he dared to raise his head and meet the principal's eyes, an ocean of emotions he couldn't begin to distinguish from one another washing over him in huge waves.

Principal Hendrickson sighed and leant forward, clasping his hands and placing them on the desk. "Anybody can be subjected to bullying, Asa, to pain, to peer pressure, regardless of gender, age or popularity. And you can't let anyone tell you otherwise."

"I think I'm starting to understand that now," Asa mumbled, a faint smile gracing his face, but there were no traces of it in his eyes.

"Is there action going to be taken?" his mother asked then, her dark eyes blazing. The worried state she'd been in was slowly dissipating as her fierce and protective instincts kicked in.

"I would suspend Carson, considering this is a serious matter," Hendrickson paused and Asa instantly knew things were only going to get worse, "But since Asa had taken matters into his own hand without coming to me or any other teacher in this school, I don't think I will be able to do so. The boy's injuries are pretty serious, and I think he'd have to take a few days leave from school too."

"It can't be that bad," Asa muttered, feeling a sense of déjà vu of when he'd said something similar to Wyatt just an hour or so ago.

"You broke his nose," Principal Hendrickson deadpanned, "and his eyes are beyond swollen. Let's also not forget about the fractured ribs."

Asa's eyes closed on their own accord, dread piercing his chest painfully as his breathing faltered. His hands tightened their grip on the chair he was seated on.

"So what's going to happen?" his father asked the question that Asa was too afraid to ask.

Principal Hendrickson cleared his throat and pressed his lips together, looking deeply conflicted. "Carson's parents threatened to press charges if appropriate action isn't taken by the school."

All the breath seemed to get knocked out of Asa, and he felt his stomach immediately coil into a tight knot of dread. This couldn't happen. It couldn't. It couldn't. It couldn't.

"But I didn't know then that it wasn't just some petty fight." The principal rubbed his eyes. "I had no clue the issue was much bigger and serious than that. So I won't suspend you like I had initially intended to, Asa."

Asa's lungs came to life, and all his muscles loosened up, as the breath of immense relief left his body. He let go of the death grip he had on his chair and leaned back, running an exhausted hand down his face.

"However, you're no longer allowed to take part in this year's interstate swimming meet."

Everything seemed to freeze around Asa.

His heart froze. The beginning of the relieved smile on his face froze before it could fully bloom. The hand he was running through his hair froze.

The world froze but time was still slipping by, not waiting for him to catch up.

"Wait wait wait." He shot out of his seat, hands shaking by his sides as he stared at the principal with utter disbelief. "You can't do that! You can't—that's not—I did nothing wrong! I did *nothing* wrong—"

"Asa!" his mother thundered, grabbing his arm and pulling him back, but he just shook it off, not looking away from Hendrickson.

"You can't take that away from me!" Asa shook his head vigorously, not wanting to listen to anything else anymore. They couldn't do this to him. They *couldn't*.

"Okay." the principal nodded. "All right, fine. I won't take this away from you. Maybe you'd like doing community service better. You know, when the Williams go ahead and press those charges against you. Maybe you'd prefer being on probation? Or is it that you're actually okay with having some sort of record staining your credibility when you apply for colleges and jobs?"

"I don't deserve this." Asa's voice shook with barely restrained anger.

"But Carson deserved to be sent to the infirmary?"

"I told you what he did!"

"And you think his parents are going to care about what their son did?" Hendrickson raised his eyebrows. "All they care about is their son's swollen face and bruising body and making the person responsible pay. If they take this to any other authority outside of this school, I won't be able to help. This is the only way I know to minimise the consequences. You need to understand that."

Asa couldn't believe what he was hearing. This wasn't happening, was it? This was his senior year. It was his last year at high school. His last ever chance to take part in this meet. He was supposed to set new records this year, achieve new milestones. He was supposed to win that championship title one last time.

"This was the first time I ever took a stand for myself," Asa said quietly, a faint tremble in his voice. "This was the first time in all my years of being put down that I fought back."

And it was true. All his fights with Hunter in the past had never been for himself. It had always been Asa sticking up for some other student who was being bothered. But never for *himself*. Never for Asa.

Today in the cafeteria though, something had finally snapped. And now here he was, paying for letting himself drown in the poison he'd allowed others pour into his veins which was eventually carried into his heart.

"You don't fight hate with hate, Asa," Hendrickson said. "Punches and blows don't solve anything. You think Carson and the other narrow-minded students like him are going to walk into school with changed mentalities? You think that fight will inspire them to have a sudden change of heart and that this city's going to become more receptive all of a sudden?"

Asa didn't say anything. He wanted to set this world on fire right now. He wanted everyone to choke on all the hate that infested this place.

"Look," Principal Hendrickson sighed and rose out of his seat, "I went through your career initiative files from last semester." He was referring to a programme their school had held during the last few months of Junior year, where the students who wanted career guidance were given tips and suggestions on which colleges to apply in order to get the best coaching in the field they wanted to major in. "And I noticed that you didn't want to pursue swimming professionally. So this could've actually been much worse, you know. You're not losing anything on a large scale by not participating in the meet this year."

But Asa felt like he'd already lost a part of himself.

"I think I'd like to go home for the rest of the day," He swallowed, picking up his bag from the chair he'd been sitting on.

197

"Sure, no problem," Hendrickson said kindly. "I really am sorry, Asa. But all this could've been avoided if you'd just come to me. Or even gone to your parents."

Asa didn't respond. He didn't even wait for his parents, as he threw open the door and stormed down the hallway, exiting the school and finding himself in the sanctuary of his truck minutes later.

But even while he drove down the streets that were scattered with autumn leaves, he found himself wishing the passenger seat wasn't as vacant and empty as Asa's heart right then.

37.
Isla Martin

Isla was worried when she couldn't spot Asa anywhere for the rest of the day.

She didn't want to be worried, but then again, lately she was feeling a lot of things she didn't want to feel.

The news about the fight had spread like wildfire, considering it occurred in the canteen in front of a very large audience. Isla had shrugged it off, aware of Asa's tendency to give in to his rash nature and let his fists speak for him, but when he hadn't turned up to History class, she knew something was off.

School was over now, but he was still nowhere to be seen, and that twisted her stomach into an anxious knot.

"He's not here," a familiar voice said from behind her, and Isla felt her blood begin to boil at the sound, the blind rage taking over whatever worry she felt for Asa.

She turned around, narrowing her eyes at Willa. "Did it sound like I was talking to you?"

Annoyance flashed across the other girl's eyes and her lips curled into a grimace. "Would it kill you to let go of your pride for one second?"

"Letting go of my pride?" Isla raised a perfectly arched eyebrow. "No, that wouldn't kill me. But being forced to make conversation with you might."

Willa swore under her breath. "I don't need to put up with this shit," she muttered. "Listen, I couldn't give two hoots about you, but I happen to be fond of Asa. Considering he spent the afternoon in the principal's office along with his parents and that I saw him leave earlier, I figured he could use his best friend and wanted to tell you about it. But seeing the complete bitch you're being right now, he actually should be better off without you."

"You don't know me." Isla seethed.

"And I don't *want* to. Now if you'll excuse me, I have people I actually care about to get back to."

"Wait," Isla begrudgingly called out, her tongue tasting bitter at having to prolong this conversation.

Willa stopped walking away and turned around, snorting. "What?"

"Where's Carmen? I need—"

"No," she began shaking her head, her tone adamant. "*Hell no.*"

Isla's eyes turned into slits, "What do you mean *no?*"

"I mean, no, I'm not telling you where to find her," Willa spat. "I have no idea what the hell went down between you and Asa that day, but I could see how shaken up about it he was. And this is the guy who's supposed to be your best friend. Carmen's my friend, and I'll be damned if I let you put her through that kind of shit."

"I'm not going to do anything to her," Isla snapped, her patience hanging by a thread and her palms curling into fists.

"Yeah." Willa scoffed. "Is that what you told yourself when you befriended Asa? That you weren't going to hurt him?" She shook her head in disbelief. "You're a goddamn train wreck, Isla. People like you do nothing but hurt all those around you, and I won't allow Carmen to be one of those people. So if you want to find her, do it yourself. I won't be one of the reasons you get more involved in her life."

Isla's lips curled upwards into a menacing smile, calculating Willa's weaknesses and aiming to hit her right there. "Is that why you had

200

to move away from your old school and come here? Your old friends felt smothered by all your overprotective tendencies?"

"Maybe I'm overprotective about the people I care about, Isla," Willa said seriously. "And yeah, maybe I suffocate them sometimes. But at least I *have* friends. And I think that says a lot."

The words were a punch to Isla's gut which caused her breathing to falter as she watched the other girl walk away.

Isla had always been the one with her finger on the trigger, the one with the power to bring someone else to their knees. But Willa had managed to send bullets flying into her skin, and Isla loathed being at the mercy of someone else's words. It brought back memories she'd rather keep buried at the darkest pits of her mind.

Memories of when she was the one on the receiving end of cruel whispers and harsh judgments, until she had eventually turned all that pain into power. She'd built a fortress around her and didn't think twice about pricking someone with her thorns before they got close enough to do any more damage to her already fractured heart.

When you were a blonde with blue eyes who liked wearing crop tops and shorts, nothing else mattered. If the world made up its mind that you were a slut, then that was what you were. Isla wasn't stupid enough to try changing people's perspective of her. Instead she learnt how to turn her heart to steel and her tongue into a weapon. And it worked.

It worked until it didn't, and she could feel her grip on reality slowly slipping through her fingers like grains of sand. Because she'd grown so accustomed to letting herself spit poison from her mouth instead of spilling poetry that she no longer knew how to utter words that weren't cruel. She'd ripped too many hearts to shreds in order to safeguard her own that she gradually forgot how to differentiate between the ones she wanted to break and the ones she wanted to protect.

Asa had never belonged to the list of people she permitted herself to break.

No, Isla had never meant to break her best friend. She was supposed to be the one who crushed whoever dared cause him pain, but had instead ended up being the one who pulled the trigger.

She was just so, *so* used to wearing a façade that she now couldn't separate herself from who she wanted to be to who she let the world morph her into. And if that wasn't proof of her behaviour heading towards a downward spiral, she didn't know what was.

After all, there was only so long someone could go on wearing a mask before it either started slipping off or, worse, becoming a part of their identity.

•　　•　　•

Isla had given up looking for Carmen, assuming she'd already left, and started to drive away from the school when she spotted her walking a few feet away.

She let her car pick up speed, before pulling up right next to her with screeching wheels and a loud honk.

Carmen jumped, her eyes widening from being startled, before her posture relaxed when she realised it was only Isla.

"Get in." Isla gestured, her voice drifting through the open window as she leaned across the seats to open the door.

"Um, no," Carmen quickly said, shaking her head. "I like walking."

Isla blinked. "Oh."

"Yeah." She offered a small smile.

"You're upset with me because of Asa," Isla accused her, knowing that it wasn't true but using her manipulative skills to guilt-trip Carmen into accepting the lift. She felt bad doing it, but as much as she liked Carmen, she cared about Asa more. And if taking advantage of Carmen's compassionate nature was the only way to learn how Asa was doing, then she wasn't going to apologise for it. There was another way, a part of her knew. She could always just go to Asa and check on him herself. But Isla Martin was a proud person, and it was that very pride that would be her downfall one day.

202

"Of course not!" Carmen exclaimed, looking shocked at the blunt accusation. "I'm not going to pick sides in a fight that I wasn't even a part of."

"Why won't you get in then?" Isla pulled her brows together, trying to appear as if she was troubled and hurt by Carmen's actions.

"I just... Never mind." She sighed heavily and walked towards the car, before getting in and shutting the door after her.

Isla fought back the smug smile that threatened to take over her face. She wasn't going to let herself feel triumphant until she'd gotten what she needed out of Carmen. The sense of accomplishment vaporised into thin air the instant she properly registered her stream of thoughts.

Until she'd gotten what she needed out of Carmen. Was that how low Isla had fallen now? Was she only going to use the poor girl and then discard her when she no longer served a purpose?

This must have been what Willa was talking about. Maybe Isla really was a train wreck. Maybe she did indeed end up hurting those around her time and time again.

"Get out," Isla whispered, her hand tightening around the steering wheel.

"What?" Carmen looked taken aback, staring at Isla as if she'd grown a second head.

"You need to leave," she said, swallowing. "I don't want to—" But she didn't continue. She *couldn't* continue.

I don't want to hurt you too, Isla had wanted to say, but long forgotten was the ability to voice out her emotions.

"Wait, Isla, I don't understand—"

"I asked you to get out of my vehicle," Isla snapped. "I really don't see what's so hard to understand about that."

She waited for the blow. She waited for Carmen to snap back at her. She waited for the look of disgust.

Nothing of the sort came. Nothing except for Carmen chewing on her bottom lip, as she examined Isla with worry and a tinge of sadness.

And somehow, that was worse than any insult anyone could've thrown her way.

"This must have been what it felt like for Asa," Carmen finally said, her voice quiet.

Isla frowned at her. "What?"

"Something happened today," she sighed, "in art class. And I reacted by pushing Asa away like the way you're pushing me away now. I didn't realise how much it must suck to have someone you care about push you away until now." She ran a hand down her face. "God, the last thing I ever wanted to do was hurt him."

Isla's mind was stuck in a loop, repeating Carmen's words over and over again: *"to have someone you care about push you away…someone you care about…"*

"Wait." Isla blinked, her throat tightening. "Did you just imply that…that you *care* about me?"

"Well, of course I do, Isla," Carmen said in a completely surprised tone. "I thought I'd already made that clear."

"I-I didn't—I just—I thought…" She shut her eyes and took in deep breaths, trying to steady herself and get a hold of her emotions. When Isla opened them back again, Carmen was watching her anxiously.

"Why are you so nice to me?" Isla asked, looking away and fidgeting with the ends of her long blonde strands.

"Because…my mum was like you," she mumbled, causing Isla's head to whip towards her in bewilderment. "Back in high school, she was that girl: the popular one, the queen bee, the one that apparently slept around too much and wore short shorts. She had it pretty bad during school, and that reputation followed her into college too, despite getting her act together and having a steady relationship with my dad by then."

"Oh," was all Isla could say. "I…well, at least she's got you and your dad now, right? She must be happy."

"The dead don't get to feel happy."

Isla's eyes widened. She was suddenly fumbling for words. "Shit, Carmen. I'm so sorry—I didn't—"

204

"Its fine," Carmen said. Something in her tone ended the conversation on the particular topic effectively.

An awkward silence fell on them, and Isla found herself searching frantically for something else to talk about.

"So." Isla cleared her throat, breaking the silence. "You push people away too, huh? When you're upset?"

Carmen shrugged somewhat half-heartedly, looking distracted, and Isla couldn't exactly blame her. "Yeah, guess so."

"Can't say I'm not surprised."

Carmen turned to look at her. "That we have something in common?" she asked.

"That you have a flaw," Isla responded.

The other girl frowned, her grey eyes observing Isla's blue ones. "Of course I have my flaws, Isla. I'm not perfect, contrary to popular belief."

"Could've fooled me."

Carmen laughed humourlessly. "You know, for someone who hates Willa so much, that's pretty judgmental of you."

Isla pressed her lips together, deciding to change the subject because there was something more important she needed to say right now. "Listen, about Asa…" she trailed off, unable to meet Carmen's eyes, "He's always the one that everybody takes their bad days out on—everybody he cares for, that is." She ran her fingers along the steering wheel. "Maybe it's because we know he'll eventually forgive us for it and always be there no matter what. Just—and I know it sounds hypocritical coming from me—but please don't be another one of those people. Everyone he loves has let him down at one point in his life. Don't add yourself to that list."

Carmen didn't say anything, but then again, she didn't have to. The tenderness that crept over her face when Asa was mentioned spoke volumes to Isla.

Maybe Asa was in safe hands. Maybe Isla needn't worry as much. Maybe—and this killed Isla on the inside—he didn't need her around anymore.

"He misses you, you know," Carmen told her softly.

Isla didn't believe that for even a second, knowing it was just Carmen being nice. Instead of arguing with her about it though, Isla just smiled and asked for her address.

After she'd dropped off Carmen and was driving herself back home, all she could think about was going to that beach bonfire tonight.

That, and getting drunk out of her mind.

38.
Letting Go

Asa was lying on his bed, hating the world—being angry at everything and everyone around him, even if it seemed illogical and plain stupid. He flexed his fingers, curling and uncurling his fists, as he lifted his hands into the air and examined the bruised knuckles. Just like that, his surroundings disappeared, and the scene encompassing those last few crucial seconds from his record-breaking race last swimming meet materialised before his eyes.

His body was moving through the water with the kind of grace and skill one could only acquire after pouring all their sweat and blood into perfecting a certain art. His hands were once again outstretched in front of him, his fingers flashing through his peripheral vision every now and then as he furiously moved closer and closer towards that finish line.

And there was that chanting from the indoor bleachers.

God, even now he could hear the sound of his school's name being roared over and over again by the other Reichenbach students and family who'd come for support.

Asa closed his eyes and smiled, almost being able to feel the wildfire that had coursed throughout his body that day when he'd been titled the national champion—something that he was never going to feel again.

Maybe Asa didn't hate the world, then. Maybe he wasn't angry at everything and everyone around him. In all honesty, it was probably himself he hated, himself that he was mad at.

But then again, what else was new?

Opening his eyes with a deep sigh, he pushed himself off the bed and headed down towards the kitchen instead. There was no point lying around and moping while feeling sorry for himself. He'd dug himself into this hole, nobody else. And he needed to own up to that.

"Oh, you're up," his mother remarked when he reached the end of the staircase which was right in front of the living room.

Asa frowned. "What are you talking about? I was never asleep."

She shrugged. "You've been in there ever since you came from school. I thought you were taking a nap."

"No," he muttered. "No nap."

His mother just nodded, looking at him wearily as if she wanted to say something more but then seemed to decide against it.

"Where's pa?" Asa asked, looking around the room curiously.

"He went to grab dinner. Friday night is takeout night, remember?"

"Right," he mumbled, hating his one-word responses but feeling restless and uneasy to hold up a proper conversation. Maybe he should take a nap. Better yet, maybe he should just call it a night and deal with the world tomorrow onwards.

He sighed deeply and turned towards his mother. "You know what, ma, I think I'll just go—"

A loud knock interrupted him and both of them turned to stare at the door with confusion.

"Are you expecting someone?" he inquired.

She shook her head. "No, and your father wouldn't need to knock." She paused, thinking for a minute. "Unless he forgot his keys like usual."

The person on the other side of the door knocked again, but this time it didn't stop. The knocking only grew louder and yet, it didn't seem urgent. In fact, it seemed almost…*sloppy*?

Asa frowned and when he noticed her about to get up from the couch, gestured for his mum to sit, deciding to check who it was for himself.

Whoever the idiot was behind the door seemed to have been placing their entire weight on it because the instant Asa opened it, they crashed into Asa and sent him flying to the floor with a painful groan. Seconds later, he felt a body collapse right on top of him, an elbow hitting him right in the ribs and making him see black dots in his vision.

Asa swore, a string of colourful Spanish words leaving his mouth in an angry fit. For the first time, his mother didn't reprimand him for it. He turned towards her for help, but she seemed to be frozen in her seat, her jaw dropped wide open at the scene that had just unfolded before her.

"Ma? Hello? Yeah, less seeing and more helping, *por favor*?"

He heard the sound of a familiar giggle, and his eyes widened when he realised who had just turned up at his place during this hour of the night.

"Isla?" he asked in bewilderment, lifting his head off the ground only to meet her messy blonde head. "Isla, what the heck are you doing?"

"You're so adorable when you speak in Spanish." She giggled again, and Asa swore some more, closing his eyes and letting his head fall back on the floor.

She was drunk. Good God, she was completely drunk.

He pushed her body off him gently and stood up before reaching down and grabbing a hold of her arms, lifting her to her feet.

"Isla." He frowned, worry and concern washing over him as he examined her for any injuries. "Where have you been?"

"You're upset." Isla pouted, noticing his anxious expression. "I'm always making you upset, aren't I?"

Asa sighed and dared to glance at his mother. He wished he hadn't done that though, because her dark eyes were narrowed into slits, and her face was twisted into a grimace.

Instead of saying anything to his mother, he directed his attention back to the drunk girl that he was struggling to keep from collapsing to the floor. "Isla, please just listen to me, okay?" He shook her shoulders, trying to get her to focus. "How did you end up here? How—"

The beach party, he suddenly realised. Hadn't Isla mentioned in school that there was a bonfire at the beach tonight? The one that he had to skip out on because he was supposed to be driving through the neighbourhood with Willa and Carmen, before everything went to hell and he'd had to come home instead.

"The beach is pretty far away, Isles," he muttered, just wishing she'd find enough sense in her drunken state to respond to him. "You couldn't have walked here—Holy shit, did you *drive* here?" His voice grew in volume as the panic took control of him. "Did you just drive drunk?!"

"Shh! The neighbours are going to hear you!" his mother hissed.

"Ma, can you please check if there's a dark blue car parked outside?" he asked frantically, tightening his hold on his best friend. Or, at least, someone who *used* to be his best friend. He wasn't too sure about a lot of things anymore.

He heard footsteps approach him as his mother walked back into the house. He looked up just in time to see her shake her head.

"No." She shot Isla a quick glance, but kept her face unreadable. "No car. Someone must have dropped her off."

"I had a ride," Isla mumbled, her words beginning to slur as she tried to stand still. "Hunter dropped me off."

Asa's jaw clenched and he wished more than ever that he was some class-A douchebag so that he could just tell Isla to get out of his house. But Asa wasn't a class-A douchebag and despite his growing rage and annoyance, he couldn't abandon her. Not when she was in such a vulnerable state.

"I can't believe this." His mother scoffed, throwing her hands into the air. "All this girl ever does is hit you below the belt every time!"

"What do you want me to do, ma?" he snapped, losing his patience and taking his frustration out on her instead. "Leave her like this?"

"Of course not!" she exclaimed, looking so angry that Asa had to swallow and blink twice. "I just don't know why you keep hanging around someone who brings you down so much!"

"She doesn't bring me—"

"Yes, she does! Your loyalty and affection are blinding you, but I'm your *mother*, Asa. You used to come to me during middle school and freshman year whenever she hurt you, remember? You used to talk to me. I don't think there's anyone who's picked on your weaknesses and insecurities the way this girl has! And whenever I tried telling you that, you would get mad at me until you no longer came to me with your problems. And now I never know what's going on with you at school!"

"Is that what this is about?" he asked, still sounding angry. Angry that whatever his mother said was true. Angrier that he could never admit it to himself. "That you didn't find out how bad things were at school until today in the principal's office?"

His mother took a deep breath, closing her eyes as she tried to get a grip of her anger. "*This*," she said, opening her eyes slowly, "is about how you always let yourself see good in someone who also has a lot of bad. And normally that's a very admirable quality, *mijo*, but not if it's making you think that you deserve what they put you through."

He turned away from his mother and looked at the girl who'd now fallen asleep in his arms. It was hard to think about how malicious Isla could be when she looked so peaceful and harmless right then.

"She has nobody else, ma," he said quietly.

"Then she should be more grateful towards the fact that you're still putting up with her," his mother murmured, patting him on the cheek gently. "Put her in the guest room. I'll let her parents know. It's too late, she might as well remain here."

211

"Thank you." He met her eyes with a sad smile.

"She's still someone's child." His mother shrugged. "I can't turn a blind eye when she obviously needs some help."

"Thanks," he repeated, before reaching down to hook his other arm behind Isla's knees and then carrying her towards the guest room.

When he looked down at her sleeping figure, the quilt pulled up till her chin, Asa couldn't help but feel a pang of sympathy and nostalgia for the girl he once used to know.

A girl that was slowly slipping from existence and becoming something else instead.

But she was still his best-friend, wasn't she? This was still the same Isla he knew.

It had to be.

Maybe his mother was wrong. Ma had to be wrong. There was a good chance Isla would eventually grow out of whatever phase she was going through right now. Whatever it was that was making her withdraw from everyone and become even colder and detached than usual.

So Asa just sighed softly and walked out of the room with a content smile on his face, knowing that come tomorrow morning, everything would be much better and they'd be able to wipe the slate clean.

Maybe, just maybe, he'd have his best friend back.

• • •

Isla winced, clutching her head, as Asa placed a mug of coffee right in front of her, steam rising up from it and mingling with the cold air.

"My head hurts," she groaned, mouth twisted into a grimace.

"That's terrible," Asa said, not bothering to hide the grin which only earned him a glare.

"Still a dick, I see," she retorted.

"Still a moody bitch, I see," he shot back.

"Asa!" his mother's booming voice sounded all the way from the living room to the kitchen they were seated in. Asa made a mental note to lower his voice.

212

"Still got the anti-cussing policy, huh?" Isla asked, lips twitching at the corners.

Asa shrugged lazily, leaning back on his seat. "That's the San Román household for you."

"Sometimes I think your mother doesn't like me much," she suddenly said, her voice quiet but also free from judgment.

He sighed deeply, running his hand down his face as a yawn escaped his mouth. "She doesn't *hate* you," he said carefully.

"But she dislikes me."

Asa pursed his lips, his head spinning as he thought about how to tackle this in the least offensive manner. "It's complicated..." he replied and trailed off, knowing he was walking on eggshells; he hated it. Lately, with Isla, taking caution was becoming necessary because he no longer knew what was going to set her off next.

It didn't use to be like that.

"How so?" She pushed, obviously not wanting to let the topic go.

"Well," he paused, running his tongue over his mouth. "She doesn't dislike you because of the reasons students at school dislike you. Ma doesn't *look down* on you, if you know what I mean."

Isla nodded and then looked away, taking a few sips of the hot drink before placing the mug back on the table and meeting Asa's eyes once again.

"She just doesn't trust me," Isla said slowly, stating an observation rather than fishing for answers.

"I—"

"With you."

"What?" Asa frowned, pulling his brows together.

"That's it, right? She doesn't trust me with you. She thinks I'll end up being more of a burden than a friend."

"Or maybe she's just speaking from the experience of the countless times you've let me down, Isles." He sighed. "So, yeah, of course she's going to be protective."

213

"It never bothered you before," she muttered. "You always come running back."

Anger flared in Asa's gut, making him sit up straight and glare at Isla with incredulity all over his face. "Always come running back?" he repeated, beyond pissed.

Isla flushed and looked away. "Okay, fine—"

"I am not your lapdog." He seethed, still finding it hard to wrap his head around the fact that she believed—she actually goddamn *believed*—he'd just let her walk over him repeatedly.

"Geez, okay!" she snapped, before letting out a groan and massaging her temples again. "God, can we just stop arguing? I'm too hungover for this shit."

"You always have an excuse when it comes to acknowledging your faults, Isles," Asa muttered, feeling tired now. Tired that he was stuck in this loop with her. Tired that they kept going around in circles, repeating the same mistakes, inflicting the same pain. It just went on and on and on.

And God, Asa was tired.

"And what would you rather have me do?" She smiled, but it was cold. And the shivers it sent through Asa's bones were anything but pleasant. "Should I mope about my flaws like you, Asa? You want me to waste away my days wondering how I'm never good enough? How I don't deserve anything good? Would you prefer if I had the self-esteem of a peanut like you?"

And Asa laughed then. It was a sad laugh nor a short laugh.

A broken laugh.

Because, goddammit, mothers knew best and his had been right last night.

"That's..." Isla cleared her throat, regret flashing in her eyes. "Listen, that's not—"

"Actually, Isla, I'm done listening," he said quietly, shaking his head. "I'm just done. Done with the constant wondering why you keep falling off the wagon and waiting for you to get your shit together so that we can be okay again. Done with always asking myself when you'd stop taking out all your frustrations on me. Done with believing there must be something wrong with *me* because even though I'm the only person who's stood by your side and never left all this time, you seem to have no qualms about breaking me over and over again. There's nothing wrong with me. There can't be. Not when it's *you* who claims to love me but goes ahead and hurts me more than anybody else ever has. That's not love. And I'm tired of you justifying yourself by using our friendship as an excuse."

Isla's hands were shaking where it sat on the table top, close to the steaming mug, and he wondered, for a second, if she was going to throw it at him.

Instead, he watched as she pushed her chair back and rose out of her seat unsteadily, pressing her lips together.

"Thank you for the aspirin," she told him in a quiet voice. "And the breakfast." She tucked a strand of her light hair behind her ear. "And the coffee too."

Asa scoffed and shook his head. "You're still not going to give me an apology, are you? Not even for the shit you just said a minute ago?" He threw his hands into the air, so many emotions washing over him at once that it was hard to focus on one particular feeling. Rage. Sadness. Nostalgia. Longing. The need to feel Carmen's reassuring hands hold his face. "Is it honestly that hard for you to just say you're sorry?" He searched her face for any signs of remorse, any indication that she wanted to apologise.

He didn't find any such signs, though. And it made him wonder if it was just Isla growing more remorseless or himself losing the ability to read her like an open book.

Both cases frightened him, but this was no longer his problem. Her burdens were no longer his to carry. And when he watched her turn around and walk away without a response, he felt a weight slowly slide from his shoulders, and he could stand that much taller now.

When he watched her open the door and slam it shut behind her, something in his chest broke away. It was as if there had been a rock lodged between his lungs, or somewhere right in the middle of his ribcage, and watching her leave was what finally loosened it. As if his heart was literally liberated by a burden that weighed far too much.

Maybe this was the hardest step in that road to self-love. Because even though he'd chosen himself, he'd also lost something big. Something that had been a part of him for so long.

Maybe learning to love yourself was never about the situations where you won repeatedly and wore a triumphant smile on your face as if you could conquer the world if you put your mind to it.

Maybe sometimes you had to lose a piece of your heart so that you could work on making it whole again.

Sometimes, no matter how much it hurt, no matter if it felt like you were using a chainsaw to cut off one of your own limbs, you just needed to let go of the things that no longer brought you peace or joy.

And as much as it pained Asa to admit it, his deteriorating friendship with Isla Martin was one of those things.

39.
Hook, Line, and Sinker

When Asa walked into school the following week, one hand loosely wrapped around the left strap of his backpack and the other hand running through his dark hair absentmindedly, he felt a hand grab the back of his shirt all of a sudden and slam him into a wall.

His bag softened the blow of his back hitting the hard concrete, and his jaw fell open, bracing himself for a punch, or a kick—something—however the second his eyes registered the familiar but angry face of Wyatt, his shoulders slumped against the wall, and a breath of relief escaped his mouth.

"You goddamn moron," Asa muttered, knocking Wyatt's hand off of him. "The heck was that for? You scared me!"

"Now you know what that feels like then," Wyatt snapped. "Do you know how many times I called you or texted you throughout the freaking weekend? The last time I saw you was in front of Hendrickson's office, and then you weren't in school for rest of Friday! I thought they'd suspended you, or worse."

"Well, depends on your definition of worse, really." He shrugged, feeling a little bitter again. "Because if worse means I'm no longer allowed to be a participant in this year's meet, then yeah, worse did happen."

First, Wyatt's brows pulled together slowly as if he couldn't begin to understand what Asa was telling him, but then the realisation eventually dawned on his face, and his green eyes widened in disbelief.

Wyatt let out a sound that was between an incredulous laugh and a scoff. "You're kidding." He shook his head and stepped back slightly. "You've *got* to be kidding."

Asa ran his fingers through his hair, looking away into the distance as he watched students enter the building in groups. "Wish I was."

"No no no." Wyatt shook his head, obviously not willing to accept the startling news. "No, they can't do that! They can't."

Asa shrugged, trying to appear nonchalant even though he knew his friend could see right through that façade. "It's all right," he lied. "I mean, our school still has a chance of winning—"

"I don't give a shit about the school," Wyatt muttered, looking away. "This meant a lot to you, didn't it?"

Asa didn't respond for a while and just stared at the side of his friend's face and it hit him then how oblivious and blind he could be sometimes. Because here was someone standing right in front of him who'd stood by his side for as long as he could remember, but someone he'd never appreciated enough, if at all.

Picking up on the lack of response, Wyatt turned back around to face Asa, confusion flickering in his eyes. "Asa?"

"Do you remember how we became friends?" Asa asked, but he didn't know who he was really speaking to, Wyatt or himself.

"Um—"

"Freshman year," he went on, watching the memory play out in his head as if it was just a moment from yesterday and not a little more than three years back. "I had entered the swimming building for the swim team try-outs."

"Yes, I rem—"

"And this particular group of other freshmen—there must have been three of them—told me that I had no business trying out for someplace where I didn't belong and that the openings on the team belonged to them already so I shouldn't waste my time hoping to get it."

"Okay—"

"And the others within earshot just looked away awkwardly because they figured it wasn't their problem and they pretended to not have heard anything… but you didn't stay quiet." Asa's vision zoned out of replaying the scene in his head and focused back on his current surroundings, his eyes meeting Wyatt's confused and surprised ones. "You told them to shut up if they had nothing nice to say and that if they so much as looked at me in the wrong manner, you would place them in a chokehold underwater."

Wyatt grinned then. "I remember that. Their expressions were hilarious."

Asa didn't register his words as he continued to speak, the words flowing out of his mouth naturally. "When I went home that day, I was so upset, and all I did was keep thinking about what they said. Ma was worried that I'd never make any friends and that maybe we'd have to move somewhere else."

"I'm not getting what you're trying to say." Wyatt frowned.

"I'm saying that I went home with their hate at the back of my mind. I'm saying I stayed up the whole night ranting to my mother about how I wished none of them would be selected for the team. I'm saying I spent so much time letting the anger in that I forgot to tell her about this one boy who'd stood up for me. And…" Asa's fingers curled around his bag's straps, his nails digging mercilessly into the leather. "And that's what I've been doing all this time too. Focusing on all the people who've stuck knives in my back rather than the ones who've *had* my back."

Wyatt opened his mouth, blinking in bewilderment, but he seemed to be at a complete loss for words. Asa didn't mind, though. Today, he'd rather do all the speaking. God knew he owed the guy standing in front of him that much, at least.

"So I want to say I'm sorry," Asa murmured, looking away from his friend and past his shoulders instead. "And *thank you*. Thank you for

219

that first time in freshman year, and thank you for all the times you've been there."

Wyatt was still not speaking. He seemed to truly be clueless as to what he should do or say which only resulted in the situation slowly beginning to grow awkward, and with that, Asa's urge to face-palm increased, too.

"Dude," Asa deadpanned finally, throwing his hands into the air. "I get that you're not like me—that you're not that heart-to-heart kinda guy—but a little courtesy would be nice anytime soon."

Wyatt snorted and looked towards his right, but the small smile on his lips didn't escape Asa's attention. "Next thing I know, you'll be asking for a hug," he muttered, a teasing edge to his voice.

"I wouldn't mind one actually," Asa said in a serious tone, but his eyes were alight with mischief.

Wyatt grinned. "I haven't seen you this carefree recently; good to know you're back."

"I'm still waiting for my hug."

"Oh, piss off." Wyatt snorted and shoved Asa playfully before walking down the hall with a smile and a shake of his head.

Despite the light-hearted moment, Asa found himself in wonder if perhaps losing something in the short run meant winning another thing in the long one.

Because even though he knew that Isla was no more a part of his life, leaving a dull ache somewhere in his chest, gaining back Wyatt's friendship felt like a breath of fresh air and for once—for *once*—he wanted to focus on the good rather than letting himself drown in the bad.

•　　•　　•

Asa was using the school's pool again.

It was a spare period, and just like all the other times, he wanted to spend it in the one place he could have a peaceful state of mind.

Even underneath the water, whilst he held his breath, a part of him still thought about how he'd had that peace of mind during the car rides with Carmen, when she used to be seated beside him.

Honestly, he'd never believed anything other than losing himself underwater could bring that sense of calmness over him. But apparently there was something else that effortlessly provided him solace, and it came in the form of a hurricane with midnight hair and thundercloud eyes that smelt like a late autumn afternoon.

There was a pressure right in the middle of his chest, but he was quite certain it had nothing to do with the fact that he'd been holding his breath for so long and everything to do with the mere recalling of Carmen's half-smile half-grin.

Needing to come up for air, Asa let his arms stop moving and waited as his body gradually dropped from the floating position, and his feet grazed the pool's floor. Even with his towering six-foot-three-inch frame standing in the centre of the pool, the water managed to reach his collarbones. That's how deep it was.

"Hey."

The voice that had materialised out of thin air made Asa gasp, and forgetting momentarily that he was standing in a pool, he stumbled backwards only to lose his balance. He fell into the water without warning, and it entered his mouth that'd opened in shock, making his lungs burn before he quickly scrambled to the surface again, coughing violently and spluttering all over the place.

"Oh my God!" he heard Carmen yell and from his currently blurred peripheral vision, saw her scramble to her feet, as if to rush towards the side of the pool he was in.

Asa shook his head quickly and gestured for her to stay back, while he still tried to catch his breath. "Don't—" He heaved, grabbing onto the pool's edge and lifting himself up halfway. "The floor's slippery—" he cleared his throat, hating the burning sensation from swallowing water, "so unless you want a concussion or a fractured skull, I'd suggest not running."

He stayed put in that position for a while, the edge of the pool wall pressing into his stomach as he kept his upper torso bent over the wall in an attempt to catch his breath. Eventually, the burning feeling in his lungs and throat dissipated, and his breathing became even once again.

There were so many questions running around in his head, bumping into each other and setting off mini explosions, but he shoved them all away to a corner of his mind. They weren't his priority right now.

No, right now, all he wanted to do was look at her. At Carmen. He just needed to allow his eyes to drink in every single atom of her being.

So he pressed his palms further against the wall and pulled himself completely out of the water, sitting there by the edge of the pool and tilting his head to the side as his eyes swept over her like they had all the time in the world.

Carmen was staring at him, her eyes slightly wide and dazed, her mouth just a tiny bit ajar like she wanted to say something but didn't know how to. Her skin was pale, almost ivory, and her dark hair and grey eyes made her look like some porcelain doll. Honestly, if she had cherry red lips, she might as well have been the real-life version of Snow White.

But the problem with having pale skin such as hers was that it was pretty noticeable when colour seeped in, and his eyes instantly picked up on the rosy tint that was dusting her cheeks and neck now.

Asa's eyes never left hers as his lips curved into a lazy smirk, knowing that she was feeling flustered about seeing him up close like this. He was so used to Carmen looking past his defences and his exterior, that he'd forgotten that she was capable of being affected by his physique too.

"Did you just come here to check me out?" He grinned.

The rosy tint of her cheeks darkened to a furious shade of red as she quickly shut her eyes and muttered something under her breath.

To Asa's surprise, she shook her head to herself, opened her eyes, and then began walking towards where he was cautiously. Once she was right next to him, she dropped her bag and seated herself on the floor, crossing her legs as her kneecaps gently brushed his legs.

"So," she said.

"So." He raised a brow.

He noticed as one of her hands reached up for the chain around her neck and began fidgeting with it.

"I have a spare right now too." She shrugged. "And I figured you'd be here during yours."

"You're on a spare too?" Asa's mind flashed back to their conversation last week when they'd had a free period together. "Another coincidence?" he asked with a touch of nostalgia in his voice.

Carmen's lips slowly curved into a small smile. "Funny things they are, coincidences."

"Hmm," he mumbled, distracted, as his eyes drilled into hers.

"I mean, it's crazy, isn't it? To think that we've been having our spares at the same time all this time. But you'd always be here in the pool, and I'd be spending my time in the art room." She looked at the floor, her brows pulling together. "Just a building apart. That had been the only distance between you and me."

All those times he hadn't acknowledged her existence, and she'd just been a building away during his spares, a few tables away during lunch, a couple of rows away during AP Lit, and just a single seat away in AP Cal.

And now... Now he could feel every inch of her being intertwined with his own existence and Lord knew Asa wouldn't change it for the world. It didn't matter that they'd been going to the same high school all this time; it didn't matter that it'd taken them this long to find each other.

They were here, together, right now. And that was all that mattered.

Carmen sighed deeply, interrupting Asa's stream of thoughts. "I'm not like you," she muttered suddenly.

He turned away from staring at the water and furrowed his brows, looking at her quizzically. "What?"

Her eyes landed on his, and something in his stomach twisted painfully. *God*, he'd missed speaking to her. Or even just having her within touching distance.

"When you're upset, you want to let someone in," she explained, her fingers curling around the pendant of her chain tighter. "You want to talk to someone. You prefer opening up. But I... I push people away. I choose to isolate myself. Suffer in silence, that sort of thing."

Asa sighed and unfolded his arms, reaching out a hand and taking one of her palms in his.

"Wow, your hand's pretty cold," she remarked in surprise.

"Because of the water," he said nonchalantly. "But, listen, you don't have to ex—"

"No, *you* will listen," Carmen said firmly, frowning at him. "You were pushed away when all you were trying to do was help, and you are owed an apology for that. So stop trying to shrug it off and let me apologise to you. You deserve that much at the very least."

Asa's breathing faltered, and he felt warmth flood his insides, because even when he didn't need her to explain her sudden change of heart last week, here she was anyway, telling him he deserved to know. Because even when Asa didn't know how to put himself first, Carmen always knew. And she never failed to do so.

And if Asa wasn't careful, he could fall in lo—

No, he decided. *To hell with caution.*

Asa was already in love with her. Hook, line and sinker. And there was not a single bone in his body, not a single fibre of his being that was going to even consider denying this fact.

I love her, I love her, I love her. He was so goddamn in love with her, and there was no other revelation that could've shaken Asa's world more.

But the storm was only momentary, lasting for a mere heartbeat, before the calm came back and took a hold of his senses. Carmen may have a mind that was made of chaos, but she brought Asa nothing but peace. And admitting to himself that he was in love with her made him feel at peace. It didn't necessarily make sense to him, not completely, anyway. But logic didn't matter to him right now.

Right now, all he wanted was to lose himself in that sense of calm and pure bliss.

"It's just…" Carmen was speaking again, completely clueless and unaware about Asa's realisation. "…seeing Hunter there, it… it took me by surprise. My extended family aren't exactly on good terms with my dad and me, especially mum's side of the family."

"Carmen." Asa held up a hand, knowing that she was speaking about something important but unable to really pay attention to anything other than the fact that his heart was about to explode out of his chest any minute now. "Um, I just—I need for you to just stop for a little while, okay?"

She blinked, completely taken aback and uncertainty flickered across her face. "Is something wrong?"

He laughed weakly, not meeting her eyes. "No no, nothing's wrong. Quite the opposite, actually. Oh God, out of all the times I could've admitted this to myself, it just had to be today and right at this moment—"

"Asa." Carmen's voice sounded slightly disappointed now, "I'm trying to tell you something important here."

He squeezed his eyes shut, wanting to throttle himself. "I know," he muttered. "And I am honestly so sorry, but I can't really focus on anything right now."

"Oh…" The dejected tone in her voice twisted Asa's heart painfully, and that was enough to make him push the realisation that he was in love with her to a corner of his mind for now. "It's just that it, you know, takes too much out of me to speak about her," she mumbled, her shoulders falling as if the world just dumped all its burdens on her back. "About Mum, I mean."

Pushing everything else away and cursing himself mentally, he angled his body towards her and forced himself to focus on what Carmen was saying. "Why?" he asked softly, his thumb drawing circles on the back of her palm that was resting safely in his hand.

"Because she's not with us anymore," she said carefully, as if she was putting much thought into her choice of words.

The cloud of comfort that'd wrapped around Asa slowly began drifting away as the heaviness began settling in its place.

"I'm sorry," he said quietly, but then cleared his throat, wanting to elaborate. "Sorry as in, I wish you didn't have to go through that. God knows I'd go insane without Ma in my life."

She cracked a smile then, the one that reminded Asa of a crack in the glass of a window. The smile that reminded him something broken had the power to illuminate, if allowed.

And he didn't truly realise how much strength Carmen West carried in her evergreen soul until that very moment when she was speaking about a bone-crushing loss but wore a smile that lit up the world in all those crushed places.

And maybe Asa just fell more in love with her for it.

40.
Because I Love You

Carmen tried not to stare too hard while Asa walked towards the bleachers to grab his towel, while she followed right behind.

But for the love of all that's holy, she didn't expect his shoulders to look that much broader now that it wasn't covered by a shirt.

Her appreciative eyes couldn't help but latch on to every single movement of his entire body: the way his back muscles bunched as he reached down to pick up his towel that was hung over one of the seats on the bleachers, and the way his arms flexed as he raised his hands to dry his hair.

A single droplet of water hanging on to the ends of a lock of his drenched hair slipped off and fell on the back of his neck, before continuing to trail down his back in an excruciatingly slow manner. It took its time as it made its descent, taunting Carmen and tempting her twitching fingers. She eventually reached out and pressed her thumb to his cool and slightly damp skin, wiping away the drop of water like she was smudging the outlines of one of her sketches.

She felt him tense under her touch, his back going completely rigid before she felt his muscles loosen up slowly and relax once again.

"I really am sorry, Asa," she murmured, her thumb drawing circles on his back, the way he'd done just moments ago on the back of her palm.

227

"It's honestly not a big deal, Carmen," he told her softly. "I keep telling you that."

"Yes, but…" She'd felt awful when Isla had snapped at her and tried pushing her away. Knowing that's how she must have made *Asa*, of all people, feel wouldn't stop eating away at her.

"But?" He turned his head to the side, glancing at her over his shoulder.

"I guess I just didn't want to be yet another person who let you down," she confessed, lifting a shoulder in a partial shrug.

This time Asa turned around completely to face her, and it didn't do her lungs and every other organ in her body any favours when he stepped closer, and took her chin in his hands.

"You could never let me down, Carmen," he told her seriously, gazing at her with an intensity that was so profound, she felt it pour into her and fill that void in her a little bit. "You only ever keep lifting me up, time and time again."

She waited for that void to drain out the emotion that was filling her up and making herself feel less fractured in her core. But the emptiness didn't come. It didn't come. And it may have been only a small fraction of that void which had been filled, but it was more whole than she'd ever felt in her seventeen years of existence.

And if that didn't speak volumes, she didn't know what did.

Asa was smiling at her with something different in his eyes this time; there was more tenderness there, but also comfort. Like the internal struggle she'd seen him go through in the parking lot the other day wasn't present anymore. As if that war which had been raging on within his soul was finally put to rest.

They say "eyes are the windows to one's soul", and something in Asa's coffee ones told Carmen that he'd found peace somewhere.

"Hey." He tapped her chin as if to shake her out of her thoughts. "Five minutes 'till the bell rings and our spare is over. I'm gonna head towards the lockers to get changed, okay?"

She nodded, her lips lifting into a small smile. "See you later, then?"

"Of course." He grinned, stepping away and grabbing his sports bag from the floor. "You aren't getting rid of me that easy." He threw over his shoulder, as he walked away.

Carmen just smiled and shook her head.

He wasn't getting rid of her that easily either.

•   •   •

It was lunch period, and Carmen was just stuffing her History textbook in her locker when a huge shadow fell over her.

She didn't bother fighting off the smile, recognising the tall frame of Asa almost immediately. Shutting her locker door, she turned around only to have her body freeze and the smile drop from her face when her eyes landed on Hunter instead.

She'd forgotten how much Hunter resembled Asa in both height and build.

But the similarities ended right there like a page that was brutally ripped off a book, as if a force had wanted to put an immediate stop right at that particular point.

Hunter's ocean blue eyes didn't hold the warmth that Asa's coffee-hued ones did. Hunter's towering height and strong physique overpowered and intimidated, whereas Asa's exact same build protected and defended instead.

Hunter may easily be considered one of the most attractive boys that walked down this school's hallways, and even though the same could be said for Asa, the latter had a beautiful soul and that triumphed over any other physical factors.

Hunter Donoghue didn't hold a candle to Asa San Román.

And here was Carmen, related by blood to one and losing her heart to the other.

"No hi?" Hunter asked, his lips pulling up into a lazy smirk.

Carmen couldn't help but recall the way Asa had smirked at her the same way in the swimming complex of the school when he'd caught

229

her blushing at his bare chest. The gesture had been teasing—playful even. But watching Hunter pour malice into it made her realise how one single gesture can radiate different meanings when the people behind them held such contrasting intentions in their hearts.

"I don't understand," Carmen said, pulling her eyebrows together. "You never used to acknowledge me in school. Why *now*?"

Hunter cocked his head to the side, not taking that calculating gaze off her or even dropping that nerve-wrecking smirk. "Because," he drawled, leaning his side on the locker next to hers.

"Because?"

Hunter didn't answer her question and just shrugged in a nonchalant manner as if he could lounge by her locker all day. "So, where's our resident saviour?"

"His name is Asa," Carmen said slowly, the corners of her mouth twisting downwards in distaste.

"Yes yes," Hunter murmured. "Your precious little Asa. Tell me, does being with him make you feel better about yourself?"

Don't break don't break don't break don't break, Carmen reminded herself. *Carmen, don't you dare break.*

Her mind kept chanting those stupid words in a never-ending loop, as if repeating those words in her head would help keep her feet planted on the ground and stop her knees from buckling underneath her while her carefully constructed world crumbled with the blow of Hunter's words.

"Does he know?" Hunter asked, eyes gleaming with the joy of a predator who'd found the prey's jugular vein, ready to sink its teeth right there. "About you, Carmen? Does he?"

Carmen felt her chest constrict at the way her name was thrown out of his mouth, like it'd burnt his tongue and left a foul taste behind.

"You know, in a twisted way, the two of you would actually be a perfect fit for each other." He laughed, as if he was enjoying an inside joke that only he knew of. "But no, I think even San Román has better standards than that. Not even he could stoop this low." Calculating blue

230

eyes fell on Carmen once again, remorseless and ice cold. "If you're thinking he'll be able to save you the way he does the other weak, pathetic students here, you're so wrong," Hunter muttered, already bored with this one-sided conversation. "You can't be saved, Carmen."

"You loved her, didn't you?" Carmen asked, voice shaking, but determined to say something despite the shattering of her heart into a thousand shards.

The smirk fell from Hunter's face, and his eyes grew even more hateful as they burnt holes into Carmen's head.

But Carmen took advantage of his momentary speechlessness. "My… my mother," she choked out, her breathing getting heavier and faster. "She took care of you, didn't she? When *your* mum passed away? She was the surrogate mother for you, right?" Her hand tightened its grip on her bag, because everything around her was swimming, and she just needed something to stay grounded.

Inhale. Exhale. Inhale. Exhale.

"Is that why you hate me so much?" Carmen asked, managing to keep her voice steady despite everything inside her being ripped apart inch by inch without even an atom of mercy. "You lost your birth mum and then you lost your aunt—my mum—who was the closest thing you had to a motherly figure? Because… because i-it was my fault, wasn't it?"

Hunter pushed himself off the locker and stepped closer, bringing his face down to Carmen's with such venom pouring out of his eyes and clenching his fists as if he wanted to pound the daylights out of everything that breathed. "Yes," he spat in a low voice so that she was the only one who could hear him. "You killed her. *You.*" And then the cold smirk returned. "Spare San Román the efforts of saving you. That boy may like broken things, but you're not broken, Carmen. You're a goddamn abomination. And anyone brought into this world the way you were, are incapable of being loved."

It's not true not true not true not true not true.

You can't cry, Carmen, don't cry please don't cry please please please.

231

She shook her head, but she no longer knew who she was trying to convince. "My dad does," she whispered. "My dad loves me—" Her voice broke, her throat tightening as the lump there just grew bigger and more painful.

"What dad?" Hunter chuckled. "Your mum's husband? Last time I checked, he's not your biological father. My heart goes out to the poor guy. You're not even his responsibility, and now you've all but turned into a burden that probably reminds him of what happened to his wife."

And then Hunter was gone before she could even catch her breath, leaving a trail of the shards of her crushed and broken heart behind him as he walked further and further away.

• • •

Carmen could hear the loud laughter and shouts in the hallway even though the door to the art room was closed.

Then again, it was still lunch and students didn't particularly mind their behaviour all too much during this time. She knew she was supposed to be in the cafeteria as usual. That she should be seated at the table next to Joyce, along with Willa and Lottie as usual.

But Hunter had thrown a wrecking ball right at her chest, and she'd lost all appetite, choosing to seek refuge in her safe haven right here.

She had her art journal out, and her charcoal pencils, sketch pens, and crayons littered both her table and the vacant desk next to hers.

Carmen's fingers put more pressure on the blue crayon she was currently using to colour in the upper half of the page as the sky on a spring morning. But as Hunter's words kept replaying in her head like a broken record, her hand movements became harsher, more forceful, and the crayon snapped into two, breaking her stream of thoughts.

"Goddammit," she cursed and grabbed the two halves of the crayon before throwing them at the wall.

The door to the classroom opened just as the pieces hit the wall and then fell to the floor, slowly rolling in the direction of the door and stopping only when they hit the intruder's shoes.

Carmen's creased forehead and deep frown instantly softened when her eyes landed on Asa who was looking at the broken crayon at his feet in confusion.

A few seconds later, his eyes slowly met hers.

"Someone's having a bad day," he stated, raising a brow.

"I'm fine," she muttered, averting her eyes and staring at the half-completed entry in her art journal.

"I'm sure," he said easily as he bent down to retrieve the pieces, but Carmen picked up on the subtle sarcasm in his tone.

"I *am*," she insisted.

Asa walked towards her, dropping the two halves of the crayon on top of her journal before dragging a chair next to her and spinning it around, sitting on it with his chest leaning against the backrest and his hands folded on top of it.

"So, I noticed you were missing in the cafeteria." He left the remark hanging, probably expecting her to tell him why she was skipping lunch.

"Not hungry." She shrugged.

She wasn't looking at him, still staring at her journal, but she could feel his eyes on her as they burned into the side of her face. She wondered if he was going to call her out on the bluff and push her for an explanation.

Instead Asa just sighed and placed his chin on top of his folded hands. "By the way, I ran into Willa." He chuckled lightly. "We totally forgot about how we were supposed to hang out last week."

Carmen looked up at him then, her eyes widening slightly as a guilty smile tugged at her mouth. "She wasn't upset, was she?"

He shook his head. "No, she wasn't. I think it was pretty obvious after the fight with Carson that I wasn't going to make it. You could've gone with her, though."

Carmen just shrugged half-heartedly in response. "Eh, wasn't in the mood then."

There was a few seconds of silence, and she knew what Asa was going to say right before he did.

"I'm guessing that had something to do with Hunter running into us?"

"Yeah." She sighed. "He really knows how to rain on someone's parade."

This time Asa's chuckle was humourless and had an edge to it. "Rain? He brings a whole goddamn hailstorm."

Carmen shot him a look. "You really hate him," she remarked.

"I do." Asa's tone was unapologetic. "But I'm also trying to let go of all the focus I used to direct towards him. All it does is bring me down."

"That's honestly good to hear." She smiled softly. "Because nothing he says to you is true, and you don't deserve to have it hanging over your head."

"Take your own advice some time."

Carmen froze, her smile slowly fading away. "What?"

Asa narrowed his eyes at her. "You *know* what. All those things he said to you the last time we were in this room together. None of that was true either. But you took it to heart, I know you did."

She looked away from him and picked up one of her charcoal pencils, flipping the page of her journal to a fresh, blank one. "You don't know what you're talking about."

"And you're upset right now, too," he continued, disregarding her attempt to sweep her misery under the rug. "So, I'm just going to stop beating around the bush and ask you point blank if he's the reason you're holed up here during lunch."

"It doesn't matter, Asa." She sighed heavily.

"It does to me," he said, his voice suddenly quiet.

Her heartbeats were skyrocketing again so loud that she was amazed Asa himself couldn't hear them.

"Because you feel like it's your job," she muttered, unsure if she wanted to steer the conversation down this road but unable to shake off what Hunter had said last week when he'd run into them in this very classroom.

Asa lifted his chin from where it was resting on top of his hands and stared at her in perplexity. "What does that even mean? My 'job'?"

Carmen pressed her lips tightly together, not at all certain about what the outcome was going to be, but she just needed to ask him. She had to know.

"Hunter," she explained, "when he was here last week...he said...he called you the resident saviour and me damaged goods."

"Carmen—"

"And then," she cut him off. "Then he said that you like broken things."

"I remember every single word he said, Carmen," Asa said through gritted teeth, an unimpressed look on his face.

"Well, good." She shifted her gaze away from him, looking down at her fingers instead. "Because I want to know if you're here, skipping your own lunch, to check up on me because you actually care or... Or because like he said, I'm just another broken thing for you to patch up." She drew in a long shaky breath, her fingers trembling as she clasped her hands together in a tight hold. "I want to know if you're saying that me being upset right now matters to you because—"

"—because I love you," Asa said, unblinking. Not a shred of hesitancy in his demeanour.

Carmen's eyes were on his so fast, she didn't know how her brain registered the sudden shifting of her sight so quickly. "What?" Her voice was so quiet, so terrified, that she wouldn't have been surprised if Asa hadn't heard her at all.

But he did. He heard her.

"I'm not here because I look at you like some stupid project, Carmen," he told her seriously but there was no mistaking the way his voice shook and how his hands were gripping the headrest of the chair like it was his lifeline. "I'm not going to try and convince you that you're not broken and that Hunter was wrong, because yes, you *are* broken." He

235

paused, hesitating, then slowly unclasped his hands and placed his palm on her wrist. "But so am I. So is Hunter himself. And Isla, and Willa, and all the other seven billion people."

"And..." Carmen swallowed. "And that's okay, right?" She tried to sound firm, because whenever she'd seen someone with a heart that wasn't whole, she loved them regardless of it. But her words sounded more of a question than it did a statement.

"Of course, it is," he murmured. "How else can the light get in?" His eyes fell on something near her journal and he nodded towards it. "Now that you're certain I'm not asking because I think of you as something to repair, mind telling me why you're so worked up that you broke the poor crayon into two?" His tone was back to being smooth, with that teasing edge to it.

And Carmen was grateful for that, because she didn't have to deal with what he'd said regarding his feelings for her just yet.

Asa must have guessed the "I love you" threw her completely off balance, because he wasn't pushing her about it, and Carmen felt her heart inflate with something so intense because of his ability to be so effortlessly selfless.

"I just had a confrontation with Hunter again," she confessed. "And he's not someone who's afraid to kick you below the belt."

He sighed. "I knew the guy had issues, but I thought he'd have *some* redeeming quality," Asa muttered. "I mean, you're his family. Regardless of how he treats me, he should be decent to you."

Carmen let out a short laugh, but there was no mirth in it. "He hates me the most, Asa."

There was a short silence before Asa spoke. "Why?"

"His mum and mine were sisters. Twins, in fact. But his died in a car crash when he was around three, and my mum filled in those shoes. I guess he grew really attached to her. But then she died, too, and he had to go through the same loss for the second time in his life."

"And he hates you because you remind him of her?"

236

Carmen didn't answer right away, because even though that was one of the reasons her presence agitated Hunter, his hatred was born from the blame he placed on her. But she wasn't ready to have that conversation with Asa right now. She'd like to tell him some day, about how Hunter was right in accusing her of killing the woman who brought her into this world, but today was not that day.

"Yeah," she answered, not meeting his eyes. "I guess I remind him of her." She didn't like lying to him, but her chest was constricting, and she just needed to let herself breathe for now.

The silence that enveloped them right then was peaceful, almost like it was consoling the two of them. Carmen let her soul float in the comfort that Asa somehow brought with him whenever he was with her. Her fingers traced the edges of her journal before she flipped back to the previous page. The sky was only half done, the left half of it bare because she'd snapped the crayon into two.

"Why'd you start a new drawing if you hadn't completed this?" Asa asked, referring to when she'd turned to a fresh page and started sketching a cracked vase.

"You saw the blue crayon," she muttered. "I have spare ones at home. Whole ones. I can't use this when it's broken into two."

Her eyes followed Asa's hand as they grabbed one of the broken halves and placed it in her palm before he wrapped his fingers around it. "It's just broken, Carmen. It doesn't mean it can't still colour."

He offered her a knowing smile as the meaning behind his words *really* began to sink in.

Lifting their joined hands, he pressed his lips against the back of her palm, speaking against her skin in a soft murmur. "And I would break every single crayon you have in your possession just to show you broken crayons can still create masterpieces as much as an unbroken one."

41.
Don't Let Me Walk Away

Asa felt his heart sink the tiniest bit when Carmen sighed and pulled her palm out of his grasp.

"How can you just say those things to me?" She sounded lost—truly lost—and it twisted his gut.

"What things?" he frowned, genuinely confused.

She closed her eyes, pulled in her bottom lip. Asa didn't know if she was calming herself down or trying to formulate her thoughts into words.

"Things like what you just said. The whole metaphor regarding broken crayons creating masterpieces, as if—as if you actually believe that I can... That I—" She didn't seem to know how to say what she wanted to say anymore but it finally dawned on Asa what the actual issue here was.

"That's what this is about," he mumbled to himself.

"What?"

"You're not questioning the whole crayon metaphor," he told her even while knowing that he was entering unpredictable territory. "You're questioning what I just admitted about my feelings for you."

"I..."

"I guess the shock of hearing me say it is wearing off and its only beginning to sink in, huh?" He laughed weakly, staring at a paint splatter on the floor that one of the art students must have caused.

"Asa—"

"It's okay, Carmen," he said gently. It hadn't been planned; he'd never *meant* to say it. And he hated putting her on the spot like that.

But Asa was and always had been a heart-over-head guy, and he had let his emotions get a grip of his tongue when the three precious words had rolled off it and out his mouth like it was only natural for him to say so.

And maybe it *was* natural. Every way his senses responded to Carmen's presence seemed like that was their sole purpose.

"I just...I don't... I don't think I—"

"I said it's okay," Asa cut in. "And I meant it. Besides, I should be the one apologising anyway. I shouldn't have just said something like that without considering if you were ready or not to hear it."

The silence that followed his words didn't feel right; it wasn't comfortable like the other wordless moments they'd shared. This one was different somehow, like there was a palpable amount of tension simmering just beneath the surface.

It was evident in the way she wouldn't meet his eyes, in the way Carmen's mouth was slightly ajar, as if a part of her was battling against saying something and the other part was fighting back.

Asa didn't particularly like it, but he wasn't one to shy away from a confrontation, whatever the outcome may be.

"Can...can I say something?" Carmen finally spoke, her voice quiet and hesitant.

No. Asa wanted to say no.

"Sure," he said easily.

"I don't want to hurt you." She swallowed audibly, the tremble in her voice unmistakable now. "But I don't know how not to do that by saying what I want to say."

I'd still be in love with you, Asa wanted to say. But something told him Carmen didn't want to hear those words right now. Hell, he didn't know if she *ever* wanted to hear him say that to her again.

"I'm a big boy." His lips curved into a smile, but his chest was constricting and stomach coiling into painful knots. "I can take it."

She offered him a small smile in return, as her eyes met his, seemingly buying his relaxed facade.

"It's just that...when you say you love someone—" she looked away, "—it's supposed to be about opening up. That kind of intimate confession should be about wearing your heart on your sleeve, baring your soul wide open for the other person to see..." Carmen's fingers found her chain, and the fidgeting began again. "But...when you—when—" she sighed deeply, "—when you told me you loved me, it didn't feel like you were *opening up* to me. It felt like you were *dumping* on me." Her fingers tightened around her chain. "And there's a difference between opening up and dumping something on someone."

If the silence was uncomfortable before, it was downright suffocating now.

For a few seconds—but really long seconds—Asa couldn't hear anything but his breathing faltering and the blood pounding in his ears.

He didn't know how he wanted to react. Scream? Pull out his hair? Tell her it was all right and that he understood? Storm out? Remain speechless as he listened to something inside him shatter repeatedly?

He didn't know. He didn't know. He didn't know.

But he managed to find his voice soon enough.

"Which is why I apologised." His tone sounded unintentionally harsh, borderline defensive even. He had taken off that armour and allowed her to see the boy underneath it, but her words seemed to be bringing those walls crashing down on him—painfully. "Because I figured you weren't expecting it, because I knew I'd put you on the spot. And for the record, I didn't plan that. It just happened, and I was just as shocked as you were when I said it, so you weren't the only one I put on the spot—"

"Why are you getting defensive?" She whipped her head around to stare at him in confusion and slight annoyance.

Asa cursed under his breath and stood up abruptly, throwing his hands into the air. "Because when someone tells you they're in love with you, you don't throw it back in their face!"

"What did you expect? For me to say it back?!" She narrowed her eyes at him, her chest heaving in a suppressed tornado of emotions.

"*Goddammit*, Carmen!" he snapped, jaw clenching, "I don't care if you *never* say it back to me. When I tell you I love you, I say it because I *do*. Not because I'm expecting something in return! And if you don't know that about me by now..." he let the sentence hang, turning away from her and pressing his lips into a thin line.

Inhale. Exhale. Inhale. Exhale.

He could feel that rash part of him clawing at the insecure parts of his mind; he could hear the whispers telling him to run. But he fought back against the voices, He resisted the temptation to storm out the door and never look back because taking down his armour was terrifying, but it was also what allowed him to be here, with Carmen.

So he fought back against the part of him that wanted to build those walls back up. He fought against it because Carmen West was worth fighting for.

Regaining his composure and breathing deeply so that the slight tremble in his fingers was no longer because of anger but due to all the raw emotion coursing through him, he walked closer to Carmen and then crouched down in front of her.

"Look." His voice was gentle as he took one of her palms in both his hands and cradled it against his chest. "I wasn't supposed to say it, not like that anyway. But you need to know it was sudden for me, too. And it was just as hard for me to realise I'd actually said it as it was for you to hear it. So I don't expect you to jump up with joy or tell me you love me in return, but *Carmen*—" There was a flash of pain in his eyes. "You don't get to analyse what I said, okay? Dissecting it and then coming to the conclusion that it was me *dumping* on you than opening up to you? That was... that was out of line."

"I'm s—"

"It's one thing for you to not be ready to accept it, but a wholly different thing to just blatantly disregard what I said like that."

"I know, I'm so—"

241

"And you didn't ev—"

"Asa!"

He stopped speaking, his mouth falling open in shock at her yelling. "What?"

Carmen let out an exasperated breath. "I'm trying to say I'm sorry and you keep interrupting me," she deadpanned.

"Oh." He blinked once. Then again.

"Yes, oh."

Asa's cheeks grew warm ,and he shot her a breath-taking smile in return. "Well then, thank you for uh, apologising."

"You know, technically speaking, I didn't apologise *yet* because you kept cutting me off."

"Eh, it's the thought that counts." He shrugged, the smile slowly morphing into a wide grin.

And when she grinned back at him then, and with that subtle shake of her head, Asa's chest didn't feel so constricted anymore.

·   ·   ·

Asa and Carmen were walking towards his red truck, the conversation flowing easily between them, when he caught her smiling to herself in an oddly nostalgic manner during one of their moments of silence.

"What is it?" he asked her, pulling his brows together.

"That dent." She nodded towards the familiar vehicle. "Just above the front left wheel. It just. I don't know. It feels nice. It's been a while since we shared a ride back home."

Asa's lips quirked up, feeling that calming wave of warmth wash over his insides just like it always did whenever Carmen talked about the little things—the seemingly insignificant things but which mattered to him because it mattered to *her*.

Goddamn, he really was in love with her, wasn't he? He bit his lip discreetly at the rhetorical question, the bursts of affection he felt for her in unexpected moments not bothering him anymore. He was about to say

242

something, but he forgot what it was as soon as he felt a strong arm fall around his shoulder and tug him closer to a body.

"Hey," Wyatt muttered, his blonde hair dishevelled and grey-green eyes looking troubled.

Scratch that. Not troubled. Asa realised his friend looked plain pissed off.

"What crawled up your…" The words died in Asa's throat when Wyatt shot him a threatening look. Instead, he just rolled his eyes and stopped in his tracks. "Why do you look like you found someone taking a piss on your doorstep?"

"Some asshole keyed my car," he bit out through gritted teeth, obviously trying hard to contain his anger. "I had to call a service and they took my car to the garage, so I'm going to need a ride."

Asa's eyes slowly travelled to a very bewildered Carmen standing a few feet away, staring at both him and Wyatt.

"Sure." Asa shrugged. "Do you know who did it?"

"If I did, I'd be sitting in a cell by now, arrested for homicide," Wyatt snapped, as if he couldn't believe Asa would ask something so stupid and self-explanatory.

Asa held up his hands in a gesture of surrender. "As if you're the type to throw punches," he mumbled under his breath, inaudible to Wyatt's ears.

"Can we get going now? If I stay here any longer, I might actually start breaking limbs in order to find out who did it."

"And I thought *I* had anger issues." Asa shook his head.

Wyatt's disbelieving stare fell on him. "Are you kidding me? I'm nowhere as violent as you!"

"Whoa. Okay, violent is a strong word."

"You know how many fights I got into this year so far? That's right, *none*. And you? God, I've lost count!"

Asa folded his arms across his chest defensively. "Keep talking and you'll find yourself walking home."

243

"Fine, *Mum.*" Wyatt mocked, walking past him and towards the truck where Carmen was still standing.

This should be fun, Asa thought as he too covered the distance to where both of them were.

He noticed Wyatt's eyes flicker towards Carmen in confusion. "Hi," he said uncertainly.

Carmen beamed at him. "Hey—"

"Yeah, I don't really care," Wyatt cut her off. "I just need you to move. You're blocking my way."

Carmen's jaw dropped open the same moment that Asa smacked his palm against his own face.

"Excuse me—" Carmen began, but was cut off again.

"Asa!" Wyatt shouted, not turning back to see Asa staring at the scene unfolding before him with weary eyes. "There's some chick leaning against the door on the passenger seat. Can you ask her to scamper off because I'm really not in the mood to be civil right now?"

This was going to end well.

"Hey, man." Asa patted Wyatt on the back. "I see you've met Carmen." He turned towards Carmen who had her eyes narrowed at Wyatt. "And I see you've met my friend Wyatt."

"I'm seriously beginning to question your choice of friends," Carmen told him, not breaking the stare-off with Wyatt.

Asa chuckled weakly. "What are you talking about? Wyatt's super friendly."

"I'd really hate to see what your version of *unfriendly* is then, Asa," Carmen said seriously.

"Why is the girl talking to you?" Wyatt asked, frowning.

"'The girl' is Carmen West." Asa sighed. "Please be nice."

Wyatt raised a brow, smirked, and then shrugged. "I can be nice," he said nonchalantly, before looking at her again. "Please crawl away from where you're standing because you're being a nuisance," he said in a pleasant manner. "Please."

Asa rubbed a hand down his face, sighing again "I don't think that qualifies as nice."

"What are you talking about?" Wyatt asked incredulously. "I even said please! *Twice!*"

"Yes, I feel really honoured," Carmen said in a flat tone. "I can't begin to imagine how heartfelt those words were."

Wyatt's eyes narrowed. "All right, listen up smartass—"

"All right," Asa intervened, wanting to bang his head against the window of the passenger seat. "That's enough. The two of you are going to play nice during the ride, or I'll kick you both out, got it?"

"Both of us?" Carmen and Wyatt asked in unison.

"Yes, Wyatt needs a ride today, so figure out a way to put up with him," he responded to Carmen first, before turning to Wyatt, "and I've been driving her back for a long time now, so deal with it."

"I have no problem." Wyatt shrugged. "Just tell her to move away and get in the back because the passenger seat is mine."

"I would have given it to you if you'd asked nicely instead of treating me with such hostility," Carmen said calmly, not moving an inch.

"I'm having a bad day, I'm in no mood to play nice."

"I'm having a bad life. You don't see me snapping at strangers, do you?"

"Guys, you're giving me a headache," Asa groaned in exasperation. "Wyatt, why don't you just get in the back—"

Wyatt shot him a look of pure betrayal. "What happened to 'bros before hoes'?"

Before Asa could say anything though, something flickered in Wyatt's eyes, and he whipped his head towards Carmen, an almost horrified look on his face. "Not calling you a hoe, sorry," he hastily said, but with sincerity. "They really need to come up with a better term."

That seemed to soften Carmen's posture, and her lips actually curved into a faint smile that was directed at Wyatt.

"Don't worry." She waved it off. "I know there was no real heat behind it."

245

"Hmm." Wyatt's eyes narrowed in speculation. "Maybe you're not *so* bad."

Carmen sighed, and her shoulders fell from the defensive stance. "Who are you dropping off first?" she asked Asa.

"Wyatt," he replied. "His house would come up before yours."

"I bet." Wyatt smirked at Asa, a knowing glint in his eyes.

Asa flushed and discreetly flipped him off when Carmen wasn't looking.

"All right then," she muttered, "You can ride shotgun. I'll just move over once we've dropped you off."

"She's very sensible, this one," Wyatt remarked, looking more amused by the second. "I approve."

"Wyatt, please, *please* shut your mouth, okay? For me?" Asa requested.

The wicked grin didn't vanish from Wyatt's face but he nodded anyway. "Cute, San Román. I'll bug you about this later, and you know me. I'm a man of my word."

Great, Asa thought.

Carmen waited for Wyatt to get into the truck and close the door before turning to Asa, "He was teasing you about me, wasn't he?"

Asa's cheeks burned, and he never wanted to punch Wyatt more than he did right then. "He was right. You *are* a smartass. Now get in."

She turned around to get into the back seat, but not before Asa saw her trying to fight off the smile on her face.

And that made a smile of his own appear.

•   •   •

"He's actually pretty friendly, you know," Asa told Carmen once he'd dropped Wyatt off, and she was back to being seated next to him, right where she fitted perfectly. "He's pretty chill and really hard to anger, but once someone *does* manage to piss him off, then it's even harder to get him to calm down. Really unfortunate timing that you had to meet him when he was pissed."

"Don't worry, I'll take your word for it," she answered, and even with his eyes on the road, Asa could hear the smile in her voice.

This was nice. Really nice. *God*, he missed this.

"Hey, Carmen?" His tone was light, airy. But his heart was doing all sorts of cartwheels inside his ribcage.

"Mmmm?"

"Don't ever push me away again, okay? Or go on avoiding me for days because now that we're doing this again" —he gestured around the truck, referring to them going back from school together after a long while— "it feels insane to think that I missed a couple of days spending this kind of one-on-one time with you."

"I won't," she promised, her voice quiet even though it was just the two of them in the vehicle. "And please don't let me push you away either. Don't let me walk away, because knowing me, I'm very liable to do so."

"I promise," he said softly, and then used his free hand to grab one of hers. "I'll hold on," —he kissed the back of her hand,— "even when you're pulling away."

"Good," she murmured, and Asa could hear the faint smile in her voice again.

The remaining duration of the ride passed by in a comfortable silence, with Carmen's hand in his and nothing but the sound of her breathing filling Asa's ears.

I love you.

He wanted to say it again; the words were skipping along the tip of his tongue, playing too close to the edge, ready to fall over and come tumbling out of his mouth.

I love you. I love you. I am so goddamn in love with you.

But Asa swallowed back the words, forced it down his throat, and crammed them into a box that he then sealed and didn't dare touch until it was okay for him to say them to her. If that time ever came.

The truck came to a slow stop right outside her house but as usual, Carmen didn't make a move to leave the vehicle right away.

It was another one of the little things Asa had grown to love about her: the way she wasn't afraid to show she preferred spending time with him. Even the stolen moments such as this, where she needed to get home and he needed to go home too but instead made time for each other.

I love you.

Carmen's grip on his hand suddenly tightened, and Asa's heart jumped to his throat in fear that he actually said the words out loud. He relaxed once he realised he hadn't.

"Asa." Her voice sounded choked, and it made him turn towards her in mild alarm.

"*Sí?*"

A ghost of a smile graced her lips at his response, but her expression turned serious within a heartbeat. "I need to say something, okay?"

His stomach jolted uneasily. "Okay." He forced a smile.

"All right, so." Carmen cleared her throat and twisted her body around so that she was completely facing Asa, her left side pressing into the back of the seat. "When I—Those things I said back in the art room. When I accused you of dumping the fact you're—that you—" There was a sound of pure frustration from the back of Carmen's throat, and it startled Asa. "When you admitted what the extent of your feelings for me were, I questioned it not because I doubt *you*, Asa, but because I doubt myself."

"What do you mean?" he asked gently.

"I mean that if you'd told me you were in love with someone, I'd have known that you meant it. *Really* meant it." There was a pause, and Asa noticed Carmen's breathing was a little louder and rushed. "But when you said you felt that way about *me*, it...it's hard for me not to question the sincerity behind your words —because—well, because it's *me*."

"Carmen…"

"I don't know how to deal with being loved by you," she said in a pained voice. "I don't know how to deal with *being* loved." She took in a deep, shuddering breath, and Asa felt his heart break for her along with it.

"What are you talking about?" His voice sounded hoarse to his own ears. He *hated, hated, hated* hearing the raw hurt in her voice. "People love you. Your dad loves you."

She let out a weak chuckle. "Because he *has* to, right? Because he raised me, and the feeling comes naturally with all those years spent by my side. That kind of love is out of duty, not choice." There was another pause. "But when you said you—when you said it, I know it was out of your own choice. Out of your free will and… I don't know how to—*I don't know.*"

"You once told me that I have a beautiful inside," he reminded her. "Do you remember?"

Carmen nodded, eyes watering and gleaming.

"And you also told me that I make this world a better place," he continued. "Do you still believe that?"

She nodded again. "And I always will."

"Okay then," —he exhaled, a tired smile crawling over his face— "because when you told me what a nice inside I have or how you think the kind of person I am makes this world a better place—if you really meant all that you said—I want you to remember that it's that same person telling you he's *absolutely* and *unapologetically* in love with your heart and your soul and your mind." He brushed his lips on the back of her palm that was resting cosily in his hand. "And something tells me you'd never doubt the sincerity of a person like that."

When Carmen smiled at him then, her lips shaking and her eyes watery, Asa fell in love with her all over again.

Carmen West had been everybody's rock for far too long, and she needed a rock of her own to hold onto now that her world was crumbling around her. And Asa would be that for her. An anchor, a safe place for her to seek solace in, a sanctuary—he'd be whatever she needed him to be 'till she picked up the pieces of her broken heart and glued them back together.

Maybe he didn't know how to fix her by himself and maybe it wasn't up to him. But what he most definitely could do without a sliver of hesitancy was love her wholeheartedly while she saved herself.

And that was what he would do.

42.
Brother Dearest

Asa had just stepped into the general boys' locker room, accustomed to using the one at the swimming pool building only whenever necessary, when all conversation suddenly stopped and every single head turned in his direction.

The soft smile that had unintentionally slipped onto his face when he replayed a conversation between him and Carmen instantly fell and he froze momentarily.

"Asa," the swimming coach called out, nodding casually at him.

"Coach." Asa nodded back, regaining his composure and stepping further in, letting the door swing shut behind him.

"We were just talking about the interstate swimming meet," Wyatt said in an airy tone, obviously trying to ease the tension that was now almost tangible in the air.

"Yeah," somebody else spoke up, "and about how Carson is not going to be able to take part in it." His tone had a bitter edge. "Convenient for you, isn't it? You've got no competition now."

Asa stared at the sophomore with incredulity, genuinely clueless as to what he was talking about. "What the hell are you going on about? Obviously, Carson can compete in the meet; you're exaggerating the damage I did to him."

Wyatt shook his head. "Gabe's not talking about Carson's injuries. Didn't you hear? Hendrickson isn't allowing Carson to enter the meet either." He didn't bother keeping the glee out of his tone, earning a dirty look from Gabe, the sophomore.

Asa blinked, obviously taken aback at this news. "I—I didn't know…" and neither did he know how to feel.

On one hand, he was euphoric something fair was actually happening, that Carson was being punished for his disgusting behaviour as much as Asa himself was being punished for getting into a brawl.

On the other hand, though—despite his dislike for Carson—Asa knew he was every bit the passionate swimmer as himself. He knew how crushed he'd felt when he was told he couldn't be a contestant and Asa didn't think he'd wish that sinking sensation upon someone else.

"I'm sure." Ronnie snorted, apparently not believing that Asa didn't know about this.

"Dude, shut up," Hayden muttered. "Carson had it coming anyway. He never knew how to keep his mouth shut."

"Well, Asa could've just thought with his brains rather than his dick that day," Gabe snapped. "Now all he's done is ruin this school's chance of winning that championship."

"Wanna say that again?" Wyatt asked threateningly, eyes narrowing into slits.

"All right, that's enough." Coach's authoritative tone cut off any further arguments. "Shit happens. Shit already *did* happen. So quit your whining. Jesus, even the cheerleaders don't make such a fuss when they lose a competition." Then he left the room.

"Cheerleading isn't even a sport," Ronnie snickered after the coach was out of earshot.

"Don't let Isla hear you say that," Asa muttered, not hearing his own words until after he'd said them.

He didn't expect the sudden jolt of pain, he really didn't. Defending her, speaking up for what Isla believed in even though they weren't on speaking terms anymore. It was so natural for him to do so, and it hit him like a punch to his gut.

Inhale. Exhale. Inhale. Exhale. "Right," one of the seniors drawled, a suggestive tone lacing his voice. "I almost forgot how quick you'd jump to your girlfriend's defence."

"She's not my girlfriend." Asa sighed, tired of having this conversation for the thousandth time.

"By the looks of it, she isn't anything to you anymore."

That comment hurt, but Asa didn't show any signs of it. He wasn't going to give anyone any more ammo to load their guns. He was done being at the mercy of whoever had their hands wrapped around the trigger. Except, he realised, he'd already given someone the ultimate power to shoot him dead when he told Carmen he was in love with her. He stamped down on the worry, though. There was no reason to be afraid, was there? Carmen's hands were safe. They were gentle. Her hands could never aim a loaded gun at him.

Asa was safe. He was *safe*.

He'd found a safe haven in her. And he was darn lucky to have done so.

"Asa's right, though," somebody else from the basketball team spoke. "Isla's out of the picture. He's got himself a new girlfriend now."

Asa's back stiffened, his muscles tensing, and the only words playing in his head were *Oh, don't you dare. Don't you drag Carmen into this.*

"I've noticed, too!" Ronnie grinned, eyes widening. "She's a senior, right? I think she's in one of my classes."

"So, is she any good?" someone whose name Asa couldn't pronounce asked suggestively.

"'Any good'?" Asa repeated, feeling sick to his stomach. He hated locker room talk.

"You know." Gabe smirked. "In the sack."

Anger flared up in Asa so fast, he thought he would explode into flames right then and there.

"Don't talk about her that way," he hissed.

"Oh, relax," Ronnie rolled his eyes. "As if you haven't thought about getting it on with her. What's her name again? Something West…Carmen, I think."

"That's enough," a low voice came from the back and Asa whipped his head around, eyes landing on Hunter who'd been seated on the bench at the corner all this while, apparently watching the scene unfolding before him without a word.

"What?" Ronnie gawked, stunned like every other person in that room that Hunter was actually not jumping at the chance to antagonise Asa, his supposed archnemesis.

"I said shut up," Hunter growled. "Or, are you fucking deaf?"

Ronnie was blinking repeatedly, his mouth opening and closing like a fish on dry land, looking so lost that he might as well have arrived on planet Earth just yesterday.

"Since when do you have a problem with us talking about girls?" one of the senior swimmers scoffed.

"When the girl you're speaking about is my cousin, you asshole," Hunter said with an edge to his voice, his tone sharp enough to cut through steel. "Mention her one more fucking time, I *dare* you."

The whole room fell silent within a matter of seconds, and everybody looked away awkwardly, suddenly finding something to fidget with or forcing themselves into conversations with whoever was near them.

But Asa wouldn't look away. He *couldn't*.

He hated Hunter, and he always, *always* would. But his eyes remained fixed on the brown-haired, blue-eyed boy as if waiting for him to turn to smoke and vanish into thin air like it would in a dream.

But it wasn't a dream, because Hunter was still seated there, sweeping his eyes over the lockers, the scattered jerseys, and the athletes in a bored manner. No, scratch that. Hunter didn't look bored—not even that, no. There was nothing there in his eyes, not a single flicker of emotion. And Asa hated himself right then. Because even though this boy had put him through hell, made him feel like he wasn't good enough, Asa felt the tiniest part of him twist in sympathy for Hunter.

He tore his eyes away, reminding himself that he was the last person Hunter deserved any shred of compassion from.

With that in mind, he walked towards Hayden and Wyatt on the other end of the locker room and soon enough fell into an effortless conversation with them.

• • •

"Hey," Asa murmured as he lowered himself into the seat next to Carmen during lunch, his voice soft enough for only her to hear.

She tilted her head towards him, a surprised smile lifting her mouth at the corners. "Hi." She tucked a strand of hair behind her ear. "This is a nice surprise."

Carmen sounded genuinely happy, and that sent a ripple of warmth through him.

"Yeah? Well, then, I'm glad you're not kicking me out."

She laughed, and Asa could picture a shooting star zooming across the midnight sky, a trail of light in its wake.

"Is this going to be a daily occurrence now?" Willa asked, raising a brow as she placed her tray on the table and sat down across from them.

"Feel free to move if it makes you uncomfortable." Asa shrugged, a lazy smile playing on his lips.

"All right, Cassanova." Willa grinned. "Play nice now. We can still vote you out of this table, you know. Carmen's the only one in your favour here."

Asa's teasing eyes fell on Joyce, the mischief in his smile unmistakable. "Joyce, you want me here, don't you? Unless, of course, you want to take my place in History class again."

Joyce's cheeks flamed red, and her jaw dropped open, appalled that Asa had the audacity to actually threaten her.

"I'll take that as a yes." He grinned, taking advantage of her speechless state. He turned towards Willa. "Guess it's a tie now."

"You guys aren't a thing, right?" Lottie spoke up for the first time, nodding towards Carmen and Asa. "Like, you aren't together or anything, yeah?"

Asa figured she was Joyce's counterpart, bold and blunt.

"No," he replied, somewhat awkwardly.

Lottie let out a breath of relief, and it rubbed him the wrong way.

"You seem relieved to hear that," Willa remarked, picking up on the gesture too.

Lottie lifted a shoulder into a half-shrug. "Well, yeah. Carmen deserves better."

All the air was knocked out of Asa's lungs as her words hit him in the chest like a ton of bricks, and Willa's spoon fell from her hand, landing on the table with a clatter, and her eyes widened with shock and discomfort.

"That wasn't a very nice thing to say," Joyce mumbled under her breath, but since silence had fallen among their table, her words were audible enough for everyone to hear.

"The truth stings. Deal with it." Lottie shrugged again.

"Lottie!" Carmen hissed, and Asa felt her tense beside him.

"What?" she asked innocently. "I mean, come on. The only reason he notices you is because you're not one of the girls who swoon over him! But the minute you start paying him attention and he's won you over, he'll drop you like a used tissue paper."

He could shake this off like he would have done once not long ago. Asa could let this roll off his back and sweep it under the rug. But he'd had enough. This time, he wanted to fight back.

Folding his arms across his chest, and leaning back in his chair, he narrowed his eyes and stared down at Lottie. "And how do you know that?"

Lottie blinked once. Then again. It was obvious she wasn't used to her judgements being questioned.

"What?" She frowned, darting a look at Joyce and Willa before landing her eyes back on him.

256

"All that you just said," he said, chin raised, voice hard. "You seem to know me like the back of your hand. How is that?"

Lottie's brows pulled together, the skin on her forehead creasing as she squinted at Asa. "Because... well, it's obvious" —she threw her hands in the air— "all you jocks are the same."

Asa nodded seriously, as if he was genuinely taking her words into consideration. "All right, all right." He unfolded his arms and placed them on the tabletop, intertwining his fingers together and leaning towards Lottie. "See, I may be good with words but numbers are never my strong point. So I can't tell you *exactly* how many jocks there are in this state alone. But I'm guessing you're smart enough to know that there are probably a couple thousand. So tell me, Lottie, are you saying you've crossed paths with every single one of those jocks? Is that what you're telling me? I mean, if you can be so sure of labelling and stereotyping every single school athlete, then you must know what you're talking about, right?"

He felt a warm hand touch his knee under the table, and he found himself appreciating Carmen's silent support more than he thought he would.

Willa laughed weakly in an attempt to lighten the atmosphere. "Oh come on, Asa. Take a joke. Lottie's just messing with you, I'm sure."

Asa's stare shifted to Willa, his eyes hardening at the edges. "A joke is supposed to be funny. Provoke laughter. Cause amusement. For *both* parties. I suggest looking up the dictionary sometimes. Because Carmen doesn't find it funny, Joyce doesn't find it funny, and I certainly don't think it's amusing that she took it upon herself to judge my intentions with Carmen."

"I didn't—"

"And you're the last person who gets to justify what she said," he cut her off. "Not after the way you treated me. And Isla. I get that you've had a difficult past, but use that pain to empathise, not attack."

"That was a low blow, bringing up my past like that." Willa glared at him, her face twisted into a grimace.

Asa smiled at her coldly, completely unapologetic. "Come on, Willa," he mimicked her own words. "Take a joke. I was just messing with you." This time, Carmen's hand squeezed his knee gently and he didn't know if she was reassuring him or if she was asking him to put an end to this right now. He figured it was most probably the latter.

So he took in a deep breath, reminded himself that these were still Carmen's friends—friends of the girl he was in love with—and let it go.

"I'm going to get my stuff for next period from my locker," he told Carmen, turning his face towards her. His eyes softened when they landed on the familiar pair of grey eyes.

"There's still twenty minutes of lunch left," she pointed out, but her voice sounded small even to his ears.

"I'll find something to do, don't worry." He waved it off, not wanting her to take what had just transpired to heart. Asa knew she had enough on her plate already as it was. This unnecessary drama was definitely something she didn't need.

"But you haven't even eaten properly." Carmen gestured towards his tray, the dismay still evident in her voice.

"Lost my appetite." He shrugged, pushing his chair back and rising out of his seat.

As he walked past her, he let his fingers graze the back of her neck and shoulders in an attempt to say that it was okay. That *they* were okay.

Just as he reached the doors of the cafeteria, he stopped in his tracks and turned around to spare her a glance, only to find her eyes already on him. The gentle nod of her head and soft smile on her face told him that she'd understood what he'd tried to say without words. And that yes, they were indeed okay.

I love you.

Even standing a good distance away from her, those three words were still aching to be released in a scream for the world to hear. But Asa

258

just closed his eyes for a brief second. He inhaled deeply, shook the words off and then walked away.

•   •   •

It was just after the final bell had rung and when the students were flooding into the hallways from every single classroom that Asa saw Hunter again. Normally, he'd have turned away. Asa would have thanked his lucky stars that Hunter hadn't seen him and just went on his way.

But so much had changed within the past two months—so much had changed *within* Asa.

And now that the question that'd been nudging him for the past few weeks popped into his head again, he found his feet taking him towards the godforsaken boy.

He was so going to regret this. But he kept walking towards Hunter anyway.

Asa stopped just a few feet from where Hunter was standing in front of his locker and rummaging through it with an agitated look on his face. And now that he was here, he couldn't understand why the hell he thought this was a good idea in the first place. He wanted someone to throw something at his face for his stupidity, preferably a chair.

"If you keep staring at me for even a second longer, I'm going to gouge your eyes out with my thumbs." Hunter's annoyed voice snapped Asa from his thoughts. "I'm not staring at you," Asa retorted, feeling all the rage he felt for this boy boil towards the surface in the blink of an eye.

"Then piss off."

"Why'd you stand up for Carmen today?" The question flew out of Asa's mouth before he could restrain it.

He noticed Hunter freeze for a moment before he quickly slipped back into that devil-may-care facade.

"I don't know what you're talking about," Hunter answered smoothly, his tone implying that he could be doing a thousand other things than have this conversation with Asa.

But Asa knew bullshit when he saw it; he'd put up with Isla for years now and during that time, he'd learnt to tell when someone was wearing a mask.

"Yes, you do," he said, sounding annoyed. "You defended her in the locker room today."

Hunter sighed, temporarily stopping the search of his locker's interior. "I wanted some peace and quiet but all the guys' voices were annoying me. So I asked them to shut up." He went back to digging through the contents of his locker, not once sparing Asa a glance. "That's all."

"Bullshit." Asa scoffed. "You spoke up because somewhere deep down, I think some part of you actually cares about her."

He saw Hunter's jaw tick, and instantly knew he'd touched a nerve. "You don't know shit," he muttered.

Asa didn't know what the hell he was doing still standing there, having what he could only describe as a twisted resemblance of a conversation with the one person who loathed him as much as he loathed them in return.

"And when I say somewhere deep down, I mean *really* deep," Asa went on, "like buried underneath all your hundred layers of tough exterior and scowls."

Hunter slammed his locker door shut at that, and the bang resonated throughout the hallway, startling most of the students and causing some of them to dare look their way while the others just picked up their pace and walked faster.

"What the fuck do you want?" Hunter asked, eyes blazing as he looked at Asa for the first time since their conversation. "For me to admit that I care about her? Well, I don't. Sorry to burst your bubble, but piss off already."

"You're lying." Asa shook his head. "Why else would you—"

"Maybe I'm just a territorial asshole," Hunter answered, taking a threatening step closer, the muscles in his jaw clenching. "Maybe it was just the sadistic part of me telling them that tormenting Carmen was *my* job. Did you ever think about that?" When Asa didn't respond, Hunter laughed darkly. "Figured so. Did you really think I cared about her? Stop being so naive and looking for redeeming qualities in me. Never gave a shit about her and I never will."

Asa should drop the topic. He should be walking away. He knew better. He was smarter than this.

But his feet stayed rooted to the spot.

"Then what about Isla?" he asked, asking the question that he'd wanted to for a while now. "I know you were the one who dropped her off at my place that night after the party. Why'd you do that if you really don't give a shit about anyone?"

A disbelieving laugh left Hunter's mouth, and he shook his head at Asa as if he couldn't digest the fact that this conversation was even taking place.

"Are you for real?" Hunter pronounced each word deliberately slow, dragging out each syllable as if he was talking to someone who was partially deaf. "I did that to get at *you*. I knew it'd piss you off. So I came to your doorstep with your best friend just to rub it in your face."

Listen to him, Asa. Listen to what he's saying.

What the hell was he thinking? That the person who'd tormented him for years was capable of redemption? Was Asa really that plain stupid and gullible?

He knew Hunter Donoghue. Known him for years. There was not a single compassionate bone in the guy's body. That didn't mean Asa didn't feel the faintest flicker of disappointment that Hunter was just cold to the bone.

"You done?" Hunter asked, his voice and expression going back to being free of any emotion. Asa didn't understand how Hunter did that. He himself found it hard to keep his emotions in check; Asa was passionate like that. But he needed to understand that not everyone was going to have the same heart or mind-set as his.

So he took a few steps back and tightened the grip on his bag's straps. "Yeah," Asa muttered, looking away from Hunter's blank stare. "I'm done."

• • •

"You're awfully quiet," Carmen commented as they drove back from school. "What's on your mind?"

Despite being distracted with all the thoughts swimming in his head, Asa's mouth curved upwards into an affectionate smile. He didn't know what it was about the question, but the way she'd asked it made his heart flutter the tiniest bit.

"Nothing," he murmured. "Just thinking."

"Of?" She turned her face to him, offering him a lazy smile.

"People, I guess." He twitched his left shoulder in an attempt of a subtle shrug. "They're never really what you expect. I mean, you have this idea of them, and they either prove you wrong by rising above your expectations, or by sinking even lower."

Carmen's smile slowly faded, and a frown replaced it. "Are we talking about Lottie here? Because I put her in her place after you left the cafeteria halfway through lunch."

Asa shot her a quick sideways glance before turning his attention back to the road. "Damn." He grinned. "I missed out on that. But, no, I wasn't speaking of Lottie. I actually ran into Hunter today."

"You ran into him?" Carmen furrowed her brows.

"Well. Okay. Didn't run into him. I walked up to him and initiated the conversation."

Amusement lit up her dull grey eyes, and she looked like she wanted to laugh. "Oh, Asa. Why on earth would you do that?"

"Learnt my lesson, don't worry."

"And? Did whatever you learn about him surprise you?"

"Definitely did," Asa said, making a U-turn. "I mean, I always thought he was just an asshole, but I found out he's actually a soulless bastard. So there's that."

"You seem disappointed."

262

"I'm not."

There was a short stretch of silence between them before Carmen interrupted it.

"He wasn't always like that, you know.""Hunter?" Asa frowned. "It's hard to picture him without his permanent scowl and murderous glare."

A light giggle tumbled past Carmen's lips. "Seriously. Since my mum was always pampering him after his passed away, we'd spend a lot of time together. Mostly it was me going over to his place. We must have been around three at the time, but I still remember snippets of our childhood. And both of us had no siblings, so I guess I always looked up to him and regarded him as an older brother, and I the little sister he never had."

Asa was finding it really hard to wrap his head around the fact that Hunter Donoghue used to have a heart in his robotic body once. Then again, nobody was born with hate and cruelty in their hearts, were they? Those traits were taught, or inherited, or even picked up from one's surroundings.

"It's...really weird to think of him that way," Asa admitted, scratching the bridge of his nose.

"Sometimes I think it was all from a past life or something," Carmen spoke quietly, her voice blending with the tranquil atmosphere inside the truck. "He'd be saying something vicious enough to rip my heart out in school, but all I would see is the boy who used to give me piggy back rides up and down the stairs of his house when I was too tired to climb it by myself. Sometimes I want to hate him so much, but I'd recall the numerous times I'd fallen asleep on the couch only for him to carry me to my room and tuck me in bed."

Her eyes were unfocused like she wasn't in the truck with Asa anymore, but in a place during her childhood when she'd known happiness and love.

263

"But then we turned six. Mum died. And that was that." She let out a deep sigh, as if it had been sitting on her soul for far too long. "Everything just went up in flames."

Asa hesitated but asked cautiously, "Why?"

Carmen was quiet for a long time; she continued to remain silent 'till they reached her place. Asa figured she wasn't going to respond, but she eventually did. "They didn't want me around anymore."

"They?"

"Mum's side of the family is the side where Hunter comes from," she mumbled, exhaustion seeping into her voice. "They flat out told my dad they didn't want anything to do with me anymore."

Asa's stomach coiled into a tight knot, feeling both anger and grief on Carmen's behalf.

"And your dad's side?"

"They love Dad a lot," she said. "They just don't understand why he took it upon himself to raise me, someone who's not even his biological daughter." Asa recalled wondering before if Carmen was adopted because she shared no resemblance whatsoever with her father. He didn't ask her any more than she was willing to offer him though, so he just allowed her to do the talking. "And they'd keep hinting at Dad to give me up to the system. I guess he got fed up with them because he no longer keeps in touch with his folks."

"No offence, but you really didn't hit the jackpot when it comes to family." Asa mused.

And to his delight, Carmen started to laugh.She was full-on laughing: her head tipped back, hand covering her mouth, and eyes crinkled at the edges as the passenger seat vibrated with her shaking shoulders.

Carmen kept laughing, and Asa kept falling.

I love you. I love you. I love you.

Asa didn't hold back this time."I *do* love you, you know," he said, gulping slightly as his voice drifted into the air and filled the space between them with an emotion so raw, so tangible, that Asa thought his heart could burst any minute.

Carmen stared at him for a while, not saying anything, before her lips slowly turned up at the corners into a smile that could only be described as ethereal.

"I know," she told him quietly, her eyes uncharacteristically bright.

"Good," he murmured, tracing a finger along the hairline on her forehead and down her temple before moving along the curve of her ear. "Because I don't think I'll ever stop saying it."

She opened her mouth then—no, wait—not opened. But her lips did part, and he heard the soft breath that spilled out of her mouth right then, and for a second—for a mere heartbeat—Asa thought she was going to say the words back.

She didn't, though. And oddly enough, Asa was okay with that.

Because he wasn't stupid; he knew she had feelings for him. He didn't know if she was *in* love with him yet, but he knew her feelings ran pretty deep. And if she needed time to navigate through those sea of emotions, then he'd offer her time.

And maybe one day she'd find her way to him the way he'd found his way to her.

For now though, everything was as close to perfect as they could be. And he wasn't going to complain about wanting more.

43.

How to Love With a Fractured Soul

Carmen realised she couldn't bring herself to paint anymore.

Well, technically speaking, she could. But it just wasn't the same for the past few days. She'd be halfway through sketching something, or in the middle of painting on a fresh canvas, then the words would float through her head and send her world spinning.

Because I love you.

Those words. Words Asa had said to her without a second thought.

Words she knew in her bones that he meant from the depths of his heart.

Whenever she recalled that moment, everything else would cease to function. And the artwork she'd been working on would seem irrelevant, almost miniscule in the face of the fact that Asa San Román— the boy with the heart of gold—was in love with *her*.

Her fingers still ached each time his words resonated through her being. There was still that yearning to put her emotions into paper in the form of a drawing or a painting.Carmen just wasn't yet able to figure out what it was that she wanted to create. Didn't know how to channel the sea of emotions she was hopelessly swimming through into art.

She was sitting on the chair by her bedroom's window, her drawing pad opened to a fresh page on the small mahogany desk in front of her, when there was a knock on her door.

"Honey?" her dad's voice floated to her ears, pulling her out of her reverie.

She stopped chewing on the drawing pencil in her hand and called back, "Yeah, Dad. Come on in." The word *dad* left a trail of bitterness on her tongue but she chose to not dwell on that for now.

The door swung open slowly and her father stepped in. His sandy hair was dishevelled and sea green eyes nervous. Then he walked forwards and seated himself on the edge of her bed.

"Drawing something new?" He motioned with his head towards the drawing book on her desk.

"Trying to," she shrugged.

"But?"

"Inspiration is down or too high. Can't really tell."

He nodded, taking in her response as his eyes swept across the room, a fond smile lighting up his face when his eyes caught the framed photograph of the two of them at the restaurant they used to visit every Friday for dinner.

They'd tried to keep the tradition alive even after her mother's death, but had only succeeded in doing it for three months. The pain had been unbearable, and everything that reminded them of her had to be erased from their lives. And so that tradition had died along with Sophia West.

"Dad?" Carmen asked gently, ignoring the pressure at the centre of her chest at calling him that. "What is it?"

Her father released a deep sigh, dropping his head as he lifted his hand to massage the length of his nose with his thumb and forefinger.

Something must have happened, Carmen realised, and it caused an uneasy sensation to erupt in the pit of her stomach.

"Your aunt called," he eventually said.

"My aunt?"

"Your mum's other sister," he muttered. "Beatrix."

This wasn't making sense. After all these years? Why was she making contact with them *now*?

"Why?" Carmen asked cautiously, dreading what the answer might be.

There was another sigh from her father. He seemed to wish that he was anywhere else but here, doing anything else but having this conversation.

"To invite us over for Thanksgiving dinner," he finally said.

Carmen's eyes were as wide as saucers, and her jaw dropped open in pure shock. This was definitely not making sense.

"*Why?*" This was the one question she was capable of asking—the only one she wanted to ask. Because her mind still couldn't find any logical reasoning whatsoever that her presence was actually asked for.

"I asked her the same thing." Dad pulled his brows together. "She said your grandma was the one who demanded it."

"But *why?*" Carmen pulled in her bottom lip, anxiety rippling through her in gigantic waves.

"I'm guessing the old age must be getting to her. Time does that to people, sometimes. They grow oddly sentimental."

"Do you want to go?" Carmen asked after a few minutes of complete silence, observing her father. Carmen didn't think it was such a great idea, but she also couldn't help but consider the fact that those people had once been her dad's family. His in-laws.

But he shouldn't have to pay for Carmen's sins.

It was honestly twisted, the way he didn't just lose his wife, but both the family he was born into and the family he married. And all because he chose Carmen over them. Years later, and he was still choosing Carmen.

That fact alone melted Carmen's heart.

"The question is, do *you* want to go?" her father turned to face her, eyes serious but kind.

"I want you to be happy, Dad," she mumbled.

He smiled at her then. The corners of his eyes wrinkled and affection lit up his face. "I *am* happy," he told her. "I have you."

But Carmen knew that'd never be enough—it couldn't. She was still a reminder of all that he'd lost.

"We'll go then," she said, her tone not hiding her uncertainty and reluctance.

Her dad pressed his lips into a thin line, and in that fleeting moment, Carmen realised she'd picked up that trait from him. And somehow that tiny realisation embedded a larger impact on her than she expected.

Because it meant that even if she wasn't his by blood, it didn't make him any less of a father to her. And neither did it mean she wasn't a daughter in his eyes.

Maybe family wasn't always about whose blood ran in your veins. Maybe it was about whose heart beat alongside yours through thick and thin.

"You sure, kiddo?" he frowned. "If you don't want to, we can stay back."

"It's Thanksgiving, dad," she said with a sad smile. "It'll be a change from spending the night just by ourselves, yeah? Plus, they're the ones reaching out this time. How long have we wished for this?"

"I don't think the others would be so thrilled." He rubbed his eyes tiredly. "It's Sophia's mum who wants us there."

"Yeah, well, grandma was always the one who called the shots in that family, yeah?" There was a touch of nostalgia in Carmen's voice, her eyes proving that she was reliving old times in her head.

Her dad just offered her an exhausted smile in response, his eyes also adorning the same faraway look as Carmen. He stood up from the bed, cracking his knuckles as he did so. "I'll let your aunt Beatrix know that we're coming then." He nodded, shooting her one last smile before leaving the room.

"Hey, Dad?" Carmen called out just as he was about to close the door.

He popped his head in through the gap of the half-open door. "Yeah?"

"I love you," she said, the left corner of her mouth lifting up in something akin to a ghost of a smile.

"I do too," he told her, eyes softening and smoothing the crease on his forehead.

But Carmen noticed that he didn't say "*I love you*" back. Just like he never did ever since they'd buried her mother six feet under when she was six years old.

The door to her room closed with a soft click, and Carmen stared at it as the tear running down her cheek slipped off her chin and fell on the fresh drawing sheet on the desk.

And then more silent tears followed.

•   •   •

It was during the third week of November, and also the last week of school before Thanksgiving holidays started, that Carmen met Isla again.

"Hey," Carmen greeted as she approached the familiar blonde in the girls' locker room, where Isla was getting ready for cheer practice.

Electric blue eyes met Carmen's and surprise flickered through them. "Carmen." Isla blinked, obviously not expecting her. "What's up?"

Carmen slid her bag off her shoulder and fished around through it before pulling out a book with deep red velvet binding that Isla had given her for this purpose. She extended her arm towards Isla, offering her the book. "Those drawings you asked for." She nodded towards the journal. "The one for your parents once you leave for college. They're all done."

The other girl's eyes widened, and she grabbed the art journal from Carmen's hands, flipping through the pages with shock and awe. "Wow, you did them all within just two months and a half?"

Carmen shrugged. "Had a lot of spare time on my hands these days." And there was also the issue of not being able to create her own works because of Asa's words building a home inside her head and refusing to leave until she acknowledged them.

It was as if they had a mind of their own, as if they purposely constructed a barrier in her mind to stop any creativity flowing through until she'd digested the words *I love you* and allowed it into her system.

But it was one thing to hear Asa say those words to her and a wholly other thing to *accept* it, to allow it into her heart.

"Wow…I—these are beyond amazing, Carmen," Isla said softly, her fingers tracing one of the sketches as if she was afraid she was going to hurt the paper. "Just—*thank you*. Thank you so much."

"You're welcome," Carmen mumbled, warmth washing through her at the fact that her drawings were being appreciated. Ever since she started sketching those photographs for Isla though, there'd been a question clawing relentlessly at her mind, and it was bothering her now too.

"Isla…" she started with a cautious tone. "Why did you ask me to draw them that way?"

Isla's eyes left the journal and looked back at Carmen, confusion swimming in them. "I told you; I wanted to give them—"

"No." She shook her head, cutting Isla off. "Not *why* you asked me to draw the photos. Why did you ask me to draw all those photos *without you* in them?"

Isla's eyes went wide and there was a flash of pain in them, but it was gone as soon as it had come.

Carmen didn't get it though. All the family photographs of the Martins had both Mr. and Mrs. Martin along with Isla in them. They looked happy enough—*genuinely* happy. But Isla had asked Carmen to sketch those photos exactly as they were with the exception of Isla's presence in them.

"Because it's a gift, Carmen," Isla finally muttered, the exhaustion seeping into her voice as she sat down on one of the benches, her shoulders drooping. "I want to present them with something, and what better way to do it than show them how their life would looked like without me in it? An alternate reality where their screwed-up daughter isn't born. A lifetime when they didn't have some whore with no future as a daughter."

And despite Carmen's reserved attitude towards Isla on Asa's behalf, she felt her gut clench in worry for the girl. Isla and Carmen might not have the same stories, but that didn't mean she didn't understand the pain and the turmoil the other girl must be experiencing.

"Don't call yourself that," Carmen said quietly, feeling a pang in her chest.

Isla scoffed. "The rest of the world does, why shouldn't I?"

"Because the minute you call yourself what they label you, you give them the power to destroy you. So, don't," she said firmly. "Besides, this school and this city aren't the rest of the world. It doesn't even cover *half* of this world. There's still so much to see, so much to do. Once you're done with senior year and leave, this will all be just some bad memory."

Isla didn't say anything for a while, but after a few moments, she eventually sighed and looked up at Carmen. "Thanks." She smiled, but it didn't reach her eyes. "For both the drawings and just you being you. But I've got to get going now. I'm co-captain, can't keep my girls waiting."

Carmen wanted to say more—she felt like she should be saying more—but she heard the tone of finality in Isla's voice. It clearly said she was done talking about it, and so Carmen didn't try stopping Isla as she rose from the bench and walked away.

Maybe some people didn't want to be saved.

• • •

The final bell rang, its shrill and sharp sound piercing the silence in the classroom and making Carmen wince. She'd never gotten used to the sound, and it still made her want to cover her ears.

Gathering her books from her desk, she slipped on her shoulder bag over her arm and headed out of the classroom, joining the stream of enthusiastic students pouring into the hallways. She was just about to turn into one of the corridors, when a firm hand wrapped around her forearm and yanked her back to a corner of the hallway, out of the way of the bustling students.

272

The first thing her body registered was that it wasn't Asa's hand. The second thing was irrational fear, a sudden overwhelming need to scream, but before she could act on her sudden spark of terror, her eyes landed on the person responsible for her mini heart attack.

"Hunter!" she gasped, all the fear leaving her in an instant. "You idiot," she muttered angrily, pulling her arm away from his grasp. "You scared—"

"Tell me you're not coming to the dinner," he said, cutting right to the chase.

Something inside Carmen deflated at his words, and it only made her angry at herself for holding onto the hope that things between them might change for the better. She felt like a pathetic little girl who don't know how to admit defeat when she'd already lost to this world ages ago.

"I could tell you that, but then I'd be lying," she muttered, a bitter edge to her voice that was completely uncharacteristic of her. But Hunter had a way of bringing out the loathing she buried deep inside her. She couldn't decide if suppressing it made her weak and hypocritical, or if letting it out of its hiding place would make her seem less like the calm and forgiving person she was seen as.

It was the calm and forgiving part of her that Asa was in love with, right? He hadn't seen her loathing, hadn't seen the parts of her she wished she didn't have to bury because she'd rather they not exist at all.

Hunter made a frustrated noise at the back of his throat, something between a growl and a sigh. Or maybe it was a suppressed swear word. Carmen couldn't tell.

"Do you go *looking* for misery?" he asked her then, impatience very much evident in his tone.

She narrowed her eyes at him. "I'm going because if it's an opportunity to reconnect with my family, then I'm going to take the chance."

"Your family." He scoffed. "*Family?* Family doesn't bring you down. They don't rip you to shreds. Which is what we've done to you in the past, so I don't get why you would accept Aunt Beatrix's invitation!"

Carmen ran both her palms down her face, feeling the agitation crawl up her nerves. "Hunter, what do you *want* from me?" she snapped, losing every ounce of patience she had when it came to him.

He clenched his jaw so hard that Carmen genuinely wondered if he wasn't hurting his teeth with the gesture.

"I want you to decline the invitation," he finally said, looking past her shoulder and into the distance. His expression was free of anger now and was back to being blank, and his voice bordered on robotic. His entire demeanour was simply devoid of any emotion. "Call Aunt Bea and tell her you can't make it."

Even after all this time, his hatred for her ran deep. So deep, in fact, that he was here, asking her to not come to a place that he was going to be in just because he didn't want to acknowledge her existence.

"I can't do that, Hunter," she said, her voice hardening with disappointment and anguish towards the boy she'd once known, the boy who'd once been the closest figure to a brother that she'd had.

"Why not?" he bit out through gritted teeth.

"Because they're not just my mum's people, they're also my dad's family. The family he married into! He might not say it, but I know he misses them." Carmen hauled her bag higher up her shoulder, feeling the strap dig into the skin of her neck. "Bottom line, I'm going to that dinner. So deal with it, Hunter. And if you're disgusted by my presence so much, then don't come."

Hunter swore under his breath and yanked at his hair, his emotionless facade breaking as the annoyance, anger and something else that Carmen couldn't identify played across his features.

"I'm not going to be there," he told her.

That stung more than she'd have liked to admit. "Fine," Carmen mumbled, unable to mask the wounded tone in her voice. "Suit yourself."

"No no." He shook his head in an almost frantic manner. "You don't understand. I'm saying I'm not going to be there. As in, the minute Dad heard you're invited, he said he won't be attending Thanksgiving, and I'm not allowed to either."

274

Carmen could only stand there and stare at Hunter, her mind completely baffled beyond belief.

"So don't go," he muttered, the hard edge to his voice softening just the tiniest bit. "Because grandma might want you there, but she's sick and won't be there for the whole dinner. She'd probably greet you, stick around for a while and then go back to being on bed rest. And after that, the rest of them are not gonna stop with the snide comments and hints. You *know* that."

"Wait." Carmen swallowed, holding up a finger, her hand shaking the slightest bit. "Wait a minute." She took in a deep breath and tried getting a hold of all her emotions because everything inside her was in utter chaos now. "Are you telling me you're here—you're actually here—to ask me not to go out of *concern*?" She kept blinking up at him, confusion pulling her brows together and creasing her forehead.

"Why do you have to go there?" He scowled, the annoyance creeping back into his voice. "Why can't you just take what I said and go along with it? Why do you need to keep digging around regarding my intentions?"

And Carmen let her heart do the talking for her. "Because I need to know that the brother who told me he'd fight off the world for me when we were just six years old is still in there somewhere."

"Well, he's not." Hunter shrugged, eyes guarded and his voice cold enough to send chills down anyone's spine. "He died a long time back."

"I don't believe that," Carmen whispered, feeling someone approach from behind.

"And *that*," Hunter said, emphasising the second word, "is why you'll always keep getting your heart broken."

His eyes then landed on something just past Carmen's shoulders, and before she could turn around herself, she felt a familiar palm slip into hers, lacing their fingers together.

She almost melted into Asa's side as he stood there next to her, realising that she didn't truly know how much she appreciated the warmth

275

he brought with him until he was right there, offering her comfort even when she didn't ask for it.

"Everything okay here?" he asked. Asa's eyes were trained on Hunter—calculating and hard—but the gentle, coaxing tone of his voice told Carmen that the question was directed towards her.

"Yeah," she said softly, smiling for the first time that day as she tilted her head back to look up at him. "It is now."

His coffee eyes shifted away from Hunter and dropped down to meet hers, the hard look instantly softening and warmth pooling into his eyes.

Carmen spared a glance at Hunter, but his face was back to being expressionless. He looked like he was going to say something, but then just shook his head and took off down the hallway.

Carmen and Asa stood side by side, hands joined, and watched him go.

"Sure you're okay, right?" Asa asked immediately, turning around to face her completely. "Because if he said something else to hurt—"Carmen shook her head, cutting him off, as her heart swelled with affection at the protective stance Asa had taken. "Quite the opposite, really," she mumbled, still distracted with thoughts about the upcoming dinner. "I think he was here because he was worried." It sounded horribly weird when she said it out loud.

"His attitude swings are going to give me whiplash," Asa muttered under his breath. "Do you know he stood up for you a few days back?"

Carmen's head instantly snapped up from where she'd been staring at the spot Hunter had stood in just minutes ago. "What?"

"Locker room," he explained. "Some of the guys were being idiots. He put them in their place."

Carmen frowned. "You discuss me in the boy's locker room?"

Asa flushed. "Of course not!" he retorted. "It wasn't my fault!"

Carmen grinned in response. "I was just pulling your leg. Relax."

And then, completely on impulse, she placed her other hand on his shoulder and stood on her toes, leaning in to place a light kiss on his jaw. "I know you'd never treat me like that," she mumbled into his skin, before pulling away and landing back on her feet.

The breathless smile he offered her right then made her heart skip several beats.

Oh God. Oh God. Oh God.

When exactly had Carmen lost her heart to this boy with the sun's glow in his eyes?

Was it when she caught a glimpse of him running his hand through his hair in the cafeteria? Was it when he handed her art journal back to her, a sincere apology on his lips? Was it when she saw him grinning with his head tipped back? Was it when he'd thanked her for existing and kissed her cheek? Was it when he told her he loved her? Was it when he touched her shoulder or held her hand during times she needed comfort?

Did she fall for him at one particular moment in time? Or did every single time he allowed her a peek into his soul add up to it?

She didn't know when it happened, and she supposed it didn't matter either.

She'd given up every bit of her fractured, ripped heart to Asa San Román, and even though she loved him with the shattered remnants of a soul that wasn't whole, she wished—oh, she *wished*—that this broken version of her would be enough.

Please, she said a silent prayer, *please let it be enough.*

44.
I'll Say It Back

Asa's eyes scanned the text he'd just received from Hayden which informed him about a party that was going to be held later on that night at the house of one of the guys from the basketball team.

He nibbled on a corner of his bottom lip, deep in thought, as he tried to decide if he wanted to attend or not.

Before, he'd have gone without a second thought, but now, parties surprisingly didn't hold the same allure for him as they once had.

Firstly, he'd matured and since then realised that underage drinking was a pretty stupid thing to do. He supposed being removed from the interstate championship had driven him to that realisation and made up his mind. It had sucked to learn that he couldn't take part in it, and he didn't want to risk getting caught with alcohol in his system and be kicked off the school's team for good in case the cops showed up.

And secondly, the girls. Parties had always been the perfect place to work his charms. But now... Now that didn't appeal to him either. This, he realised, had a lot to do with a certain girl who had midnight hair and eyes that never failed to pierce his soul.

He wasn't going to touch another girl when he knew his heart belonged to someone now. Hell, he hadn't so much as flirted with anyone for a long time now.

And Asa definitely wasn't complaining. Why should he? With Carmen, every little thing was always more. *She* was more. And he'd drop just about everything just to keep getting his fill.

He let out a sigh and used his thumb to swipe the pop-up text away from his home screen.

He'd just decide on attending it or not later. Even if he didn't want to drink or have an intense make out session for one night, he still did want to spend some time out of school with Hayden, Wyatt, and a few other guys who he could tolerate.

It'd been a while since he hung out with the guys, and oddly enough, he kind of missed it. He also desperately needed some kind of normal after 1) losing his best friend, 2) getting kicked off the one competition he'd been looking forward to his entire life, and 3) telling the girl he was in love with how he felt about her in the bluntest way.

It was ironic, really, that the three things he least expected to happen turned out to be the very source of his growth.

Shaking his head to himself, he slipped his phone into his pocket and turned around, only to find Carson approaching him.

For the love of God. Couldn't he just catch a goddamn break?

None of the bruises were visible on his face anymore, and his eyes had healed from the swelling, but Carson's slightly crooked nose still told a story of him getting it broken.

You took away my chance of participating in the meet," Carson said, eyes fixed on Asa with a steely resolve that only meant trouble.

"I took away mine too," Asa told him matter-of-factly. "Sucks, I know."

"Yeah well, that spot was never yours anyway," he bit out. "But I deserved to be there. And *you* took it away." He stepped closer, and jabbed Asa's chest, pure rage radiating off him in waves. "Because you went crying to the principal and your parents like the pathetic piece of shit that you are."

Asa didn't want the words to get to him; he didn't want to allow them inside his head only to engrave themselves into the walls of his mind while they plotted to antagonise him later.

But he was finding it really hard to do so.

It hadn't been weakness, had it? When Asa had come clean about the bullying?

He'd done what he had to do in order to make surviving school easier. Had that been pathetic?

Stop it, he chastised himself. *Stop it. Stop it. Stop it.* He just wanted to stop letting them get to him. Wanted to stop with all the self-doubt already.

"You'll pay for it," Carson then said, his voice low with the promise of retribution. "One way or another, you're going to pay. I'm going to *make* you pay."

Asa wasn't new to trouble; all throughout his life, his impulsive nature had always guided him to it. And more often than not, he'd found himself in one confrontation or another.

But something in Carson's voice—not the words, but the tone in which he delivered them—unsettled Asa. And that was saying a lot.

He kept his cool, though. He didn't let himself rise to the bait. "You can pull the same shit you did in the cafeteria that day." Asa shrugged. "It won't matter. Because I'm not going to let you provoke me into throwing the first punch. Not this time."

Carson's answering smirk intensified the uneasy feeling in Asa.

"Asa, Asa, Asa." He sighed, shaking his head in mock disappointment. "I don't have to get to *you*, in order to get to you, do I?" His smile widened. "Give Carmen my regards."

All sense of self-preservation that kept Asa in check instantly drained away from his mind and body, and he took a threatening step closer, balling up his fists, when Carson held out a hand and spoke again.

"Think carefully about what you're going to do right now," he said. "Because one more misstep on your part, and my parents aren't going to give you the courtesy of going to Hendrickson first." He cocked his head to the side, angling his jaw towards Asa. "Go ahead. Punch me. I'd love to slap you with a harassment charge."

Asa's fists clenched even harder, his fingers digging into the skin of his palm, as he tried to hold in his temper. He took a few steps back because the closer he stood, the higher the chances of him choking the other boy.

Carson seemed to view Asa backing off as a victory. "That's what I thought," he muttered, a triumphant glint in his eyes. "You can't do shit with the school already keeping a close eye on you. Have a great day, Asa. You never know when shit is going to hit the fan."

•   •   •

All throughout his fourth period class, Asa's mind was running at a thousand miles per minute.

He wasn't much of an overthinker; he'd never been one. Asa had always been the act-now-suffer-the-consequences-later kind of guy. Now, though, all he could do was overanalyse every possible scenario that Carson's threat could lead to. And it scared Asa, because he'd never felt this way before. If he was half as smart as he usually was, Asa would shrug off Carson's words and label it as nothing more than an empty threat.

But Asa wasn't feeling so smart right now. What was logic and reason in light of the girl he loved being used to get back at him?

"I'm not talking to a wall, Mr San Román," the teacher's words fell on his ears, snapping him out of his thoughts.

Asa's eyes widened as he tuned back into his surroundings and registered the fact that every single head in the classroom—except for Hunter's, *of course*—was turned towards him.

"Um…" Asa looked past all the amused students and turned his attention to the teacher. "I—I'm sorry, was there a question? I didn't catch it."

The teacher muttered something under his breath and shook his head to himself before turning back to the board. "Don't zone out during class again. I need each and every one of you to focus."

Asa nodded hastily even though the gesture couldn't be seen with the teacher's back now turned to him. "Sorry," he called out, ignoring the mortified burn creeping up the back of his neck.

The teacher continued with the lesson and all the students shifted their focus back to the task which was given to them. Asa released a breath of relief.

There was a soft tap on his shoulder from his left, and he tilted his head to meet Wyatt's inquisitive eyes.

"Everything all right?" he mouthed.

Asa started nodding about to falsely reassure him, when he stopped and decided to just let Wyatt know that no, everything was not all right. It was about time Asa started letting someone else in anyway. So he shook his head and gestured with his hand that he'd talk to Wyatt later.

The unabashed honesty from Asa seemed to surprise the other boy, but he just nodded and offered Asa a thumbs-up.

Fifteen minutes later, once the bell rang, Asa found himself walking down the hallway with Wyatt at his side.

"So," Wyatt started. "What's up?"

Asa's mouth curved into a wry smile. "Want me to answer that literally?"

"You could try." Wyatt shot him a sideways glance. "But I'd have to punch you." And then, he grinned.

"Yeah," Asa muttered distractedly. "Wouldn't want that now."

"All right, seriously," Wyatt said, the amusement beginning to fade from his usually cheery voice. "What's going on?"

"It's lunch now, right?" Asa nodded towards the school's main doors. "Let's head out."

Wyatt raised a brow. "Don't want to spend it with Carmen?" He sounded confused.

"Dude, it's one lunch period. It's not like I can't be away from her for thirty whole minutes."

"Could've fooled me."

"Shut up."

The light banter between the two lasted 'till the moment they were seated at a table by the window of some fast-food place.

"So, Carson's back," Wyatt announced, grabbing the ketchup dispenser and squirting some onto his plate of potato wedges.

Asa's eyes met his and narrowed in suspicion. "How'd you know I wanted to talk about him?"

Wyatt rolled his eyes. "Do I look like I was born yesterday?" He dipped a wedge into the sauce and chewed off the upper half of it.

"You act like it sometimes," Asa deadpanned, snatching the other half of the potato wedge and tossing it into his mouth.

Wyatt snorted and leant back in his chair, raising his brow as he regarded Asa. "Stop beating around the bush and tell me what happened."

Asa mumbled something under his breath and picked up his fork, playing around with the lasagna on his plate. "He blames me for not being allowed into the meet."

"When has he ever owned up to his own mistakes? Of course he was going to find someone else to pin his loss on."

"I'm not worried about him blaming me," Asa explained. "I just can't help but think about what he's going to do *because* he blames me."

This time, Wyatt frowned. "He didn't explicitly tell you he was going to do something to you, did he?"

Asa shook his head. "Not to me. He did say that he could get to me another way, though. And then he mentioned Carmen."

Realisation flickered through Wyatt's eyes, and he chuckled lightly under his breath, which only confused Asa. "So why are you worried?"

Asa blinked, staring at Wyatt as if he'd sprouted another head within the blink of an eye. "What do you mean why I'm worried?" he repeated, wanting to smack his friend on the head. "It's pretty self-explanatory."

"Yes." Wyatt nodded slowly. "He threatened the girl you care about. But *why* are you worried?

283

A string of curses left Asa's mouth in one single breath, impatience flaring up in him. "Maybe because I'd like to put a stop to this whole thing once and for all?" he snapped, unable to understand how Wyatt didn't find the seriousness in all of this.

Wyatt sighed and looked at Asa like he was dealing with a five-year-old. "Did you ever stop to think that's what Carson probably wants? For you to make the first move?"

"I don't care if I'm giving him the upper hand by letting him provoke me into doing something stupid. I'm not standing by as he takes a swing at Carmen just to knock me off."

"You mean, *if* he's going to do that."

Asa shook his head again, more frantically this time. "You weren't there, man. He meant whatever he said."

"No, Asa, it was an empty threat," Wyatt said firmly. "Just deconstruct the threat using simple logic without letting your feelings for Carmen get in the way."

But that was the problem right there—all that occupied Asa's mind was the thought of her getting hurt because of his own mistakes.

"Yeah, I'm not sure how to do that right now," he muttered, looking away from Wyatt and focusing on the few vehicles that passed by the window they were seated at.

"All right, tell me, when do you think the guys got to know about Carmen?"

Asa's mind immediately flashed back to a particular moment in school and realisation dawned on his face. "The locker room, when Ronnie mentioned it in front of all of them."

"Exactly."

"But Carson wasn't there at that time." Asa pulled his brows together.

Wyatt only shrugged in response. "Not important, someone would've just told him. But that's not the point here, Asa. If he heard about that, then there's something else he'd have definitely heard of too."

Something clicked in Asa's mind. "Hunter's threat," he mumbled, more to himself than to Wyatt.

"Bingo." Wyatt grinned. "Now Carson can be an idiot with no filter on his mouth sometimes. But I think you and I both know even if he did try to mess with you, there's no way he's stupid enough to piss off both you *and* Hunter." He popped another one of the potato wedges into his mouth. "Like I said, it was an empty threat. No way in hell he's actually going to act on it."

That actually made sense—a *lot* of sense.

Asa's relentless worrying seemed utterly nonsensical and stupid now that Wyatt had helped him see past the surface of Carson's words.

"Why'd he make the stupid threat anyway?" Asa cocked his head to the side. "If he was never going to live up to it?"

"I'm guessing he was counting on your rashness to do the rest of the job," Wyatt said in a somewhat soft tone. "He must have known you would let it get to your head."

Asa dropped the fork into the plate and leaned back in his chair, feeling his shoulders drop as he ran a hand through his hair. "I need to seriously get my shit together," he muttered harshly, angry at himself for letting his emotions get the better of him. He wondered if being a heart-over-head kind of guy did more damage than good. "Maybe I should take lessons from Hunter and learn how to become a goddamn robot."

Wyatt pressed his lips together, chewing on the inside of his cheek as he mulled over something in silence.

"No...," he finally said, meeting Asa's eyes with a small smile of his own. "No, you shouldn't have to change that part of you because people do horrible things sometimes. Besides," —he took a gulp of his water— "I think it takes a certain kind of courage for someone to wear their heart on their sleeve, the way you do."

Asa scoffed lightly. "Fat load of good it's done me."

"Yeah," Wyatt replied. "It got you Carmen, didn't it?"

Asa's eyes snapped to his with lightning speed, a whole ocean of emotions flooding through him right then as the reality of Wyatt's words hit him.

Because that part of him—the part that allowed himself to be vulnerable—was what Carmen's eyes had seen and told him made the world a better place. There couldn't be anything wrong with him just because he had no qualms about opening up his heart to this world, right?

No, there had to be something wrong with the people who shamed him for it.

An odd sense of calm washed over him gently right then, the sensation being a high contrast to the sudden crashing of emotions just minutes before.

He met Wyatt's eyes again, grateful that he had someone who could use his mind when Asa himself couldn't.

"Thanks, man," he said softly, short and sincere.

Wyatt grinned. "Dude, if you're going to be thanking me each time I save your ass from doing something stupid, *thank you* is soon going to become the most frequently used phrase in your vocabulary."

Asa just rolled his eyes in response, slipping back into their light banter as the seriousness slowly dissipated, and Carson's threat was no longer hanging over Asa's head so heavily anymore.

"You just proved there was a reason I kept you around." Asa grinned, that playful edge in his voice reappearing as they stood up and began to leave. "Good timing too. I was about to give you the papers terminating our friendship."

"Give me a heads-up next time you want a brovorce so that I can lawyer up."

"What the heck is a brovorce?" Asa asked in bewilderment as he opened the door of the diner and stepped out into the chilled air.

"Divorce, but, you know, between bros."

"You're such a goddamn idiot, Wyatt."

"Hey, you were the one who mentioned you pulling paperwork terminating our friendship. Might as well put a name on it."

"Why do I always get stuck with the weird ones?" Asa muttered under his breath.

"Because the weird ones are the best ones." Wyatt grinned, clapping Asa on the back as the two of them took off down the street to walk back to school.

Asa didn't say anything to that, but the affectionate smile on his face spoke volumes on its own.

• • •

When they reached school, there was still about five minutes of lunch remaining. Wyatt and Asa parted ways, the former heading off towards a different hallway with the latter taking off in the direction to his locker.

Asa was still walking between the rows of lockers when Carmen appeared from the other end, her head bent slightly as she stuffed a textbook into her shoulder bag.

She hadn't seen him yet as her eyes were focused down on her bag as she zipped it close whilst walking, but Asa didn't bother calling out her name or alerting her of his presence. He just picked up his pace, taking quick strides towards her as his heart started beating irrationally fast and his breathing faltered.

It was only when he was a few steps away that Carmen looked up and saw him. Her eyes widened, a smile forming on her lips as she opened her mouth to speak. "Hey, we missed you at lu—"

Whatever she was about to say got cut off as Asa wrapped an arm around her waist, pulling her flush against his body in a tight, bone-crushing embrace.

He couldn't care about being gentle, not right now. The hug was sudden and rough and hard enough to knock the breath out of both of them, but all that mattered was that she was here.

Carmen was *here*, safe and sound, in his arms, and that was all that he needed to steady the insane *thumpity-thump* of his heart.

His other hand slipped into the long strands of her hair, his fingers running through the silky locks in a soothing manner.

She was here. She was here.

"You're okay," he breathed into her hair, his voice hoarse. *"Estás bien, estás bien."*

Asa could hear her say something against his chest but her voice was muffled due to how tightly he was holding her to him.

He didn't let her go for several more heartbeats, before he realised that he was probably cutting off her air supply. He loosened his hold on her, but not pulling away or removing his arm from around her small waist.

"You were saying something?" he murmured, looking down at her with such intensity in his eyes. His heart felt like it could explode from all the overwhelming emotions right then.

For a moment, it looked like he'd rendered Carmen speechless. Her head was slightly tipped back to look up at him, her chin was still grazing his chest, and her eyes were wide and bright, so many conflicting emotions flickering through them.

He didn't think he'd ever found her more beautiful than he did in that very moment, in another one of their tiny infinites.

I love you.

"What was that for?" she asked him softly, her tone awestruck and…happy.

"I don't know," he mumbled, "I just—I just needed to—to—oh, I don't know, Carmen." He pressed his forehead against hers and let his eyes flutter shut. "I just don't want to ever let go of you."

"Asa?"

"Mm?"

"We're standing near the lockers," she told him. "People might stare at us."

"I don't care." He shook his head against hers. "I don't care about anything but you and you and only *you* right now."

"Asa?" she called after another beat of silence had passed.

"Yeah?" His voice was only audible to her ears.

"One of these days you're going to tell me you love me again," she whispered, and he felt cold fingertips touch his jawline, leaving nothing but a burning sensation in its wake. "And I'm going to say it back."

Asa's eyes flew open, meeting a pair of silvery ones that reminded him time and time again of the calm before the storm. Right now, he felt it stir up a whirlwind of emotions in the pit of his stomach.

"You do that." He smiled, his voice rough and thick with emotion. "And I'm going to kiss you 'till you forget how to breathe."

45.
Sexy Is An Attitude

He didn't know how it happened, but when the last bell for the day had rung, Asa found himself standing by the main doors of the school along with Wyatt, Carmen, Hayden, Willa, Joyce and Lyra.

It was the weirdest bunch. That, he had to admit. A group of completely mismatched people, and yet somehow, complemented each other perfectly.

"Hey, there." Lyra grinned as her eyes fell on Carmen, before shooting Asa a discreet smirk to which he just rolled his eyes. "I've been dying to bug Asa about you, but now that you're here, I might as well get to know you directly."

"Hey back." Carmen smiled, her voice strong and clear as always.

It never failed to amaze Asa how Carmen's appearance was so deceiving. She looked like someone who was very withdrawn from society—but whenever she spoke, it was always with such confidence and pleasantness. He admired that about her, how she was bold in her own soft, gentle way.

"Tell me Asa's bringing you along tonight," Lyra gushed. "We could—"

"Wait wait," Carmen interrupted, furrowing her brows. "What's happening tonight?"

"Nothing," Asa answered. "Just some party. That I haven't even made up my mind about, by the way." He directed the last part to Lyra.

"I'm going." Willa shrugged. "Joyce is and there's no way I'm letting her go by herself. Like, who even knew she'd like parties? All she does is blush every time someone speaks to her."

"I'm standing right here." Joyce huffed, eyes darting around the entire place while her cheeks reddened.

"I know, sweetheart." Willa rolled her eyes. "Would you rather I say that behind your back?"

Asa smiled, shaking his head subtly. From the number of times he'd interacted with Willa, he'd come to realise she was quite protective of the ones she cared about. It made sense then that she would attend the party Joyce wanted to go to.

"I don't need to talk to people in parties," Joyce explained, uttering more than just the usual three or four words Asa was accustomed to hear from her. "Everyone's too drunk to pay attention to me—or too busy dancing and having a good time themselves."

"So, you like dancing?" Asa grinned, which seemed to cause Joyce's eyes to widen and hesitate in her reply.

"Um…Yeah," she muttered. "Both Carmen and I do, actually."

Surprise flickered through Asa's eyes, his lips twitching in amusement at the new piece of information. Carmen just kept surprising him.

"Hey, Asa!" Lyra called from his side, making him turn away from Joyce and look at her instead.

"So, Carmen's coming." She winked, slipping an arm through Carmen's as if they'd been close friends for a handful of years rather than having met just minutes ago.

Asa frowned. "The party?"

"Yeah." It was Carmen who spoke this time. "I remember going to one, like, last year or something. I kind of liked it, actually. Dancing is always so liberating." She smiled wide at that last part, her eyes creasing at the corners—a sign that she was genuinely happy about the idea of going out tonight and letting loose.

For one wild second, Carson's words resonated through Asa's mind, but he pushed it down, reminding himself of what Wyatt had told him earlier today.

Carmen wasn't just the girl *he* was in love with; she was also someone who mattered to the seemingly heartless Hunter. So there was no way Carson was going to incur the wrath of two boys who were infamous for the notorious brawls they got into.

"Cool," Asa said nonchalantly. "Guess I'll be coming too."

Carmen's answering smile almost stole his breath away. "That'd be perfect."

"Don't you trust us to be good company?" Hayden asked, looking genuinely curious.

"No," Asa deadpanned. It was a lie, though. Hayden, Wyatt and Lyra were three of the most laid-back people he knew, but there was no way he could not attend that party and be at peace.

Even if Wyatt had done a pretty good job of ripping apart Carson's threat with logic and reason, Asa couldn't completely shake it off. It was always better to be safe than sorry, though, and going to that party wasn't going to cost him anything now, did it?

"Carmen can ride with us then." Willa offered, shooting her a smile. "And you too." She nodded towards Lyra.

Lyra grinned in response, "Thanks, girl. The name's Lyra, by the way."

"Wait, how far is the party from my place?" Carmen asked Asa, pressing her lips together.

"Not that fa—What? Wait a minute. No! You're not walking to the party that late in the evening— you'll freeze." Asa shook his head vehemently, wondering if Carmen deliberately wanted to fall sick sometimes.

"I'm a winter baby." She shrugged innocently. "The cold is my friend."

"Yeah, Asa." Wyatt grinned devilishly. "Let the girl do what she wants."

Asa shot his friend a dirty look. "Don't you go encouraging her. You're just as reckless as she is."

"Excuse me?" Carmen raised her brows. "*You're* talking about being reckless?"

"I agree with Carmen here." Wyatt nodded vigorously.

"Amen," both Hayden and Lyra chorused.

"You're all traitors, the entire lot of you," Asa muttered.

"Come now, Asa." Carmen smiled cheekily. "It's not their fault they like me better."

Joyce snorted before erupting into laughter and then covering her mouth in embarrassment.

"You, with the purple highlight." Wyatt nodded towards Joyce. "You're allowed to laugh for heaven's sake. I know we look rough around the edges, but I promise we don't bite."

Joyce's cheeks were on flames by now, mumbling something incoherent in an offended manner.

"Guys, we shouldn't be loitering around here now that school's over," Hayden said, interrupting the conversations they were having amongst themselves. "Besides, if we're all going to the party, shouldn't we be heading back home now?"

"Dude." Wyatt looked at him incredulously. "School let out only a few minutes back. We have a few hours before we need to even *start* getting ready for the party. Your sense of timing is insane."

Hayden only scowled at him in return. "But we have homework, don't we? Don't you guys want to get it over with before you leave for the night?"

"Are you shitting me right now?" Lyra muttered, sounding like she wanted to smack her own forehead.

Both Wyatt and Asa groaned in unison, "Come on, man." Then Asa threw his hands in the air. "It's Friday!"

"Yeah." Wyatt nodded. "Plus it's the last day of school for Thanksgiving. We have holidays for a week and a half before we need to hand in those assignments anyway."

293

"Life—especially the academic aspect of it—is much easier when you're not procrastinating, you know," Hayden pointed out, completely serious.

"Ladies and gentlemen, Hayden Burrows, your resident fun police," Wyatt drawled, rolling his eyes.

Asa chuckled, pushing himself off the wall as he realised there were only a handful of students remaining apart from them.

"Guys, we should probably get going, though." He sighed, running a hand through his hair. "Guess we'll all see each other in a couple of hours, then."

There were murmurs of agreement, a few exchanges of goodbye thrown into the mix, and before he knew it, Asa was walking beside Carmen across the parking lot.

•   •   •

"Hey, Carmen?" Asa asked after a while, keeping his eyes on the road as he drove.

"Yeah?" She was looking down at her art journal opened on her lap as she furiously sketched something in it—Asa was dying to know what it was, but he forced himself to not even dare sneak a peek.

"This party tonight." He casually brought it up, keeping his entire demeanour relaxed and nonchalant. "You really wanna go? Or was it Lyra just being her persuasive self again?"

He heard the scratch of the pencil against paper stop then felt Carmen's eyes on the side of his face. "Lyra wasn't pushy," she said, sounding somewhat surprised at the topic. "I actually don't mind a good party once in a while."

He nodded slowly. "All right then, as long as *you* want this."

He heard a sigh leave her mouth and then a soft *thud* as she placed her journal on the dashboard.

"Come on, Asa," she mumbled. "You think I didn't notice you frowning when Lyra mentioned I wanted to go?"

"Why can't you notice the other stuff?" Asa grumbled good-naturedly. "Like how sometimes I reach for your hand on instinct, but quickly pull away before I can hold it?"

That earned him a playful smack to his shoulder.

"Come on, Asa. I'm serious. What's going on?"

"Nothing," he reassured her easily. "I was just worried about whether you were going out of peer pressure. That's all, okay?"

It wasn't exactly all there was to it, of course, but he didn't really think it was necessary to mention Carson right now. He'd never seen Carmen put herself out there the way she had today when she admitted she found dancing a form of liberation.

She deserved this. She deserved a night with no worries and burdens weighing over her head. Because even though she'd mentioned to Asa about her plans for Thanksgiving dinner and never spoke about it again, he could tell the anxiety was getting to her.

Carmen West deserved the world, and if all she was asked for was one night of dancing and letting go, then she was going to get it, everybody else be damned.

"Okay." She exhaled heavily, obviously not buying what he said completely, but she did not push him further. "And by the way, Asa?"

"Yeah?" He spared her a quick glance, meeting her eyes briefly— which was ridiculously enough to make his heart flutter—before he directed his attention back to the road.

"Next time, don't pull your hand away. Feel free to hold mine whenever you want."

The gigantic smile on Asa's face lasted the whole ride back, and even though he thought it was impossible to love her any more than he already did, Asa felt his heart fall a little deeper.

When they reached Carmen's place and she was just about to get out of the truck, Asa placed a hand on her shoulder.

She turned around, the skin on her forehead creased to form a tiny *v*. Instead of just asking him what it was, Carmen tilted her head a slight fraction, knowing he'd understand the gesture.

"When you, uh, when you reach the party with the rest of the girls, let me know okay? I'll come get you at the door."

Carmen's lips twitched, amusement dancing in her otherwise inexpressive eyes as she observed Asa.

"Asa San Román." The way his full name rolled off her tongue drove him insane. "Are you scared some other guy is going to run into me and sweep me off my feet?"

Asa's eyes softened, and he reached for her face, grazing his knuckles along her cheekbones with a certain kind of tenderness he'd never displayed before.

"I'm not worried about that," he told her, his voice barely audible. "I know where I stand with you; you've made it pretty clear."

"Good," she whispered. "And you should know that I feel just as confident with where I stand in your life. I trust you, Asa, so if you're worrying about what I think about your history with girls, I need you to let that worry go."

And just like that, Asa was reminded of why he loved this girl with such intensity.

Because Carmen managed to voice out an internal struggle of his that he hadn't known how to deal with. But here she was, reading between the lines of what he was saying and letting him know that she understood.

"You never fail to amaze me, you know that?" He chuckled lightly, using his other hand to tuck a strand of her hair behind her ear.

"I know that now," she replied, an uncharacteristic teasing glint in her eyes that told Asa she must be in an exceptionally good mood. "Also, Asa, could you do me a favour?"

He turned serious within a blink of an eye. "Anything, tell me."

Carmen tapped his hand caressing her ear. "Please don't tuck my hair behind my ear again. I prefer when it falls around my face."

For a few seconds, Asa could only stare at her and then he was laughing. He was laughing so hard his stomach hurt and his vision actually blurred.

"Not sure if I should find this offensive or funny," Carmen told him with a sigh, but there was no mistaking the look in her eyes as she watched him laugh

And it was the memory of that look that Asa knew would make his heart swell during the simplest moments of his life.

He knew that look—he wore it himself every time she gave him one of those rare half-grin-half-smile of hers. Or when she was utterly engrossed in one of her art journal entries, with her brows pinched together and her bottom lip completely pulled into her mouth.

It was the look of someone losing more of their heart to the other person.

•　　•　　•

The front gardens of the house the party was being held in was clean and completely litter-free.

The backyard, though, was an entirely different story. There was a hedge running along the sides and the back of the two-storey house, so the host seemed to have no qualms about students discarding beer cans, bottles, tissue paper and food wrappers on the ground since that area was shielded from prying eyes.

Asa noticed there weren't any of the traditional red cups, which meant that there was no beer keg. He figured that explained why there were glass bottles and cans scattered instead.

"You made it." Ronnie's voice fell on Asa's ears just as he began climbing the backyard patio steps. He had to cross the bricked area to get to the open double doors of the house's back entrance.

"Yes, I *am* standing here, aren't I?" Asa cocked a brow.

"You've got guts, coming to a party." Ronnie raised the beer bottle in his hand, tipping it in Asa's direction, and then took a swig.

"Yes, it must take a lot of guts to come to a party," Asa said flatly, sarcasm heavy in his tone.

Ronnie, despite being intoxicated, seemed not to appreciate Asa's mouthing off. "You know what I meant. This isn't school grounds. No rules or regulations to protect you here."

"Yeah well, Ronnie, the thing is, rules and regulations never protected me much in school either, did they? *I* protected myself. And by the way, what the hell is your problem anyway? I get why Carson hates me; that's the only emotion he's capable of besides anger. But I've never done anything to you."

"Are you kidding me?" He scoffed. "You're always walking around like a self-righteous prick who thinks he's better than the rest of us. Like you're better than me."

"Oh, wait, I just remembered why I can't stand you." Asa held up his hand, as if thinking hard about something. "Ah, yes, you're the one with an endless supply of sexist comments. Right. Well, have a great night, Ronnie, because if you're done trying to scare me off—and failing miserably, might I add—I'm gonna go ahead and join the life of the party in there."

Without so much as another glance back or waiting for the idiot to respond, Asa strode into the house, the fast-paced beat of the music filling his ears almost instantly and making every nerve in his body thump with the catchy rhythm.

He had just squeezed his way through a small throng of seniors when Hayden approached him from the other end, waving his phone in the air as he walked closer.

"Lyra texted," he said. "They're here."

It hit Asa right then that tonight would be the first ever night he'd be spending with Carmen outside school and the realisation alone set off mini explosions in the pit of his stomach.

He didn't even bother suppressing the grin that spread across his face as he followed Hayden back to where he'd entered the house from.

As soon as those doors opened, loud arguing fell on Asa's ears—apparently the girls were having a really passionate debate about something—but he tuned it all out as his eyes zeroed in on Carmen and hers found him at the exact moment.

Her face lit up instantly, and she began walking towards him, as Hayden left his side and joined whatever debate was going on amongst Willa, Joyce, and Lyra.

"Hey, you." She grinned once she was close enough.

"Hey," he murmured, sweeping his eyes over the plain black turtleneck she wore and the dark jeans she paired it with.

"What?" she asked suspiciously, tilting her head back a little.

He shook his head, unable to hide the small smile tugging at his lips. "I've never seen you completely in black."

"Oh?"

"Yeah, it, uh… it actually looks really good on you." He shrugged, ignoring the burning sensation in his cheeks.

But he was right, though. With her endless dark hair flowing freely down her back and the turtleneck hugging her petite frame, the colour really complemented her ivory skin tone and made those silvery-grey eyes of hers pop out. She looked almost exotic, but in a very ethereal kind of way.

Only Carmen could have that touch of grace to her posture which made her seem like someone from out of this world. Not necessarily the drop-dead gorgeous type, but someone who claimed your attention anyway by the way she effortlessly carried herself.

Asa figured that, in a way, being a small-framed, reserved and all-around quiet person who could still pull off being bold and be in her element was its own kind of sexy. She set her own trend, this Carmen West. And Asa loved that about her. Heck, forget love. He was goddamn proud of the way she defined herself, something he had struggled to do for a long time.

"Thanks." She laughed, the rotating disco lights casting shadows across her face that seemed to pull Asa in even more.

He reached out and hooked his forefingers through two of the belt loops on her jeans, yanking her forward until she stumbled and fell against him.

299

"What was *that* for?" she grumbled, rubbing the tip of her nose that had bumped into the hard planes of his chest.

"I just wanted to," he said, unhooking one of his fingers from her jeans and wrapping his hands around her waist instead. He noticed how her clothing clung to her like second skin.

"Did you have to yank me though?" She grinned, that teasing glint in her eyes appearing for the second time today, which told Asa she was definitely enjoying herself right now. "What happened to being gentle?"

His hold tightened around her waist, pulling her impossibly closer to his body until he was sure every single muscle of his had memorised the feel of her body against him. "*Gentle—*" he leant forward, dropping his voice to a low rumble "—is overrated."

Asa knew the faint dusting of pink in her cheeks weren't because of the red disco lights this time.

"Besides—" he paused, deliberately dragging his eyes over every inch of her face "—I like seeing you up close like this." He unhooked his other finger from the belt loop and lifted that hand to her face, skimming the skin just underneath her eyes. "This...eyeliner...it suits you."

"Asa." Carmen's grin seemed to widen. "I have a feeling I could wrap myself in seaweed and you'd still tell me it suits me."

"You're that confident?" His lips lifted into a half-smirk, eyes alight with mischief.

"No." She shook her head slowly, eyes crinkling at the edges. "You're just that whipped."

And despite his growing fondness for this new side of her, surprise flashed across his face. "Damn, you weren't kidding when you said the dancing atmosphere put you in a more relaxed mood." He pressed her closer to him. "I like this more open, laid-back version of you. The attitude's kind of sexy, to be honest."

Carmen raised a brow in response. "We definitely need to go dancing more often, if it means you're going to be more unrestrained with your speech."

300

"Carmen West." He looked at her with a devilish smile. "You asking me to talk dirty to you?"

He ended up getting shoved hard in the shoulder, sending him stumbling back as he erupted into laughter. Just as he regained his composure though, Joyce walked up to them and curled her hand around Carmen's arm.

"We're gonna hit the dance floor, you coming?" she asked, the excited smile on her face not wavering.

Carmen nodded, flashing her friend a smile of her own. She then turned towards Asa. "You joining us?"

He snorted, stifling another laugh. "I can't dance to save my life. You go ahead." He smiled at her in reassurance, ignoring the small flash of worry he felt right in the centre of his chest as he watched her go with the other three girls.

He didn't feel like smothering her by hanging around too closely during the one time she wanted to let loose and just have fun.

After standing there for a few more minutes and making sure she was all right with her group of friends, he turned around and started heading further into the house, deciding to find his own group of weirdos to hang out with.

A small sigh fell past his lips as he pushed his way through dancing bodies, silently wishing that tonight would provide Carmen with that sense of freedom she was looking for, and hoping against hope that his demons didn't find their way to her tonight.

Carmen had been through enough, and she didn't need to start paying for his mistakes, too.

46.
Kiss Me Right

Asa and Wyatt were laughing hard with a couple of other guys as Hayden told them about a prank that had gone terribly wrong last Halloween.

"You know," Wyatt said, leaning into Asa's side so that Hayden wouldn't hear him. "He's a pretty happy drunk. I forget he always has a stick shoved up his—"

"I can hear you, asshole!" Hayden yelled from where he was sat, causing Asa and some of the guys to snicker.

Wyatt just raised his hands in surrender, leaning back in the beanbag with a sheepish smile. "You know that somewhere deep down I love you," he said smoothly.

"I bet." Hayden snorted.

Asa leaned back in his chair, a lazy but content smile on his face because the night seemed perfect so far. He didn't know the last time things had gone so well without it being interrupted by something terrible happening, but he was trying not to let his wandering thoughts tamper with his good mood.

He was, however, beginning to get thirsty, so he pushed the chair back and stood up. "I need a drink," he said, flexing his arms as he rose. "Please tell me there's something that's not spiked."

"Yeah, there's a white icebox down in the kitchen," one of the guys within earshot called out. "All canned soft drinks."

Asa shot a grateful smile towards the guy as he walked past. "Thanks, man."

He stepped into the marbled kitchen, stopping in his tracks as his eyes searched for the icebox. He found it easily, considering it was pretty huge and propped up against the corner of the pantry cupboards.

Opening the box, Asa found a few unpacked cartons of fizzy drinks sitting between the pile of ice cubes. He pulled out the Pepsi pack and placed it down with a heavy thud on the counter, kicking the lid of the icebox so it fell shut. Despite the number of times Asa had used his hands to throw punches hard enough to break noses, he couldn't seem to tear the goddamn polythene of the sealed carton.

"*Joder!*" he swore under his breath, growing extremely frustrated as the only damage he'd done so far to the packaging was a few dents.

There was an impatient sigh from next to him and before he could turn around, an arm shot out and yanked the carton from Asa's grasp.

"Couldn't have used a fucking scissor," Hunter muttered under his breath as he easily ripped off the tightly-packed polythene. Grabbing one of the cans from the pack, he shoved it into Asa's chest, sending him stumbling back due to the force.

Asa blinked at the carton that Hunter had opened within a matter of seconds, then looked down at the drink in his own hands. "You know..." He shifted his eyes from the drink to Hunter. "Only you can pull off helping someone out and being a goddamn dick at the same time."

"I wasn't helping you out. I was getting impatient of waiting for you to open the stupid thing because I wanted one myself."

Asa raised a brow at Hunter's empty hands. "So where's your drink then, if you weren't really helping out?"

Hunter's jaw ticked, and he forcefully wrenched a can from the pack for himself, which caused the rest of the cans to tumble over and fall, the sound of it muffled by the music.

Asa just shook his head in exasperation and kicked open the icebox, dropping all the extra cans into it before shutting the box.

"And since when do you even attend parties?" Asa furrowed his brows. "The last one you came to was around three months ago."

"You keeping track of my extracurricular activities, San Román?" Hunter cocked a brow, juggling his can of soft drink in the air.

"No," Asa shot back. "I just no longer had to keep looking over my shoulder, wondering when you'd show up and ruin the night for me whether it was something you'd say or do, like another round of punches." Asa's grip on his drink tightened. "I preferred the punches over the words, by the way. The punches healed."

Something flashed across Hunter's eyes, but it was gone before Asa could take in another breath of air. He seemed like he was struggling to say something. It wasn't that he opened and shut his mouth repeatedly—no, Hunter was more composed than that. But there was a tensed air about him in the way his shoulders were squared and his mouth was pressed into a thin line.

When Hunter did finally part his lips to say something, his eyes landed on something in the distance instead. His eyes hardened, a look of incredulity and rage crossing his face.

"That's Carmen," he stated in disbelief.

Asa didn't turn back to see for himself, figuring that Hunter probably caught a glimpse of her dancing there with the other girls. "Yeah, so?" He lifted a shoulder into a shrug.

Hunter's glare fell on him, making Asa feel wary all of a sudden. "You know." He chuckled darkly. "I heard this dude mention something about Asa's girl being here, but I shook it off because even though I knew you're a reckless idiot, I didn't think you were brain dead as well."

Asa slammed his drink down on the countertop and took a threatening step closer, squaring his shoulders and straightening himself to his full height. It was the exact same stance as Hunter's and gave him no advantage whatsoever.

"Watch... your... mouth," he bit out, eyes flashing and daring Hunter to say something else.

Then again, Hunter had never been one to back down from a challenge either. So Asa wasn't surprised when the other guy chucked his own drink to the side, the can rolling down the counter 'till it hit the wall.

"You brought her here!" Hunter snapped, fists clenching at his sides, a gesture that genuinely shocked Asa. Even though Asa himself tried to keep his temper in check occasionally, Hunter had never been one for self-restraint. "Here where half the guys are ones you've pissed off at some point and the other half hate me."

"She need—"

"And guess what you and I both have in common, Asa?" Hunter stepped closer, shoving at Asa's chest. "*Carmen fucking West.* And you brought her here, handing her over on a silver platter."

"Would you stop being so ridiculously paranoid?" Asa retorted, beyond pissed now. "You think that way because if it was *you* in their shoes, *you'd* have done something horrible like using somebody's loved one in order to get back at them! Goddamn, *puta*. And the only one with that exact same mentality here—who would actually stoop low enough to get at either you or me through Carmen—is Carson who doesn't hate *you*, by the way, just me. So he's not going to do anything either."

"How do you know that?"

"Because I do," Asa hissed, wanting to throttle Hunter for digging a mountain out of a mole hill. "Because Carson's the only one who even thought to go there and cross that line."

Hunter's eyes narrowed in suspicion. "How do you know that?" he repeated his earlier question, but with a cautious tone this time.

"Well, he—" Asa stopped abruptly, knowing that he'd walked into this one and was probably digging his own grave.

"He what?" Hunter's voice turned to steel.

"Oh, you know." Asa tried shrugging it off, but obviously failed spectacularly at his attempt to do so because Hunter's furious expression only seemed to grow darker.

305

"No." Hunter forced through gritted teeth as if he was restraining himself from throwing all the knives in the kitchen at Asa. "I *don't* know. So tell me."

Asa sighed heavily, pinching the bridge of his nose. "Look, he was just trying to get in my head, okay—"

"Did he threaten her?" Hunter asked, a short laugh of disbelief escaping his mouth. "The bastard threatened her, didn't he?" He shoved Asa aside and began walking away when Asa grabbed his arm and yanked him back.

"Where are you going?" he asked, frowning at the moron.

"Where do you think, dumbass?" Hunter snapped, snatching his hand out of Asa's tight grasp. "Rip his lungs out. Maybe even force it back down his throat."

When he tried moving again, Asa stepped in front of him, blocking his way. "That's a lot of anger from a guy who claims not to give a shit about Carmen at all."

A frustrated growl rose from the back of Hunter's throat. "Move out of my way, Asa. I'm not doing this with you right now."

"Oh no, this is actually the perfect time to do it," Asa snapped back, exhausted with Hunter's inconsistent attitude.

Because one minute, he was tormenting Asa and the next, he was doing him a simple favour of getting him a drink. The other minute, Hunter was breaking Carmen's heart and the next one, he was ready to break the limbs of anyone who so much as thought of hurting her.

"You know, maybe it's you I should be punching the living daylights out of." Hunter seethed, "Considering you're the one who brought her here despite Carson directly approaching you about her."

"Then go ahead and punch me!" Asa glared, curling his palms into fists. "Because I won't fight back. If it helps you to curb your anger and stop you from creating a scene here with Carson, then go ahead. Take it out on me. We can go out the back and you can punch me to your heart's content, but you're *not* ruining Carmen's night by causing havoc here."

306

Hunter continued to glare at Asa, his jaw clenched, for several beats longer before he eventually let out a breath and his shoulders relaxed as he stumbled backwards. Hauling himself up on top of the counter, Hunter leaned his back against the wall as his legs hung over the edge.

"You really need to work on your anger," Asa told him seriously.

Hunter didn't respond to that.

"She always did like dancing," he finally murmured, and it took every ounce of self-restraint in Asa to not choke with shock at the fact that Hunter was using a tone of voice that wasn't cutting or venomous.

"Yeah, I just found out earlier today," Asa replied, somewhat awkwardly. He didn't know how to deal with this version of Hunter.

Asa liked sticking to the image of Hunter he had in his head—the cold-to-the-bone, remorseless, piece of shit bully who'd made Asa's life a living hell for a long time. That was the only version of Hunter that mattered to Asa, the only version he'd ever known and impacted his life to a great extent. He didn't want to know if there was a heart underneath all that cruel exterior. Asa didn't want to know if Hunter was capable of an emotion as simple as caring for Carmen.

It was always easier to believe someone you hated with every fibre of your being was some sort of machine. A robot.

It was easier to not give them an identity, to not acknowledge that there's a chance they can feel too. It was easier to view them as a monster. And Asa never wanted to see Hunter as anything more than the monster that he was.

"I want to hate you," Asa told him suddenly, causing Hunter's eyes to snap towards him. "I really want to."

"You should," Hunter replied matter-of-factly, as if that was the most obvious response.

Silence fell among them, but the air was filled with words. And they kept piling atop one another until the atmosphere in the kitchen started to suffocate Asa. He knew he needed to get out of there. Fast.

He grabbed his drink and was about to turn around when Hunter's voice made him stop in his tracks.

"I lied to you the other day."

"When?" Asa asked, feeling bitter as old memories began to resurface. "When you told me that I don't belong and never will?"

Hunter's eyes broke contact with Asa's, and he stared at the refrigerator magnets on the opposite end of the kitchen.

"When you confronted me at the locker," he said. "And asked me about Isla. I lied then."

Asa's anger simmered down as the confusion took over. "Isla?"

"I didn't drop her off at your place because I wanted to hit you where it hurt." Hunter's eyes remained fixed on the magnets, not wavering nor twitching. "I was the first one to leave the beach that night; I couldn't stay any longer. But I noticed that she was completely wasted and some of the guys were staring meaningfully at her."

The silence that followed was deafening, but Asa remained rooted to his spot, knowing that there was more that Hunter wanted to say.

"I know I've done..." Hunter paused again, as if looking for the right term, "...things. Horrible things. Crossed so many lines. But I don't know, I couldn't leave her there knowing that she was in no state to give consent and could possibly be taken advantage of. It was only after one of the guys there tried making a move on her that I grabbed her and drove to your place. I know I've done things I can't even digest anymore, but I'd like to think I haven't sunk so low that I could just turn a blind eye to what was happening."

Asa didn't really know what to think. Or say. Or *if* he should even say anything.

"Why drive her to my place?" he finally asked, picking the one question he knew wouldn't lead to any bursts of anger.

"Got the address from Hayden. I don't know. Didn't want to drop her off at hers in case she got into trouble with her folks."

Asa was supposed to hate him. Hunter was this big, bad monster in his head, and he wanted the image to remain that way. But with each minute that passed, Asa's carefully constructed picture of Hunter Donoghue was coming undone.

"Thanks, then," he muttered, looking at the can in his hand. "For looking out for her." And Asa truly meant it, right from the depths of his heart that still loved Isla. He was about to turn away yet again when Hunter's voice stopped him.

"And, Asa?"

"Yeah?" he asked with nonchalance, hoping his voice won't reveal how insane he found all this.

"I lied about the other thing too," Hunter said, jumping down from the countertop and dusting off nonexistent dirt from his shoulder.

"What other thing?" Asa asked, wondering what other curve ball Hunter was going to send his way.

"About you not belonging," he said quietly. "You've always belonged." And then Hunter was walking past Asa, muttering under his breath, "It was me who never did."

•   •   •

Asa stood on the second floor of the house, leaning on the banisters as he watched the makeshift dance floor below with thought after thought racing through his head. Then he pushed everything that had just taken place in the kitchen to the furthest corner of his mind, not wanting to drain himself mentally right now. Sighing to himself, he shook his head and was about to head back down when he caught a glimpse of a familiar body.

Carmen was there, right below him, dancing without a care in the world and a giddy smile on her face.

The view twisted his heart painfully. He wanted to keep her happy like that, always. But he knew that once tonight was over and come morning, Carmen's shoulders were going to be weighed down by burdens he couldn't even start to comprehend.

"You know," Carson's voice came from beside him as he fell into step next to Asa and looked down at the dancing bodies as well. "I didn't get it at first, what you saw in the girl. I mean, she's not exactly the prettiest face in school, is she? But tonight, with those figure-hugging clothes she's got on—"

"Finish that sentence, and I will break your jaw," Asa said in a deathly quiet voice, no mistaking the promise in his words. For a fleeting second, he wished he had just let Hunter deal with Carson.

"It's not like it's a crime to use my eyes, is it?" Carson smirked, taking a gulp from the glass bottle in his hand.

"Keep talking. I'd love a reason to punch that smirk off your face," Asa muttered, his gaze following every movement of Carmen's hands and sway of her hips.

"Relax," Carson said, sounding like he was enjoying himself. "I'm just here to enjoy the party, just like you. Just like Carmen. Nothing's happening tonight."

"Nothing is happening *ever.*" Asa pushed himself off the banisters and turned to face Carson. "So keep your empty threats to yourself. Now, if you'll excuse me, I'm going to spend the rest of my night with someone who doesn't pollute the air I breathe."

Asa descended the stairs, eyes fixated on Carmen, but slowed down in his strides when he noticed she was speaking to a guy Asa had seen around school occasionally.

Now, Asa wasn't that batshit possessive kind of guy, but he really, *really* didn't appreciate it when the other guy wasn't even paying attention to what Carmen was saying, but was dragging his eyes over her body instead.

Asa knew firsthand that every single syllable that spilt out of Carmen's mouth were nothing short of pure gold, and that boy over there wasn't even focusing on anything she was saying.

Moron, Asa couldn't help but think.

By the time Asa reached Carmen, the boy was gone.

"Hey." Asa smiled, his hand instinctively going to rest on the small of her back as he leaned in to peck her temple.

"Hey." She grinned, her cheeks looking flushed and her eyes bright with delight after all the dancing.

310

"You're having a great night, aren't you?" Asa couldn't help the smile that crawled over his face at seeing her so happy and carefree.

"One of the best," she said, and then completely shocked him by stepping closer and winding her arms around his waist, resting her chin on his chest and tilting her head back to look up at him. "I've been dancing away to my heart's content."

"And making new friends too, I've noticed." Asa raised his brows, lips curving into a semi-smirk.

Carmen raised her brows at him. "I thought you didn't get jealous, Asa," she remarked, clearly amused.

"I'm not," he told her truthfully. "But it doesn't mean I have to like it when they look at you like a piece of meat. You're more than what is underneath those clothes."

When Carmen offered him one of those breathless smiles of hers, he felt his heart leap to his throat.

"Asa?"

"Tell me."

"I've had a great time so far but can I ask you for something now?"

"Anything." He traced the apple of her cheek with his thumb, registering for the first time the velvety texture her skin was blessed with.

"Take me away from here," she breathed, gazing up at him with a burning intensity in her eyes. "I just want to spend the rest of tonight with you before I need to go home."

Asa leaned down and pressed his forehead to hers. "I thought you'd never ask," he mumbled, releasing a relieved breath. "Come on. I want to get out of this place, too."

•   •   •

"So," Asa exhaled loudly, once the two of them stepped out of the house and the cold November air rushed at their faces in full force. "Where do you want to go?"

Carmen rubbed her hands over her face, running her fingers down her hair and shaking it, causing the dark strands to fall around her in

311

gentle waves. "Honestly? Anywhere," she told him, lifting one corner of her mouth into a slanting smile. "I just want to spend the time with you."

Asa's breath hitched, and he prayed it didn't show in his expression how much her words impacted him. "You keep saying things like that to me, and I'm going to lose my mind."

"Sanity is overrated, anyway." She shrugged, biting down on a smile.

God, he didn't want this night to end. Asa didn't think he could ever get enough of Carmen when she was like this.

"All right, smartass." He rolled his eyes. "But I'm coming up empty here too. I've got no idea what to do."

"Let's just go for a walk then."

Asa shook his head in disbelief. "You always find a way to come back to that, don't you?" Despite his words though, he began walking across the front lawn of the house they'd just left, beckoning Carmen to follow. "You and your walks."

"Fresh air," she told him as she fell into step beside him. "I hear it's healthy."

"Really?" His voice dripped with sarcasm. "I never knew."

"Which is precisely why I just told you."

Asa huffed, shooting her an unimpressed look from the corner of his eyes. "Always got to have the last word, don't you?"

"Don't blame me for being able to pull one over on you."

"Please." Asa scoffed, the mischief seeping back into his tone. "There are other ways I can shut you up, and they don't involve words at all."

That seemed to shut Carmen up, and Asa couldn't help but shake with silent laughter as they walked down the quiet streets, the pale glow of the lampposts casting soft shadows on their skins.

"Asa? How are we going back?"

"Dad dropped me off on his way out somewhere, but my place is still pretty close by," he replied, rubbing his palms together for warmth. "We can get my truck from there and I'll drop you home."

"All right," she hummed, and stepped closer to him, their arms brushing together deliberately, but neither of them feeling uncomfortable about it.

They walked further down the streets, and even though Asa knew Carmen wasn't familiar with these surroundings the way he was because she lived on the other side of town, he also knew she trusted him to walk her through this neighbourhood.

That meant a lot to him more than he could ever say. He didn't know why it mattered exactly, but it was the little things when Carmen trusted him that always warmed his insides.

"Hey, what's that?" Carmen asked after some time, pointing towards an area in the distance where tiny glowing lights were visible.

"A park?"

Carmen shot Asa a flat look, making him raise his hands in surrender. "I know that's a park, Asa," she said. "I meant why are there fairy lights strung along the branches?"

"They normally do that around here," Asa told her. "The lights go up around the time school holidays for Thanksgiving starts, and they remain there 'till the New Year."

"Do you like parks, Asa?"

"Not really? I mean, I'm not a nature person."

"Well, pretend to like them for tonight because we're going in," she said, grinning.

Asa laughed and nudged her shoulder with his. "I don't have to pretend, Carmen. I may not be a nature person, but I'm definitely your person which means I'm going to love every moment I get with you, okay?"

He saw her lips twitch before they curved upwards into a soft smile, and she turned her face to meet his eyes. "Okay, Asa," she murmured.

They entered the gates of the park, heading down the winding cobblestone path that began right at the entrance itself.

Asa let his eyes sweep over the thick branches, well-maintained grass, and the soft yellow fairy lights that were wrapped around alternative branches, providing an almost celestial-like vibe to the place.

As they kept moving forward, he felt Carmen's palm brush against his gently before she laced her fingers through his, and giving his hand a light squeeze. Asa felt her tug at his hand, motioning him to sit down with her as she lowered herself onto the grass.

"That's the third time you've done it tonight, you know," he told her softly, holding onto her hand tighter as he crossed his legs on the ground.

Carmen's confused gaze landed on him. "Done what?"

"Made the first move," he mumbled, feeling kind of embarrassed that he was paying attention to the miniscule details. When Carmen continued to stare at him in perplexity, he sighed and scratched the back of his neck with his free hand. "At the party, just before we left it, you hugged me. And then when we were walking down the streets, you stepped closer to me and now, this." He lifted their joined hands, warmth flooding his cheeks. "You initiated the handholding."

"Um..." Carmen looked conflicted. "Are you saying you don't like it? Because I thought—"

Asa shook his head, stopping her from saying anything else. "I *love* it when you make the first move," he explained, smiling contently at her. "It's just that it's usually me initiating the physical gestures, whether it's hugging you, or kissing your palm, or touching your face. And this is nice. You making the first move is nice."

She continued to stare at him, but this time, no traces of her previous confusion was evident. Her expression was almost tender, a myriad of emotions flickering in those thundercloud eyes of hers. Her ivory skin was now dusted with a golden glow due to the fairy lights strung all around them and it made Asa rethink this world's definition of beautiful.

"Asa," Carmen finally said, her tone cautious and slow. "Do you remember what I told you at school?"

314

Asa's heart was pounding in his chest. *Thud. Thud. Thud. Thud.* It was so loud, almost deafening, that he didn't understand how the rest of this city couldn't hear it.

"Yes." He let the word out of his mouth in an exhale. "I do."

"Good," Carmen whispered, the conflict in her eyes slowly fading away as she looked into his eyes like she was peeking at his soul instead. "Because I want you to tell me you love me now."

"One of these days you're going to tell me you love me again."

"And I'm going to say it back."

Her words floated through Asa's head, causing his stomach to coil into an unbearably tight knot. He shifted his position on the grass so that he was leaning his back against one of the tree trunks, Carmen sitting just a few inches away, the sole object of his sight and attention. "All right, Carmen," he smiled, his voice as gentle as the rustle of the tree leaves.

And then, he reached forward and circled an arm around her waist, hoisting her up without any warning and dragging her on to the top of his lap so that she was sitting sideways on his legs.

A gasp left her unsuspecting mouth and her eyes widened just the slightest bit as she clutched his arm for support to steady herself.

"Asa! What—"

"I love you," he said roughly, his calloused thumb grazing the curve of her bottom lip. "I told you so the first time in the art room, then that time in my car, and I'll keep saying it for as long as you let me." His eyes kept looking between her eyes, at her lips, memorising every inch of her face like he wasn't ever going to see her again. "God, I *love* you."

"Every time you say it, I need to catch my breath." Carmen laughed weakly, but Asa could hear her breath faltering and then quickening as she leaned into him.

She brought up her hand to his face, dragging her fingers down his cheek and along his jawline, and Asa wondered if she was pouring the galaxies that ran through her veins into his skin with every single touch.

"I love you too, you know," she breathed, her voice trembling as the words came tumbling out her mouth and floated to Asa's ears. "I don't know exactly when I fell in love with you, but I only remember that I did. And I'm here, Asa. I'm here—with you—and I'm telling you that my heart is yours for the taking."

For a while, Asa couldn't really say anything. There was no way he could formulate the jumbled mess of emotions crashing through him into words, be it in English or Spanish.

"You do that. And I'm going to kiss you 'till you forget how to breathe."

"And you..." He trailed off, clearing his throat as he clung to what was left of his voice. "You remember what I also told you?"

Carmen nodded slowly, her grip on Asa's collar tightening.

His voice dropped a few octaves, turning raw and husky in a matter of seconds. "Turn around." He tugged at one of her legs, and she obliged, turning fully on his lap to face him until both her legs were on either side of him and her chest was just a breath away from his.

His arms found her waist again, and he couldn't help but fall in love with the way his palms fitted so perfectly around the curve of her hips. He pulled her forward until she was completely pressed against him, and then leaned forward. "I'm going to kiss you now," he said.

He felt one of her arms go around his neck and the other grab a fistful of the front of his button-down. "I want you to," she told him, her breath fanning across his face.

Now that he'd got permission, there was nothing holding him back.

Asa closed that gap between them, angling his face as he inched closer, and brushed his lips against hers in the faintest of kisses. He pulled away the tiniest bit, before leaning in again and repeating the gesture, his lips caressing hers in a barely-there manner.

"Asa," Carmen muttered, breathing heavily. "Stop treating me like a porcelain doll, and kiss me right."

A laugh was making its way up Asa's throat, but it never spilled out of his mouth. He tightened his hold on her body and then crashed his lips against hers in a full, all-consuming kiss.

316

He was kissing her for the first time and so was she, but to anyone watching, they might as well have been kissing each other for the last time. Their hold on each other was ironclad, almost like they were afraid that if they loosened their grip, something was going to pull them apart.

"*Te amo*," Asa gasped as he pulled away to catch his breath. "*Te amo, te amo, te amo.*" The words kept tumbling past his lips without control, as he peppered kisses all over her face, from the skin between her brows to the bridge of her nose to the corner of her mouth.

Carmen smiled, her eyes shining as she pressed her forehead against his, her chest heaving as hard as his. "I love you too," she sighed against his lips.

Asa might be the embodiment of the sun in Carmen's eyes because of all the warmth he brought her, and Asa might compare Carmen's presence to that of the moon for all the times she'd been a beacon of light for him in the dark.

Bur right then, right there, in a heart-stopping moment that'd become one of their many infinites—as their bodies melted into one another's, and their lips found their way home to each other—they might as well have created an eclipse of their own.

47.

Binary Pairs

The funny thing about kissing Asa was that while the act of kissing someone was meant to make you short of breath, the intimacy of the moment reminded Carmen this was the same person who reminded her to live.

The same person whose name on her tongue was enough to fill her lungs with air and allowed her to just *breathe*.

Breathe because the storm didn't last forever, the nightmares would be gone by the time the night had passed and the sun had risen. And Asa. Oh, Asa was proof that morning came and always would.

And Carmen loved him for it—with her heart and soul.

Asa's hands seemed to be glued to her waist, as if that had become the favourite resting place of his palms now. But Carmen wasn't complaining; she was used to being regarded as some fragile piece of ceramic because her gentle heart was seen as a form of innocence and gullibility. But the way Asa's fingers dug into her hips through the material of her turtleneck, the way his lips kept claiming hers in rough, hard kisses, told her that he didn't think of her as fragile or weak.

It was exhilarating, knowing that Asa was a perfect gentleman during school, but was purely driven by passion alone when it came to this. And knowing that it was her who was bringing out this more unrestrained, raw side of him made her nerves buzz with an electric charge that brought every single atom of her being to life with even the faintest touch from this boy with coffee eyes and golden skin.

"You were right," Carmen breathed out when they pulled apart again after losing all sense of time somewhere between kisses.

"About?" His chest heaved against hers, and Carmen could feel his heart thumping along with her own.

"Gentle being overrated." She chuckled under her breath, letting her eyelids flutter shut and just enjoying being in his arms.

"Mm-hmm." He was obviously distracted, his fingers busy entangling her hair and pulling her head back and her collar down as he dragged his mouth down her throat. "God, I should've done this ages ago," he groaned into her neck. "Should've just kissed you senseless in the parking lot that day."

Carmen tried to find her voice, to force her brain to form words and coherent sentences amidst the explosions in her head. "Don't be silly," she said and gasped as he tugged at her hair harder and placed open-mouthed kisses at the base of her throat. "We couldn't have ever done this at school."

Asa snapped his head back, pulling away from Carmen and staring at her with a wounded look on his face.

"What are you talking about?" he asked, eyes wide and lips swollen, causing Carmen's gut to clench painfully. "I want to be able to kiss you any time I want."

She raised her brow, not hiding the obvious amusement on her face. "And you can," she told him. "But we're not going to have intense make out sessions in front of people."

"So I *do* still get to kiss you then?"

Carmen shrugged, suppressing the smile tugging at her lips. "Sure. You know, those quick pecks on the mouth. A chaste brush of the lips. We can totally do that."

Asa's jaw dropped open, shooting her an incredulous look as if someone had just told him the Earth was flat. "There's only one way I know to kiss my girl." His eyes dropped to her lips for emphasis before he dragged them back up to meet her eyes, "And it's anything but chaste."

"And what way is that?" she murmured, drawing lazy patterns on his left cheekbone with her index finger.

"The knee-buckling, make-your-world-spin kind of way." He grinned wickedly. "The only way I'm going to kiss you is by pretending each time is the last time I'll ever get to do so."

Carmen shook her head with a ghost of a smile, feeling her hair swish against her back as she did so, before she sighed in contentment and tucked her head under his chin. She smiled to herself and relished the feeling of melting into his body, the way her small frame fit cosily against his broad one. As if nothing could get to her past him.

They sat there for a while, no words being exchanged. The only sound that filled the air around them was each other's breathing, which was no longer ragged and heavy, but slowly calming down and regaining its natural rhythm.

Carmen's eyes flickered upwards, finding a gap between the thick branches and leaves that allowed her to catch a glimpse of the dark sky stretching out endlessly above her and Asa. There weren't as many stars as she'd have liked to see, but they were enough to make the sky look like someone had strung fairy lights on it.

"Do you know about binary pairs?" she asked softly, listening to the sound of his steady breathing.

She felt his hand shift and start stroking her hair, running his fingers from the roots right down to the tips. "As in, the one to do with computers?" he asked, and she could hear the confusion in his voice. "The ones and zeros?"

Laughter fell past her lips, light and breezy. "No." She traced her finger along his collarbone, hearing his breath hitch at the contact. "I mean the stars."

She felt Asa shake his head as his chin moved against her temple due to the gesture. "I haven't." He pressed his lips to the top of her head. "But I'd like to hear about them from you."

Carmen snuggled further into his chest, shifting her gaze back to the tiny bit of sky she could see. "So the stars have a system, and the binary pairing is a pretty common one where only two stars belong in one system."

"System?"

She nodded against his chest. "Yeah," she murmured. "They orbit around the same centre. In their own little world, belonging only to their system."

"That seems nice," Asa commented. He stopped his kneading of her hair and started massaging the back of her head.

"It is," she said. "There's the primary star which shines the brightest. And the secondary star which is the dimmer one. You wouldn't be able to tell by just looking at the sky from here, though. Any of those stars above could actually be a binary pair, instead of a single star. When we look at them from here, it appears as one star because the primary star's brightness allows the secondary one to seem just as bright to our eyes. Kind of like it's lending its light to the dimmer one." She tore her gaze away from the sky, looking down at the grass, her smile fading.

"You... You sound almost sad about it," Asa stated, confusion finding its way into his voice again.

Carmen could honestly blame Asa if he found her extremely weird to be getting sad about something as beyond her control as the elements of space.

"I don't know," she muttered, her voice sounding deflated to her own ears. "I mean, they're not equal, are they? One's brighter while the other one's light is dimmer as if it's a given that they can never shine as equals. That one of them will never shine as great as the other because it was created that way."

There was a stretch of silence as Asa's hand paused in its soothing movements against her scalp. "Carmen," he said after a while, his tone gentle now. "I'm not sure we're speaking of stars anymore."

Carmen remained quiet for a while, wondering how exactly to put her thoughts into words. "I just... I..." She paused, took a deep breath, and then told herself this was Asa, and that she could say just about anything she wanted. "I wonder sometimes if human souls are like that too."

"Working in a system?"

"When they find that one soul they connect with on a deep level, yeah. Except the system would instead be a relationship." Carmen titled her head back, gazing up at Asa as he bored his eyes into hers. "But there's that one soul that's born dimmer, incapable of shining as bright as the other because it was fractured the second it came into existence, just like the secondary star."

At first, Asa seemed perplexed, the crease between his eyebrows increasing until something registered in his eyes and then his expression grew angry.

"Don't say that," he told her, voice firm but also pained. "You're anything but a fractured soul. God, *Carmen*, every single word that comes out of your mouth is literally gold, okay? You make me question what it even means to be beautiful every time you do something that's insanely kind, because that's who you are. Your compassion makes you the strongest person I know, and if that isn't the personification of light, then I don't know what is."

Carmen shook her head slowly, not taking her eyes off him. "Asa, I'm not looking for assurance," she told him truthfully. Because Carmen West didn't need to be told otherwise. She'd long since accepted her fate and needed to learn to live with the fact that some people just would never shine that bright. "I've just had this on my mind for a while now and felt like telling you. That's all."

"Yeah, well, screw the stars," he muttered. "I'm not in love with them, I'm in love with you. And that's all the light I need."

Carmen beamed at him, her eyes shining as she leant forward and brushed her lips against his in a fleeting kiss. "You're going to be the death of me, you know," she mumbled against his mouth.

"Took the words right out of my mouth." He smiled, leaning his forehead against hers.

They remained there like that, forgetting about the rest of the world for a few more heartbeats.

•　　•　　•

"Hey, Dad?"

Carmen's dad looked up at her from the pancakes stacked on his plate. "Yeah?"

She dug her fork into her own breakfast, gripping it hard as she tried to keep her eyes fixed on him, instead of looking away.

"Um," she said and then hesitated. "I kind of have a date tomorrow night."

It had been two days since Carmen had told Asa she loved him back. Two days since he kissed her under a tree wrapped in fairy lights, Two days since he drove her back home and told her he wanted to take her out somewhere.

Her dad blinked, opened his mouth, and then closed it. Then opened it again. "Oh, that's, uh, nice. That's nice, yes." He looked down, narrowing his eyes really hard at the pancakes like they were going to offer him some sort of advice. "Wait." He met her eyes. "Is this the same guy who drives you back daily?"

Carmen nodded, holding her breath as she hoped against hope that her father wouldn't make an objection like he'd done that day when he met Asa for the first time.

"All right." He nodded, looking down at his food again, but not touching it. That upset Carmen.

"Dad." She pressed her lips together, softening her tone as she tried to make him understand. "He's...he' not like that. He's good to me. You need to trust me when I say that."

"I do trust you," he said eventually.

"And I trust Asa." Carmen offered her father a small smile. "So you've got nothing to be worried about."

He glanced at her, his forehead creased. "I'll always be worried about you," he muttered, but Carmen relaxed once she saw him fight off a smile. "So. The name's Asa, huh?"

323

"Yeah." Carmen shrugged, struggling to keep herself from grinning at the mere mention of his name.

"Well, make sure you come back at an appropriate time, yeah?" Her father shot her a quick smile. "I don't want you returning home all by yourself too late in the night. It's a safe neighbourhood but I don't want to take any chances."

Carmen stared at her dad, her lips pulled down into a frown. "What do you mean I'll be returning home by myself? You'll be here, right?"

"Honey, it's a Monday. I'm on call tonight at the hospital, remember?"

"Wait, that means you won't be here to greet Asa when he comes to pick me." She tried to ignore the sudden wave of disappointment that washed through her, dampening the excitement she'd felt since this morning at the idea of going on her first date with Asa.

It must have shown in her tone or her expression, because her dad smiled apologetically at her. "I'm sorry, love."

This wasn't his fault, she told herself. It was his job, his commitment. There were lives depending on him tonight, and he needed to be there, at that hospital.

That didn't mean it didn't hurt, though. So she forced a smile on her face and waved it off. "It's all right, Dad. I get it, don't worry."

"Maybe some other time, then? Something tells me he's going to be around for a long while. You wouldn't have gotten involved unless you were serious about this guy."

"We *are* serious," she told him, her cheeks beginning to hurt due to the forced smile still plastered on her face.

Her dad nodded and seemed to look relieved. "See? I'll get to meet him on another day. Don't worry about it. You have a good time tonight."

Carmen waited then. She waited for the hundred and one questions fathers bombarded their little girls with when it came to a boy.

Those questions didn't come, though.

Because he didn't want to know. He just wasn't involved in her life the way she liked for him to be.

It stung, yes. But Carmen tried to tell herself it was just the impending "family" dinner that was getting to her father's nerves. She knew that must genuinely be one of the biggest reasons he was so distracted lately, but she doubted he'd have asked more about Asa even if the dinner wasn't happening.

It was only when her dad had finished with his breakfast, kissed her goodbye on the cheek, and left the house for work that Carmen let her shoulders drop with a heavy sigh. She let the fork drop to her plate, not really feeling like she wanted to eat anymore, and stared at the empty chair across from her where her father just sat moments ago.

"His name's Asa, Dad," she said to the vacant spot, her voice quiet. "His parents are originally from Mexico, but his dad is half-Dominican. He loves swimming, by the way—" she laughed weakly, feeling stupid for doing this, "—but he doesn't want to pursue the sport as a career. He says he likes the idea of a legal career, though. Probably become some hotshot lawyer." Carmen laughed to herself at that last part, but the sound quickly turned hollow and empty, echoing through the walls of a place that was feeling less like a home and more like a house as the years passed by.

Her throat tightened, a lump forming at the back of it. "What am I even doing?" she muttered to herself, shaking her head in disappointment. "You're not even here, Dad. You haven't been here for a while now."

Ignoring the sound of her heart breaking all over again by yet another man who was supposed to be her family, she grabbed her plate and began cleaning up.

• • •

Carmen's fingers ran over the different fabrics of the clothes hanging in her closet, the blouses and skirts swaying gently as she released them from her temporary hold.

325

What was exactly acceptable to wear on a first date? She knew that she didn't put much of an effort when she went to that party two nights back, but she didn't really care because she'd felt comfortable in a simple turtleneck and jeans. It kept her warm and allowed her to dance freely.

But tonight was going to be different. She was going out with the sole purpose of spending the night with the boy she loved, and that meant putting in an effort.

Not wanting to dwell too much on it, she pulled on a pair of unused black jeans, ripping off the price tag still attached to it, and chucked it across the room.

Her hands were just about to reach for the cream-coloured camisole when her eyes caught a flash of black and she recalled Asa's words which now resonated in her head.

"I've never seen you completely in black."

"It, uh, it actually looks really good on you."

A fond smile crawling across her face, she reached for the black camisole instead, feeling the silk slide smoothly across her skin as she slipped it on. Carmen would have been contented to go out with him in just those clothes, but wearing a sleeveless top would be plain stupid considering the November air was growing harsher by the day. Her gaze flickered to the clock and saw she had only about fifteen minutes left. She quickly threw on a red bomber jacket and paired it with a grey scarf around her neck.

After applying some eyeliner and brushing through her hair until she was satisfied with her appearance, Carmen spared her reflection one last glance and then headed out towards the living room, only to hear the doorbell ring.

Her heart instantly leapt to her throat at the sound, and her feet picked up speed until she was practically skipping towards the door. Wrapping her palm around the doorknob, she pulled it open to find Asa standing on her front porch, a make-your-heart-skip-a-beat smile on his face.

"Hey," Carmen breathed out, her mouth stretching into a wide grin without her being conscious of it.

"Hey you." He smiled softly, his eyes drinking her in as if they were capturing this particular moment and committing it to memory. "You're wearing mostly black," he commented, biting down on a corner of his mouth to obviously suppress the huge smile that was threatening to take over his face.

"Someone once said it looks good on me," Carmen said, stepping out of the house and locking the door before slipping the key into her pocket.

"That someone was definitely right," Asa replied, slipping his hands into his pockets, a gesture that caused Carmen to take in his appearance.

The cream-coloured crew neck sweater he wore hugged his torso, defining every single muscle from his broad shoulders to his sculpted chest and leaving very little to Carmen's imagination. It was crazy, honestly, the way she'd always known that he had the looks that caught every eye and a body that made heads turn and yet it was the one aspect of his being that she'd never really given much thought to.

She'd fallen in love with the way he uttered her name as if there was a constellation waiting to be named after her.

She'd fallen in love with his mind, the same one that recited a seventeenth-century quote to her in his truck.

She'd fallen in love with his heart, the very one that returned her art journal purely out of the belief that she deserved her kindness back.

And she'd fallen in love with his soul, a soul strong enough to make a confession of being in love with her even when she was just a broken version of herself.

After all that—after telling him she loved him back, after being kissed by him 'till she was gasping for air—here she was, now beginning to fall in love with his body, too.

327

Realising she was probably staring at his form for a little too long, Carmen looked up at Asa to find his eyes already on her, causing her cheeks to grow warm.

"You don't blush often," he told her, voice serious. "But when you do, I swear to God it drives me insane."

"Were you born with that smooth tongue or did you have to pick up lessons along the years?" Carmen asked cheekily, lifting a corner of her mouth into one of her signature teasing smiles.

"Does it really matter?" Asa asked, that mischievous glint present in his eyes as his lips formed a lazy smirk. "Because you weren't complaining about my smooth tongue that night in the park."

Carmen's jaw dropped as all words abandoned her, and something like fireworks erupted in her stomach. "Asa!" she hissed, wishing the ground beneath her feet would just crumble and drag her down with it.

He laughed and pulled both hands out of his pockets, walking towards her and pulling her into a tight embrace. "I'm sorry," he said, the ghost of his laughter lingering in his voice. "And, listen—" his voice dropped to a soft murmur, and he kissed the tip of her nose, "—I just wanted to tease you, but if those sort of remark make you uncomfortable, then tell me, okay? And I won't make them anymore."

Carmen's expression softened and she lifted a hand to caress his cheek. "The comment was out of the blue. It just shocked me, that's all," she reassured him. "But don't worry, it doesn't make me uncomfortable."

"All right then." He grinned before pulling back and frowning slightly. "Wait, why'd you lock your door?"

"Dad's not gonna be home tonight." She sighed. "Night shift. He'll probably come in around seven in the morning tomorrow."

Asa was looking at her intently right then, making Carmen feel funny on the inside. "What?" she asked, not breaking eye contact even though she wanted to because of his scrutinising gaze.

"You sounded a little bitter," he remarked, lifting an eyebrow.

328

"It's nothing." She shook her head. "I'm just being unreasonable, that's all."

"Missing your dad isn't unreasonable, Carmen," Asa said, leaning down to kiss the top of her head. "I'll get to meet him some other time. It's not like I'm going anywhere."

Carmen smiled contently and slipped her arm through his, pulling him along as she began walking down the porch steps. "Come on," she said in an upbeat tone. "Tonight is yours and mine, everything else can wait."

"I like the sound of that," Asa said, pulling her in closer to his side as they walked towards his truck. And even if she wasn't looking at him right then, Carmen could still hear the grin in his voice.

48.
Mi Amor, Mi Cielo, Mi Sol

Carmen knew that there was no such thing as a perfect person, but she was beginning to believe perfect nights existed. Because, honestly, there was no other word she could take from the entire English vocabulary that would better describe their date so far.

Since Asa was aware of Carmen's love for nature, he'd decided against taking her to a restaurant and instead brought along a picnic basket then drove her to the public park in her neighbourhood.

"Pick a good spot," Asa said as he killed the engine and they climbed out of the vehicle. "We're in your territory now and I don't really know the places around here."

Carmen shot him a confused smile. "Why did you bring me here then? We could have gone to a place you were familiar with."

"Tonight is about the both of us," he told her, grabbing the picnic basket from the back of the truck while she carried the blanket and the mini icebox. "You like nature and spending your time in fresh air, so we're at a park, one where you're comfortable with."

"And which part of this night is about you?" She smiled at him, touched at his thoughtful gesture.

He held up the picnic basket with a grin. "Mexican food—home-cooked and a hundred percent guarantee to make you fall in love at first bite."

Carmen snorted, the laughter escaping her lips before she could help it. "Tell me you didn't actually cook for me."

"Of course not. I bugged the daylights out of my mum to prepare all this. She made a huge fuss and all that, but it was just a cover. Secretly, she was thrilled that I was keeping her involved in my love life."

Something ugly reared its head inside Carmen. Here was Asa, gushing about a parent who wanted to know about the girl he was seeing, whilst her own father had not shown even a shred of interest today. She pushed the thought away. *Dad's working,* she reminded herself. His patients needed him.

They managed to find a good enough spot in the park, and Carmen proceeded to spread out the blanket while Asa set down the icebox and began unpacking the picnic basket.

"You know, I've never had Mexican before," Carmen mused out loud as she sat down.

"We talking about food or guys?" Asa raised both his brows, fighting off a smile.

Carmen just shot him a look of disbelief, feeling her stomach jolt and the tips of her fingers tingle whenever Asa made a remark like that.

"Both," she mumbled, trying to ignore the blush as she reached forward to open the icebox.

"You're blushing again," he grinned, seeming extremely satisfied with himself.

"I thought seeing me blush drove you insane."

"Yeah, and you told me sanity is overrated anyway."

"That has to be crossing a line of some sort," Carmen grumbled. "Using my own words against me like that."

Asa's lips slowly pulled up into a smirk as he leant back on his arms and cocked his head to the side, his eyes burning into Carmen's. "*Oh,*" he said in a low voice. "I plan on crossing lines all night long, *mi amor.*"

Carmen sunk her teeth into her lower lip, biting down on the smile really hard because yes, she *loved* it when he spoke to her that way.

331

"Come on." Asa laughed, shaking his head to himself and shifting from his position. "Let's start with the food or I'll end up spending the rest of the night finding ways to make you blush."

"You know, I don't think people come to the park with food and blankets at half past eight in the night," Carmen said, sounding amused.

"We'll just have to make history then," Asa told her, catching her eyes and offering her a tender smile. "Besides, the park is very well-lit with all these lampposts and garden lights. It might as well be late noon or something."

Carmen hummed in agreement, her eyes instantly widening as soon as one of the food containers was opened and the aroma hit her nose.

"Now," Asa declared grandly. "Let me introduce you to some fine cuisine."

And so Carmen let herself be taught about how *gorditas* were best served with potatoes and that *frijoles* were just plain disgusting—in Asa's opinion, anyway—which was why he hadn't let his mum add it to the mix. Carmen also learnt that *pozole rojo* was Asa's absolute favourite, and according to him, no one made it as good as Iliana San Román did.

Asa's eyes were lit up with a pure kind of innocence, making the golden embers stand out even more than usual. He rambled on and on about how he believed tacos were overrated and that *elotes* tasted much better without the mayonnaise and sour cream, the enthusiasm never leaving his face or voice as he allowed Carmen to step into his world.

And even as her ears registered his words, her heart was absorbing everything else: the rushed tone of his voice as if he'd never be able to say all that he wanted to before tonight was over; the way his lips remained stretched into a wide, excited smile; and the way his entire face seemed to light up when he spoke so passionately about something he loved.

"And, I mean, who would even want to eat that, right? It even smells—" Asa was cut off when Carmen grabbed the back of his neck on impulse and pulled his face down to press her lips against his.

332

She rose to her knees from her sitting position, curling her entire arm around his neck as she kissed him deeply. The moment didn't last for too long, though, as she pulled away after a few more seconds.

Asa blinked, staring at her in a dazed manner as he brought his hand up to touch his bottom lip. "What was that for?" he asked in a surprised tone, genuine happiness evident on his face.

Carmen lifted her shoulders helplessly. "You were being cute."

Asa only grunted in reply, averting his gaze, but Carmen caught the way his lips twitched—a telltale sign of a smile being suppressed.

That only caused a smile of her own to sneak its way onto her face.

•　　•　　•

As it turned out, Asa was also obsessed with ice cream.

After they had left the park, Asa drove them to a self-service ice cream parlour and had gone crazy trying out toppings of various flavours and types until he realised he couldn't force himself to eat his horrible concoction.

Carmen watched him dump his paper cup into a bin and serve all over again, all the while struggling to contain her laughter because she had repeatedly told him the toppings he'd chosen didn't blend with one another at all. He'd told her something about being adventurous and trying out new things.

"Just plain old cookies and cream," Asa said with a sigh as he walked to where she was standing, holding up his freshly served ice cream.

"Aw, really? What happened to being adventurous?" Carmen asked, feigning pity.

Asa shot her a half-hearted glare. "Don't."

"Now, now." She grinned. "We can't all be experts at both Mexican cuisine and ice cream. Don't be too hard on yourself." Carmen pressed her lips together, trying her hardest not to laugh at the wounded look on Asa's face.

"You're being awfully cheeky tonight," Asa muttered, eyes softening as they swept across every inch of Carmen's face.

"Means I'm happy." She smiled, reaching out and slipping an arm around the crook of his elbow as they walked towards the exit and left the parlour.

They decided to leave his truck in the parking lot, opting to walk around the block with their ice cream cups rather than having it inside the crowded parlour.

Asa went on to tell her about the time he'd made breakfast for his family for the first time ever and his mother had come into the kitchen with a baseball bat, thinking a burglar had broken in.

Carmen listened as he told her about his mother's huge vendetta against cursing whilst she herself did it relentlessly. And not once did Carmen find herself without a smile on her face. She loved to hear him speak about his family, about his trips to Mexico for their Independence Day, and the crazy pranks his cousins would pull on each other.

Somewhere along the way, Carmen realised he was doing the talking for both of them because he knew she wouldn't have much to say about her own family. And if it was even possible, she fell that much more in love with him.

They dumped their empty ice cream cups into a street bin and walked back around the block to return to the parking lot, Asa's arm now draped over Carmen's shoulders as he tucked her into the side of his body.

"So how come you don't have a phone?" Asa asked, frowning slightly.

"I've got no use for it," Carmen replied, pinching her brows together. "I mean, all everyone uses it now for is the social media applications, right? I can't see myself opening up a Facebook or Twitter account, unless I wanted to take nature photographs or share my paintings and stuff."

"Um, you'd use an Instagram account for that, rather than Facebook or Twitter," Asa told her, amusement dancing across his face.

"Same thing, right?" Carmen sighed. " Just pictures being posted everywhere."

"Fine, forget the social media, but what about keeping in touch with your friends?"

"I have this thing called a landline, you know." Carmen rolled her eyes. "Joyce contacts me through that. Willa and Lottie aren't exactly the friends I take back home with me after school."

Asa stopped in his tracks, removing his arm from around Carmen's shoulders and shooting her a deadpan look. "Do I really have to spell it out for you?"

Carmen tilted her head at him, confusion flickering in her eyes. "What are you talking about?"

Asa grumbled under his breath before throwing his arms into the air. "Me! I'm talking about *me*. How am *I* supposed to keep in touch with you?"

Understanding dawned on Carmen's soft features, and a sheepish laugh escaped her lips. "Oh," she mumbled.

"Yes, *oh*," Asa mimicked, shaking his head fondly as he watched her.

"Well, then, I actually do have a phone. I mean, Dad got me one two months back but I haven't used it yet. It's still in the packaging." Carmen grinned a little too wide, shrugging in an apologetic manner.

"God, you're such a dork." Asa grabbed the back of her neck and tugged. "Come here." She stumbled forward at the same time that he stepped closer, bending his head to place a messy kiss on her mouth, a smile still on his lips.

Then they headed back to the parking lot, the sound of the flickering lamppost above them blending in with their giggles while they kept sharing quick, short kisses and grinning against each other's mouths, tripping over their own feet like love-struck fools as they walked.

•   •   •

Asa's eyes flickered to the clock on the dashboard of the truck just as he parked in front of Carmen's house. The numbers read ten minutes to eleven.

335

There was a long, deep sigh from next to him, and he turned to look at Carmen who was stretching her arms above her with a giddy smile on her face.

It made his heart skip a beat, which was actually pretty terrifying because he didn't think he'd ever felt his heartbeat skip so far in his entire life.

Until now, of course. Until Carmen goddamn West.

"Asa." His name tumbled out of her mouth in a soft breath, as if speaking his name alone seemed to make her feel content.

"Mm?" His response was distracted, almost barely-there, as his eyes zeroed in on her lips yet again.

He'd lost count on the number of times he'd kissed her tonight, and yet here he was, craving more. It was crazy to think that he'd fallen in love with her without wondering what her lips would taste like, what her skin would feel like.

But now that he knew what it was like to run his fingers through her endless midnight hair; now that he knew about the wildfire capable of coursing throughout his entire body at having her body pressed against his; now that he knew the mind-blowing sensation of having her lips tucked between his own, it was all that consumed his mind.

Ah, crap, he thought. He really wanted to kiss her again now.

"Tonight was perfect," she mumbled lazily, looking up at him with dazed eyes. It was the first time Asa had seen a pair of grey eyes look so warm.

You're perfect, he wanted to say, but kept his mouth shut before he made a fool of himself.

"I'm glad you think so." He smiled back. "Because I just had the best night ever." He paused and reconsidered his statement. "Well, second best, actually."

"What's the first?" Carmen pulled her brows together.

"The night you told me you loved me back," Asa murmured, his heart fluttering ever so slightly.

"Because I told you I love you or because you finally got to kiss me?" She bit her lip and wiggled her eyebrows.

Ay, Dios mío.

"*Carmen*," he gasped, breath hitching and the words in his head tripping over one another as his mind reeled from discovering this new side of her—a side that Asa was pretty confident only he had the privilege of knowing.

"What?" she asked, her mouth curving into an impish smile, that teasing glint in her eyes from the night of the party making its appearance once again.

"You—that." Asa paused, and then swore under his breath. "You have no idea what you're doing to me."

"I think I have a pretty good idea." She grinned at him and then started to open the car door. "Walk me to my door?"

"As if you even had to ask." Asa scoffed, getting out of the vehicle himself. "You know by now I'm a perfect gentleman."

Carmen climbed up the front porch steps and then turned around to face him, lifting a brow in amusement. "In school, you mean, and in public. But I know what you're really like when it's just the two of us, and *gentleman* is the last word that comes to mind."

Asa was seeing stars. He had to be by this point.

"You make one more suggestive comment," he said warningly, "and—"

He stopped, because the lack of a car in her driveway reminded him of something.

"Wait a minute, your dad's not home." He grinned, squaring his shoulders and stepping closer to Carmen.

"Yeah. I did tell you."

"Yeah. Which means he's not pulling the typical dad move and watching us from behind a curtain." Asa's eyes were zeroed in on Carmen's now, inching closer and closer towards her as she slowly backed away.

"You sound happy about that."

"Oh, I am," he said in a gruff voice. "Because now I can do this." He grabbed both ends of her scarf and tugged her forward. "And this," he breathed out, as he lowered his head and grazed his teeth across her bottom lip, hearing her breath hitch at the contact.

"Asa," Carmen gasped against his mouth, her breathing growing ragged and heavy.

"What?" he mumbled into her skin as he left a trail of kisses down her throat and neck. "Where are all your smartass remarks now?"

His right arm curled around her waist and he used his left one to cup the back of her head as he walked forward 'till her back was pressed against the wall of the house, both of his hands behind her lessening the impact of her body hitting the hard surface.

"Carmen Carmen Carmen," Asa breathed heavily, leaning his forehead against hers, a smile playing at the ends of his mouth. *"Mi amor."* He kissed her forehead. *"Mi cielo."* Then he kissed her cheek. *"Mi sol."* He kissed her other cheek and then dipped his head, kissing her on the mouth with everything he had, not wanting this date to end at all.

"Asa." Everything that left either Carmen's or Asa's mouth was a gasp now, every single syllable short of breath and thick with emotion.

"Tell me."

"I'm so happy right now," she told him, her breath still faltering as she grabbed a fistful of his sweater.

Asa kissed her forehead again. "I'm happy that you are. You deserve the world."

"No, you don't understand." She began shaking her head frantically, her voice trembling. "I'm happy, so goddamn happy, Asa. And I… I don't—this is too unreal. I haven't been this content and at peace in, like, forever and I just… Maybe I'm being irrational, but I can't shake the feeling that this will all just get ripped away from me."

"Carmen—"

"And—and—and—" Her hold on his sweater tightened, and Asa watched in horror as she looked up at him with scared, watery eyes. "I did have true happiness once, you know. I remember what it was like to

338

have known love. It feels like a lifetime ago, but I remember. I remember what it felt like. And I also remember what it was like to have it all snatched from my grasp within the blink of an eye when my mum died."

"*Mi amor*, I need you to breathe, all right? Please just take in deep bre—"

"I thought that feeling was gone forever, that I'd never know what it'd be like to be loved irrevocably, and I have it now, Asa. I have it with *you*. But happiness has never stuck with me before; it's always so fleeting. So temporary and—"

Asa grabbed her chin and lifted her face to look at her with determined eyes. "We are *not* temporary," he said firmly, making sure she understood how serious he was, and then rested his forehead against hers again. "I can feel your heartbeat," he mumbled after a while, focusing on the accelerated beats of her heart since her chest was firmly pressed against his own. "It's skyrocketing. Just like mine. Try and tell me that's temporary."

"I'm sorry," she said in a small voice, looking away.

"For?"

"Panicking. Breaking down on you like that."

"If not me, to whom are you going to break down on?" He kissed her temple. "You're always being brave and strong for everyone else. Let me be the one person you don't have to put on a mask for." He kissed the bridge of her nose. "Let me in, Carmen. No matter what, always let me in."

She gave him a tiny smile, but it was enough to send a wave of warmth through him and calm his insides.

"I will," she promised, releasing the death grip she had on Asa's sweater and relaxing slowly as the panic faded away.

"Carmen?"

"Yeah?"

"There's something I've been wanting to tell you all night."

"What is it?"

"You were wrong the other night," he said softly. "About the binary pairs."

"I was?" she sounded confused.

"Well, no, not really. You were right. But also wrong."

A short laugh fell past Carmen's lips. "That makes no sense."

"You said that there was a primary star in the system and a secondary one whose light was dimmer. Well, I went back home and did some reading about the whole binary system."

"And?"

"And, as it turns out, in certain cases both stars *do* have equal brightness." Asa smiled, the corners of his eyes crinkling as he did so. "And then there's a type of a binary pair called close binaries." He cupped her face, running soothing circles on her cheek with his thumb. "They say that both the stars in that particular system have the ability to transfer their mass from one to the other, almost like giving each other parts of themselves." Asa pulled her in for a tight embrace, hugging her so hard that he might as well have kept all the broken pieces inside her firmly held together. "And I think that's pretty darn amazing," he said into her hair.

Carmen didn't respond, but the way her hands tightened around his torso, the way it screamed *never let me go never let me go never let me go* as she returned the hug, spoke volumes to Asa.

"So, see," Asa murmured, stroking her hair gently. "Two stars can shine equally bright. And the next time you compare stars to souls, just remember that they *can* be equals." He pressed his lips to the top of her head, breathing in her scent and enjoying the sense of calm it brought him. "Life finds a way to beat the odds, Carmen. You just need to know where to look."

49.
I'll Stand by You

The rest of the days passed by in nothing short of pure bliss, and before long, Thanksgiving had arrived too, and the reality of it all hit Carmen in the face like a bucket of iced water.

Her father had grown even more withdrawn than ever, filling in for more shifts at the hospital. Carmen would wake up most days to find himself already gone which eventually cut down their time usually spent together during breakfast.

The logical part of Carmen told her he needed space to think, to come to terms with the fact that he was stepping foot in the family home of his wife's side after so many years. He was probably anxious to the bone of meeting the people who were once his people too.

But another part of Carmen couldn't help but wonder if perhaps it was she that he was avoiding. That maybe staying in the same room as her was becoming too much for him.

Everybody had their breaking point. Everybody had to hit rock bottom one way or another. Maybe her father's time was now. And maybe, after hitting it, he'd be able to dust himself off and start over.

Maybe next time around, they'd do things right.

So many maybes. And Carmen's heart swelled with the realisation that Asa was the one thing in her life that was definite. He was her rock, her solid ground that kept her feet rooted when everything seemed to spin around her.

Warmth washed over her at the thought and a soft smile found its way on her face.

There was a loud knock on her bedroom door, causing Carmen to reach towards the speakers and turn down the volume of The Script resonating throughout her room.

Normally, she wasn't the type to play music really loud but this evening she needed a distraction. Anything to drown out the rest of the world for the twenty-five minutes she took getting herself ready.

Walking towards the door of her room, she pulled it open and began to speak. "Dad, we still have time before we need to—"

Asa stood there instead, leaning sideways on the doorframe with a small smile on his face.

Carmen blinked repeatedly, trying to understand what her eyes were seeing.

"Asa? What even—how are you—wait—"

Asa rolled his eyes and pushed himself off the wall, standing up to his full height. "Am I allowed to come in?"

Carmen couldn't speak; she could only stare at him with her mouth agape, so she just nodded wordlessly, stepping aside to let him in. She was about to shut the door when Asa stopped her.

"Don't." He shook his head. "Your Dad's orders. Leave the door open."

Carmen flushed but obliged anyway, not wanting to push her dad's buttons on the one day they needed to stick together more than ever.

"What are you doing here?" she asked in a bewildered tone. Nevertheless she was unable to help the pleased smile from forming on her face.

"You're going to that Thanksgiving dinner," he said, shrugging. "and I know I can't be there with you tonight, but... I don't know, just wanted to see you before you go."

She felt a fist squeeze her chest painfully tight as his words registered in her head. "You're here as moral support?" She tilted her head to the side, gazing at him with a tender expression.

His cheeks coloured ever so slightly, and he scratched the back of his neck. "Well, yeah, I mean... I know it's not going to mean much when you're actually there at that dinner, but—"

"It means the world that you dropped in to check on me, Asa," Carmen murmured, stopping his train of thoughts.

He stopped fidgeting and shot her a relieved smile, before shrugging and seating himself on the edge of her bed.

Carmen shook her head to herself and moved towards the mirror, picking up her eyeliner and applying a thin coat of it. She could feel Asa's eyes watching her but didn't comment on it, feeling oddly comfortable with him in her room, on her bed. With Asa in there with her, the house felt more like a home than it had in the past few years. And the depth of that realisation, the implications behind it, and the way it emphasised on the intensity of her feelings for him terrified Carmen.

"You're wearing a dress." Asa observed and was surprised, trailing his eyes down her body.

"I try avoiding it when I can, but I just want tonight to go smoothly." Carmen sighed, dropped the eyeliner on her dresser and evaluated her appearance. She'd adorned a deep burgundy dress, the kind that hugged her torso but flowed freely from her waist. "They're all pretty—what's the word?—aristocratic people. Don't think they'd appreciate me showing up in a pair of skinny jeans and a bomber jacket."

She met Asa's eyes through the reflection in the mirror and watched his lips turn down into a frown.

"You've always had a huge heart," he said. "But you've never been a doormat. You made that very clear when I took your journal when we met. Why on earth would you wear a dress if it's not what you want?"

Carmen's shoulders slumped. "It's just a dress, Asa. If it helps me blend in and not stick out any more than I already do, I'd feel more comfortable."

Asa stared at her for a couple more minutes before sighing in defeat and walking up to her, wrapping his arms around her waist from behind.

"I just wish they could see you for you," Asa murmured, resting his chin on her shoulder as they both stared at each other through their reflections. "You're amazing as you are and shouldn't have to feel uncomfortable around people who supposed to be your family."

Carmen's hand reached up to ruffle the top of his hair. "I'm comfortable around you, Asa," she told him quietly, her voice serious. "And you *are* family to me."

The purely affectionate smile he offered her right then awoke butterflies in the pit of her stomach, and she felt their wings graze her insides as they took flight.

"I love you," he said softly, turning his face to press his lips against the side of her head.

"I know," she told him, searching his eyes with her own but finding nothing but sincerity there as he uttered the words. "And I love you too."

He grinned at her response, pecking her cheek quickly before pulling away. "I'm gonna head home now, all right?"

"Wait, you didn't tell me how you got Dad to let you come in here." Carmen raised a brow.

Asa chuckled. "Just told him the truth. That I wanted to see you off because I knew you were nervous about the dinner."

"Oh," Carmen mumbled, feeling that familiar sense of warmth that only Asa could bring flood her insides.

"Yeah." He yawned, bringing up his hand to cover his mouth. "Sorry, stayed up all night yesterday to finish this book and then got dragged out of my bed by Wyatt to go to the Thanksgiving football match this morning."

Carmen laughed lightly. "I didn't know Wyatt was interested in football."

"He isn't a diehard fan." Asa grinned. "He *does* hate the rival school though so he wanted to watch ours kick their ass."

"And did we?"

"Yeah." Asa nodded, then paused as his lips twisted into a small frown. "Our team captain was completely off his game today, though."

"Team captain," Carmen repeated, her tone guarded. "That's Hunter."

Asa nodded, averting his eyes and looking around her room instead. "Yeah, he seemed super distracted today."

There were a million questions flying through Carmen's mind, so many worried remarks sitting on the very tip of her tongue. But she kept her mouth shut, knowing it was pointless to ask Asa about Hunter's mental state. Asa wouldn't know, and neither would he appreciate her concern over someone that he loathed with every single cell in his body.

"Never mind that now." He waved it off, smiling at her reassuringly. "He's not your problem. You've got enough on your mind for tonight." He leant forward and placed a quick kiss on her temple. "Good luck with everything at the dinner," he told her. "I really hope things go okay for you."

Carmen offered him a grateful smile. "Thank you, Asa. Now go on and get some sleep. You look like shit."

He rolled his eyes, but shot a smile in her direction anyway before leaving her room and closing the door with a soft click.

•　　　•　　　•

Carmen pressed her lips tightly together as her father parked the car in the driveway of the large house, right behind a dark blue Land Rover. There were few other luxurious cars parked in front of them, making Carmen's stomach coil into knots at the fact that there would be at least three other families in there already. Both Carmen and her dad sat there in the car for what felt like hours but were actually a couple of minutes. Painstakingly long minutes.

"All right," her father breathed out loudly, drumming his fingers on the steering wheel while his knee bounced anxiously. "Let's go. Come on."

Carmen clutched the door handle like it was her lifeline—as if it was Asa's hand—and breathed in slowly.

Inhale. Exhale.

I love you, Asa had told her today just before she left the house to come here.

Inhale. Exhale.

She could get through tonight. Carmen could do this. And if she ever felt her breathing falter, all she needed to do was think of him. She'd think of Asa or recall something he'd said to her and then she would be able to breathe again.

"Yeah." She exhaled slowly, turning to her dad and smiling tightly. "Yeah, let's just go in."

Her father led the way to the front steps of the house, and Carmen trailed behind him, both of them too much of a bundle of nerves to be saying anything to each other.

She watched as the large oak doors were opened by someone from the help (most probably the housekeeper) and Carmen stopped in her tracks, the reality of the situation hitting her a little too hard, like a swift kick to her chest.

"Carmen?" her dad called out tentatively, watching her with cautious eyes while she stood at the foot of the steps, not making a move to climb it.

"Um." She swallowed. "Why don't you go ahead, Dad?" She rubbed her palms together, the chilly air seeping into her bones despite the cardigan she wore over her dress. "I'll be there in a minute."

He opened his mouth, as if to say something but then closed it, offered her a strained smile and allowed the housekeeper to usher him in.

As soon as the door closed and Carmen was left by herself, she let her shoulders drop and started pacing around, frantic words and phrases spilling out of her mouth in her frenzied state. She felt a presence behind her just as a hand touched her elbow, causing her to jump away and whip her head around, pulling a muscle in her neck as she did so.

Her breathing came to an abrupt stop as her eyes landed on a dishevelled Hunter; his breathing was ragged as if he'd run all the way from his home. Carmen decided it was possible because she couldn't find a car that just arrived, and neither did she hear the sound of any vehicle before he approached her.

His dark brown hair, which sported highlights of a lighter shade of brown, was a mess—another reason to believe he'd run all the way here.

"Um." Hunter shifted on his feet awkwardly as Carmen continued to gape at him. "I'd really appreciate it if you quit with the gawking and just say something instead."

"What—what are you doing here?" she asked incredulously, looking around him as if the answer would materialise out of the thin November air.

"Apparently there's a thanksgiving dinner being held here," he responded, the sarcasm heavy in his tone. "Shocking, huh?"

Carmen shot him a disapproving look, feeling that spark of irrational annoyance flare up in her whenever she was in Hunter's presence.

"You told me you weren't coming," she reminded him.

"I did."

"You said your dad didn't allow it once he learnt about me being invited."

"Yup."

Carmen frowned deeply, knitting her eyebrows together in extreme perplexity. "But you're here?"

"I am."

Carmen let out a frustrated sound from the back of her throat, wondering how one person could effortlessly get under her nerves the way Hunter did.

"You know," he said, slipping his hands into the pockets of his hoodie. "You're always so calm and relaxed but whenever it's *me* you're talking to, all your patience seems to just run out."

"That's because it *does* run out," she told him flatly, noticing at the same time that her breathing was still not back to its natural pace. She didn't know if it was a trick of the lighting around the exterior of the house, but Hunter's usually guarded eyes seemed to soften the tiniest bit.

"All right." He shrugged. "Go ahead. Go on. Say whatever you want. Let it all out. Might help with the nerves."

"My nerves are fine," she mumbled, just wishing for Asa's warm, protective arms to be wrapped around her right now.

"Sure they are," Hunter muttered under his breath, but Carmen heard it anyway.

"Really, Hunter." She pressed her lips together, squinting at him and trying to decipher his thought process. "Why are you here?"

A part of her—a tiny, *tiny* part—felt the beginning seeds of hope plant themselves right in the middle of her chest. Maybe she wasn't dead to Hunter after all.

He didn't respond to her question, and instead just sighed and attempted to fix his hair. "Come on, we can't stand out here forever."

He began climbing the steps, but Carmen remained rooted to the spot.

Hunter must have noticed the lack of a presence behind him, because he then looked over his shoulder and upon finding her still standing there, stopped in his tracks.

"You're going to just freeze to death," he deadpanned.

"Would be doing you a favour, right?" she asked quietly, swallowing past the lump in her throat. God, she hated being vulnerable in front of him.

With Asa, it was different. Carmen could wear her heart on her sleeve and cut open her chest for him to take a peek at her soul. But opening up with Hunter, letting her emotions show around him, made her feel weak. Pathetic even. Like she needed to be tougher in his eyes. As if her bones needed to turn to concrete and her tongue to steel.

Hunter visibly flinched at her words, but the momentary display of emotion was gone as soon as it had come.

"Don't be an idiot," he muttered, averting his gaze. "Just come in."

"No."

Hunter's eyes snapped back to hers, incredulity written all over his face. "What do you mean *no*?"

"I mean no," Carmen bit out, feeling that same old bitter feeling run through her veins as she struggled to keep her normally calm composure.

Hunter swore under his breath and looked away, jaw clenching angrily. "You're never this difficult," he snapped. "With anyone. Ever. Why do you have to act this way now?"

"And how exactly would you know that, Hunter?" Carmen laughed darkly. "How would you know whether I get difficult from time to time or not? Because you've been there by my side all these years? Because you've stood by me? Because you've been my *brother*?"

Carmen's eyes stung, and she could feel the prickling sensation behind them—tiny little needles jabbing at her tear ducts endlessly while she struggled to get a grip on her emotions.

The frigid facade that Hunter seemed to always be wearing crumpled at her words, turning to ashes and dust then getting carried away with the wind.

But that vulnerable moment of his lasted for a fleeting moment, gone within a blink of Carmen's eyes. She watched as Hunter's expression just hardened, turning to stone before he turned back around and stormed towards the doors, leaving Carmen standing alone in the dark.

Why did it hurt even twelve years later? Hunter had abandoned her a lifetime ago, left her alone in the dark when she'd needed him the most, so how come watching him walk away hurt her just as much as it did the first time?

349

She watched him raise a fist to knock on the door, his clenched fist hanging in mid-air. She watched him bend his head and tilt it to the side as if he was having a debate with himself in his head, watched him kick the wall next to the door in frustration.

And then she watched him actually turn back around with a conflicted expression on his face.

After few more beats of hesitation, Hunter sighed and slowly walked back down the steps, coming to a stop directly in front of her. "What do you want from me, Carmen?" he asked quietly.

Her throat seemed to tighten at the same time the lump lodged there grew even larger, making it indefinitely harder for her to get the words out.

"I want you to tell me why you're here," she told him in a small voice, feeling like the five-year-old kid who had to go and confess that she'd broken one of his Marvel action figures when she'd tripped down the stairs with it. She'd expected him to be angry, then, to throw a tantrum and forbid her from touching any of his belongings ever again.

He hadn't, though. He'd been too worried about whether she'd hurt herself from the fall. Then he stole some candy from the hidden stash before sneaking in to her room in the middle of the night to cheer her up.

It was how she felt again right now, standing in front of him, wondering if he was going to lash out and tell her to leave him alone.

Instead, his shoulders slumped forward slightly and he ran a hand down his exhausted face. "You know why I'm here," he finally said, looking at her for the first time without any coldness to his demeanour.

Carmen shook her head. "I need you to say it."

Annoyance flickered across his face for a brief moment, and he looked away, swore under his breath, and then looked back down at her again.

"I didn't." He stopped himself, seeming to struggle with something that Carmen couldn't exactly see. Hunter closed his eyes, breathed in deeply until he finally exhaled in a calm, steady manner.

When he opened his eyes, Carmen knew it was no longer a trick of the lighting; there was an almost tangible softness in his eyes. The normally cold blue irises of his looked like they actually held a certain kind of warmth in them now.

"I didn't want you to be alone," he eventually said, his voice barely above a whisper as if he was so frightened of someone hearing his vulnerability.

And right then, right there, in that single moment, Carmen caught a glimpse of the little boy she'd known once—a boy she had shared a strong bond enough to call him her brother. She clung to that sliver of hope with every jagged piece of her cracked heart.

"Come on." He beckoned with his head towards the doors, something like the tiniest hint of a smile tugging at his lips. He held out his arm for her, and Carmen hesitantly hooked her elbow around his, feeling like she was testing uncertain waters with no lifejacket, no guide—nothing. Nothing but the ghost of a childhood her soul still ached for.

Hunter rang the doorbell, and Carmen instinctively tightened her hold on his arm, acknowledging that she was about to step into the lion's den, but also acknowledging that someone was willing to step into it with her, *for* her.

"Hunter," Carmen said quietly while they waited for someone to answer the door. "Thank you."

"*Don't.*" He squeezed his eyes shut, as if her words pained him too much. "Don't thank me, Carmen. You of all people don't get to thank me."

The large door opened just then, and Carmen offered a warm smile at the same woman who'd opened it for her father, before crossing the threshold and stepping into the house with Hunter.

"I've got twelve years of owning up to do," he told her, his voice holding a certain kind of exhaustion she hadn't heard before. "So don't show me gratitude for doing something I should have done in the first place. Which was to have your back, through thick and thin."

And those seeds of hope embedded in Carmen's chest began to show signs of growing.

50.
All Those Broken Hearts

When Carmen's eyes landed on the grand staircase a few feet away from her direct line of sight, she could almost see the ghosts of the four-year-old versions of both her and Hunter.

They were struggling to climb those steps, clinging to the banisters like it was their lifeline then those ghosts turned into their five-year-old selves, and Hunter and Carmen no longer needed to wrap their fingers around the banisters. Then they were six-year-olds, running down the stairs and chasing each other while Sophia West screamed at them to be careful.

"Carmen?" Hunter's tentative voice pulled Carmen out of the flashback, and the ghosts of their six-year-old bodies vaporised into thin air and the yells of her mother turned distorted, fading into the background.

"Nothing's changed," Carmen murmured, feeling a physical pain in the middle of her chest as if someone was squeezing the life out of her beating heart.

"A lot has changed." There was a sad smile on Hunter's face.

"Yes," she said. "But... it also hasn't. Everything is right where it used to be. The walls are still the same colour and none of the fancy stuff are taken down."

The Rutherford family home was a mansion with no qualms about its ostentatious appearance and Carmen remembered every single

353

holiday spent within these walls. Her mother, who was born Sophia Rutherford, had always managed to drag both Carmen and her dad here on holidays because it was an unspoken rule that the Rutherfords celebrated together as a family.

Changing one's surname after marriage didn't permit her to break this rule, so even after Sophia Rutherford had become Sophia West, the tradition continued.

It had been the least ideal place for a child, what with its fine ornaments and fancy furniture. But Carmen hadn't been alone then. She had Hunter, and the two of them together had always found a way to survive and make the best of it.

In a way, Carmen supposed they'd been each other's escape—a form of liberation from their suffocating upbringing and the extravagant lifestyle.

And when Carmen's mother had passed, she'd broken free of the hold this place had on her. She'd found permanent liberation with her father, a few towns away. But Hunter had remained and Carmen was beginning to realise the shackles they had on him, too.

Carmen wondered then, if perhaps in the eyes of the six-year-old Hunter, it had been *her* who'd abandoned him.

"Carmen?" Hunter's voice was calling her again.

She tore her eyes away from the awfully large staircase, suddenly feeling like the world around her had grown infinitely large or was it that she only felt small? That she'd shrunken considerably to a mere speck of dust? Perhaps it was both.

This place and the people that came with it always made her feel small. Unwanted. Unloved.

And she could feel all her confidence leaving her bones through the gaps between her fingers like grains of sand. Gone was the almost eighteen-year-old who'd grown to accept the lack of belongingness. In her place was the little girl who'd spent a good part of her life wondering what she'd done wrong. Carmen didn't feel so strong anymore, and the panic was beginning to sink in.

"Carmen?" This was the third time he'd called her by name, and it didn't fail to shock her that Hunter's tone was actually... *patient.*

"Sorry." She cleared her throat.

"We need to head into the living room," he said, trying to smile but failing, which was okay because Carmen didn't think she would be able to muster up a smile in return.

"All right." She nodded, taking in a deep breath and squaring her shoulders. "Yeah, all right."

"And one more thing."

Carmen met Hunter's eyes. "What?"

He seemed to hesitate then sighed heavily. "I'm going to need you to let go of my hand before we enter the room."

She felt her heart sink right down to the soles of her feet, as if whatever fragile thread was holding it in place was mercilessly severed with a single swift flick of a knife.

Carmen nodded, trying not to show her disappointment. She wasn't supposed to rely on him like this, anyway. Besides, it would have been a big step on his part to attend this dinner he was specifically told not to. It was perfectly fine for him not to be one hundred percent willing to let the rest of them know he wanted to stand by her side.

She felt Hunter pull his arm away and then step directly in front of her, crouching down slightly as if he was about to speak to a child, and Carmen supposed, in a way, she must've reminded him of a lost child right then.

"Not because I'm having second thoughts," he told her, as if able to read her mind. "But I don't want them seeing it as you needing support."

"I do need the support," Carmen said without hesitation, feeling no shame in admitting that she needed help sometimes. "Not really feeling all that in my element right now."

"How you feel doesn't matter," Hunter said bluntly, making Carmen involuntarily wince. "What matters is you do not appear weak because that will only give them incentive to pick on you."

"You think I'm weak?"

Hunter snorted. "Are you kidding? You survived me in school. You accepted this stupid invitation. You're here. Maybe a little rusty and a little bent out of shape, but you're still here, standing on both feet. Heck, I'd say you were baptised by fire itself, Carmen."

Carmen cracked a smile at that, feeling the constriction in her chest loosen up a little, and then followed Hunter through an archway in the wall next to the staircase which she could remember led to the living room.

While Hunter pulled off the casual demeanour, strolling into the room like he belonged there, Carmen's body was tensed and her muscles were as stiff as lead.

And so upon finding only one other person there, a sigh of relief fell past her lips, a sigh so heavy that it caused this particular person to whip his head towards the two of them.

Cole Rutherford's eyes glided right over Carmen, as if she wasn't even there. Then again, she would rather not be acknowledged than be seen and antagonised.

The twenty-six-year-old pushed himself off the wall, slipping his phone into his pocket as he approached them. The expensive suit he had on looked like it was tailored just for him, which it probably was.

"Hunter," he greeted in that low voice of his. "I thought Uncle Grayson said you guys won't be able to make it tonight." Uncle Grayson. As in Grayson Donoghue, Hunter's dad.

"Yeah." Hunter shrugged nonchalantly. "Had a change of mind."

Cole lifted a brow, a knowing look in his eyes. "So why isn't your father here?"

Carmen's chest constricted again. She didn't want Hunter to pay for choosing to stand by her. She knew what his father could be like.

"You should probably ask him," Hunter replied coolly, not appearing the slightest bit worried. Carmen wondered how good of an actor he was, because he'd have to be insane not to be worried about going against the wishes of Grayson Donoghue.

"I will." Cole smiled, but without any warmth to it. "Should I also ask him if his son is accustomed to bringing the trash *into* the house rather than taking it out?"

Trash. He'd called her trash.

Trash.

Carmen thought she shrunk a little bit more.

Hunter's forehead creased, his eyes looking genuinely confused as he stared at Cole. "What are you talking about? I didn't drive you here. You came by yourself."

Carmen's heart jumped up from her feet to her throat as she looked at Hunter with wide, flabbergasted eyes. Was he flat out *defending* her? To *Cole's* face? Cole Rutherford, who Hunter used to look up to back when they were kids?

Cole's face flushed, the tips of his ears growing a deep shade of red. "Careful, Hunter," he said in a low voice. "You don't want to sabotage that shot at a football scholarship, do you?"

Carmen watched as Hunter tensed, his body going rigid and lips forming a thin line at the barely-veiled threat.

"I trusted you with that," Hunter said slowly, his voice sounding almost urgent. "Don't you dare hold it against me."

Cole smiled coldly, and his grey eyes—a physical feature that almost all Rutherfords had, including Carmen—flashed with warning. "Should've thought about that before you took the pills then."

Hunter's face completely drained of colour and the two of them watched as Cole turned around with that air of superiority and walked away, all the while not even sparing a glance at Carmen.

"Hunter, what was he talking about?" Carmen asked with a frown. "Why would you have problems with the scholarship? You're easily a top pick for any college."

As if her voice was all that it took to remind him of where they were, Hunter snapped out of his troubled state and squared his shoulders

357

again, offering Carmen a strained smile. "It's nothing you need to bother yourself with. Don't worry." He waved it off. "It's just Cole and his empty threats."

Carmen forced a smile in return and let it go, but deep down she knew just as well as Hunter that Cole wasn't the type to make empty threats.

"There you are," a woman's voice floated towards them and Carmen turned to find her mother's older sister, Beatrix Rutherford, approach her with her father trailing behind.

"Dad." Carmen blinked in surprise. "Where were you?"

"He was with your grandma," Aunt Beatrix said, watching Carmen intently. Something flashed across her eyes as she continued to stare at Carmen, but it was gone as soon as it had appeared. "She asked for both you and your dad, needed to speak to you about... well, I don't really know what about."

"Why?" Carmen asked, unable to help the overwhelming curiosity, losing control over the questions colliding into each other in her head. "Why *now*?"

Her aunt shrugged. "Must be the old age." She paused. "She's sick, too. Might not be long 'till she... you know. Yeah."

It was a shame, really, that Carmen's presence was required by someone nearing death, someone who wanted to leave this world without a guilty conscience.

"I see," Carmen said with a small nod, at an utter loss on how she was supposed to respond to that.

Aunt Beatrix lifted a brow. "That's it? You're not sorry to hear she's ill?"

Carmen didn't respond right away, wondering what should be the diplomatic approach to that question.

"Well..." She hesitated, making sure to sound polite and reasonable. "There are people dying everywhere. It's just the circle of life. I can't be feeling sorry for everyone who's about to leave this world."

Something twisted in Carmen's stomach, and she winced as the words replayed in her head, making her realise how cold they actually sounded.

Her aunt's lips formed a thin line. "She's not just anyone. This is your grandmother. Your mother's mother."

Carmen inhaled sharply. She may be able to tolerate the casual mention of her mother most of the time, but not when it was done so in this house. Not amongst these people. Because with them, there was always some messed-up implication or the other behind it.

"I never had a grandmother," Carmen told her aunt, feeling the panic and the need to just crawl into a hole beginning to take a firm hold of her. But it was true, wasn't it? The only person she'd had so far was her father—and now Asa too.

She'd never had grandparents, or aunts, or uncles. She'd never known what that was like.

"Carmen." Her father's voice was almost neutral, if not for the subtle warning in it she picked up on.

That made her a little angry, but more than that, she felt cornered. Ambushed. Her dad should have her back, right? If things started going south tonight? He had to.

"That's all right, Jonah," Aunt Beatrix said to Carmen's dad, not taking her eyes off Carmen. "The girl is right after all, isn't she?"

Before anyone could say anything else, Hunter cleared his throat from next to Carmen, breaking the tensed silence. "Hey, Aunt Bea." He smiled easily, stepping forward and placing a quick kiss on her cheek. "You look lovely as usual."

Carmen saw her aunt's eyes soften the slightest bit and she offered Hunter a half-smile. "Tell me your father knows you're here."

"He's not at home." He shrugged. "And what he doesn't know can't hurt him."

"Another client meeting?"

"Don't know. I stopped asking a long time back," Hunter muttered, stuffing his hands back into his pockets.

Aunt Beatrix looked like she was about to respond to that, but then seemed to have a change of mind as she cleared her throat and turned towards the archway instead. "Well, now that everyone's here, let's start with dinner, shall we?"

Carmen furrowed her brows and turned as well, trailing behind her aunt as they headed into the dining room. "Wait, it's just us and Cole? I thought—"

"Oh, no no." Aunt Beatrix shook her head. "The others already arrived before you. I'm guessing they've already taken their seats at the table."

At that, Carmen's stomach knotted painfully, and she almost reached for Hunter's hand, but then recalled his words and stopped herself just in time.

Instead, she curled her fingers into her fists, and used the pain of her nails digging into the flesh as an anchor while walking towards the large dining area.

• • •

Nothing had happened so far.

Carmen kept her head down, focusing on nothing but her food which was insanely delicious that it almost made her forget where she was. Almost.

She was grateful towards the fact that it wasn't dead silent but that most of them were actually talking amongst themselves, not too loudly but enough for there to be a steady chorus of chatter around the table. Besides, her heartbeats were deafening enough to reverberate throughout the entire mansion, and she was glad no one was forcing her to speak over that noise in her head.

Everything was going as smoothly as she could have hoped for, really.

Until her father's pager was alerted and everything went straight to the pits of hell.

Bleep. The sound ripped through the soft murmur of the dining room, making Viola Rutherford(Cole's mother) squeal and drop her fork with a loud clatter against her plate.

Felix, who was only five and a distant cousin of Carmen's, jumped back in his chair and shot out his arm to steady himself, knocking his father's wine glass in the process, the deep red liquid trickling down the surface, staining the pretty tablecloth.

Carmen's mouth fell open at the mess, and she turned towards her left only to find Hunter struggling to contain his laughter, ducking his head, his shoulders shaking silently.

"What the hell was that?" someone hissed from the opposite end of the table.

"I'm sorry, that was my—" Carmen's father pushed back his chair and stood up, taking a few quick sips of water, "—my pager. I'm sorry, but I need to make a call to the hospital."

Carmen's mind was a blank slate. It was as if all logic and reason was instantly wiped out as she fumbled with her chair and struggled to push it back and get out of it, too.

"Well, I'll come with you to the hospital—"

"Don't be silly," Aunt Beatrix chided Carmen. "You can't just leave during the middle of your meal. And do you really want to spend the rest of Thanksgiving in a hospital?"

"But I need to leave with Dad—"

"To the hospital?" Viola snorted, not even looking in Carmen's direction. "What an inconvenience! Let your father do his job without throwing a tantrum, foolish little girl."

"Viola!" Aunt Beatrix hissed, glaring at the other woman who just sniffed and stuck her chin further into the air.

"That's enough," Carmen's father muttered, rubbing his temples with his eyes shut in exhaustion. "I'm not going anywhere. I just need to step outside to make a call because the cell reception inside is too weak. It's probably nothing; I get alerts like this on a daily basis."

361

He walked past Hunter and Carmen, nodding at his daughter reassuringly as he mouthed, *It won't take too long*, just before he stepped out of the dining room.

His words did nothing to calm Carmen down, though. She'd been there several times when her father was paged, and the calls usually lasted for at least thirteen minutes or so because he was always being asked to hold the line 'till he connected with whichever nurse had sent the alert.

"Go on then." Aunt Beatrix nodded towards Carmen's plate, her tone not unfriendly. "Eat. You heard your father. He's not going anywhere."

But Carmen's appetite seemed to have vanished into thin air along with her ability to appear composed and unfazed.

"You know," Cole began to say, leaning back in his chair comfortably and looking at Carmen for the first time that night. "If it does turn out to be something serious, he's going to have to attend to his patient and leave you here."

"I'll leave with dad then," Carmen said decisively, staring right back at him.

"Your house isn't even on the way to the hospital," he pointed out with a slight scoff. "Are you just going to linger around in the emergency unit, then?"

"If I have to, yes."

Cole's mouth twitched before pulling up into a cold smirk, reminding Carmen of that lunch period when Hunter had found her by the lockers and offered her that very same smirk before telling her that she was the one to blame for all his misfortunes. The lunch period when she'd hidden away in the art room where Asa had later found her.

Looking at Cole now and noticing that cold gesture Hunter himself had thrown her way time and time again made Carmen sick to the stomach.

Suddenly, it didn't seem enough that Hunter was here with her. He'd put her through hell—through seven levels of it over and over and over again. Him being here just wasn't enough.

362

And just like that, she felt rage start to bubble up in her veins. Because Hunter being here didn't erase everything else he'd put her through.

"Your father's doing a noble job, you know," Cole said, the smirk never leaving his face. "He's saving lives. If he has to go and save one tonight, then let him. Don't you already have enough blood staining your hands, Carmen?"

The rage flew out through her fingertips, leaving her bloodstream and something much darker and bitter flowed through her instead. Carmen couldn't name it, but it was turning her bones cold and cutting her chest open wide, leaving an empty, aching hole right there where her heart should've been. It was something that made flowers wilt and ripped the wings off butterflies and allowed frost to spread over souls.

The instant those words left Cole's mouth, Carmen felt like she was dying. Except that she was still breathing which was somehow worse.

Someone else dropped something this time. Was it a fork? A spoon? A glass? It came from next to her. Perhaps it was Hunter. Maybe he dropped something. But Carmen was too still. Too frozen. She couldn't make her muscles move. Couldn't check for herself what and where the sound was.

Maybe it was just the shattering of what was left of her heart. Or the exploding of what little sanity she had left. She didn't know. She didn't know. She didn't know.

She didn't know anything but that her lungs were having trouble functioning and her heart was going to burst out of her ribcage in an excruciating manner. She didn't know anything but the stabbing of a hundred needles behind her eyes.

Her ears seemed to have tuned out, not registering anything that was happening. But nothing *was* happening. There indeed was an eerie silence that had fallen among everyone in that room and Carmen was conscious enough to acknowledge it was that fleeting sense of quiet and calm before the storm truly began. Before it hit them and created havoc and left them with nothing but the remnants of what was once been.

But this was okay, she tried to reassure herself. This was okay. Because Carmen West had grown up with a storm raging inside her head the second she was born. It had created explosions in her head and burned down her hopes to ashes and tossed all her love to the wind—and she survived.

She survived almost eighteen years. And she'd survive tonight.

She wasn't the kind of girl who ran away from the storm. She was Carmen goddamn West, the kind who had hurricanes named after her.

"Cole." Aunt Beatrix began slowly, her hands shaking as she withdrew them from the tabletop and hid them on her lap, away from calculating eyes. "Let's just try to have a peaceful dinner—"

Viola snorted, cutting through Beatrix's voice obnoxiously and amplifying the tension in the air. "Peaceful," she muttered sardonically. "*Peaceful.* You say that like this family is supposed to find peace with that—" Viola gestured with her hand in Carmen's direction, not dignifying her with even a glance, "—that *thing* in this house. At our dinner table."

Carmen's eyes flickered towards the clock. Only two and a half minutes had passed since her father stepped out of the house. She still had a long way to go.

But it was okay. Because if she truly believed Asa was proof that morning came and took the nightmares with it, then Carmen perhaps should allow herself to believe that she was proof storms never lasted, and that the sky cleared once again for a brand new day.

So she sat back in her chair and took the hits and the blows. She wouldn't defend herself because every single word that flew out their mouths were hauntingly true, and there was nothing she could say to dispute them.

But she would also never let them see her break.

This would pass. Tonight would pass. She just needed to hold on for now.

"I'm sorry," a voice whispered from next to Carmen and she turned around to see Hunter, no longer laughing about the spilt wine but

364

whose face had gone white and completely drained of blood. "I'm *so* sorry. I'm sorry I'm sorry. I—"

Carmen stared at him in confusion as the apologies kept tumbling out of his mouth uncontrollably, audible enough only to her ears as arguing ensued over the rest of the guests.

Some of them were more than eager to rip Carmen to shreds; others just wanted the dinner to go by without any disturbance and were asking each other to shut up; and the rest just continued with their meals, blissfully ignorant.

But Carmen drowned them all out. She got rid of the noise and focused on what mattered.

"Hunter? Why are you apologising?"

He squeezed his eyes shut and clasped his hands together in an attempt to stop the trembling. "I was supposed to—I'm supposed to—I came here because—God, I'm so sorry." He opened his eyes and tilted his head towards her, his blue eyes filled with so much anguish that it shot daggers right at Carmen's heart. "I was supposed to be strong for you," he admitted quietly. "But I can't. Everything is so *loud*. And I... I don't know."

And she understood. Carmen understood.

Because while the others sat there, trying to pull at Carmen's strings and unravel her, they were also breaking Hunter. After all, Sophia hadn't only been Carmen's mother, had she?

All of them were so buried deep with their hatred and disgust for Carmen that they didn't see their words were killing one of their own.

So she reached out and slipped her hand into his, squeezing gently. "I'm not your burden to carry, Hunter. You're not supposed to be strong for me." She blinked once, offering the tiniest of smiles. "But we can be strong for each other."

The tremble in his hands slowly subsided, and he squeezed back, wordlessly telling her that even if everything else went to shit and blew up in their faces tonight, they still had each other. She wouldn't have lost *all* her family.

"—was her fault!" Ethan Rutherford, Cole's father, thundered as he glared at Aunt Bea. "Our dad must be shaking in his grave," he spat. "Knowing you brought his daughter's killer to sit with us at the ta—"

"Shut up."

Hunter's voice was low and could be easily drowned out by their uncle's roaring, but it still rose above the noise with that subtle get demanding undertone that nobody but Hunter Donoghue could pull off.

Carmen realised that, right now, maybe he needed to be that ruthless boy she'd seen walking down the school hallways. Maybe the only way he knew to fight back was to become the person he was fighting.

"What?" Ethan Rutherford raised a brow.

"I asked you—told—I *told* you to shut up," Hunter said indifferently, his eyes on their older relative but his hand still in Carmen's.

"Don't you speak to my dad that way," Cole snarled.

Hunter snorted. "Like I give two shits about what you want."

"Watch that mouth of yours, boy," Viola said sharply, glaring at Hunter. "You speak to my son with respect!"

"You always let your mother do your talking for you?" Hunter cocked his head, never breaking the stare-off with Cole.

But that smirk on Cole's face only turned sharper. "At least I have a mum, Hunter. You, on the other hand..." He let the words hang and even though Carmen saw no change in Hunter's exterior, she felt his hand tighten around hers. "You lost both, didn't you? Which person loses *both* their chances of having a mother, seriously? It's like some horribly written joke. But maybe it's just you. Maybe you tend to bring in a whole lot of bad karma just like how you dragged in that stray with you tonight."

"She's *not* a stray!!" Hunter snarled, eyes flashing as he yanked his hand out of Carmen's grasp and stood up from his seat, slamming both palms against the tabletop, the sheer force of the gesture sending a shockwave that rattled every little thing on the table.

Carmen's breathing faltered, beginning to feel the panic at how things could start spiralling out of control.

"She is as much a part of this family as I am," he continued, the tone of his voice more restrained, that flash of anger subdued for now. "Same blood that runs through her veins runs in mine. In yours. In anybody's born into this family."

Viola gasped, as if hearing something inhumane spill out of Hunter's mouth. "*Same* blood?" she spluttered, looking horrified. "Same what? Do not compare my son to that piece of filth. My boy is pure. *Good*. He doesn't have tainted blood. He doesn't have a rapist's blood in his system!"

Only seven minutes had passed. Her dad was still outside, still on the line with the hospital.

But Carmen was feeling the life drain out of her now, and she didn't know how much longer she could keep up the nonchalance.

Tainted blood.

Carmen's skin felt heavy now, and there was bile rising up the back of her throat. What was that emotion which was currently burning through her? The feeling that made the hair on her skin rise and had her throat in a tight fist and made her stomach churn. What was that? Self-loathing? No.

Disgust. It was disgust.

Carmen no longer felt like she was home in the body that she came in. *"Tainted"*.

She was going to be sick.

It was loud sobbing that snapped Carmen out of her downward spiral within those milliseconds. Beatrix was crying.

Carmen watched as the woman slouched back into her chair and covered her face with one hand, tears streaming down her face. Despite everything, Carmen felt her heart break yet again.

Hunter had lost his mother and Carmen had lost hers, but Beatrix Rutherford had lost both her sisters, and she was now forced to watch the memory of one them being dragged through the mud and spit on.

"It wasn't her fault," Hunter gasped. He seemed to be having trouble catching his own breath after the curveball that Viola had thrown at him. That rough-around-the-edges, tougher-than-steel exterior of his was crumbling down, falling apart to nothing.

There was only so much even he could take. He was no longer the ruthless boy who Carmen used to watch walk down the hallways but he also wasn't the lost little kid who'd apologised just minutes ago for not being strong enough.

He seemed to be something in between now, as if he was stuck floating between identities different halves of him wanted to claim.

Still, Carmen said nothing. She wondered if that was the masochist in her, if it was that ugly, dark part of her rearing its head after being dormant for so long. That part of her she could never learn to love.

"No, I suppose you're right," Cole drawled, eyes gleaming. "It wasn't *Carmen's* fault that dear little Aunt Sophia was raped, was it? No, that was all on her. I mean, that woman had a reputation, didn't she? Wild cheerleader during her high school days and whatnot."

Nobody saw it coming, but Beatrix's hand came crashing down against Cole's cheek in an ear-splitting slap, the sound ricocheting off the walls of the large house and bouncing on everybody's nerves.

"Don't... you... dare," She bit out each word, her eyes red and cheeks stained with tears that kept flowing despite her rage. "She was my sister! My baby sist—" Her voice broke and she choked on her own words, the gut-wrenching sobs making it harder and harder for her to speak.

Everything was swimming around Carmen.

She was there, but she also wasn't. She felt someone wrap their hands around her forearms and haul her out of her chair. and guide her away from all the chaos. She felt the floor beneath her feet, saw the walls and the framed paintings and the elegant chandeliers whizz past her as whoever was pulling her picked up their pace.

And then she was out in the chilly night air, taking in huge gulps of breath. It was cold outside, but somehow it was also warmer than it was in there with all of them.

"I'm never stepping foot in there ever again," Hunter said in gasps, his hands leaving their hold around Carmen and clutching his knees for support as he bent over and clenched his jaw. "Never again."

Carmen was still saying nothing. What was there for her to say, really?

Maybe she was still in shock. Nothing seemed to be working in her; her senses registered absolutely nothing.

"What are you guys—" Carmen's dad stopped short, pausing in his steps towards the house, when he saw the state both she and Hunter was in.

His mouth parted as if to ask if something had happened, but the words didn't come. Instead, realisation dawned over his face and then his eyes hardened.

"Are you going to be okay on your own for a while longer?" he asked Carmen. "I need to go do something I should've done a long time ago."

The disappointment hit first, a huge wave of it, dragging down whatever remaining composure Carmen had left. And then came the anger.

"Am I going to be okay on my own?" She let out a short, humourless laugh that took both Hunter and her dad by surprise. "I've been on my own for a while now. I didn't have you in there with me, and I don't need you now."

Hurt flashed through her father's eyes but he didn't say anything. He turned to Hunter instead.

"Here." He tossed the car keys towards Hunter. "Take her home, will you? I'm going to end this once and for all." And with one last glance towards his daughter, he walked past them and back into the godforsaken house.

Even her father didn't get it. She didn't want to be defended in a place where she knew she was never going to be accepted. She just wanted a warm pair of arms around her and a safe place to break down against. She didn't want a father. She needed a dad.

Twelve years after the tragedy, and he still couldn't grasp that fact.

"It wasn't true," Hunter murmured from next to her as they settled into the car, hesitating before awkwardly patting her shoulder in an attempt to be comforting. "Her death isn't on you."

Carmen laughed. She didn't know why, but she was laughing. She was laughing so hard that she even doubled over and clutched her stomach, ignoring the panicked look on Hunter's face. And then somewhere in between, a laugh broke, splitting right in the middle and turned ugly, clawing at Carmen's throat and ripping through her very existence as it turned into a sob.

One soul-crushing sob after another fell past her lips, her shoulders shaking violently against the passenger seat as the universe she carried on her shoulders came crashing down with full force.

"Hey, hey," he mumbled softly, rubbing her arm gently, his voice thick and hoarse. "Those animals that hurt your mum, it's on them, okay? Not you, Carmen. Never you."

Carmen wiped a hand under her eyes, but the tears didn't stop, and she eventually gave up trying. "You say that like she died because of the rape, Hunter," she told him in a small voice, her words wobbling with her soft cries. "It wasn't that which killed her, was it?"

Another sob escaped her, sounding like it came from deep within the hollow in her chest, where her heart was supposed to be.

One of her hands flew to her mouth, as if covering it would stop the guttural cries that kept spilling out. "She survived the rape, Hunter." She wept, her vision completely blurred as the tears came down in torrents. "She survived it; she had *me*. And then she went on to live for six more years. And you know what took her life?"

Hunter didn't respond, but he could no longer look Carmen in the eyes.

"*I* did," she breathed out, wishing it would just stop hurting so damn much. Everything hurt. Too much. "Six years of watching me smile and laugh and talk and walk and just existing—*that's* what killed her. Because every single time she looked at me, she had to relive the worst night of her life over and over again. Until it became too much."

"Carmen." Hunter struggled for words. "Carmen, please stop. Don't."

"I was a reminder of her life being ruined." She sniffed, wrapping her hands around herself as the sobs subsided and the cries grew silent. "And she couldn't kill me for it, so she just killed herself."

Carmen West may have a thunderstorm in her eyes and a touch of galaxies in her veins, but she was also a human. And unlike raindrops and stars, humans weren't beautiful to look at when they fell.

And right now, Carmen West was falling.

51.
Achilles' Heel

Carmen's eyes seemed to have finally run dry, the tracks of her tears on her cheeks still pretty much apparent as she tucked her feet under her and nestled further into the couch.

"You should probably eat something," Hunter said, stuffing his hands into his pockets and looking around the house he hadn't stepped foot in for almost twelve years. "You didn't have much back there."

Carmen sniffed, running a hand under her eyes to get rid of any wetness remaining there.

"Not hungry," she muttered, her voice so hoarse it made her tone sound more clipped than she intended.

"Water, at least?" he offered cautiously, still not sitting down as he observed her. "Your—"

"Don't want anything." There was that part of Carmen emerging again, the part she loathed. The part that shut down on everyone and pushed people away when she was in agony.

And right now, she was in agony. So much so that it was almost unbearable. She wanted to hug herself so tight in hopes that it would somehow glue back all her shattered pieces.

She couldn't *breathe*.

How was it that emotional pain impacted her physically, anyway? How did it manage to suffocate her?

Everything hurt: blinking hurt. Speaking hurt. *Existing* hurt.

And she didn't know what to do with all that pain filling up every little crack and dent in her heart.

"So that's what you're planning on doing?" Hunter asked, raising a brow as he stood behind the couch opposite her, folding his arms on the headrest. "Giving the silent treatment? Starving yourself? Refusing to even drink anything?"

Carmen's eyes flashed with warning once they met Hunter's ones. "Don't push me."

"Right," he drawled, his eyes flashing back at her with a look of pure defiance. "Because you're going to give me a piece of your mind if I push you too much. Because for once in your life you're actually going to put someone in their place after wronging you."

"Stop it, Hunter. I mean that."

"Well, go ahead, show me what you've got then—"

"Stop it—"

"—I mean, you are Carmen West, right? The girl who's always smiling, always letting things roll off her, the one who's always unfazed and nonchalant —"

"Shut up!!" Carmen bellowed, jumping from the couch and hurling whatever her fingers could grasp in Hunter's general direction.

The TV remote flew a good distance past Hunter's head, crashing into the wall near the entrance of the living room, the batteries falling out and rolling away as few pieces of the device broke and scattered across the tiled floor.

"What the hell do you want from me!" Carmen's eyes flashed, every bit of that storm in her coming to life and engulfing her as a whole.

"This," Hunter replied, not appearing the least bit stunned as he gestured towards her. "I want you to stop shutting down. I want you to stop blocking out all the bad shit. Scream at me. Yell at me. Throw whatever at me. Go ahead. Punch me while you're at it. But don't go crawling back into that shell of yours."

Carmen let out a laugh of utter disbelief, throwing her hands up into the air. "Is that what you'd like me to do, Hunter? You'd like me to let you in?"

Hunter tilted his head slightly, his eyes narrowing the tiniest fraction. "Yeah," he eventually said. "If it takes you screaming your lungs out at me, then so be it."

"I can't believe you," she muttered under her breath, shaking her head to herself.

"Why is it so hard for you to believe—"

"I did let you in!" Carmen's voice was thunder as wave after wave of buried, restrained pain from a lifetime ago came undone and crashed over her. "I *did* let you in once." She bit out, her breaths coming in harsh gasps. "And do you know what you did? You took all that love and trust and admiration I had for you and walked right out of my life with it. And then—do you know what you did after that, Hunter?—you threw it all back at my face in school. You turned all that affection into something ugly and used it to drag me down time after time."

"Carmen—"

"I did let you in, Hunter." Her voice cracked, like that split in the sky when lightning struck. "And you repaid it with pain and my heart torn to shreds."

Asa. She wanted Asa. She wanted his rough fingers running through her hair, his hands cradling her waist, his chest shielding her in a bone-crushing embrace, his terms of endearment tumbling out his mouth as he murmured them against her skin repeatedly.

She wanted the one person in this world who made her realise what home was supposed to feel like.

"Fine." Hunter snapped, eyes hardening but not before Carmen noticed a flicker of hurt there. "Don't let me in, then. At least let me call that perfect little boyfriend of yours."

Carmen froze, momentarily losing track of her thoughts regarding Asa and wondering how, even after all this time apart, Hunter could read her like an open book.

374

"Come on," he muttered, sighing in defeat. "He'd be better at this whole comforting thing anyway. I'm not the sentimental type. Can't do this heart-to-heart shit right now."

Carmen's mind flashed back to when Asa had hugged her after their date on the porch when she'd started panicking—how he'd wrapped his arms around her in an ironclad grip as if he wanted to force back all her broken pieces together.

She wanted to feel that again, to get lost in his warmth, to see that tenderness in his coffee eyes every time he stole a glance at her.

But...

But Carmen had just fallen and crash-landed on the cold concrete with everything that made her whole now lying around in fragments. And she just needed to gather those shards of her entire being and sew them back together before raising herself up from rock bottom.

It was tiring—this constant act of coming undone and patching herself back into something whole. But she knew what it was like to have been condemned before being given a chance, and Carmen wasn't about to do the same and give up on herself.

"I can't do that," she mumbled under her breath, letting her body fall back into the soft cushions as all the energy drained away from her bones.

"Why not?" Hunter asked, that sour look still on his face.

"Because..." Carmen pressed her lips into a thin line, feeling her chest tighten with something she couldn't explain. "He, uh, he doesn't— he doesn't *know*."

At first, confusion swam in Hunter's eyes then understanding dawned on his features. Carmen watched as his expression softened and the annoyance slipped away from his demeanour. Pushing himself off the other couch, he walked towards Carmen and then dropped down next to her, leaning back against the cushions and tipping his head back on the headrest.

"Then let him know," Hunter said, shrugging as he kept his eyes fixed on the ceiling.

"No," Carmen said hastily, eyes widening and her heart jolting sharply in her chest. "No, don't be ridiculous, Hunter. I can't do that—I mean, Asa and I—we—things are good, okay? Really good. I love what he and I have but... Letting him see this part of me, telling him about where I come from—I can't—it... it's just going to make..." Carmen sighed heavily, feeling weighed down by something she couldn't touch. "I...I feel like what we have is *pure*, you know? And I don't—Hunter, I can't let that part of me taint it," she finished saying in a small voice.

"It's not a part of you, Carmen," Hunter told her quietly. "It *is* you. You need to stop pretending like it's a piece of cloth—like it's something you can take off whenever you want."

"I'm not sure if you're trying to make me feel better or worse."

Hunter sighed and shot her a flat look. "What I mean is, you're keeping your birth at an arm's length instead of owning it and letting it sink in—*really* sink in."

"I'm fine." Carmen looked away. "It's worked this far, and I've always managed to pick myself back up."

"Maybe, but it's also acting as a barrier when it comes to you letting Asa all the way in."

Carmen stiffened, and Hunter seemed to notice it, because he turned to face her with a weary expression, as if expecting her to lash out at him again.

"You know nothing about Asa and me," she muttered, curling her fingers into her palm.

"No, I don't," he replied easily. "And do you know why? Because I wasn't around—because I wasn't a part of your life. And do you know why that was? Because I put up a barrier that didn't allow you all the way in. And that cost me you, Carmen." Hunter averted his gaze, jaw clenching. "After that, it was a downward spiral. Shutting down mentally, closing off and pushing away people—it all became so easy, almost as natural as breathing. If you let this keep dragging you down, it's going to cost you Asa. And then more."

Carmen blinked back a fresh set of tears, her throat tightening and making it even more painful to speak. "I don't know how to—how would I even say it? How am I supposed to actually say the words—I don't…"

"See," Hunter murmured, the uncharacteristically soft tone of his voice catching Carmen off guard. "The problem isn't that you think he's going to love you any less. It's that you've never actually said the words out aloud. And saying them would make it all real and you're not ready to accept that."

Despite the harsh, bitter truth in his words, Carmen chose not to confirm them and instead looked at Hunter through the corner of her eyes. "You can't know that," she said quietly.

"Yes, I can," he said, smiling sadly. "Because when you broke down in the car just an hour ago as we were leaving the dinner, I wanted to tell you that I never meant any of those things I said to you. I wanted to tell you that you're so much more than a broken heart, that you weren't an abomination, that I'm sorry, that I lo—that you matter to me. I wanted to tell you how I wish I could take everything back. But I couldn't bring myself to say any of that."

Carmen's vision blurred as she tilted her head up to look at Hunter, the tears gathering at the corner of her eyes. "Why not?"

"Because," he paused, breaking the eye contact and looking down at his hands, "the minute I tell you that I care, that I'm sorry, that I *do* accept you as one of my own, that I never meant for all the hurt I caused—it will become real. Everything becomes real. It becomes real that I caused you so much pain, that I let you down, that I was supposed to be your brother and protect your heart from getting broken, but instead, I went ahead and broke it before any other man ever had the chance to. And once all that sinks in, I'll be forced to accept it… and I don't think I could ever live with myself after that, Carmen."

Carmen couldn't recall the last time she'd been rendered speechless but oddly enough, she found it touching, even more so that this was coming from the ice king himself.

"I...don't know what to say." She blinked, a tiny smile tugging at her mouth.

"Say that you won't make this easy on me," he replied, a corner of his lips lifting in something of a smile. "That you'll make me work towards earning your trust back because I want to deserve it. Rather that than you giving it to me out of that forgiving heart of yours."

"Kind of hard when I can't find it in me to hold anything against you anymore." Carmen grinned, her first real smile during the whole night.

"You can't just forgive me that easily, Carmen." Hunter sighed, looking troubled. "Or anyone for that matter."

"You're not anyone." She nudged him with her elbow. "You're like my—what's that phrase again?—ah, yes, Achilles' heel. That's what you are."

Hunter frowned, looking even more unimpressed by the second. "You do know his heel got him killed, right?"

Carmen blinked at him, furrowing her brows together. "Wait, that phrase actually means something? I thought it was a fancy way of referring to someone's blind spot or weak point."

Hunter snorted loudly, surprising both Carmen and himself with the suddenness of the gesture, causing them to dissolve into laughter.

Warmth blossomed in her chest at the simplicity of that moment—two people who'd suffered just as much tonight but who had also found a way to make each other laugh.

"Hey, Hunter?" Carmen spoke into the silence that had fallen amongst them, the ghost of her laughter still lingering in her voice.

"Yeah?"

"Thank you," she said softly.

"For?" His forehead creased ever so slightly, never the one to display his emotions to their fullest extent.

"When I was five, this classmate of mine—I think his name was Ben—used to follow me around all the time and spend every single lunch hour with me. You hated it. You never liked it much when someone took up too much of my attention away from you. And one day, you hid his

378

favourite action figure he always brought to school so that he would waste the entire period looking for it while you finally got to spend that time with me."

Hunter's face flushed and he scratched the back of his neck, suddenly looking like he wanted to be anywhere else. "I forgot about that," he muttered. "But, yeah, I remember now. I didn't know that you knew I was the one who hid his toy."

Carmen grinned. "Of course I knew. It was such a typical move of yours. You used to be so possessive back when we're kids."

"All right, all right," he grumbled. "I think I'm more mature than that now."

"You are." She smiled, hesitating briefly before she leant sideways and rested her head on his shoulder.

Hunter froze for a few seconds and then seemed to relax, allowing a small breath of relief to leave Carmen's lungs.

"That's why I was thanking you," she mumbled, her eyes drifting shut as the exhaustion of the night caught up with her. "Because I know you're not Asa's biggest fan and that you're finally getting to spend some time with me after all these years. But you didn't let that territorial nature of yours to stop you from putting my needs first when you offered to call Asa tonight." She subconsciously snuggled further into his side, a yawn escaping her mouth. "So thank you."

She heard Hunter mutter something inaudible under his breath and smiled to herself, the last thing floating through her mind as she surrendered to sleep being the wish that this newfound happiness would last.

•   •   •

Breakfast the next morning was tensed.

Carmen sat on one end of the medium-sized table, and her father on the other, both staring down at their food listlessly.

Hunter—who had passed out on the other couch last night while he waited for Carmen's dad to show up after she'd fallen asleep—seemed to either not notice the awkwardness or he was deliberately not acknowledging it.

Carmen figured it was probably the latter; the boy had an infuriating ability to remain stoic regardless of what the situation was. The earth could split open and he'd still remain unfazed.

She supposed that was another one of their similarities. Carmen too had a tendency to wear nonchalance so well that it drove Asa insane sometimes.

The mere thought of him lifted her lips into a soft smile.

She knew she'd seen him just yesterday, right before she left for the god-awful dinner—but it felt like forever with everything that had happened.

"Carmen," her dad finally spoke, making the smile on her face drop and her head snap towards him.

"Yeah, Dad?" she asked, her words a little rushed because she wasn't expecting him to say anything.

"Your phone was ringing when I got home last night," he said, letting his fork fall back on his plate. "The two of you were completely out of it so you must have not heard the calls, but it was Asa."

"Asa?" Carmen furrowed her eyebrows.

"Yeah, I answered it and let him know you were asleep. I think he might drop in today—he even asked if it was okay with me." Carmen's dad smiled at the last bit, seeming pleased, and she held back a smile of her own, making a mental note to congratulate Asa on actually making progress with her father.

Hunter just snorted at that and rolled his eyes, earning him a kick from Carmen under the table.

His eyes met hers and he lifted a brow. "Seriously? What are you, eight?"

"I was going to ask you the same thing," Carmen said sweetly, before dropping the facade and shooting him a deadpan look. "Behave. Asa's not even here and you're already acting like a jerk about it."

"Please." Hunter scoffed. "As if he wouldn't do the same if the tables were turned. In fact, he probably has a life-sized poster of me in his basement which he uses to practice throwing darts or something."

Someone cleared their throat, and both Carmen and Hunter turned to face her father. "I'm going to be up in my room in case you kids need something," he said awkwardly, obviously wanting to get away from the conversation the other two were having.

"Sure, Dad." Carmen smiled, before looking away quickly, finding it difficult to maintain eye contact with him after last night's events.

Hunter just nodded, leaning back in his chair and offering her father a single wave of his hand as he walked out of the kitchen.

"You have a Jonah West-sized chip on your shoulder," Hunter remarked once Carmen's father was out of earshot.

"Shut up," she mumbled, pushing her plate away. "I can't believe I told him I didn't need him." Carmen shuddered at the memory, recoiling on the inside as her words replayed in her head.

"Even the great and mighty Carmen West is allowed to make mistakes," Hunter muttered, yawning as he stretched his arms above his head. "So quit your whining and stop beating yourself up about it."

"You really do have a way with words," Carmen said distastefully, throwing him an unimpressed look.

"I don't sugarcoat." He shrugged.

She just hummed in response and let herself drink in the sight right in front of her, wondering if a few weeks ago she'd have allowed herself to believe in the idea of Hunter and her reconnecting.

Hunter's palm came crashing down on the table with a loud bang, causing Carmen to jump back in alarm and snap out of the trance she was in.

"Are you insane?" she hissed, feeling her heartbeat return to its normal rate after that momentary scare.

"You were staring. It makes me uncomfortable. Your boyfriend did that once while I was looking for something in my locker, and I told him I'd carve his eyes out."

"Oh, God." Carmen pinched the bridge of her nose, closing her eyes for a brief second. "You *are* insane."

"Well, obviously. I totally didn't tell my father about where I was going to be last night and then I stayed over here—even if that bit was unplanned." He let out a low whistle. "Hell awaits me once I get back home."

"I'm sorry," Carmen began, frowning. "If—"

"Shut up," he snapped. "I don't want to ever hear you say those two words to me. I'm the last person you need to be apologising to—about anything."

"I don't think anyone else can be nice and rude at the same time the way you can," she commented seriously, shaking her head.

Hunter raised both his brows. "You know, Asa also said something along those lines at that party two weeks back. Something about me being the only person who can pull off doing something nice and acting like an asshole at the same time."

"For someone who hates Asa so much, you sure do remember the things he does and says."

"What can I say? The guy knows how to leave an impression." As if on instinct, Hunter's hand reached up to his jaw, rubbing it with a scowl on his face. "Asshole even broke my jaw once. *Shithead.*"

"Yeah? What did you do to provoke him?" Carmen scoffed, rolling her eyes good-naturedly.

But the light-heartedness of the moment faded away as Hunter's expression darkened and a muscle in his jaw ticked.

"Nothing I'm proud of," he said quietly, looking away. "He was defending someone I was giving a hard time. I deserved the punch."

Carmen's heart sank and her gaze fell to her hands, watching as they drew lazy patterns on the surface of the table. "Listen, Hunter," she began to say, taking in a deep breath, "I—"

"Your father mentioned Asa calling you last night," Hunter interrupted, and Carmen tried to ignore the disappointment that washed over her. "Don't think I've ever seen you around with a phone in school before."

Carmen debated responding to his obvious attempt at changing the subject by either ignoring it or pushing him about the other thing. But they'd only just found some sort of common ground, and she wasn't about to disrupt that.

Letting out a deep sigh, Carmen settled back into her chair and decided to go along with it. "That's because I never used to have a cell. Activated it only recently."

It was the first thing she'd done the night of their date after kissing Asa goodbye on the porch. She headed straight to her room, rummaged around in her closet for the sealed box, tore away the packaging, and pulled out the shiny new phone.

Hunter was about to say something else when Carmen's phone buzzed and she looked down at the screen to find the pop-up text;

Asa: *I'm here ;)*

The wink in the text was enough to send up a flare of heat through Carmen, colouring her pale cheeks with a burning sensation only Asa could stir up in her. But then Hunter cleared his throat, and the realisation that it wasn't just her and her dad in the house hit her with full force and the phone almost slipped from her grasp.

Her father did say Asa was going to drop by. She just didn't expect for him to arrive at this time of the morning.

"He's here?" Hunter asked, voice and face free of any emotion as he stared at Carmen.

She nodded uneasily, fingers curling around the device in a tighter grip. "Yeah, um, he's here…"

"And you'd like me to leave," Hunter finished for her, a tight smile on his face.

"Don't do that," she murmured, looking at him with pleading eyes. "I just don't think it's the best idea for the two of you to be under the same roof."

Hunter didn't say anything and just shrugged and stood up from his chair, grabbing his empty plate and leaning over to take Carmen's too. "Well, don't keep him waiting. I'll just wash these and be on my merry way. I need to change out of these clothes anyway."

Carmen mumbled *thank you* to him as he turned on the tap and then directed her attention towards her phone to reply to the text.

Feel free to let yourself in :D, she texted.

Smiling to herself as she clicked on the *Send* option, she looked up to see Hunter place the dried plates on the rack the same instant she heard the soft thud of the front door closing.

"Carmen?" Asa's voice floated to her ears and the sudden overwhelming emotion that came crashing down on her like an avalanche nearly knocked all the breath out of her.

Hearing his voice after what felt like an eternity made her want to cry out of sheer joy. She didn't understand how he could impact her that way.

Losing her composure, she sprang out of her chair and ran towards the entrance of the kitchen just as Asa stepped into it to check if she was there.

Her chest collided with his painfully, making the both of them stumble until a familiar pair of strong arms went around her waist, steadying her and regaining their balance. Asa chuckled, the sound emerging from somewhere deep in his throat and reverberating through his chest, lighting up yet another spark in Carmen's being that could never be extinguished.

"I missed you," she mumbled into his chest, sighing against the soft fabric covering his skin.

"We literally saw each other just yesterday," he murmured, looking down at her with that same old mischief swimming in his eyes. "Don't tell me you can't stay away..." The words died in his throat, his voice trailing off as he looked up and took in the person standing a few feet away, leaning against the sink.

Asa looked like he genuinely believed he was hallucinating, and he remained motionless, with that perplexed look on his face for several seconds before something changed in his expression, as if it was only then that it dawned on him that he wasn't seeing things, but that Hunter Donoghue was *actually* standing there, a short distance away from them.

The look of utter shock and disbelief that crossed his face twisted Carmen's insides, in a manner that made the butterflies in her stomach drop dead rather than take flight.

"Um..." Carmen trailed off, not having any idea where to even begin. "So, Hunter here—"

"—was just about to leave," Hunter cut in, his blank stare fixed on Asa for a while longer before he tore his eyes away and looked at Carmen instead. "See you around, cuz."

Carmen bit down on her lip before beginning to pull away from Asa. "Wait," she called out just as Hunter pushed himself off the sink and started moving towards them. "Let me walk you to the door."

Before she could move away completely though, Asa's arms tightened around her and pulled her back into the space she'd just created. "Not necessary," he mumbled, dropping his mouth down to her ear and placing a soft kiss there. "Hunter can walk himself out, I'm sure."

"Actually," Hunter's voice rang out sharply, causing Asa to raise his head back up and narrow his eyes at him. "Hunter would very much like Carmen to walk him to the door." His mouth twitched, his cold blue eyes staring down Asa as if daring him to say something.

The minutes passed by in tensed silence, before Carmen regained her composure and shrugged out of Asa's hold, causing him to look at her with an unreadable expression—which was scary in itself because she was always able to read Asa.

"Just wait here, okay?" She forced a smile onto her face, clasping her hands together. "I'll just see him out and come back to you."

Something flashed in Asa's eyes but it was gone as soon as it had appeared, not sparing Carmen any time to decipher what the emotion was. "Yeah." He smiled, but it didn't seem to reach his eyes. "Of course, go ahead. I'm not going anywhere."

Carmen shot him a small smile and waited for Hunter to walk past them before heading out of the kitchen behind him.

"That was unnecessary," she muttered under her breath, folding her arms against her stomach.

"True," Hunter replied casually. "And I don't really need you to walk me out, so you can head back now."

Carmen stopped in her tracks and shot him an incredulous look. "Then why did you—"

"I just like sticking it to him whenever I can," he said, slipping his hands into the pockets of his hoodie and throwing a devil-may-care grin at Carmen over his shoulder.

She sighed exasperatedly and scratched her forehead. "You really can be an ass, you know."

"I do know that" he threw open the door and stepped out, turning around on the porch to face Carmen, "just not towards *you*. Not anymore."

Carmen fought against the smile tugging at her mouth, but it eventually won the battle and crawled across her face with a nostalgic sort of fondness as she shook her head at him.

"Just go, Hunter." Carmen shoved him lightly, the ghost of a smile still on her face as she closed the door and leant against it for a few breaths.

And then, she started making her way to the one boy whose presence she'd never grow tired of.

52.
Crash and Burn

Inhale. Exhale.

Inhale. Exhale.

Asa tried to get a firm grip of his surroundings, to calm himself down and not let the outrageous situation he had just walked in on get the better of him.

There was an explanation as to why that piece of shit had been there, standing just an arm's length away, in Carmen's goddamn house. Asa was sure there was an explanation—there *had* to be. An explanation that was along the lines of Carmen feeling forced to invite Hunter in, that she had done so against her will, because Asa's mind couldn't think of any other possible reason than that.

There was no way the girl he'd surrendered his heart and soul to would open the doors of her home to the one person who'd broken those very parts of Asa time and time again.

"Hey." Carmen smiled as she walked in through the opening in the wall that led to the kitchen.

Asa swallowed and forced a smile on his face, looking up from where he was sitting on one of the dining chairs. "Hey back."

"You okay?" she asked cautiously, stepping closer until their knees were brushing and running her hand through his hair.

Asa wasn't sure how he wanted to answer that. Before, he'd have just admitted what was going on inside his head, not letting anything hold him back when it came to her. But now...

This feeling of uncertainty in their dynamic was new, and it made him falter in his response. But those few seconds of hesitation was all it took to cause a sudden shift in the atmosphere.

Carmen's smile faltered, and her hand froze in Asa's hair, fingers pausing in their act of caressing his soft cinnamon-coloured locks.

"Yeah," he eventually responded, but it was a little too late and the two of them knew it. "I'm—I'm okay."

Too late. Too late. A few seconds too late.

"Okay," Carmen murmured, and she tried to smile—she did. Asa could see that.

But he could also see the caution in her eyes. The reluctance there. And that space between them expanded a little more.

"I, uh, I called you last night, but it was your dad who picked up," Asa said, desperately needing something else to take away the burning need to have his questions answered.

Why was he here, Carmen? But Asa didn't ask.

"Yeah, Dad told me," Carmen said, pulling her hand away and seating herself on top of the dining table, letting her legs dangle off the edge.

And despite the unasked questions, despite the unsaid words, despite the underlying tension, Asa's heart still skipped a beat when Carmen's kneecaps brushed against one of his arms resting on the tabletop. Ironically, the feeling also left him bitterer towards the whole situation.

Why was he here, Carmen? But Asa didn't ask. *Did he hurt you?* Still he didn't ask.

Asa didn't ask because he knew he wasn't going to like the answer. Something had seemed odd about the entire ordeal, and now that he thought about it, he realised what it was that he found so perplexing.

388

Carmen's eyes hadn't been filled to the brim with grief like that day he'd caught her hiding away in the sanctuary of the art room after Hunter had confronted her and left her feeling like a lost cause.

No, when Asa had walked in here and looked into her eyes, he'd found the same old pair of thunderclouds gazing back at him, free from sorrow, free from grief. They hadn't held the look of a broken heart like they usually did whenever she spoke of Hunter.

And that struck Asa as odd because that was all Hunter Donoghue was capable of inflicting—*pain, pain, pain.* So even though Asa's tongue ached with the need to spit out the question; even though his throat felt full with words struggling to be thrown out, he kept his mouth sealed tight.

Why was he here, Carmen? But Asa didn't ask. Asa didn't ask because he'd seen Carmen and Hunter interact, and there was no hostility there. And he didn't want to dwell on what that exactly meant. Not yet.

"Yeah," he muttered, distracted. "He said you were asleep."

"Mm-hmm, it..." Carmen hesitated, fidgeting with her hands. "It was a long night."

Asa's posture softened, and he pushed anything related to Hunter to the furthest corner of his mind, allowing no room for anything other than pure concern for Carmen.

He pulled his chair closer to the table and leaned in 'till his torso was caged in by both her outstretched legs.

"How'd it go?" he asked softly, lifting a hand and wrapping his palm around the back of her neck, using his thumb to draw circles under her jaw.

Carmen's shoulders slumped forward and Asa watched exhaustion creep into her eyes, killing the brightness in them bit by bit.

His chest hurt. It physically hurt to watch the light literally drain away from the eyes of the girl he was so hopelessly in love with.

"Not well." She laughed weakly. "Good news is, that was my last straw. I'm never taking a chance on them again, so that's one less burden for me, I suppose."

"You know, you once told me that I'm always bending myself and that if I continued to do so, I'd eventually just snap and break."

Carmen's eyes met his and Asa leaned in further, the gesture coming naturally to him. He rested his forehead against hers and circled his other arm around her waist, pulling her forward, closer to the edge of the table—closer to him.

"You keep letting the world rest on your shoulders and it'll eventually become too heavy for your back, *mi amor*," he murmured. "That's where the bending starts. And then will come the breaking." He tilted his head and slid his cheek down hers, stopping when his mouth touched her neck and placed a lingering kiss there. "So let it go. All that dead weight, everything that drags you down, just let it go."

"I don't think I can," she said quietly, circling her arms around Asa's neck and clasping her hands together behind it.

"You can." He smiled, kissing her neck again. "If you're strong enough to let the weight of the world in, you're strong enough to let it out too."

"You really believe that?" she asked him, tilting her head to the side and pressing her lips in a tight line.

"Yes," he replied without any hesitation. "That's one of the things I love so much about you—you're not the kind who lets the world take away from you, but the kind who gives back instead."

Carmen offered him a soft smile at that, and Asa's chest tightened painfully when he saw a spark of brightness flare up in the grey of her irises.

"My fourth grade teacher used to tell us something like that that every single day without fail," she reminisced, a nostalgic look on her face. "She used to tell us that we shouldn't allow the world to change our smiles, but let our smiles change the world. Can't remember whose quote it was."

"I can't remember either," Asa said, trying to search through his memory for a famous name. "But it's true, you know. Once you learn to let go of all the extra weight, there's more room for letting in the other things."

"The other things?" Carmen knitted her brows.

"Yeah." Asa shrugged. "The little things. The simple things. People too."

"People?"

"Yeah, Carmen. People. The ones who love you, the ones who genuinely care, the ones who'd bring down the moon to your fingertips just to see your face light up."

There was a pause, not just in their conversation, but in the air around them. And then a few more beats of silence passed.

Carmen unclasped her hands from around Asa's neck and leant back, a frown tugging at her mouth. "You think I don't let people in?" she asked, something unidentifiable flickering in her eyes. Asa wasn't surprised, though. So much about her was indecipherable to him.

As much as he was certain that she could read him like an open book, he was also certain that she only ever allowed him glimpses of her pages.

"I think," he began cautiously, "that you don't let me in. Not the way *I* let *you*."

One of Carmen's hand wrapped around herself and her other one reached for that chain around her neck, igniting a spark of frustration in Asa's gut.

"I let you in," she defended herself. "There's nobody else that I've let this close to me but you. I mean, you literally have the power to crush me if you want to and I wouldn't hand over that kind of emotional power to just anyone, Asa."

"That's not letting me in. That's acknowledging the fact that you're in love with me," he pointed out gently, his heartbeats picking up speed as the panic regarding the direction this conversation was heading towards infiltrated his bones.

Asa noticed Carmen's fingers tighten around the chain resting on her neck, and he clenched his jaw, fighting the urge to yank her hand away and hold onto it with his own, reminding her that she could use him as an anchor instead of the goddamn chain.

But that was Carmen West, always using inanimate objects as her solid ground, as her rock. Whether it was the godforsaken chain, or her art journal. It was always the things without life, without a beating heart that she ran towards.

And Asa was always standing right in front of her with an outstretched arm, waiting and waiting and waiting for her to just reach out and take it in hers. And Carmen was always looking right past it.

"It's the same thing!" She threw her hands into the air, and jumped down from the table, folding her arms across her stomach defensively.

Asa didn't understand why she was slipping into a defensive mode. This was the same girl who had never failed to speak with her heart on the tip of her tongue, who had never been afraid to say whatever was on her mind.

But that had been when Asa was falling for her and now that he had, there seemed to be some kind of barricade blocking Asa's access to every fibre of Carmen's being. Asa sighed and lowered his head into his hand, a palm running down his face with restrained exasperation.

"No, it isn't," he muttered, his words sounding muffled through the gaps between his fingers. "You know it isn't."

"What do you want from me, Asa?" she asked, sounding tired all of a sudden.

"*You*," he told her softly, removing his hand from his face and looking right at her. "I want *you*."

"And you *do* have me!" Carmen exclaimed, unfolding her arms and moving towards Asa again, kneeling in front of him and taking his hands into hers. "You have me, Asa."

"Do I?" he asked quietly. "Do I really?"

"What does that even mean?"

"What happened last night?" he asked, drilling his eyes into hers. "You said it went bad."

392

He felt Carmen tense, felt her hands about to let go of his, but he grabbed them and held on. She'd warned him about her tendency to pull away from people and then to push them away too.

He had promised her, that day in his truck, to never let go, and this was him living up to that promise. This was Asa holding on even when Carmen was pulling away from him.

"It went bad, Asa," she said, voice thick and trembling slightly. "It was horrible. I hated it. Is that what you wanted to hear me say?"

"I couldn't sleep," he told her, feeling the spark of frustration grow into a fire inside him. "I was so worried for you because I knew how Hunter made you feel at school. And knowing you were about to be sitting at a table with a whole family made up of people like him was driving me out of my mind. Because all that kept running through my head was me being safe at home while you were out there all alone—"

"I wasn't alone," Carmen said softly, running her thumb against the back of his palm in a comforting gesture. "I wasn't alone, Asa. You had nothing to worry about, okay? I'm sorry if I scared you or—"

"I don't want you to be sorry, Carmen!" Asa snapped, losing his composure, and he watched her flinch, surprise flickering in her eyes at his outburst. "I want you to understand where I'm coming from. Because all I wanted to do last night was wrap you in my arms and never let go. And when I finally do make it here the first thing after breakfast, I find that son of a—" Asa stopped his rant, grinding his teeth together and looking away with an unmistakeable glint of anger in his eyes.

"Is that what this is about?" Carmen mumbled. "Hunter?"

Asa let out a hollow laugh, noticing Carmen wince at the coldness in it. "I'm going to take a few wild guesses here, Carmen, so correct me if I'm wrong, all right?" He whipped his head towards her, mouth set in a grimace. "It was too early for Hunter to be paying you a visit, although why he'd even visit is beyond me. And then there were his clothes which looked wrinkled as heck. My conclusion? He slept in them. See, now all that I can think of is the fact that he stayed over. Am I getting anywhere? Or is my theory just batshit crazy?"

Carmen didn't say anything at first and just watched him silently.

"Yes," she finally said. "He stayed over last night."

"And he was here because he came back with you from the dinner?"

"Yes," she answered, eyes guarded as they observed Asa.

"So that's why you don't want to talk about last night with me?" Asa asked, unable to help the hurt from seeping into his voice. "Because you'd already talked it out with him? Because *he* was there for you?"

"Asa." Carmen swallowed, her grip on his hands tightening. "Please. You need to understand. It was too late to call you or—"

"Bullshit," he cut her off, anger and hurt dissolving into one and spreading throughout his body like wildfire. "I would have been there for you regardless of what time it was, you *know* that. I'd have run out of the house, jumped into my goddamn truck and made my way to you within a heartbeat. You *know* that, Carmen."

He searched her face, her eyes for anything—*anything* at all. Some sort of clue, something that would give him an inkling of what was going through her mind right then. That goddamn beautiful masterpiece of a mind he'd fallen head over heels for, but a mind that he was beginning to realise he didn't really know all that well.

And that terrified Asa. Because he'd given her every single inch of him, but she'd only ever allowed him a few stolen glances into her being.

There were times—rare, oddly intimate moments—where Asa found himself comparing Carmen's existence to that of the moon, the way she was a beacon of light in all the dark places.

And it was ironic, really, that he'd never considered her to be a crescent, just that tiny sliver of her entirety, allowing only a fraction of her to be seen.

They'd been in pure bliss, tucked away in their own little world where they could pepper kisses on each other's skin while they giggled with the euphoria of young love, where they could talk about binary pairs and how they would have each other no matter what.

394

But that was a sugar-coated world, tied up in a pretty little bow and now reality was crashing down on them—on *him*—and Asa was flailing around with no sense of direction.

Another heartstring yanked out.

"Asa." Carmen broke the silence, her voice shaking now. "Just... Just *listen*, okay?"

Again, Asa laughed, no traces of humour whatsoever. "I'm always listening, Carmen," he murmured, pulling his hands away from her grasp. "You just never do the talking."

"I need him," she whispered, as if scared to tell Asa that.

"And I need you," he simply said.

"Okay, okay," Carmen breathed out, relief evident in her tone and in the smile growing on her face. "That's good. Because you do have me, okay? You *do*. Making place for Hunter in my life doesn't take away the room for you."

"See, that's where I'm having trouble understanding things, Carmen." Asa threw his hands in the air, rising up from his chair and kicking it back. "When did Hunter even come into this? Into us?"

"He doesn't have to come between us, Asa!" Carmen stood up, too, shooting Asa a look of anguish. "He doesn't have—"

"Let me ask you something, Carmen. What do you see when it comes to me? What comes to your mind when you think of us? Where do you think we're going with this?"

"Forever," the word spilled out of Carmen's mouth, a freight train with no brakes. Asa noticed the surprise cross her face before she relaxed, as if accepting it. "*Forever*, Asa," she told him softly. "That's all I see with you and I. You can call me crazy if you want. You can try convincing me that this is puppy love or—"

"I won't try convincing you that because this isn't some passing cloud," Asa's voice didn't waver, the sincerity ringing through his words and echoing off every syllable as his eyes burned into Carmen's. "It's different with us, and the two of us know that. Our perspectives, this kind of intensity—it comes with a certain level of maturity, not age. And I'm in for the long haul, Carmen. You're a part of my life, okay? Which means that everything about you becomes a part of me too. And Hunter? I can't see him anywhere in that life."

"He's my family, Asa." Carmen bit her lip, eyes growing watery. "Please."

"But you said I was your family too." Asa's voice broke, every ounce of anger fading away and the raw hurt rising to the surface. "That's what you said, Carmen. Before you left for that dinner, you kissed me and you told me that I was family to you. You *said* that. Why would you say something like that to me if you never meant it?" How could Carmen claim that Asa was family and go ahead and welcome with open arms someone who'd broken him in indescribable ways?

A single drop escaped the pool of tears gathered at the corner of Carmen's eyes, slipping down her cheek before she hastily wiped it away.

It hurt Asa to watch, but right now everything was hurting for him.

"I did mean it," she said in a thick voice, as if it pained her to get the words out. "I meant every word I've ever said to you, Asa. You are family, and I *do* love you but I love Hunter too. I can't help that."

"How can you even *say* that?" Asa asked, his voice a mere whisper of disbelief. "He's a monster. Do you know the kind of shit he's done to people? The hearts he's broken? The minds he's messed around with? The way he mercilessly kicks someone below the belt at their most vulnerable point just so that he can see them break?"

Carmen closed her eyes, stumbling back a few steps as if she wanted to *un*-hear all that Asa just said.

"Things are different now," she looked at him pleadingly. "*He's* different now—"

"And that's supposed to change all the damage he's already inflicted?"

"He's trying, Asa!" Another tear trailed down her cheek, and he had to look away. "He knows he's done wrong by me—"

"Done wrong by *you*?" Asa shot her an incredulous look, eyes hardening. "By *you*?" He chuckled darkly. "I cannot believe you right now," he muttered under his breath. "Done wrong by you—"

"Asa, he just needs time—"

"Goddammit, Carmen!" Asa slammed his fist on the table, making the salt and pepper bottles rattle. "You were basically his sibling! No matter what he did to you, there was a part of him that knew this and held back from tormenting you to his fullest capabilities! But you know who got the brunt of it all? Me. *Me.* He ripped me apart, tore down my defences. *God*, he was ruthless. Every goddamn time I thought I'd gotten my shit together, every time I believed I'd grown another new layer of thicker skin, he would come along and burn it down to nothing. He made me *feel* like nothing. And do you know the one thing that has kept me going all these years in school? The fact that once I was done with high school, I was also going to be done with that horrible excuse of a human being. And you... Carmen, I don't want to be done with you once senior year is over. I don't want to be done with you when college is over. I don't think I ever want to be done with you, but Hunter being back in your life—coming back as a *sibling* nonetheless—that's not me getting rid of him. That's him being a part of my life even after I leave this shitty town and all the shitty memories with it."

"Asa," Carmen choked out, the tears freely streaming down her face now.

The saddest part was that this was the most Asa had ever seen her react or reveal her genuine emotions. He wondered how much more there was to learn about her.

"Asa, please don't make me choose," she pleaded, shaking her head slowly as she tried furiously to stop the tears.

"I won't do that to you, Carmen." Asa smiled at her sadly. "I love you, remember?"

Something in Carmen's expression broke, and for the first time ever, Asa saw a pure kind of vulnerability in her eyes. But it was too late. Too late.

Asa had been standing with that outstretched hand for a little too long now, and it was beginning to hurt. Perhaps it was about time he stopped waiting for her to take it because she didn't look like she was about to do so anytime soon.

He looked away, his heart hurting as he uttered the next words. "I won't make you choose," he paused, letting the words hang in the tensed air between them, "but I need to be able to choose for myself. And a future with Hunter in it is not a life I want."

"I love you," Carmen blurted, her words shaking and tripping over each other like the tear tracks on her cheeks that kept colliding into one another. "I love you, Asa. I meant it the first time, I meant it yesterday, I mean it now and I'll mean it tomorrow. Just...just stay, okay? We—"

"Why, Carmen?" He tilted his head, looking at her helplessly. "Give me a reason to stay. Because you won't tell me why you want him back in your life all of a sudden. You won't tell me what really happened at the dinner last night. You won't tell me what's wrong—what's *really* wrong. You won't talk about anything when it comes to you. You won't let me all the way in!"

"It's not easy!!" she screamed, her expression crumpling and a sob escaping her lips.

"It's never easy!!" he yelled back, wanting to just reach into his chest and rip his heart out because *oh god, it hurt it hurt it hurt.*

It hurt too much. And he didn't want to feel—not anymore.

"It wasn't easy for me to let you in either, Carmen," he said in a pained voice, feeling his own eyes prickle. "But I did because of the simple fact that I trusted you and that I love you. I wanted you to know me, to see my world." His voice cracked towards the end, the rest of his words leaving his mouth in pure anguish. "And all I can think of right now is that you don't want me to be a part of your world. That you're not willing to let me *know* you."

"It's not like that, Asa." She swallowed audibly, running a hand under her eyes messily. "It's not you, it's me."

398

"Don't give me that!" Asa retorted, wanting to shove his fist into the wall behind him and watch the pieces fall away as a hole formed over there—much like the one currently growing in the centre of his chest. "Don't give me that "it's not you, it's me" bullshit. You can do better than that."

"Fine, Asa," Carmen spat back, her eyes flashing with something that Asa could only compare to a strike of lightening. "You want the truth? The truth was that it was Hunter I needed last night, and he was there."

Her words were a jagged-edged knife being shoved into his chest—impossible to pull out without taking chunks of his heart with it. And God, was it tearing him apart brutally on the inside.

Asa opened his mouth to say something but had to close it again because there was this lump in his throat and he didn't know why it was there but it felt like a thousand needles stabbing him, which was making it near impossible for him to speak.

"Wait," Carmen mumbled, her tone losing its venom and staring at Asa with a frightened look in her eyes. "Wait. That wasn't—I didn't mean—that's not what I meant, Asa. I'm so sorry, that's not—"

"He broke you," he told her with a slight tremble in his voice. "He broke you time and time again. He hurt you. He left you. And I was the one who stood by your side, Carmen. I was there to help you pick up the pieces. But *he's* the one you turn to when you need someone?"

"He understands, Asa!" Carmen gestured desperately with her hands. "He knows what it's like with that side of the family. He gets it—"

"—I want to understand too, Carmen!" Asa kicked the chair further away, a frustrated growl leaving his mouth. "I want to know how to be there for you. I want to know what brings you pain, what makes you upset. I want to be that safe place for you to fall into when the going gets rough. I want you—*all* of you. But if you can't open up to me, if it's him you're going to keep turning to in times of need... Then, Carmen, I—I really don't get what my role in this relationship is."

"I just don't want to lose you," she said softly, silent tears spilling out the corner of her eyes uncontrollably.

"You're shutting me out because you don't want to lose me, but we're in this position because you won't let me in, Carmen. Why is that so hard for you to grasp?"

"Please." She shook her head fervently, the raw fear in her eyes unmistakeable now. A part of her must have figured out how this was going to end, but Asa couldn't backtrack. It was too little, too late. "I love you."

"What's that even supposed to mean anymore?" he asked, voice strained and lifeless now. "You say those three words like it's an instant remedy. Like it can fix just about anything."

"I'm saying it because it's true." She sniffled, eyes red and puffy, killing Asa a little more on the inside. "I do love you. Is that not enough?"

Asa didn't respond right away, drawing in a deep breath and letting the air fill that aching, hollow cavity in the middle of his chest, right in the core of his entire being. And for one last time, he let reality punch him in the gut.

"No, Carmen," he said quietly, the last remaining heartstring snapping into two and shattering whatever hope he'd been clutching onto. "It isn't enough."

He saw her recoil, backing away a few steps as if his words had physically knocked her off balance.

"How can you say that to me?" she whispered, looking at him with so much hurt in her eyes. He wanted to scrub, scratch and rip that look out of his memory for good.

"Because you say that you love me but you don't live up to it." He looked down at his feet, feeling the lump in his throat grow even more painful. "You say that you love me, but here you are, ready to welcome with open arms the one person who'd made it his life's mission to make mine hell."

"Don't say that." She shut her eyes, as if it hurt too much for her to hear him say it. "Don't say that I don't mean it when I tell you that I love you."

"Then prove me wrong, Carmen." There was a sense of pleading in his tone. "Tell me you'll let me in on what's really going on with you."

Carmen averted her gaze, focusing on the wall next to Asa. "I don't know."

I don't know. I don't know.

And those three words sealed the deal.

Because Carmen hadn't said *"I need time".* Or *"I'm not ready".* She'd said *"I don't know"* and those set of three words held another meaning entirely.

"Yeah, 'I don't know' isn't good enough for me," he muttered, the fight in him draining away; Asa was done. "You could have asked for time and I'd have handed it to you without blinking an eye, but *'I don't know'* tells me you haven't even considered letting me in and that just means we are always going to crash and burn, Carmen."

Asa spared her one last glance, committing every single minute detail to memory—those long midnight locks of hair his fingers were going to ache to get tangled in, the stormy eyes his own ones were going to beg to look into, the ivory-toned skin his lips were going to miss caressing, the slender curve of her waist his hands were not going to cradle again.

And then Asa's feet were carrying him out of the kitchen, every single step he took twisting that jagged blade further into the cavity in his chest.

His fingers wrapped around the doorknob once he'd reached the front door and was just about to open it when he heard footsteps behind him.

"That's it, then?" Carmen asked bitterly, her voice sounding more broken and lost than ever. "You're just going to give up on us? Walk out on me? Because you don't like Hunter?"

"I didn't storm out when I saw Hunter here, Carmen," he told her matter-of-factly, no longer having the energy to navigate the swirl of emotions inside him, sticking with the nonchalance instead. "I stayed. I asked you why it was that you suddenly needed him again. I gave you the chance to tell me what was happening, and you didn't take it. This isn't just about him—it's about us. Yeah, it may have started out with me not being happy about seeing him here, but it also hit me how much I don't really know you."

He twisted the knob and pulled the door open, stepping out into the cold November morning—at least, he knew it was supposed to be cold—but Asa felt nothing in that moment, nothing but the emptiness in his rib cage where his heart used to dwell.

"So, no, I'm not walking away, Carmen," he murmured, not turning around to look at her. "You're not giving me a reason to stay, even after I asked you for one."

And then he was walking past the porch where he'd kissed her breathless, where he'd murmured *"Mi amor, mi cielo, mi sol"* against the warmth of her skin, where he'd been foolish enough to believe they were a binary pair capable of giving parts of themselves to each other when it was obvious now that he was the only one who'd ever done the giving.

He'd poured parts of himself into her with every touch, every embrace, every kiss, every "I love you", but she'd never trusted him with parts of herself. She'd never allowed herself to be vulnerable in his presence. And Asa was paying for it because all those bits he'd given away were no longer with him. He felt incomplete, knowing he could never patch himself back without those pieces.

He climbed into his truck, ignoring the empty passenger seat, the goddamn autumn leaves scattered all over the streets and trying not to think about the fact that while he was here, he'd left his heart back there. And that he was probably never getting it back.

53.

The Pain Death Leaves Behind

"It's going to cost you Asa."

Those had been Hunter's words.

And what had Carmen done? She'd tossed them to the wind and went about with a blindfold hoping that her feet wouldn't waver on the path she was walking on. The blindfold was removed now, and all that greeted Carmen was the sight of Asa on one path and herself on a completely different one.

Not parallel paths—no. Because parallel roads never met, did they?

Asa and Carmen had met though, had crossed paths. Had lingered around even. So, then what were they?

Intersecting lines? Roads that cut into each other at a certain point before heading in the opposite directions forever? The kind that never met again?

No, Carmen refused to believe that. She didn't want to even entertain the thought that Asa had been nothing more than a passing cloud, a ship that had stayed in one harbour for too long and had to sail away now.

There was a museum in her head, with walls the shades of brown and gold, with seventeenth-century quotes engraved into the frames of every masterpiece he'd inspired her to make.

And Carmen didn't know how to burn that down; she didn't want to choke on the ashes of its remains.

But she then realised Asa hadn't known about this museum, had he?

She'd never shown him. Never allowed him even the tiniest peek at those paintings she'd created using the sun's glow from his eyes, the honey from his voice and the gold from his heart.

His heart that had opened its doors for her three months back, ever since that moment under that tree in the parking lot when he'd given her journal back. A heart that had done nothing but give and give and give without asking for anything in return.

His heart that, for the first time, had asked her for something in return just a moment ago—a tiny infinity ago. His heart that had asked for a piece of her heart in return.

And Carmen didn't even give what it wanted, she wasn't able to give Asa what he wanted.

They always spoke about how much courage was needed to take the leap and fall headfirst into love, but they never spoke of the rare kind of bravery it took to let someone love you back. A form of bravery that Carmen was beginning to realise she didn't have.

She'd been the wings of those who'd forgotten how to take flight, a rock to hold onto for those who'd felt the ground beneath them crack wide open. She'd allowed her bones to carry fragments of the people she crossed paths with. But she'd never given any room for anybody to do the same for her in return.

She didn't have it in her to let someone be her wings while she found her own pair and worked on fixing them. She didn't have it in her to let someone be her solid ground when it was *her* world falling apart. And she most certainly didn't have it in her to allow someone else to carry fragments of her heart in their bones.

Carmen only knew how to take, never to give.

And the problem with takers was that they never knew where to draw the line, where to set the limit. Until, eventually, the givers said enough.

Asa had said enough.

He'd forgotten to take his heart back, though. Because she could still feel its beats pulsing through her own veins, its steady *thumpity-thump* echoing within the walls of that museum in her head.

He'd cut open his chest and handed his heart over to her on a silver platter, and now it just sat there in Carmen's shaking palms, and *oh God oh God oh God*, she didn't know what to do with it anymore.

She didn't want to feel its warmth, its weight, its tremble. She didn't want Asa to let her keep it.

But she should've known. Asa San Román always had a tendency to wear his heart on his sleeve and place it in the hands of whoever could inflict the most damage on it with the blind trust that they wouldn't.

It was funny, really, how even now Carmen could read him like an open book. How she knew him like the back of her hand even in his absence.

And she'd never given him the chance to know her as intimately.

Was she sorry about the pain she'd caused? Yes. Was she sorry about her inability to wear her heart on her sleeve? She didn't know. She didn't think so. Perhaps not.

Carmen waited for the need to apologise for it, but no such thing came. How was she supposed to apologise for who she was? Ever since she could remember, she'd had her heart under wraps. There was no one who'd ever asked her to open up, no one who told her she was worth knowing underneath all that gentle exterior and the smiling face.

The art of self-preservation was all she'd ever known throughout her entire life. Did she really have it in her to start taking those defences down?

"Honey?"

Her dad's voice sounded from somewhere behind her, and Carmen turned away from where she was standing, staring at the door that

Asa had just walked out of several minutes ago. She saw it in his troubled eyes, in his sad smile.

"How much did you hear?" she asked, voice hoarse and drained, the evidence of all the unsaid words streaming down her cheeks.

"Enough," he answered softly. "You guys weren't exactly whispering. And my room isn't soundproof." He offered her a wry smile, but the worry in his eyes remained.

"Fighting is normal." Carmen swallowed. "It happens." When her father's eyes only grew more worried, she began to fidget. "It *does*," she insisted, an irrational sense of anger simmering inside her.

"That didn't sound like just a fight, Carmen," he told her slowly, hesitancy evident in his demeanour.

Her father was right. It hadn't been a fight, it had been an ending. It was love in the cruellest form, ending before it had a chance to begin. The start and the finish lines just blurring into one another's edges until it wasn't possible to tell them apart.

Crash and burn. They'd always been a train wreck waiting to happen. And now that the collision had occurred, Carmen was desperately looking for the parts that could be salvaged, still blind to all the other damage lying around.

"I'm sorry," her father said, a crestfallen expression on his face.

She didn't have the energy to look confused, to even begin to understand what that apology meant. "For what, Sad?" She sighed, looking around and realising she no longer recognised these walls, the furniture. It was a house. A house. Carmen was tired of waiting for it to become a home.

"For letting you lose both parents the day your mother died," he told her, shoulders sagging as he lowered himself to the last step of the narrow staircase and seating himself there.

"Mum didn't *die*," Carmen said, devoid of all emotion. "She killed herself."

Her father flinched, a shadow passing over his features and clouding his eyes. "Nobody saw it coming," he whispered, a haunted

406

expression on his face. "One day she was with us and the next she wasn't."

"Nobody ever sees the bad stuff coming." She didn't know who she was speaking to anymore, her eyes growing unfocused and staring at nothing in particular. "It's like a car crash. Nobody sees it happen until after the damage is done. And after that, what can apologies even do? You just stand on the sidelines and watch the car burn."

Her father frowned, pulling his brows together slightly. "You have a choice there though, Carmen. You either watch it burn, or you run towards it and try getting the person trapped in there out."

Carmen's eyes zoomed back into focus and flickered towards him. "Won't you burn your hands in the process?"

Her father smiled. "Would you be able to live with letting them burn out of self-preservation?"

Carmen realised she had been in a burning car for a while now—and she still was, choking on the fumes, inhaling the smoke, trapped beneath the flames.

Was she going to be able to live with herself if she gave up on her salvation? If she condemned her own self just like everyone else?

Could the shell of the person she was now shove her hands through all that damage and try dragging out the person she was underneath all that wreckage?

Perhaps the key to letting someone else in was allowing herself to let in the potential to be the person she could be. Because keeping out the pain and the loss and the devastation was not a method of easy breathing; it was holding her breath as that pressure in her chest just grew larger each day. Building walls was easy and it kept away all the hurt, but Carmen was beginning to realise it also kept away all the love.

And that had been Asa's only crime—loving her when she didn't know how to let that love get past her walls.

•　　　•　　　•

Asa's hand hesitated, hanging in mid-air, before he finally gave in and knocked on the door.

407

Mrs. Martin's face greeted him, her mouth forming an exhausted smile as her eyes landed on him, recognition flickering through them.

"Asa." She smiled warmly. "It's been a while."

Asa swallowed past the lump that had been lodged in his throat ever since two days ago, when he'd walked out of Carmen's house.

"Hey, Sarah." He smiled easily, nostalgia sweeping through him at the sight of someone who'd been like a second mother to him during his friendship with her daughter. "Is Isla home?"

"Isla?" she repeated, sounding almost sad. "Not Isles anymore, huh?"

Asa offered her a sad smile, a dull ache settling in his chest at the memory of the girl he'd once considered family. The loss didn't hurt anymore, but there was a bittersweet throbbing that arose occasionally on moments such as these.

"I'm sorry for how things turned out," Sarah Martin said, opening the door wider and allowing Asa to step in. "Sometimes I feel like you were the last piece of good she had in her life."

"She didn't want help, Sarah," Asa murmured, his tone kind.

"I know, son." She sighed. "And I don't blame you for choosing yourself." She shrugged, but her eyes looked tired, worn out.

Asa wondered what it must be like for her to have a daughter and yet not have her at the same time.

"Go ahead." She motioned with her head towards the direction in which Isla's room was. "You know where to find her."

Asa shot her a small smile. "Thanks, Sarah."

His knuckles rapped on the familiar door, before dragging his fingertips down the hard surface, a thousand different memories spent in this house flashing through his head.

It swung open, leaving Asa's fingers touching air instead as his eyes met a pair of electric blue ones. They widened, shock passing through them before going back to being cold and detached.

"Can I come in?" he asked, shuffling on his feet uncomfortably.

Isla didn't say anything and just went back in and dropped down on her bed. But she'd left her door open so Asa took that as permission to enter.

His eyes scanned the room, frowning when he noticed all her posters were taken down and empty beer bottles scattered on one corner of the wall next to her bed.

"You've been drinking," he remarked, a sinking feeling in his stomach as his eyes flickered to Isla who was watching him silently.

"If you came here to judge—"

"No," he quickly said, shaking his head. "No, of course not. That's not why I'm here."

"So why are you here, Asa?"

He pressed his lips together, his mind racing a hundred miles before he sighed heavily and sat himself down on the swivel chair across from her.

"You took down all your posters," Asa commented, tilting his head to the side.

"Yeah, well, Arctic Monkeys no longer interest me," she muttered, leaning her back against the headrest of the bed.

"What happened to all the photographs? The ones of all your cheerleader competitions?"

"I quit the squad." She shrugged. "Doesn't matter anymore."

"Oh." Asa looked away, the sinking feeling in his stomach becoming more prominent.

"*Don't.*"

His eyes travelled towards her again. "What do you mean?"

"Stop worrying." She sighed. "Stop *feeling* for me—I'm not your problem anymore."

But Asa had loved Isla Martin once, thought of her as family even. Asa's heart still loved the people he'd once loved, even if he no longer had room for them in his life. Even if he had to take the longer route just to avoid bumping into them and risk seeing familiarity and nostalgia in the eyes of someone who was now a stranger.

"You weren't a problem," he murmured. "Not at first. You were a friend then. My *best* friend."

"Beginnings are always happy, Asa."

Asa, not Ace.

He waited for the pain, but it didn't come, and in a way, it made him feel at peace. He no longer needed her the way he used to before.

"The middle is supposed to be better," he mused out loud.

"The middle is where everything starts going south." Isla laughed humourlessly. "And when that happens, the end becomes inevitable, right?"

Asa's forehead creased, looking at Isla with perplexity. "Where did we go wrong?"

"Not we," she said quietly. "Me. You remained loyal 'till the end, until you decided enough was enough."

"You're not angry?"

Isla's eyes met Asa's, surprised flashing through them. "At you finally learning how to choose yourself? Of course not, Asa. I was frustrated it took you long enough to take a firm stand, but... but at the end of the day, all I did was take from you. And takers never know when to stop."

"You said." Asa hesitated, "You said I should've just learnt to have thicker skin and let things go…"

"And that should've been your first red flag," she said, dropping her eyes to her hands as she picked at a few loose threads on her bedspread. "There isn't anything wrong with you just because you can let in emotions. It's the people who tell you that you need to change your softness who have something wrong with them."

"And what is wrong with people like that?" Asa asked quietly, looking down and pulling his brows together. "Why do people who are so detached set their eyes on people who like wearing their heart on their sleeves?"

"Because their exterior is hard. They let the world turn them cold, instead of fighting back to remain soft and warm. And people like you, who have fought back and keep fighting back every day, remind people like me of our weakness. Of our inability to be soft despite what the world throws at us." Isla narrowed her eyes at him, the wheels in her head obviously spinning. "Asa, why are you asking this?"

"I... I want to understand," he mumbled, shifting his gaze from the floor to her face.

Isla let the confusion on her face show. "Understand what?"

Asa's mind flashed with snippets of the morning two days back, his chest constricting and squeezing the air out of his lungs at the memory.

"Hunter," he replied.

Isla's curious expression morphed into one of shock and then transformed into anger.

"What is *wrong* with you?" she hissed, throwing him a look of utter disbelief. "You just jumped out of the frying pan by getting out of that negative environment with me! And you want to head into the fire now?"

Asa sighed exasperatedly, rubbing a hand down his face. "I'm not going to become best buddies with him, Isla. I just need to understand—"

"What?" she snapped. "Understand *what*, Asa? Why he put you through what he put you through? So that, what? You can start the journey of forgiveness?" She laughed sardonically. "Right. And here I was, actually feeling proud that you learnt to let go of the things that made you unhappy. But no, you're just trading one toxic person for another."

"I need to know whether he has any good in him, Isla. The way I found good in you," Asa muttered, feeling tired all of a sudden. He felt tired a lot these days.

"Why?" she asked, her tone pained. "You owe him nothing. *Nothing*! He doesn't deserve to have you look for any redeeming qualities in him! Why do you do this to yourself again and again? Why can't you just keep away all the hate and the bad?"

"Isla, I'm not asking because I want to forgive him or make room for him in my life..." Asa pressed his lips together, the skin on his

411

forehead growing more creased by the second, "I just need to know how anybody could see anything redeemable in him. And considering both you and Hunter are basically two sides of the same coin, there's no better person to ask."

"You're asking the wrong person, Asa," she said softly, the angry scowl on her face fading. "Because it wasn't me who saw anything redeemable in myself—I still don't. It was you who saw the good in me, and I don't know how you did it. The only person who can give you the answer you want is the one who stares back at you in the mirror."

"Yeah." He chuckled without mirth. "I'm a lost cause."

"No." She smiled, and for a fleeting moment, Asa saw the old Isla in there. "*I'm* a lost cause. *Hunter's* a lost cause. Not you, Asa. You're a compass. The only reason I didn't start spiralling sooner was because you gave me some sense of direction."

"But it wasn't enough," he concluded, sadness swimming in his eyes.

Isla shook her head slowly, swallowing and turning away. "That isn't on you. You can't force someone to change. They need to want that change for themselves, Asa."

"Why don't you want that change?"

Isla stared back with vacant eyes, and Asa realised he didn't recognise the girl in front of him. Not anymore.

"I'm tired, Asa," she eventually said, sliding down the headrest until she was lying on the bed. "Just tired."

Asa sat there in the silence, watching as Isla grew drowsy and thinking back to Carmen's words of her unwavering faith in Hunter.

Eventually he rose from the chair and walked towards her bed, pulling the sheets over her sleeping body. Asa thought about the last time he'd tucked her in, back when she'd stumbled drunk into his home.

He sighed and leant down, placing a light kiss to her forehead before standing to his full height and walking away.

Before he could move, however, Isla's hand wrapped around his wrist, stopping him in his tracks.

412

Asa turned around to find her eyes half-open, struggling to fight sleep. "I'm sorry, Asa," she mumbled, her eyes falling shut again. "I'm sorry for all the pain."

His throat tightened, a prickling sensation behind his eyes as he tore his gaze away from Isla.

Asa had gotten the closure from her that he'd so desperately needed. Despite her flaws, Isla had come through for him on that. It didn't erase all the times she'd broken his heart, the times she'd fallen off the wagon and dragged him down with her. But he could close this chapter of his life for good now. This was one place he didn't have to visit anymore, one part of his past he no longer needed to look back on.

With one last glance towards her, Asa stepped out of the room and let the door close shut.

He no longer knew her, and she no longer knew him. And they were both better off this way.

•   •   •

It had been four days since Carmen had heard from Asa.

Four days since she asked herself whether she wanted to climb out of that burning car.

Four days since she decided to stop cutting her fingers on the shards of their failed relationship in a futile attempt to salvage it.

Train wrecks weren't salvaged. They were swept away, and they were cleaned up. And if there happened to be survivors, they were told to take time and rest, to nurse their wounds back to health. To allow themselves to heal.

But this wasn't her first, was it? The first train wreck had been her mother's suicide, and Carmen had never allowed herself to heal from it. And as much as she wanted to patch herself together after she'd lost what she thought would be a forever kind of love, there were still older wounds that needed tending to.

Maybe that had always been Carmen's problem. She kept gluing back the pieces despite the knowledge that it was just a matter of time 'till she fell apart and broke again.

It wasn't because she was weak. It was because she kept building back herself on a shaky foundation, a foundation that had split wide open when her mother died. And if Carmen wanted to pull herself out of the burning car, if she wanted to raise herself back up, she needed to make sure her feet had solid ground to stand on.

Carmen had hit rock bottom, and she could either see it as the death of who she was or the awakening of who she could become.

Did she want to grab onto that potential to be someone whole? Yes. She wanted to know what it'd be like to stand on a steady foundation. She wanted to know how it would feel to be able to let in love, and joy, and peace. She wanted to stop being so alone.

Carmen wanted to know who she could be once she'd broken free of the chains she let her past bind her with.

"What are you doing?"

Carmen didn't respond right away and kept looking down at the photo album she'd dug up from the storage room that had been locked for a good many years now.

"I look a lot like her," she whispered, as if too scared to disrupt the silence, as if the moment was too sacred for there to be any interruptions.

"You do," her father said, his voice shaking the slightest bit.

Carmen felt the words rise to the tip of her tongue, felt them dance along the curve of her lips. But she held them back. Pushed them down her throat, pressed down on them 'till—

No.

No, wait.

Did she really want to bury the question? Or would she rather have it answered regardless of the response?

Would it be safe for her to open up? She needed to if she wanted her question answered. Right?

But letting herself ask that question might put her in a vulnerable spot. And that vulnerability might bring in a lot of pain—*too much* pain.

But, a voice in her head said, a voice that sounded like a boy with coffee eyes and cinnamon hair, *But wouldn't that vulnerability also give you closure?*

It might bring Carmen pain, but it also might bring her peace. And Carmen was growing tired of the chaos in her bones and the storm in her soul. She *wanted* peace.

So, swallowing audibly and keeping her eyes fixed on the photographs, she let the words crawl back up her throat again. "Is... Is that why you can't—why you can't... " She squeezed her eyes shut, trying to steady her breathing. "I look a lot like her. Is that the problem why you can't love me?"

She felt her father sit down on the floor next to her, their backs pressed against the couch while the album lay opened at their feet.

"Honey, what sort of question is that?" He sounded horrified. "Of course I love you."

Carmen didn't remember crying in her life, not in the last twelve years. But something in her had broken during Thanksgiving night. And it was getting easier to let her pain spill down her cheeks.

Maybe it was because of all the pain that sat there, gathering and piling atop one another. It had become a volcano, and the thing about volcanoes was that they had an ending point. And after that, came the eruption, the spewing out of all that which was buried too deep.

"You never say it." She looked up at him through a watery vision. "Not after she died. In fact, I can't remember you saying it before also. Back when she was still with us."

So many emotions flitted across his face, all battling against each other for dominance. But his eyes. His eyes looked haunted and so full of pain. And Carmen wondered if there was a volcano in his heart too.

"It's not—it's not easy. I know that is no justification of me making you feel unloved..." her father trailed off, looking down at the photo, "I know you said apologies don't matter after the crash has occurred, but I *am* sorry, Carmen. I am so goddamn sorry. I let you down, I let you lose your dad the same day you lost your mum, and I could never

415

stop saying sorry for that. Making you feel like you weren't loved—like you didn't have a home—that's not—that." His voice cracked, unable to remain steady as the tremble in it grew worse.

"She never said it either." The words were flowing freely from Carmen's mouth now, all of them coming out in breaths, in a rush, as if there was not enough time to say all she wanted to say. "Mum, I mean. I don't remember every single moment from my childhood but I can recall her not saying those three words to me. Then again, I can't blame her, can I? I was her nightmare in the flesh."

"Honey, she loved you—"

"No, she didn't!" Carmen sobbed, her voice breaking at every syllable. "She *didn't*, Dad! You don't kill yourself because you love someone!"

Her father blinked back tears of his own, his mouth opening and closing like a fish on dry land. "Don't say that. *Don't say that.* She had you, didn't she? She decided to—"

"*Why* did she have me?" Carmen wiped her cheeks, turning to face her dad. "If it was so hard for her to love me—if it was so hard for her to go on living while I also breathed—then why did she even choose to have me? She could have saved herself a lot of pain. She could've saved *you* a lot of pain. And she could've prevented me from being born into a world of misery."

"She didn't have it in her, love," her father said softly, a single tear trickling down his face. "She couldn't bear to go through with an abortion."

Carmen scoffed, the bitterness and anger rolling off her in waves. "You know Cole's mum once told me I should feel lucky that Mum didn't get rid of me—that she chose to bring me into this world." Carmen shook her head, running her palms over her cheeks again. "Is that what I'm supposed to do, Dad? Feel grateful? Because I don't feel grateful. I *don't*. Does that make me a bad person? I—I don't know. I feel angry, though. Angry that she was a coward. She couldn't live with the guilt of having an abortion so she brought me into this world. Angry that she

416

couldn't be a mother even after making that choice to have me. Angry she couldn't love me the way a child is supposed to be loved."

"Carmen—"

"No, Dad," she cried. "She was a coward. She *was*! She couldn't deal with the guilt of getting rid of me, and she couldn't deal with me being alive, either so she took the easy way out! She didn't once stop to think about what that would do to you, to Hunter, to the rest of the family. She didn't care about the burden she was placing on *me*. *She just didn't care!*"

Carmen thought she'd known pain and anguish. But this—this was a human fist shoved into her chest, nails digging into her skin, tearing through the flesh and the bones, piercing her veins and dragging her heart out.

Her whole body racked with the sobs, her wordless cries of *"Please hold on please hold on please hold on"* shaking her shoulders violently as if they were finally getting rid of the universe that sat perched upon those bones.

Was this what letting it all out felt like? Because it hurt too much. *Too much.* Letting go of pain wasn't supposed to hurt you. The irony in it was twisted, another one of life's sick jokes.

"And you know what the worst part is?" Carmen sniffed, running a hand under her nose. "I feel like shit because of my anger towards her. I feel like a horrible, horrible person because I hate her more than I miss her, Dad! And I don't know how to live with that."

"Shh, shh, come here." Her father scooted closer, wrapping his arms around her. Carmen let herself melt into the embrace, tucking her head under his chin. "You're not horrible, Carmen. You're *human*. And Cole's mum doesn't get to tell you what you're supposed to feel. You just feel what you feel. Emotions don't come with instruction manuals, love."

"I hate Mum." She wept into her father's chest. "I hate her. I hate her *so much*. I hate that she makes me feel so much anger towards someone I'm supposed to mourn, and what I hate even more is that at the end of the day, I don't think I really hate her at all."

"You have a heart that is far too beautiful to be consumed by hate, honey," he murmured, rubbing a soothing hand down her back. "And I don't know what to tell you to take away the pain your mother left behind, but I can tell you that I love you. I can assure you that you are loved. I loved you long before you came into this world. I loved you since the moment your mother conceived you—that's nine months of loving you long before any other person in this world has. You are loved, baby girl, you are loved." His arms tightened around her, and Carmen felt one of his tears fall against her cheek, colliding into one of her own.

"You are *loved*—" her father sighed into her hair, "—and don't you ever forget that."

54.
Because It Was Real

Carmen didn't know how much time had passed with her lying there, wrapped and safe in her father's embrace.

"I'm sorry," her dad said after several minutes, breaking the silence that had fallen among them.

"For?" Carmen pulled her brows together, her eyes feeling heavy now.

"You never being able to open up before the way you did right now, for never giving you an opportunity where you could've learnt to vent or let people in." He sighed a deep sigh like it came from somewhere rooted within his soul. "I shut myself off and you learnt to do the same and now…. Now you're struggling and in pain. This is all my doing."

"Dad?" Carmen pulled away and looked at him with a certain level of seriousness she knew she hadn't displayed before. "What happened with Asa wasn't your fault."

Her father sighed and reached forward, picking up the photo album and flipping through the pages. "Maybe not entirely," he muttered. "Not *directly*. But…I had a hand in it, didn't I? The kind of environment you grew up in, that restriction on displaying your emotions. The Rutherfords did that ever since I can remember. And after your mum died, I did it too."

Carmen shrugged. "I suppose it was easier… to block out the pain, the guilt."

"I suppose it is," he agreed, his eyes glazing over. "Maybe that's why I threw myself into the shifts at the hospital so much, because there, I could keep saving lives. Every day, every hour. But it doesn't work that way, does it? I must have saved countless people by now, but it still doesn't take away the hole in my life where Sophia used to be. It doesn't take away the guilt that I couldn't save her, my own wife."

"I think…" Carmen paused. "I think I understand that she was in a lot of pain. But she didn't just rid herself off it. She passed that pain on to everyone else when she decided to end her life. And I think it's that part I don't understand. I don't understand why she'd pass on that pain to all those who loved her, to those who'd never done her wrong." Carmen looked down at her hands, running her forefinger against her palm. "It makes me wonder: who was she really punishing?"

"You keep asking yourself questions like those and the only thing you're going to get in return is more unanswerable questions, Carmen."

"I need to learn to put this whole thing to rest, don't I?" Her lips curved up into a shaky smile. "I can't keep letting it have such a huge hold on me, Dad. It's not letting me connect with anyone—with Joyce, or Willa. I even met this other girl, Lyra, who seemed really nice, but I never made a move to let that acquaintance progress into a friendship because that would mean opening up myself to them and letting them in. Showing them parts of my world, my life."

"You connected with Asa, though," her dad commented, curiosity evident in his tone as he shot a look from the corner of his eyes at Carmen. "How'd that happen?"

A ripple of pain tore through Carmen, forcing her to tear her eyes away from her dad's.

"He was different," she whispered, an image of him grinning with that trademark mischievous glint in his eyes flashing in Carmen's mind.

"Different how?"

Carmen didn't answer that immediately, taking her time to gather her thoughts that seemed to be running wild lately and formulating them into words and coherent sentences. Sentences that would do Asa justice. That she could give him at least, for now.

"It was effortless," she eventually said, feeling her stomach tie into a gigantic knot before it slowly loosened up and untangle itself, soothing her insides. "Getting to know him, growing attached to him and then eventually falling for him... it was so *effortless*."

Her dad tilted his head to the side, frowning slightly. "Then why did things go wrong?"

Carmen smiled sadly. "Like I said, falling for him was effortless. So much so that I forgot that relationships weren't."

"Honey, you were in no position to get involved in a relationship. Not yet, anyway. Falling in love is one thing, but pursuing that is a whole other matter. Why would you let him think you were ready when you weren't?" Her father's brows were pinched together, a whirlwind of worry and grief swimming in his sea-green eyes.

Carmen looked down at her lap, playing with her fingers, the guilt and shame overwhelming her all of a sudden.

"Because—" she paused to steady her trembling voice, her breaths turning heavy "—because he told me he loved me in a time when I needed to hear it, and it felt...it just felt nice to be loved. I'd lost Mum, lost Hunter, was slowly losing my dad. And then this boy—this amazing boy who always gave up on himself but never on others—comes strolling into my life one September afternoon and makes me feel like I'm actually the centre of someone's world. *His* world. And after feeling unloved for so long, I didn't want to let go of that. Of *him*. I couldn't."

Her dad didn't say anything for a while, keeping his mouth pressed into a firm line for several seconds. He didn't look too happy though, Carmen noticed. And she didn't blame him.

"Carmen," her dad finally said, voice gentle but stern at the same time. "The boy loves you. He really does. It was obvious from the fight itself." He searched Carmen's face for a brief moment, and she wondered what it was that he was looking for. "But if you've never loved him, if it was his attention and affection for you that you loved instead, then you need to let him know. The pain your mother left behind has caused enough scars and inflicted enough hurt. Don't let an innocent get caught in the crossfire of the war this family's fighting."

There was life's cruel sense of irony again. This whole thing had started when Asa had made Carmen a casualty of the battle he was fighting inside his head the instant he took her journal.

And now it was coming to an end because Carmen had dragged Asa into a war that had been raging within her soul for a while.

"He's going to hate me," she said, voice thick with so many emotions. Emotions that she had never let Asa see. Emotions that could've prevented a lot of pain if she had let them out sooner..

"Maybe," her father said. "But if you keep one foot out the door and one foot in, if you keep dangling maybes in front of him, then you're not letting him grow as a person. You're clipping his wings, love. So if you really care about him, if anything you felt for him during the months you've known him was real—even if it was for just a single moment or just a cluster of seconds—then let him go. Set him free, Carmen."

She thought about Asa, then, of his fingers brushing against hers as he placed the broken crayons into her palm; of his lips against her cheek in the art room when he'd thanked her for existing; of his arms wrapped firmly around her as he'd corrected her theory regarding binary pairs.

He had loved her, hadn't he? He had. Even when she didn't give him every single piece of her, he'd found the strength in himself to love the broken version of her soul.

And she was now going to repay that love by crushing him.

"How did I get here, dad?" Carmen mumbled, shaking her head to herself. "How did I get to the point where I made such a selfish decision?"

"Because you're human," he replied, placing a gentle hand on her shoulder. "And it's okay to want things. Yes, you went about it the wrong

422

way, but you now have a chance to make it right. So do it. Do right by Asa. Let the boy go, Carmen."

Coffee coloured eyes flashed in Carmen's mind. Eyes that had looked at her with amazement, with tenderness. With love.

Eyes that would soon look at her with pain and hatred.

But this was the bed she'd made, and she was going to need to learn to sleep on it, whatever the consequences.

Even if it meant giving up the one real thing she'd ever known.

•   •   •

By the time December rolled around, school had started too, everyone's short break for Thanksgiving coming to an end and their lives falling back into their normal schedules.

Asa's world, however, didn't feel normal.

What was normal supposed to mean anyway? Because yes, the sun was still in the sky, and the weather was still chilly and the school hallways were still the same and Monday morning blues were visible on every student's face.

But there was also that pressure right in the middle of his chest where his lungs met. It had been there since the fight with Carmen, as if he'd been holding his breath ever since. And there was that cavity in his chest, a hollow space in his ribcage where his heart used to be. A heart that refused to come back to him despite his pleas.

So, again, what exactly was he supposed to consider normal anymore?

Because when he saw the world around him now, he saw a frozen sun with frost spreading over it. He saw wilted flowers and when night fell, he saw a cracked moon with a split running right down its centre. He didn't see the world anymore, all he could see was that painting from Carmen's journal.

She'd stormed into his life like the hurricane that she was, and redefined his version of normal. It was still the same world, but he'd grown so used to seeing it through Carmen's eyes that he didn't know how to view it any other way now.

423

Asa hadn't seen Carmen today, not yet. Then again, they'd never usually run into each other in the mornings. It was always during lunch and spares and the rides back home.

It was lunch now, though. And Asa's mind was literally blank, rendering him ridiculously incapable of making up his mind on where he was going to spend it.

Because he knew the instant he stepped into that cafeteria, his eyes would search for the head with endless midnight hair, and he wasn't ready, not yet, to look into those thundercloud eyes. He wasn't ready to get struck by a lightning bolt they would send his way. He wasn't ready for that to kick-start his lungs and allow him to release the pressure in his chest. He needed that pressure for a little while longer, just a little while. It reminded him that things had been real. Once.

"Mr San Román?"

Asa snapped out of his reverie with a start, darting his eyes towards his AP History teacher who was looking at him curiously.

"Not planning on going for lunch?" the teacher asked, cocking a brow.

"Sorry," Asa mumbled, yanking his bag from the ground next to his chair and swinging one strap over his shoulder, letting it dangle crookedly against his back.

He walked out of the classroom and into the crowded hallways where everyone was rushing about, either running towards their lockers to stuff their materials in or heading in the direction of the cafeteria. Asa kept his head down, brows slightly pulled together and his mind a million worlds away.

Then he bumped into something hard, making him stumble back a few steps.

"Sorry," he quickly apologised, lifting his head back up, "I didn't..." The words died the second his eyes met Hunter's icy ones. But something else caught his attention right then—the dark colouring on the lower part of Hunter's jaw, a bruise that was at least a day old.

"Whoa, what happened?" Asa asked, his brows furrowing further as he stared at it.

"Why the fuck do you care?" Hunter snarled back, distaste evident in his tone.

Asa knew that right then, Hunter's anger wasn't necessarily directed at him, but at whoever had thrown the punch. That didn't mean he had to be okay with being treated that way though. So Asa just shook his head to himself, wondering yet again what redeeming qualities Carmen saw in the asshole, and began to walk away.

He didn't get to go that far though, because Hunter's hand grabbed his forearm and yanked Asa back.

Asa sighed in frustration. "Okay, I'm really not in the mood for a fight. Just forget I asked anyth—"

"Happened yesterday during practise," he muttered. Asa was confused for a split second before Hunter pointed towards the bruise. "Lost my temper with the quarterback."

"I'm guessing he's in worse shape," Asa commented dryly, knowing what it was like to be on the receiving end of Hunter's anger.

Hunter frowned slightly at that. "Not really... I think I kind of held back."

Asa's eyes flickered towards the wall at the other end of the hallway. "Why?"

Through his peripheral vision, Asa saw Hunter shrug. "Don't know." His tone remained nonchalant, "He was my teammate? I'm his captain and, I don't know, just didn't feel right to have to raise my fist to someone who was supposed to look to me for guidance."

Asa's eyes left the wall, landing on Hunter's ones again instead.

"Okay," he said, nodding curtly and stepping around Hunter to either head towards his truck or find sanctuary in the pool. But before he could put much of a distance between them, Asa felt Hunter's hand grab his arm again and pull him back so that they stood face-to-face once more.

For the love of God.

"Seriously?!" Asa hissed, yanking his arm out of Hunter's grasp. "Why do you have to literally *yank* me back? Call my name if you need to stop me, like a normal person would."

"I didn't start it," Hunter said, ignoring whatever Asa had just said.

"Didn't start what?" Asa snapped, still annoyed.

"The fight," Hunter answered matter-of-factly, blinking once. "He was trying to undermine my position as captain because he's the quaterba—doesn't matter. What I'm saying is, he threw the first punch. I, uh, I didn't initiate it."

Asa stared at Hunter for a few seconds, adjusting the strap of his bag over his shoulder in an attempt to have something to do other than just stand there like an idiot.

"That, uh, that sucks," he eventually said, uttering each word at a slow pace because the weirdness of this entire conversation was starting to get to his nerves. "Is that why you seemed so pissed? Cause it was your own teammate who took a swing at you?"

Hunter's eyes hardened, the scowl returning. "No," he said tersely. "The coach threatened to bench me during the final game of this season if something like that happened again. Can't have that, not with all those scouts attending."

Asa frowned, momentarily forgetting his animosity towards the boy in front of him. "But you said the other guy started it."

"Doesn't matter," Hunter muttered. "I'm team captain. It's my job to make sure shit doesn't hit the fan within our own team."

"Right." Asa nodded, looking away again and shuffling on his feet awkwardly. "Right."

"Yeah." Hunter narrowed his eyes at Asa slightly. "Just needed to say that I didn't, you know, start it."

Asa met Hunter's blank stare, unsure on how to respond to that, but before he could even decide whether he wanted to offer some sort of response or just walk away, Hunter was already turning around and taking off down the hallway.

426

"Hey," a familiar voice said from behind Asa a few seconds before he felt a hand land on his shoulder.

"Hey," Asa greeted back, tilting his head to the side, and watched as Wyatt stepped into the space beside him.

Wyatt frowned at the retreating figure of Hunter and then turned to face Asa. "You okay?" he asked, glancing at Hunter's back again with something like worry in his eyes.

Asa's mouth twitched, before forming a small smile. "Relax," he said. "He didn't hurt me."

Wyatt's worried frown didn't fade, and he stepped forward, pressing his index finger into Asa's jaw and turning his face to the side, examining the other half of Asa's face for any evidence of a fight.

"Dude." Asa laughed, shoving Wyatt's shoulder playfully. "I'm serious. The conversation was pretty civil."

"Civil?"

"For the most part."

Wyatt stared at Asa for a while longer before visibly relaxing and slipping back into that easygoing demeanour. "So," he said in an upbeat tone. "The cafeteria's in the other direction." He pointed over his shoulder with his thumb.

"Not hungry," Asa muttered, the moment of lightheartedness dissipating at the mention of the cafeteria. And just like that, it all came crashing down on him again. One moment of peace was all he wanted. One moment free of reminders. But Asa wasn't allowed even that.

Wyatt's eyes narrowed, turning serious again. "You're not jumping at the chance to spend it with Carmen," he stated, rather than framing it as a question, the corners of his mouth turning down.

Asa's chest clenched. "No," he said, that dark cloud which had been following him around since a week ago now enveloping him as a whole. "No, I'm not."

Whatever lingered of Wyatt's usual carefree attitude drained away and he lifted his hand to his forehead, scratching the skin above his right eyebrow as he looked away.

427

"Um," he started. "What happened?"

"Look," Asa hesitated, "you don't have to. If it makes you uncomfortable—"

"Why?" Wyatt scoffed. "Because I'm a guy, and we don't talk about feelings?" He slapped the back of Asa's head lightly.

"No." Asa snorted. "I was just giving you a way out in case you start regretting it later on."

"I won't," he promised. "Let's hit the rooftop."

"You do know getting caught could land us in deep shit, right?"

"Asa, if you're going to pretend like you care about detention, at least do a convincing job of it."

Asa smiled to himself, but didn't say anything else as they snuck into the stairwell that led to the roof and found themselves standing on the vast expanse of concrete.

"All right then." Wyatt sighed, dropping his bag on the dusty ground. "Spill."

And so Asa did.

•   •   •

It was several minutes later when silence fell among them.

Wyatt pursed his lips, staring into nothingness as he leaned over the railings and folded his arms on top of them, apparently lost deep in thought.

Asa, however, was facing the opposite direction, his back pressed against the metal bars that wrapped around the perimeter of the roof, staring down at his feet that kept tracing nonexistent patterns on the ground.

"You're quiet," Asa remarked, unable to take the silence anymore.

Wyatt sighed from next to him, shooting him a sideways glance. He opened his mouth, as if about to say something to Asa, but then closed it—only to open it once more and shut it again.

"Do you know what I think?" he finally asked, averting his eyes back towards the view of the parking lot and neighbouring streets and buildings that being on the rooftop provided.

"What?" Asa asked, his right foot drawing horizontal lines in the dirt now.

"That I will never understand why you let Isla into your life," Wyatt replied, his forehead creasing.

Asa's foot stopped moving, and his head snapped towards his left, staring at Wyatt incredulously. "What does that have to do with anything I just told you about Carmen and me?"

"Listen," Wyatt unfolded his arms and turned towards Asa, leaning his side against the railings, "I'm saying that you found it in you to see the good in her when nobody else could, that I'm sure she herself couldn't. Hayden thought you were batshit crazy for sticking by her side for as long as you have; Lyra wasn't very impressed either but she never commented on it; and the others who knew you on the surface and probably wanted to get to know you better? Yeah, they probably never made a move to build a bridge with you because they wouldn't have understood your loyalty towards Isla either."

"I'm still not getting the point, Wyatt."

Wyatt sighed heavily, shoulders sagging as he offered Asa a small smile. "It takes courage, I think, to be able to have faith in someone the rest of the world has condemned as a lost cause. I don't think I have that courage. I don't think I *want* to, either. That's extra weight I don't need in my life. But you took it on, Asa. Even when you knew people considered you hopeless and downright stupid, you stood by Isla for as long as you could anyway. And I think it's rare to come across someone like that. But you—you got lucky. You found Carmen. You found someone who could understand you in a way nobody else can, and I think that's pretty goddamn rare."

"Because she has the same faith in Hunter that I did in Isla?" Asa asked slowly, furrowing his brows and pressing his lips together.

"More or less." Wyatt shrugged. "And you can understand her in return—where she's coming from, why she chose to believe in someone you think is a lost cause. Carmen and you are the perfect fit if I've ever seen one before, so it just makes no sense that the two of you aren't grabbing onto each other with both arms and choosing to never let go."

"But that's the problem, Wyatt," Asa stressed, running a hand through his hair in frustration. "I don't get *why* she'd choose to want him in her life. When I befriended Isla, it was at a time when she was in a good place, so I'd already known who she was capable of being. It was later on when she eventually began spiralling. And I couldn't abandon her at a time of need so I stood by her.

"But Hunter's done nothing so far to redeem himself, has he? He's not even tried apologising to me. All I've seen is the rage and the cruelty. So yeah, when Carmen just announced out of the blue that she wanted to reconnect with him, it hurt. Because she was the one I took down my walls for—walls that she knows *Hunter* made me build around myself."

"This," Wyatt gestured wildly between the two of them, "*this* is the problem. You're supposed to be having this conversation with her. With Carmen."

Asa chuckled humourlessly. "You think I don't know that? I could even run to her right this second and spill my heart out. But if I start talking, then I'm going to be the only one doing the talking. She's not going to open up in return. I might as well take my chances talking to a wall and expecting it to respond."

"So what's the problem then, Asa?" Wyatt frowned. "Hunter or Carmen's inability to let you in?"

"Don't they kind of go hand in hand?"

"Well…" Wyatt's forehead creased. "Would Carmen deliberately hurt you?"

"No." The response was swift and sincere. That was one of the few things he never had to question when it came to Carmen.

430

"Then it doesn't matter. Hunter doesn't matter. And you don't need to go looking for any reason to have faith in him. You don't owe him that. But you can have faith in Carmen instead. Have faith in the fact that if she wouldn't do something to deliberately hurt you, there's a pretty valid reason why she wants Hunter back."

Asa was quiet for a while, letting Wyatt's words float around in his head and wondering what it'd be like to tell Carmen it didn't matter, that they could get past this and go back to how things were at the beginning.

It was a comforting idea, that. It felt so easy to do, too. But that wasn't how these things really worked, was it?

"I could do that, you know," Asa murmured, looking down at his feet. "I could just put my faith in her and disregard Hunter."

"But?"

"But the minute I do that, we're going to fall into a cycle. She'll do something that I'd never be able to understand and then expect me to have faith in the fact that she knows what she's doing. It would only allow her to never let me in."

"Are you sure about that, though?" Wyatt frowned. "About her never going to let you in?"

"I asked her," Asa said, sighing. "Before I walked out, I asked her if she was ever going to let me in. I didn't ask her to let me in right then and there. I asked her to tell me if she was ever planning to."

"And she said she needed time? Because you could give her—"

"She didn't ask for time." Asa's eyes flickered to Wyatt's, confusion and hurt swimming in them. "She said she didn't know."

Wyatt winced, his head jerking back at the secondhand punch-to-the-gut. "Ouch," he muttered, averting his gaze.

"Yeah."

Silence fell on them once again, this time stretching for a little longer than before. A small part of Asa knew lunch break was already over by now, but the more dominant part of him simply didn't care just then.

"Hey, Asa?" Wyatt spoke after a while. "How'd you fall in love if you never got to know all of her? Like how does that work?"

"Because when you fall for someone, it's never for every single part of them," Asa said seriously, his voice low. "You fall in love slowly, one piece of them at a time. You never get all of someone at the beginning itself. Whether it's one week from now, or a month, or even a year, there'll always be something you haven't yet discovered in the person you love. There's still another piece buried in them that's going to make you fall a little bit more. The start of a relationship doesn't mean the end of falling in love."

"So even if she didn't let you all the way in..." Wyatt let the question hang in the air between them, tilting his head to glance at Asa.

"Even if she didn't let me all the way in, it doesn't mean I fell in love with an illusion or a mirage. Whatever pieces of her she gave me, they were real. Her not opening up to me doesn't invalidate my feelings. It just doesn't let me love her the way she deserves to be loved. It creates a barrier in our relationship that sort of leaves us...*stagnant*. We couldn't move forward. And you know me, I don't do half measures. I *can't*."

"But it was real." Wyatt smiled, eyes warm.

Asa let out a small laugh, and even to his own ears, it sounded a little broken. "Of course it was real," he murmured, feeling that hollow space inside him ache for a fleeting moment.

It was real. Asa knew it was real.

Because the pain was real.

That knife with the jagged edge twisting into his chest was real. That emptiness in his rib cage where his heart had once been was real because Carmen goddamn West was real. And when you fell in love with someone as real as her, there was just no going back.

"Look, man," Wyatt sighed heavily, debating with himself for a few seconds before speaking again, "I'm not a romantic, just a good listener, really. But I'm also smart enough to know that this world lacks realness right now. Genuineness. So if you're lucky enough to stumble across something as real as what you have, then you don't let that kind of shit slip through your fingers. You fight for it. You hold on and you never let go."

"Even if it feels like I'm the only one fighting?" he asked quietly.

Wyatt shrugged. "You can't fight by yourself forever. She'll either join you or tell you there's nothing left to fight for. But yeah, until one of those two happens, you keep fighting."

Asa thought about Carmen, then: her hands on his face, asking him to tear down his armour because she believed there was beauty in what was inside; defending him from his own self; and her thumb caressing his cheek when she told him that he made this world a better place.

And it hit him then: the cold unforgiving truth that there was no letting go of the one person to whom you've showed your soul.

55.
The Unforgiving Truth

That dark cloud which had been hanging over Asa and following him around for the past week seemed to dissipate momentarily—not completely gone, but lingering in the distance. But he was still thankful because that gloomy haze seemed to have stopped clouding his vision and allowed him to see things a little clearer.

The chat with Wyatt seemed to have released some of that pressure in Asa's chest, allowing him some breathing space. Asa found that he could walk a little straighter, a little taller—like the whole world wasn't about to cave in around him just then.

It wasn't so much about that he was actually considering the possibility of them having another shot together, but the simple discovery that Asa didn't *need* Carmen to relieve that pressure in his chest.

Yes, she might have put it there and she might have been the one who made him feel like he'd been holding his breath ever since that god-awful morning after Thanksgiving. But letting some of that hurt out, opening up to Wyatt—*that* was what made him feel like he could breathe a little again.

So yes, it was nice for him to know he didn't depend on her, but the fact still remained that if he could choose, he would choose for her to be the one he spilled his heart to. And he'd keep choosing her.

Asa was choosing her now. He was choosing to plant his feet into the ground and to fight. Because, after all, their foundation had always

434

been solid, hadn't it? They'd started off right. It was only somewhere along the middle that they'd started to crumble. A place where Asa knew he wanted to keep going and Carmen couldn't make up her mind. That was what had hindered the progress of wherever it was that they'd been heading towards.

Asa's mind kept flickering back to that morning, wondering if maybe he could've approached the matter in a gentler manner, if maybe he should've subdued his usual aggressiveness.

Perhaps he should have toned down the yelling. Perhaps he shouldn't have allowed much of his hurt to be seen so that Carmen wouldn't have the guilt factor added to everything else she seemed to be going through.

But these were all things that were of a fixable nature. They—Carmen and Asa—were fixable. He should know. He'd been broken one too many times only to patch himself together, and something told him Carmen had done so too.

The morning of the fight was fixable. Because if Asa went to her now, without feeling ambushed the way he had when he'd run into Hunter there, he knew they could have the same conversation again with the benefit of a clearer mind.

Carmen would've also had time to think things through by now, and if he were to ask her once more whether she would be willing to let him in sometime in the foreseeable future, then maybe the two of them weren't so hopeless after all.

They were fighters, the two of them. And so he knew—he *knew*—that they had it in them to work this out.

Love alone may not be enough but if he loved her and she him, then didn't that mean there was still something worth fighting for?

Asa hadn't seen Carmen so far today but school was almost over now, and he was glad he didn't have anything for last period.

He was even more grateful towards the fact that it was one of those days when his spare period fell on the same hour as Carmen's. And didn't she always spend hers in the art room?

He hesitated once he reached the familiar classroom and it struck him right then, in that split second, that the walls of the room he was about to walk into probably knew more of Carmen than he did, that it held pieces of her that he'd never so much as get a peek into.

It was kind of sad.

But he shook it off, and with his heart in his throat, pushed the door open.

She wasn't there.

The empty classroom greeted him, all the chairs tucked under the tables and supply closet closed; there weren't any materials out, nothing to imply that Carmen had been there.

Maybe she was still making her way to the class or she decided she didn't want to spend her spare in the art room today.

Asa didn't really know why she wasn't there, but maybe that should've been the first red flag, because if Carmen wasn't there yet, it either meant that she hadn't attended school or that she was deliberately avoiding him—two scenarios that were completely unlike her.

But Asa gave her the benefit of the doubt and shook the unsettling feeling off.

He stood in the doorway for a few more minutes before turning around and letting the door close shut behind him, when he bumped into someone.

Asa's body must have registered who it was before his eyes did, because his right hand instinctively went around the shorter person's waist and steadied them. And even during the heartbeat that it took for Asa to drink in Carmen's face, his hand was somehow pulling her closer against him at the same time.

But that was always how it had been so far, right? His senses were always aware of her presence before he ever had a chance to see her for himself.

Whether it was his eyes beginning their search for her the instant he stepped into the cafeteria, or the way he breathed easier when she was just an arm's distance away, or even how he felt a wave of warmth wash over his insides when he felt her eyes on him.

Why was he still surprised by it all? Hadn't he already acknowledged Carmen was in his bloodstream and there was no flushing her out of his system?

"Hey," he breathed, face tilted down as his eyes searched hers for something—anything—but they just stared back, unblinking.

Those eyes of hers looked just like they would any other day, but Asa was beginning to realise it wasn't that they held no particular emotion in them. It was that they were guarded.

But that was okay. It was okay. Nothing time and effort couldn't mend.

"H-hi." Carmen blinked, obviously taken aback at running into him. But it was only a matter of seconds before she regained her composure, and then her hands came to rest on his hips as she straightened herself and found her footing.

Carmen stepped back, clearing her throat, as she removed her hands from his body, causing his to fall away from her waist too.

"Um." She tried to smile. "I went to the pool. Thought you'd be there cause it's a spare period."

"You went looking for me?" he asked with a tilt of his head, a fluttery feeling in his chest. She was here. Carmen was *here*. And that gaping hole in his chest didn't feel so hollow anymore. It still hurt, but in the most beautiful way possible—if that even made sense.

She nodded. "Yeah, I wanted to talk to you."

Asa offered her a small smile. "Good," he murmured. "I wanted to too."

He moved his hand behind him, feeling around for the doorknob without taking his eyes off her, eventually succeeding in getting the door open and pressing his back against it as he stepped aside to let Carmen in.

She walked past him, their torsos and arms brushing together for a fleeting second before the moment was gone and then she was inside the room, with Asa following right behind.

"Listen..." Asa sighed, sitting on the edge of one of the tables and scratching the back of his head. "About last week." His voice trailed off when he lifted his head and met Carmen's eyes.

Because it felt like—literally felt like—an eternity since he'd last seen her and the sudden overwhelming wave of affection and longing that hit him right then made him falter in his speech.

His chest swelled, feeling like it was about to combust with all the emotions blending into one gigantic knot there. But one emotion—*one single emotion*—stood out from the rest that were colliding into each other within him.

And it was that heartbreaking but also heart-mending emotion that made whatever he'd wanted to say slip away as he leant forward and wrapped his hand around Carmen's forearm.

Asa slid his hand down her arm slowly, feeling the smooth skin under his rough and calloused palm, stopping its descent only when he reached her wrist. He unwrapped his hand from around it and then laced his fingers through hers, before tugging her forward closer to him.

Carmen looked like she wanted to say something, but he watched her snap her mouth shut when he rested his forehead against hers. Asa lifted his other hand and ran his thumb along the apple of her cheek, feeling his breathing grow heavier.

"I'm sorry," he murmured, cupping her face with both hands and raising his chin to place a lingering, heartfelt kiss on her forehead. "I shouldn't have yelled." He winced at the memory, and then brushed the tip of his nose against hers. "I'm sorry."

"You're sorry?" Carmen frowned, blinking in confusion.

"Not for what the fight was about," he told her, a hesitant smile on his face. "But the way I approached the matter." He pressed his lips together, thinking through what he was about to say instead of letting his emotions get the better of him this time. "I just—that morning, I came

438

over to make sure you were doing okay, but then Hunter was there and everything else just flew out of my mind. I don't—I think I—I just felt cornered, I guess? It was like a sudden slap to the face, seeing him there, and the disbelief and anger took over my want to make sure you were all right…"

"Asa—"

He shook his head, wordlessly asking her to let him just say whatever he needed to say. "No, I just—I wanted to make sure you didn't feel like I was coming down too hard on you—or—or that I was pressurising you to tell me everything then and there. Because that wasn't my intention, you need to believe that. I wouldn't… wouldn't intentionally put you on the spot like that—"

"Those are all fixable things, Asa," Carmen muttered, averting her gaze.

"Yes." The word left Asa's mouth in a breath of immense relief because *yes yes yes* they were on the same page. "And we can do that, I know we can. So if you need time to start letting me in, then—then it's okay. It's okay. But just tell me that its time you need. Tell me that, and we can get through this, okay?"

He watched as Carmen's lips parted, that happy twinkle in her eye lighting up the way it did the night of the party and then again on the night of their date. He watched as her face softened and a smile began to form on her lips.

And then Asa also watched as the smile froze midway as if it was severed by a startling realisation. He watched as the tenderness in her expression morphed into a guarded one instead, and then saw that spark he'd ignited in her grey irises fade out and die.

That should've been the second red flag.

But hope was a dangerous thing, and Asa clung to it like it was a lifeboat instead.

Carmen's eyes filled with a tangible kind of sadness, and she closed them with a deep sigh, shaking her head that was nestled in Asa's hands. Then, ripping apart that lifeboat inside Asa into smithereens,

439

Carmen placed both her hands on each of Asa's and pulled them away from her face.

There was a sinking feeling in Asa's stomach but his grip on that lifeboat tightened. For a brief moment, he wondered if perhaps they weren't on the same page after all. If it was just him grasping at straws in the wind now.

"You're right," Carmen told him slowly, as if she was fighting to keep her voice steady and neutral. It disappointed Asa, that even now when they're trying to talk it out, she was masking her feelings.

But he pushed away the disappointment, reminding himself that this was probably new to her, that she needed to adjust to the whole notion of talking about what she was really feeling.

"I do need time with the whole letting-other-people-in issue…" Carmen's tone was cautious, as if she was weighing each word before they left her mouth, and Asa wanted to hug her, to tell her she didn't need to walk on eggshells around him of all people.

"Okay," Asa whispered, nodding his head while his lips stretched into a tiny, endearing smile. "Okay, Carmen. See, this is good. It's good. You're telling me what you want. That's all I could ask from you. That's all I needed you to say the morning after Thanksgiving."

But when he noticed the sadness in her eyes only grew heavier, it began to get harder to ignore those red flags.

"Asa," she struggled to say, her voice tight and pained, "Asa—we—that's not the problem. My need for time to open up completely isn't…it isn't where we went wrong." Carmen shook her head and took a step back. "That's not the problem," she repeated.

Asa's brows knitted, the *v* on his forehead becoming prominent as his confusion increased and his mind replayed every single second of their fight with utmost clarity.

"Is this about Hunter, then?" he asked quietly, turning his face the other way and pursing his lips for a while before he met her eyes again. "Because if it is, well, I—I can work on that. I'm not saying I can forgive him. But I can tone down on my hostility towards him when we're in your presence." Asa paused, looking down at his lap and scratching the rough material of his jeans near his kneecap. "That whole scene in the kitchen when you offered to walk Hunter to the door, that, uh, it won't happen again." He looked back up at her and shot her an apologetic, lopsided smile. "Well, at least I'll *try* to behave."

Carmen just stared at Asa, the look on her face being the *definition* of heartbreak as he watched her resolve to remain neutral and unfazed began to crumble.

"Carmen…?" he began worriedly, dread pooling in the pit of his stomach and leaving his bones cold at the same time.

She shook her head in response, as if she simply couldn't bring herself to speak yet. And when she did finally manage to find her voice, Asa wished he could un-hear the helplessness and remorse woven through every word that fell out of her mouth.

"That's not the problem either, Asa," she said in a voice that was barely above a whisper. And then something in her expression broke, and she squeezed her eyes shut, shaking her head repeatedly as apologies after apologies kept tumbling out her mouth uncontrollably.

"Oh my God," she was muttering frantically to herself. "What have I done? What have I *done*? I'm so sorry, I'm *so* sorry. I didn't —Asa, I'm so goddamn sorry—"

"Hey." Asa jumped off the table and moved towards her, placing his hands on her shoulders in worry. "Hey, look at me. Look at me." He took a hold of Carmen's chin but she still wouldn't meet his eyes. "*Mírame. Mírame*, Carmen."

Carmen grabbed Asa's hand which was cupping her chin, her fingers holding on to it so tight he wondered if their imprints would be left around his wrist. Her eyes met his, and the raw but unidentifiable emotion in them knocked the air out of Asa's lungs.

"I did something," Carmen told Asa in a barely audible voice, her breaths sounding laboured even to his own ears.

Asa frowned, tilting his head slightly to the right as he observed her. Why did she sound so scared and worried? There wasn't anything

441

truly terrible that Carmen could've done to elicit such a deep sense of remorse from her.

Whatever it was that she'd done, she was probably allowing her mind to make it seem worse than it actually was because Asa knew that at the end of the day, Carmen did what she did because she felt it was for the best. Her decisions were never selfish. Of that he was much certain .

"It's all right, *mi amor*," he said softly, running his other hand down the length of her hair comfortingly. "Nothing you did could be so bad that it'd be unforgivable in my eyes."

Her eyes grew the slightest bit watery at the edges, but Carmen seemed to have a stronger grip on her emotions this time around because she didn't cry. Not a single tear was shed, her resolve as unwavering as Asa's feelings for her.

Maybe that should've been the third flag. He was fighting to keep their relationship, while she was fighting to keep her composure.

"I didn't mean it," she eventually said, the words almost muffled by the choked tone of her voice.

Asa's frown deepened. "Didn't mean what?"

Carmen's chin shook in Asa's grip as her bottom lip trembled, causing the bubble of dread in his gut explode and trickle down his bones, flushing out any warmth that resided there.

"What I said that night." Carmen gulped, blinking back tears as she struggled to maintain her calm guise. "I shouldn't have said it... I—" Her voice cracked and she snapped her mouth shut, pressing her lips tightly together.

Asa's mind flashed back to the morning of their fight, trying to pinpoint anything Carmen had said that was possible of placing her in such obvious conflict. But nothing stood out to him as something she'd want to take back; nothing she'd said that day was so cruel that she'd apologise this profusely—

And then it hit Asa.

Carmen wasn't talking about the morning of the fight, was she?

"I shouldn't have said it that night."

442

Night.

What night was she referring to?

"Night?" He blinked, staring at her with a blank face.

Was it possible to see hearts break in the eyes of people? Because Asa thought he just saw Carmen's crack in the way her eyes filled with anguish.

"The night of the party," she explained, the words sounding as if she'd held her breath while speaking them.

What had she said during the best night of his life? What had she said that held so much significance that she now wanted to take those words back?

"Carmen." He smiled in confusion. "There was nothing you told me that night that you need to take back, okay? You didn't say anything wrong at all, nothing to apologise for regarding that party. It was perfect, *mi amor*. Perfect. Nothing you said or did back then had any problem."

Carmen's grip on Asa's wrist tightened, if that was even possible.

"Yes," she whispered, voice shaking as swallowed audibly. "Yes, it had."

Asa's brows pulled even closer together, and a small laugh left his mouth. "Love, trust me, you didn't say anything wrong during that party. I would remember, okay? I'd remember because I can recall every single millisecond of that night. How could I not? It was the night you told me you were in love with—"

The realisation slammed into Asa like a truck full of explosives, cutting off his oxygen, stopping his heart and shattering the ground beneath his feet, all within the blink of an eye.

Time could freeze, right? Didn't time have the ability to just *stop*? It had to, it just *had* to.

Because that's what it felt like to Asa right then.

Everything was so still; he would be able to pick up on the sound of a pin dropping to the floor.

But everything was also spinning. So did time really freeze? Because Asa was still frozen, and his mind was just utterly and hopelessly blank right then. But his eyes could still see Carmen's mouth moving, his wrist could still feel the pressure of her fingers, and Asa could definitely feel his heart breaking, breaking, breaking.

It wasn't the kind of heartbreak where it just snapped into two or three. No, Asa felt his heart crack right in the middle and felt those cracks slowly spread over his heart until it was only a web of raw hurt and agony.

Then he felt pieces of his heart begin to crumble—piece by little piece breaking away and falling to the shaky ground beneath his feet.

"I love you too, you know." Carmen had said that, hadn't she?

"I'm here, Asa. I'm here, with you, and I'm telling you that my heart is yours for the taking." She'd said that, she had. Those were her words. *Hers.*

Carmen had to have meant them. You wouldn't tell someone you loved them unless you meant it. That kind of cruelty wasn't something Carmen West was capable of. No. Asa refused to believe that. Then why was she saying she wanted to take back what she'd said?

"Asa." Carmen's voice sounded like it was coming from behind a wall partition, like it was something familiar but foreign at the same time. Something Asa had known but no longer recognised.

Asa couldn't respond. Everything was spinning. But everything was so still.

"Asa." Her voice was louder this time, and he felt a tug at his wrist.

The reminder of the physical contact sliced through him and his hand that was caressing her hair fell limply to his side. Asa let go of her chin, feeling like his fingers were set on fire at the touch and tried pulling his hand from her grasp.

Carmen's grip only grew more firm as Asa stepped back, his breath suddenly coming in harsh gasps. He put more force into his actions before managing to yank his arm back from her hold.

Disbelief. Hurt. Denial. And an ocean of emotions he'd never be able to name crashed over him in a single monstrous wave, causing him to stumble backwards.

"Asa?" Her voice was becoming clearer to him now, and he could detect the plea in it. "Asa, say something. Please."

But all Asa was capable of in that moment was to shake his head slowly to himself and stare at her with confused, horrified eyes.

'I don't care if you never say it back to me. When I tell you I love you, I say it because I do. Not because I'm expecting something in return."

Asa had told her that seconds after he'd told her he was in love with her, right here in this very room.

He'd told her he never expected for her to say it back. So why did she when she never meant it?

"Asa, you need to unders—"

"I told you that I didn't tell you I was in love with you just so that you could say it back someday." The words were leaving Asa's mouth, but he didn't feel like he was the one currently occupying his body.

"I know," Carmen said in a small voice.

"I told you that I just wanted you to know that you are loved," he continued, but the voice didn't belong to him. "You were the one who told me that you'll say it back to me one day."

Carmen's expression crumpled, dissolving into one of fear and guilt. "I know," she whispered, never taking her eyes off Asa.

"And even then, I never asked you when exactly you were planning on saying it back. I was content with the fact that you actually wanted to do so in the future."

"Asa, I'm s—"

"Don't," he cut her off, shaking his head. "Don't tell me you're sorry. I'm sick of hearing you say those two words." Asa's hand fumbled around for his bag, fingers trembling. "Your words mean nothing to me," he whispered, too stunned to speak any louder. "Not after this. Not anymore."

"Asa," she choked out. "Asa, please. Let me explain at least? I didn't do it to hurt you, I didn't. I'd found something that felt really good and I just didn't want to lose it—"

"But you've lost me now," Asa's voice remained a whisper, his head swimming while everything else around him remained still and composed. "If you had never said it back, maybe it would've stung a little at first, but it would definitely have passed. I would've been okay. But this." He kept shaking his head as his hand finally landed on his bag and held on to it as tight as humanly possible. "You—you told me. You told me you loved me. Why would you—why?"

Carmen's eyes were pleading as they looked into his. "I know my words don't mean anything to you anymore." Her voice sounded broken. "But it wasn't all a lie, Asa. I had strong feelings for you, I *still* do. It just wasn't love yet. I lost myself in how good and real it felt that before I could fall in love with you, I fell in love with the fact that you loved me instead. That's where the problem was: I couldn't give you what someone only in love with you would be able to."

Was that even the truth? Asa didn't know—not anymore. He could no longer recognise the person standing in front of him. He wouldn't stop shaking his head, not willing to listen, believe, digest that he was the only one in love this whole time.

Reality didn't make sense anymore.

"Asa?" Carmen asked tentatively. "Please say something. Yell at me. Shout. Please. I'd take the yelling and the screaming, but don't stay silent. Please."

She wasn't in love with me. She wasn't in love with me. She wasn't in love with me, Asa thought.

Carmen West wasn't in love with him.

This was worse than unrequited love. This was the person you were irrevocably in love with telling you they loved you back and then ripping that sacredness away.

"Asa, just say anything—"

"I hate you," he whispered.

Carmen recoiled, her entire body moving back as if she was physically pushed by an unseen force.

"Don't say that." She shook her head, a horrified expression on her face. "Please don't say that to me."

Asa walked backwards, the last few pieces of his heart drifting down to the floor where a hundred different feet would walk over them someday.

He didn't take his eyes off her as his hand moved towards the door, searching for the knob.

He found it the same instant he heard the last bell of the day ring, a brutal reminder that the rest of the world was still going on. Time was still ticking and the universe didn't stop for Asa to learn how to breathe again.

"But I have to hate you, Carmen," he told her in a pained voice. "Because if I don't start hating you, then I'll go on loving you—" Asa's voice broke and he turned around, vision blurring with unshed tears, "—and I don't want to love you. Not anymore. It hurts too much."

And then Asa was running out of there, away from the hurricane that was Carmen West, out into the cold December air, and towards his truck—where he'd no longer find sanctuary but the ghost of a girl with midnight hair and thundercloud eyes haunting the empty passenger seat.

56.
Breaking Free

They never tell you about boys like Asa San Román.

People always warned you about the heartbreaker who was constantly looking for the next girl to damage, or the one who was only interested in your body and a good time, or the one who had a superiority complex.

But they never told you about boys like Asa.

The kind that didn't do half measures, the kind that believed in giving all or nothing, the kind that knew what he wanted and wasn't afraid to fight for it even if he was going to be the only one fighting. The kind who gave and gave and gave without asking what the other person was willing to offer.

The kind that when he loved, he let himself fall hook, line and sinker.

The kind that eventually realised there was poverty in allowing his heart to give pieces of itself away too many times.

The kind who one day said enough, and then plucked his presence out of your life, leaving coldness where he'd once brought warmth.

The kind that loved you too much, that the only way he knew how to cope after losing you was to turn all that love into hate.

And Asa now hated her.

He had been the embodiment of the sun's warmth, and Carmen had let herself soak in it for as long as she was able to until she decided to leave, taking all that warmth with her and turning the place he'd used to occupy in her life cold.

Asa's absence was cold in the way he never met Carmen's eyes in the hallways, in the way they would walk past each other with the faintest brush of their arms as if they were nothing but strangers walking in opposite directions.

As if his laugh wasn't Carmen's favourite sound, as if his voice wasn't one that she'd recognise anywhere, as if every time she caught herself staring all she'd hear in her head was a breathless *"mi amor mi cielo mi sol"* followed by a pained *"I hate you I hate you I hate you."*

Carmen didn't know how to describe it, that feeling in the pit of her stomach when she had to catch herself before heading towards his locker, or before she'd accidentally think of winding her arms around his neck and kissing him on the jaw.

She didn't know what to name that disturbing knot in her chest every time she couldn't do something, because she needed to remind herself they were strangers now.

Strangers who'd once been intimates.

Strangers who knew the feel of their bodies pressed so hard against each other that they would've moulded into one. Strangers who knew the taste of each other's lips, who knew how their fingers had found home getting tangled in each other's hair.

Strangers who knew the warmth of each other's embrace, who knew one's obsession with the season of autumn and the other's love for Harry Potter. Strangers who knew one's love for art and the other's addiction to ice cream.

They'd been strangers once before, but it only hurt this time around—which begged the question: what was really meant when someone called someone else a stranger?

Did they mean *"Oh, I've never met them before, but I think they're in my Calculus class"?–* or did they mean *"I used to know them, used to think they were a forever love, but we can't be in each other's presence now"?*

Carmen didn't want to be a stranger in Asa's eyes, but he'd been selfless for so long that if making her a stranger was what he wanted, then she needed to accept that he had all right to do that one thing for himself.

•   •   •

The rest of the month didn't fly past.

It took its time, the sun rising all too fast so that Carmen couldn't lose herself to the comforts of sleep and the moon embracing the sky excruciatingly slow so that the hours in between dragged on forever.

By the time New Year's Eve rolled around, Carmen's mind had gained some sort of clarity. She was ready to accept the fact that she couldn't do the healing process alone. She needed help. Help that she was pretty sure her father himself wasn't in the best position to offer.

She'd spent the better half of the last two weeks weighing the pros and cons of deciding to get therapy, and honestly, it all boiled down to one thing: the simple fact that Carmen was going to need to open up to a stranger, someone who she wasn't supposed to form an emotional attachment with because they were only going to be temporary. Someone who was going to be gone once Carmen was better and ready to fight her battles by herself.

But she knew she was strong enough to take the next step. She knew she had it in her, and truthfully speaking, Carmen wanted to stop living in the past because the present kept slipping through her fingers, and it kept altering her future with each moment she missed.

She needed to get back some control of where her life was heading. But it wasn't just going to come to her, was it? She needed to fight for herself, for that hopeful future.

It stung to know that Asa wouldn't be a part of that future, but Carmen tried not to dwell on it too much. Because if she did, all she'd feel was guilt and a tugging at her heartstrings that she wasn't able to understand.

450

A loud bang from the kitchen snapped Carmen out of her reverie, and she sighed from where she was lying sprawled out lazily on the sofa.

"Try not to break everything in there!" Carmen called out, shaking her head and reaching forward to grab the TV remote. Her father had to get a new one because she'd chucked and broken the older remote at the wall next to Hunter's head after Thanksgiving.

"The things in the kitchen just never cooperate with me!" Hunter yelled back, sounding aggravated.

"That's probably because you've never let yourself be acquainted with the kitchen!" Carmen flicked through the channels, all of them playing some sort of New Year's special movie.

The smell of popcorn wafted over to where Carmen was, and she looked up just as Hunter kicked her legs off the couch to make room for himself, holding a large glass bowl in his hands.

"It's not my fault my father has a whole army of helpers to take care of everything in the house," Hunter said, seating himself next to Carmen as she herself got into a sitting position and crossed her legs on the couch. "They look at me like I'm a nuisance every time I try stepping into the kitchen."

"Yes, it must be terrible to have someone do everything for you." Carmen laughed lightly, digging into the popcorn and grabbing a handful.

Hunter was quiet for a while before he responded, "When you have enough people who you've never seen before come and go…well, home just stops feeling like home, you know? It's as if—as if *I'm* the outsider there, if that makes sense."

Carmen offered him a soft smile. "It makes perfect sense."

Hunter was about to smile back, but then he just rolled his eyes and leant back into the cushions. "Yeah, yeah, that's more than my dose of deep conversation for one night." He snatched the remote from her grasp and began looking for something good to watch.

She sighed and reached for another handful of popcorn, wondering if her father was having a pleasant enough time at his colleague's New Year's Eve dinner party. They'd both planned to go together, but Carmen had had a change of mind at the last minute, suddenly craving to just stay back home and take a break from the outside world.

Her dad had offered to stay back too, but it wouldn't have been the best thing for the two of them to cancel at the last minute, and besides, this was the first time Carmen could remember her father actually feeling ready to mingle with a group of people so she had wanted him to go. It didn't matter that he wasn't with her right then. It meant more than she could ever say that he was actually willing to stay back and spend the night with her. It was more effort than she'd ever seen from his side in a really long while.

"There's nothing good going on," Hunter muttered, tossing the remote onto the coffee table in front of the couch. "We should just binge-watch *Daredevil* like I suggested."

"I'm not into TV shows." Carmen frowned, speaking through a mouthful of popcorn and earning a disgusted look from Hunter which she just ignored.

"You'll like this one, trust me," he told her and then suddenly knitted his eyebrows together as if something occurred to him just then. "You know, whenever I watch it, the dude sort of reminds me of San Román."

"Asa," Carmen corrected, feeling that tug at her heartstrings again. "He hates being called by his surname."

Hunter grinned. "I know."

Carmen averted her gaze, focusing on filling her palms with another helping of popcorn. "Why, uh, why does watching it remind you of him?"

"Don't know." He shrugged. "Must be the whole saviour thing. Dude can't turn a blind eye to injustice, can he?" And then Hunter's expression darkened. "Perfect little Asa."

452

Silence fell over them and Carmen's hand froze, before she inhaled deeply and let the popcorn fall back into the bowl.

"Don't do that," she muttered, looking Hunter directly in the eyes.

"What?" His blank stare was fixed on the television screen, but Carmen could tell he wasn't paying attention to what was playing.

"Belittle him that way," she said, her voice firm. "Mock him. Don't do that. He's got his flaws too. He's aggressive and he can be a hothead sometimes. He tends to let hate get to him a lot, likes to speak with his fists whenever he can, but at the end of the day, his heart is always in the right place. And that doesn't make him perfect. It just makes him a better person than either one of us."

At the last part, Hunter's gaze fell on her and something in them softened. "Don't lower yourself to the same level as me," he said quietly. "You made a bad choice in telling him you were in love with him when you weren't and letting him believe that you were ready for a relationship, but that doesn't make you anything like me, Carmen. Don't let yourself think like that."

Carmen just stared back at him before dropping her eyes and grabbing some popcorn. "Yeah, well, he hates you, and now he hates me too. We're on the same level in his eyes."

"I'm sorry," Hunter said after a while, frowning slightly as he observed her.

"Don't be." She sighed. "If I had let it go on any longer—"

"Not about the way things ended," Hunter interrupted her, shaking his head. "But for the part I played in putting you in a position where you needed to look for love in someone else."

A frown crawled over Carmen's face at that, the tugging in her chest growing painful now. Something about the way it was worded didn't seem right. She hadn't *looked* for love in Asa, had she? It hadn't been like that.

"I didn't have to look for love when it came to him, you know," she looked down at her hands, greasy fingers playing with each other, "it

453

was just *there*. As if he was just saving it all for me and wasn't shy about showering me with it whenever he could."

Hunter's eyes narrowed, and he cocked his head to the side as if analysing her. "You have feelings for him," he stated, not really questioning it.

Carmen's eyes snapped to him in surprise. "Of course I do. Why on earth would you think otherwise?"

His mouth turned down in confusion. "So…can't you—can't you just ask him to wait 'till you're ready to begin a relationship?"

"After everything that I've done, do you really think he's going to believe a word that I say?" Carmen shook her head, turning away and staring into space. "It's one thing to not tell someone you're in love with them when they've said it to you. But to say it back and then tell them you never meant it? No, Hunter, I can't. I can't ask any more of him. Time is all that he's given me, and I just proved to him he put all that effort and trust in someone who didn't deserve an ounce of it. He has all right to feel the way he's feeling now."

"But he's in love with you."

"It'll fade," Carmen muttered, feeling her chest squeeze, "It has to."

Hunter let out a short laugh. "Is that what you're hoping for, Carmen? That your feelings will fade?"

She pressed her lips tightly together, not looking at him. "Yes," she eventually replied. "It will."

Through her peripheral vision, she saw Hunter place the bowl from his lap onto the coffee table and then turn around sideways so that he was completely facing her. "And what if it doesn't?" he challenged, his eyes drilling holes into the side of her head. "I'm not good with all this couple shit, but I'm smart enough to know there's an alternative to every situation. So, tell me then, what if your feelings don't fade? What if it just grows, Carmen? Because that can happen, right? Once you're in a better place than you are in right now—"

454

"I thought you said you were done with heavy topics for tonight."

"Shut up," he snapped, making Carmen flinch but before she could say anything else, he was speaking again, his tone merciless and harsh. "Don't try to shut me out when I talk about something you don't like hearing! I had thought that you'd have learnt your lesson about pushing people away by now, especially since it cost you the possible love of your life."

Carmen froze, the air leaving her lungs at the brutality of his words and that icy tone he'd just used on her, causing her to just blink at him in stunned silence. Something must have shown on Carmen's face though, because Hunter's demeanour instantly softened and regret flashed across his face.

"Hey," he murmured, shifting closer. "I didn't—it wasn't supposed to come out sounding like that, okay? I'm, I'm sorry—it's just…" he trailed off and Carmen watched him struggle, jaw clenching and relaxing again and again until he just sighed heavily. "This is new. Trying to be supportive—just being there for you… Being civil towards you—it still feels like a dream sometimes and I'm just. I'm still getting used to it."

And maybe Carmen did get it because how long had Hunter spent hidden behind his walls? Behind a hard as steel exterior? And, now, here he was, trying to be soft for her, trying to soften *himself*.

After a long moment, Carmen just exhaled softly and relaxed against the cushions. "Its fine," she mumbled. "I just don't want to think about the alternative, that's all."

"Well." He shrugged. "I'm going to make you think about it anyway. Because you convincing yourself of something not going to happen, doesn't mean it won't happen, Carmen."

"Don't," she said quietly, the word falling past her lips in a plea as her eyes closed momentarily. "Please don't. I know you're trying to help, but I just need you to be here for me, okay? None of that tough love right now. I just want you to be here, that's all. Just this once."

455

Hunter seemed to debate with himself before his shoulders slumped in defeat, and he sank into the couch. "All right, Carmen," he said softly. "I'm here. You've got me."

Carmen's eyes opened, and she met Hunter's blue ones that, for once, didn't look like a frozen river but a gentle sea. "Thank you," she murmured, shooting him the tiniest of smiles.

But even after Carmen closed her eyes again to welcome sleep, it was a pair of coffee-coloured ones that stared right back at her in the darkness.

And in that darkness, she heard it: *"mi amor mi cielo mi sol"*.

And like a loyal shadow, the rest followed.

"I hate you. I hate you. I hate you".

•   •   •

Somewhere along the first week of January, Carmen found herself seated on a rather comfortable sofa, not that it did much to ease her nervousness.

The small room was decorated in soft tones: cream walls, two identical sofas of a very light shade of grey with cream-coloured throw pillows on them that were separated by a small round coffee table.

The window on the wall towards Carmen's left had a white frame, with white curtains swaying gently and brushing against the tiny flower pots that sat on the ledge at the bottom of the glass.

She didn't know what an office of a therapist was supposed to look like, but she figured this was good enough. It did feel somewhat cosy after all.

"So, Carmen," the woman sitting on the other identical couch opposite Carmen spoke. "What brings you here?"

Gloria Jacobs was a thin, wiry woman but quite tall too—just not so much that it came off as intimidating. She had skin that reminded Carmen of dark chocolate, and her eyes were just as rich, almost fading into black. Her dark hair with caramel lowlights was pulled back into a bun, with a few loose strands framing the side of her long, oval face.

"Carmen?"

"Sorry," Carmen mumbled, feeling flustered. "I—uh, I spaced out for a moment there. What was it that you asked again?"

Gloria smiled pleasantly. "What brings you here, to my office?"

"I don't know." The words left Carmen's mouth before she could think them through, but it was pretty obvious to both of them in that room that she was lying, that she did know why she wanted to be there.

Gloria relaxed into her seat, left leg folded over the right one and her hands resting atop one another above the armrest of the sofa.

"You don't know?" Gloria's tone was like everything else about her: dainty and laid-back and like she was in no hurry to get anywhere.

When Carmen realised that her tongue wouldn't move, that everything that she'd planned on saying once she got here had frozen somewhere down her throat, she pressed her lips together in a firm line and dug her fingers into the cushion she was sitting on.

Open up, Carmen. Tell this woman. Tell a complete stranger about twelve years of torment, about almost eighteen years of pain and guilt, she told herself.

"Okay, Carmen." Gloria nodded once. "Can you tell me what changed? What made you decide to come for therapy now?"

Carmen's brows furrowed, and the wheels in her head began spinning, thoughts racing each other like mini rockets in her head.

Why had she decided to get help only now? Was it shame that had prevented her this whole time? Why *now*? What was it that made her decide enough was enough? That she needed to flush out the poison her past had left behind?

"I—I found someone," Carmen told her, tone uncertain and shaky but Gloria wasn't frowning or looking at her oddly so Carmen went on. "Someone from my past. They—they came back into my life, and I think—well, certain memories came back with them too. And it's getting harder to just sweep it all under the rug, I guess."

"And this is what made you decide to come here? This certain someone was the trigger?"

457

"No," Carmen whispered, her sight becoming unfocused as she stared off into nothingness. No, that couldn't be right. Hunter had been back into her life for quite a while now, and yes, his sudden reappearance did remind her of times they spent together in the Rutherford mansion, but she hadn't thought about letting herself heal then.

So, what was it?

"Thanksgiving?" Carmen's frown deepened, noticing that her response sounded more like a question than a direct answer.

Gloria seemed to find that particularly interesting. She leant forward slightly and narrowed her eyes in the most subtle manner—the gesture was so discreet that Carmen would've missed it if it weren't for the fact that she was focusing on every single movement—even the slightest twitch—of this woman.

"What about Thanksgiving, Carmen?"

"Horrible," she answered, spitting out the first word that came to her mind. "It was when everything changed. When everything I tried so hard to push back to the furthest corner of my mind, it just...everything just exploded, I guess."

"Okay, Carmen." Gloria offered her a pleasant smile again. It was the only way Carmen knew how to describe her smile: pleasant. "Is that what you want me to help you with? You want to stop pushing away things that you find...horrible?"

Carmen's eyes snapped to hers, confusion creasing her forehead. "You're not going to ask me about Thanksgiving?"

Gloria smiled again and gave a small shake of her head. "We'll get there, don't worry. Right now, we're still in our first session. So, tell me. What is it that you hope to get out of all this?"

That was one answer Carmen didn't need to think about; it was why she'd come after all. "I want to be able to let people in," she said tentatively. "To just be able to get along with people better, whether with peers, or...or even form actual friendships. To just—just be able to *connect*."

458

And so, it went. Simple but probing questions were thrown here and there while Carmen did most of the talking, trying to explain over her jittery nerves and racing heartbeats, almost to the point where her words tripped over each other and she had to get a hold of herself before proceeding with her response.

Carmen was certain it hadn't taken too long, but when their time was up, it almost felt like she'd spent an eternity in that room.

Did it always feel this way? *Would* it always feel this way? Because it seemed sort of silly, being here and talking to someone she didn't know about her issues.

Carmen also felt kind of stupid, really. What if Gloria had tended to people with much severe problems? What if she thought Carmen was just lost and making her life seem more suffocating than it actually was?

"Carmen?" Gloria called, looking at her with shrewd eyes. "Is there something on your mind?"

Carmen opened her mouth, then closed it, only to open it and shut it again. "I—uh," she hesitated, "well, I was wondering if—I know it's still our first session and it's too soon to tell—but—but do you think I could get better? Make actual progress?"

Gloria didn't answer right away, but when she did finally respond, that small pleasant smile was gracing her lips again. "I think that you know *why* it is that you're here—what it is that you're hoping to get out of our time together. And that's good. Quite good, actually."

Carmen smiled then, feeling something inside her start to crumble, not in the manner where she could feel everything inside her break and fall apart, but in the sense that something within was breaking free.

And she couldn't remember the last time she'd felt such genuine, soul-satisfying hope.

57.
Ghosts From The Past

Asa smiled at the camera, the forced gesture hurting his cheeks and the flash blinding him momentarily.

"Perfect!" Lyra squealed, grinning so wide that Asa found it miraculous her face didn't split open.

"That's the sixth attempt of yours to take a selfie of us," Asa remarked dryly, watching as Lyra's fingers swept across her phone's screen, trying to decide on a filter.

"Haven't you heard?" She grinned, eyes still fixed on the device, "sixth time's the charm."

Asa snorted. "You mean third time's the ch—"

"Oh, can you not rain on my parade?" She shot him an annoyed glare before going back to upload the photo on one of her social media accounts with the tag #EighteenthBirthdayBash, causing Asa to roll his eyes.

"If I remember correctly, this is *my* parade," he told her with a raised brow. "Which, by the way, you weren't supposed to organise because I told Wyatt and Hayden I wasn't exactly up for any celebrations."

Lyra closed down the app she was using and turned the phone's screen off before tucking it into her back pocket and frowning up at Asa. "You know, everyone here's having a good time but the birthday boy himself," she commented.

Asa sighed, eyes sweeping over all the nameless people dancing to the deafening music reverberating throughout Lyra's house, plastic red cups being passed around every other minute or so.

This used to be his kind of scene. Once. But it no longer held the same allure.

"Well," he paused. "Thanks for going through all the trouble to throw this whole thing on my behalf." He offered Lyra a tight smile and walked around her, heading towards the balcony upstairs in a sudden need for fresh air.

When Asa finally managed to squeeze his way through the crowd and sneak into the balcony, he noticed there were water droplets scattered all over the wooden railings. His eyes flickered upwards on instinct and watched as it continued to drizzle, the breeze occasionally spraying some of the raindrops his way.

Did Carmen like the rain?

Asa had never got around to asking her that, and now he wished he had.

He supposed she wouldn't. After all, she enjoyed walks, didn't she? She loved visiting the local parks and just sitting there. And the rain would've been more of a hindrance in her eyes.

But then again, Carmen probably wouldn't mind it too much. She loved nature just as it was, didn't she? She would have continued to love it: heat, rain or snow. She had always been so ready to walk during the chilly weather without so much as a sweater, that he was certain she would gladly do so even while the sky was pouring down from above her too.

That seemed more like Carmen, always ready and willing to accept things as they were without wanting to change a single element.

Asa wondered why she couldn't love herself as much as she loved everything else around her.

A strong gust of wind blew past, spraying some of the rain right into his eyes and ruffling his hair. Asa blinked, his vision becoming slightly blurry before he rubbed the raindrops from his eyes and looked down at Lyra's front lawn with a clearer sight.

461

A girl squealed, drawing Asa's attention, and he watched as she ran down the grass, with her friend yelling something from behind, both of them running to take shelter under the veranda as the rain grew heavier, no longer a drizzle now.

Asa wondered if Carmen would be the kind of girl who ran away from the shelter and towards the rain instead.

He could see her doing something like that. He could also see himself following her into the downpour, not really too bothered about getting soaked. He just wanted to see that spark of life in Carmen's eyes and her lips stretch into a carefree smile.

Asa also found himself wondering what it would've have been like if she was here now. He wondered what it would've been like to grab her hand and lead her to the lawn, to stand down there on the grass and kiss her in the rain.

Stop it, he chided himself. *Stop thinking of Carmen. You're supposed to hate her. So hate her.*

An aggravated sigh left his mouth.

"Bailing on your own party?" He heard Wyatt chuckle from behind him. "That's new."

"Well," Asa shot him a sideways glance as Wyatt stepped into the space next to him, "technically, its Lyra's party. And Hayden's. And yours. I didn't know about it until tonight."

Wyatt huffed, shoulders slumping slightly in defeat. "Yeah, we thought it was worth a shot."

"A shot at what?" Asa asked curiously.

"Providing you with some form of distraction," Wyatt replied, scratching the back of his head sheepishly.

Asa blinked. "I don't need any distractions."

Wyatt snorted. "Of course not. Swimming seems to be doing that for you."

"What do you mean?" Asa turned to face him fully, mouth pulling down into a frown at the corners.

"Just that you've been throwing yourself into it a lot lately. A lot more than usual, that is. You spend every single spare period in the pool, and then on the weekends, you're busy at that local swimming club." Wyatt lifted a shoulder in a half-shrug. "Don't you want to catch a break or something?"

"Nope." The response was quick, just like all of Asa's conversations were now: flat, ingenuine and no thrill of trying to read between the lines.

Wyatt sighed and was about to say something when his expression suddenly brightened and he grinned at Asa. "Wanna go get ice cream?"

And despite himself, Asa's lips curved into a smile. "Ditch the party? Hayden and Lyra would kill us."

Wyatt's grin only seemed to widen. "That's the icing on the cake for you."

Asa laughed, before stopping suddenly and shooting Wyatt a confused smile. "Wait, what's the cake then?"

"The privilege of my presence, obviously."

Asa snorted, lifting his hand to slap the back of Wyatt's head before shaking with silent, affectionate laughter, and then they were sneaking out of Lyra's house, climbing into Asa's truck and driving down the rainy streets.

Once they'd found a good enough ice cream parlour, Asa and Wyatt walked back out, each carrying a waffle cone that had three layers of ice cream, all in different flavours of their own pickings.

Wyatt got into the driver's seat this time around, telling Asa he should just enjoy the object of his obsession without being bothered to keep an eye on the road at the same time.

Asa laughed, his first genuinely carefree and unrepressed laugh in what felt like forever, but got into the passenger seat nevertheless, because he indeed would rather enjoy his treat than be distracted with the task of driving.

Conversation flowed easily between them, and then the topic switched to swimming and the upcoming meet.

"Coach is going crazy, man." Wyatt chuckled. "He's driving us insane too."

"Well, obviously." Asa sighed contently, too engrossed in the ice cream to be thinking of anything else. "It's his last year at the school, isn't it? He's retiring after our batch graduates."

"I know," Wyatt muttered. "I don't want to let him down either. Now that you and Carson are officially off the participants list, he's been on my back every single day."

There was that bittersweet throbbing in his chest again at the reminder of what he lost, but Asa also felt an odd sense of peace at the fact that it wasn't eating away at him the way it initially had.

"Don't worry about it," Asa said, shooting Wyatt a look and then knitting his brows together. "You know, I may not be able to take part in it but I *can* help you."

Wyatt's face lit up with that megawatt grin of his. "Yeah? That'd be perfect, man. Thanks."

"Don't mention it..." The words died in Asa's throat, and whatever feeling of content he'd just been experiencing—any ounce of bliss he'd just had—faded away and left a trail of coldness in its wake. Wyatt had turned into a street that would get them away from any traffic, and Asa recognised it as the one that Carmen and he had walked along to get to the parking lot from the self-service ice cream parlour on the night of their date.

Asa's eyes searched desperately for a particular lamppost amongst the row of them dotting the sidewalk and there it was. *There it was.*

The lamppost that kept flickering on and off over and over again (unlike the other ones that operated perfectly), emitting a sort of buzzing noise each time the bulb went off and came back on.

The lamppost that he'd kissed Carmen under.

And then his eyes trailed down the path, and he could see it now: the moment from their night materialising right in front of his eyes like he'd been standing from the outside back then and watching it happen instead of taking part in it himself.

There they were—Carmen and Asa—with their arms wound around each other, sharing quick kisses as they tried to get to his truck without tripping over each other's feet and stumbling to the ground.

He could hear it now: her giggles dissolving into his light chuckles and then the sound was gone, getting carried away with the wind, never to come back again.

The ice cream turned to sand in Asa's mouth, and just like that, the hollow feeling in his chest returned.

•   •   •

"Something happened today," Carmen told Gloria during one of their sessions with a bounce in her knee, feeling sort of accomplished about what had happened.

Gloria's smile widened, seeming to pick up on Carmen's good mood. "Yeah?"

Carmen nodded, feeling at ease with herself after the many weeks she'd sat on this very couch, in this very room. "I, uh, well, there's this girl—her name's Joyce. I've known her since sophomore year but every time she's tried reaching out, I just shut her down, you know. Her birthday invitations, sleepovers or just an afternoon of hanging out."

"And you accepted it this time?"

"No." Carmen's lips twitched and then a smile broke out on her face. "I *made* the offer this time. I asked her if she would like to go watch a movie or something."

"That's great, Carmen." Gloria nodded approvingly. "Really great."

Carmen smiled softly, then looked down at her hands. "She's, she's nice. A good person, I suppose. I think she was surprised I was making the first move to actually be more than peers, to be something like friends."

"You're making an effort, that's what counts."

Carmen merely shrugged in response, humming softly.

"Carmen?" Gloria's voice broke the brief spell of silence that'd fallen over them.

"Yeah?"

"Why do you fidget so much with that necklace you wear? I've noticed you always reach for it when you're anxious or uncomfortable."

Carmen didn't respond, not right away at least. She didn't think anyone would actually ask her that.

"Um," she began, and then paused to collect her thoughts. "It belonged to my mother. It—it reminds me to hold on. That no matter how bad things get, I need to keep holding on."

The older woman's eyes narrowed slightly as she observed Carmen for a few seconds. "Hold on to what, Carmen?" Gloria then asked. "Do you use the necklace to hold on to yourself? Or to your past?"

Carmen averted her gaze. "What difference does it make?"

"All the difference," Gloria told her. "Holding onto yourself means using your own self as an anchor, letting yourself believe that you alone are enough to pull through something, but holding onto your past is allowing your misfortunes to define you. If so, then that necklace is no longer an anchor, is it?"

"No," Carmen whispered, throat tightening. "No, it becomes dead weight."

Gloria smiled. "So why do you hold onto the necklace?"

"I guess it...It reminds me of all the pain. I want it to be a reminder that I survived all these years, but whenever I look at it, all I do is remember the bad."

"Maybe sometimes you can't change things, Carmen," Gloria said softly. "Did you ever consider that? That maybe the necklace won't become an anchor, but it'll always remain a dead weight?"

"You think I should get rid of it?"

"Do you *want* to get rid of it?"

"I want to be happy."

466

"And what does that mean to you, Carmen? What does being happy mean?"

Carmen's eyes flickered towards the window to her left, watching as raindrops raced each other down the glass, blurring the view of the streets outside it would've otherwise provided her.

"Being able to let the good things in, I guess," Carmen murmured eventually, sighing as she relaxed into the cushions. "And learning how to let go of all that brings me down."

"So, what's the problem, Carmen?"

Carmen's stomach knotted, her breath faltering as it hit her again and again and again like a punch to the gut. "I'm supposed to let in the good things," she said in a low voice, regret lacing every word.

"Yes…" Gloria frowned, looking at her curiously.

"There was something good I'd found, something that genuinely made me happy…" Carmen's heart paused, then resumed, stopped, then restarted all over again as the sudden realisation struck her like an arrow to the chest. "And I—I didn't know how to let it in… So I let it go instead."

●　　　●　　　●

January came to an end a little faster than Carmen expected and for that, she felt a little grateful. But it also meant that Gloria had to always keep the window shut now, because unlike the on-and-off drizzles in the previous month, February brought with it a constant downpour.

"Tell me about the boy."

That threw Carmen off guard, and it took her a good two minutes to regain her composure as she stared at Gloria with hesitancy in her demeanour.

"My cousin?" Carmen asked, all the while knowing exactly who it was Gloria was referring to. And that it most definitely *wasn't* Hunter.

"No, not him. You told me he was your Achilles' Heel, one of your weakest points." Gloria's dark eyes examined Carmen's face for a fleeting moment. "I want you to tell me about the other one, the one who you said was a source of strength."

467

"I don't see the point in me talking about him. He's not the problem here."

Gloria smiled, her eyes patient and knowing. "You wouldn't be here if you knew exactly what your problems were, would you?"

Carmen huffed, a panicky feeling washing over her. She didn't want to talk about Asa. She *couldn't*.

And that was exactly how she knew she *should* talk about him. But her lips remained shut, sewn together with threads made of steel.

"Why don't you like talking about him, Carmen?"

"There's nothing to talk about," she replied matter-of-factly.

Gloria lifted both her brows at that. "No? That's interesting, considering it took losing him for you to decide to get help."

Carmen's eyes tore away from watching the heavy shower outside and snapped to Gloria's, her breath hitching.

"No, it isn't. I'm here because of what happened at Thanksgiving."

A soft sigh left Gloria's mouth and she leant back in her seat, cupping her chin as she peered at Carmen.

"I thought we've been through this Carmen," she said gently, but her voice still managed to be firm, not allowing Carmen to find a way out of this conversation. "*Yes*, you let in everything that you'd kept buried about your past after what happened at Thanksgiving. And *yes*, that was what made you realise you needed to talk about it to someone like me, but you didn't take that step, did you? Even after that night, you didn't tell your dad you were thinking of getting help."

Carmen shook her head, fingers playing with each other as she felt a lump rise in her throat. "No," she said hoarsely.

"So what *did* finally make you take the next step? What made you realise you didn't want to go living like that for the rest of your life?"

Carmen's vision blurred and that lump in her throat grew to the point that it became quite painful. "Losing him," she choked out. "Losing Asa made me decide enough was enough."

"So, tell me then, Carmen." Gloria's tone was gentler this time. "If he was an important person to you that losing him was a wakeup call, do you really believe there's nothing to talk about when it comes to him?"

"No," Carmen mumbled, then surprising herself and Gloria too, she suddenly cracked a smile. "I could go on talking about him, to be honest."

Gloria tilted her head to the side. "Is that why you're here? For him?"

Carmen's smile faded, and she knitted her brows together really hard, feeling her stomach coil into a tight ball before the truth dawned on her. Clarity uncoiled the knot in her stomach, easing her nerves and allowing Carmen's lips to form a peaceful, self-content smile.

"No," she said softly, but decisively. "No, I'm here for *me*. I want to get better. I don't want to live in the constant fear of losing someone and cutting off everyone I meet from my life before I've even given them a chance. Just because there's a possibility that they may get close enough to hurt me."

"And is that why you let him go? Because you were scared he might one day hurt you?"

Carmen's lips twisted into a frown, her forehead wrinkling. "No," she said carefully, considering her response. "I let him go because I'd *already* hurt him. And I didn't want to keep dragging him down with me just because I was too caught up in my past." Carmen pressed her lips into a thin line, forcing the words out even when she wasn't sure how she felt getting to the part of her life where Asa was involved out into the open. "I felt stuck, like I was in limbo. But he was in a place where he'd already started to grow as a person, and I didn't want to be the one holding him back."

"And why do you think you'd be holding him back? Because you weren't sure if you'd make any progress with dealing with your mother's death?"

"Because I wasn't in a place where I could've given a relationship what I needed to give it, I guess," Carmen paused then sighed. "But he was ready to give his all, and I let him believe I was ready too. So that when I couldn't live up to it, well, I think it made him feel like...like I didn't value him as much."

The heavy rain outside seemed to fall back into a calmer shower, the droplets no longer hitting the window like tiny bullets. It cast an odd sense of tranquillity over Carmen's state of mind just then.

"What made you feel like you couldn't offer to that relationship what you needed to, Carmen?" Gloria tilted her head to the side, her rich eyes boring into Carmen's. "Or to any other kind of relationship in your life, whether it was friends or even your father, for that matter? Was it the circumstances of your birth? Did you maybe think that your mother being raped meant you didn't deserve anybody's affection?"

This was something that had plagued Carmen's mind a lot for as long as she could remember—during sleepless nights, when she was adding a new entry into her art journal, or moments when she'd sit back and watch students stand in groups, so unapologetically comfortable around one another.

And now that she was being made to say it out loud, she felt surer than ever about her answer.

"I don't think so, no."

This seemed to catch Gloria's attention because there was something akin to surprise on her face for a brief second before it disappeared. "So that part of your past doesn't bother you?"

"It," Carmen frowned, opening her mouth and shutting it again, repeating the action at least three times before she finally found the right words, "I mean, I don't hold my mum accountable for that or anything. I know she's not at fault there and—and ultimately, I hate whoever hurt her that way. I've—I've never dwelled too much on what it meant, I guess. Never looked at myself as something that was the result of a rape."

Gloria tapped her chin with her forefinger, her face unreadable as she just looked at Carmen unblinkingly. It was a few minutes before she spoke again. "All right, Carmen." She nodded in something that looked like approval. "You seem to be pretty confident about that. So what aspect of your past do you feel is a burden? If it wasn't the circumstances of your birth, then what do you think blocks you from opening up to people?"

And there it was. The core of all the pain and the guilt that had crept into the crevices of Carmen's entire being.

"Mum's death," she said quietly. "Sometimes I feel like visiting her grave or something. But then I ask myself if she'd want that because I—I feel like *I* was the reason she chose to leave and—and it made me wonder if perhaps going to her resting place would somehow be considered a disturbance. Because she wanted to get away from me, right? And I—I don't want to take that away from her by going anywhere close to where she's found her peace."

"So you blame yourself for your mother choosing to kill herself?"

Carmen shifted in her seat, not meeting the woman's eyes, but she nodded stiffly regardless.

"And is that why you keep people at bay?" Gloria asked, lacing her fingers together and placing them atop her raised knee. "You're afraid that your presence in their lives would do them no good because you believe your own mother didn't want you?"

Carmen swallowed audibly, feeling like there were a bunch of needles pricking the back of her throat. "It's just…if I could cause *so much* pain to someone when I was just a six-year-old, then—then how much pain would I be able to inflict *now*? How far off the edge would I end up pushing someone one day?"

Gloria didn't say anything for a long while, letting the words and their implications hang in the air between them.

"So which is it, Carmen?" she eventually asked. "Are you afraid you'd hurt someone the way you believe you hurt your mother? Or are you afraid you might hurt someone the way you believe your mother hurt *you*?"

The silence dragged on, heavy and thick, as if every single thing around Carmen was waiting, as if the universe itself had just hit pause for her to release the breath she was holding.

"The latter," she finally said in a rushed exhale. "For so long, I've been angry at her, blaming her for making such a selfish decision to leave us behind, to leave by passing all that pain on to us. And I was so afraid to do the same thing to someone else. So scared that I might put somebody—who cared about me—in a miserable place because I decided to make a selfish choice."

"I see," Gloria murmured after a while, the concentrated expression on her face dissipating as she once again slipped into that laid-back posture.

Carmen's eyes met hers. "See what?"

"Why it's so hard for you to speak about the boy," she replied. "You think you made that selfish choice when it came to him, that you did to him the one thing you were so afraid of doing. You told him you were in love with him when you hadn't reached that point yet because you wanted to keep him around, and you believe you've done the very thing your mother did." Gloria paused. "You think you made a choice that worked in your favour, but in doing so, you put someone who loved you in a place of misery."

Carmen didn't bother fighting off the tears that gathered at the corner of her eyes. "Yes," she said in a hushed tone. "But that's not the only reason."

"Not the only reason what, Carmen?"

"Not the only reason I don't like speaking of him."

There was a short pause. "Oh?" Gloria raised a brow. "What else is there?"

"Talking about him makes it...real," Carmen said quietly, her heart beginning to race like all those raindrops sliding down the window.

"Makes the fact that you did the one thing you never wanted to do real?"

Carmen shook her head. "No...It makes the fact that I'm actually getting better real. That I'm making progress here becomes real." She ran an exhausted hand through her hair, feeling the long strands fall over her shoulders. "Coming here for the past ten weeks has allowed me

472

to open up more than I thought I'd be able to, and after each session, I'm able to let a tiny part of my past go. To let go of some portion of all that dead weight. And whenever that happens, it gets easier to let something else in. Whether it's me telling my dad about my day, or talking to Joyce about my favourite bands, or even feeling comfortable about going bowling with her and Willa on the weekends."

Gloria's eyebrows furrowed ever so delicately and she blinked once. "And this is what you wanted, right? To let yourself open up so you can form real connections with people?"

Carmen nodded slowly. "Yes. Yes, it is. I can't even begin to say how much lighter I feel on the inside already."

"So, then what's the problem?"

"I…" Carmen hesitated, curling her palms into her fists and feeling the tips of her nails being pressed into her skin. And then she lied, hoping her tone was convincing. "I guess that I never really thought of myself in a place where I could learn to let myself be happy. Where I'd want to stop letting my past have such a huge hold on me."

But those weren't the words that Carmen had meant to say initially. That wasn't the problem. That wasn't what had recently begun to plague Carmen's mind.

No, the problem now was that it was also becoming easier to let in all those moments of both emotional and physical intimacy with Asa. It was becoming easier to accept the fact that he'd only ever had her best interests at heart.

It was becoming easier to accept the fact that Asa San Román had been (and maybe *still was?*) in love with her.

And it terrified Carmen more than anything else in the world to realise that she could truly begin to let herself be loved with such intensity by him—only now, only *after* she'd let him go.

58.

The Thing About Redemption

The last week of February and the first week of March seemed to blur and blend into each other that it was difficult for Asa to pinpoint exactly when one month ended and the other began.

Months, years, what did it matter? Hadn't Asa already once acknowledged that his life was measured by lifetimes instead? And hadn't he decided he'd lived two lifetimes: the world before Carmen West and then the one with her?

He supposed this was the third one: the world *after* Carmen West.

There was that hollow feeling in his chest again. Asa wondered how it was that something so empty could weigh so much.

Asa had also begun wondering about a lot of things lately, especially about how they never really told you about girls like Carmen West.

Sure, he'd heard of the ones who couldn't commit to one man, the ones who were just interested in the size of your wallet, or even the ones who only wanted what was underneath your clothes.

But no amount of books he'd lost himself in spoke about girls like Carmen goddamn West.

The kind that was an artist, whose fingertips turned everything they brushed against into something magical. The kind whose heart was a masterpiece that no kind of art could compete against.

The kind that reminded you of the moon, always ready to shine her best against the darkness, so much so that you forgot it had different phases, and she only let you fall in love with half of them. Then you spend the rest of an infinity wondering what the other half was like. The kind that planted seeds inside the crevices of your heart, mind, and soul with every precious word that fell past her lips. The kind that made those seeds flourish and grow with each kiss until you could feel the roots dig deep into the core of your being and build a home inside you. The kind that one day decided you weren't a home but a temporary resting place, and so when she left, she also left behind that home you'd let her build in the centre of your chest.

And so, each time you felt her absence, the emptiness of that home, all those roots embedded so deeply within you being torn to shreds at her departure, it would finally dawn on you why storms were named after people.

Because after all, that was what Carmen was. A hurricane. The type that came with a beating heart trapped inside it.

Traces of the havoc she'd wreaked were evident in every silent ride back home from school, in the absence of the smell of paint mixing with the scent of his watermelon gum, in the way he wanted to tell her about how he had to skip the scene of Sirius Black's death again even though this was probably his hundredth time reading the series.

Sometimes Asa would be so lost in thought that he'd see her across the hallway and almost wrap his arms around her from behind before burying his face into the crook of her neck. Almost.

But he'd always catch himself in time. And then the realisation would hit him as if it was the first time all over again: *She wasn't in love with him. She wasn't in love with him. She wasn't in love with him.*

And even though Asa could swear on his life that his heart had already been shattered into smithereens, he'd feel something in him break a little more.

•　　•　　•

After helping Wyatt with his training for the meet during after-school practises, Asa found himself walking back towards the main school building to grab his bag from the locker as Wyatt waved goodbye and got into his car to head back home.

Asa turned down the hallway, so used to the directions by now that he didn't even have to watch where he was going. He'd just gotten his bag and was about to walk away, when he heard a commotion from the direction of the boys' locker room.

Recognising most of the aggravated voices, Asa approached the small crowd that had gathered there, choosing not to make his presence that obvious as he observed the scene with a frown.

"…was my call!" Hunter's icy tone was one that Asa would recognise anywhere, even if he didn't hear the entire thing he'd just said.

"Says who?" a boy who was a foot shorter than Hunter, but a little broader, with a scowl firmly etched onto his face, snarled back.

Asa recognised him as the quarterback. It suddenly dawned on him that this was probably the one who'd managed to throw a punch at Hunter a few months back. He probably wouldn't get so lucky the second time around. Hunter wasn't the kind to let someone catch him off guard twice.

"Says my fucking title as team captain," Hunter spat back, balling his fists and squaring his shoulders but not stepping closer in a threatening manner that would've implied he was looking for a fight.

Asa didn't *want* to believe Hunter was holding back, that he was actually showing self-restraint. But he also couldn't deny something that was as obvious as daylight.

"You keep undermining me in front of the team every single chance you get!" Hunter hissed at the other guy. "I'm not going to just watch you ruin everything I've worked my ass off to achieve because you've got some complex problem. It's senior year, college scouts are going to be there, and I'm sick of you trying to challenge every word that comes out of my mouth."

"Yeah, and I'm sick of you looking down on me all the time but you don't hear me complaining, do you? So why don't you just run along and go cry to your mum about it."

Hunter visibly froze at the insult, his face draining of all colour.

The words weren't aimed at Asa, obviously, but he held his breath anyway, feeling the secondhand punch to the gut that the blow of that remark would've undoubtedly thrown at Hunter.

Asa didn't know much, but from what little Carmen had said, he knew enough to be certain that the death of Hunter's mother was a sore topic—especially that he'd lost *both* of them.

And then it all happened in really slow motion.

Hunter shook off that brief moment of stunned silence, and then one of his fists was raised into the air.

"The coach threatened to bench me during the final game of this season if something like that happened again."

Hunter's words were suddenly fresh in Asa's memory, as if that conversation had only taken place yesterday and not a few months back.

"Can't have that, not with all those scouts attending."

Asa's muscles tensed as he watched Hunter's fist drop lower and lower, every millisecond feeling like they were minutes instead.

Hunter deserved to get benched if he loved the sport so much. He did. How many students had he been merciless towards before?

How many long-lasting scars must he have inflicted and on how many people? Didn't he deserve to lose what was probably one of the handful of things he actually gave a shit about? Didn't Hunter deserve a dose of his own medicine?

But then Asa was suddenly in a chair in the principal's office with his parents by his side and he could hear Hendrickson's voice as the words floated around in his head: *"However, you're no longer allowed to take part in this year's interstate swimming meet."*

The memory dissolved into nothingness, blending into the scene currently playing out right in front of Asa's eyes.

None of the other boys seemed to be doing anything, and even though he didn't understand why, Asa's feet were suddenly moving towards them.

He managed to get in between Hunter and the other guy, fast enough to place his palm on the other guy's chest and shove him out of the way to break up what would've led to a fight, but Asa wasn't fast enough to jump away himself or dodge the punch which now landed on his own face instead of who it was intended for.

Hunter's fist struck the side of Asa's face, hard knuckles colliding into his lip and jaw, making his bag slip off his shoulder and sending him stumbling back a few steps—a result of both Asa's surprise at his own actions slowing his usual reflexes and Hunter's inability to stop the momentum of the swing.

Pain flared in the bottom left of Asa's jaw before shooting up in the entire side of his face. He lifted his fingers to his busted lips and felt something warm and wet trickle down his chin.

"Hijo de puta!" Asa hissed as he pulled back his fingers from his face and saw the red liquid smearing them.

Without waiting to see how much bloodier his split lips could get, he shoved past Hunter, barrelling into the shoulders of whoever was in his way as he stormed into the locker room and headed straight towards the row of sinks lining one of the walls.

Asa winced as he took in the reflection of his bloody mouth from the long mirror that hung above the sinks, spanning over the entire length of that wall. His eyes fell on a faintly discoloured patch of skin near his jaw where he was certain a bruise was going to form by the time morning came.

And this time he couldn't even blame Hunter. That only pissed Asa off more.

What had he been thinking?

"What the hell were you thinking?!" Hunter's voice thundered throughout the locker room as he slammed the door open. Asa turned just in time to see the prick throw his bag (which he must've picked up from

478

where it'd fallen) in his direction, watching as it skidded across the floor and stopped right at his feet.

Asa shot Hunter a heated glare and snatched his bag from the floor, placing it on one of the benches between the lockers before going back to the sink and turning on the tap.

"*Pendejo*," Asa muttered under his breath as he tried splashing water on the cut.

"Swear at me in Spanish again," Hunter threatened, narrowing his eyes at Asa. "Go on, I fucking dare you."

Asa turned around fully to face Hunter and looked him straight in the eyes. "P-e-n-d-e-j-o," he said unflinchingly, deliberately dragging out each letter as he spelled them. Then, he let his mouth curve upwards into a smirk.

Hunter's jaw clenched, and Asa watched as his palms curled into fists, shooting Asa a look that would've killed if the particular saying was actually true.

And then, he stormed towards the storage cupboard in the corner of the room, yanking the doors open with unnecessary force and grabbing something that Asa couldn't see.

Hunter marched back towards him and shoved the object into Asa's chest, the unexpected gesture catching him off guard once again and causing him to stumble backwards slightly.

Asa looked down to see a fresh roll of tissue paper in his arms, and he took it with a scowl, turning back to the sink as he soaked a few tissues and began to dab at his bleeding lip.

"You're welcome," Hunter said in an annoyed voice as he moved back and leant sideways against one of the sinks, observing Asa with a scowl of his own.

"Oh, yeah," Asa retorted sarcastically. "*Thank you*. I was totally in the mood for a busted lip and a bruising jaw."

"I didn't ask you to intervene," Hunter snapped. "He asked for it anyway!"

Asa laughed disbelievingly. "You know, maybe I *do* deserve this," he gestured wildly to his face, causing a few water droplets to fly around him, "—for actually feeling the tiniest shred of empathy and stopping you from doing something completely stupid only to get punched and then have you mock me for it!"

Hunter's scowl lost some of the heat behind it as it morphed into something like a frown instead. "Empathy?" he asked in confusion, but the annoyance and anger still lingered in his tone.

"Yes," Asa told him, throwing the used tissue papers into a bin nearby. "Empathy. The ability to put yourself in someone's sh—"

"I know what empathy fucking means!" Hunter spat, looking like he wanted to throw something at Asa.

Asa shrugged. "Could've fooled me."

"You're making me really want to slam my fist into your face right now," Hunter said in all seriousness.

"You've never held back before," Asa muttered. "What's stopping you now?"

Hunter pushed himself off the sink and stepped directly in front of Asa, frustration swimming in those icy blue eyes. "When are you going to stop holding that against me?"

"When all the shit you put me through stops hanging over *me*," Asa said in a steely voice. "Just because you haven't done anything recently doesn't erase everything else you already have done!"

"Oh, come on!" Hunter growled in irritation, kicking the leg of a bench nearby. "It can't be that hard for you to let go of—"

Asa's head whipped towards him, warning flashing in his eyes. "Don't you *dare*," he said in a low voice, shaking with repressed anger. "Don't you *dare* belittle the things you did, the things you said. You don't get to decide if it's easy or not for me to let go of it all. You don't get to decide how much damage you've caused to someone. That's like setting a person on fire and telling them how loud they're allowed to scream." Asa stepped away from Hunter and looked him dead in the eyes. "When someone tells you that you hurt them, you either apologise or you ask

480

them what you can do to make it better. You don't tell them they're not supposed to feel the way they feel."

A muscle in Hunter's jaw ticked as he looked away. "You're telling me you've never done things you regret?"

Asa scoffed, shaking his head to himself. "Hell yeah, I've done plenty of shit that I regret. I've gotten into numerous fights sticking up for the other students who get picked on here. I once took Carmen's journal and kept it as leverage. I let Isla's negativity blind me so much to the point that I completely disregarded Wyatt, Hayden and Lyra who were always there as great friends. I let myself be so consumed by all the hate Carson threw my way that I lost my chance to participate in the meet this year.

"These are all things I regret, Hunter. But you know what? My heart was always at the right place. My intentions were never malicious. And *still*, I tried making amends for them. But you," Asa let out an exhausted breath and dropped down on the bench his bag was placed on, "you always looked to hurt people, Hunter. You wanted to break them just because it made you feel powerful. And I don't see you trying to make amends at all."

"I can't just turn over a new leaf overnight!" Hunter snapped, meeting Asa's eyes once more.

"I know *that*," Asa snapped back. "But you haven't even started to show any signs that you *want* to turn over a new leaf!"

Hunter threw an incredulous look in Asa's direction. "Are you fucking blind? Did you not see me there at Carmen's that day? What do you think I was doing there?"

"I think that you were trying to get back somebody that means something to you," Asa replied in a flat tone, cutting straight through the bullshit. "I think that you were making amends in a place where you were emotionally invested. Where there was something in it for you. Where you had something to gain, which was a place back in Carmen's life." Asa leant forward, placing his elbows on his knees and narrowing his eyes at Hunter.

"You want redemption so bad, Hunter? Do you really want to make amends? Then you start with doing right by the people who you

481

have nothing to gain from. Do right by those who you have no personal ties to. Apologise to the ones who you've hurt just because of the fact that they exist. It needs to start with selfless choices, Hunter. Because what you're doing with Carmen serves no one but you, and that's not redeeming yourself. That's just hiding behind the one person you know who doesn't look at you like you're a monster."

There was a deafening pause in the semi-civil-semi-heated conversation between both boys, broken only when Hunter sighed heavily and seated himself next to Asa, keeping a good distance between them.

"Is that what you want me to do?" Hunter asked with an even voice, but there was an odd touch of gentleness to it that Asa had never heard before. Albeit it was very faint, it was there nonetheless. "You want me to apologise to you?"

There was another long pause, the tensed air not allowing Asa's fists to unclench just yet.

"No," Asa finally muttered. "Because it won't make a difference to me anymore. And to be completely honest, I don't think I can forgive you." He cast a sideways glance at Hunter to find his eyes already on him. "You want to see me as a bad person for it, then go ahead. If it makes things easier for you to paint me as the bad guy, do it. But I'm not going to apologise for who I am. Not anymore." Asa averted his gaze, staring straight ahead as he uttered the next words. "I don't have a heart as big as Carmen's, Hunter. I can't forgive that easily."

Another pause.

"What if all the others I apologise to never want to forgive me as well?" Hunter finally asked, voice quiet.

"That's the beauty of redemption, Hunter." Asa sighed. "You apologise because you're letting the person you wronged know that you have it in you to acknowledge what you did to them, not because you're expecting their forgiveness in return. I might not need the closure from you, but there might be others out there who do."

Asa remained seated there for a few moments longer, before grabbing his bag and rising up from the bench, heading towards the door.

"Hey, Asa?" Hunter's voice stopped him just as he was a few feet away from the door.

Asa stopped and looked at him over his shoulder. "Yeah?"

"Thanks."

"For?"

The corners of Hunter's lips twitched but he stubbornly kept them fixed in a thin line. "Taking a punch so that I wouldn't get benched," he said matter-of-factly. "You know, *empathising*."

Asa offered him a curt nod, forcing himself not to smile at that last bit, and then turned back around, covering the distance towards the door. But just as his palm wrapped around the knob, Hunter called his name again.

"Asa, one more thing."

He pulled the door open and stood there, tilting his head to the side so that Hunter would know he was listening.

"It won't work."

"What won't work?" Asa asked, turning his face around completely to look at Hunter, a confused frown on his face.

"Your plan to cope with Carmen's absence by hating her," Hunter murmured, eyes drilling into Asa's. "Trust me, I tried to do it too. I tried it for twelve years, in fact. Didn't work out so well. I somehow managed to find my way back to her." The corners of Hunter's eyes softened ever so slightly. "And so will you."

59.

Find My Way Back To You

Joyce was sitting crossed-legged on Carmen's bed, flipping through the pages of a celebrity magazine she'd brought with her.

"Dude," she said suddenly, not looking up from what she was reading. "Did you listen to Swift's new album? *Reputation*?" Joyce grinned to herself and shook her head. "Incredible doesn't even begin to describe it."

Carmen frowned from where she was sorting out the clothes in her closet according to their colours.

"No," she called over her shoulder. "She's good, I guess, but I wouldn't say I'm a fan. Besides, I'm very picky when it comes to music. I don't listen to anything out of my comfort zone."

Joyce looked up from the magazine with knitted brows. "What do you listen to?"

"The Script," Carmen answered, placing a deep red turtleneck above a small pile of other red tops she had. "Mumford and Sons. Sometimes even Bastille."

"Ah." Joyce clicked her tongue. "I've listened to some of The Script but haven't heard of the others. By the way, if you're into that kind of music, I think you might like Birdy too." She seemed to ponder over this for a little while. "Yup, definitely seems like your type."

Carmen nodded and offered her friend a small smile. "Will check it out once I'm done sorting these clothes."

"Don't worry about it." Joyce grinned and pushed her magazine aside before jumping off the bed and walking towards Carmen's dressing table where her phone was. "I'll just send whatever songs of hers I've already downloaded into my phone to yours."

"Thanks." Carmen's smile widened.

"Yeah, no problem. Try listening to "Wings", it's my personal favourite from her original works. And as for her covers, you should try the ones she did for Passenger's "Let Her Go" and Ed Sheeran's "The A Team". She did them better than the original singers, in my opinion."

Carmen stopped whatever she was doing and shot Joyce an amused look. "You're pretty enthusiastic about everything related to music, huh?"

Joyce grinned back at her and proceeded to tell Carmen about how she wanted to create her own YouTube channel one day and start doing covers of her own. In return, Carmen told Joyce about wanting to go to an art school.

The rest of the evening passed by with both girls making light conversation, talking about the little things, the ordinary things. And the smile never left Carmen's face.

By the time Joyce left, night had already fallen, bringing along with it a heavy rain. Carmen stood by the front door for a few more minutes, relishing the cool wind against her face and the occasional spray of water that was sent her way.

Sighing softly, she stepped back and shut the door, heading towards the kitchen to make herself some coffee before she retreated up to her room.

Once she'd made it to her room with a steaming mug of coffee in one hand, Carmen reached for her phone on the dresser and clicked on one of the songs Joyce had sent to her;

…staring at the bottom of your glass, hoping one day you'll make a dream last…

The low, rich voice of Birdy filled the room as Carmen moved around, clearing away any remaining clothes that she'd pulled out of her

485

cupboard. It was when she started clearing away all the art supplies scattered on her desk that Carmen's heart nearly stopped.

She had her mug to her lips, sipping on the warm liquid while her other hand tried to carry all the twenty or so paintbrushes, when her wrist knocked into a pouch and sent it over the edge of the table, letting a few crayons roll out of it.

Her eyes fell on the broken halves of a blue crayon.

Time stopped.

"It's just broken, Carmen. It doesn't mean it can't still colour."

Carmen's breathing came to an abrupt halt.

"And I would break every single crayon you had in your possession just to show you broken crayons can still create masterpieces as much as an unbroken one."

There was a jolt in her chest, and it felt like everything inside Carmen just collapsed into a heap.

And then the paintbrushes in her hand were slipping past her shaking fingers, dropping to the floor of her bedroom with a loud clatter.

Carmen's heart was pounding, pounding, pounding.

Thud. Thud. Thud.

But Birdy's voice was somehow floating above the roaring in Carmen's ears.

...you only need the sun when it starts to snow, only know you love him when you let him go...

Her feet stumbled back, hands trembling as the coffee spilt from her mug and the ceramic went crashing to the floor, shattering into the tiniest fragments as the sickening realisation slammed into Carmen again and again.

The entire world seemed to have stopped on its axis, the only sound being Carmen's uneven breathing and Birdy's soulful singing.

...and you let him go, and you let him go, and you let him go, and you let him go...

●　　　●　　　●

As the days dragged on, Carmen found it increasingly harder to let her creative juices flow, the allure of art seeming to have lost that spark which had been burning brightly all throughout her life.

Right then, she was seated in the school's art room, staring at the blank canvas in front of her, wondering which shade of green she wanted to use. Her eyes swept over the palette, wondering if there really was that much of a difference between colours. Green was still green, regardless of it being mint or jade. Who the hell cared about shades anyway? It just made painting more complicated a task than it needed to be.

Her eyes skimmed over the shades of blue. They were still just blue. To hell with baby and royal. Why did it matter?

Why had it *ever* mattered to her? Carmen couldn't remember what all her fascination with colours and their various shades had been about before. It certainly didn't make much sense to her now.

Her gaze slid over, landing on shades of red, of yellow, of br—

Of *brown.*

And suddenly, shades mattered.

Because that one right there—yes, the corner most one—it was the caramel-like tone of the apple of Asa's cheeks, right where his skin was a bit lighter near his cheekbones. And the other shade of brown on the other corner was of Asa's hair: a deep, rich colour that looked like grounded cinnamon.

Carmen's eyes fell on another shade, one that was of Asa's eyes, reminding her of coffee beans in their most exquisite form. Then another shade which reminded her of his eyes again, but when they were illuminated by the sunlight that sometimes fell on Asa's face in the most perfect angle, making his eyes look like grounded coffee being blended into water, an almost liquidised gold.

And then Carmen's hand was reaching for a brush, her hand flying as she splattered the blank canvas in front of her with all the pieces of Asa, the way those pieces seemed to still linger in every nook and cranny of her life, paint splatters that she could never erase.

And then Carmen remembered.

487

She remembered why colours mattered, why shades of them mattered; why art had always, *always* mattered.

Carmen remembered because Asa was art himself, the one masterpiece she never truly allowed herself to appreciate and cherish when it had been within her grasp, just waiting for her arms to reach out and take a hold of it.

Asa San Román was a thousand shades of brown and gold, and Carmen West had turned him grey.

"Carmen." She heard a familiar voice from behind her, and she turned to see her art teacher standing there with a puzzled look. "What are you trying to paint?"

Carmen's eyes flickered back to the indecipherable piece she'd just created. Then again, indecipherable to whom exactly? Beauty was always in the eyes of the beholder and the same notion applied to the interpretation of art too.

"I don't know," she murmured.

This seemed to amuse the teacher. "You always give me that answer when I ask you what the meaning behind your works are."

Carmen couldn't exactly name it, but something about that remark got to her. Maybe it was how her teacher still held onto a shred of hope that Carmen would one day offer a genuine response, or maybe it was the sudden realisation that she had been closing herself off to people even in these small ways.

So, when the teacher turned to begin walking away, Carmen spoke. "Warmth," she said, making the teacher stop in her tracks and turn back around.

"Warmth?"

Carmen gestured to the half-dried painting in front of her. "It's supposed to be warmth," she said softly. "Like, if warmth had a colour or could be turned into art, this is what I believe it would look like."

And if warmth was a person, Carmen knew what he looked like too.

Carmen had known warmth. Had known it in its purest form. And truth be told, she missed it.

She missed *him*.

"That's…that's actually pretty deep," the teacher said, mouth lifting into an appreciative smile. "Quite the perceptive mind you've got there, Carmen."

She just smiled in response, watching as the teacher walked away and headed towards another student, probably asking them what the story behind their painting was.

Asa's and Carmen's story couldn't be narrated through one single painting though. No, a museum would be needed for that.

A museum where everything that hung on its walls were timeless and spoke of ancient souls and were simply magical, forever preserved for future generations to discover and marvel at.

But is that what Carmen wanted? To let them be nothing but a part of history? For her to watch him behind glass doors? Didn't she want to be lacing her fingers through his instead? To stand beside him? To feel that certain warmth only he was capable of spreading through her?

No, Carmen decided. She didn't want to watch him from behind glass doors. She didn't want to marvel at him like a common stranger.

She wanted him. Not the way he made her feel—but *him*.

She wanted his beautiful mind, his heart of gold, his courageous soul—every crack, crevice and jagged edge of Asa's entire being.

Carmen had to hit rock bottom to climb back up, and maybe it worked the same way with relationships too. Sometimes two people had to crash land before they could soar. A big *maybe*. And an even bigger *sometimes*.

But Asa had once told her that life always found a way and that she just needed to know where to look. Carmen was willing to take a leap of faith towards the possibility that the two of them together could just be the one in a million that found a way.

She wasn't going to wait for life to find that way for her. She was going to put herself out there and pave a path with her own two hands and feet. Because the problem wasn't that Asa and Carmen were the wrong fit. They'd been the perfect fit, just with horrible timing.

And Carmen wanted to believe that the right people with wrong timing could be lucky enough to find their way back to each other.

It was a belief she was ready to fight for. A belief she was ready to wage war against the whole universe for.

• • •

Carmen was *so* not ready to wage that war. She was standing a few feet away from Asa, watching as he grabbed a book from his locker and stuffed it into his bag and all she could do was stare.

She wondered if it was an old classic or if he was just rereading the Harry Potter series all over again. And if it was the latter, she also wondered if he had to skip the death of that Black character, a scene that Asa had once mentioned was unbearable.

She almost started walking towards him right then, but caught herself before she could get any further. Every time her feet took one step forward, all that echoed through her head was a brokenhearted "I hate you".

Part of Carmen was hesitant because she didn't know what to expect if she actually did approach Asa. She'd never been on the receiving end of his cold shoulder and wasn't particularly enthusiastic about finding out what that'd be like. And the other, much smaller part of her, she wondered if perhaps he truly *did* hate her, not that she could ever blame him if he did. Or even worse—that he'd fallen out of love with her. Carmen didn't think she'd be able to bear that.

"Go on. Speak to him," a familiar voice said from beside Carmen and she tilted her head to find Wyatt looking at her, no traces of his usual happy-go-lucky nature.

Carmen swallowed, then looked away from him and towards Asa again. "He said he hates me," she said in a small voice.

"I didn't know he said *that* to you," Wyatt muttered, looking at Asa too. "But it's in Asa's nature to feel every single emotion so deeply. So if he said he hates you, those words came from a place of so much pain."

490

Carmen looked down at her feet, the merciless claws of guilt digging into her insides and tearing away at her.

"I'm not saying that to make you feel worse," Wyatt told her. "I'm telling you that because if he was *that* hurt, then it's because he loved you in equal measure. And all that love can't have simply vanished into thin air. So go to him."

"Do you..." Carmen hesitated, not feeling too comfortable about voicing her thoughts to someone she didn't know well, but she reminded herself that this was good. That letting someone in on how she felt could actually help her right then. "Do you think he'd want to talk to me?"

Wyatt looked away from Asa and met Carmen's eyes. "If you're asking me if he's going to go easy on you, then the answer is no. Forgiveness isn't Asa's greatest forte."

Carmen sighed tiredly. "That I know."

"But..." Wyatt knitted his brows as he tilted his head slightly. "Despite all the ways he's going to try to infuriate you or give you the cold shoulder, I think that, at the end of the day, he does miss you."

Asa was closing his locker now, completely oblivious of the two people observing and having a conversation about him.

"Well..." Carmen huffed out a deep breath, making up her mind as she took out her phone and sent a text to her dad, asking him not to come and pick her up. "Guess I'm going to have to find a way to put up with his hostility until he cracks. It's not like I don't deserve it," she muttered the last bit to herself.

Wyatt chuckled, the seriousness in his posture fading away slightly. "Good luck with that. You'll need it."

They stood there for a second longer, but Carmen snapped out of her uncertainty when Asa started to walk out of the school building, deciding to take that leap of faith. Turning to Wyatt, she threw him a quick goodbye and then picked up her pace before breaking into a sprint as she ran towards Asa.

Always towards Asa.

Carmen had made up her mind to fight for him. She wondered if perhaps her mind had already been made up ever since that instant her soul had struck a match with his, igniting a spark in each other that just wouldn't die.

•   •   •

Carmen found herself standing in front of the building that housed the school's indoor swimming pool, a separate block that was within Reichenbach High's premises but a minute's walk from the school itself.

She'd seen Asa disappear into it a few minutes ago, and instead of following him in and doing whatever it was that she felt she was supposed to do, she was standing out with her feet glued to the spot.

It had dawned on her just as she was about to open the door that she didn't exactly have some master plan. Carmen was utterly clueless as to what she would do once she found Asa.

"I'll hold on, even when you're pulling away."

Asa had given her his word, hadn't he? And he'd lived up to that promise, too because he had come back after the fight that November morning. He had come back to her.

And maybe it was time Carmen did some of the holding on now. Maybe it was time she showed him that walking away wasn't the only thing she was capable of.

And so with her heart in her throat, Carmen gripped the handle of the door and pulled it open. Having come here a few times before when her spare periods had fallen on the same hour as Asa's, Carmen had no trouble making her way towards the bleachers that surrounded the pool. Her eyes swept over a few guys in swim trunks who were seated, either scrolling through their phones with a towel hanging over their bare chests, or just jogging around as a warmup exercise before they dived into the water.

Carmen couldn't find Asa, but then again, she could see only a handful of the swimmers here, so she figured he was in the changing rooms with the rest of them.

492

The thought hadn't finished crossing her mind when she felt someone touch her waist from behind in an attempt to get her attention.

It was too light a gesture, the fingers just brushing her hip for a fleeting second so Carmen couldn't tell if it was Asa's hand or not. She would have definitely recognised the familiarity of his touch had it lingered for a moment longer.

The face that came into view once Carmen turned around wasn't Asa's. But it was a face she was familiar with nonetheless.

A face she'd seen in the hallways, in the cafeteria, around the parking lot. And definitely a face that didn't place a smile on Carmen's.

"You lost?" Carson William's smooth-as-honey voice, accompanied by the usual raspy undertone, fell on Carmen's ears as he directed the question at her.

Carmen's lips parted, as if to respond verbally, but she settled to just shaking her head instead.

Carson leant back on one of the metal bars that ran down from the highest row of the bleachers to the bottom, acting as a divider for each block of seats.

His eyes dropped from hers, travelling down the length of her body as the ends of his mouth stretched into a barely-there kind of smirk.

"So, Asa huh," he commented in a low voice, looking back up at her again. "What is it with you? You prefer Hispanic meat?"

"Excuse me?"

"You know," he said in a dismissive tone. "Out of everyone in the school, you go for the Mexican trash—"

"All right, let me stop you right there." Carmen's eyes narrowed, her voice firm. "You're not even half the man that Mexican trash is. So before you open your mouth and spit out opinions that aren't required, I suggest you take a good look at the mirror and start worrying about what kind of person *you* are."

Carson's smirk widened and he cocked his head to the side before taking a step closer to Carmen. "You talk to Asa that way?"

Carmen stood her ground, not backing away even though she felt her stomach coil into a ball of discomfort. "No," she said matter-of-factly. "Then again, when Asa starts to speak, it isn't utter bullshit that spills out."

Carson's eyes narrowed now, and he took one more step closer to her. "You know, for someone who's supposed to be a goody-two-shoes, you sure have a mouth."

An incredulous laugh fell past Carmen's lips. "I choose to be kind because I *want* to, Carson. Because it makes me happy." She looked him straight in the eyes then, making sure he felt the promise behind her next words. "But if you think I'm going to stand by and watch someone have a go at the people I love, you have no idea who I am. I can be fierce, and I'll be so without apology."

Carson seemed like he was about to say something else but an unfamiliar feminine voice cut through the air, grabbing both his and Carmen's attention.

"Coach needs you," the girl with shoulder-length honey hair and small, round grey-green eyes told Carson, walking towards them in one of those full body swimsuits, "*now.*"

Carson muttered something under his breath, shot a glance towards Carmen, and then began walking in the direction of the changing rooms reluctantly.

"Sorry about that," the girl said with a small smile, approaching Carmen and dropping down on the nearest seat on the bleachers. "He's a dick."

Carmen's eyes widened with mild surprise as she blinked at the girl. "You did that on purpose?" she asked. "So the coach didn't really call for him?"

The girl grinned and shook her head. "A girl's gotta do what she's gotta do. I'm Marlene, by the way."

Carmen laughed lightly, shooting her a smile of gratitude. "Thanks, Marlene. I'm Carm—"

"—Carmen." She nodded. "I know. You here for Asa?"

Something fluttered in Carmen's stomach at the mention of him, taking her by complete surprise.

"Yeah," Carmen replied, her voice carrying an odd softness. "Yeah, I'm here for Asa."

Marlene smiled, her eyes examining Carmen's face for a moment. "You know." She chuckled lightly. "I actually used to have a major crush on him."

"Oh?" Carmen blinked, taken aback and completely unsure how to react.

"Yeah... Maybe more than a crush, I don't know. He's the kind of guy you could actually get into a steady relationship with so that was like a bonus."

"Bonus?"

Marlene's face flushed and her cheeks turned a beet red. "Um, well, you know...we, uh...Asa and I— we sort of..." She shrugged awkwardly. "You know..."

Oh, Carmen thought.

"You've got nothing to be worried about," Marlene said hastily. "That was long before you were in the picture. Besides, I haven't fallen so low that I'd actually go after another girl's man." She smiled warmly at Carmen. "I'm just saying that he's a good guy. A little bit of a magnet for trouble obviously, but you know, he has a good heart. I'm just happy he's found someone."

"Uh..." Carmen hesitated. "We're not really together anymore."

Surprise flashed across Marlene's eyes, and her mouth dropped open slightly. "Oh," she muttered, sounding a little disappointed. "That sucks. I mean, I don't know you personally, but I've seen you around before and you seem like a really nice person. I was happy that Asa found someone like that, you know."

Carmen shifted on her feet, eyes flickering towards the pool, wondering when Asa was going to show.

"Um, thanks I guess?" Carmen smiled uncertainly, adjusting the strap of her bag on her shoulder. "If—if you don't mind me asking. Why is it that you never made a move to ask him out? If you knew you'd have liked to be involved with him on a more serious level?"

"Isla." Marlene sighed, shrugging and running a hand through her short hair. "I mean, she was such a toxic presence in his life, you know? And I didn't want that baggage following him into my life too. My older sister fell into an unhealthy relationship, and it took her a really long time to finally get away from it. I just didn't want to have to deal with any kind of toxic shit after seeing what she went through."

Carmen frowned, letting Marlene's words float around in her mind, not really understanding how one thing led to the other.

"But..." Carmen furrowed her brows. "But your relationship would have been with Asa, not Isla."

A scoff escaped Marlene's mouth. "Come on. Back then, there was no Asa without Isla. The two were a freaking package deal. If you wanted one in your life, the other came along. No questions asked." She shook her head, a small sigh leaving her lips. "I'm not the kind who does half measures. If I'm going to get involved in a relationship, I'm in for the long haul. I knew Asa was the same too, so it'd have been perfect. But I also didn't believe it was worth the burden Isla would've placed on us, you know?"

And like the crack of dawn, that road towards convincing Asa they were worth a second chance became clearer.

Carmen may have walked in here with no plan whatsoever, without the faintest clue about how she was going to approach Asa or how she was going to prove to him that she wanted to make things work between them, but the conversation with Marlene right then had just enlightened Carmen, and she knew what she had to do.

It was a small step, a baby step, but it was a step forward nonetheless and that was what mattered. And now that Carmen knew where to start, she was going to see it through 'till the end.

60.
A Piece of Me

By the time Asa walked out of the changing rooms with Wyatt in tow, Marlene had left the bleachers and hit the pool. Carmen could see her lithe body moving through the water with enviable grace.

While Wyatt was in his swimming trunks, Carmen noticed that Asa wasn't, and then she remembered that he probably didn't need these extra practises because he was no longer taking part in the interstate competitions.

Maybe Asa was just here for his friend, as a gesture of support. It seemed like the sort of thing Asa would do.

Carmen saw him laugh as he spoke to Wyatt, watched Asa's cheekbones rise as the corners of his lips stretched into a wide grin, and noticed his eyes literally glow with mirth.

There was that tugging sensation in her chest again. As if Carmen was being thrown off a cliff and being yanked back up with a rope before she could hit the ground.

Familiar coffee eyes met hers, and time seemed to just...*stop* for the two of them right then.

Nothing mattered. Nothing mattered but that Asa was there— *right there*—standing a few feet away from her, and that his eyes were burning into hers with the kind of intensity poets bled on paper to describe.

And then the moment was gone, the warmth draining out of his eyes, replaced with nonchalance instead.

It was such a tiny gesture, but quite a significant one, and even though it hurt Carmen to have him mask his emotions in front of her, she couldn't help but wonder if that was what she'd put him through each time she pushed him away and shut him out.

Carmen stood up from her seat hesitantly, unsure of how he was going to react. She'd barely taken a step forward when Asa already resumed walking in the direction he'd been heading towards, completely ignoring her.

She faltered in her steps at the obvious hostility, but didn't stop as she forced her legs to carry her over towards him.

Carmen cut into his path, coming to stand right in front of Asa and forcing him to stop in his tracks.

He wouldn't meet her eyes, his jaw clenching as he determinedly kept his stare fixed ahead of him, on whatever was behind Carmen.

"Uh." Carmen cleared her throat, clasping her hands together and shifting on her feet. "I, um, c-can I speak with you?"

There was a beat of silence. Then another.

Wyatt cleared his throat awkwardly, scratching the back of his head. "I'm...I'm gonna go—I'll leave you guys to it." He was just about to move and head towards the pool, when Asa's hand shot out and grabbed Wyatt's arm.

"Where are you going?" Asa frowned at Wyatt, his voice sounding tensed. "I'm supposed to help you get ready for the competitions."

"I know," Wyatt responded calmly. "And that's exactly what I'm going to do. I'm gonna practise."

Asa nodded curtly. "Great, then let's get started. Come on." He moved closer, walking around Carmen and completely disregarding her presence, as if she was just a piece of rock blocking his path that he needed to sidestep.

"No," Wyatt called out almost instantly, causing Asa to stop in his tracks once again. "I don't need you every single practise session, and I think I can handle myself for today, so you can leave."

Carmen saw Asa's eyes narrow at his friend, shoulders squaring in a subtle manner. "Leave?" He lifted a brow. "I've got nothing better to do, might as well spend my time helping you."

"Asa." Wyatt shot him a look.

"Wyatt." There was warning in Asa's tone.

A loud sigh left Wyatt's mouth, and he fixed Asa with a hard look. "I'm going to go hit the pool, got it? And I don't want to see you there. I mean that, Asa." He broke the stare and looked at Carmen, offering her what she supposed was a reassuring smile. "All the best," Wyatt mumbled to her under his breath before walking away from the two of them.

Carmen shifted her body around to face Asa, watching wordlessly as he glared at Wyatt's retreating figure before turning away abruptly and making his way towards the door of the building in quick, long strides.

She took off after him immediately, not hesitating, not pausing for even the briefest moment to second guess herself.

"Asa!" Carmen called after him as she picked up her pace, struggling to catch up with him.

The second she pulled open the door to step outside, a blast of cool air rushed to Carmen's face and the smell of damp earth wafted to her nose.

Asa was standing just an arm's reach away, a frown on his face as his eyes darted around the parking lot with agitation. His eyes flickered up towards the sky and upon noticing the dark clouds, his frown only deepened.

Taking in a deep breath and ignoring the erratic beats of her heart, Carmen slowly approached Asa. Once she was close enough, she cleared her throat in an attempt to compose herself, hoping that she could get through this without losing her mind or tripping over her own words.

"Listen, Asa, I—"

"Your dad. Is he coming to pick you up?" Asa suddenly asked with a clipped tone, startling Carmen and making her blink repeatedly at him before responding.

"W-what? My…Uh, no. No, he isn't. I to—"

"Stay here," Asa ordered, still refusing to look her in the eyes. "I'll bring the truck around."

"I thought you hated me." Carmen raised her brows, looking at him through the corner of her eyes.

Asa clenched his jaw, his shoulders stiffening. "I gave you the first ride back home long before we were even friends," he told her. "It had been a simple, civil gesture back then just like it is right now. You don't have to read anything into it because it means *nothing*."

And then he was walking into the rain, towards the parking lot, heading in the direction of wherever his truck was.

Carmen released the breath she'd been holding in, feeling her shoulders drop slightly at the realisation that Wyatt hadn't been kidding when he said Asa was going to be difficult to crack. Of course, Carmen had known it too. Asa wasn't one to forgive easily. But truth be told, she never expected him to have such a strong resolve.

The sound of an approaching vehicle caught Carmen's attention, and her eyes landed on the familiar red truck that set off the tugging sensation in her chest again.

Sighing softly, she left the shelter that the roof of the building provided and went into the light downpour, running down the steps as she felt the wind whip her hair back and the raindrops kiss her skin, causing an exhilarating sensation to course through her veins.

Asa leaned over the seats and opened the passenger door for Carmen, allowing her to get in right away instead of getting any wetter in the rain.

"I love the rain," she said in a rushed exhale, the lingering exhilaration doing the talking for her.

500

"I know," Asa muttered, driving them out of the school's parking lot.

"You do?" Carmen shot him a surprised look, knowing she hadn't ever told him that.

"Lucky guess." His tone remained clipped and detached.

Carmen looked away, not liking the disappointment or the sinking feeling in her stomach at being given the cold shoulder by Asa himself of all people.

The ride was uncomfortably silent, the air so thick with tension and an undercurrent of something much stronger, yet also somehow so fragile that Carmen could have cut through it with her fingernail in order for it to explode.

"You, uh." Carmen broke the silence, then stopped, feeling nervous all of a sudden. "You didn't ask me why I'm getting a ride from you today instead of my dad."

"I would have, but that would imply I actually cared," Asa responded easily enough. "And I don't."

The remark stung, but Carmen let it roll off her knowing that this was just Asa's hurt doing the talking for him. Broken hearts did and said whatever it needed to for self-preservation. She would know. She'd know better than most people.

"But you knew Dad was picking me up these days?" Carmen asked, something like awe lingering in her tone.

Asa's brows furrowed in confusion, but other than that, he didn't give much away. "Yes."

There was a fluttery feeling in Carmen's chest near her left breastbone, upon hearing that Asa had actually cared enough to make sure she had a ride back home.

"Well, if you're not going to ask, I'm still going to tell you." Carmen shrugged, deciding she might as well spit it out now. "I asked him not to come."

Asa's eyes were still fixed on the road, not giving Carmen any signs of acknowledging what she'd said.

501

"Because I was hoping that we'd be able to do this," Carmen went on, gesturing to the truck and the space between them.

Asa didn't respond.

Carmen sighed heavily and ran a hand down her face in mild frustration. "Because I miss you, Asa." Putting into words what she was feeling was refreshing in a way she'd never known—terrifying in the moments before she spoke them and soul-satisfying once she'd got them out. "I miss you, okay?"

"Okay."

Her breath hitched at the outright dismissal of her words, of her attempt—regardless of how tiny it was—to voice out what she was feeling.

"I'm trying to tell you how I feel, Asa," Carmen said, feeling frustration simmer in the pit of her stomach.

"And I recall telling you that your words mean nothing to me. Because when it comes to you, Carmen, words are just that: words."

Carmen's chest clenched at the reminder of what was probably one of the worst days of her life. The image of Asa's face flashed in her mind, the look of utter disbelief, that heartbreak in his eyes where warmth was supposed to be. *She* had put him through that.

It had been words with which she'd let him believe she was ready for a relationship back then, and it had been words with which she'd ripped away that belief from right under his feet.

Sadly, it was only words that she had right now too. Except, this time, she hoped Asa would be able to see that it came from a place of vulnerability and raw honesty.

"Hunter told me what you did for him last week," Carmen said after a few minutes of heavy silence.

"Yeah, well." Asa shrugged, his hand tightening around the steering wheel. "Didn't do it for you."

"I know," Carmen told him softly. "You did it for him."

And that makes my heart fall a little bit more.

502

But Carmen decided now wasn't the best time to say anything she hadn't planned on telling him.

"Is that why you're here?" he asked, shaking his head to himself slightly. "To thank me for Hunter?"

"No," Carmen murmured, her eyes drifting towards Asa's profile. "I didn't know what I was going to say to you, but then I ran into Marlene and…"

Asa's head tilted towards her, not exactly taking his eyes off the road, but the gesture was enough to let Carmen know that he wasn't expecting her to say *that*. It was more acknowledgment than he'd shown her the whole ride so far.

"We, uh, we started talking and…" Carmen shrugged despite knowing that Asa couldn't see the gesture. "And something just struck me when she mentioned that she was afraid to get involved with you because of Isla."

Asa brought the truck to a stop, and Carmen's eyes flickered to the windshield, only then realising that they'd already reached her place.

But Carmen didn't make any move to leave Asa's presence. Not yet.

The silence stretched on, unnerving and making Carmen's heart do somersaults in her chest. How was she supposed to word it? How was she supposed to start? Did she slowly build up to it?

"He was the first person to tell me he loves me," Carmen blurted, her tongue not waiting for her frantic thoughts to catch up. The words had slipped past now, and there was no taking them back.

Asa's forehead creased, and he turned his head to finally meet Carmen's eyes for the first time that day.

Something happened. There was an explosion in Carmen's chest.

It was as if a barrier had burst wide open and all the caged butterflies had broken free and they were now flapping their wings in every single crack of Carmen's being—and the feeling was driving her insane.

503

Was this what it was like to truly open yourself up to the emotions a certain someone could make you feel? To let in everything that one single person was capable of sending your way?

"Uh," Carmen paused to clear her throat, "Mum and Dad. Well, I had a complicated childhood so—so it was hard, I guess, for them to tell me they loved me. And the rest of my relatives, well, they pretended to just not notice my existence." She looked down at her lap, her hands toying with each other. "But Hunter, he, uh, he just...he would just casually say those three words to me, you know? When we were playing together or when we were about to say goodbye for the night and go back to our own homes. I mean, at his age, all the guys tried to act cool and not hang around their little sisters or any girls for that matter. But he never cared, you know? He wasn't afraid to show that I mattered to him, that he'd rather spend his lunch breaks at school with me than the other guys."

Carmen sighed deeply and tilted her head back on the seat, letting her eyes flutter close for a brief moment.

"But," she opened her eyes and pulled her brows together, "but then he grew up and was no longer the boy who wasn't afraid to show love. In his place was a brick wall, closed off to everyone, not showing even a sliver of emotion. I don't know why. Maybe it was because I knew him in a way nobody else ever did, but the minute I saw the tiniest crack in his armour, I just held on to it with both hands and didn't want to let go. I couldn't give up on the one person who made me feel belonged when I was a kid."

When Carmen turned to look at Asa, she found his eyes already on her. They were conflicted, confused, hurt, angry—a myriad of emotions that kept crashing into each other and fighting for dominance.

"Why?" he asked quietly, shaking his head at her like he genuinely didn't understand—*couldn't* understand—what she was doing. "Why *now*, Carmen? Why are you even telling me this?"

"Because I'm tired of looking at you from across the hallway and feeling myself lose you all over again," she told him, her voice growing hoarse. "And this is me trying to give you a piece. Trying to let you carry

504

something of mine with you. You must have wondered why I just welcomed Hunter back with open arms, and while I am honestly sorry for doing so without ever considering your feelings, I do want you to understand where I was coming from. And that it wasn't a place of me wanting to hurt you, but from a place where the six-year-old in me just wanted her brother back."

Carmen watched him for a moment longer, searched his eyes for something—*anything*—but she came up empty. But that was okay. It was okay because Asa had crossed the entire bridge towards her time and time again, not stopping at a midpoint and waiting for her to meet him halfway. But Carmen was standing at that midpoint now. She was telling him that she was ready to walk that bridge too.

And if Asa needed time to process the fact that Carmen was now willing to build the very bridge that she'd burnt to ashes, then she supposed he wasn't asking for too much.

Carmen had taken that first step; she'd shared with him the very first piece of herself. She was finally finding her way back to him, and it was both the ending of one thing and the beginning of something else all at the same time.

So, with her heartbeats a little steadier and her breathing a lot more calmer, Carmen climbed out of the truck and began walking towards the familiar door of her home, away from Asa.

And she hoped and hoped and hoped it'd be the last time she'd ever walk away from him.

•　　•　　•

"What are you doing?"

Carmen looked up at Hunter's voice, the small smile on her face stretching slightly further.

"Breaking my crayons." She grinned at his incredulous expression.

Hunter blinked once, dropped his stare to the colouring sticks in Carmen's hands and the ones scattered over her desk, and then met her

505

eyes once again. "I can see that," he said slowly. "So let me repeat my question, *what* are you doing?"

Carmen shrugged, exhaling loudly, and as she did so, a wave of self-content washed over her, making her feel a little lighter on the inside than she had in the past few months.

"They're a reminder," she responded.

"Of the fact that you can break things?"

Carmen smiled again, the memory slowly unfolding and playing out in her head, and she could swear that she felt it right then: the ghost of Asa's hand brush against her fingers from the time when he had placed those broken halves into her palm.

"Of the fact that broken doesn't always mean completely useless," she told him softly. "And shouldn't be assumed as trash."

Hunter's brows furrowed, ocean blue eyes narrowing at her curiously as he leant his shoulder against her doorframe, with one hand still clutching the handle.

Carmen sighed. "I mean, these can still colour, right?"

"You're weird," he told her seriously. "But I happen to like you, so I guess I've got to tolerate your philosophical moments."

"Please," Carmen let out a tiny snort, "you *love* me."

"Yeah?" His lips twitched at the obvious repression of a smile. "Says who?"

"Says the fact that you stay over every single time your dad is out of town," Carmen told him with a raised brow. "And your dad's out of town *a lot.*"

Hunter offered her an exaggerated roll of his eyes. "Well, get used to it. Because you're not getting rid of me anytime soon, if ever."

"I *don't* want to get rid of you," Carmen said warmly, noticing that he didn't exactly acknowledge the fact that he loved her. Surprisingly enough though, Carmen wasn't upset about it.

She didn't doubt it anymore; Hunter did love her, even while struggling to break down that steely armour he'd grown so used to enveloping himself with. And Carmen was okay with letting him take his own time to grow comfortable with the shift in their relationship compared to how it had been the beginning of senior year and all the times before that.

"Don't you miss your home, though?" she asked in an attempt to change the topic, moving to sit on her bed with her legs outstretched in front of her and her back resting against the headboard.

Hunter pushed himself off the doorframe and hesitated before stepping into her room, a piece of cloth balled up in one of his fists. Placing the maroon material on her desk, he dragged the chair towards the bed and stopped right across from her before dropping down on it.

"Home is wherever you are," he told her with a simple shrug of his shoulders, but Carmen noticed he looked slightly tensed, almost as if he didn't particularly like admitting that.

And for some reason, Asa's face flashed through her mind: hurt, disbelief, betrayal, heartbreak.

"Don't," Carmen said quietly, causing Hunter's eyes to snap towards her. "Don't let me have such a huge place in your life. Asa did, and all it brought him was pain."

"Well," Hunter paused, observing Carmen for a while before smiling softly, "you're worth the pain."

Carmen pursed her lips, looking at him with slight weariness, not truly believing what he was saying. And as if trying to prove its point, her mind replayed the very words Hunter had uttered to her in the school hallways when he'd walked in on Asa holding her hand.

"You know, in a twisted way, the two of you would actually be a perfect fit for each other."

Carmen didn't say anything and just watched Hunter with a conflicted heart and sad smile as his words from what felt like a lifetime ago resounded in her head.

"That boy may like broken things but you're not broken, Carmen. You're a goddamn abomination."

Hunter had said that to her, he had. But it was also Hunter who was telling Carmen now that she was worth the pain. He was telling her that *he* believed that.

It was hard to digest what he was saying now when he'd unblinkingly ripped her heart to shreds before. Carmen wondered if it was the same for Asa. She wondered if he, too, doubted Carmen's words when she'd opened up to him about Hunter a few days back.

But maybe, just maybe, Asa would come to realise that the cracks that Carmen had inflicted upon his heart were capable of being sewn together by only her. Just like Carmen was beginning to realise Hunter's words now was drawing out the venom of his previous ones that'd crept into her being.

Because sometimes, and only sometimes, the ones who broke certain parts of your heart were the only ones who could truly help you patch those pieces back together. The ones that could cause that kind of damage were sometimes the very ones you allowed to step across your threshold, the ones you deemed were worthy of the pain they'd brought. The ones you loved more than you hated despite what they had done to you.

Carmen was ready to fully acknowledge and accept the fact that she wanted to love Hunter more than she hated all the pain he'd brought, and she could only hope with every fibre of her being that Asa could find it in him to love her more than he hated what she'd done as well.

"Hunter, it's okay." The words left her mouth before she could truly register them.

His observant gaze turned puzzled and he knitted his eyebrows together. "What's okay?"

"Us," Carmen told him softly, leaning forward and slipping a hand in his. "I forgive you, you know. It's okay. *We're* okay."

Hunter just continued to stare at her, his Adam's apple bobbing as the conflict in his eyes grew. His mouth fell open, slightly moving as if he was just about to say something to her, before he seemed to have a change of mind and clamped it shut.

508

"What is it?" Carmen asked with a gentle tone, knowing that he was only finding it difficult to say whatever he wanted to, because it was important, because it mattered to him.

"Uh, I…" Hunter cleared his throat and leant back in the chair, fixing his gaze on one of the legs of the bed. "How come you never asked me why I had a sudden change of heart? Why I wanted to stop holding Mum's death over you?"

Carmen's heart clenched at how Hunter still referred to her own mother as mum.

"I didn't want to push you," she admitted with a sheepish smile. "You always get annoyed when asked to talk about feelings and all that…" She shrugged, letting the sentence hang in the air.

Hunter's gaze softened and he lifted one of his legs, placing it on the bed and nudging her foot with his. "You ask me whatever you want whenever you want," he muttered, looking away again. "I promise to try and not snap."

Carmen's chest swelled with affection and she offered him a small smile. "Okay then." She nodded towards the piece of clothing on her desk that Hunter had brought in with him. "Can you tell me what that is?"

Hunter chuckled lightly and then reached behind his head to grab the cloth before throwing it straight at Carmen's face.

She took a hold of the dark red material once it slipped down to her lap and began to stretch it out. "What on earth is this?"

"My jersey," Hunter mumbled under his breath, lifting one tensed shoulder in an awkward shrug. "The first away game of the season is just around the corner and, well, I'd like it if you were there, wearing my number."

Carmen's eyes grew wide as she stared at him in a mixture of awe and bafflement, before she looked down at the front of the jersey in her hands and saw the number *17* in big, white lettering with the team name *Vikings* above it in a much smaller font.

509

Turning the jersey around, she found the same number printed on the back, but this time with Hunter's last name, *Donoghue,* sewn above the *17* instead of the team's name.

"I know a lot of guys give it to their girlfriends, but…" Hunter scratched the side of his head. "But you know me, I'm more of a family guy than the romantic type. Can't deal with all that lovey-dovey shit." He looked like he wanted to add something else but hesitated and pressed his lips together.

Carmen waited as a beat of silence slipped past, and then Hunter spoke again:

"Football and you—they're the only aspects of my life that matters. So it only makes sense for you to have my jersey number."

Carmen bit her lip, and she didn't know if it was to stop the gigantic smile from breaking out on her face or to prevent happy tears from pooling in her eyes.

"I…" Carmen blinked, glancing down at the maroon-coloured piece of clothing and then back at Hunter's composed expression. "I don't know what to say."

"You can say that you'll wear it," he remarked, lifting a brow.

"Of course, I'll wear it, you idiot." Carmen laughed, affection lacing her voice. "Thank you," she mumbled in a softer tone. "This means a lot because I know how much you've loved the sport ever since we were kids."

It looked like Hunter wanted to say something again, but this time he refrained himself for good and just settled for a small smile in Carmen's direction.

"He'll come around, Carmen," Hunter said with a small sigh after a minute or two had passed.

Carmen's eyes snapped up from examining the jersey, and she frowned at him curiously. "What?"

"San Román," Hunter shrugged. "I don't know if you'll ever end up together or not, but he will forgive you, that much I'm certain of."

510

Carmen's eyes dropped back to her fingers that were playing with the lettering on the dark red material in her hands. "You don't know that."

There was another sigh from Hunter. "Yes, I do," he muttered, rising up from the chair and beginning to walk towards the door. "Because the one thing he and I have in common is our love for you, even though it's on two completely different levels. Either way, he would know what I know: that you're worth the pain."

"What does that even mean, Hunter?" she sounded tired and worn out now. "That I have the ability to hurt someone so deeply but it should be okay because it's coming from me?"

He offered her a small smile. "No. It means that you have a significant place in his life. And now you get to decide what you want to fill that place with."

Carmen then understood what Hunter was trying to tell her. She had never fought back with him because she always believed *he* was worth the pain. And in doing so, she let him continue to hurt her. And hurt her. And hurt her.

Until Hunter had decided he didn't want to just be someone who was worth the pain because if he had that significant a place in Carmen's heart, then he was also capable of bringing *that much* joy. And here he was, trying to fill that place with something other than agony and negativity.

And Carmen supposed she had places to fill too—places that she had rendered empty.

Because when it came down to it, Carmen didn't want to be someone worth the pain when she could be someone who washed it away instead.

And maybe that was what love was.

61.
I Want You To Stay

The stadium was packed with students by the time Carmen and Joyce arrived. Making their way through a sea of people to get to the stands, Carmen's eyes swept across several faces; some she recognised but most she didn't. It made sense as this was an away game, and it was the students of the school to which this stadium belonged to that filled most of the seats.

"There they are!" Joyce suddenly shouted, having to raise her voice considerably in order to be heard over the roar of the crowd.

Carmen felt Joyce tug at her hand as she picked up her pace and pulled her along, heading towards one of the stands at the right part of the stadium. She noticed Willa seated there, along with a few other girls from their year that Carmen shared some classes with but didn't really call friends.

Still, they were better off being seated with students from their own school than amongst the competing teams.

When they were close enough, Willa jumped out of her seat and threw her arms over both Carmen's and Joyce's shoulders and pulled them in for a quick hug, yelling in their ears, "Finally! Keeping these seats for you guys wasn't fun."

People were still flooding the bleachers though, so they broke the group hug and quickly settled down into their seats so as not to block anyone's way. Three or five more minutes passed before the already noisy stadium erupted into excited screams and deafening cheers from both schools upon seeing the teams enter the field.

Everyone was on their feet with lightning speed, hollering out either particular players' names or just their team's name, proudly showing their support. Despite knowing pretty well how the sport was played, Carmen wouldn't call herself a huge fan of it, but the enthusiasm pouring out of every other person in the stands was flooding the air and it was hard not to feel the positive energy fill her up, too.

Carmen smiled to herself, sweeping her eyes over the stands, the field, the food stalls. She inhaled the air filled with the smell of popcorn and cheesy fries and even the slight tinge of sweat that coated the hyped-up atmosphere and realised she was actually quite happy right then, in that moment.

The smile on her face didn't waver, remaining there on the edge of her lips even as they all sat back down while the match started.

• • •

As the halftime approached, Carmen turned towards Joyce, about to state that she was thirsty and offer to get something for her too. But Joyce had already turned towards her and was already speaking before Carmen could say anything.

"All this screaming is making my throat hurt! I'm going to get a soda and maybe even a snack or two," she rose from her seat and looked down at Carmen, "you coming?"

Carmen grinned and stood up, sliding off her shoulder bag to leave it on the seat so it'd be obvious that space was already taken. "I was actually about to ask you the same thing," she told her friend as she grabbed her purse from the bag, "come on."

Apparently, a lot of other people had the same idea as them, because it was taking forever for them to descend the steps and head towards the food stalls. When they did manage to push past the crowd however, the sight of the long queue at the cheesy fries stand made Joyce groan with frustration.

"Maybe one of us should get the fries and the other should go to the soda stand," Carmen suggested. "It'll take too long otherwise."

Joyce mumbled something under her breath and gestured for Carmen to leave. "I'll get the snacks, you get the sodas."

Nodding her head in agreement, Carmen turned around and began walking towards where she could see soft drinks and bottles of water being sold.

It was only after what felt like hours that Carmen started walking back to the seats with two cans of sodas in each hand, not spotting Joyce anywhere near the food stall and assuming she'd already left once she'd bought the snacks.

She should've just kept walking forward, but for one split second, her eyes swept over the crowd once again, and Carmen halted in her steps when her sight fell on a familiar figure standing by the corner of the bleachers, right where the gate to the exit of the stadium was.

Isla hadn't noticed her though; those electric blue eyes of hers was trained on something in the distance. Curious now, Carmen followed her line of sight, and her eyes landed on the group of cheerleaders on the field who were taking a break themselves now that it was halftime.

Carmen watched as one of the girls chucked a water bottle at another cheerleader, and another member of the cheer squad massage one of the girl's necks. There was a kind of unity there, the same kind she'd witnessed between players of a football team whenever she'd watched the games with Hunter back during happier times.

Her gaze returned to the familiar stranger by the bleachers.

There was a twist on Isla's mouth, something between a frustrated scowl and a sad smile. Carmen thought it looked more like sadness than anything else. She was still debating on what to do when a pair of electric blue eyes snapped to her own grey ones.

Carmen froze for a moment, feeling like a deer in headlights and then, uncertainly, she raised one of her hands that was still holding the soda can into the air and waved.

514

Isla's face remained unreadable as she visibly hesitated for a brief second, before leaving the stands and walking towards Carmen.

"Hey," she said easily, a small lift to her cherry-stained lips. It was one of those smiles offered out of courtesy, Carmen could tell. But she returned a genuine one anyway.

"Hi," Carmen greeted back, the condensation on the cans now making her palms uncomfortable. She tucked them under her arm and rubbed her damp hands against the rough material of her jeans.

"I didn't peg you for a sports kind of person," Isla muttered, glancing at the field before looking at Carmen again.

"Just here to show my support." Carmen smiled. "Won't say I'm a diehard fan."

Isla hummed in acknowledgement and looked away again, staring at the field— or maybe nothing in particular.

Carmen's eyes, however, remained fixed on the girl's face, finding it hard to recognise her as the same person she met more than half a year ago.

"You've gotten a haircut," Carmen said softly, repeating the very first words she'd spoken to Isla around seven months back. Without really registering what she was doing, Carmen lifted her hand and grazed her fingers across one of the uneven locks that fell just above Isla's right cheekbone.

Blue eyes flashed to her own ones again.

"What?" Isla blinked, a little startled.

"Your hair." Carmen gestured with her free hand towards Isla's shaggy strands. "It's different now. Did you cut it yourself?"

This time, the smile that Isla offered was genuine, and yet, sadder than when she'd been staring longingly at the cheer team she'd once captained.

"You noticed," Isla mumbled, but it sounded like she was speaking to herself more than she was addressing Carmen.

"You noticed". Those were the exact words Isla had responded with back then too.

515

Something nagged at the back of Carmen's mind—but it was a wisp of smoke, floating around aimlessly, something she couldn't quite grasp to make sense of right now.

"Yeah." Carmen shrugged. "Falls around your face differently."

Recognition flickered in Isla's eyes; she was recalling their first ever conversation, too.

Isla's smiled widened the slightest bit. "Makes my cheekbones more prominent?" she joked, repeating Carmen's comment about her haircut back then.

Carmen let out a short laugh, but didn't say anything as her eyes roamed over the platinum blonde mane that was cut in uneven lengths, no longer flowing below Isla's shoulders but stopping just past her pointed chin. It didn't make Isla's cheekbones look more prominent, it made Isla look...*messy.*

"It was nice running into you," Isla said after a few minutes, breaking the silence that had fallen between them. "I'll s—" Her eyes fell on what Carmen was wearing, and they flashed with surprise before going back to being impassive.

Carmen looked down at herself, forgetting for a moment what would be so extraordinary about her clothes when she suddenly remembered she was wearing the jersey.

"Past few months have really been about huge changes, huh?" Isla mused, eyes fixed on the lettering of the jersey.

"I guess." Carmen shrugged, not knowing what else to say. Hunter's name wasn't printed on the front, but she had a feeling Isla knew whose number she was wearing anyway.

Isla opened her mouth, raised her eyes to Carmen's, dropped her gaze back to the *Vikings* printed on the front of the dark material, then met her eyes once again. "I hope he doesn't let you down," Isla finally said, her voice sounding oddly thick with emotion.

Carmen blinked, obviously taken aback. There was probably a thousand things she could've said in return. Instead she just smiled softly and said, "I hope so too."

516

Isla's eyes grew glassy, and she tore her gaze away, tilting her head back and looking at the starless sky. Carmen looked up at it, too.

It must have been raining heavily somewhere else, because there was a flash of lightning in the distance. Then they heard the low rumble of thunder.

"You're a good person, Carmen West." Isla sighed heavily, a ghost of a smile on her lips.

Carmen's eyes left the sky and found the side of Isla's face.

"So are you, Isla Martin."

Another beat of silence passed, and Isla shook her head before turning to face Carmen. "Let me walk you to the bleachers," she offered before frowning slightly. "You should've gone to get the drinks with a friend or two. It's not the best idea walking alone in this crowd here. The guys from this school don't have the best reputation, you know."

Carmen waved her off. "It's all right, really. I can—"

"It's *not* all right," Isla said patiently. "You're wearing the jersey of the opposing team's captain. Not the smartest idea, Carmen."

Carmen didn't argue any further, allowing Isla to escort her back to the bleachers and leave her side only once she'd seen Joyce and Willa seated a few rows above.

•　　•　　•

There was still a few minutes for halftime to be over, so it was still nearly impossible for Carmen to push her way through the groups of people chatting excitedly in between rows of seats, moving from one corner of the bleachers to the other in order to greet their friends.

Carmen was just a few feet away from reaching Joyce when she got sandwiched between the backs of two students who obviously didn't care about making room for people to walk through as they remained standing instead of settling in their seats.

Gritting her teeth in frustration, she was about to ask one of them to move when an eerily familiar hand grabbed a hold of hers and pulled her forward, away from the suffocating position she was stuck in.

Carmen didn't have to look to know who it was; she'd recognise the feel of his calloused palm and firm fingertips wrapping around the skin of her wrist anytime, anywhere.

In any version of an alternate reality, she'd know his touch, his warmth. She'd know the sudden unsteady beats of her heart, the knot in her stomach as if all the butterflies had gathered right in the centre of it. She'd know *him*.

It felt like another eternity in which she steadied herself and dared to meet his eyes.

And, there they were. Liquidised gold.

Carmen's heart skipped a beat.

It took copious amounts of willpower to suppress the giddy smile that was threatening to take over her face.

"Um." She paused. "Thanks."

Asa's eyes narrowed the slightest bit. It would've been only natural to miss the gesture, but Carmen's senses were tuned into everything Asa-related right now..

He offered her a curt nod and moved back a few steps, letting her walk past him to where her bag was occupying her seat.

"You definitely took your time," Joyce said incredulously once Carmen was close enough. "Seriously, I was beginning to think you got lost and was about to come look for you."

"Nah, just ran into Isla." Carmen shrugged, handing Joyce one of the fizzy drinks that wasn't as chilled now as it was when she'd bought it.

Surprise flashed across Joyce's face, and her mouth made an inaudible "oh" but she didn't say anything else and Carmen was thankful for it. In the recent months, she'd come to realise that Joyce didn't really have a narrow-minded perspective, that it wasn't in her nature to stereotype or generalise people.

Joyce just had a pliable mind, and it was easy for other people's attitudes to rub off on her. Despite that weakness, she was actually a pretty great person, and Carmen appreciated that.

518

Popping her own can of soda open, Carmen's eyes sneaked a glance at the tall frame just an arm's length away, his mop of cinnamon hair looking almost glossy under all the stadium lights.

"How long has he been here?" Carmen found herself asking Joyce.

"Asa?" Joyce furrowed her eyebrows. "He was already here with Wyatt and Lyra by the time I came back with the fries. They were chatting with Willa and the rest of the girls. I don't know, maybe they were on the opposite side of the stadium before the halftime and decided to be seated here instead."

"Makes sense." Carmen nodded absentmindedly. "The opposite side is filled with a majority of the other school's students."

"Right." Joyce snorted, munching on cheesy fries and rolling her eyes. "That's why he's here, because he didn't like the seating arrangement."

Carmen paused midway of bringing the can to her lips and frowned at her friend. "He didn't come from the opposite end of the stadium just to be near me." Joyce opened her mouth to say something when Carmen cut her off. "I mean, he *is* the kind of person to do something like that, but he's not my biggest fan right now, so it just seems unlikely."

"The heart wants what it wants, Carmen," Joyce said dramatically before releasing a sigh. "And right now, mine wants more cheesy fries."

Carmen laughed lightly and shook her head, before gesturing towards the direction of the food stalls. "Do you want me to come with you?"

"Umm…" Joyce kept humming as she scanned the area around them and then stopped as she suddenly noticed something in the distance. "Nope! Seems like Lyra and Wyatt are heading in that direction. I'll just catch up with them."

"Sure?"

"Yeah, thanks!" Joyce flashed her a toothy smile and then hurried down the steps to join the other two who were already descending the bleachers.

She didn't see Asa with them though, which was odd since he'd been chatting with them just minutes ago.

Carmen had barely finished thinking it when she felt a presence near her and before she could look up, that presence was filling in Joyce's vacant seat.

Asa seemed comfortable enough seated towards Carmen's right, his legs outstretched in front of him and fingers tapping away at his phone.

Carmen blinked, forgetting how to breathe for approximately three to five seconds. And then she turned back towards the field where the teams were gathering to resume the game, finally registering in her mind that Asa was indeed sitting beside her.

The game didn't seem to matter anymore, and Carmen's fingers kept tracing the rim of the can, her stomach too knotted for her to be able to even drink anything.

"Hey, Asa!" Willa called from Carmen's left, and Carmen felt Asa turn his face towards her.

She didn't register Willa's words—or anything else for that matter—because Asa had shifted in his seat and was now leaning across Carmen to be able to communicate with Willa better.

Carmen's sight was blessed with a direct view of Asa's side profile, his slanting cheekbones just a few breaths away from her lips. She watched, with fascination, as his strong jawline twitched and clenched with every word he spoke. There were a few dark strands of hair that'd fallen over his forehead, brushing the tips of his left brow.

He was just a breath away. Just a breath away. And yet, somehow, she was miles apart.

Carmen's attention snapped back to her surroundings when Asa was beginning to pull away and his face was slipping past her line of sight. Something seemed to catch his attention though, because he suddenly stopped halfway, and when Carmen turned to look at him, she found his eyes fixed on the jersey she was wearing.

A beat passed. Then another.

"Um…" Carmen trailed off awkwardly, clueless as to whether she should say something or not.

"Our school's team actually has pretty cool jerseys," Asa commented, pulling his eyes away from the material swallowing Carmen's small frame. The jersey was almost twice her size.

"Yeah…," Carmen said distractedly before clearing her throat and speaking in a clearer tone. "Yeah, it does." There was a pause after that, but it felt more like a breakneck speed than a pause. As if everything had gone still at the suddenness, at the abrupt halt, and was waiting for one of them to give into the overwhelming silence.

"Uh…" Carmen hesitated, the words in her head tripping over one another and falling into a nonsensical heap as something in her rushed to offer some sort of explanation. She felt an irrational need to justify herself. "He, uh, he wanted me to wear it, and, well, I mean, this sport means everything to him, you know. And it's the first away game of the seas—"

"You don't…" Asa's voice was oddly gentle, before he pressed his lips together, clenched his jaw, and let out a small yet heavy sigh. Slowly, his eyes met Carmen's.

Her heart skipped another beat, but it hurt a little this time around.

"You don't have to explain," he eventually said, his voice quiet yet audible over the shouts and loud conversations around them.

Carmen didn't realise she'd been holding her breath, until he'd spoken those words and she exhaled what seemed like all the air she had left in her lungs.

"Oh?" It fell past Carmen's lips sounding like a surprised question than an acknowledgement.

Asa's gaze shifted to the grounds in front of them, and Carmen followed his line of sight. Both of them watched a very familiar figure, who was as tall as Asa but with a slightly larger physique, move around the field like a graceful predator who was on a mission to own the night.

"I get it now," he murmured, his eyes still following Hunter's movements on the field, "you love him, as I once loved Isla."

Carmen was holding her breath again, but this time she didn't seem to know why.

"I...I—yeah." She looked away just as Asa's eyes landed on hers once again, and she resumed toying with her soda can.

The minutes ticked by after that, and when Carmen realised that Joyce wasn't back yet, she swept the stands and then spotted her a few rows down, speaking to a few other familiar faces.

Asa shifted in his seat next to Carmen, catching her attention.

"Once, uh, once Wyatt or Lyra comes back, just let them know I left, yeah?" he asked, not facing Carmen fully, but tilting his head in her direction to show that he was addressing her.

Carmen's stomach sank to her feet. "You're leaving?" She couldn't help but ask, somehow managing to conceal the disappointment in her voice.

Asa stood up, slipped his phone into one of his pockets. "Yeah. I was actually supposed to get dinner after the game with Wyatt and Lyra. But I'm not feeling up to it anymore. Just let them know; I'll drop them a text anyway."

"Say something say something say something goddammit say something just say anything," she frantically thought. *"No no no no don't say anything don't make yourself look like a fool—*

Say something say something tell him how you feel say anything just open up to him, Carmen—"

"Asa, wait!"

Asa was just about to step down to the row of seats below the one they were on, when Carmen leant forward in her seat and shot her arm out, wrapping her fingers around his arm and tugging it.

He stopped dead in his tracks and his eyes snapped to hers with the speed of lightning, then dropped to his hand where her fingers were making contact with his skin.

"Shit shit shit what are you doing you idiot, you absolute idiot," she chided herself.

Carmen quickly pulled back her hand and self-consciously cradled it with her other palm, tapping one of her feet nervously against the ground.

He was staring at her with a mixture of hesitance and confusion, those warm eyes of his, questioning and curious.

"I, uh, I—I would actually—" she tried to say. *Oh for God's sake, Carmen,* she told herself. "I mean, what I'm trying to say is that…that it'd be nice if you, um, if you could stay."

The pause that followed her words was the loudest silence ever, and the shouting and screaming from the stands faded away to nothing.

"What?" Asa blinked, his forehead creasing as he continued to stare at her.

Carmen placed her palms on her knees and prayed he didn't see the way she gripped them so tight in order to steady her erratic heartbeats and faltering breaths.

"I said…" she began slowly, "that I'd like you to stay."

Something like surprise flickered in Asa's eyes but he covered it up quickly. The slight tremble in his voice when he uttered the next words however, he wasn't so quick to conceal. "You do?"

There was a pang in Carmen's chest, right where her heart resided. "Well, I don't want you to leave."

He turned his body around to directly face her. "Which one is it? You want me to stay, or you don't want me to leave?"

She knew what he was asking, and they weren't the same thing.

Did she want him because she chose to have him, or did she want him simply because she didn't want to deal with an empty space he'd leave behind?

Carmen looked into his eyes, saw his guard up, and then lifted her lips into the softest of smiles. "I want you to stay."

Something in Asa's posture seemed to soften, a very subtle gesture, but Carmen was drinking in all the little things. Then he stepped back up and settled into the seat next to her.

"Well, I guess I could put up with the rest of the game for tonight," Asa remarked with a casual shrug of his shoulders, sparing a glance at Carmen briefly before looking away again.

"I suppose you could," she murmured back, her eyes watching the players move around the field as it began drizzling and a ghost of a smile graced her lips.

62.
Just One Night

"You actually understand what's going on?" Asa asked after fifteen minutes or so of silence.

When Carmen looked at him in confusion, he gestured towards the game being played in front of them.

"Football?" she asked, a corner of her mouth lifting into a smile. "Yeah, used to watch it a lot back when I was a kid."

He nodded, humming in acknowledgement and then shifted his gaze back to the field.

A few beats of silence passed before Carmen turned her face towards Asa and picked up the conversation. "Wait, do you mean that you don't get the game?"

"No, I do get it," he said, leaning backwards and relaxing against the seat, as his gaze remained on the field. "Sort of, I mean. Wyatt's a fan. I'm not. He just makes me tag along with him to watch the games. But I don't know, I just forget the football terms and roles of the different players easily." He paused, smiled to himself, and then shook his head. "Swimming is so much simpler, honestly."

Carmen stared at the side of Asa's face as he said that, wondering if maybe sitting on these stands and hearing the crowd roar and their school's name being chanted during every achievement reminded him of what he was missing out on this year.

"I'm really sorry that you can't be a part of the meet, you know," Carmen told him seriously.

Asa's eyes snapped to hers, mild surprise evident in them.

"Thank you?" He sounded unsure of what he say. "I don't think you've ever brought it up before."

Carmen's shoulders lifted into something resembling a shrug, seeming to be at a loss herself. "I don't know... I guess it just didn't click for me to ask you about it or we just never had any conversation that could've led to the topic."

"Maybe," Asa murmured, and then dropped his eyes to his lap as one of his hands began picking at the material of his dark jeans. "But you could have still asked," he added in a quieter voice.

Carmen's breath caught in her throat and without permission, her mind raced through various times she'd spent with Asa. Had she never inquired him about his feelings? Had she never asked him if there was something on his mind, bothering him?

He always seemed so put-together in her eyes—he was her solid rock—that somewhere along the way she forgot he needed some solace too.

"I'm sorry," Carmen said, the apology genuine and raw on her tongue. "It never—I never—I don't know why I didn't—"

"I hate it when you apologise to me," Asa suddenly said, stopping his fidgeting with his jeans and raising his head to meet her eyes. "I really do. All I want to do when you apologise is tell you to stop saying sorry because...well, I don't even know why. I just feel like I shouldn't be someone you need to be so sorry around."

Carmen's eyes stared right back at his as she drank in his words and let it flow through her. "Then..." she started hesitantly. "What do you...what kind of 'someone' do you want to be to me? Who do you want me to see you as?"

Asa's brows furrowed the tiniest bit and Carmen's eyes watched his lips part slightly, the wheels in his head turning as his eyes kept flickering between Carmen's own ones.

"Your favourite hiding place? Your panic room? I don't know how to put it into words, Carmen." He shook his head, his eyes never leaving hers, but also somehow leaning in even closer, leaving the rest of the world behind them. "Just somewhere that you can scream into all you want, pour out your heart whenever you feel like it's getting too heavy and trust that every word you spill would never leave that room. Just for you to know that whatever pieces you give me would be for my eyes only; that I wouldn't dare give those pieces to anyone else; that I would keep them safe. I just want to be—" He came to an abrupt stop as realisation flickered in his eyes. The next words he uttered weren't even words, but a single shaky breath; "I want to be your art journal." One of his hands left the arm of his seat and reached towards Carmen's cheek, before he froze and pulled away, his fingers curling into his palm as he did so. "Am I asking for too much?"

It was a genuine question, not a rhetorical one, not a mocking one, not a self-sympathising one. Asa wanted to know—to *really* know—if he was asking for more than Carmen could ever give.

Carmen's mouth parted, her throat constricting with all the raw emotions that were pouring out of Asa's very being and filling her up from the inside. She felt an odd prickle at the back of her eyes but furiously blinked it away and swallowed past the painful lump in her throat.

For a painful moment, she wished he would love her less. It made her want to cry—the intensity of his feelings for her. To this day, she wasn't able to understand it, how he loved her when she wasn't even the whole version of herself.

And when she continued to look at him then, she knew right down to her bones that he was indeed the safest place she'd ever known. After all, Asa *was* warmth. And if Carmen did choose to put her trust in his hands, she knew he'd hold on to it with a death grip and never let go.

But, above all, Carmen *wanted* to let him in. She wanted him to take a sledgehammer to the dam built inside her heart and just let all the pain, and the hurt, and the guilt rush out of her system.

Asa wasn't asking for too much. He was asking for the *one* thing Carmen wanted to give him but just didn't know how to. So with her heart in her throat, Carmen slowly lifted a trembling hand and placed it atop one of Asa's, the inside of her palm resting gently above the back of his. "No," she told him softly, and he heard her. Even with all the background noise, he heard her. "You're not asking for too much, Asa."

His eyes fluttered shut, a few breaths passed, and when he opened them again, they were a shade darker. "I've missed hearing you say my name in that way," he mumbled.

Carmen frowned in confusion. "What way?"

"Like it means something to you."

"You've always meant something to me," she told him in a hoarse voice.

Asa didn't say anything for a few heartbeats, and instead just watched her with thinly veiled caution in his eyes. And then something in his composure cracked, and exhaustion flooded his face, so many emotions flitting across his sharp features that Carmen couldn't pinpoint them as they all rushed to form whirlwinds in his eyes.

"I want to believe you," he told her, and she heard the underlying helplessness in his voice. She heard the slight tinge of fear and the doubt. "I really do."

"But?" Carmen asked in a quiet tone, tearing her eyes away from his, because the heartbreak imprinted on every inch of his face was more than she could bear.

"But I gave you a loaded gun once," he said. "And I'm wondering if I'd be a fool to give you a second."

Carmen had no response to that.

•   •   •

Asa supposed he'd spaced out and lost all sense of his surroundings because suddenly the stadium erupted into the loudest of cheers that night and all around him, people had jumped to their feet. It was absolute pandemonium.

It didn't take him too long to realise the cause of the celebration when he saw that the students who were cheering and on their feet were ones he'd seen around occasionally in their school hallways. Asa trailed his eyes towards the field where the red and white jerseys of the Vikings could be seen running around the ground, victorious grins slapped on the faces of the football players of his school.

Without meaning to, his eyes drifted towards the familiar boy who was the team captain. Asa didn't think he'd ever seen Hunter happy. But right now, the usually cold and impassive boy had a grin on his face and a kind of pride in his eyes that Asa knew too well from experience. It was probably something only an athlete would be able to recognise.

Asa caught a glimpse of the Hunter that Carmen seemed to adore so much, and Asa wondered what kind of damage must have been done to him in order for that boy to have grown thorns in every corner of his being.

"Well," Carmen said from beside him, a soft smile on her face as she watched the players on the field celebrate for a few seconds longer before turning to face Asa. "I should probably start heading towards the parking lot."

Was his time with her over already? It was too soon. He wondered if any amount of time spent in her presence would be enough.

"Oh?" He raised a brow, masking his unwillingness to let her go. "Your dad's here?"

Carmen wrinkled her forehead. "No." She shook her head. "I came with Joyce."

Asa's eyes scanned the bleachers, but it was hard to spot anybody since people were abandoning their seats now that the game was over.

"I don't see her anywhere," he pointed out, squinting as he kept looking for the familiar mop of brown hair with a purple highlight.

"Yeah, I have no clue where she is either. But we agreed to meet by her car in the parking lot."

Asa's frown deepened, and he glanced at Carmen. "Is that even safe? You don't know this school, this neighbourhood."

529

"It's not like it's going to be deserted." Carmen shrugged. "There'll be plenty of people about."

Asa's eyebrows knitted together as he stood up from his seat, casting one last sweep over the stands. "Still," he muttered, scratching the side of his head uncertainly. "Let me walk you to her car at least."

When Carmen didn't respond, he shifted his body to face her and found that pair of thunderclouds he'd grown to love already examining his face with a kind of look he couldn't decipher.

And it was so easy, in moments like these, to get lost in her eyes and allow himself to be whisked away by whatever he found in them. This time though, Asa wondered if maybe it wasn't such a bad idea to be more cautious. After all, what harm could come from deciding to guard his heart? He'd experienced his fair share of consequences of leaving it unshielded and naked on his sleeve.

And although Asa was by nature a heart-over-head person, he decided a little self-preservation seemed sensible enough this time around.

"Okay, Asa," Carmen finally said, her voice so soft that it was almost carried away by the sudden gust of wind that blew past. Both of them snapped their eyes to the sky at the same time when they heard the rumbling of thunder; it sounded much closer now.

"It's probably going to start raining again." Asa sighed, stepping back and gesturing for Carmen to walk forward. "It's been raining every night for the past few weeks."

"Hmm." She nodded in agreement, slinging her bag over her shoulder and walking past Asa, her arm brushing against his torso with what little space the rest of the crowd allowed them.

For that tiny heartbeat, all Asa could do was watch—and *feel*. Whether it was the top of her head grazing along his chest, or her arm pushing into the hollow right beneath his ribcage as people squeezed past and pushed them closer together, or the length of her leg pressing against his. And though he couldn't put it into words, there was something hauntingly beautiful about the way the wind picked up the hair strands covering the side of her face that was in his line of sight and letting them fall behind her shoulder.

His eyes trailed down her profile, the way her eyes fluttered shut when a sudden spray of water hit her as it began drizzling; the way her lashes formed dark crescents that stood out against the ivory of her skin; the crease on her forehead that only deepened as more students began flooding the exit gates.

It was funny, really, how he could be stuck in the midst of a massive crowd that was trying to get home or find some temporary shelter from the rain, but all that his eyes sought out was her.

Asa didn't understand, and he wondered if he ever would.

"Wow, I didn't expect it to be this crowded," Carmen interrupted his stream of thoughts, her voice louder than usual as she tried to speak over the loud chatter of everyone else. "I feel like we've been standing on this same spot for ages now."

"High school football is a pretty big deal around this town," Asa said easily enough, his voice not giving away the vulnerability that came with being around Carmen.

A few more minutes passed and the two of them had finally made it to the exit when something caught Asa's eye.

He didn't stop walking—his hand hovering over Carmen's lower back, but not actually touching it as she walked ahead of him—when Isla's eyes met his from where she remained seated at the top row of one of the stands.

Her eyes flickered to Carmen, who hadn't noticed her yet, before landing once again on Asa. And then Isla blinked once, slowly, and nodded with a faint smile on her face.

Was that approval? Encouragement? Support? Was that Isla telling him she was glad to see them standing side by side again? Asa didn't know, but that moment seemed to hold some kind of significance that he couldn't describe yet.

Isla's figure kept growing smaller the more Asa and Carmen continued moving forward, but he didn't look away yet and parted his lips, about to mouth a silent goodbye to her when suddenly the bleachers disappeared from view and was replaced with a small stretch of wall and then the open space of the parking lot. They'd finally made it past the exit gate.

He swallowed back that goodbye and breathed in the fresh night air.

Out here, it was cooler and the atmosphere was free from the stench of sweat, smell of junk food and the humidity that came with so many bodies being in close proximity.

"You see Joyce yet?" Asa asked, tucking his hands into his pockets because he didn't want to give into the urge to hold hers.

He watched Carmen chew on one corner of her lip, those eyes of hers scanning the area around them as she turned her body around in a full circle. "Nope." She shook her head. "Her car's right there, though."

"We'll wait there then." Asa shrugged, his eyes following the direction Carmen's hand was pointing in. "Come on."

Carmen seemed to hesitate for a second—just a second—before she began walking towards the dark grey vehicle. She looked like she wanted to say something but Asa didn't push; he didn't know what pushing was going to achieve this time when it hadn't worked so well before.

An uncomfortable silence passed before she finally spoke. "You don't have to…I mean, you can leave you know. It's—it's really all right. She'll be here any minute."

She wasn't looking at him though, her eyes fixed on her left foot drawing patterns on the ground, and the only sound filling the space between them was their breaths and the soft crunch of gravel.

"Carmen," he said carefully. "Look at me."

Her foot paused in the middle of a pattern and was raised a few inches off the ground. Tilting her head towards him in acknowledgment, but not meeting his eyes yet, she let her foot fall back flat on the gravel.

"Are you not…" The words trailed off Asa's tongue, slipping back down his throat and choking him. But he ground his teeth together and

532

forced them out. "Are you not comfortable with being alone with me anymore?"

Startled eyes met his, bewilderment flashing through them and the genuine look of shock told him that he was wrong. "No, of course not," Carmen said incredulously. "Why would you think that?"

Asa opened his mouth to say something, stopped himself, and then sighed. "I don't know, you seem to be a little off now that we're not in a crowded place and it's just the two of us. Or am I just reading too much into things?"

Her eyes left his once again and went back to tracing the invisible patterns her foot began recreating. The sound of gravel crunching filled the distance between them again.

A beat of silence passed. Then another.

Asa didn't push. He waited.

"I…" Carmen began after a while, pausing to swallow and hesitate. "I don't want you to have to put yourself through being in my presence out of courtesy. I mean,… waiting here with me is… it's nice. It's considerate. But if it's making you unhappy to be around me, I'll be safe. Joyce will be he—" Carmen stopped speaking as her eyes seemed to register something in the distance. "Oh, look. She's already here!"

Asa looked over his shoulder and spotted Joyce walking towards them while talking to another girl, her forefinger wearing the key ring of what was probably her car's as she kept twirling it in the air. He turned his face around to look at Carmen, a million things running through his head now that his time with her was really coming to an end. With every step Joyce took in their direction, there was another addition to the list of things Asa wanted to suddenly tell her.

Carmen stepped away from him, adding another mile to the space between them.

"Bye, Asa." She offered him a small smile, but it didn't reach her eyes. She took another step back. "I'll see you around school, maybe." She tried to widen her smile, but the corners of her lips seemed to wobble and she dropped it, turning her head away and taking another step to open the passenger seat of Joyce's car.

And the passenger seat in Asa's truck remained empty.

He turned around, mumbling "Bye" to the spot where she'd been standing just seconds before, and then started making his way towards his truck. He pulled a hand out of his pocket to text Wyatt and Lyra, letting them know that he was heading straight home.

Behind him, he heard the fading voice of Joyce greeting Carmen and then the opening and closing of another door which was probably the driver's side of the car. And then he heard the engine start.

Asa closed his eyes and shook his head to himself. Tonight wasn't the right time for them to talk anyway. It was too crowded, too chaotic. It was a freaking school game for heaven's sake. They would've felt rushed and in a hurry to get the conversation over with. They didn't have the entire night to themselves.

He'd have given her this night though, if she'd only asked.

Asa didn't hear the sounds behind him until the footsteps had caught up with his, but before he could turn around, a body brushed against his side and a hand was pressed flat against his chest, stopping him in his tracks.

Carmen's eyes were shut as she inhaled deeply, looking completely out of breath and struggling to regain her composure.

Asa's eyes widened and his head whipped around to look over his shoulder where he saw Joyce's car pull out of the parking lot and disappear from view.

After blinking several times like a complete idiot, he turned back to face Carmen. Midnight hair, eyes that reminded him of rainy skies and the occasional skip of his heartbeats. God, it really was her.

"What...what are you doing?" he asked hoarsely, his disbelief ringing clearly throughout his voice.

"You didn't answer me," she told him, still sounding a little breathless from running all the way towards him.

"What?" He stared at her.

"I asked you if you were staying by my side out of courtesy and because it was the considerate thing to do," Carmen explained, referring to when they'd been waiting for Joyce. "And you didn't tell me that I was right."

Asa stared at her harder, wondering if she'd truly lost her mind.

"That's because you weren't right," he eventually told her, his shoulders still tensed from the shock of seeing her come back. "You were wrong. I just wanted to spend whatever little time I had left with you. Not because it was the considerate thing to do. I don't look at you as a burden, Carmen. Never have, never will."

He watched Carmen swallow, watched her blink a few times and then she let out a short, nervous laugh. "Okay," she breathed, almost muttering to herself. "Okay, that's good. I was hoping that was the reason because then... Then it means that you won't mind giving me a ride back?" She ended it questioningly, almost as if she was afraid to come to conclusions about his feelings for her anymore.

"Why?" He couldn't help but ask that. He was so confused right now. He didn't mind, of course he didn't, but he just couldn't understand what was going through her head right then.

Carmen smiled at him, but it looked nervous, very unlike the usual steady ones he'd seen her offer him before. "Just...just go with it for now? The small steps first? I, uh, I don't know how to put it, but—"

There was a sudden flash of lightning, and Asa saw Carmen's eyes instantly shut. He didn't react to it though; he was already looking right at the eye of the storm—fallen in love with it even. Then came the ear-splitting crack of thunder, and with it, the sudden downpour that the past few hours had been showing signs of.

Asa didn't stop to think twice. He grabbed a hold of Carmen's arm and began pulling her towards the other end of the parking lot where his truck was, the droplets of water pelting down on them and everyone else who hadn't left the venue yet.

"It's just rain," he heard her say from behind him as he picked up their pace. She sounded like she was smiling.

She really was insane.

"I prefer getting soaked under my shower, not in the middle of a parking lot," Asa said.

"You're no fun." She sighed contently, her words and her tone not at all in sync with one another.

"I don't want to catch a cold either," he pointed out.

"Wimp." Carmen sniffed, and Asa stopped dead in his tracks before turning around to look at her, finding that cheeky twinkle in her eye he hadn't seen since forever.

"What did you just say?" He snorted, letting out a disbelieving laugh.

"Nothing," she quickly said, and then nudged his foot with hers. "Don't you want to keep moving? We're only getting more soaked."

"I'm not a wimp," Asa grumbled under his breath before beginning to walk them towards his truck again.

A part of him wondered if this had to be wrong on some account. If it was even considered normal for the two of them to be able to banter this way after all that remained unspoken between them. After all the pain and the misery that had happened. But Asa also couldn't deny that it was only so, *so* natural for them to fall back into step beside each other, in every sense of the way.

He wondered if someone watching from the sidelines would understand, and then he realised it wouldn't matter if they didn't. Whatever transpired between Asa and Carmen remained between them, and the rest of the world didn't get to have a say in it.

Asa stopped in front of his truck, digging the keys from his pocket and hesitating when he was about to unlock the door. The rain didn't pause along with him; it kept pouring down in torrents, but he didn't care right then.

"Asa?" Carmen asked with a small frown, looking at him quizzically and blinking away raindrops from her eyes.

He watched her for a moment, just like he had when they'd been making their way to the exit gates. He saw her blink again as a drop of

536

water fell into her eyes; as tiny droplets hung off her dark lashes before they fell onto the curve of her cheek and trailed down her face; and as locks of her hair got plastered to her face, looking like dark brush strokes against a white canvas.

"This doesn't seem strange to you?" he finally asked, ignoring the rain, ignoring the rest of the goddamn world, ignoring everything that just wasn't Carmen West.

"What?"

"Us." He shrugged. "*This*." He gestured between them. "I once thought it'd be nearly impossible for us to even be in the same room again. But he we are."

Carmen smiled softly. "Here we are."

He took a step closer to her, and Carmen took a surprised one back. He paused in his tracks, forehead creasing at her retreat, before he took another determined step forward so that he was right in front of her. Carmen tried stepping back again, but seemed to realise she couldn't put any more distance between them when her back hit the surface of his truck.

"Carmen," Asa said patiently, his eyes not looking away from her face. Stepping even closer, he placed a palm against the vehicle, on the space next to where she was leaning against it, and crouched down slightly to meet her at eye level.

He brought up his left hand to place it next to Carmen's other side but thought better of it and let it fall back. It was a small gesture, yes, but he hoped she'd see it as him not wanting her to feel trapped or caged-in from both sides, and that he was still offering her a way out if she wanted it.

He had meant it when he said he wanted to be her art journal, and journals were supposed to be a form of liberation, not suffocation—*love* wasn't supposed to be an act of suffocation. And he needed to show her that. Even more, Asa needed to show her that *he* understood that.

"Carmen," he called again. "Look at me."

She didn't seem to acknowledge him right away, but eventually those eyes of hers flickered towards his and standing this close to her, Asa could hear her inhale shakily.

"You keep asking me to look at you," she said in a hushed breath.

"And you keep avoiding looking me in the eye," he murmured back.

Asa's eyes followed a drop of water that slid down the tip of Carmen's eyebrow and trailed down her temple, before slipping past her shoulder bone and disappearing into the neckline of the jersey she wore.

"You said—" Carmen began speaking but then came to an abrupt stop. Her eyes darted towards the space next to Asa's right, and then to his left. She was refusing to make eye contact again. The same girl that always had an unwavering ability to look deep into someone's eyes was now faltering, and that troubled Asa.

"Yeah?" he urged gently, knowing by now that with Carmen, patience was a key factor when trying to communicate with her.

Carmen sighed, shaking her head and lifting a hand to wipe away the raindrops that'd gotten into her eyes. "You said you gave me a loaded gun once."

Their eyes met for a split second, and then she was averting her gaze again. Asa resisted the urge to take a hold of her chin and turn her face towards his.

"Yes, I did," he said in a cautious tone, pulling his brows together. "What about it?"

Carmen inhaled deeply, and then let out a heavy, shuddering breath. Her eyes met his again. "You also said you'd be a fool to hand me a second one." And then she went back to staring at something in the distance or nothing at all in particular.

Asa opened his mouth, about to repeat his earlier question out of confusion but his puzzled state lasted for only a mere heartbeat, before it dissipated and something seemed to dawn on him.

The realisation was watching a sunrise from a hilltop, or witnessing a sunset at a beach, or even laying out on the roof of a car and stargazing, breathtaking at first but too beautiful that it eventually made the heart ache. Because how could such beauty be real?

This time, Asa reached out a shaky hand and placed his fingertips on her chin. "Carmen," he said softly, and then turned her face to meet his eyes. "*Carmen*," he repeated, his breathing still on hold. "Are you trying to tell me you want me to give you that second gun?"

She hadn't ever explicitly asked him for a second chance, had never really told him she felt enough towards him that she'd genuinely want to try again.

He was too afraid to let himself dare, to let himself hope that perhaps Carmen believed they were worth fighting for.

Asa's eyes never stopped searching hers, though he couldn't really tell what it was that he seemed to be looking for. But they looked so vulnerable right then, and it struck Asa that he'd never seen her in such a brutally raw state before, not like this.

"I want…" Carmen paused, swallowed, blinked really hard, and Asa wondered if all the drops of water streaming down her face belonged to the rain and not her own eyes. It was hard to tell. "I want you to give— to give me this one night." Her tone was cautious, each word dragged out with deliberation and anxiety.

"That's all I'm asking from you." She smiled shakily. "This one night from your life, Asa. Let me have it. And whatever I can give you, I'll give. You asked me to trust you so here's that trust, take all of it. Take the pieces I'm willing to let you have tonight. And…and after that, after everything's out in the open, you can leave. If you decide that you'd rather we went our separate ways, then we'll say goodbye and that will be it, Asa. That'll be the end of the road for us."

Carmen pushed herself off the truck and filled whatever space was left between them. "But if you decide to come back to me, if you decide to stay—" Her voice broke and she lifted a trembling hand to brush her cold fingertips against the length of his eyebrow. "Then I just want you to know that there's always a place in my heart and my soul for you."

Asa's lips parted with a rushed breath tumbling out, his throat constricting painfully and his eyes feeling like there were a thousand needles stabbing it from the behind.

I'm still in love with you. Six words. How easy it would've been to let them fall past his lips. So, *so* easy.

And yet, Asa resisted. *Self-preservation*, he reminded himself. He needed to guard his heart, didn't he? Not bolt it shut permanently, but protect it in what little ways he was capable of. He didn't have to say the words, but he also owed it to himself to have this conversation, to finally just sit down and fill that distance between them with the words that were never spoken.

"Okay, Carmen," he said then, a small smile of his own tugging at the corners of his mouth. "Okay." He breathed, hearing the crack of thunder above them and closing his eyes shut as an unfamiliar feeling flooded through him, offering his body warmth during the heavy downpour.

"Tonight is yours," he promised, grazing her cheekbone with his thumb. "So take it."

And for the first time that night, Asa saw some of that storm inside her eyes give away to the calm.

Right then, right there, with the moon as their light and the rain as their only witness, the two of them took that leap of faith towards the idea that maybe, just maybe, it was okay to believe in soulmates.

63.

Through Your Eyes

Rain was still pouring down in torrents when they arrived at Carmen's house.

Asa killed the truck's engine, cutting off the usual soft roar of the vehicle and enveloping the two of them with a heavy silence instantly.

Biting the corner of her bottom lip and ignoring the weight of all the unsaid words pressing down on her chest, Carmen glanced at Asa. "Sorry about your truck," she muttered, referring to both the driver and passenger seats that had absorbed the rainwater from their soaked clothes. "Your seats are ruined."

"Nah." Asa clicked his tongue, eyes flickering from the road ahead to the empty house beside them. "She's been around for a long time now," he said with an odd touch of warmth to his tone, patting the dashboard of the truck fondly. "Survived worse than a bit of rain."

Carmen offered a small nod in acknowledgement, before folding her hands over her chest and rubbing her arms.

"You're cold," Asa commented.

"You did make us stand in the rain back there in the parking lot."

"I recall you telling me it was just rain and proceeding to call me a wimp for not wanting to get drenched."

"But I wasn't the one who ended up drenching us," Carmen pointed out, raising a brow. "That was all you."

Asa's eyes narrowed and he looked like he was about to shoot something back at that, but then seemed to have a change of mind. "I'm too cold to argue about this right now. Can we just go in already, please?"

Carmen suppressed a smug smile, and turned to open the door of the passenger seat, bracing herself for the pelting down of raindrops the second time that night as she made a dash for her house.

"I'm definitely going to catch a cold after tonight," she heard Asa exhale loudly from behind her, having reached the porch steps at the same time as Carmen.

"Would be worth it." The words slipped out of Carmen's mouth with a light laugh before she realised it. Her hand suddenly paused in its act of unlocking her front door and she raised her chin to meet Asa's eyes.

He was already looking at her.

"It *is*," he told her, voice soft yet serious.

Carmen's heart skipped another beat that night. Or maybe it was several beats. She couldn't keep track anymore. Averting her gaze, she focused on unlocking the door and letting themselves in.

Once they'd entered her house and she let the door swing shut behind them, Carmen sighed. "I already feel warmer now that we're indoors." She lifted a hand to wipe away all the stray droplets of water on her face before running her palm over her head and pushing back all the wet strands of hair. She was dragging her palm back down over her cheeks, when her eyes suddenly made contact with Asa's.

Carmen froze momentarily, taking in the fact that he was watching her wordlessly, with an unreadable look on his face. "What?" she asked softly, the corners of her mouth twitching.

Asa pressed his lips together and slowly shook his head.

Carmen observed him for a few more seconds before her eyes dropped to his torso, noticing how the soaking wet material of Asa's button-down clung to his body like a second skin, stretching over his broad shoulders and down the defined planes of his chest.

"You probably need to change," Carmen said quietly, silently praying that her voice was as steady as she wanted it to be.

"I do," he said matter-of-factly. "It's starting to feel uncomfortable. Not to mention, cold."

"Right." Carmen cleared her throat, blinking twice and tearing her eyes away. "Right, of course. Uh, you —you can follow me up. There's probably something of Dad's you can wear." She turned towards the direction of the small staircase built along the side of one wall, and she felt Asa follow right after her.

"I've seen your dad only once," Asa said, and the sound of his voice gave away just how close he seemed to be standing behind her. "Twice, actually. That day when I dropped you off, and on Thanksgiving. I really don't think anything of his would fit me. He has a narrower frame than mine."

Carmen sighed and scratched the bridge of her nose. "I don't know," she muttered. "We'll see. There has to be something. Do you need to change your jeans too?"

"No," Asa replied. "They haven't absorbed as much water as my shirt. I don't mind staying in them."

"All right…" she mumbled under her breath, trying to recall if her father had any baggy shirts or t-shirts that would fit Asa. Carmen was just about to pass the guest bedroom and walk right into her dad's when she suddenly stopped in her tracks and headed into the guest room instead.

The room had never been used before and was always kept shut, collecting dust and cobwebs until the past few months, when Hunter had started staying over each time his dad was out of town.

Carmen was sure that her cousin left a few spare clothes around and sure enough, when she pulled open the large chest of drawers placed against the far side of the wall, she found a pile of folded tees inside.

Grabbing one off the top, she walked back out and handed it to Asa, hoping he'd just take it without asking any questions as to whose it was. "Here you go, that should fit you just fine."

Asa took the t-shirt from her, a distracted expression on his face. He looked like he was a million miles away from here. "Thanks," he muttered under his breath, eyebrows furrowed together before he seemed to snap out of his reverie and glanced down at Carmen. "Where do I change?"

"Um…" Carmen trailed off uncertainly, her eyes flickering between the different doors in the hallway, suddenly forgetting to form coherent words as her brain picked that moment to freeze over. "I, uh, you…"

She watched the uncharacteristically serious expression on Asa's face slowly morph into one of light amusement and then she saw that long-forgotten mischievous glint in his eyes, a look that Carmen thought she'd never see him wear again over the span of the past few months.

She watched him lift a hand towards his neck, his forefinger scratching the hollow at the base of his throat where both collarbones met, and then he slowly trailed downwards before coming to a stop at the topmost button of his shirt and popping it open.

Carmen's body froze but at the same time, her brain decided to do her a favour and kick-start. "What are you doing?" she blurted, her eyes widening.

"I asked you where I'm supposed to change," he told her in a casual tone, and then dragged his index finger further down, unfastening the second button with a barely-there kind of smirk and revealing a sliver of his chest. "And if you're not going to respond, I might as well undress here."

Carmen gaped at him, flabbergasted for a whole three seconds before her senses came crashing down over her again and she huffed, turning around and throwing open the door to the guest bedroom.

"There!" she exclaimed, pointing towards the open room, heat spreading over her cheeks and neck like wildfire. "You can change in there for heaven's sake!"

Asa's lips twitched and let his hand fall to his side before pushing himself off the wall and walking towards the guest room. "See," he murmured, stepping past her. "All you needed was a little bit of motivation."

544

"Just shut up and get changed," Carmen said exasperatedly, pushing him further into the room with a gentle shove and then walking towards her own bedroom, the tiniest of smiles gracing her lips now that Asa had somehow managed to break the uneasiness that'd been hanging over them since the ride from the stadium to here.

And as Carmen stepped into her attached bathroom, stripping off her wet clothes and putting on dry ones, she couldn't help but wonder if that was what Asa had intended all along, if the little stunt he'd just pulled was to remind her that he wasn't as serious in nature as he was playful and laid-back.

It seemed like something he would do for her. The thought alone made her chest flood with a particular kind of warmth that only Asa could radiate.

Opening the door of the washroom and stepping out, she found Asa leaning against the open doorway of her room, eyes scanning the walls, her dresser, her wardrobe and everything else as if he'd never been in here before.

"Asa, what are you doing?" Carmen asked, tilting her head slightly.

"Was waiting for you to be done." He shrugged, leaning away from the wall. "Can I come in?"

Carmen blinked, not responding for the first few seconds as she felt sharp pangs of regret and dismay right in the pit of her stomach. This was the same Asa who had once felt comfortable enough to pay her a surprise visit on the day of Thanksgiving, the same Asa who didn't have to ask her if she would like him entering her room because he'd already known the answer.

And here he stood—the very same Asa—just no longer confident in his instincts when it came to her.

"Of course you can come in," she told him in a hoarse voice, looking away from those eyes of his and picking up a fresh towel, making herself look busy while she smoothened its creases and folded it.

Just as she hung it over the back of the dresser's chair, she felt a hand touch the back of her elbow gently and Carmen turned around to find Asa incredibly close, lesser than even an arm's length away.

His eyes were trained on his feet, brows pulled together in deep thought as he took another step closer before allowing his hand around her elbow to trail down further and wrap around her wrist.

"Did that…" He raised his head to meet her eyes, a small frown on his lips. And then, bringing a hand towards her face, he used the back of his knuckles to stroke her lower jaw. "I didn't make you uncomfortable, did I?" He cocked his head to the side. "There, in the hallway? I wasn't trying to make you uneasy. You just seemed to be spacing out and worrying, so I wanted to break the ice."

A smile broke out on Carmen's face, giddy that even after all this time, she still knew him. She'd been right when she'd assumed he was just trying to keep the atmosphere light-hearted for her benefit.

Her mind flashed back to the evening of their date, when he'd shown up on the steps of her front porch with that mischievous shimmer in his eyes and that devilish grin on his lips. He had made a sarcastic remark, though Carmen couldn't remember what it was. And in return, she had asked him, "Were you born with that smooth tongue or did you have to pick up lessons along the years?"

He'd grinned at her then, and she'd known there was a witty response to her question already sitting at the tip of his tongue.

"Does it really matter?" Asa had smirked at her. "Because you weren't complaining about my smooth tongue that night in the park."

Carmen remembered the furious blushing she'd endured, the speechless state she'd been left in. And then she remembered him shedding off that cocky demeanour as his natural instincts had taken over, instincts that needed to ensure she was at ease, at comfort. "I'm sorry," Asa had said, ever the embodiment of warmth. "I just wanted to tease you, but if those sorts of remarks make you uncomfortable, then tell me okay? And I won't make them anymore."

Looking at him now, standing right in front of her, that same hint of concern in his eyes and the same gentleness in his tone, Carmen knew any pain she'd caused him hadn't taken away the beautiful person he was beneath all that flesh and bone.

And *God*, did she love him for it.

"I know you were only trying to make light of the situation," she told him with a soft smile. "You don't have to explain."

He watched her for a moment, as if wanting to confirm for himself that she was at ease, and then released a small sigh. "Good," he mumbled, a corner of his mouth lifting up slightly into something similar to a smile.

His gaze travelled upwards, landing on her hair which was still pretty damp since Carmen hadn't got a chance to wipe it yet. Asa ran his fingers down a few locks and then pulled his hand back, looking down at the tiny water droplets he found there.

"You haven't dried your hair yet," he pointed out, rubbing his fingertips together. "You're going to give yourself a really bad headache on top of that cold, you know." Unwrapping his fingers from around Carmen's wrist, he leaned forward and slipped his arm underneath hers, reaching for the towel she'd hung over the chair behind her and then walked over to the bed.

Carmen watched as he settled on the mattress, leaning back against the headboard with his legs crossed on the bed and patting the spot right in front of him. "Come on then," he said, not taking his eyes off hers.

Bewildered, she walked towards Asa, stopping just as her knees brushed against the bedframe and looked at him curiously. "Asa, you don't—I can dry my own hair, you know."

Asa sighed deeply and stretched his hand out towards Carmen, the inside of his palm turned upwards, silently asking her to take it. "I want to take care of you right now," he said quietly. "Please just let me."

Carmen had taken care of herself for so long now, and she didn't think Asa understood to the fullest extent what his words were making her feel.

She slipped her palm into his without blinking an eye, letting him pull her up onto the bed, and settled on the space in front of him, bringing her knees up to her chest and loosely wrapping her arms around them.

"Um," Carmen started, her eyes trained on her intertwined fingers resting atop her knees, her voice beginning to tremble slightly, "So...I—I guess that tonight I wanted to—to..." She let out a frustrated breath, knowing that she had so much to say to him, but not knowing how to begin. There was really no way she could think of to start this conversation.

"We have all night," Asa murmured from behind her, his hand taking a hold of a few locks of her hair and starting to dry it with the towel. "Just breathe for now."

Carmen seemed to relax at that, her shoulders sagging forward slightly and her fingers loosening their painful grip around each other.

Asa continued to thread his fingers through her hair, separating it into portions and wiping each one thoroughly before letting it flow down her back along with rest of the dried strands. Carmen's eyes fluttered shut, a small sigh of content escaping her lips at the soothing movements.

It was a few minutes later when Asa finally stopped. "There you go," he mumbled under his breath, chucking the towel away and gathering her hair into a neat pile before pushing it to the side and letting it fall over her right shoulder. "All done."

"Thanks," Carmen whispered, eyes still closed.

Asa hummed in response, and Carmen felt the back of his fingertips trail down the length of her spine in one single feather-light stroke.

After a while, Carmen spoke, "You're quiet."

She felt him shift behind her, and opened her eyes to see both his legs stretch out on either side of her, no longer in the crossed-over position they'd been in earlier. Carmen's cheeks grew warm; it felt more intimate this way.

"I told you," he said in a voice so quiet that she wouldn't have heard it if she wasn't seated this close to him. "Tonight is all yours. So, you do the speaking, and take as much time as you want to. I'm not walking out that door until you've said all that there is for you to say." Asa's hushed words could've easily got lost in the space between their bodies, but somehow that only added to the sensation of the two of them being the only ones in the world that night. "Even if I have to stay here 'till sunrise."

A small laugh fell past Carmen's lips. "Dad would probably be back by sunrise." She suddenly lifted her head from her knees and turned her body around slightly, shooting a curious look at Asa over her shoulder. "Wait, don't you have to be home?"

Asa's hands were crossed behind his head, his eyes never leaving Carmen's as he responded, "Was supposed to stay at Wyatt's anyway, so there aren't going to be at least three dozen worried calls from Ma."

"I guess your dad's pretty chill then," Carmen stated.

Asa shrugged. "He trusts that I'll be able to handle myself."

"But your mum's always worried about you?"

Asa nodded, affection pooling in his eyes. "Always." He chuckled. "But she has a temper. She's borderline insane when I sometimes turn up home late and couldn't drop her a message either 'cause my phone died or I'd just forgotten to do so."

"And you don't get frustrated with her during those times?"

"Sometimes I do," he admitted sheepishly, unfolding his arms and letting it fall down by his sides as he picked at a loose thread on a pillow. "But then I remind myself that all that anger comes from a place of worry, and that worry from a place of love. Aside from dad, if it's not her feeling protective over me, who else is supposed to? She's a mother; she'll always have those maternal instincts. I should be grateful I get to have one when there are other kids out there who don't."

Asa inhaled sharply, his hand freezing and letting the thread slip through his fingers as he snapped his head towards Carmen. "I didn't— *Joder!* —Carmen, *shit*, that's not—I'm going to shut up, okay? I'm so, *so* sorry. I just didn't think—I was speaking about ma and I—"

"Don't stop," Carmen whispered, shifting her body around sideways so that she could get a clearer look at him. "I want you to speak about her...I want... I want to know... to know what it's like."

Asa's eyes softened—his entire posture softened—and Carmen watched him hesitate for a split second before he reached out and wrapped an arm around her waist, tightening his grip just a little bit more as he pulled her towards him until she was resting sideways against his chest. Carmen closed her eyes, whatever nervousness she'd been feeling earlier crumbling to dust and floating away as her heart grew lighter in weight.

She felt Asa's other hand slip into her hair, cool fingertips massaging her scalp in small, inconsistent circles.

"She loves cooking," Asa told Carmen, not asking her if she was sure she wanted to hear him speak about what it was like having a mother around. He didn't question, didn't make her second-guess, he just obliged, trusting that Carmen knew what she wanted. "And she takes a hell lot of pride in it, too. Anyone mentions anything about how she's just giving into a gender role about women being cooks, they better start preparing to get their asses handed to them. With extra whipped cream on top." He let out a chuckle at that, fondness evident in that small sound itself. It made Carmen smile and made her chest warm all over.

"She's passionate about everything. I suppose she lives by the motto "Go big or go home". Every little thing she does, she does it by pouring her blood, sweat, and tears into it. So when she's mad, she's a spitfire on the loose. And when she's stubborn, there isn't the most valid and logical argument you could lay out before her; it's not going to change her mind. Same thing with forgiving too; she's a pro at holding a grudge. She'll be cursing you to the pits of hell while making the world's best enchiladas. The woman's crazy."

Asa sighed, his breath fanning the top of Carmen's head and fluttering a few strands of her hair ever so slightly. "But when she loves, she does so with every inch of her existence. She'll give and give and give, until she forgets how to stop giving." His fingers trailed down Carmen's

550

scalp, tangling themselves in her hair as he messed around with her dark locks. "She's the kind of person who never makes you doubt the intensity of her love, even if it does make you question her sanity from time to time."

"Sounds like someone I know." Carmen smiled, tilting her head up to look at Asa.

His eyes met hers as he looked down at where the side of her face was pressed against his chest. Carmen's ear was right next to his sternum, and she could her the faint *thumpity-thumps* of his heart. The calming effect it had on her was indescribable.

"I'm not stubborn," he pointed out, a small smile on his lips. "And my cooking skills are nonexistent. Unless its normal stuff like sandwiches. But Ma says I'm a disgrace to the Mexican cuisine."

"I meant the part about not forgiving easily—"

"I am *not* as bad as my mother. She would literally take her grudges to the grave—"

"—and the part about loving wholeheartedly and irrevocably."

Asa's mouth snapped shut at that, and he stared at Carmen, surprise flickering in those eyes of his.

"And you're passionate too," Carmen pointed out. "It's like you feel so much you don't even know what to do with those feelings sometimes."

"I can handle my feelings just fine," Asa muttered, punctuating his words with a gentle pull of Carmen's hair. "Just not when it comes to you," he admitted in a small voice.

Carmen stopped breathing for a moment. And then her heart went into overdrive.

"Why do you love me so much?" The question slipped past her attempts to stop it, her voice cracking as she searched Asa's eyes relentlessly for an explanation.

She felt him freeze beneath her, his arm tense around her waist, his fingers grow slack and loosen their grip on her hair.

And then, after a moment, he exhaled.

He exhaled as if he was breathing out all the air that was left in his lungs, and if it were possible, he pulled Carmen even further into his body.

"I don't know, Carmen," he told her earnestly, voice thick with emotion. "I don't know how to tell you in words. I only know how to show you. And even then, it couldn't possibly reveal even a third of what I actually feel."

And maybe that was it, the one thing that was their biggest difference and also what allowed them to complement each other so well—he didn't have the words to tell her he loved the midnight shade of her hair and could only show it by running his fingers through them. And she didn't know how to show him how obsessed she was with the gold of his eyes, but could only talk about them in pure poetry.

But words could only prove so much, and actions didn't always speak volumes. There had to be a little bit of both.

"All I know," Asa spoke again. "Is that the world was black, white and a couple shades of grey. Then you happened. And now leaves aren't just leaves, September isn't just a month, rain isn't just rain, autumn is no longer just another season, and art isn't just art. You change the world, Carmen West. And all I want to do is see it through your eyes."

And Asa had done it; he'd managed to gather 'a little bit of both', managed to arrive at that balance. He'd found the words to say to her.

If she uttered those three words now, would he believe her? Carmen couldn't help but wonder as she stared into his eyes, all words abandoning her at his confession. But three words remained; three words sat at the tip of her tongue, begging to be released.

Not yet, she told herself. She still had a lot she needed to say.

There was another pull of her hair. "Say something." Asa smiled, but it looked a little uneasy.

"You wouldn't believe me if I told you," Carmen whispered in a haunted tone. "Not tonight, anyway."

Asa untangled his fingers from her hair and used his knuckles to stroke her cheekbone. "Then tell me something I can believe," he whispered back, never breaking eye contact.

Carmen paused to gather her thoughts, running her mind through every possible way she could just to start this conversation but coming up empty each time.

"I don't know where to start, Asa," she told him in an apologetic tone. "I'm sor—"

"Shh." He shook his head, placing his finger on her lips. "No more apologies for tonight, remember?" He took his finger away, dragging it down her bottom lip as he did so. "Just…just start at the point that you feel is the beginning."

Carmen's thoughts floated to tonight's game, when she'd finally found the courage to run after Asa. The football field flashed in front of her eyes—the passionate players, the wild crowd, and the hyperactive cheerleaders.

"She was popular," Carmen began, averting her gaze from Asa's and trailing her eyes over the patterns her fingers had started to trace on his chest. "Dad said she was popular because she had a fierce spirit and a kind smile, but my aunt Viola used to say Mum's popularity came from her ability to seduce anything that walked."

"Your aunt is an idiot, no offense."

"I honestly don't mind." Carmen sighed, her mind flashing back to the wretched night of Thanksgiving. "She wanted to have fun, I guess. Didn't want to settle down until she'd lived her life to the fullest and tried everything that her heart desired. At least, that's how Dad put it." Carmen's hands stopped drawing invisible patterns on the t-shirt Asa was wearing and instead grabbed a fistful of it and tucking her head underneath his chin. "She had a reputation though, amongst the guys during high school. And despite meeting Dad in college, despite falling in love with him and leaving her old ways behind so that she could get involved in a serious relationship, that reputation still followed her. People never really let her forget."

Asa's hand went back to her hair, his long fingers stroking it all the way from the roots down to the tips.

"And just like the boy who cried wolf, nobody believes a slut when she cries rape." Carmen laughed darkly, the bitter sound scaring her own self. Almost on instinct, she tilted her head back and glanced at Asa; he didn't seem shocked or scared of her, though.

"Dad had gotten into a student exchange program at that time, and he wasn't at campus with her, so everyone thought she'd taken that chance to cheat on Dad. They didn't believe her. Told her that she was only accusing the guy of rape because she hadn't expected to get pregnant and a baby was something she wouldn't be able to hide from my dad. They said she was just looking for a scapegoat, that the pregnancy was a result of an affair, not an attack." Her grip on Asa's shirt tightened. "A lot of people sympathised with Dad. They felt even sorrier for him when he believed my mum. They thought he was too in love with her to see reason."

There was a long stretch of silence, before Carmen felt Asa's fingers take a gentle but firm hold of her chin, urging her to meet his eyes.

"Carmen," he said in a cautious tone, releasing her chin and using that hand to brush away stray strands from her cheek. "The pregnancy... the child..."

"Yes," she answered the question that he was too much of a soft-hearted person to blatantly ask. "And you can say the words out loud, Asa." She let go of the death grip on his t-shirt and brought her hand up to his face, tracing the curve of those slanting cheekbones. "I don't really have a problem with the circumstances of my birth. I don't see myself as some aftermath of a college horror night."

Asa's mouth slowly stretched into a soft smile, those eyes of his growing almost dusky as he continued to gaze her with a mix of pride, sorrow and... and something else raw and unfathomable.

"You are crazy strong, I hope you know that," he mumbled, caressing the apple of her cheek with the delicacy of a feather.

Carmen's mouth twisted into a slight frown. "I don't always feel strong though."

554

"So?" His finger traced the curve of her ear. "You're allowed to break."

An image of broken crayons flashed in Carmen's mind, causing the edges of her mouth to curve up into the tiniest of smiles.

I love you. Three words sat on the tip of her tongue. But would he believe her? Would he, really?

"It was after she died that things really exploded." Carmen sighed. "That family was fractured when Hunter's mum died in a horrible accident. And when mum also died, that fracture spread, I guess. It spread until the whole family just cracked and broke apart. There was no place for me there and where I wasn't welcome, Dad didn't want to stay either."

A few more beats of silence passed, and Carmen found herself enjoying these little quiet pauses, breathing in his scent and soaking in the comfort of his strong arms while his fingers continued to thread through her hair and his other hand remained secured around her waist, holding her against him.

She liked this. She liked how he knew her enough to know that this wasn't her unloading all the extra weight on him, that this wasn't her looking for comforting words or testaments of her self-worth or even advice on self-love. Asa seemed to understand the fact that all she wanted to do—really wanted to do—was let him *in*.

And Carmen appreciated that more than words could say.

64
Three Words

The silence stretched on, calming and comfortable. They weren't saying anything, but Asa's lips still wore the ghost of a smile as he leant his head back on the bedframe and played with Carmen's hair.

"Carmen," he said after a while. "How come you know so much about what happened to your mum?" He leaned away from the headboard and looked down at Carmen. "I mean, I guess you would have gotten answers about your birth from your dad but the circumstances of her attack? The judgment and accusations she had to face? Those were long before you would've been born. And I know it's not my place to say this, but your dad must have been smoking something to tell you all the details of her suffering."

There was a light slap on his leg followed by Carmen sighing. "Dad's not an idiot. He knew that all the shaming my mum was put through wasn't something that I needed to know. I had a right to know about my birth, why my biological father wasn't in the picture, why my relatives weren't very welcoming of me. And so he gave me the answers I needed. But the other things—the things about my mum's reputation, about how she was shunned—those I learnt from my extended family." There was another heavy sigh from Carmen. "I mean, I was a kid back then. It wasn't hard to eavesdrop whenever I heard my mother being mentioned in conversation. And—and I don't know, the looks Cole's mum used to give me made me feel like I was doing something wrong, so

I was always careful about what I said and how I acted. Until I just grew used to keeping to myself and not speaking much at all in that house.

"I guess Dad finally saw how unhappy I was there," she continued. "And decided to move back here. But I still remembered the looks, the bitterness when they spoke of my mother…and I just grew up thinking she must have done something bad in order for them to feel that way about her. Turns out she didn't do anything bad, the only thing that was so wrong in her family's eyes was my existence. I suppose they believed — *believe*—she should've lived…and that I should be the one buried six feet under."

On instinct, Asa's arms tightened their hold around her, as if there was any chance of protecting her from the damage that had already been inflicted on her. "It wasn't your fault if your mother died giving birth to you, Carmen," he sounded almost angry. Angry for Carmen. Angry at the rest of the world for taking away a little girl's childhood because of something way beyond her control. "She chose to have you, didn't she? Why would anyone in their right minds possibly blame you?"

There was a pause in the air.

It wasn't one of those comfortable ones. It wasn't one of those small stretches of silence that punctuated every little confession that spilled out of Carmen's mouth. This was different. Asa felt Carmen tense under his arms, squirm for a bit, and clench her fist around the material of the t-shirt he was wearing.

"Mum…" Carmen cleared her throat before continuing. "Mum, she didn't—she didn't die during—it wasn't because of childbirth."

Asa's brows knitted together, the hard frown on his face deepening even further. "Oh?" he asked, perplexed. "Then that's all the more reason why they can't blame you. People really blow my mind sometimes."

"They can," she said in a small voice. "Blame me for her death, I mean. I—I'm not saying they're right in doing so or that I'm justifying their words or their actions but—but I can see why they'd think that I'm the one to blame."

557

Asa opened his mouth, about to ask her why she'd let herself think that; how exactly her mother died that it continued to haunt her to this very moment; how come it was so hard for her family to accept her mother's passing away if death came for everyone at one point in their lives. Wasn't death natural?

And then he clamped his mouth shut, because Asa wondered if perhaps the death of Carmen's mother wasn't due to natural circumstances. If maybe the reason Carmen seemed to be in so much pain and carry heartbreak in her eyes was because she'd inherited that pain from someone who'd left it behind for her.

Asa's eyes landed on Carmen and for the third time that night, he watched. The roots of her hair on her forehead seemed to have formed tiny beads of sweat, her palm that was resting on his arm felt clammy, her eyes kept darting in all directions as she kept opening and shutting her mouth with a kind of desperation on her face he hadn't seen before. Subtly, he shifted his hand that was loosely hung around her neck and moved it lower, lower enough that it slanted across her chest and he could feel the pulse of her heart.

It was beating fast. *Too* fast. And something told Asa it had nothing to do with their close proximity.

His eyes trailed over her face once more and swept over her obviously distressed posture.

Was he, someone who claimed to love her, going to actually put her through saying the words when it was so blatantly visible how much she was struggling right in that moment? Was Asa really going to ask that of her?

He wasn't an idiot. He could come to a vague conclusion as to how her mother died. And whether Asa was in love with her or not, he didn't think he'd want to put anyone through actually speaking out the words. Hell, as much as he despised Hunter and as much pain as that boy had caused him, Asa didn't think he'd ever do that to him either. There were some lines you just didn't cross.

And so, Asa lifted an arm from around her and placed it on her cheek, tilting her face towards him. "Carmen," he said gently, with a small nod of understanding. "It's okay. You don't need to tell me right now if you can't."

Surprise flashed across her soft features, before confusion settled into the depths of her eyes, filling it to the brim. "But—but..." She shook her head, sitting up straight and leaning away from his embrace. "I need to let you in. I need to tell you. You said I didn't open up much, that we couldn't work if I remained closed off. I need to do this, don't I? I don't want to leave you in the dark. Not anymore."

Something inside Asa hurt. It hurt so much to know that the way he'd delivered his words made her think he needed absolutely every single piece of her that she had to offer. That wasn't what he'd asked for: it wasn't what he'd meant.

"Carmen," he murmured, running his thumb across her forehead and down her temple. "I asked you if you were ever going to let me in, and you told me you didn't know. And so I walked out." Asa lowered his head, brushing the tip of his nose against hers. "But you're here. And you're giving me a way in. This is all that I ever wanted. This is all that I asked for—for you to show me you're *willing* to actually open up and let me in. I never demanded for you to tell me all that there is to know within a single night itself. I just needed a sign, some sort of proof that you were actually willing to do some of the giving too."

He angled his face and then pressed his lips to her cheek. "I open up quickly. You don't. I get that. People have their own pace when it comes to letting others in. I just never knew if you were ever going to do so when it came to us. You're showing me now that you do want to make this work, that you want me to understand, and as long as that's the case, as long as you're making the effort on your part, I don't see why we can't go at your pace."

He smiled down at her, trailing his finger along her jaw. "Everyone's always talking about taking things slow when it comes to the physical aspects of the relationship, always preaching about being patient with your partner until they're ready to take things to the next level and not to force them into doing something that they're not comfortable with…but nobody ever warned us about this—" he gestured between the two of them, "—about patience being needed for someone letting you in mentally and emotionally too. That forcing someone to open up is just as bad and pressurising as forcing them into doing something physical. But making you feel pressured is the last thing I ever want for you in this relationship, I need you to believe that."

"I do believe that." She smiled back at him, and then leant forward to kiss his jaw. "I do," she breathed, her voice so quiet that Asa felt her words against his skin long before he heard them. "But to be fair, I should've come to you sooner and told you I needed a little space to figure things out, that I needed to get some professional help so that I could come to a point where I could make a completely rational decision. I didn't though, did I? I just went ahead and crushed your heart because I was still too scared of getting help, scared of admitting to myself that I *needed* the help. It was only after I lost you that the magnitude of the situation really sunk in…and I knew I needed to do something or else I'd lose myself forever."

Carmen ran her fingers through her hair, pushing away strands from her face and furrowing her eyebrows as she stared at her index finger drawing soft circles on Asa's cheek. "But even after seeing someone, I knew I couldn't just come to you. You probably needed time to cope, too, and it was only fair that I gave you that space to decide for yourself what you wanted. In the meantime, I figured I needed other relationships in my life too if I ever planned on making one work with you. I had to build other bridges, to put myself out there before I approached you. Otherwise, I would just become used to your presence and yours alone, and I didn't want this to get toxic. I knew it wouldn't be a healthy choice for me to continue keeping other people at bay and only making room for you in my life. I needed to make friends, try connecting further with acquaintances, try reconnecting with Dad."

Carmen's eyes flickered to Asa's. "Does—does that make sense?" she asked in a somewhat timid voice. "I—I know I'm speaking too much, that I'm saying a lot. That I'm probably repeating the same point over and over but I want to know if you—"

Asa gently brushed his thumb along her lower lip with a small nod of his head. "Perfect sense," he promised. "I'm glad you found it in you to finally make a stand and show priority towards your health. I wish things had transpired differently, that your path towards finding yourself and starting to heal all those old wounds didn't have to include breaking my heart. You made a choice, a terrible one, with painful consequences. But you've always accepted me for who I am, always shown a genuine interest in where I come from, always been ready to remind me to love myself and that I'm worth more than I let myself believe. And I don't want to be that person who forgets all the good that comes with knowing you, just because of one bad choice."

He brushed away the hair from her forehead and placed a soft kiss there. "I don't want to let that one choice you made define you for the rest of your life, Carmen. I don't want to let it define my perspective of you. You're so much more than a single choice made in a confused and lost state of mind."

"Thank you," she told him softly, sincerity swimming in her eyes, and for the first time since Asa had known her. He saw it. Asa saw those three words dancing around in those pools of raw emotions and unknown depths.

A part of him, however, was thankful when she didn't utter them, because it had been a long night, and so much that had remained unsaid between them were out in the open now. The air around them was crackling with an overwhelming amount of feelings clashing into each other, setting off mini explosions. If she'd said the words now, he didn't know if he'd be able to truly let himself believe them. It would've been a little too soon.

So he just buried his nose into the crook of her neck and breathed in the scent of damp earth, wind and rain that was still clinging to her hair and skin. Carmen was going to tell him she loved him one of these days, he knew that. And on that day, Asa would let himself believe her, before telling her still loved her back too.

For tonight, however, this was enough.

* * *

Asa's eyes landed on the clock next to Carmen's bed, sitting on top of the small desk with a lamp right next to it. It read 01:00 A.M. in red neon lights. His gaze travelled back to where she was sound asleep in his arms, a single strand of dark hair resting across her face and her breathing steadier than it had been when she'd been reliving her childhood or lack thereof.

He wished he didn't have to see the beaten-down and worn out part of her, wished he didn't know it even existed. He wished it had never happened to her, that she didn't have to go through what she went through. He thought he'd seen how ugly the world could be, thought he'd seen the worst of it—but it had still taken away her innocence and made her see things that she shouldn't have had to.

But at the same time, wasn't everything that had happened so far turned Carmen into the person he found himself falling in love with? Because despite everything, she refused to let the world turn her bones to steel, her heart to stone and her tongue to a sword.

Compassion, empathy—these came from places of suffering. And Carmen had seen suffering. That was what made her into the person she was today, the person Asa had loved and will probably continue to love for as long as time allowed.

He didn't love the girl she could've been; he loved the girl that wanted to stick her hands out and dig her way up from beneath all those broken shards and rubble. He loved the girl with the dents and the scratches and the bruises and the scars. He loved the girl who carried an unimaginable amount of light within her, but he understood now that it shone from a place of cold and empty darkness.

And somehow, that made Asa love her even more.

The world broke everyone at one point, but so very few had the strength to pick up the pieces and fit it together, knowing the cracks weren't a symbol of weakness but a testament of *I survived, I survived, I survived.*

Asa didn't need to save Carmen. She'd learnt how to pick herself up and she had survived a long time ago. And for someone who always felt the need to be someone's saviour, loving Carmen—loving a survivor—was a form of liberation.

Carmen set him free, and Asa gave her a sense of direction. It was as extraordinary and as simple as that.

•   •   •

After gently moving out from under her and placing her head on a pillow, Asa grabbed the blanket folded at the foot of the bed and draped it over Carmen's sleeping body, letting it fall just underneath her chin. He leant down for a quick peck on the forehead, trailing his thumb over her eyebrow affectionately one more time, before switching off the lights and heading down the stairs.

It was dark down here, too and as Asa was walking past the living room, having to cross it in order to get to the front door, his ears caught the faint sound of the television that was on, and he faltered in his steps.

For one panicky moment, he thought it was Carmen's dad, but when the light from the screen fell on the person in front of it, allowing Asa a glimpse of the familiar mop of brown hair laying against the sofa's headrest, he relaxed.

The relief lasted only a while though, before Asa started feeling slightly anxious again. Running into Hunter here hadn't been part of the plan. At the school cafeteria, or in the hallways, or even during parties, crossing paths with him wasn't all that huge of a deal, but here, in times like these, when it was just the two of them, Asa truly didn't know how to handle the situation, and it made him uneasy to the very core.

"I don't know if you're enjoying the view from behind." Hunter's slow drawl floated over the couch and towards Asa. "But it's beginning to make me uncomfortable."

And just like that, the uneasiness dissipated and was replaced by the usual wave of annoyance that washed over Asa every time Hunter opened his mouth.

Rolling his eyes to himself, Asa walked forwards and past the sofa, coming to a stop only when he was at a considerable distance from the idiot.

"You don't seem surprised to see me here," Asa remarked, sticking both hands in his pockets.

Hunter's eyes were glued to the television, the ongoing action on the screen casting various shadows and lights across his face, obscuring the colour of his eyes in the dark room. It made him appear more intimidating than usual.

"Your truck's out the front, genius," he muttered, raising the beer bottle to his lips and taking a swig. "Doesn't take rocket science to put two and two together."

It was becoming quite apparent that Hunter didn't know any other language than sarcasm. But, for one wild second, Asa wondered if the feeling of discomfort was mutual, and this was just Hunter's way of covering up his awkwardness compared to Asa's natural response which was to freeze and falter.

A beat of silence passed, heavy with a palpable kind of tension.

"Congrats on the win," Asa said suddenly, rushing to fill in the silence because his feet were still not moving. "I'm guessing that you managed to put the quarterback in his place? You know, the one that you almost took a swing at."

"You mean the one that you just had to get in the way of?" Hunter's lips twitched, traces of a smirk appearing on his face.

Asa ignored the remark, eyeing the bottle in Hunter's hands. "Shouldn't you be out celebrating with the team?"

"I was." Hunter shrugged, eyes still following every moment on the screen. "But eventually got bored and came home. Besides, this is my idea of celebrating: *Daredevil* on repeat, popcorn, and a drink."

"*Home?*" Asa blurted, unable to stop himself in time and completely taken aback at Hunter addressing this place as home.

For the first time that night, Hunter's eyes flashed to Asa's. They almost looked like glass paint in the dark, illuminated by nothing but the light from the television.

"Does that bother you?" he asked in an even voice, his tone giving nothing away.

Asa was even more bewildered than before. "What?" He frowned, pulling his brows together and staring with utter perplexity at the boy seated in front of him.

Hunter sighed and placed the drink next to the small bowl of popcorn on the coffee table, before grabbing the remote and hitting pause.

Asa didn't want Hunter to pause the episode, as pausing implied the beginning of a conversation. And Asa didn't want a conversation; he just wanted to congratulate the other boy on the win and keep going on his merry way.

"Carmen wanting to reconnect with me," Hunter explained. "Me choosing to be back in her life." His eyes narrowed the slightest fraction as he leaned further back into the couch and regarded Asa. "Does that bother you?"

Asa opened his mouth to answer when he realised that he actually didn't have a very good response to that. Clamping his mouth shut, he allowed himself to think his words through before saying anything. Speaking to Hunter was walking on a fine line between civility and war; it was tiptoeing around a minefield, the smallest misstep and everything would explode in both of their faces.

"Carmen loves you," Asa finally said, his tone cautious but steady. "A lot, it seems. Your presence in her life makes her happy. And I care about her being happy."

"That's not answering my question," Hunter said matter-of-factly.

Asa bit down on the inside of his cheek, willing himself to not lose his temper.

"Your presence in Carmen's life does not necessarily mean you being a part of my life," Asa told him, not breaking eye contact. "As long as there are clear boundaries between you and I, there's no reason for me to feel bothered by you and her."

Hunter stayed silent, observing Asa for a moment longer before he shrugged and ran a hand through his hair. "Fair enough," he said eventually, but there was something else in his tone—just a tiny hint of it—that Asa couldn't put his finger on.

"Hey—" Hunter suddenly sat upright, eyes narrowing and nose crunching in confusion "—are you wearing my t-shirt?"

"Are you out of your goddamn mind?" Asa snorted, wondering if the boy had truly lost his mind. "Why the hell would I even want to wear your—" He stopped abruptly, suddenly recalling Carmen handing it to him hours before. Asa had wondered how it had been an almost perfect fit for him. Now it made sense.

"I'm going to kill her one of these days," Asa finally said in a flat tone, looking down at the t-shirt with a disgusted face.

"That's my favourite one, too!" Hunter exclaimed, looking genuinely miserable and just flabbergasted. "Now I have to fucking burn it."

Asa's head whipped towards him, a deadpan look on his face. "Burn the t-shirt? I have to bleach my whole body once I get home!"

"Asshole," Hunter muttered.

"*Pendejo*," Asa returned.

Hunter sighed like he was dealing with a child. "What have I told you about swearing at me in Spanish?"

"To not do it?"

That earned Asa a glare, not that he particularly minded or was intimidated by it, of course.

A few more beats of silence passed, but the underlying tension wasn't as overwhelming as it had been minutes back. The awkwardness remained though, doubling, then tripling in its magnitude, until Asa just needed to get out of there.

Was it shame he felt when in Hunter's presence? The inability to accept that someone who was a stranger had somehow had a huge impact on who Asa was today? The knowledge of the fact that the boy in front of him knew all of Asa's weakest spots and how to press them?

"I need to go," Asa said, holding his breath and releasing the words in a rush. "Congrats on the win again." He turned around, heading straight towards the door and pulling it open, taking in huge gulps of the cool night air as soon as his feet hit the floorboards of the porch.

He didn't hear the door swing shut nor did he turn around to check if he hadn't pulled it after him, when he found Hunter's foot in the doorway, stopping it from closing fully.

Hunter held a finger up, cutting off whatever Asa was about to ask him in confusion. "I need to say something," he told him.

Asa blinked. "I was just inside. Could've told me then."

"I wanted to," Hunter said curtly. "And was just about to when you started taking off."

Asa stuffed his fists into his pockets again, irrational anger simmering inside him. He didn't want this. Didn't want to have to speak to this person standing in front of him.

But Asa was also not walking away.

Why was that?

"I know you said that it wouldn't make a difference to you anymore whether I had this conversation with you or not," Hunter began, stepping over the threshold and closing the door behind him. He moved towards the railing of the porch and leant his back against it, crossing one leg over the other and folding his arms across his torso. "You also said you no longer needed the closure." Hunter held his gaze.

"I don't," Asa said stiffly, grounding his teeth together.

"I call bullshit," Hunter stated easily enough. "But for your sake we'll say you don't need it anymore and that I'm doing this for me."

Asa furrowed his brows together, frowning hard as his perplexed state only grew worse. Every time he thought he had Hunter figured out,

567

another layer was peeled off and he got another peek beyond the surface of the cold shell.

"I don't have a problem with who you are, never did." Hunter shrugged indifferently, but this time Asa's eyes caught on to the façade. It was crumbling now, ever so slowly. This—whatever was happening now—seemed to matter to Hunter, despite the nonchalance he was trying so hard to feign.

"With who I am?" Asa asked.

"Yeah—" Hunter nodded "—with where you come from. With your language. Your skin. Your identity. Whatever." He shrugged again. "Doesn't matter to me."

Asa was feeling a little dizzy with all the questions that were storming his mind right now, but he kept his lips sealed because Hunter looked like he had more to say.

"I only picked on you for them because it was easy to," he said slowly, wincing when the words spilt out of his mouth, apparently only realising how blunt they sounded once he heard himself saying it. "Sounds harsh, but I'm not going to bother sugarcoating. Too much has happened for me to downplay things. I'll say it like it is. And when I say you made it easy for me to identify all your breaking points, I don't mean it in the sense where I blame you or where I'm trying to tell you that you contributed to the shit I put you through."

Hunter exhaled, looking away and running his hand through his hair before bringing it down over his face again. "I mean it in the sense that I saw weakness and I was terrible enough to feed on it." His eyes met Asa's once again. "There were cracks in the wall you'd started building around you because of all the hate you got from other people, and instead of helping you mend those cracks, I decided to take a hammer and keep swinging at those spots 'till it was *you* who broke."

Asa could hardly do anything else but blink repeatedly, his brain and every other sense deciding to hibernate during that conversation.

"Why…" Asa cleared his throat, forced himself to sound composed. "Why are you telling me this?"

568

Hunter tilted his head to the side, narrowing his eyes slightly as he studied Asa. "Because you told me that redemption starts with the people I've wronged. That it starts with me making things right with people I have no personal ties to, in places where I don't have any personal gains…" Again, he shrugged. "So here I am, at that starting point."

If Hunter seemed to be doing a lot of shrugging tonight, it seemed like Asa was doing a lot of blinking. As if each time his eyes shut and flew open within a matter of seconds, the scene before him would vaporise. As if it would turn to smoke and float away like one of those phantom effects they showed on screens.

"I don't know what I'm supposed to say," Asa said slowly, uncertainly.

Another shrug. "You can walk straight to your truck and drive away. I'm not telling you this because I expect you to respond. I don't expect your forgiveness, or your empathy, or even your understanding. I owed it to you, and closure is probably the only thing I can give you that would mean anything anymore. I'm just stating the cold hard truths here, San Román." He unfolded his arms from across his chest and placed them against the railing. "I don't give a shit about your race. It makes no difference to me. And I wanted to let you know that the only reason I picked on you for it was because I saw how much it broke you when others made racist comments at you. I saw your insecurities form, saw them pile up, and I took pleasure in kicking you where it already hurt."

Hunter swept his hair with his palm again. "That's all I needed you to know. That it wasn't that I thought there was something wrong with you—" and then, in an uncharacteristically soft voice, he added, "—because there really isn't."

Was it pathetic on Asa's part to admit to himself that he appreciated the gesture? That it *did* mean something to him? It wasn't that he was still looking for validation—not anymore. Never again. But—but, still, there was perhaps a small void that he could now fill up. Another chapter of his life that he could close now and not look back on.

569

Asa had satisfied his pride when he'd told Hunter he no longer needed the closure, that it wouldn't make a difference to him whether he got any or not, but he was somehow glad that Hunter had taken down his own pride and decided to give Asa some of that closure anyway.

Averting his gaze, Asa found his eyes sweeping over the dark streets, illuminated only by the soft glow of the streetlights. His sight followed the sway of the trees under the gentle wind, and he watched the droplets of water that still sat on the leaves from the earlier downpour fall to the ground as the breeze shook the branches.

He shuffled on his feet, hesitated, then moved forward until he too was standing in front of the railings that wrapped around the porch. "Yeah," he finally said quietly. "You were a terrible person. I'd go as far as to saying that you even broke me." Asa sighed, looked down at his hands as they brushed away fallen leaves from the surface of the wooden bars. "But the breaking was also what *made* me—"

"Don't," Hunter hissed, the word coming out with such venom that it made Asa stumble back wearily. But when he glanced at Hunter, the loathing and anger he saw on his face wasn't directed at Asa. Hell, he wasn't even looking at Asa.

"I didn't make you," Hunter bit out. "I *broke* you. *You* made yourself. Don't give me that credit; I never understood the logic behind all those sayings about how you're supposed to be grateful towards your tormentor. It's bullshit. Just plain nonsensical crap. Sometimes there isn't some huge backstory towards why someone hurt you. There always isn't some heartbreaking tragedy that makes someone inflict all their suffering on you, too.

"Sometimes people are just ugly. Sometimes people are just rotten. Sometimes they just take sick pleasure in watching others hurt. Sometimes they feel powerful in being able to cause all that misery and fear. There isn't always something more beyond the surface of an angry and hateful person. I'm not going to use whatever I went through as a justification for who I am, who I used to be. Carmen went through the very same things, but she didn't allow herself to turn into a wretched thing, did she? We make our own choices, Asa."

Hunter sighed heavily, as if he was releasing so much, *too* much. "She chose to let it make her; I chose to let it break me." He knitted his brows together, looking down at his feet. "And you chose to let it make you, eventually. *You* picked up your pieces, *you* glued them back together, and *you* patched yourself up. You. It was all you. *You* made yourself. So don't tell me that hurting you was a way for you to build yourself. You wouldn't have had to do any building if there hadn't been any breaking in the first place. Don't give me credit. Don't give Carson any credit. And don't ever give the other Hunters or Carsons you'll run into somewhere down the road any credit either. Because as much as it sucks, there are more Hunters and Carsons out there that you're going to have the misfortune of meeting."

Asa remained quiet for a while, taking in all the words, letting it sink in his mind, allowing it to flow into all those places that still needed a little bit of lighting within him. "Well," he finally said, clearing his throat. "I guess it's safe to say that I'd rather have the misfortune of running into a Hunter than another Carson."

Hunter snorted from next to him, muttering something under his breath and shaking his head to himself. He tipped his head back, stared up at the sky scattered with stars and exhaled slowly. "You're actually an okay person, San Román."

Asa hummed in response, still feeling all sorts of bizarre about the entire conversation. "And you're actually capable of being less of an ass, Donoghue."

Silence filled the space between them, because, yes, space still existed between both of them. They were two sides of the same coin, weren't they? The realisation hadn't hit Asa until now. They were both boys that had been dealt the short end of the stick, that the world had done injustice to when they were growing up. They were both boys whom the world had peeled off its mask for, to whom places infested with hatred and cruelty were shown at too young an age.

But only one boy had taught himself to spin gold out of it, while the other learnt to turn everything he touched into steel.

"That's all I wanted to say," Hunter spoke after a while, pushing himself off the wooden railings and rubbing the back of his neck. "I wanted to start making amends. I just didn't know *where* to start or *how* to start or *who* to start with until that day in the locker room, after you took that punch." He shifted on his feet. "So thanks, I guess, for giving me some sort of direction."

At those last words, an old memory played in Asa's head and he couldn't help the chuckle that escaped his mouth.

"What?" Hunter narrowed his eyes.

"Just remembered something that Isla once said," Asa muttered. "About me being a compass."

"She isn't entirely wrong," Hunter said, looking away. "I don't think Carmen would've made the decision to get help until she'd lost you. So, in a way, you nudged her into that direction."

Asa glanced at Hunter, and for a moment, the scene of watching him grin with victory on the football field after winning the game flashed in his mind. It made him wonder of the boy he had once been—long, long back.

"I'm sorry, you know," Asa eventually said in a quiet tone.

"For?" Hunter looked utterly confused.

"Carmen's mum," he answered. "Your aunt."

Hunter stiffened, the muscles on his jaw tensing, before he looked away. Still he didn't entirely relax. "She wasn't just my aunt," he finally responded. "She was a mother to me too."

"Carmen mentioned that once, I think."

"Hmm."

Asa observed Hunter for a while, before stating, "You love her."

The way Hunter's features softened at the statement is something that Asa would probably need to commit to memory, because he didn't think there were many things that could evoke such an emotion from him. "Carmen?" A corner of Hunter's lips actually lifted into something

572

resembling a smile. "With *all* of my heart. Sometimes I think she's the only one reminding me there's a human underneath the machine I've become."

"You should tell her that some time," Asa remarked. "If you already haven't."

"One day," Hunter promised. He met Asa's eyes. "You'd have made a great friend, you know. Someone I could've once identified with, a time before I lost myself. But… but I can also see why we can't be friends. I get it. For Carmen's sake, however, acting civil towards each other isn't too much, is it? We can learn to coexist."

"Coexist," Asa murmured, watching a drop of rainwater from a leaf on a nearby bush trickle down the stem and spill into the damp soil. "Seems fair enough."

Hunter nodded, then turned, slipping his hands into the pockets of his hoodie and started walking away.

Asa heard the footsteps stop, and he turned around to see Hunter walk back towards him.

"Something else you need to say?" Asa asked, raising a brow with amusement.

"Just one thing," Hunter shrugged. "Before I forget." He took a step closer, and looked Asa dead in the eyes. "I *am* sorry." Three words uttered as clear as day and with all the sincerity that was humanly possible. "I realised I never really said the words, and I wanted to get it out, because we're probably not gonna have an actual conversation ever again after this." He offered Asa a tight smile, hesitated as if there was something else he needed to say, and then walked away.

Hunter stepped into the house and closed the door shut.

And somewhere in the back of Asa's mind, a door was being shut too. A chapter was being closed and sealed, no longer an open wound.

•   •   •

Asa's grandpa had once told him that his rash nature and tendency to act on impulse would get him in trouble one day.

And perhaps his grandpa had been right the whole time, because Asa's recklessness extended all the way to the manner in which he carried his heart and how he let himself fall head over heels, feeling every single emotion so very deeply.

And it did get him in trouble, all right. But Asa was beginning to realise love was sometimes worth that trouble. He realised that Carmen West, the hurricane with a beating heart—who had thunderclouds for eyes and the midnight sky for hair and who painted broken moons and frozen suns—was indeed worth that trouble.

EPILOGUE:
An Art Journal

Late April

Isla's funeral was a quiet, simple event.

That didn't go to say it wasn't crowded though. Because it was. Almost the entire school seemed to be there, along with her family and other relatives that Asa had never seen before.

It was a sea of black clothes, pale faces, and puffy red eyes.

Asa didn't know what he looked like. Asa didn't know what he was supposed to feel.

He'd lost the Isla he knew a long time back—long, long before she'd taken her own life. Asa had already dealt with her loss, with her absence from his life. He'd grown accustomed to that space in his life that she had once occupied.

And yet there was something about death that made it all permanent.

Asa couldn't cry because his heart had already mourned losing her when she'd been alive.

"He'd already lost her. He'd already lost her. He'd already lost her. He'd al—" Asa squeezed his eyes shut. He'd already lost her, hadn't he? So why did it hurt so much now?

A warm hand slipped into his, soft palm caressing his own rough one.

He glanced sideways to find Carmen standing by his side, a tired smile on her face, her eyes a little hollow.

Asa blinked. "Carmen," he said hoarsely, sounding like he hadn't used his voice for days. "What are you doing here?"

"Where else should I be?"

Asa shook his head, his mind averting its attention from the pallbearers carrying the coffin towards the spot that was chosen for Isla. "You aren't supposed to be here," he told Carmen, eyes softening. "I thought we'd agreed already. If Isla knew about the nature of your mother's death, she would never have wanted you to attend this funeral too. Not when it would mean making you relive your worst memory."

Carmen had already lost someone to suicide, and Asa thought she had every right to sit this one out. That was a kind of selfishness that had to be permitted, right? He didn't want to know what it must be like for her to have to see another family crumble and break the way her own did.

"I'm sure she was the kind of person who would've understood," Carmen said in a small voice, her grip on Asa's hand tightening. "But I didn't want you to be alone."

Carmen's palm slid down his, her fingers finding home in the spaces between his own ones. She locked their hands together, never letting go.

"I'm selfish enough to put my emotional state of mind first and avoid this funeral," she murmured, then met Asa's eyes. "But still selfless enough to keep the panic attack at bay and be here with you."

"You're having panic attacks?" Asa's breathing faltered.

"Had it the day mum died," she replied matter-of-factly. "And then had it the night of Thanksgiving when I was about to fall asleep." She shrugged. "I've been feeling like I'm going to get hit with one ever since I woke up this morning."

Asa frowned hard. "You really shouldn't be here." He sounded almost pleading.

576

"I want to take care of you right now," she told him, repeating his words from a memory that seemed to be a lifetime away now. "Please just let me."

And so he did.

They stood there together, side by side, under a cloudy, pale blue sky. The sun peeked out from behind the fluffy clouds every once in a while, the light spilling through the cracks in between branches and leaves that hung above them.

Asa watched as they lowered the casket into the ground. Asa felt as the dirt in his fist made an imprint against the inside of his palm before he dropped them into the grave. He listened as a mother's strangled cry flooded his ears and ripped out his heart.

And all along, Carmen never let go of his hand.

Both of them stood and watched: Asa, unable to cry, because he no longer knew the person being buried into the ground but now suffered a new kind of heartbreak he'd never imagined experiencing; and Carmen, who was too still and too frozen, because she may be physically here but her mind had taken every other part of her to many years back, to another funeral just like this one, except it had been raining heavily that evening.

The grief was overwhelming, unbearable even, hitting the two of them in completely different ways.

Still, they held on.

•   •   •

Late August

It was a bright sunny afternoon, and Carmen was seated in a familiar room.

Gloria had changed the curtains. Gone were the plain white ones. It was a gold, cream, and white polka-dotted one that swayed in front of the window now. And there seemed to be two new additions to the collection of flowerpots that sat on the ledge at the bottom of the glass.

Carmen's eyes swept over every inch of the room, a small smile playing on her lips. "I like the curtains," she told her therapist softly. "And the flowers are great, too."

"I'm glad you like them, Carmen," Gloria replied, that same laid-back tone present in her voice, consistent as it had been since the very first day Carmen had stepped foot into this office.

"Whenever you speak, you sound like you have all the time in the world," Carmen said suddenly, clapping her hands together and grinning at Gloria. "Like you're in no hurry to go anywhere. I like that."

Surprise flickered in those rich, dark eyes of the older woman sitting across her. "Thank you," she said pleasantly, shaking off the surprise. "I'm happy you're more comfortable here than you were in the beginning."

Carmen shrugged, the smile not leaving her face as she noticed that Gloria no longer had those caramel lowlights in her dark hair. She still wore it in a bun, though, letting the usual few strands fall loose and frame the side of her long face.

Carmen realised Gloria was actually a very beautiful-looking woman, not the kind that you noticed right away, but the kind that artists would appreciate because of the strong bone structure in her cheeks and jaw.

"You have nice bone structure too," Carmen blurted, playing with her fingers, the stupid grin from her face not fading away.

If Gloria was also surprised by this remark, she hid it well. But she did raise a brow in amusement. "You seem to be in quite a good mood today."

"I had an epiphany recently," Carmen said. "Or at least, I realised something."

"Oh?"

"Yeah," she murmured, looking down at her clasped hands and toying with her fingers on her lap. "That I was wrong before."

"When?"

"When I let myself believe I didn't love him."

Gloria leant back against the cushion, folding one leg over the other and regarding Carmen with a composed face. "Really?"

Carmen narrowed her eyes. "You don't seem all that surprised that I'm saying this," she pointed out suspiciously.

"I'm your therapist, Carmen," Gloria stated, the pleasantness in her tone always consistent. "You've been coming to me for months now. You've even graduated high school. That's how long you've been coming here. I was just waiting for the day you realised it on your own and told me about it."

"Oh," Carmen mumbled, averting her eyes and letting them wander around the soft tones of the room. Her gaze landed back on the window, where sunlight was streaming through the glass and into the room, flooding the entire place within those four walls with so much light. The irony wasn't lost on Carmen, as this was also the same place that held all her darkest thoughts.

Yet here she was, watching the sun illuminate every single inch of it.

"I kind of miss the rain." She found herself saying with a soft sigh. The downpour had stopped for a while now, taken over by the clear skies and the blinding sun.

"I'm more interested in what you have to say regarding your epiphany." Gloria smiled.

Carmen's eyes met the woman's for a brief second, and she looked away again.

"They say you are what you read," Carmen started, pulling her eyebrows together as she pieced the words together in her head first. "That it is the society you grow in that has a huge role in your perspective of things, influencing your thoughts and your actions."

"It's true," Gloria said carefully. "To a certain extent."

"Do you know what they tell you when you're growing up?" Carmen's smile was partly sad, partly bitter. "Do you know what they teach you about love? What they repeat over and over again like a mantra until it's the only thing that pops in your mind whenever someone tells you they love you? Do you know what that very first seed is? The one that they plant inside your head that your insecurities water for the rest of your life?"

Gloria shook her head. "What do you think it is, Carmen?" Her voice was oddly soft. "I'd like to know."

"The fact that you cannot love someone else until you love yourself."

A pause.

"You think it's not right?" Gloria asked.

Carmen's eyes flashed, every bit of thunder and lightning coming to life in them. "I *know* it's not right." Her voice shook, as if every single shackle that had bound her was snapping into two. As if those wings she'd never been born with were finally battling their way from underneath her skin and bones, refusing to stay chained any longer. "It's *bullshit*. And I want to rip those words apart with my own hands and set them on fire until they're nothing but ashes. Until they're no longer out there to control somebody else's heart the way it did mine."

Carmen inhaled shakily, unable to contain all the fury, all the cries of someone wronged, and the inability to do anything but feel all the emotions run through her like wildfire, igniting all the rusty corners inside her with angry sparks.

"I loved my dad long before I even understood the concept of loving myself, and this was when he was still estranged and distant from me. I loved Hunter, the very person who made me miserable, long before I knew what it was to love myself. Hell, I loved my mother. *My mother* who broke me more than anybody else in this entire world—the same mother who was supposed to love me unconditionally but left me to suffer the consequences of her actions. I loved her too. *Even* her." Carmen leant forward, looking Gloria in the eyes as if she was speaking to the world itself. "And I loved Asa," she said in a voice that was forged from iron. "At a time and place in my life when I hoped to go to sleep and never wake up, when I didn't want to kill myself but wished to die anyway. I

580

loved Asa then, just as much as I do now. Loving myself was the last thing on my mind, but *God*, I loved him to the brink of insanity."

"They say you can't love anyone 'till you love yourself." The words spilt out of Carmen's mouth like poison ivy, dripping with the bitter aftertaste of bad blood. "They told me I couldn't love anyone 'till I loved myself. What does that even mean? That I am not capable of an emotion so pure just because I have a rough past? That I don't have it in me to offer love to somebody else because I have a few bruised knuckles and a bloodied fist? That I cannot make room for people in my heart just because it was a fractured one? That I am not fit to love another soul because I had trouble finding the light in my own?"

Carmen's fists clenched, wave after wave of righteous anger washing over her with each breathless second that ticked by. "They tell me that I cannot love someone else 'till I love myself," she repeated, her voice a hiss, a reminder that she was a hurricane. "Are they telling me my insecurities make me unworthy of helping someone else get rid of theirs? Are they telling me that the nights I spend staying up and crying to myself are nights I cannot spend running my fingers through someone else's hair and whispering into their ear how I think they make my world an amazing place?"

Carmen exhaled. She exhaled as if she was gathering all the remnants of those wretched words still left in her bones. She exhaled as if she was coiling them into a tight ball with angry fists. She exhaled as if she was hurling them out of her system with all the power love allowed her to feel.

"I didn't know how to love myself," she said quietly, the storm having calmed down and floating around like a gentle breeze now. "And there are going to be days when I'll forget how to do so. When I might fall again, where I might crash, where I might break. But I will still love the people I love with every single fibre of my being. And nobody gets to tell me otherwise.

"Not loving myself made me unready to get involved in a relationship. Not loving myself made me slow and weary when it comes to

581

opening up and letting people in," —Carmen paused, then breathed— "but love exists even when you aren't in a relationship. Love exists even when you're struggling to spill your darkest secrets to someone else. My scars, my insecurities, my flaws—they do not determine my ability to love another heart, another soul. Just how I act on it."

The silence that fell on the two of them in that room was like the aftermath of a hurricane: dead quiet with the shock of witnessing the violent emotions fly past in strong bursts; messy with all the anger that'd been released from the inferno inside Carmen's heart.

Wow, Carmen mused to herself. *That felt good.*

She tipped her head back on the sofa and breathed in deeply, wondering how things would've transpired if she hadn't let herself believe that she was incapable of loving someone just because she had dents and scratches on her being.

"What are you thinking about?" Gloria asked after a while, breaking the stunned silence that had wrapped around them.

"Alternative scenarios," Carmen replied. "If I hadn't let myself believe that what I felt for Asa back then wasn't love, if I hadn't let myself believe that I was someone too damaged to feel such a deep sense of connection to him, then maybe... maybe I wouldn't have had to let him believe it, too. I wouldn't have to tell him that I wasn't in love with him, because that wasn't true, was it? I was in no place to get into a relationship, true. But I *did* love him. I just let the world dictate my feelings for me." Carmen smiled sadly, scratching the side of her nose. "It would've saved the two of us a lot of pain."

Silence fell on them again, and Carmen appreciated that Gloria didn't feel the need to comment on what she'd just shared. The never-ending possibilities of what ifs wasn't something she wanted to navigate through, despite bringing it up occasionally.

"Gloria," Carmen said in a quiet, serious tone after a while.

"Yes, Carmen?"

"The first month that followed Isla's death, Asa took it really hard," Carmen muttered, looking down at her hands again. "I think maybe a part of himself thought he was to blame, as ridiculous as that sounds. It took some time, but his parents and I eventually got through to him and made him see that sometimes you couldn't help people, no matter how much you wanted to." Carmen pulled in her bottom lip, lost in thought. "There's this saying, isn't there? About how you could bring a horse to a lake, but you couldn't force it to drink. It's the same way with people too, isn't it? Because Asa's friendship with Isla had grown rocky a long time before he met me. He tried to stick by her, but she just didn't seem to want the help and preferred to push him away in every turn. Isla should've wanted it for herself to be saved in order for her to actually be saved."

Carmen gulped, her voice beginning to tremble as she spoke the next words like each syllable was porcelain. "So… is it okay for me to—to think that it was the same case with my mother?" She leant further back into the cushions, curling in on herself like a little child. "Maybe…maybe it wasn't *completely* my fault? Maybe my mother didn't *want* to be saved? Maybe giving up was her choice? And…and even if I was a contributing factor towards her ending her own life, I guess I wasn't the sole reason, right?

"I spent nights by Asa's side telling him how Isla's death wasn't something he could have ever foreseen. And I'm beginning to wonder if the same words I'd comforted him with are the words I need to be telling myself each time I laid the blame on me for mum."

Carmen was always painting Asa in shades of gold and plucking out the thorns from Hunter's being. And maybe, just maybe, it was okay if she could give some of that love that she showered everyone else with towards herself, too.

•   •   •

Late September

Carmen had officially met Asa's parents around a month back, at a fancy little family restaurant for dinner, much to Mrs. San Román's dismay that the first time she was meeting the love of her son's life was at a place where she couldn't exhibit her fine culinary skills. She had assured her that it was fine, that Mrs. San Román could cook for her some other time. And here she was, to live up to that promise.

This was different than their official introduction to each other though; that had taken place somewhere a dozen other families had entered and walked out from. This was Asa's *home*. The *San Román* home.

This was another level of intimacy that had Carmen's stomach swamped with butterflies.

The door swung open just as she was about to knock it.

"Hey." Asa grinned, the rays of the setting sun slanting across his eyes in just the right angle and making Carmen forget how to breathe for three whole seconds.

She narrowed her eyes at him. "I didn't even knock yet."

His excited grin softened, turning almost sheepish. "I was waiting for you."

"Oh," Carmen mumbled, a faint blush spreading across her cheeks.

Asa snorted and shoved her forehead with his palm, making her stumble backwards a few steps. "Don't flatter yourself. I was crossing the hall when I heard a car pull up. Figured it was you being dropped off."

The smile dropped from Carmen's face and she shot him a dirty look, before tiptoeing and attempting to look past his broad shoulders. "Why are you at the door?" she grumbled. "Isn't there somebody else in the house who can welcome me better?"

"Don't be silly." Asa scoffed, that devilish grin on his face only widening further, before his arm suddenly shot out and grabbed Carmen by the waist, pulling her into the house and kicking the door shut. "Besides," —his voice dropped to a low murmur as he dipped his head down and pressed her against the door— "who else in this house can give you a better welcome than this?" His lips found hers for one heart-stopping moment, the hand he had on her waist tightening its grip and squeezing her hip slightly.

"Your parents are here." Carmen's words were breathless as she uttered them against his mouth.

Asa hummed in response, brushing his lips against hers. "All the more reason to do this now." He kissed her again. "You know, considering they're going to be there all throughout dinner, and I'm going to have to keep my hands to myself."

"You're such a pervert sometimes." Carmen sighed, a smile forming on her lips.

"You love me, anyway."

"You know I do."

Asa's grin dissipated, a gentle smile crawling across his face instead. "I never get tired of hearing you say it though. And you tell me you love me at least thrice every single day."

"Good," —Carmen raised herself on her toes and kissed him on the jaw— "because I'm probably never going to stop."

Asa lifted a hand, trailed a calloused thumb along the curve of her eyebrow, never taking off his intense gaze from her. "I can't wait 'till dinner is done, and I get to have you all to myself."

Something exploded in Carmen's chest, gut—*everywhere*. She ignored the heat flooding through her and stepped away, knowing that if they didn't force themselves to move, they'd remain glued to each other against the front door all night long.

"Come on." Carmen tugged at his hand. "The sooner we get dinner over with, the sooner you get to have me all to yourself."

"I like the sound of that." That impish grin was back on Asa's face, setting off little fireworks in the pit of Carmen's stomach.

"Of course, you do," she replied with a good-natured roll of her eyes, slapping him on the chest.

"*Por dios!*" a woman's voice rang out from somewhere in the house. "Would you bring her in already?"

Asa's and Carmen's laughter dissolved into one another's, the massive grins on their faces never fading and making their cheeks hurt in the best way possible.

"Come on." Asa laced his fingers through hers, starting to walk forward when he noticed the small paper bag in her other hand. "What's that?"

"Seeds," Carmen answered.

Asa stopped in his tracks. "Seeds?"

"Mhmm." she nodded. "I need to bring something, right? This is the first time I'm coming to your place. I mean, the first time I'm here when your parents haven't gone out on their date nights or something."

Asa cocked his head to the side, amusement dancing in his eyes. "Aren't flowers the normal thing to bring?"

Carmen shrugged. "You would've put them in a vase and watched them die in a matter of days. After which you'd need to get rid of them." She held up her hand with the brown bag and shook it gently. "I don't want to give you something that dies."

A beat passed, but Asa seemed to be at a loss for words.

"Um, I mean…" Carmen waved her hand in the air. "You already have a well-maintained garden. These would just be an addition. And they'll keep growing."

She couldn't read Asa's eyes again; there were too many emotions flying through them. Too many. Carmen wondered if he himself knew how to distinguish all that he was feeling from each other.

"I love you so much," he whispered, tilting his head ever so slightly as if he was still trying to come to terms with the fact that she was indeed real.

"I love you too, Asa." She gave his hand one gentle tug, and then they were walking towards the living room together, fingers intertwined and their steps in sync with each other's.

Always towards Asa.

But maybe Carmen needed to amend those words. Maybe it needed to be always *besides* Asa.

•   •   •

Dinner had been pleasant. More than pleasant, in fact.

586

Asa thought it'd probably been one of the best nights of his life yet, all because of nothing but the mere simplicity of it. Another infinity added to the list of other infinites he'd been experiencing ever since Carmen West had walked into his life with her midnight hair and thundercloud eyes.

His eyes landed on her, watching as she laughed with his parents as they told her about something embarrassing that'd happened on their date night last week. There was a flutter right in the middle of Asa's chest, and it intensified until he thought it was going to sprout wings and fly right out of his body.

It shouldn't be humanly possible to feel *this* much, to have emotions run along such boundless depths.

Carmen caught his eyes, and the fluttery sensation exploded, spreading through every part of him until it was filling him up. He was afraid it was going to swallow him whole. It shouldn't be humanly possible to love this much. It *shouldn't.*

And yet Asa's heart continued to disagree.

It was a while before they finally excused themselves, and Asa was wrapping his fingers around her small wrist, leading her into the privacy of his room.

As soon as he kicked the door shut behind them, he took a hold of the shoulder bag slung on Carmen's arm and chucked it to the side.

"Hey." Carmen frowned. "I have things in there! You can't just throw—"

Asa's lips found hers in an almost ravenous manner and cut her words off, his hands sliding up her neck until they were cupping the back of her head and his thumbs were caressing the skin underneath her jaw.

He felt the momentary shock dissipate from her body as she began responding to him, one of her hands coming to rest on his waist and the other clenching a fist around the front of his shirt.

Carmen's words were the only thing resonating in Asa's head: *"I don't want to give you something that dies. I don't want to give you something that dies. I don't want to give you something that dies."*

587

Those words were fuel to the raging inferno beneath Asa's ribcage, until the flames were roaring high and loud, pulling the two of them in, encaging the two souls, but not burning them. After all, he loved her and she loved him, and there was no way to burn something that was baptized by fire itself.

Eyes still closed and the kiss still unbroken, his feet began moving forward, directing them away from the door and further into his room, until he felt Carmen come to a stop when the back of her legs hit the frame of the bed.

Asa pulled away from the kiss, his breath coming in gasps as he rested his forehead against hers. "I never get tired of this," he mumbled against her mouth.

Carmen seemed a little too dizzy to speak and just offered him a dazed nod of her head.

Asa hesitated for a single heartbeat, before he slowly dropped his hand from the side of her face and tugged on the cardigan she was wearing. "Can I take this off?" he asked in a voice so quiet, it might as well have been the wind.

Carmen nodded.

He reached out, about to remove it from around her shoulders, when he stopped. "No," he murmured, losing himself even more to the flames blazing around them. "I want to watch _you_ take it off." He dropped his other hand from her face and took a step back, not daring to break eye contact with her. "Take it off, Carmen."

There was no hesitation on her part, but Carmen still took her own sweet time in slipping the cardigan off her shoulders. Asa's eyes followed her movements as the fabric fell past her arms, revealing the thin straps of the silky camisole she wore underneath, the dark material contrasting with her pale skin in a painfully sinful manner.

Carmen let the cardigan fall to the floor, and Asa reached out this time, trailing two fingers down the silk, wondering if the skin beneath the fabric was just as smooth in texture. He placed a hand on her waist, right where the hem of the garment she wore met the belt loop of her jeans.

"Is this okay?" he asked, never taking his eyes off hers as he slowly slipped his hand under the camisole and dragged it up her side, stopping only when his palm met the curve of her hip and made itself comfortable there.

Carmen nodded again.

"And this?" He let his other hand graze along the skin on her other side too, the movement causing her camisole to ride up her torso as he dug his fingers into the dip in her waist.

Another nod from her.

"Good," he said in a husky tone, realising that the silk she wore didn't even hold a candle to the feel of her skin against his.

Asa took a step closer to her, angling his head and lowering his lips to meet hers again, when she cleared her throat and held up her forefinger.

"Can… can I?" Carmen asked with a slight tremble to her voice, as she hooked her finger around one of the buttons on his shirt and tugged.

Asa smiled, the edges of his lips lifting up with tenderness as he gazed down at her. "Go ahead, *mi amor.*"

He felt her hands work on the buttons, her fingers popping each one open with shaky hands, while he held her eyes with a heated gaze, not daring to blink, not daring to miss even a second of this.

He felt air hit his naked chest when his shirt came undone, but Carmen's eyes were still glued to his, and that made his heart race like never before. He felt her hands sweep across his shoulder blades, dragging down the sleeves until his arms were exposed. And then the piece of clothing fell to the floor.

Carmen didn't make a move to step any closer, but her hands came to rest on his hips, and he felt her palms slide up his chest, her soft fingertips tracing every dip, dent and curve of his muscles.

It was when she dug her nails into his shoulder and raised herself on her toes to kiss his neck that Asa finally lost it.

Asa's eyes flashed and within the blink of an eye, he stepped closer, one of his hands grabbing Carmen's waist in an iron-tight grip and pulling her flush against his chest. The camisole she was wearing did nothing to conceal the raw feeling of both their torsos pressing into each other, every hard plane of his chest digging into every soft curve of hers.

His other hand slid up her back in an excruciatingly slow manner, the tips of Asa's nails grazing her skin through the flimsy material, before his fingers slipped into the strands of her hair, tangling themselves into her long, dark locks.

"I could get used to this," he told her in a rough voice, eyes flickering to her lips and then back to her eyes.

"So could I," she breathed out, the edges of Asa's abs carving themselves into her own body as he pulled her impossibly closer.

His voice dropped a few octaves. "I like the sound of that."

Asa's eyes fell on her lips again, and this time he didn't look back up at her within a matter of seconds, allowing his heated gaze to linger on her mouth intentionally.

"Of course, you would." She lifted her lips into a smirk, rolling her eyes.

"You speak too much, you know that?"

"And you're not doing such a good job of shutting me up right now," she told him breathlessly.

"No?" he murmured, tilting his head as his eyes continued to memorise the curves and dents of her lips.

The fire around them continued to roar and engulf the two of them as if it was burning away all the pain and the anger and the regret, cleansing them of the past few agonising months. They felt the heat seep out of their bones, trailing down their skin until it turned to smoke and dissolved into the air, getting carried away forever.

Carmen shook her head, feeling Asa's fingers tighten in her hair. "No," she whispered.

Asa started moving again, pushing her backwards as his arm clung to her waist like it was coming home after being away for far too long.

And then Carmen was being pushed past the bed and against the wall, Asa's hand behind her back preventing the blow of the hard surface against her body. Carmen's heart fell a little more right then, because even

590

when caught in the heat of the moment and being driven by the intensity of their situation, he was still taking care of her.

"I don't think I've ever told you how much I love kissing you," Asa said hoarsely, curving his body further into Carmen's. "Or how much I enjoy it when you run your fingers through my hair." He dropped his forehead to hers, the side of his nose massaging hers, as his lips remained a breath away from her own. "Or how the curve of your hips are my hands' favourite place."

Fireworks. Those had to be fireworks—the things that were exploding in the pit of Carmen's stomach, in the middle of her chest, and in every dark corner of her mind.

He pressed her further against the wall. "You drive me insane, Carmen West, and all I want to do right this moment is kiss you and kiss you and kiss you until you forget your own goddamn name."

"I told you this on the night of that party," Carmen mumbled. "But you're just so whipped." A light, silvery laugh escaped her lips.

Asa raised his brows. "You know, just for that comment, I'm not going to kiss you for the rest of tonight."

Carmen hummed in response before she lifted her hands, sliding them up the hard indents of Asa's chest, sweeping them over his broad shoulders and then lacing her fingers together at the back of his neck, playing with the strands of hair there. Leaning forward and dragging her chest up against his own, she rose on her feet and angled her face upwards, covering his mouth with her own in a knee-buckling, soul-satisfying kiss.

Asa clung onto his resolve to not engage in it for a few more seconds, before that resolve shattered and went up in the flames of the fire consuming them in that moment. Then he was responding to the kiss with just as much fervour, if not more, his chapped lips hungrily enveloping Carmen's soft ones.

"Asa," Carmen gasped as she pulled away mid-kiss, needing to do something before they got carried away. "Asa, wait."

He groaned into her mouth. "Right now?" he grumbled. "What is it?"

"I need to give you something."

Asa's brows furrowed and he took a step back. "Okay?"

"Um" —she pushed herself off the wall and stepped around him— "it's in my bag. Just wait here."

Asa dropped down on the bed, resting his elbows on his knees, as he watched Carmen head towards where her bag was lying on the floor before she picked it up and dug something out of it.

"Here," she said softly, seating herself down next to him on the bed, their thighs pressed against each other's. He looked at her hands, where a deep red, leather-bound spiral book was.

"What is that?" he asked curiously.

"An art journal," she told him, a tender smile lighting up her face.

Asa's confusion only grew. "Your journal is blue. Did you get a new one?"

Carmen shook her head. "No. This one's yours..." She paused. "At least, the one that you inspired me to create anyway."

Asa stared at her with awestruck eyes, rendered speechless like so many other times she'd managed to do to him. "I... Carmen, I don't—I don't know what to say."

"Don't say anything." She smiled.

Asa swallowed and looked down at the book in his hands before flipping it open. His eyes landed on the first page, sweeping over the calligraphic writing engraved into the rough texture of the paper;

To Asa,

Who is the definition of warmth,

And the memory of a sunrise,

And proof that nightmares end because morning comes.

Heart thumping wildly, Asa turned to the next page. His breathing faltered when he realised it was the same painting he'd accidentally seen from Carmen's own art journal back when he'd met her.

But, it wasn't the exact same. The moon wasn't cracked, and its brilliance against the night sky almost stole his breath away. The sun wasn't frozen, and the gold that was splashed across the paper seemed to crawl up Asa's skin. And the flowers. Oh, the flowers were no longer dead, but full of life and rich in every possible colour.

And then his eyes fell on the girl right in the centre of it. She was still torn between both halves of the page, a part of her belonged to the daylight and the other claimed by the darkness. But this time, the girl wasn't faceless. She had a pair of eyes, a nose, eyebrows, and a mouth. This time, the girl had an identity.

Carmen was telling Asa she'd found herself.

He was about to turn the page, when Carmen's hand covered his own, stopping him from doing so.

"Later," she said, tilting her head to the side. "I want to tell you something now."

Asa closed the journal and placed it on the bedside table, before turning his body around to face her and giving her all his attention. "*Sí, mi amor?*"

Carmen shuffled closer, lifting her legs and placing them on the bed until her kneecaps were resting on top of Asa's thighs. "I'm still learning," she mumbled, and Asa saw a faint blush spread across her cheeks. "So I'm probably going to trip and make a lot of mistakes…but just bear with me."

Asa's lips stretched into a smile, curious and amused. "I'm here, Carmen. Just go ahead."

Carmen inhaled deeply, pressing her lips together before letting out the breath and clearing her throat. And then in a voice as soft as a spring breeze, she spoke to him. "*Eres el sol de mi vida.*"

The smile was instantly wiped away from Asa's face, his breath hitching and eyes widening, every single word in both English and Spanish failing him. "You are the sun of my life," she had said.

"*Con sólo escucharte, con sólo mirarte, mi día está complete.*" She smiled, running her fingertips along his jawline as she told him that just hearing him and seeing him made her day complete. *"Tú enciendes estrellas en mi interior…"* He lit up the stars inside her. *"Y nadie me mira como tú."* And nobody looked at her the way he does.

She leant forward and brushed her lips against Asa's, who was stunned into absolute silence. *"Te amaré para siempre."* Caressing his cheeks, Carmen promised to love him forever, and she believed she just might.

Asa continued to stare at her, blinking occasionally as his mouth kept opening and closing in an utterly bewildered manner. Again, the mix of emotions flitting across his features was impossible to read, and the silence stretched on.

"Asa?" Carmen laughed gently. "Say something."

That seemed to snap him out of his trance because within a heartbeat, his hands were cupping her cheeks again, and Asa was kissing her: rough, and hard, and insanely passionate. Carmen's back hit the bed and Asa hovered over her, not breaking the kiss, craving her taste more than air in that breathless moment. He tilted his head, angling his lips to deepen the kiss, his tongue grazing her bottom lip before slipping into the warmth of her mouth. Carmen's hands slid up the length of his bare back, her nails digging into his skin as she dragged her fingers upwards and tangled them in the dishevelled locks of his hair.

And then the heated kiss dissolved into a sensitive one, his inability to put into words what he was feeling seeping through his frantic movements into every caress, nibble, and pull of her bottom lip.

Slowly, but eventually, the urgency of the moment melted away, too, and surrendered to the one emotion that bound both their hearts together, the one feeling that worked as a tether between the very core of their beings. It spread through them like the dawn of a new infinity, the beginning of another lifetime, flushing their insides with a warmth so pure, so beautiful that it was heartbreaking and soul-mending at the same time.

It didn't matter that they were going to different colleges, that they were going to have to work in great distances. Nothing else mattered in that single heartbeat, in that breathless cluster of seconds, but the fact that it was now turning into yet another one of their infinites. Yet another painting to be hung on the walls of the museum Carmen had built in her mind for the boy who was a thousand shades of brown and gold.

They were a forever kind of love, and no amount of distance could take that away.

Carmen laughed breathlessly, the genuinely happy sound startling her for a second. "What's my name again?" she murmured, closing her eyes for a brief second.

Asa chuckled, the sound reverberating through his chest and seeping through Carmen's skin, tugging at her heartstrings in the most achingly pleasurable way possible.

"Mi amor," he whispered, his ragged breaths fanning across Carmen's skin as he kissed her forehead. *"Mi cielo."* A kiss on the bridge of her nose. *"Mi sol."* He rested his forehead against her temple before pulling away and gazing intensely into her eyes. *"Te amo,"* he promised. *"Te amo mucho."*

"I love you too, Asa San Román." She grinned, brushing her thumb across his cheek and seeing the raw emotion flickering in the depths of his eyes. Carmen wanted to keep that look in his eyes forever, to see genuine and heartfelt happiness light up every inch of his face forever. She'd fight for that, she knew she would, and this was a battle she wasn't about to lose.

She'd lost Asa once, and she wasn't about to let him slip through her hands the second time around. Because when you found that certain someone whose soul was able to spark a fire in yours, you held onto them with both hands, and you never, never let go.

THE END

595

BOOK YOU MIGHT ENJOY

BUBBLE TEA GIRL
Althea Liu

"Friendship is something you need to nurture over time. It's not something that happens overnight."

When Julia, a designer and writer of witty one-liners for a local fashion boutique, meets the socially and fashion awkward Weilian, she thinks she is nothing but trouble.

Weilian, who looks like she has been kidnapped off a rural worker truck, works at the Bubble tea store across the boutique. She comes near Julia's shop day after day. The more Julia starts trusting Weilian as a friend, the more her socialite friends wantonly gang up on her.

Julia suddenly discovers that her fashion ideas are now the talk of the town, but somebody else swiftly skyrockets to fame with it. Julia is now frantic and desperate. She didn't do all the work for someone to use her ideas and claim them as her own, taking her dreams and her career with it.

Will getting the fame due to her satiate her hunger for revenge? And can a friendship be regained from a betrayal with another betrayal?

Grab a copy and witness how Julia secretly carries out her revenge that leads to her malefactor's undoing in Althea Liu's Bubble Tea Girl.

BOOK YOU MIGHT ENJOY

BAD GIRL IN DISGUISE
Angie Wu

"I come here to forget—to forget my problems and be myself, even if it is just for one night."

They say good girls always get the interesting bad boys. And the bad girls will get the boring good guys.

Opposites attract, right?

But that's not the case for Jesse Marks. She is a bad girl. She defies stereotypes and breaks the rules. She owns a gigantic motorcycle and sneaks out to clubs every night.

At school, she disguises herself as a good and nerdy student; she's the teachers' favorite. Nobody can know about her true personality.

However, her facade slowly fades away when the bad boy, Lucas Johnson, arrives at the school she studies.

Problems start to arise. Terrible pasts make their way back. Horrible decisions are made. Secrets will be unveiled.

How will it affect Jesse's life? How will she deal with all the obstacles coming her way?

This young adult romance story is not for the faint-hearted. Grab a copy now!

ACKNOWLEDGEMENTS

Thank you first and foremost to my Wattpad readers, who read the original draft of Through Your Eyes, the unedited, typo-filled version and loved it anyway. It is because of the lot of you that I never stop writing. Thank you for always, always encouraging me and motivating me and sending me private messages on the site to let me know that I have made a difference in your life with my writing. That is all that I have ever wanted. Know that you have made me the happiest writer on the planet.

Thank you to my agents AJ, Precious, Winnie, and the rest of the team at BLVNP, who literally turned a dream of mine into reality. Thank you for making me believe in miracles once again.

Thank you to my family; to my mother who read me bedtime stories and made me fall so passionately in love with words. To my little sister who supported me endlessly and fell in love with this story even during the times I began doubting it. And my big sister, who doesn't forget to tell me how proud she is of me and keeps pushing me to reach new heights.

Thank you to my other family; Amanda, who never failed to tell me I was going to become a published author one day even though I never believed her at the time; Shavi, who is my daily dose of sunshine that I grow to appreciate more and more every single day, and Mishka, for reminding me to love life and do what makes me feel free.

Thank you to Kiara, without whose endless encouragement to go ahead and post this story on Wattpad, it would still be sitting in my drafts. Thank you to Rithini, for being my biggest motivator – and to Bogas, and Sul, who are always there to cheer me on.

And last but not the least, thank you to Tay, my source of unwavering support who puts up with my spam of texts at past midnight whenever inspiration strikes or a new plot crosses my mind. Know that even though you live continents away, you are forever close at heart.

AUTHOR'S NOTE

Thank you so much for reading *Through Your Eyes*! I can't express how grateful I am for reading something that was once just a thought inside my head.

Please feel free to send me an email. Just know that my publisher filters these emails. Good news is always welcome.
ali_merci@awesomeauthors.org

Sign up for my blog for updates and freebies!
ali-merci.awesomeauthors.org

One last thing: I'd love to hear your thoughts on the book. Please leave a review on Amazon or Goodreads because I just love reading your comments and getting to know you!

Can't wait to hear from you!

Ali Merci

ABOUT THE AUTHOR

Ali is a passionate reader and writer. She's also a lover of literature and iced coffee with a slight obsession for chocolate cake and Marvel superheroes! During her spare time, you will most probably find her drawing Mandalas or Bohemian doodles, staring at pictures of abstract art on her phone, or even browsing through Latin origins of random English words. She's also a huge fan of courtroom dramas, redemption character arcs, angsty romance, and protagonists that know there's strength in kindness and compassion.

www.ingramcontent.com/pod-product-compliance
Lightning Source LLC
Chambersburg PA
CBHW031019030726
47497CB00004B/927